To Sandy,

Hope you enjoy the books!

From Shell —

Leila Audrey Kantor

THE ENIGMA JOURNAL

LINDA AUDREY KANTOR

iUniverse, Inc.
Bloomington

The Enigma Journal

iUniverse books may be ordered through booksellers or by contacting:

iUniverse
1663 Liberty Drive
Bloomington, IN 47403
www.iuniverse.com
1-800-Authors (1-800-288-4677)

ISBN: 978-1-4502-9313-6 (pbk)
ISBN: 978-1-4502-9311-2 (cloth)
ISBN: 978-1-4502-9312-9 (ebk)

Printed in the United States of America

iUniverse rev. date: 3/4/2011

To my cousins and friends, who made my childhood far more fun than it would have been without them; to my parents, who did their best for me; to my wonderful family, Colin, Christopher, Laura, and Joshua, who listened to me talk about this book for a decade; and to Margaret, who taught me I had worth.

Contents

Summer 1944

Uncle Jack

When I was very young, I never realized my life was different from other children's lives, or my father was different from other fathers, or my lack of a mother was a subject that should be discussed. I accepted the components and boundaries of my existence the way any innocent does: absolutely and without question.

My earliest recollection is of splashing in a washtub beneath a clothesline lined with waving sheets. I'm giggling and mounding my hair in a soggy heap atop my head. Bubbles are rising toward the sun, and I'm trying to grab them before they float away. Rover, my border collie, is popping the bubbles in his mouth and making the strangest contortions from the taste. A man is kneeling next to me, laughing. I feel my head being pushed toward the water, and I'm afraid I'm going under, but his voice soothes as gentle hands rinse the suds from my hair. Then I'm dried with a white towel, scratchy from the clothesline, dressed in a yellow shift, and carried upstairs in the big house to take my nap.

I still remember, after all this time, the warmth and breadth of the man's chest, the faint tick of his pocket watch, the crisp starch of his collar, and the hardness of his shoulder on which I had rested my head.

I remember, too, how the man had gone by the time I awoke from my nap.

For five years, I've received letters from him with precise regularity. At the beginning, he wrote a single page with words printed large and without embellishment, enclosed within the more expansive letters he sent to Gramma. His letters remain a single page, unless I've been naughty, but now he uses script.

His most recent letter, dated August 1, 1944, is on my dresser next to the chalk horse I won at the carnival last summer, shooting wooden ducks with the fake gun.

The letter reads:

Dear Baby,

I trust you are being good for Gramma. She reports that you loathe your vegetables and you despise washing the eggs. The last is understandable. You'd think the hens would be more considerate than to dirty their own eggs, but they don't seem to care. You need to continue this task and stop your complaining. Not every duty in life is pleasant. And you also need to eat your vegetables so you grow up fine and tall. You don't want to end up a "gnome," do you? (I don't mean literally!) Look up "gnome" and use the word properly in your next letter.

About the previous matter, I will tell Gramma to let you hate one vegetable. Whenever she serves it, you can make a big fuss, scrape it off your plate, and feed it to the hens. But you can't change your mind daily. Pick one and stick to it, and the rest you must eat.

I hope you're enjoying your last weeks of summer before school starts.

Love, Daddy

His letter arrived from Italy a week ago, and I haven't yet replied. I detest writing him because he doesn't seem real to me. He's a shadow on the periphery of my life, a nuisance, an obligation. But I won't get my supper tonight until I do, because one of my chores is to stroll down our driveway every Sunday evening to pop our weekly letters to him in the mailbox for Mr. Story to collect on his Monday morning route.

Already I can smell Gramma's chicken roasting in the woodstove, the delectable scent wafting up the stairs into my room. She'd likely serve mashed potatoes, gravy, applesauce, and biscuits with honey, all of which I approve, plus an absolute slew of god-awful garden vegetables, of which I do not.

"Abby, are you finished yet?" Gramma called from the bottom of the stairs. "It's time to walk our letters down. Supper's almost done."

"Just about, Gramma." I picked up the fountain pen Daddy had sent for my eighth birthday, yanked a sheet of stationary from my bureau, and started in.

Dear Daddy ... I stopped, out of steam already.

I never knew what to write. The safe things I could tell him seemed so boring. The fun things could get me in trouble. Gramma didn't keep a yardstick behind the dining room door for simply measuring. She'd never whacked me with it, although she'd often threatened to. Others were starting to join her chorus, Uncle Jack in particular. One of these days, my luck was sure to run out. Whatever I wrote to Daddy would inevitably circle back to bite me.

While I was thinking, I drew a sneaking cat on my bare knee. On my ankle I drew a complacent mouse. I wondered how long the ink would last before wearing off. Depending on her mood, Gramma would either take a scrub brush to me immediately or wait until my Saturday night bath. Even I knew it wouldn't be proper to have cartoons decorating my leg at church. I sighed and resumed my letter in the safest manner possible: I made nice things up.

Gramma tucked my fabrication within her own letter and affixed a stamp. I sealed the envelope with spit and raced it to the mailbox. I'd no sooner returned to our yard when Uncle Jack drove up in his gray Ford. After the dust settled, he and Aunt Annie got out. I glanced expectantly toward the backseat, but no more bodies emerged.

"Hey, where's Darrell?" I demanded. Not only was Darrell my favorite cousin, he was my best friend. I didn't care a whit about his twin brothers, Duane and Dennis. We tied them up whenever possible.

Uncle Jack glared at me. "Good evening to you too, Miss Abigail."

As usual, I'd forgotten my manners. "Good evening, Uncle Jack, Aunt Annie." I felt myself blush.

"And the same to you, Abby." My aunt smiled her forgiveness, took a covered dish from the trunk, and headed for the house.

My uncle didn't smile. Rather, his disapproving gaze swept over me and lingered on my artistic efforts. I braced myself for a reprimand, but for once he let it slide.

"So, I guess Darrell's not coming then?" I asked.

"Obviously not. He and the twins somehow neglected to weed the garden. Snuck off fishing instead. So tonight they'll get sandwiches and tomorrow they'll get extra chores. No work, no pleasure. You understand how it is, don't you, Abigail?"

I nodded and made my escape.

I understood perfectly. Uncle Jack was the law, and the law always won. That my cousins had failed to follow his orders explicitly struck me as amazing. Equally amazing was his thinking that sandwiches were a punishment. Most sandwiches contained no vegetables except lettuce, which was similar to grass, and everything alive ate grass. A sandwich with Darrell was highly preferable to partaking of Gramma's succulent chicken with my uncle hovering nearby.

Whenever my cousins ate at our house, we four kids sat in the kitchen while the grown-ups supped in the dining room. Tonight, being alone, I'd be eating with the adults. The instant Gramma announced supper, I dove for the chair between her and Aunt Annie. Then my aunt slid over for some inexplicable reason, and my uncle assumed the chair next to me, watching, correcting, and judging.

I had to keep my elbows off the table, chew with my lips pressed firmly together, swallow before I spoke, and request a dish to be passed instead of helping myself. I had to avoid slurping, burping, and the other thing. The other thing would result in no dessert, even if I let one rip by accident.

By contrast, expelling gas was a considerable source of amusement when it was just us kids in the kitchen. "Barking spiders," Darrell termed it; I preferred "sauerkraut perfume." While neither twin had a pet name for this particular breach of social etiquette, both tended to contribute generously. If too generously, a punch from Darrell would be forthcoming.

While Gramma didn't condone barnyard behavior during meals, she didn't demand absolute perfection. An occasional fart could be forgiven, if not ignored.

Not so around Uncle Jack. I'd have thought we were dining at the White House with President Roosevelt himself. It was all so stifling. It was so much to remember. I found myself thinking if Daddy was similar to his younger brother, I was fortunate to have an ocean and a continent separating us.

When Gramma got up to serve coffee and dessert, my beets still remained where my uncle had plopped them on my plate. The beet blood had seeped into the remnants of my mashed potato dam, but I'd gobbled the decent food before the dam had been breached.

I poked a beet slice tentatively with my fork. Purplish red rivulets trickled from the wound. My stomach churned a warning. Gramma had never made me eat beets. Uncle Jack probably knew I detested them, which would be all the more reason to give me plenty.

I was in one hell of a jam. I couldn't eat my beets, and I couldn't leave the table until I had. No matter how long I took, my uncle would sentence me to my chair, contemplating a putrid pile of bleeding beets. A reprieve from Gramma might be forthcoming after he and Auntie went home, but that wouldn't be for an hour or two. In the meantime, I'd miss dessert.

"Having a problem with those beets, Abigail?" Uncle Jack asked. He produced his pipe from a vest pocket, added some loose tobacco, tamped it down, and struck a match.

Fortuitously I remembered my father's latest letter. "Daddy said I could pick a vegetable I hate and I wouldn't have to eat it. I can prove it too. I can show you his letter."

"I hardly … want to see … anything from him." Uncle Jack timed his phrases between pulls on the pipe. Pipe lit, he called toward the kitchen, "Annie, please bring back the zucchini and beans. Our niece dislikes the beets."

I was determined to survive his malicious attempt to poison me. Aided by copious gulps of milk, I choked down everything he dumped on my plate. He watched, seemingly amused, so I had no opportunity to feed my napkin or the floor rather than myself.

I'd no sooner vanquished the odious items and was dabbing my mouth with my napkin, when a horrific image flashed through my mind: cauliflower! I'd made a horrendous mistake in picking beets as my most hated vegetable. How could I ever, *ever* eat something that looked exactly like brains? The contents of my stomach wiggled like worms. I swallowed desperately against the inevitable.

"May I be excused?" I begged, bile rising in my throat.

Before my uncle could reply, I bolted from the table, raced outside, and heaved. Chunks of chicken plopped to the ground amid green clumps of beans and yellowish zucchini slime. I vomited again, more forcefully this time. Then I rinsed my mouth at the pump and finished my interrupted journey. Slamming the outhouse door, I slumped against the wall and bawled. Periodically I paused to wipe my eyes with a paper wrapper from the box that had contained Empire Delicious Apples, Best in Washington State, placed strategically between the big hole and the little hole. When my sobs subsided into intermittent hiccups, I blew my nose in the last of the blue wrappers.

I hated Tyrant Jack. And I hated Annie of the Red Hair and Timid Gramma for condoning his abuse of me. When Daddy returned, would he treat me in the same abhorrent manner as did his evil brother? More than likely!

Nobody loved me. Nobody understood. Nobody cared.

Nobody.

At dusk, I emerged. The gray Ford remained parked in our yard, so I couldn't go inside the house. I didn't want the tyrant to see me. I didn't want anyone to see me.

I stood in the deepening gloom at the edge of the grove and pondered what to do. I considered crawling in the haymow to sleep with the cats ... no, I wasn't good enough for them. I'd slide down the coal chute and curl up with Rover ... no, there wasn't enough room. I'd lie down in the slough and let the badgers eat me ... yes, that's what I'd do. I'd disappear off the face of the earth and they'd all feel bad.

Or would they?

"Remember Abby?" someone might say, during a future Sunday supper. "You know; the one Jack force-fed like a goose till she puked. Whatever happened to her? Vanished that night into thin air. Never even found her bones. Those badgers make quick work of a person. Here at night, gone by morning. Or maybe it was gypsies ... I heard of a snatching once by Madelia ... oh, but this is wonderful coffee! Coffee's so scarce these days, with all the rationing. May I have another cup?"

As I eased by the woodshed, I heard someone clear his throat.

"Come here, Abigail." The voice, as always, was deep, commanding.

I walked as slowly as I dared to where the tyrant was perched atop Gramma's woodpile, smoking his pipe.

"You certainly make a spectacle out of yourself," he scolded. "Throwing up perfectly palatable food and then howling about it. I never heard such a damn conniption in an outhouse before in my entire life!"

I refused to give him the satisfaction of agreement.

"You better have gotten it out of your system … have you?"

I nodded without looking at him.

"Good … so, why don't you climb up here and keep me company?"

I had as much desire to keep him company as I did to pull out my own toenails, but I had no choice in the matter. I sat as far away from him as possible, wrapped my arms around my bent knees, and willed myself not to cry again.

"You don't like me, do you?" he said.

I shrugged.

"What's that supposed to mean? Answer me, one way or the other."

"Do I have to tell the truth?"

"You just did."

I felt bad then, not for him, but for me.

We sat, together but separate, in silence. Then, as I feared he would, he slid an arm around me and drew me close. I resisted as long as I could, but something about the faint tick of his pocket watch and the slight crinkle of his shirt as he breathed stirred within me a dim recollection, a loneliness, an emptiness—one that I did not, could not, comprehend.

"Uncle Jack?" I said.

"What?"

"Tell me about my mother."

He stiffened and took back his arm. "That's an odd topic for a lovely summer evening, Abigail. Don't you already know enough?"

"No. I want to know everything."

"That's impossible. Besides, I have better things to do."

Rebuffed, I drew away from him and tighter into myself. Out of the corner of my eye, I watched the curl of smoke from his pipe rise and fade away. I wished he would rise and fade away too.

After several minutes, he set aside the pipe. "What do you already know?"

"Her name was Ellen and her parents died of the Spanish flu," I began. "She took a train from New York City and got adopted by a banker and his wife because they didn't have kids. Gramma says some orphans never get adopted, so she was lucky somebody wanted her. After she grew up, she married Daddy, and I was born. That's all I know. Gramma said to ask you the rest."

"It hardly seems necessary. You already know quite a bit."

"No, I don't," I said. "I don't even know what she looked like. Tell me something about her … please?"

"Oh, all right … well, if I remember correctly, her hair was similar to yours, but she had green eyes instead of brown. She was slender and tall, every inch a lady."

"Then she was pretty?"

"Some might think so … I remember she dressed exceptionally well."

"In fancy dresses?"

"That's what exceptionally dressed ladies wear."

"Oh." I had hoped Mother would've been a tomboy like me. I deplored wearing dresses. Overalls and a cast-off shirt from Darrell suited me better.

"Not all the time," he clarified. "She dressed for the occasion. For instance, she might have worn slacks and a nice blouse, if she were woodpile sitting with us right now."

I tried to imagine my mother woodpile sitting with us. I tried to imagine my mother putting her arm around me instead of him. I tried to imagine having a mother.

"Anything else?" he said. "It's getting late, and I don't like leaving your cousins alone after dark."

"They'll be all right. Darrell can watch the twins."

"Two against one."

"But the one is smarter than the two together."

"That sounds like something Darrell said."

"It is," I admitted.

"I thought so … all right, what else? Make it quick."

I started with the basics. "So what did Mother like to do? Did she like to read?"

"Yes, and she liked card games and dancing … horses too."

"Horses?" I was terrified of horses.

"She had one growing up and another after she married, I believe."

"I wish I could ride," I found myself saying.

"I'll teach you," he offered. "But first you have to overcome your fear. A horse can sense when you're scared, and you'd find yourself on the ground."

"Maybe next year … for now, I just wish I had a picture of Mother on a horse. Do you have one?"

"No."

"I've never seen a picture of her. Why doesn't Gramma have pictures of Mother?"

"Why don't you ask her?"

"I have, and she won't tell me."

"Maybe she doesn't know what happened to them."

I looked at him hopefully. "Oh, so there were some pictures?"

"I suppose … at one time."

"Maybe Daddy took her pictures along with him to Italy," I said. "Maybe he even took their wedding picture. Do you think so?"

"How would I know? Ask him, not me."

"I have, and he won't say. I'd so love a picture of her."

"I imagine you would, Abigail … now I really have to be going."

I grabbed his sleeve. "No, please don't go. Not before you tell me how she died. Just tell me what happened and why she isn't in the cemetery with everyone else."

He frowned and settled again. "I didn't know you realized that."

"Realized what?"

"That her grave isn't in the cemetery."

"Of course I noticed!" I wondered just how stupid he thought I was. "I'm almost ten, and I notice lots of things. Why, Gramma and I go out there to put flowers on the graves of Grandpa Walter, Great-grandma Elsa, Great-grandpa Friedrich, and their little baby with no name who never saw the light of day—"

"Sounds like you're learning the family history."

"Yes, I know how the baby died before it came out," I boasted. "Gramma's told me stories about a whole bunch of other people too."

"What did she say about your mother's death?"

"Nothing. That's why I'm asking you."

"I see … and who else have you asked? Have you asked Annie?"

"Yes."

"And what did she say?"

"She said to ask you."

"Good, she's finally stopped gossiping. Never thought I'd get her trained." He smiled.

"Are you kidding me?" I said. "You can't train people like you train your horses, Uncle Jack. Even I know that!"

"Don't bet on it. Consistency, discipline, and high expectations; works equally well on horses, kids, or a wife … all right, maybe not the wife." His smile faded, all signs of humor gone. "Now you listen to me. You're not to bother folks with all your questions."

"Why not?"

"Because I said so … and because it's pointless."

"Why is it pointless?"

"Because they don't know what happened."

"Why don't they know?"

"They weren't there."

"Who was there? Were you there?"

"Change the subject. I'm done talking about this."

"But she was my mother!" I protested. "Why can't I know what happened to her?"

"I didn't say you couldn't, but it won't come from me. Ask my brother. It's his decision what to tell or not tell you."

I rolled my eyes in exasperation. "I have, but he never tells me anything. All Daddy ever writes is how to behave, what to do, what words to look up, what to eat—" I stopped, wishing I hadn't mentioned the vegetable incident.

"I see … so I'm your last hope?"

"Yes."

He tapped the tobacco out of his pipe and slipped it into his pocket. "I'll say this much, Abigail. Your mother isn't in the cemetery because she died far from here, and the circumstances surrounding her death are subject to interpretation. Come on, let's go inside. It's your bedtime, and Annie and I have to be getting back before the twins tear the house apart."

"Subject to interpretation" … what did he mean by that? From my bedroom window, I watched the tail lights of his car fade into the night.

Looking up, I surveyed the crescent moon playing peek-a-boo with the scuttling clouds and the pinpricks of countless stars dancing across the expanse of darkened sky. Lost in thought, I listened to the wind wafting my lace curtain along the sill and the leaves of the cottonwood trees outside rustling in subtle harmony with the lace curtain.

And somehow the sounds transformed into the swish of my mother's gossamer nightgown against the wooden steps as she padded softly upstairs. She carried a letter, glaring white as bone in the reflection of the moon.

Letters

My spirits rose the next morning along with the sun. Three whole weeks of summer remained before school started, Gramma was making pancakes for breakfast, and I'd awoken with a wonderful idea.

I cheerfully composed my next letter to Daddy before my idea evaporated.

Dear Daddy,

Tell Uncle Jack to leave me alone. He gave me such a licking last night down by the woodpile so no one could hear and stop him, all because I didn't want to eat the vegetable I hate most, which you said I didn't have to. Afterward he said some mean, nasty things about Mother. I think he'd gotten into Gramma's hooch and it made him talk wild. He talked so wild he scared me, even more than the licking scared me! Please write back and tell me the truth about Mother so I can try to forget the ugly stuff he said about her.

Your adorable daughter, Abby

P.S. "Gnome" means a little troll person, as in Uncle Jack is too tall to be a gnome, but he sure is a witch.

I could hardly wait for my father's reply!

Uncle Jack kept his word and assigned so many chores to Darrell and the twins to punish them for going fishing that I had no one to play with all week.

But being alone didn't bother me particularly. I explored the slough for the hundredth time with my Red Ryder BB gun, but didn't shoot anything. I chipped an arrowhead from a flint stone and fashioned a bow from a willow branch. I massacred bugs with hot water. Salt did them in too, but Gramma had hidden the box from me. I slid down the haystacks so often the hay began sliding with me, so I had to stop before Ole, our hired man, tattled. I built a raft to use when the spring rains flooded the slough, but it came out crooked. I hoped Darrell could fix it when he found the time, so I set it aside.

In my quieter moments, I cut the Tarzan comic strips from the *St. Paul Pioneer Press* and pasted them in my scrapbook before Gramma donated our newspapers to the paper drive. Brown County had a monthly quota of forty-seven thousand pounds of paper, she said, and we had to do our share. When

I hoped that keeping my Tarzan clippings wouldn't cause Brown County to fall short of its goal, Gramma just smiled.

In the evenings, while she crocheted or mended, I finished *Tarzan of the Apes* and started *The Son of Tarzan*. I didn't understand all of the vocabulary used by Burroughs, but I could get by, so I didn't bother looking anything up. Daddy was sure to cover the words I didn't know soon anyway.

The weekend finally came and with it my obligatory Saturday night bath in preparation for church on Sunday. My cat and mouse drawings had already faded, so a bit more coaxing with a soapy washrag did the trick.

While Gramma and Aunt Annie attended services faithfully, dragging me and my cousins with them, Uncle Jack seldom passed through the vestibule of the New German Lutheran Church. He said he didn't believe in God, but I suspected he was afraid God didn't believe in him.

Neither Gramma nor Auntie could keep track of us kids without him, so Darrell and I always had fun after church. Once we locked Duane and Dennis in a basement closet that held the altar cloths and communion cups. When we shut off the light and ran away, we were stunned when their shrieks carried clear to the choir loft and the belfry beyond! I got off with just a scolding from Gramma, but Darrell got worse from Uncle Jack when he got home.

On this particular Sunday, Reverend Richter's interminable sermon finally droned to a close. I'd been yawning and fidgeting the whole ten minutes he'd gone overtime, anxiously anticipating an afternoon visit to my uncle's so I could play with Darrell.

Uncle Jack was a gentleman farmer, Gramma explained to me once, which meant he rented out his two hundred and forty acres of prime Minnesota farmland instead of digging in the earth himself. In a further effort to keep his hands clean, he employed Charlie Kopischke to care for the livestock and help with the horses. While Charlie was a few bales short of a wagonload, my uncle had little choice but to hire him since most of the mentally and physically able men in our community were either tending their own farms or gone to the war.

Uncle Jack didn't go to war because he was a farmer with three kids and an ulcer, which he said he got from the twins. With little to do, he spent his time breeding and training horses. He sold them to Canada for their mounted police force or to anyone who could pay, although I'd heard he'd given several to injured soldiers in our community.

Their house had started out much like ours: a white clapboard farmhouse built in the 1890s, with the living rooms downstairs, the sleeping rooms upstairs, and a wraparound porch front and side.

That was before Uncle Jack started modernizing. Now the house was a virtual paradise, boasting two indoor bathrooms with commodes that flushed and store-bought toilet paper. Aunt Annie's kitchen held all the latest conveniences. Even my cousins' bedrooms were nicer than mine. Rather than faded linoleum and mismatched bureaus, their rooms had carpet and matching mahogany furniture.

But it was the living room that truly captivated me. In 1936, my uncle had paid a carpenter to remove the ceiling and plaster the walls clear to the pitch of the roof. Now fifteen stuffed animals were mounted along those walls, all staring down with their glass eyes. A piano stood in one corner, which no one could play except my aunt. A locked gun cabinet held rifles and shotguns of various calibers. A bookcase featured whitened skulls, teeth, and claws, plus numerous books about Africa. One book was personally autographed by President Theodore Roosevelt himself! An imposing framed photograph of T. R. and his son Kermit, posing on the back of a dead buffalo, hung above the bookcase.

Uncle Jack loved Africa, and he was a wealthy man: those two facts were plain, even to me. But he didn't spend nearly as much money as he used to, Gramma said, since he'd stopped gallivanting off to the Dark Continent.

Now he spent mainly on his horses and his clothes. He dressed like a dandy; I'd overheard that comment in town last year. Rather than wearing overalls, flannel shirts, and sturdy shoes, Uncle Jack favored jeans and starched shirts in black or khaki, often paired with a vest. He alternated between English riding boots and intricately tooled cowboy boots with matching belts. The boots and belts were specially made in Chicago and sent to him. He probably had the shirts sent from there as well, because I never saw anything even close in Gramma's Monkey Ward's catalogue. He replaced an item when it showed wear and that was about the extent of his spending.

But Aunt Annie seldom saw anything she didn't like, so his money went flying out the door with regularity, and their house filled up over the years to nearly overflowing. Not that she spent all his money selfishly. Gramma said both church and library benefited mightily from Uncle Jack's largesse because of my aunt's insistence. And needy children in our town always enjoyed a good Christmas. Sometimes I worried my aunt would spend my uncle out of money just when I wanted something so grand that Gramma couldn't buy it for me, but Darrell dismissed my concern, saying I always worried about the dumbest things.

Once I asked Gramma how Uncle Jack got so rich while we stayed so poor. She said we were as rich as we needed to be and someday things would even out. Aunt Emma said my uncle had gotten his money in Africa, but she had no idea how.

Darrell and I theorized that his dad had turned into a brigand and stole diamonds or gold. We were constantly on the lookout for hollows in trees or loose siding on outbuildings where he might've stashed the booty. We never found a thing, but we never gave up looking.

Uncle Jack ran low on money once, or so Aunt Emma reasoned, because he returned to Africa just before the war. Since the war, he'd stayed home, but mysterious packets, resplendent with exotic stamps, continued to arrive periodically from Nairobi. Whoever got the mail that day would place the packet reverently on the dining room table. There it would remain until my uncle took it upstairs to open in private. Darrell and I speculated endlessly as to what those packages contained.

After enduring church and a lingering supper, we kids were primed to play. Darrell chose cowboys and Indians. We lured the twins to the barn and tied them to a post. Then we danced around them, waving real hatchets and whooping about taking scalps. When Darrell accidentally swung his hatchet too close, Duane screamed. Dennis chimed in. Darrell gave them both a quarter to shut them up. I was glad Uncle Jack was rich so at least my cousin *had* two quarters.

Six cars were parked in the drive by the time we came back to the house. Several opened jars of hooch sat on the kitchen counter. Darrell took a swig when the twins weren't looking. So did I. Rhubarb—delicious! Gramma was playing dominoes with her church cronies. Aunt Annie was playing euchre with three neighbor ladies. All were enjoying their crystal glasses of hooch, judging from their giggles. Uncle Jack was pouring whiskey for the men. He glanced up as we slunk through the dining room, but he didn't say anything.

Upstairs, Darrell and I told ghost stories and scared the twins sufficiently to cause nightmares. Then we played hide and seek. After exhausting the hiding possibilities, we slid down the steps in a cardboard box. That was a hoot until Dennis flew past the landing, continued down the next section of steps, burst through the downstairs door, and landed in a rumpled heap nearly beneath the dress of one of Gramma's elderly friends.

That got Uncle Jack's attention. "Stop that damn nonsense before you knock somebody down!" he yelled at Dennis. "Go to bed, you and Duane!" Eying Darrell and me, he added, "Pipe down or I'll see you later."

"Yes, sir," Darrell said. He cast a conspiratorial glance toward me.

Now we could engage in our favorite quiet pastime: Snoop. Darrell was Sherlock and I was Watson, and together we could find anything, anywhere. The house was crammed with nooks and crooks, crannies and crevices, dead ends and promises. There were more boxes, trunks, and chests than could be counted. Snoop and Company was always making new discoveries.

We started in familiar territory: Uncle Jack and Aunt Annie's bedroom. Darrell pocketed a pack of Camels plus two quarters from the nightstand tray to compensate for the ones he'd given the twins.

"Won't he miss it?" I asked.

"What, the money or the smokes?"

"The money."

"Nope. He's worth thousands, maybe millions. What's a couple of quarters?"

"Two weeks' allowance for me."

"Glad I'm not you."

"Thanks, you're all heart."

Darrell briefly rummaged in the nightstand. "Hey, look at this: Snoop Exhibit Number One."

"What's that?" I said. "An ugly little balloon?"

My cousin smirked. "It's no balloon, you ninny. It's the reason they didn't have more kids after the twins … think I should poke a hole in it?"

"Sure." I had no idea what he was talking about.

He rolled the rubbery thing around in his palm and then put it back. "Nope, bad idea. Too many brats in this house already. They'd sure be surprised, though … come on, Watson; I've something else to show you."

I followed him to the hall as he shut his parents' door behind us.

"Look what I noticed the other day." Darrell pointed to a chimney cover high on the wall.

I shrugged. "It's a chimney cover. So what?"

"Well, there's no reason for it to be there since the stove pipe got removed when Dad installed the furnace. The hole should've been plugged and papered over when the wallpaper was replaced last spring."

"Maybe the paper hanger forgot."

"No, Dad wanted it this way or it would've been redone. I was thinking about it the other day, and I noticed the wallpaper looked worn along the edges, so I checked into it—"

"And?"

"And it's loose! There's something wrapped in brown paper behind the cover. I know because I took a peek without you the other day."

I was suitably impressed. "Maybe it's the diamonds, Sherlock!"

"Or gold, Watson, a whole bag of gold—"

"Or a big pile of paper money—"

"Maybe not money, but a map to the treasure—"

"Stop blabbing and let's have a look!"

Darrell got a chair from his room, climbed up, and removed the chimney cover while I stood watch. He tossed me down a small packet and together we raced to his room.

I undid the wrapping, but anticipation died when I saw the contents. "Why, it's nothing but letters and a picture."

Darrell looked equally crestfallen. "No diamonds … no money. I thought for sure we'd found the gold."

"Or at least the map to the gold," I said. "Well, we didn't. Snoop Exhibit Number Two is a bust. We better put this back before somebody notices."

Darrell deliberated a moment. "No, I think we should read some of the letters first, since we went through all the effort. Maybe there'll be a clue somewhere."

"Good idea, Sherlock." I started to hope again.

The letters had no envelopes, but were simply bundled and tied with a blue ribbon. I eased off the ribbon and unfolded the first letter. The handwriting was elegant, containing many swirls and flourishes.

"Read it out loud," Darrell said. "You read squiggles better than me."

My precious darling,

I hope this method of communication works out. Remember to send your replies only to my box and destroy my letters after you read them and we'll be safe forever. No one must ever find out. We both have too much to lose.

Oh, darling, you can't even imagine the turmoil I've endured lately, just thinking about you and you so far away! Will things be better by the time I see you again, or will things be worse? I have no idea, darling.

Try not to be alarmed, but nearly all the time I am watched. Love, the knife that cuts so shallow but so deeply at the same time. I am suffocating from love. And I must return love in kind; smile, laugh, or the jig's up. Be caring, be submissive, or the jig's up. I can hardly perpetuate the pretense, but I shall, darling, I shall! In a few short months, I'll see you again and I can hardly wait. Already I can hardly sleep for thinking of you. At long last, I will be experiencing Africa with you—

"Africa?" Darrell said.

"That's what it says. Maybe we shouldn't read this stuff, Darrell. Maybe we should put it back and pretend we never found it."

"Too late for that. Finish it."

I repeated the last sentence before continuing.

At long last, I will be experiencing Africa with you. Perhaps between the hunts and the celebrations and the confusion of traveling to and fro after the game, we can steal a private moment for ourselves. Our tents will never be far apart and—

My cousin was shaking his head.

I hesitated. "I don't recognize the next few words, Darrell."

"Skip it then."

—of whether or not our bodies touch—

"Damn!" Darrell said.

—and yet I know we shall remain forever joined in this tragic, impossible love that we feel for one another.

"That's all there is to this one," I said.

"How's it signed?"

"There's no name."

"How about a date?"

"No date."

Darrell scowled. "Something's going on, and it has to do with Africa. If I were older, maybe it'd make more sense, but I know I don't like it. I don't like it one bit."

"Neither do I … what do you think it's about?"

"I don't know … unless there's someone in Africa that Dad's been seeing. Maybe that's why he went again before the war. Maybe those packets from Nairobi aren't money. Maybe they're more love letters, because he won't let Mom touch them and he never says a word about them afterward."

Uncle Jack's interest in anyone but Aunt Annie was unthinkable, inconceivable. I felt compelled to uphold his honor even though I detested him. "But what makes you think these letters are even written to him?"

Darrell looked at me with distain. "Who else would they be to? Mom's never been to Africa, so nobody's writing her … no, these letters were written to Dad. And he sure didn't want anybody seeing them, because they didn't jump in the wall and hide behind a chimney cover all by themselves."

"You're right," I murmured. My mother's unexplained death, my uncle's mysterious wealth, and now letters linking him to a unknown woman in Africa … what other perplexing secrets might the Stahl family possess?

Hastily we skimmed the rest of the letters, but they were in a similar vein. No signatures, no dates, no anything. Next we studied the photograph.

"It's Dad, all right, but it was years ago," Darrell decided. "He's thinner and he didn't have a mustache yet."

"But who's the lady?" I said. Shadowed by a hat, her face was turned toward my uncle as they stood together in front of a native hut.

"No clue. That stupid hat covers half her face."

"Some ladies like to keep the sun off their complexions."

"I guess … hey, look at this, Watson!"

"What?"

"There, behind and between the two of them."

I squinted again at the photograph and saw a second man in the distance, partially hidden by another hut. He held a rifle to his shoulder. The barrel pointed directly at Uncle Jack and his lady companion.

I gasped. "Why, he's aiming his gun at them! Do you think your dad ever knew?"

"Not at the time, or he wouldn't be smiling for the camera."

"However bad this looks, it must've turned out all right," I said. "Your dad never got shot or he wouldn't be alive today."

"But what about the lady?" Darrell challenged. "What if the man was aiming at her instead of Dad? Maybe he shot her instead. Or maybe he didn't shoot either of them because he only was trying to scare them. There's no way of knowing what happened next, is there?"

"No," I breathed. A mystery was one thing, but a photograph of an imminent crime was quite another matter!

"Hey, I just heard a door slam downstairs." Darrell cast a worried glance at his own door. "The party must be breaking up. Hurry, let's get this stuff back!"

I reassembled the packet, hoping it looked the same as when we'd found it. Darrell returned it to the wall and set the cover in place.

I took his arm as we descended the stairs. "Don't worry … whoever wrote those letters, it was long before your mother. Your dad would never do anything wrong."

"Of course not."

"And however bad that picture looked, it must've turned out all right."

"I sure hope so."

"We'll never know for sure, though."

"Yes, we will. One day we'll know … Abby?"

I paused on the landing. "What?"

"Why do you suppose Dad kept all those letters but only that one picture?"

Fire

I WENT GIDDY with excitement when my letter from Daddy finally arrived. He'd tell me about Mother! He'd protect me from Tyrant Jack! Such a wonderful day!

Abigail, he wrote, not *Dear Baby.* I had a sinking feeling already.

Never have I been so ashamed of you. What is going through your mind that you would lie so? You know what happens to liars. You are an insolent (look it up) and deceitful (look it up) child who deserves the harshest of punishments. If I were not so far away, I would see to it personally. About the Sunday night in question, my brother was neither drunk nor did he administer a spanking to you, although I now wish that he had. As it is, I've written your grandmother about what to do with you. In your next letter I expect a full explanation and a heartfelt apology.

Sincerely, Father

P. S. concerning your feeble attempt at humor in your sentence containing the word "gnome," a male witch is called a warlock. Jack may be many things, but that certainly is not one of them.

Never had he written me so cruelly. I crumpled his letter and flung it in my wastebasket. I saw no need to explain why I sought information about Mother, of whom he hadn't written a single syllable. And until he did, I'd provide no apology. In fact, I wouldn't write him ever again. Let him rot in Italy, if that's where he preferred to be!

Gramma was unusually quiet during supper that evening. What had he told her?

Darrell called shortly after I finished the dishes. He wanted me to meet him at the stone pile so he could show me his new pony. I was out the door in a flash. After Daddy's chastisement, I needed cheering up.

So did Darrell. I expected him to be thrilled about Peaches, but he seemed in the doldrums himself.

"She's a pretty little horse," I said, hoping to start a conversation.

"She's part American quarter horse and part something smaller," Darrell said. "She's gentle, so you don't have to be afraid to ride her."

"I will if you're with me."

"Suit yourself."

His thoughts were elsewhere. Nothing I said perked him up. I was about to go home when he suggested we ride to their farm and talk things over in the haymow. After a short ride on Peaches, who didn't frighten me at all, we were comfortably nestled in the hay.

Darrell lit one of the Camels he'd swiped from the nightstand. "There's something you should know, Abby."

"And what's that?" I helped myself to a cigarette. Darrell held the match for me like Humphrey Bogart had for Ingrid Bergman in *Casablanca.*

"A couple of days ago, when everyone was out of the house, I went to read those love letters again. They were gone."

I inhaled sharply. "Gone?"

"That's what I said."

"Are you sure? Maybe they just slid down the wall. Did you check?"

"I reached as far as the crosspiece. They weren't there. I think Dad figured out we'd found them, and he took them away."

"But nobody saw us that night. I know it for a fact. And I wrapped everything up like we'd found it, and you put it back exactly the same way, didn't you?"

Darrell avoided my eyes.

"Well, didn't you?"

"I thought I did, but now I'm not so sure."

"What?" I said through my teeth. "*What?* What'd you forget to do?"

"I think I forgot to put away the chair."

"You forgot the chair? You left the damn chair right under that chimney cover? That's like leaving a sign with an arrow pointing up! You idiot! You moron! You nincompoop!" Name-calling didn't seem sufficient, so I punched him.

He punched me back. "I said I *might* have forgotten. You're as guilty as me, remember? Picking a fight won't help anything."

I rubbed my arm. *Bogart would've never hit Bergman,* I thought, *but Bogart was a gentleman. Darrell was a jerk.*

"I know it won't help," I muttered. "And if you even care, it hasn't been a good week for me either." I told how I'd written a white lie to Daddy, trying to learn more about Mother, but he'd gotten mad and now Gramma was watching me.

Darrell said he felt the same way. Something was hanging in the air, words unspoken. He was afraid of being alone with his dad. He was afraid of an accusation blindsiding him—an accusation for which he'd have no answer. For the first time since its conception, he said, Snoop and Company had gone too far. We'd found something truly disturbing. But now that we had, we couldn't ignore it.

"You're absolutely right," I said. "No matter what, we'll—"

A loud whinny from below interrupted my affirmation. We inched forward and peered toward the stable, where Uncle Jack was circling a mare on a long tether. She was a beautiful Arabian with wide-set eyes, flowing mane, and up-flung tail. She pranced and danced, pausing periodically to snort and shake her noble head at her master.

"I never saw that one before," I whispered. "She's beautiful."

"She came on the same truck as Peaches," Darrell whispered back. "Dad named her Banat er Rih. Supposedly it means *Daughter of the Wind*, but it probably doesn't. Did you know that George Washington rode an Arabian mare named Magnolia during the Revolutionary War, and Napoleon had one named Marengo?"

I blew a puff of smoke in his face. "Well, aren't you a regular history lesson today."

Darrell reddened. "So stay stupid, stupid."

I stuck out my tongue. Then I watched my uncle mount the Daughter of the Wind. She shied to one side, her dainty hooves upturning minute clouds of dust. He reached down and stroked her neck. She calmed and he put her through her paces. She trotted quickly, picking up her feet as though she deigned to put them on common earth. He sat easily in the saddle, reining her in a large circle. He held his crop but did not use it; I'd never seen him use it on a horse. After several minutes, he reined her in, shoved open the stable gate with his boot, and repositioned himself. At his command, Banat broke into a gallop. Horse and rider raced amid the outbuildings, scattering chickens and ducks alike in a frenzied cacophony of cackles and squawks.

Upon his third circling of the yard, he pulled her to a halt under the mow door. Darrell and I slunk down and watched him through the loose hay. He squinted, searching the spot where we'd been visible seconds earlier. Apparently satisfied, he gave Banat rein and they were off again, down the driveway this time.

"Do you think he saw us?" I asked, sitting up.

"Don't know." Darrell snuffed his cigarette in the sardine can ashtray and lit another. "So what if he did? We're allowed to be up here."

"But he looked suspicious." I helped myself to a second cigarette.

"He always looks suspicious. Don't worry about it."

I was about to reply when a yowl resonated across the farmyard, a blend of squalling baby and an animal caught in a leghold trap. "What's that?" I said.

"Cats!" Darrell yanked me to my feet. "Come on, I bet old Jake's back! It'll be the catfight of the century!"

We scrambled down the mow ladder. Rounding the corner of the barn, we saw two tomcats squaring off. We hunkered by the rock pile to watch.

"In the far corner, we have the challenger, Jake Werner," Darrell intoned into his cupped hand, imitating the sportscaster he admired on the radio. "Jake's weighing in today at about thirteen pounds, covered in large yellow stripes, and he's primed to kill. Around the catfighting world, ladies and gentlemen, he's known as a mean, ugly bastard. He's only got one eye, and all bets say he's about to lose the other one going up against the current world champion. In the near corner, we have the undefeated Big Blackie Stahl, weighing in at about twelve pounds, black as pitch and a heart to match, with claws that love to tear, that love to rip, and here we go—"

With unnerving howls, the two tomcats lunged at each other, spitting and clawing. Big Blackie came down on Jake Werner, but Jake twisted and his claws raked Blackie's belly, and Blackie let out a snarl. Blackie's head went under Jake's throat, and it looked to be a good hold, but during the ensuing roll in the dirt, Blackie was thrown clear. With his ears laid back, his shoulders hunched, and his eyes glinting hate, he pounced on Jake's back. This time it was Jake who howled. Squirming free, he whirled about and pinned Blackie against the ground with both paws and his huge mouth. The situation looked precarious for Big Blackie Stahl.

"Scat, you devil!" Darrell heaved a stone at the cats. The missile fell short, but the thump scared Jake sufficiently that he released Big Blackie and fled into the cornfield.

Blackie, looking disorientated, staggered to his feet. He spat at us, slunk off to a nearby lilac bush, and began to lick himself.

"He'll be all right," I said. "Good thing you threw that rock, though. If you hadn't, we might be burying him in the grove today."

"Who cares?" Darrell grumbled. "Damn stupid cat."

"You just hate cats … hey, what's that noise?"

"What noise?"

"That noise … listen."

From the direction of the barn came a faint crackling, like paper being crumpled. The sound grew, not merely in intensity, but seemingly in momentum. I glanced at Darrell, who had cocked his head to listen.

His face went pale beneath his farmer's tan. "It's the hay, Abby! It sounds like the hay's on fire!"

"No, it couldn't be!"

We ran through the double doors and saw that the hay near the bottom of the ladder was alive with the crackle of hungry flames. Rolls of heavy, dark smoke churned up the ladder to the haymow. Within minutes, the barn would be completely engulfed.

"Water! Get a pail of water!" Darrell shouted.

"It's too late!" I wailed. "A little water won't help!" The fire was spreading exponentially and the pump was twenty feet beyond the barn.

"Well, do *something*!"

"Like *what*?"

"How should I know?" Darrell's face contorted with helplessness and horror. He flailed his arms like a madman and kicked furiously at the burning clumps.

"Stop it! You're making it worse!" I grabbed his arm, but he shook me off. Then the smoke changed direction from the suction of the wind through the barn, temporarily blinding me. I doubled over, coughing.

"Let's get out of here!" Darrell pulled me outside and sprinted for the grove.

I cleared my lungs and followed. As I raced past the house, I caught a glimpse of Aunt Annie standing on the side porch, waving her apron over her head. Beyond her, I saw Uncle Jack cropping Banat furiously across the flanks as he rode the mare toward the inferno.

Darrell stopped running near the line fence. He slumped to the ground, covered his head with his arms, and cried. When he'd sobbed himself dry, he blew his nose with his fingers, a habit I found revolting, then walked to where I'd been waiting.

"We might as well go back, Abby," he said, his voice flat. "There's nowhere we can hide that Dad won't find us, nowhere at all. After the fire truck and the neighbors go home, we'll be in for it."

I held tight to a shred of hope. "How can you say that? Nobody saw us do anything. Nobody knows how the fire started. I don't even know myself."

Darrell's mouth gaped. "Are you kidding me?"

"No, I'm not kidding. Why should we be blamed? Maybe lightning—"

"Without a storm?"

"Maybe lightning bugs—maybe fireflies, maybe—maybe—"

"Bugs don't start fires, you dumbbell. It's us and our damn cigarettes. Dad will figure it out. He figures everything out."

I stared at him as I realized that my cigarette had vanished somewhere between the barn and the cat fight. I remembered it dangling from my lips in the haymow and then—? Dear God in heaven, I'd torched my uncle's barn!

Would Reverend Richter preach a sermon about me on Sunday? Would Daddy fly home to punish me the minute he heard? Would Sheriff Branson haul me to reform school? Would Gramma sell me to a caravan of gypsies? Worst of all, what would Uncle Jack do? He scared me on a normal day! I burst into tears.

"Stop your blubbering," Darrell said.

"You cried and I wasn't nasty to you," I sobbed. "You probably think I'm taking all the blame for this, but I'm not!"

"Wasn't my cigarette that set the hay on fire."

"Oh, yeah?"

"Yeah ... I still had mine while we were watching the cats."

"No, you didn't. You were imitating that sportscaster. You can't do that with a cigarette in your mouth."

Darrell frowned as if trying to remember, but I remembered clearly.

"Besides, who stole the Camels and then gave them to me?"

"You didn't have to smoke them."

"If I hadn't, you would've made fun of me ... I'm going to tell, Darrell. I'm going to tell everything you did, because I'm not taking all the blame for you!"

"And I'm not taking all the blame for you! I wasn't alone in that damn haymow! I wasn't smoking by myself! This time you won't weasel out with your lies and your phony tears! This time you won't get a scolding or a couple of old lady swats from Gramma! You'll get a hard licking from Dad, same as me!" Darrell's rant ceased abruptly.

His eyes reflected resignation ... and abject fear.

My own resignation. My own fear.

"Will it hurt bad?" I managed to ask.

"Terrible ... we're dead meat."

Dread seized my insides like a cold hand reaching from a tomb. I could foresee my fate already: *Abigail Stahl, dead at nine. Smoker, barn burner. Gypsies didn't want her. Uncle cleared of wrongdoing. Too bad, so sad ...*

After an hour or two, when more waiting accomplished nothing and the inevitable had to be faced, we headed back.

It seemed a very long walk.

Meandering curls of smoke still rose from the blackened beams and rafters, but most of what had been the finest barn in Brown County had been violently consumed. The fire truck remained parked in the yard, but the volunteer firemen had been roundly defeated and were in the process of rolling up their hoses.

Neighbors grouped in twos and threes, watching the proceedings. Aunt Annie sat on the back steps, holding her face between her hands. Gramma was trying to console her.

Only the twins looked happy. They looked downright anticipatory as they scampered toward the smoldering barn. Dennis carried two long twigs and Duane a bag of marshmallows.

For a moment I wished I were as brainless as them ... or as innocent.

Darrell and I snuck in the house, climbed the stairs to his room, and closed the door.

Taking no further notice of me, he jammed his hands deep in his pockets and started pacing. "We're dead … we're dead … we're dead," he kept repeating. The litany continued until the screen door opened downstairs and voices began to fill the house.

Darrell emerged from his trance. "Time to pee!"

"But I don't have—"

He jerked me into the hall bathroom and flipped up the toilet seat. "Don't look."

I turned away while Darrell took his piddle.

"Your turn."

"I said I don't—"

"Do it!" His eyes flashed.

Maybe he knew something I didn't, so I forced a tinkle. I was yanking up my panties when we both heard an angry voice downstairs, louder than all the rest.

"Where are those kids?" Uncle Jack was shouting. "Anybody seen those fool kids?"

A moment later, he came bounding up the steps. We heard him go directly to Darrell's room, and then, finding no one, he burst into the bathroom.

I'd never seen my uncle in such a state. Always meticulous, his clothes were torn and filthy. His face, streaked with soot and sweat, accentuated the whites of his eyes. His lips curled tightly over his teeth as he uttered a single word—"You!"

He grabbed us by the scruff of the neck and marched us downstairs. The neighbors assembled in the kitchen parted way for us like the Red Sea had for Moses. Conversation ceased as everyone turned to stare. Out the back door, across the yard, into the woodshed. He flicked on the light and slammed the door behind us with awful finality.

Darrell stood rigid with his back against the wall, his face ashen. I took my place beside him.

Uncle Jack lost no time launching into his tirade. He paced back and forth in front of us, not abjectly as my cousin had done, but purposefully. Watching him made my skin crawl and my stomach shrivel, but he demanded that we look at him every second. I disobeyed once and he yelled, "Abigail, eyes front!" and chucked his riding crop under my trembling chin.

He demanded to know what kind of fool we thought he was, and what made us think we could get away with what we'd done. He said he thought he'd smelled cigarette smoke when he rode past the barn, and he knew we'd swiped his Camels from the nightstand. He suspected we'd done it before, so he'd baited a trap for us, and we'd fallen for it hook, line, and sinker. And we'd been up to no good lately in other areas as well, and he didn't have to be the sharpest pencil in the box to put two and two together.

With every shouted phrase, he rapped the riding crop against the side of his boot. The effect was mesmerizing. A shout, a rap. More pacing. A shout, a rap. When he finally stopped, the silence was palpable. I could actually hear Darrell swallowing.

"Turn around, Abigail. Nose in the corner." Uncle Jack pointed to where he wanted me.

From behind me, the horror began.

"No … no, please, Dad … no," Darrell whimpered. "Oh, God, I'm so sorry … no, not this … don't do this …no, please, don't!"

"Stop sniveling. You deserve this—and more!"

Darrell again begged for leniency. Uncle Jack made no response. Amid the shuffling, I heard the metal buckles of my cousin's overalls scrape the wooden floor. The buckles scraping the floor could only mean—

A soft, whirring sound culminated in a harsh crack as my uncle brought down the hard leather of the crop across *my cousin's bare bottom.*

Darrell shrieked.

I clutched the wall for support and prayed for deliverance. It seemed as though Darrell screamed nearly forever before he was sent, bawling, to his room to rub his rump in private and to contemplate his sins.

Then it was my turn.

"Come here, Abigail." The voice was ominous, lethal.

I couldn't move. I couldn't breathe. When steely fingers clamped around my arm I would've peed on myself, had I any left in me.

I found myself sprawled over a large toolbox near the center of the room, my hands pinned behind my back as I was held in place. My uncle had left my clothing intact, but two layers of thin cloth likely didn't help much.

The first swing of the riding crop seared my bottom. I screamed. Before he could administer the second, I panicked, my terror giving me strength. I squirmed, struggled, and flailed my legs.

"Stop that!" he ordered.

But I wasn't listening. When I doubled up my knees so that my shoes protected my rump, making further punishment impossible, he released me. As I started to slide off the toolbox, my knees straightened as my feet sought the floor. Too late I realized his ruse when his boot clamped across the back of my ankles. Seconds later, I found myself in the same position as before: helpless as a newborn kitten, but not nearly as meek.

I'd never imagined anything could sting as much as that damn riding crop, and I heard myself screaming the same as Darrell had.

Finally my uncle paused for a moment. "Had enough? Have you learned your lesson yet?"

"Let go, damn it!" I screeched.

"You brat! How dare you talk to me like that!" And he took up the crop again.

That time I was beyond feeling. I was beyond everything. All I could hear was screams, as from very far away. When he held off the second time, I couldn't stop screaming. He said something and I couldn't make out the words. I feared he would resume, but instead he held me to my humiliating position until my screams lessened and I started to sob.

"Breathe, Abigail!" I heard him say.

I caught my breath between sobs. I felt numb except for the part that hurt. He released me. I slumped to the floor.

He stalked to the door and opened it. "Get out, Abigail. Get off my farm."

I struggled to my feet and ran. Straight to Gramma's car I ran, throwing myself onto the backseat. She'd been waiting for me.

I bawled all the way home.

And Gramma harangued me in German all the way home.

"Du dummes Kind!" She threatened me with one hand while driving with the other. *"Schlechtes, schlechtes Mädchen!"*

When she was really angry, English failed her. But I understood enough. I was a stupid child, a bad, bad girl.

The moment we got inside the house, she sent me to my room. In blessed privacy, I knelt on my bed, eased down my overalls and panties, and surveyed the damage in my dresser mirror.

It was substantial.

Gramma retired to her bedroom minutes later. The slam of her door was unmistakable. She wanted nothing more to do with me. No one did.

I crept downstairs and took the ice tray out of the freezer compartment. As quietly as possible, I popped the cubes into a basin, pumped water from the cistern, located a clean washrag, and took everything back upstairs.

I washed the tears from my face and blotted my neck and arms. I rested the rag in the icy water while I changed into my nightgown. Then I wrung out the rag and lay on my stomach on the rug next to my bed. I bunched up the nightgown around my waist and placed the cold rag across my bottom to draw the heat from my skin.

Gramma always used an iced rag when I'd bruised myself, and I hoped her technique would likewise alleviate the pain of Uncle Jack's licking. It did … a little.

I dipped and wrung out the rag numerous times that summer night as

I lay on my stomach on the floor of my upstairs bedroom, chastened and miserable.

Would Gramma, or anyone, ever love me again?

Lavender Ink

For the rest of the week I stayed in my room, except for meals and chores. I was beyond embarrassed; I was mortified. Gramma remained unsympathetic. I longed to call Darrell to ask how he was faring, but I would've died if my uncle had answered, so I didn't.

On Sunday, however, my seclusion ended when Gramma hauled me to church. At least I could sit again without wincing. A wave of whispers accompanied my entrance. I dove for the nearest pew and hid my face in the church bulletin.

"There's that Stahl brat," the parishioners were murmuring behind their flowered hankies and leatherette Bibles. "Looks fairly normal, doesn't she? But looks can be deceiving. Even the Good Book tells us so. About time Jack ripped into her, not that it'll do any good. Destruction in a dress; that's what she is. Probably has matches tucked inside her anklets … oh, what hymn did they say?"

Uncle Jack appeared at the last possible moment, herding my cousins down the aisle like sheep. Aunt Annie trailed behind. Darrell made no eye contact although he passed right by me.

Reverend Richter's sermon was on raising children. Spare the rod, spoil the child … no surprise there. Benediction over, I was heading to the car to wait for Gramma to finish chatting when I felt a familiar, heavy hand on my shoulder.

"Abigail," Uncle Jack said, "I want a word with you—in private. Meet me on Wednesday by the rock pile just before supper. And don't call Darrell in the meantime. He's not allowed to talk to you. Understand?"

"Perfectly," I muttered.

Later that afternoon, Gramma asked for my letter to Daddy. I said I didn't have one.

She said to hurry up. I said I wasn't going to hurry up.

She said I wouldn't get my supper if I didn't write my letter. I said I'd starve to death if that's what she wanted.

She got so mad she lapsed into German. I stayed mad in English, informing her that I'd never write to Daddy again because he didn't care about me, nobody cared about me, and I had better things to do.

That comment earned me five whacks with the yardstick. I didn't bother crying. After what Uncle Jack had done to me, her efforts were pathetic and I told her so. She burst into tears, which rattled me, but not enough to apologize for my sass.

I was stomping outside when I heard her ask central to ring up my uncle. I tore back in the kitchen, broke the connection, and announced that I'd changed my mind. She hung up the earpiece with a look of triumph that made me cringe.

I was in an absolutely foul mood when I scribbled:

Dear Daddy,

Darrell and I got bored last week so we smoked some Camels we swiped (I like Lucky Strikes better) up in Uncle Jack's haymow and burned down the whole damn barn. You can get the details from anyone who was there. Gramma says I should make restitution (my new word this week), but since I don't have any money, I guess it's up to you.

Here are my sentences using correctly the vocabulary words from your last letter. You're right, I have been insolent, but I'm no longer being deceitful. I'll tell you everything exactly the way it happens from now on. I think it's you who's being deceitful, with your refusal to tell me anything about Mother.

Hope you're having fun there in Italy, killing Nazis or whatever you do.

Your incendiary (my second new word) daughter, Abby

My father would blow his stack when he read my note, but to try to hide the incident was futile. He'd hear about the fire from Gramma, Uncle Jack, and half the town. But there was nothing he could do about it except dash off a terrible letter that would've frightened me in the past, but the thought of which no longer bothered me.

I felt strange inside, all nasty and rotten. Darrell once compared the feeling to being like pond scum. Pond scum was smelly and ugly, but it always rose to the top.

I'd undoubtedly bottomed out. But my rise was postponed when Gramma forced me to wash the entire week's worth of eggs by myself after supper. She usually helped, although it really was my job, and she'd bring down the radio to pass the time and make popcorn afterward.

This time I was denied both radio and popcorn. A maelstrom of rancorous thoughts swirled through my mind as I sat alone in the dank basement with rags and basins of water, scrubbing hen shit off eggs, drying and packing them into cartons for Ole to sell in town.

Savagely I flung an egg against the cellar wall. It did my heart good to see the shell explode and the yolk ooze down the wall and puddle on the floor. I was tempted to fling every egg, one by one, against the wall. Only the nightmarish recollection of Uncle Jack, wielding his riding crop, stayed my hand.

Monday and Tuesday crawled, but abruptly it was Wednesday. I was queasy with trepidation. I had no idea what my uncle wanted, or why he wouldn't say his piece at church, or over the telephone, or simply shoot over in his gray Ford and have it out.

He might have more in mind than talk. Both my behavior and my attitude since the fire had been less than exemplary. I pulled on four panties under my thickest jeans before heading for the rock pile to meet him.

After a while, when he didn't come, I began to hope he'd forgotten. Then I saw him, astride Banat, nearly a mile away. I took a pee so I'd be ready for anything. As he neared, I saw he was clad entirely in black, the better to intimidate me.

I curled up on my boulder as he dismounted, covered my head with my arms, and made myself small. His boots crunched along the rocks, then stopped.

"It's hard to talk to you if you won't look at me," he said.

I waited.

"And it's doubly hard if you won't respond."

I stayed quiet.

He slapped the riding crop against the side of his boot, hard.

I flinched.

"Oh, so that's it. You're scared, aren't you?"

"Yes … "

"Good. If you're scared, maybe you'll stay out of trouble. Or have you already been up to more mischief?"

How should I answer? Did he already know about my latest antics? Sometimes Gramma told him everything, sometimes nothing. I decided to offer a blanket apology without going into specifics.

"I'm so sorry about everything, Uncle Jack." I looked at him with all the pathos I could muster. "And I'm especially sorry about your barn. I swear to God I didn't mean to burn it flat to the ground."

"I know you didn't, or I wouldn't have anything more to do with you." He sat down across from me. The crop he placed by his side. "But regrets won't build a barn or replace the hay. And hay's scarce because of the drought. I'll probably sell the Angus and start over in the spring."

"Don't do that. Please don't sell the cattle."

He frowned. "Why should you care?"

"I care a lot. If you sell the Angus, I'll never see Copper again."

"Who's Copper?"

"That little red calf that was born last spring. You know, Daisy's calf. She runs up to the fence when she sees me—"

"Don't tell me you've made a pet out of a calf that'll get sent to market, either now or later?"

"Yes, but I'd rather have later. After all, you keep some of your cows for years. And I know Copper will be a good mother someday."

"She's a runt and she's red, Abigail. She's worth nothing to me."

"Well, she's worth something to me," I said, stung by his harsh words. I'd learned only recently that cattle taken away on the truck were destined for the plate and not another pasture.

"So what? Actions have consequences, Abigail. You and Darrell smoked in my haymow and everything went up in flames. The barn's gone: my problem. The hay's gone: my problem. Now the Angus will have to go: still my problem. And Copper will go: your problem. Your pet will leave with the rest and you'll never know where she went or how long she lived."

The tyrant had spoken. Copper would die and I would be the cause of her death. What more could he do to punish me? Make me eat her? I blinked back bitter tears.

He dug out a half pack of Camels, tapped one out, and lit up. I did my best to withstand his scrutiny without withering.

A minute passed.

"Hell, I won't sell all the Angus," he decided. "If I can't find enough hay for all of them, I'll still keep Copper, Midnight, and a few more to keep them company."

"Thank you." I hoped he wouldn't change his mind later. "Copper will make you glad you spared her life. She'll have lots of black calves; you'll see … who's Midnight?"

"She's my pet, the lead cow, the one with the bell. Why do you suppose she's long past her prime and I've never gotten rid of her?"

I dared my first smile in a week. "Oh, I didn't know. I didn't know she even had a name."

"Of course you didn't." His mood darkened again. "I have secrets too."

I wondered whether he was referring to secrets I already knew about or others. I wondered whether he'd truly forgive the trouble I'd caused him. I wondered whether he'd let me smoke as long as I stayed away from hay.

"Promise you won't smoke again," he said.

"I promise."

"Good. Then my other buildings might survive your childhood."

I lowered my eyes. "You must hate me now."

He took a long draw on the cigarette and exhaled. "Hate's a strong word, Abigail. Of course I hate your carelessness and your total lack of judgment.

Who wouldn't? But no, I don't hate you personally. Now, to get to the point for our meeting. It's time you came to live with Annie and me."

The words hit me like a tornado out of a clear sky. I reacted the only way I could: I began crying.

"Guess I don't have to ask what you think of that idea," Uncle Jack said.

I wept with gusto. I wept to change his mind. Tears, snot, drool. Nothing was too extreme. If he didn't reconsider, the Princess Abigail would languish as a hapless prisoner in Tyrant Jack's castle until the Flying Knight, also known as Daddy, came back to rescue her, and that might take years!

If I'd only cried when Gramma whacked me instead of giving her so much lip, if I hadn't smoked and incinerated my uncle's barn, if I'd been more amiable instead of constantly carping and complaining, Gramma would still love me.

"Maybe it was a good thing when Annie and I only had sons." Uncle Jack skewered me with one of his disapproving scowls as he dug a handkerchief from his pocket. "Boys don't bawl as much as girls. You're a regular Niagara Falls."

His comment made me so mad I stopped howling. "Why can't I ... stay with Gramma? Is it too late ... for me to change?" I blew my nose and mopped my eyes.

"What are you talking about?"

"How I've acted lately." I hiccupped. "Gramma's been telling on me, hasn't she? I'll change. I'll be good—"

"Oh, so you *have* been acting up? What now? Did you set fire to the chicken house? Garage? Shed?" His eyes narrowed. "You'd better confess, because I can find out."

"Nothing as bad as that." I hiccupped again. "Just little things ... things I don't even remember. Please let me stay with Gramma. I'll be good. I want her to love me. I don't want her to give me away."

"Oh, so that's what you think? Well, you're wrong. Your moving in with us was my idea, not hers. But she's growing old and you're growing up. You're still good company to her, for the most part, but you've developed quite a mind of your own lately. Your latest shenanigans are especially troubling."

"I said I was sorry."

"But are you truly repentant?"

I detected a slight uncertainty in his voice.

"Like what Reverend Richter preaches?"

"Yes, like that."

"Yes."

"So … if I leave things as they are, you'll behave yourself from now on?"

"I'll never give Gramma any more trouble," I stated.

"And me?"

"You neither. I promise."

"You often promise one thing and do another, Abigail."

"Not this time. This time, I mean it."

"You'd better."

"I do."

"I'll hold you to it."

"I know."

He studied me for a long moment. "Fine, I'll leave things as they are for now. But if circumstances change, or if you misbehave in any way, you'll find yourself under my roof faster than you could ever imagine. Is that clear?"

"Yes." I experienced a momentous wave of relief.

He snuffed out the cigarette. "I should've known you'd react this way."

"I'm sorry. I just thought I'd always live with Gramma until Daddy came back … he is coming back, isn't he?"

"If he's lucky."

"Do you know when?"

"After the war ends."

"I don't understand why he never comes back to see me."

"He did, about five years ago. He stayed nearly a month."

"I can't remember back that far. I think I remember his voice, but I'm not sure … why hasn't he come back since then?"

"He's busy. He has a very important job, over there in Spinazzola. It's a lot of responsibility for one man."

"But Carol Jensen's dad comes back to see her. He's a colonel like Daddy." I meant to sound bitter because I was. "Having a very important job is no excuse."

"No, it's not."

"Do you know why he hasn't come back?"

My uncle paused. "I have an idea."

"What is it?"

"I can't tell you."

"Is it my fault?" I worried. "Is it something about me?"

"Don't be absurd."

"Then why?"

"I said I'm not telling you. I've only a guess and I won't repeat a guess."

"But—"

"No more arguments. Accept your life as it is and stop your digging … oh, don't give me that glum look, Abigail. You think nobody cares, but you're wrong. I'm sorry you have to grow up this way, but it could be worse. You have family who loves you, and I'll always make sure you're cared for. It's my duty."

I already suspected he considered me a duty, but hearing the words hurt. They hurt enough that I got up. "I'm going home," I said.

"Not yet. Sit down."

I sat, hating him.

He reached in his shirt pocket and produced an envelope. "Here's the second reason I wanted you to meet me today … go ahead, take it."

The envelope, with my name printed in lavender ink, glistened white as bone in the late afternoon sun. Hesitantly I took it from his hand and opened it. A locket on a golden chain and a single sheet of stationery fell to my lap.

Curious, I pried open the locket's tiny clasp. Inside were spaces for two photographs. One side was empty. The other was of a young woman with dark hair. Her expressive eyes were framed by daintily arched brows. A corsage graced her shoulder, and her slender neck was encircled by pearls. She looked pensively at the camera.

"Who is she?" I asked.

"Your mother."

I was astounded. "Mother? This is my mother? But you said you didn't have any pictures of her!"

"You misunderstood. You asked whether I had a photograph of her on a horse. I said I didn't, because I don't."

"But where did you get this one?"

"It doesn't matter. Just be happy I had one to share with you."

"I am … oh, I am." I caressed my unexpected treasure. "You don't know how much I've wanted a picture of her."

"Oh, but I do know." He turned away and lit a new cigarette.

I focused on the photograph of the mother I'd never known. I memorized her face—so open, so kind. Her eyes, her mouth, her nose—all similar to mine. Even her hairline had the same cowlick. I seemed to be looking into myself, at who I would become.

Without a picture, I'd had difficulty comprehending Mother's existence. Now she became real to me. Her eyes looked back at mine. Her lips were poised to speak. I felt her presence. She seemed inside me. I shivered.

"Read the letter," he said gently.

I eased open the folded page and read the words printed in lavender ink.

My dearest Abigail,

I have put this in safekeeping for you in case I do not see you again. One does not know what lies in the future, and I wanted to write this letter so I can somehow touch you through my words although I cannot take you in my arms.

If you are reading this, a long time has already passed and I've been gone many years. Be assured that the day you were born was the happiest day of my life. I cared for you when you were little the best as I was able, and I loved you more than life itself. I would've given anything to see you grow into a fine young woman.

Because of cruel circumstance, this has been denied me. But if it be God's grace, I will be watching over you from heaven. Be good, my precious child, and be kind to your father, your grandmother, and to your uncle and aunt.

You have my love, for all eternity.

Your mother, Ellen Elizabeth Coetzee Stahl

I began to cry long before I finished reading, and somehow—I couldn't recollect afterward how it happened—I crept onto Uncle Jack's lap, where I wept into his shirtfront. It was as though the emptiness inside demanded the nearest entity to gather me up, to envelop me, to comfort me. My loathing of him vanished in the face of such need, and the racking void within me necessitated my nearly unbelievable action.

"Are you all right now?" he said, after I quieted.

"Yes," I lied. I had a locket and a letter instead of a mother. I had multiple letters instead of a father. How could he even ask such a question? But there was nothing he, or anyone, could do about it.

So I folded my letter along its old lines, tucked it into the envelope, and stuck it deep in my pocket until I could get home and put it somewhere safe.

I was about to slip the locket over my head when I saw him looking at it like one kid looks at another when he offers a bite of his last piece of candy or half of his last stick of gum, being polite, but hoping the other kid will decline his offer and tell him to keep the whole of it.

I curled the chain around the locket as I held it one last time, and offered it to him.

He shook his head. "No, keep it. It's yours."

"But I want you to keep it safe for me." I pressed the locket into his hand. "I'd probably lose it before I get home. Take it back until I'm older. Just let me see it whenever I want."

He slipped the chain over my head in one deft motion."No, you won't lose it. You'll get it home just fine."

"All right … thank you." I tucked the locket beneath my shirt so it couldn't swing freely.

"One more thing," he said. "You're not to talk about or show that locket to anyone. It must stay a secret between you and me."

"Why?"

"Because knowledge of it would cause problems."

"What problems?"

"That's for me to know … it just would. Trust me."

I had no one to trust but him. "I won't tell anyone."

"Good. But if you break your promise, that locket will be taken from you and your quest will end."

"What's a quest?"

"Don't be coy with me, Abigail. I'm talking about your desire to learn everything about your mother. Keep our secret, and I'll tell you more when the time is right."

"When will the time be right?"

"When I decide it is, and when you're old enough to understand."

"Oh," I said, disappointed. "What about the letter? Can I show that to anyone?"

"You can show it to your grandmother. And if you absolutely must, you can show it to Darrell … yes, you can talk to him again. The two of you can put your heads together and wonder about it day and night, for all I care, but the locket must stay a secret."

I promised again.

He took the riding crop and stood up. "Come on, I'll take you home. It's past supper and your grandmother will be worried."

"You've already missed your supper."

He smiled. "No, I haven't. They wait for me because I'm the boss." He swung me up on Banat before I could protest and mounted himself. "Ready?"

I wrapped my arms around his waist and steeled myself against my fear. "Yes."

Banat took off at a gallop. Her pounding hooves navigated field and gully, ditch and driveway. Too terrified to beg him to slow down, I held on for dear life. He set me down in Gramma's yard and rode off again. I heard him laugh for the sheer joy of riding as he encouraged Banat to run as fast as she wanted. As they skirted the barn, a gust of wind sent his black hat rolling.

"Your hat!" I ran to rescue it from the dust.

By way of a reply, he waved.

I held his hat, warm from the late afternoon sun, warm from him. I watched as horse and rider headed for the straggly line of cottonwoods rimming the slough. I stood there for several minutes after they disappeared, thinking. Then I put the locket in my pocket and went inside the house.

Gramma was sitting at the kitchen table. "I waited supper for you."

"Thank you, Gramma." I saw our plates already served up with second plates inverted over them to keep the food warm. Quickly I took my place.

"What did Jack want with you?" she asked.

"Can I tell you in the morning?" I was unable to speak of it so soon.

She nodded, folded her gnarled hands, and bowed her head. *"Komm Herr Jesus, kehre bei uns ein. Lass diese Geschenke zu unserem … Segen sein."*

I dutifully ran the English version past God: "Come, Lord Jesus, be thou our guest. And let these gifts to us be blest … amen."

Gramma reached across the table and patted my arm. "If you prefer, Abby, you needn't tell me at all. Everyone's entitled to a secret or two."

When I climbed the stairs that night, I took Uncle Jack's black hat along. Sitting cross-legged on my bed, I traced the creases of it with my fingertips and wondered how it would be to have two parents, or even one. Eventually I hung the hat on my bedpost. I would return it in the morning.

Then I copied Mother's letter so I could show Darrell without jeopardizing the safety of the original. The locket I taped to the underside of my bottom dresser drawer, where it would be hidden but accessible.

Forcing my thoughts ahead, I re-read some of Daddy's past letters, seeking clues about him. But he seldom mentioned anything tangible: little about the war, where he lived, what he saw, what he did, and nothing of his heart.

No, my letters were comprised simply of words: words of instruction, words of expectation, words to look up, and words of censure. I had no mother. And, for all practical purposes, I had no father. All I had were words.

Still, I couldn't help speculating. Was Daddy like Uncle Jack? Or was he completely different? I couldn't even visualize him. The only photograph I'd ever seen of him hung above Gramma's bed, taken when he'd first joined the military, at age twenty-six, nearly twenty years ago. Where were his baby pictures, his school pictures? Gramma had owned a camera for decades. So had many of our other relatives. To my knowledge, no one had photographs of either of my parents. It made no sense.

But my uncle *had* produced a photograph of Mother after he'd pretended ignorance the night we sat together on the woodpile. His insistence on secrecy suddenly bothered me. Who would take my locket if I blabbed? Was possession of the locket inherently dangerous?

Uncle Jack knew all the answers. I was certain of it.

But he wasn't talking … yet.

Sugar

UNCLE JACK HAD guessed correctly. I was on a quest. A snippet of information here, a bit there, another letter, a second photograph, a misspoken word, and one day the pieces of the puzzle would drift together and I'd be able to color in all the pages of my life.

Gramma showed the merest hint of surprise as she read my mother's letter the next morning.

"So, what do you think?" I asked.

"I never knew this existed … how did Jack come by it again?"

"He didn't say. He had it and he gave it to me, that's all."

Gramma's wrinkles knitted together in a frown. "Did he say why?"

"No. Why would Mother write me a letter like this?"

"I have no idea."

"Maybe she thought something bad would happen to her," I wondered aloud. "Did something bad happen right after she wrote it?"

"I wouldn't know because I don't know when she wrote it." Gramma took a cake pan out of the cupboard and rifled through a drawer.

"Maybe she died soon afterward. Was she sick?"

"Not that I knew."

"Or did she die in an accident?"

"So many questions for so early in the morning!" Gramma said. "I'm looking for my cake recipes and you're not exactly helping, are you?"

"No." I didn't feel like helping either, if she wouldn't divulge anything.

"Oh, here they are, under the potholders … would you like carrot cake or white?"

"Carrot." Vegetables in desserts were to my liking.

"Get the mixer out for me, would you?"

I hoisted the heavy mixer onto the counter. "Maybe you don't know how she died, Gramma, but you must know something. How come nobody wants to tell me anything?"

"Now where's that egg separator hiding? I saw it just yesterday." She fumbled amid the utensils in the exact drawer the egg separator had been in since I could remember.

"The damn thing's right here, Gramma!" I grabbed it and slapped it on the counter.

Her eyes narrowed behind her bifocals as she shook a forefinger at me.

"So help me, Abby, how many times have I told you not to swear? Must I get Jack involved? He'd put an end to your dirty mouth, once and for all!"

"No, don't tell him," I said, distraught at my blunder. "I'm sorry. I won't do it again." One night of lying on my stomach with a cold rag across my rump was enough!

She sighed and began cracking eggs for the cake. I repeated how sorry I was, as though repetition equaled sincerity. I found the rest of the ingredients without her asking. I washed the mixing bowls and measuring cups without being told. I waited until she seemed receptive to further questioning.

"You were going to tell me about Mother."

"I don't know if I should."

"Why not? What's the harm?"

"No harm, I suppose, but I never knew her very well."

"Then tell me what you do know ... please, Gramma?"

"I guess that would be allowed. Let me think ... well, I remember she stayed with me for several months when your father was gone that time. She was pleasant but quiet, at least around me. She kept mostly to herself, upstairs in the room you have now. She wrote letters and she read ... oh, where'd I put the spatula? The one with the green handle."

I found it and urged her to continue.

"She went to church, always dressed to the nines. She gardened, but only in the mornings. Even then, she'd wear a hat to keep the sun off her face. Imagine that, living on a farm and concerned with such niceties, *Eitle Frau!*" Gramma chuckled.

Vain woman? I'd understood the words. Apparently Gramma hadn't liked my mother ... interesting. "So what else did Mother like to do?" I asked.

"Not much. Some afternoons she'd go riding. Evenings she'd work on her cross-stitch, but she never finished any. Such a waste of time and thread ... oh, I just remembered. Annie called this morning. She's low on eggs again. Take three dozen and make sure they're clean."

My errand was my dismissal. The subject was closed.

Darrell was idling in the tire swing when I trudged up Uncle Jack's drive. He promptly informed me of the terrible fight his parents had had during the night. Only rarely did they disagree, as his mom usually agreed to whatever his dad wanted. Even if he did rile her Irish temper, she'd simply throw her purse at him or put her hands on her hips and yell, "Get over it, Jack!" She'd look so comical because she was so petite that she could generally start him laughing.

But last night had been no laughing matter. At first, Darrell thought the fight was over the construction of the new barn, but the arrangements were already made, and his mom was more than capable of overseeing things while his dad was gone, and—

"Gone?" I said. "Where's he going?"

"Africa. I didn't know myself until this morning. He's packing right now … hey, where're you going?"

"To talk to him!" I hollered over my shoulder as I ran for the house.

Aunt Annie stood in the kitchen, mixing batter in a large bowl. I set her eggs on the counter. She acknowledged me with a nod. She appeared to have been crying.

I slipped upstairs. The door to the main bedroom was ajar. Uncle Jack was stuffing clothes into a canvas bag. I tapped on the door. "Can I come in?"

He glanced up. "No."

When he turned to get something out of the dresser, I eased inside.

He whirled around at the click of the latch. "I told you no. Don't you ever listen? Don't you ever learn? Now beat it before I beat you!"

Yesterday those words would've sent me fleeing, but today another fear was stronger than my fear of crossing him. "Uncle Jack, please, I have to talk to you—"

"I don't want to talk." He jammed a shirt in his bag. "I've said everything I'm going to say, and you'd damn well better—"

"Are you coming back?"

There must have been an expression on my face that gave him pause. "What kind of a question is that?" he said.

"You know what I mean. Daddy left, and I don't know if he's coming back. Mother left, and she never came back."

"Oh, so you think I'll pull another vanishing act? I'm amazed you care, Abigail. For as hard as I've been on you, I'd think you'd want me gone and gone for good."

"No, I'd rather you stayed home." I knew Gramma relied on him. Aunt Annie relied on him. Even I relied on him, when no one else knew what to do. He held things together, kept things running. In his absence, everything would fall apart, go amok.

"Well, that's a surprise … to answer your question; yes, I plan to return. As to when, I haven't the vaguest idea. When the situation is straightened out, I suppose."

My antennae shot up like a bug's. "What situation? I thought you go hunting in Africa."

"Not this time. Business calls me away, urgent business."

"What business?"

"My business, little girl, not yours."

"Are you sure you didn't give me Mother's letter and locket in case you don't come back?"

"I gave them to you because I thought you should have them. Nothing more, nothing less."

Another worry occurred to me. "But how can you go with the war going on?"

"It's no longer active in that part of the world. Besides, I have my ways. I always have my ways. Now leave me alone. I need to finish here and I can't think with your yapping."

I tried a different tack. "Then take me with you. I'd love to go to Africa."

He shook his head. "Don't be ridiculous."

"Please?"

"No. You're staying home where you belong."

"Well, if I can't go this time, can I go next time?"

He stuck a final shirt in the bag and closed it. "Tell you what. I'll take you when you're old enough to hunt. I'll take you when you're old enough to engage in a genuine conversation with me instead of your childish nagging. Is that good enough for you?"

"Yes," I said. "Just promise you're coming back this time. You always make me promise."

"Fine, I promise. I'll return as long as the mambas don't get me."

"What's that?"

"Snakes. Or I don't fall out of the mokoro—"

"What's a mokoro?"

"A dugout canoe, young lady of a thousand questions; or drown in the swamps or get eaten by crocodiles. What do you think it's like going to Africa? Do you think I hop a train in one continent and hop off again in the next? I get to where I'm going by any means possible and nothing's too unusual or too dangerous to accomplish that." He looked at me wearily. "Wipe that concern off your face, Abigail. I feel like I'm a dead man already."

I started sniffling. "But so many bad things could happen to you over there, Uncle Jack. Africa's a million miles away, and I'm so scared—"

"Stop being scared. You'll never amount to anything if you're always scared and you're always crying. But if it makes you feel better, I won't be near any mambas, and I won't be in a mokoro. I'll be in whatever has four wheels and enough petrol to get me where I need to go. I won't even be in a jungle. I'll be in the heart of civilization, or what passes for civilization." He glanced at his watch. "And I'm about to miss my train. If you won't leave my bedroom, little girl, then I will." He shoved his documents in his pocket, grabbed his bags, and went downstairs.

I followed helplessly. My uncle was intent on his own course. He would go and never be heard from again. I paused by the grandfather clock and watched as he set down his luggage behind my aunt, who was washing dishes.

"Annie, I'm leaving now," he said. "If you refuse to come along, you'll have to hitch a ride to town and fetch the car later."

She ignored him.

"All right … so be it."

She turned, her green eyes blazing. "Damn you, Jack Stahl, and damn your sugar! Damn you both to hell!"

He took a step backward like he'd been hit. Then he strode from the house with his bags. I heard the car door slam, the engine start, and with a roar he tore down the drive.

Aunt Annie, oblivious to my presence, ran after him. "Don't go, Jack! Don't leave me like this! I didn't mean it! I love you! Damn it all, I'll always love you!" But her pleas were met by a cloud of billowing dust arising from the parched driveway. She collapsed in one of the rockers on the porch and shook with sobs.

I joined Darrell in the tire swing. For a long time, we didn't say anything.

Darrell spoke first. "She never swears. I can't believe she said 'damn.'"

"It gets worse." I repeated what I'd heard in the kitchen.

"Sugar?" Darrell said. "Mom said that? That's the strangest thing. Did she damn everything else rationed too?"

"No, just sugar."

"That's so weird. And damning somebody to hell is serious. It's not like saying 'damn lousy weather.'" Darrell's bottom lip trembled. "I don't think Dad's ever coming back."

"He promised me he would."

"Then he told you what you wanted to hear. Even Mom thinks he's gone for good."

"I hope you're wrong." I looked down, my own lip trembling.

"There's another reason I think Dad's not coming back. He never said good-bye. He never leaves, even for a day, without saying good-bye and telling me and the twins to be good. Today he didn't say a word. He got one of those mysterious packages from Africa a few weeks ago too. He seemed really upset afterward."

"He said he had business in Africa," I said. "Some situation needed his attention. Maybe that's what upset him."

"Business?" Darrell slid out of the tire swing. "What business could he possibly have in Africa in the middle of a war, unless—"

"Unless what?"

"Unless it has something to do with—with—"

"With what?"

"I'm not sure, but I think it's a mystery for Snoop and Company!" Darrell slipped into his alter persona. "Remember those letters that talked about meeting him in Africa—"

"But they were old letters—"

"We don't know how old, Watson. And the picture of the lady—"

"We couldn't see her face."

"I'm not talking about *who* she is. I'm talking about maybe she's still *there,* waiting for him. Maybe he's going to her and he's never coming back. Or maybe he'll break off with her and then he will be back, and everything will be fine again."

"That makes no sense, Sherlock," I argued. "Your mom damned the sugar. What's sugar have to do with some lady?"

"Because that's her nickname!" Darrell crowed. "Some men call their wives or lady friends 'Honey' or 'Cookie.' Why not 'Sugar'?"

I wouldn't have made the leap from a baking ingredient to a lady in a thousand years, but somehow it made sense. Then I realized I hadn't told Darrell about my peculiar meeting with his dad the previous evening. I kept mum about the locket, but I spilled the rest and produced the copy of Mother's letter.

"That's it!" Darrell's eyes shone with excitement. "That's the connection we've been missing!"

"What connection? You're talking in riddles."

"Think about it, Watson. Dad gives you a letter nobody knows he has. Supposedly it's from your mom, to be given to you years after her supposed death. He hands you the letter one day and tramps off to Africa the next. Coincidence? I don't think so!"

"I still don't understand."

"Think about it. What if that letter was written so you'd never come looking for her? She could be alive right now! Maybe she's been living in Africa all these years. Maybe she ran away because your dad was mean to her. Maybe she's been writing my dad—and in the last letter, she said she was tired of waiting for him. So now he's gone to join her. Maybe Mom knows what's been going on, and that's why they were fighting all night—"

"That's too many 'maybes,'" I scoffed. "My mother is dead."

"But there's no proof, is there? Nobody seems to know how she died, or at least they're not saying. She's not in the cemetery, is she? Maybe the whole thing's made up so nobody would come looking for her."

"You've lost your mind," I said, my own mind reeling.

"Oh, yeah? So why aren't there photographs of her? Did she destroy them before she ran off so it'd be harder for the cops to find her? Or did your dad burn them because he was so mad she ran off?"

My hands clenched. "Shut up, Darrell! My mother would never run off and let me grow up without her. She said so, in her letter. Say you're sorry before I punch your face in."

Darrell threw up an arm in response to my threat. "Sorry … you're right. I shouldn't have dragged your dead mom into this."

"No, you shouldn't have." I lowered my fists and took a deep breath. "I bet there's no lady at all. I bet your dad really has business in Africa. Nobody ever tells us anything."

Darrell nodded. "That's for sure. We're always the last to know … not having him around for a while will be nice, though. No more lickings, chore lists, or jumping every time he hollers. Mom doesn't get as excited about every damn thing like he does."

"I hope he comes back," I found myself saying.

My cousin's eyes shifted toward my aunt, still in her rocker, still weeping. "I hope he does too … oh God, I hope he does too."

The way things had turned out, I was glad I'd forgotten to return Uncle Jack's black hat. At least it stayed where I put it, and it didn't leave me. It would hang on my bedpost until he came back … if he came back.

Autumn 1944

Billy Hartmann

Snoop and Company had no opportunity to pursue either *The Case of the Missing Mother* or *The Mysterious Trip to Africa* because the start of school interfered with further sleuthing. Although it was inevitable I'd spend nine months enduring what I already knew, I hadn't done a thing to prepare.

I was surprised, therefore, when Gramma bustled into my room carrying a large sack. Inside I found blouses, sweaters, skirts, jumpers, outerwear, and shiny leather shoes. A second, smaller sack held school supplies for the entire year. I looked to her for an explanation.

"Jack thought it was high time you had store-bought clothes so you'd be up with the town kids," she said. "While you were visiting Ruth the other day, Annie and I went shopping with the money he left us. Your cousins got new clothes too."

"Oh," I said. Anything Gramma had sewn in the past had been adequate.

"You could be more enthusiastic," she added. "It's nice of Jack to think of you with all the problems he's had lately in Africa."

My ears perked, but she didn't let slip another syllable about Africa or my uncle's problems. Instead she turned the conversation to how I'd destroyed his barn, causing him no end of trouble and expense.

"I told him I was sorry, Gramma," I said for the twentieth time.

"Sorry is as sorry does. You say one thing and do another." Her tone softened. "Well, what would you like to wear for your first day of school? I'll iron it up."

I gave her something off the top of the pile to get rid of her. Then I wondered why Uncle Jack had to provide for my school needs this year. Daddy always sent extra money in August for that purpose. Had he forgotten me? Or disowned me? I calculated the days since I'd mailed my snotty letter. His reply was long overdue. And Gramma hadn't made me write him since!

I intended to dash off an apology, but I ran out of time. I took an extra bath, although I'd had my weekly just two nights ago, and Gramma again washed my hair. While it dried, we enjoyed caramel popcorn and apple juice on the porch and watched the sun set.

The wind picked up and gradually turned to the northwest. Gramma said summer was over. The weather always changed the first weekend of September; a person could actually smell the difference in the air.

That night, as she tucked me in bed and kissed my forehead, she said it was sad that my father was missing yet another milestone in my life.

By choice, I thought, and reached for my panda.

A new teacher had moved to town for my fifth-grade year. She introduced herself and printed her full name on the blackboard so we kids could memorize the spelling.

But Miss Frieda Fuhrman was hardly new. She looked as old as the hills and as wrinkled as a raisin. She had bluish gray hair that frizzled on the sides, steel-rimmed glasses that kept sliding down her nose, and a no-nonsense black dress long out of style.

She said she'd been teaching fifth grade for nearly forty years and had seen everything kids like us could do. She'd lost both her parents this past year and had moved to our little town to live in the house she'd inherited.

Billy Hartmann, champion wiseass of our class, piped up and said that losing one parent was understandable, as he lost things constantly, but losing both parents in a single year seemed downright careless.

Titters rippled through our classroom. Our third-grade teacher, a novice, had been reduced to tears by Billy Hartmann on the first day of class two years ago. Our fourth-grade teacher, a battle-hardened veteran of primary education, had had her nerves rattled by him as well. Control of our class for the entire year depended on cowing Billy Hartmann.

Miss Fuhrman pushed up her glasses and eyed Billy. "Come here, young man."

He strolled to the front of the classroom as a malicious smirk spread across his ruddy face.

Miss Fuhrman's eyes went cold as granite in winter. She looked him over from head to toe, stepped back, and scrawled a tight circle on the blackboard with chalk.

"Mr. Hartmann," she said, "you will press your nose within this circle. You will stand here for half an hour. If I hear more lip out of you today, tomorrow, or the remainder of the year, you will be further humiliated in more degrading ways than you ever thought possible."

We kids collectively sucked in our breaths, awaiting his reaction.

Billy's little pig eyes narrowed. He swallowed hard. He clenched and unclenched his fists. He took a hesitant step toward the blackboard, then another. When his nose was firmly within the prescribed circle, our class began to breathe again. The impending crisis had been efficiently dispelled; Miss Fuhrman was truly in charge.

I was particularly relieved. I hated Billy Hartmann. He'd started taunting me about my lack of parents last year. Billy's folks were nothing to brag about, Gramma said, so I assumed he'd looked around until he found someone who had none at all.

After his morning run-in with Miss Fuhrman, I knew he'd look for trouble in the afternoon, and I intended to stay well out of his way. But my good intentions were not enough. I'd no sooner finished the chicken sandwich, apple, and cookies Gramma had packed in my new lunchbox, washed down by nearly cold milk from my new thermos, when Billy Hartmann zeroed in on me like a fly to a cow patty. Ruth and Karen, my so-called friends, deserted me in an instant.

"Everybody seems to be leaving." Billy's mouth curled downward.

"I'm leaving too." I reached for my lunchbox.

He snatched it before I could and held it aloft. "Hey, what's this? A brand-new lunchbox?"

I tried to remain calm. "Give it back."

"Maybe I will and maybe I won't. Would your granny get mad if you got it all beat up the first day of school?"

"No."

"Bullshit. Grannies hate things getting busted up. So how come you're still stuck with the old bag anyway? How come your hero daddy didn't come back last summer like you said?"

"He's busy. There's a war going on, if you don't know."

"Oh, I know … I know lots of things."

I got to my feet. "I'm sure you do. Now give me that. I have to go in."

He grinned and held my lunchbox behind him. When I tried to grab it, he said something that drained the blood from my face.

"That's not true!" I hissed. "You take that back!"

"I'd take it back if it weren't true, but it is."

"Is not! You're lying!"

"Are you calling me a liar?"

"Yeah, because you are. You lie about everything and you're lying about this!"

"No, I'm not. It's true. It's really true and everybody knows it, except you."

"I hate you, Billy!" Adrenaline pumped words into my mouth faster than was prudent. "You say things like that because your dad's a damn drunk and he beats on your mom and he ought to beat more on you—"

I never saw his fist coming. My mouth exploded as a spurt of hot blood shot past my lips. I reacted the only way I could: I jumped him.

In a heartbeat, we were down on the grass, punching, rolling, and screaming. When his hand flicked past my mouth, I latched onto one of his grimy fingers and bit down hard. He yelled and slammed me alongside the head with his free hand and I lost my grip. I tried to scramble free, but he caught me so hard in the stomach I nearly lost my breath. Then he pinned me between his knees and pummeled me, and all I could do was shriek.

Darrell ran to my rescue and yanked him off. Billy let fly a string of cuss words. The two of them went down in a clench, punching and swearing. They were pulled apart, with difficulty, by Mr. Ennis and Mr. Anderson, teachers from the adjoining high school, who together patrolled our playground for an occasion such as this.

Miss Fuhrman arrived in time to help me to my feet. "Are you all right, dear?" She wiped my sticky hair from my face and slid a comforting arm around me.

I spat a glob of blood on the ground. "I think so."

"Oh, what has that horrible boy done to you? Here, hold my hanky over your mouth. Are your teeth intact? Is anything broken?"

I shook my head, aware of spectators standing in a loose circle around us, staring as though we were freaks in a sideshow. Fights were rare at our school, as the participants were automatically hauled to the principal's office, and no one wanted that.

Mr. Anderson told everyone to scat. The show was over. He took Billy and Darrell by the arm and ordered me to follow him. He was personally escorting the three of us to Mr. Kessler's office.

Mr. Kessler was the bane of any miscreant. I'd heard all the rumors and I believed every one. His eyes could drill through a kid's head and read mischievous notions as clearly as though they were printed on a blackboard. His vise-like fingers gravitated spontaneously toward the necks of troublemakers. He kept a Board of Education in his desk drawer that exactly covered the contours of a kid's bottom. And if he were caught in a disciplinary dilemma outside of his office, he wore a snappy leather belt that slipped off as easily as snot to a sleeve. Mr. Kessler was the underlying reason Billy Hartmann had pressed his nose inside Miss Fuhrman's chalk circle for a half hour that morning.

Mr. Anderson conferred briefly with Mr. Kessler as we waited in the outer office.

"I'll get you both for this," Billy snarled.

"Touch Abby and I'll bust your chops," Darrell said. "You don't scare me worth shit."

"Quiet, Darrell, somebody will hear!" I gave my lip a final dab with Miss Fuhrman's hanky. The split felt like a chasm beneath my tongue.

Mr. Anderson returned, wedged himself between Darrell and Billy, and ordered me into the inner sanctum.

My heart hammered a staccato beat as I closed the door behind me. Mr. Kessler hunkered in his swivel chair like a gigantic bear about to spring. His eyes appeared abnormally large behind his thick glasses. He tapped on the surface of his desk with a beefy forefinger. I looked furtively for the Board of Education, but did not see it.

"Sit down, Abigail." Mr. Kessler motioned to the chair in front of his desk. "Are you looking for something?"

"No, sir." I assumed my seat for the inquisition and swung my eyes forward. Too unnerved to look directly at him, I fixed my gaze on a photograph on the wall that I assumed was of his wife and children.

"So, are you all right?" he asked.

"Um ... yes, sir."

"Nothing broken, nothing loose?"

"Not that I can tell."

"Good. But stop at Mrs. Benson's office after you leave, just to be sure. That lip looks like it could use some mending."

I nodded.

He shifted his weight. "Now, young lady, tell me what that fight was all about."

I shook my head.

His finger stopped its idle tapping. "Let me rephrase the question, in case you didn't understand. What started that fight out there?"

My eyes filled. The photograph shimmered. "I can't tell you."

"You mean you won't."

My voice broke. "No. I'm truly sorry, sir, but I just can't."

The chair creaked as the bear leaned back. He pressed his fingertips together. I watched the fingers moving in and out, a mirror image. It reminded me of the child's rhyme: *See the church, see the steeple, open the door, see all the people.* I stifled an insane urge to giggle.

"You're aware that I can make your visit with me this afternoon quite unpleasant, aren't you?" He leaned forward and stared at me.

I nodded in terror.

"Well, then?"

"I can't. It's too awful."

"What's too awful?"

"I'm sorry, sir. I just can't say."

"Did Billy threaten you in some way?"

"No, sir."

"Tell me what then, so I can fix it."

"I can't," I whispered.

"I'm not asking you again, Abigail."

I remained silent.

Abruptly the bear opened the center drawer of his desk. I shut my eyes and clutched the arms of my chair. No one, except Uncle Jack that one time, had ever seriously laid into me, and here I was about to get paddled at school!

"What's wrong with you? Open your eyes."

The words of the bear cut through the darkness. Fearfully I opened my eyes. He'd taken a pen from the drawer and was writing something.

"Give this to my secretary on your way out," he said. "And see the nurse before you go back to class."

I took the note and fled. Twenty yards down the hall, in another room, I stopped to allow Mrs. Benson to wash my face and apply iodine to my lip, which started to throb dreadfully during the process. She clucked sympathetically as she applied cold compresses to my remaining facial injuries: three large purplish bruises and a welt on my chin.

I examined my face in her mirror when she finished. Considering I'd been beaten by a bully who outweighed me by twenty pounds, I felt I was in reasonable shape.

As I walked past the office on the way back to my classroom, I heard Billy Hartmann getting it. The definite whacks of the paddle and Billy's squawks could be plainly heard through two closed doors.

Despite my split lip, I smiled grimly. *He deserved every bit of it,* I thought, *for saying that my father had killed my mother.*

June 17, 1935

I FOUND MYSELF quite the celebrity at school in the following days. That I'd attacked the most hated bully of our class, and survived, made me the focus of much discussion and downright awe. Ruth and Karen offered their apologies for deserting me. I remained aloof. Darrell hovered protectively. Mr. Kessler made random visits to the school yard, ostensibly to smoke. Billy Hartmann stayed a far distance, glowering.

I fared less well at home. Gramma demanded to know what instigated my foolhardy confrontation with Billy. I refused to tell her. She called Mr. Kessler, from whom she learned nothing. She gave me a final chance to confess. When I yelled that our whole family was one big fat secret and why should I be the only one expected to spill the truth, she sent me to bed without supper. At midnight, I raided the refrigerator. She found out in the morning, but she let it go.

While the days passed tolerably, the nights were unrelenting agony. Alone in the darkness, with nothing to distract me and hold back my fears, I suffered. The murky recesses of my mind screamed for an explanation, and I had none.

How could Billy Hartmann have said such a thing? It had to be a lie! The handsome soldier in the portrait above Gramma's bed simply couldn't have killed his own wife, my own sainted mother! But Billy had heard the lie from someone. Such hateful words did not appear in the mouth of a ten-year-old out of a void.

Or was it the truth? Was I the only one who didn't know? The photograph of the man aiming his gun toward Uncle Jack and his lady companion took on new significance. Was she my mother? And the tall man in the distance my father?

On Sunday afternoon, I finally caught Darrell alone. As we sat together in his tire swing, I revealed Billy's accusation, along with my own suspicions.

He said we needed to check into it because rumor is usually based on fact. Going back to the time of my mother's death might yield some clues. Since I hadn't found out much, his own brilliant intervention was sorely needed: Snoop was on the job.

"Thanks, but I wish you'd stop talking like my life is a game," I said. "This is my real mother and my real father. You're not Sherlock and I'm not Watson, and we should stop pretending."

"But if you don't pretend, how can you avoid being hurt?" Darrell said.

"I guess you're right."

"Of course I'm right. I didn't tell you before, but I've been snooping ever since Dad left, trying to find those love letters."

"And have you?"

"No, but I found a key that was really well hidden. I tried nearly every lock in the house before I figured out it fits the cedar chest. I didn't open it yet because I was waiting for you. Mom's making supper and the brats are at the Werners, so right now's a good time."

I slid out of the swing. "Well, let's go."

We slipped upstairs undetected. Darrell took the key from my uncle's dresser in the main bedroom and opened the cedar chest.

"Phew, smells like old people." Darrell wrinkled his nose as the stale aroma of antiquity wafted upward. "Come on, help me look."

I knelt by the chest and helped him rummage through its contents. Photographs, many of people unknown to us, were piled on one side. Marriage and birth certificates, diplomas, and miscellaneous documents were strewn on the other. Nothing seemed to pertain to either of my parents.

"Here's the prize, I bet!" Darrell produced a worn Bible from the bottom of the chest.

"What good is that?" I scorned. "It's in German."

"For being my cousin, you're sure stupid." He flipped through the pages. "See?"

On a memorial page, decorated with flowers and cherubs, I saw Mother's full name and the date of her death: June 17, 1935.

"Then she really is dead," I said.

"Don't give up hope yet, Abby. Writing doesn't make it so. It could be part of the cover-up." He returned the contents to the cedar chest and the key to the dresser.

I was in no mood to argue. "Okay, so now what?"

My cousin smiled confidently. "So now we'll look for an obituary. No telling what we'll find in the newspaper office. Snoop and Company is poised to crack the case."

I'd never thought of doing that. I was beginning to respect Darrell.

The next Saturday, as we approached *The Weekly Times* office while Gramma and Aunt Annie were shopping, my palms began sweating and I felt dizzy.

"What's wrong?" Darrell asked, noticing. "Are you sick?"

"No, but I'm nervous."

"About what?" Darrell frowned. "Get hold of yourself. Remember, we're doing a project about stuff that happened on June seventeenth here in our town. Mr. Post hates kids. He won't want us digging around, so I'll have to convince him. You better not barf or fall over during my spiel."

"I won't." I clutched our Big Chief tablets and newly sharpened pencils we'd brought to add credence to our story.

Mr. Post reacted with annoyance when we interrupted him setting type. Darrell said his piece and promised to put everything back, nice and neat.

"You better, because I know your folks," Mr. Post growled.

"We know … thank you, sir."

Darrell hustled me down the basement steps before the editor changed his mind. My apprehension rapidly gave way to anticipation. Looking up, I saw the back editions of the newspapers were stored in boxes stacked on wooden shelves. Paper labels, yellowed from age, marked the contents. Recent years were pristine, but beyond a decade or so, the boxes were falling apart.

"Just look at this stuff," I marveled. "Forty, fifty years of old papers. Why do they keep them? What good are they to anybody?"

"So people with questions can find answers, you dumb bunny. Good thing you have me, or you'd never figure anything out." Darrell located the appropriate box and opened the lid. Dust motes whirled in the stale air. He sneezed and wiped his nose on his sleeve. "God, the dust down here is giving me fits! Here's June. Look through this one while I look in the next one. The obits are on page two."

I looked and found nothing. Neither did he. We took another from the box, then another. In the July twentieth issue I found it. Reading aloud, I pronounced the unfamiliar words as best I could:

Mrs. Ellen Coetzee Stahl, age 26, died June 17, 1935, in Kenya. Graveside services were held with internment in the Coetzee family cemetery. Pallbearers were Mr. Jackson Stahl; assisted by Kaninu, Wainaina, Kinanjui, Farah, and Knuth, all laborers on the farm.

Ellen was born April 8, 1909 in Kenya. Immigrating with her parents, Johann and Mary Coetzee, to this country in 1913, she lived in New York City until coming to Minnesota in 1919. She was united in marriage to Mr. James Stahl, formerly of Adrian Township, on September 2, 1929. She accompanied her husband as he pursued a career in the military, living in various states. She enjoyed reading and traveling.

She is survived by her husband, James, and a daughter, Abigail. She was preceded in death by her parents in the epidemic of 1918, a brother in infancy, and by her adoptive parents, Charles and Tillie Rausch of New Ulm.

So young, she now resides with the angels.

My throat tightened. Mother's presence pressed upon me more menacingly than when I'd been given her letter and locket. I shuddered. "Darrell, I have to get out of here—now!"

"It's all right, Abby." He steadied my shoulders. "School projects never get anyone worked up. Don't give us away."

I took a deep breath. "I won't … I'm okay."

"Good." He sliced the obituary from the page with his pocket knife.

"You shouldn't be doing that, should you?"

"How else can we study it? I can't remember all those dates and names from just one reading."

"Neither can I," I murmured. "Africa … Mother died in Africa."

"If she died at all."

After church the next day, Darrell studied the copy I'd made as we sat in the shade of the elm nearest the parking lot while we waited for Gramma and Aunt Annie to finish chatting.

"Dad was a pallbearer at your mom's funeral, so he was already in Africa when she died," Darrell said. "Nobody travels clear across the world to attend a burial."

"So?" I said.

"So he must know what happened."

"He said he didn't. Her death was subject to interpretation, whatever that means."

"It means everybody has their own opinion." Darrell looked thoughtful. "But I'd think Dad would know what happened, since he was there."

"Maybe he didn't see it. He told me to ask Daddy, so Daddy must know … your dad wouldn't lie to me, would he?"

"I don't know, but it still doesn't make sense. Dad must have a good idea of what happened. Deaths don't get covered up. An investigation would show the facts. Why all the secrecy? Unless Dad's hiding something … or covering up for somebody."

I flared at the insinuation. "Are you saying Daddy's responsible, that what Billy Hartmann said—"

"No, I'm just trying to make sense of it. I didn't tell you before, but I hadn't really expected to find an obituary. I'd think printing one would lead to more questions rather than fewer, unless—"

"Unless what?"

"Unless it was printed so folks would believe your mom died so nobody would ever come looking for her."

I rolled my eyes. "You're back to that again!"

"Well, I'm not giving up the idea. As head of Snoop and Company,

Sherlock must explore all possibilities … and I just thought of some other things too."

"Like what?"

"All the other people mentioned at the funeral were natives who worked on the farm. What farm? The Coetzee farm? What happened to the other Coetzees? None of them are mentioned. And if there was a Coetzee farm, was it small or big? Maybe the Coetzees are rich. It says she was buried in the family cemetery. Nobody here gets buried in a family cemetery anymore unless they're rich. And how did your mom find her relatives in Africa after being in this country so long? We're missing a link, Watson, and I bet it has something to do with Dad going back to Africa this time."

That night my mother appeared in my room. I saw her clearly, dressed in a shimmering gown, her dark hair drawn up in a twist, her throat encircled by pearls. I smelled her perfume and felt the drift of her diaphanous sleeve upon my cheek as she floated ethereally past my bed. She opened my window without touching it and peered into the darkness. She stood there so long I was able to rouse myself and speak to her.

"Who are you looking for?" I heard my voice, but it came from somewhere else, somewhere very far away.

Without turning, she raised her arms in supplication. "Your father," she said.

Birthday Girl

I KEPT MOTHER'S visit secret. Had I told, Darrell would've ridiculed me and Gramma, being of the opinion that nocturnal visitations were the devil's doing, would've hauled me to Reverend Richter, who scared me as much as did Mr. Kessler. I anticipated Mother's return for several weeks, but when she didn't come, the events of ordinary life took precedent.

Uncle Jack's barn got erected by a crew of Mennonites from Iowa, the neighbors sold Aunt Annie enough hay for the livestock to survive the winter, and Copper matured into a nice red heifer that Bob the bull would notice in the appropriate season.

The rest of September and most of October passed swiftly. *The Case of the Missing Mother* went dormant. Darrell said we weren't giving up solving the mystery; we were simply resting.

That was a poor choice of words, I said, because rest was in short supply around Gramma. Each morning, I had to tidy my bedroom, dump my wash water, and empty my chamber pot. After school, I had to feed Rover and the cats, haul the slop jar to the pigs, burn the trash, and dump whatever remained on the junk heap. After supper, I cleared the table and washed the dishes. On weekends, I helped Gramma mop, vacuum, and dust. In the time remaining, I washed the eggs and ironed.

Darrell was kept as busy as me, although Charlie worked far harder for Aunt Annie than he'd ever worked for Uncle Jack. Either he felt sorry for her or he just liked her better than he did my uncle. After all, who didn't?

Not a peep had been heard from my uncle in over two months. It seemed as though the Dark Continent had opened its carnivorous jaws and swallowed the man whole.

One afternoon in late October, while practicing with our BB guns during a rare respite from our chores, Darrell and I decided to do what Uncle Jack did each autumn: pheasant hunt. When we presented our idea to Aunt Annie, her eyes nearly dropped from her head.

"Why, you're only nine and ten," she said. "You'll shoot your heads off!"

"I'm almost ten," I reminded her. "I won a chalk horse at the shooting gallery when I was only eight."

"And I'm nearly a year older than Abby," Darrell said. "Davy Crockett hunted bears when he was my age."

The chalk horse was a fact, but I wasn't certain about Davy Crockett.

Aunt Annie held fast for as long as she could, but eventually she caved. "All right, fine! Darrell, get your .22 and the extra one for Abby, and I'll see what you can do."

While she sat in judgment from the comfort of her lawn chair, coffee cup in hand, we propped empty cans on fence posts and plinked them with the .22's. We began at ten yards, increasing the distance in increments of five until we proved we were proficient at fifty.

"Good enough?" Darrell asked.

"Pick those up," she told us. "Twenty-four thousand cans provide enough tin for a Flying Fortress." She folded her lawn chair and went up to the house.

"What does that have to do with pheasants?" Darrell said to me.

"Both fly."

Minutes later, she returned with Uncle Jack's 20 gauge for Darrell and her own diminutive .410 for me, plus a pouch full of shells.

"That's your gun, Mom?" Darrell questioned. "Since when were you interested in guns?"

She told him to stand aside and pitch a can in the air. As the can rotated far over our heads, she raised the .410 to her shoulder and peppered it full of holes. "Since before you were even a thought … any more questions?"

Darrell grinned. "Nope."

We thought our lesson would be over in minutes, but it lasted all afternoon. She demonstrated how to carry our weapons, how to walk abreast, how to cross a fence, when to flip off the safety, and how to shoot.

"Carry your gun across your body, up and away from your companion," she instructed. "Keep the safety on till you're ready to shoot. Stay behind Rover and he'll get the pheasant up for you. He's not a true hunting dog, so he won't point and freeze. He'll just nose it out and scare it into flying. Then your reflexes kick in. Your thumb slips off the safety and your finger finds the trigger. When your eye is on the pheasant, the gun goes off and the bird drops. It's as simple as that."

As simple as that? When she threw leftover shingles from the barn roof into the air in front of us, I missed most of the time. Darrell was only slightly better.

I paid close attention to every nuance and suggestion for improvement, but Darrell rapidly lost interest. Noticing his inattention, she broke off a willow branch and whacked him across the legs. Darrell was wearing cutoff overalls on this particular Indian summer afternoon, and the switch left an angry red mark on his bare shins.

"I hate to use the same tactic on you that your father does, Darrell, but apparently it's the only way to reach you. Start listening or you'll be helping Charlie in the horse barn while Abby and I go hunting."

Darrell remained stoic. She hadn't hurt his hide nearly as much as she'd hurt his pride, but his attention span lengthened significantly.

We practiced and practiced. We shot up the box of shells, then several more. My aunt said it was fortuitous that my uncle had hoarded so much ammunition before the war started, or we'd be out of luck.

On Sunday, we laid aside our guns and attended church. On Monday and Tuesday, after school, our lessons continued. On Wednesday, she graduated us, with a heartfelt prayer for our safety.

Finally we were on our own.

Darrell and I hunted on clear, crisp mornings, plodding down the picked corn rows with Rover, who found a new lease on life whenever he put nose to chilled ground.

Gramma furrowed her brow at every outing, saying we were far too young to hunt without adult supervision, but Aunt Annie reminded her that we'd been shooting BB guns and .22's for years. We'd passed her instruction and what happened now was up to us, and God.

We were careful beyond careful.

In three Saturdays, Darrell got five pheasants and I got three. I felt I would've surpassed him if my gun had a bigger pattern, but Darrell maintained that pure, raw talent had downed the birds.

Aunt Annie snapped our picture after each event. We held our shotguns and our pheasants, our weary faces sporting ear-to-ear grins as Rover snored in the background.

I couldn't help but wonder whether Uncle Jack, a continent away, had likewise managed some hunting after his covert business had been concluded.

And my heart ached a little, deep inside me.

The first real snow of the season came the night before my birthday, in the second week of November, hard streaks of wet that hit the frozen ground like globs of spit. Accompanying the snow was a fierce wind that beat against the storm windows and rattled the doors in an effort to get inside.

By morning, the world was silent, white, and very cold. After devouring a birthday breakfast of pancakes and sausage, I crunched down our long driveway to wait for the bus. My legs turned numb inside my snow pants and my fingers soon lost feeling, but I thawed by the time the bus rolled into town.

Gramma and Aunt Annie arrived at my classroom between our geography and science lessons, laden with nectar and cookies. My classmates sang "Happy Birthday" and presented me with cards they'd made, except for Billy Hartmann, who gave me nothing.

Gifts were optional, but Karen gave me an Indian arrowhead she'd found on their farm, and Ruth gave me fingernail polish. Miss Fuhrman presented me with an autograph book so I could better remember my school year. Then she appointed who should clean up the crumbs, and my school party was over.

For the rest of the day, I watched the clock, anticipating the big party awaiting me at home. I was not disappointed. As the bus dropped me off, I spied a red banner billowing from our mailbox, an open invitation for neighbors to drop in after supper for birthday cake. Someone had tacked another banner above our front door. Inside, the dining room was resplendent with red and white crepe paper streamers. A glass platter held sweets, and Gramma's best china graced the table. Arranged on the oak buffet was every birthday card I'd ever received for every birthday I'd ever had. My grandmother never threw out anything she deemed sentimental, and at times like this it showed.

She was nowhere in sight. "Gramma?" I called.

"I'm down here, Abby." Ascending the basement steps slowly, she carried in her apron an assortment of vegetables from the root cellar.

I made a face.

"There's more to a birthday supper than sweets, but tonight you don't have to eat anything you don't want to," she said.

"Thank you, Gramma."

"But don't complain if you get a stomachache."

"I won't … everything looks so pretty."

She smiled pensively. "It does, doesn't it? Annie helped this afternoon, or it never would've gotten done. You need to thank her."

"I will … what's the matter, Gramma? You look sad."

"Oh, I was just thinking of how many birthdays you've had already." She began peeling a potato. "Time is going by so fast."

"Is that all?" I knew contemplating the past was a common trait of old people and nothing to worry about. "So, who's coming to my party?"

"Not so many this year … Annie and your cousins, Vic, Emma, and Virgil. I invited Ben and Evelyn too, but she called this morning and said Judy came down with chicken pox. I hope you're not too disappointed."

"It's okay, Gramma," I said. I hadn't had chicken pox yet, so it was for the best.

Uncle Vic was Gramma's cousin, but I called him uncle because I didn't know what else to call him. He was tall and stringy, and he kept a wad of tobacco tucked in his cheek unless he was eating. Gramma thought his habit disgusting, but I thought it was swell.

Aunt Emma was short, round, and told the funniest stories. She baked the best birthday cakes in the world, and I knew she'd create something special for me.

Their son Virgil had been in the infantry until most of his left foot was blown off storming the beach at Normandy back in June. Now he walked lopsided but managed to drive and farm. He could wiggle his ears, imitate anything, and blow his nose louder than anyone.

"Your father sent a present you can open with the rest," Gramma said. "But you can read his letter now. It's by the radio."

After ignoring me for nearly three months, Daddy had remembered my birthday! I grabbed the letter and ran upstairs to read in private.

Dear Abigail,

It has been several months since I've written you. Perhaps you've noticed and wondered why … or perhaps not.

I confess I was most disturbed by your last letter. Your arrogance (look it up) and your audacity (look it up) were nearly unbelievable. And your flippant (look it up) description of your transgression (look it up) was thoroughly appalling! To put it bluntly, Abby, you have been a very naughty girl and you have made me very angry.

A shiver shot up my spine. It was not what I wanted to hear on my birthday.

In fact, I was so angry that I needed considerable time to pass in order to know exactly what to do and how to respond to you. I hope, in the meantime, you have come to the realization that what you did was very wrong and you have made amends (look it up) to your uncle for the trouble you've caused.

I've written and offered to pay for half the damages incurred (look it up). Half seemed fair, as Darrell was equally to blame. This your aunt has accepted in my brother's behalf, as she writes that Jack is off to parts unknown. As I am far from wealthy, this will be a hardship for me, but as your father I must assume responsibility for what you've done. You can never repay me, of course, but you can make things right with me by stopping immediately all your foolishness and mischief. I do not want to hear of anything you've done wrong from now on!

These are my directives. You are not to smoke. You are to stay away from my brother's new barn. You are not to swear in a letter to me, ever again. At home, you are to help your grandmother in every way possible. At school, you are to stay out of fights. You are to study hard and be the best you can be.

In addition, I expect your weekly letters to resume immediately, chronicling (look it up) your efforts toward those worthy goals.

So many orders. So little fun. So many vocabulary words to look up in Gramma's dog-eared dictionary and use appropriately in my next letter. I propped myself on my elbow and read on.

Regarding the day at hand, and I'm sure this is the part you're waiting for: I wish you a very happy birthday. I cannot believe you are already ten. When I went away the last time, you were only four, a raven-haired, dark-eyed little waif (look it up), all jabber and giggles. You had more energy than a tub full of puppies. You climbed trees faster than the squirrels, and you fell out of them too.

Do you remember tying your doll to one of the cats to give her a ride? Needless to say, that dangling doll scared that cat out of eight of its nine lives! It showed up later with the string still tied around its belly, but your doll was gone forever. I had to drive you to town for a new one to dry your tears.

Later that same month you befriended Benny. Remember him? He started out the runt but he grew bigger than the other ducks because you fed him all the time. I wouldn't let you bring him inside because of the messes all ducks make, so the next thing I knew you had cut two holes in one of my socks, put his legs through, slipped the rest over his tail like a diaper, and he was quacking all over the house!

Do you remember me reading you fairy tales out on the porch before I left? Already you were picking out words you knew. Now you can read and write nearly anything you wish and Mother reports you are turning into quite the young lady.

Apparently I hadn't been the only one telling Daddy what he wanted to hear. Wearing my store-bought clothes with Ruth's polish on my fingertips hardly made *me* a lady! I resumed reading.

I am hopeful the war will end soon. The Krauts are on the retreat and peace can't be far behind. Then I'll return and see for myself how you've grown and who you have become.

He'd never mentioned coming home before. I was beyond surprised; I was shocked. But what truly shocked me were my conflicting feelings. I both anticipated and dreaded his return. A murderer couldn't have written this letter, reminiscing about when I was little. He couldn't have done what Billy Hartmann said … or had he?

In honor of your birthday, I've sent some presents I bought here in Italy as well as something I made. I hope you enjoy them. I regret missing yet another milestone in your life, but I expect to be present for your next birthday. We can make up for lost time then.

In the meantime, I'll be anticipating a letter from you shortly. You would be wise not to disappoint me.

Love, Daddy

Cognizant of the threat, I stared at his signature. Who are you, Daddy? What are you? When you return, will you be all I want? And all I need? What if I disappoint you? Or worse, if you disappoint me? I sighed and tucked his letter next to Mother's letter. In that way, my parents were together again: letters in a drawer.

Aunt Annie and my cousins arrived at five o'clock. Darrell carried in a graniteware roaster containing two roasted pheasants and a capon. When my aunt raised the lid to check on it, the delicious aroma caused me to salivate.

My cousins, dressed in their church clothes, looked scrubbed and uncomfortable. Dennis said it was my fault. Darrell told him to shut up. Dennis stuck out his tongue. Darrell knuckled him in the ribs. Dennis ran to my aunt. She marched him to a corner of our living room, where she ordered him to stand until suppertime.

Darrell circled a forefinger near his ear. "She's going haywire," he whispered to me. "Dad better come home and spank the brats before she falls apart." He arranged the Chinese checkers on the rug in front of the oil stove in the living room, far from the bustling kitchen. We let Duane play because we could beat him.

At a quarter to six, Uncle Vic, Aunt Emma, and Virgil arrived with my cake, several presents, and something wrapped in brown paper.

"Where's the birthday girl?" Aunt Emma hollered.

"I'm right here, Aunt Emma!" I abandoned the game and ran to her. She scooped me up in her ample arms, smooched my face, tousled my hair, and wrinkled my dress, all in five seconds flat.

She gave my cheek a playful tweak. "Oh, you won't believe what your silly uncle got for your birthday. You just won't believe it."

"I bet I know."

"No, you don't, not in a thousand years."

"Yes, I do. It's a can of Copenhagen."

She threw back her head and laughed. Uncle Vic laughed too. After catching her breath, she gave me a final squeeze and went to help in the kitchen. Uncle Vic went with her to amuse the womenfolk, or so he said.

Virgil herded us kids back to the living room and we played his favorite game. We'd name something and he would imitate it. We were laughing so hard our sides ached when Duane requested a cow giving birth to triplets. Virgil was emitting some truly ghastly bovine noises when Gramma called everyone to the table.

My birthday feast was scrumptious. I stuffed myself on pheasant, chicken, and mashed potatoes, richly smothered in gravy. I avoided the turnips and beets. I did eat two carrots.

Uncle Vic passed the object wrapped in brown paper. The grownups filled their glasses with chokecherry wine. Virgil shared his with me, over Gramma's protests.

Amid much fanfare, Aunt Emma brought my cake to the table, ablaze with ten red candles. I shut my eyes, wished for Daddy and Uncle Jack to come home safely, and blew them out with one breath. After my birthday song, Virgil teased me about giving me a birthday spanking, but I knew he was just fooling.

Neighbors and church friends joined our festivities after supper. After the extra people went home, Uncle Vic produced the wine again, and my party continued happily as before.

We were laughing and talking so loud that no one heard a car drive up and leave again. No one heard the back door open. No one heard him enter the house. He just appeared, as though from nowhere, when Aunt Annie screamed.

Conversation ceased. Our startled eyes followed her as she ran to him and covered his lips with her own. She was laughing and crying simultaneously when Uncle Jack pulled her off, complaining gruffly, "Enough, woman, let me breathe."

Gramma's eyes welled. "Thank the Lord, Jack, you've made it home!"

He comforted her with a long hug. "Of course, Mother. Was there ever a doubt?"

Then Darrell and the twins encircled him, jostling for attention. For all their complaints about him, they looked pathetically relieved to have him back.

I understood. He was their father, their sun, the center of their small universe. And where was my own father on this, my tenth birthday? I remained sitting at the table, consumed by jealousy.

The conversation soon degenerated into incomprehensibility as my cousins tried to tell him everything that had happened since he'd been gone.

"Whoa, there!" Uncle Jack said with mock sternness. "I appreciate all the attention, boys, but I'm only one person and you're landing on me like bees on a hive. We'll do this later, when I'm more rested. I'm not going anywhere again for a long time."

"Then you took care of things?" Aunt Annie asked.

He nodded.

"And you did well?"

"We'll talk later, Annie … good to see the rest of you folks again."

Uncle Vic stepped forward and clapped my uncle on the shoulder. Virgil did likewise. Aunt Emma enveloped him in a bear hug like she gave everyone else.

"Goodness gracious, Jack!" she exclaimed. "You're nothing but skin and bones under those heavy clothes you're wearing."

He shrugged. "I've lost a bit."

"Looks like more than a bit," Gramma said. "What happened? Weren't they feeding you over there?"

"I've had plenty, Mother … nothing to worry about."

"A strong wind could blow you away. I'll go fix you a plate."

"Don't fuss." He handed his overcoat and scarf to Darrell. "I ate earlier on the train, and I'm too tired to eat more tonight."

I noticed how his shirt hung slackly and his belt had been tightened two notches. His wavy auburn hair, always worn longer than was common, reached nearly to his shoulders. His mustache needed trimming. He needed a shave and probably a bath. But the finely chiseled features that made my uncle a handsome man remained. The rest could be rectified. My prayers had been answered: the owner of the black hat was back.

"You are terribly thin, Jack," Aunt Annie said. "Have you been sick?"

"Yes, and I suppose I'll have to tell you about it, or you'll barrage me with questions all night." He settled in the easy chair in the living room as the rest of us followed. "Ah, this feels wonderful … could I get a cup of coffee? Cream only."

"I'll get it," Aunt Emma offered.

"I've had a fever. African tick fever, it's called, although the name could refer to a dozen diseases they have over there. I got it hiking in the tall grass after—"

"Jack, you didn't!" Aunt Annie admonished. "You went hunting, on top of everything? You promised me you wouldn't."

"No, I never promised," he said irritably. "I said I didn't expect to, but when I found someone who'd take me to a safe area, I went for a few days. I sure as hell wouldn't go all the way to Africa and not even try, Annie. Do you want to hear about it or not?"

"Of course I do." She sat on the arm of his chair and draped an arm across his shoulder.

"As I was saying, the fever is carried by a tick, hardly big enough to see, but what havoc it causes. I didn't notice the bite until a red ring formed around the site, like a bull's-eye, and soon I was burning up."

"Wasn't there a medicine that could've helped?" Gramma asked.

"Medical supplies these days are rare or nonexistent, Mother. I either lived or I didn't."

Aunt Emma returned with his coffee. "Thank God you made the right choice."

"Thanks." I saw his hand shake as he stirred in the cream.

"So what happened then?" Uncle Vic prompted.

"Nate, my guide, got me back to the village and we waited it out. First the aches and pains came, worse than any influenza, followed by fever. Nate said my eyes went glassy and my face turned blotchy. Then the headache started. Felt like a spike being driven into both temples. Nate said he'd heard of a man who'd shot himself because of it. The poor fool was so sick he couldn't even accomplish a good suicide. Died later in Joberg. Nate said if it came to that he'd shoot me himself."

"No!" several of us said, myself included.

"He was kidding." Uncle Jack sipped his coffee. "At least I think he was … well, I'm here and that's all that matters."

Aunt Annie caressed the back of his neck. "Yes, that's all that matters."

He ignored her and focused his dark eyes on me. "And there she is, the birthday girl, waiting patiently to open her presents while everyone is making such a fuss over me. Come here, Abby. Sit on my lap like a good girl and tell me how you've been … Annie, take my coffee back to the kitchen. It's not agreeing with me tonight."

I sat awkwardly on his lap, wishing he hadn't asked me to do that in front of his own kids, but I couldn't think of a graceful way to decline. "I thought you'd forgotten about me," I said.

"I told you I'd be back. Didn't you believe me?"

I admitted I'd had doubts.

"You can believe what I say. I'd hoped to be back sooner, but at least I arrived in time for the presents." He took from his pocket a small package, gaily wrapped. "Add this to your pile."

"Thank you." I started to cry.

"Now what's wrong?"

"I miss Daddy. I wanted him here for my birthday."

"You're missing someone you don't even remember? Self-pity on your birthday is so inappropriate, Abigail. You should be thankful for who's here, rather than fret about who isn't."

"I guess so." I tried to wipe away my longing for a father along with my tears.

"So, what have you been up to lately?" he asked. "Have you been behaving yourself?"

What could I say? I couldn't tell him about finding the German Bible or Mother's obituary. I couldn't admit I knew he'd been in Africa at the time of her death. I couldn't confess why I'd fought Billy Hartmann, although he'd probably be informed about the fight itself. I could tell him about slaving away to help Gramma, but he wouldn't be impressed. Kids were supposed to work hard for their elders.

That left pheasant hunting. Brightly I launched into how Darrell and I had practiced, and how we'd taken his shotguns and walked the corn rows with Rover—

"You kids took my shotguns out, loaded?" He looked astounded.

"Sure, how else could we kill anything?" I boasted. "We blasted eight in total and Auntie cooked two tonight. They were yummy!"

"So my wife gave you a few hours of instruction and turned you loose?"

"It was far longer than that." I realized his reaction was one of anger, not awe. "She taught us for three whole afternoons, and she taught us good."

"Three afternoons be damned! Three years would've been more appropriate. You've no business at your age even touching a shotgun. I'll have a word with her about this."

"Please don't do that. It wasn't her fault, Uncle Jack. She didn't want to, but we nagged her into it."

"Naturally. But you won't be nagging me, so don't plan on hunting again in the near future. Thank God you didn't kill each other!"

Darrell had been eavesdropping. "We were real careful, Dad."

"I'll also be having a word with you. I assume this pheasant business was your brilliant idea?"

"No, it was my brilliant idea," I said, taking the blame. Not even a tyrant would punish a birthday girl.

My uncle seemed taken aback. "Is that so? Are you turning into some kind of little huntress?"

"Maybe."

"Then I'd better stay home and keep track of you. No one else seems able to."

I smiled my agreement. Darrell mouthed "thanks" before resuming the checkers game.

"So, while we're waiting for the women to finish in the kitchen, why don't you bring your gifts in here?" Uncle Jack said.

I slid off his lap, got my presents, and arranged them on the coffee table, finishing precisely when everyone had reassembled. I started with the smallest, which made my uncle's gift first. I unwrapped a beautifully carved elephant.

"It's ivory," he said. "I thought you'd like something from Africa since you want to go there someday."

"Thank you, Uncle Jack, it's simply wonderful!" He seemed to expect a hug, so I gave him one.

Uncle Vic's gift was indeed a can of Copenhagen.

"Open it," Uncle Vic said when we were done laughing. I did, and discovered a violet sachet to tuck in my dresser drawer to sweeten my clothes.

"You didn't think he'd give you the real thing, did you?" Aunt Emma teased. "Just so you know, that's the second sachet. The first I had to throw away because it sucked up the nasty smell and stunk just like the snuff."

"Some folks might prefer the sweet smell of snuff over the nasty smell of violets," Uncle Vic said, and we laughed again.

Aunt Emma gave me a Scottie dresser dish containing bows, ribbons, and barrettes. Now my hair wouldn't have to be so unruly, she said.

Virgil gave me an anthology of Edgar Rice Burroughs's Tarzan stories. I let out a whoop of joy and gave him a squeeze that made him blush.

My cousins gave me a new domino set because I'd lost the double sixes months ago, and dominoes just didn't play right without the double sixes.

Aunt Annie presented me with my first vanity set: a tortoise-shell brush and comb, hand mirror, cologne, and dusting powder. I thanked her while hoping I wouldn't be expected to use it anytime soon.

That left Daddy's present, but Gramma said to save it for the very last. She wanted hers to come next, explaining that it was hidden in the fruit cellar because it was too big to wrap. Virgil volunteered to get it while I waited with my eyes covered. When it was time to look, I was overwhelmed at the sight of a gorgeous blue and white bicycle, with chrome trim and a little basket in which to haul things.

"It's fabulous, Gramma! Where'd you get it? Nobody can find a new bike these days!" I hugged and thanked her until she went misty on me.

"Your aunt found it," Gramma said as though that explained everything.

It did. Aunt Annie seldom ran out of sugar, coffee, butter, or anything else rationed. She bought under the table, I'd heard, but it must've been a pretty special table to have produced a bicycle.

I thanked her so profusely that she confessed the bicycle wasn't new. I said I didn't care. To me it looked new, and it would ride the same as if it were.

At last I'd come to Daddy's present. Uncle Vic used his pocket knife to cut away the wrappings. Inside the large box I found several smaller packages, each individually wrapped.

Again I started with the smallest. The first box contained a charm bracelet. Charm bracelets were all the rage at school. I'd never wanted one, but Gramma probably told Daddy I did. As I passed it around so everyone could see, Uncle Jack reached in his pocket and put something in his mouth. He did not look well.

My next present was a diary, followed by a matching scrapbook.

"I don't think your father wants you to fill it with Tarzan comics," Gramma said. "Some of your best drawings or mementoes of your school year would be more appropriate."

"But I draw terrible and I'd rather not remember my school year," I said.

Everybody laughed except Uncle Jack. He sat with his head against the back of the chair, his eyes partly closed.

The next box held a drawing of a little girl, simply framed. The girl was standing in a shadowed room, gazing out a window toward the sunset. She was holding an apple and looked rather melancholy.

"That's an odd birthday present," Aunt Emma opined.

Aunt Annie peered over my shoulder. "Why, it's an original pastel. See, here's the artist's name in the corner: J. A. Stahl … oh, Mother; James did this?"

Gramma adjusted her glasses. "That's his signature, all right. He hasn't done anything artistic for years, to my knowledge. To think he'd have started again, and in the middle of a war."

I embraced the picture and felt closer to my father than I ever had.

The last box was the largest. To everyone's puzzlement, it contained a hat, stuffed with newspaper to maintain its shape. Somehow it seemed familiar, with the braid along the brim and the strawflower decorating the band.

"That looks like one your mother had once," Gramma said to me. "I wonder where your father found another so similar?"

"It's not similar, Mother. I think it's the same one," Aunt Annie said. "See? Look at the wear inside the band … Ellen wore this gardening, from what I remember."

Gramma looked more closely. "Oh, I believe you're right. What was he doing with this in Italy, of all places?"

"He probably took some things of hers back with him after—after what happened," Aunt Annie said. "Try it on, Abby, unless it bothers you."

"No, it doesn't bother me." But it did, and I took it off again.

"You won't be wearing that for a while, Abby," Aunt Emma said. "It's way too big. Since he's kept it all these years, why didn't he keep it until it fit?"

I couldn't hazard a guess, but a piece of the puzzle had unexpectedly fallen into place. The lady with Uncle Jack in the photograph Darrell and I had found was Mother. And the tall man aiming his gun at them? I couldn't bear thinking about it. I looked at Uncle Jack to gauge his reaction, but he'd fallen asleep.

Gramma followed my line of vision. "Oh dear, Jack's plumb wore out. It's time to call it a night." She shooed everyone out within minutes. She wouldn't even permit Aunt Annie to rouse him from his slumber. No, she'd watch over him herself and drive him home in the morning. She covered him with blankets and set a pillow on the davenport, in case he awoke during the night and needed to stretch out.

I washed up, changed into my flannel nightgown, got my goodnight kiss from Gramma, and went upstairs. I hoped I wouldn't lie awake half the night wondering what Auntie meant when she referred to "what happened." Had it been a slip of the tongue or did she know more than I'd thought?

After I went to sleep, I hoped I wouldn't dream about the hat, or the photograph, or Mother, or Daddy. No, I would dream a dream befitting my tenth birthday. I would dream of a perfect life with perfect parents, and I would star in my perfect dream.

The last time I saw Gramma, she was sitting in her rocker near Uncle Jack, watching him as he slept. She would stay awake as long as she could, and then she'd sleep with her bedroom door ajar so she could hear whether he needed anything.

She would've done the same for me. She would've done the same for any of us.

Tales of the Bwana King

I SNUGGLED DEEP into the down comforters that kept me from freezing in the unheated portion of our home. For a few awful minutes, I'd be so cold my teeth would chatter. Then the comforters would reflect my body heat and I'd turn toasty. My toes curled around the hot water bottle Gramma had tucked between my sheets. Soon I was asleep, grateful my uncle had returned, anticipating a bright tomorrow.

At four o'clock, I awoke with a stomachache. I'd eaten far too many sweets. I pulled on my chenille robe and went downstairs.

I broke a film of ice on the water pail and dipped my cup to drink. The cold made my teeth tingle. I dipped another cupful and stirred in a teaspoon of soda to settle my stomach. I didn't want to wake Gramma just to hear her say, "I told you so."

Ice crystals clung to the windowpanes, forming lovely etchings of which Jack Frost would've been proud. One resembled Pegasus winging his mythical way over Mount Helicon, but the real world beyond was dark and foreboding. The north wind howled, vibrating our front door in a ghostly cadence.

I shivered, shut off the light, and started upstairs. But something seemed amiss. I walked back into the living room. Moonlight shimmered through the frosted windows, dimly illuminating Uncle Jack as he lay sprawled on our davenport. I bent down to listen, but I couldn't hear him breathe.

"What are you doing?" he said.

I startled. "I couldn't hear you. I thought something was wrong."

"Nothing's wrong, and you wouldn't hear me. I don't snort, honk, or otherwise engage in auditory excess."

He was referring to Virgil, who made more noise by simply existing than anyone else. That was one of the many reasons I liked Virgil, but his attributes were clearly lost on my uncle.

"I'm sorry for bothering you," I said. "I'll go back to bed now."

"Not just yet." He switched on the floor lamp. "I don't feel well. In fact, I feel like hell. Be a good girl and make me some tea."

I hesitated.

"Well, what now?"

"I don't know how. I can make coffee, if you like."

"Then your grandmother hasn't taught you what you need to know," he snapped. "Or, more likely, she's tried and you've refused to learn … I don't believe you anyway. Any fool can make tea."

So I was a fool. I stuck out my lip, just a little, so he wouldn't see. Why was he being so mean to me? Could I help that Gramma only drank tea when she had a sore throat, and she always made it herself?

Uncle Jack sighed audibly. "Boil water in the damn teapot. Take it off the burner. Add some tea to the damn tea ball. You know what a tea ball is, don't you?"

I nodded.

"Put the tea ball in the hot water for three minutes. Dip it up and down. Then take it out. Pour the tea in a cup and bring it to me. And bring me some damn crackers too. I'm running on empty … any questions?"

I shook my head. His liberal use of "damn" indicated his level of irritation, so I'd paid close attention. I made his tea and found the crackers. When I brought them to him, he was huddled under all the blankets in Gramma's rocker, which he'd pulled nearer the stove.

"Thank you," he said.

"You're welcome." I turned to go.

"Abigail."

I looked back reluctantly.

"Yes, I'm talking to you. Come here and sit down." He indicated the davenport with a tilt of his head. "I want to talk to you."

"But it's four in the morning."

"Smart girl. She can tell time. Now sit."

I clutched my robe around me for warmth and sat down. The kitchen had been chilly enough to see my breath. The living room wasn't much warmer, and my uncle's demeanor seemed colder than the air. I shuddered.

He offered me one of his blankets. I wrapped it around myself silently.

"In Africa, I was king," he said. "Bwana want, Bwana get. Boy go, boy fetch. Chop, chop. Boy move slow, boy get beat. Boy look crosswise, he gone. No other job around so boy move good. Hot fire at dawn. Hot tea, rusks, mealie meal. Good lunch in cool box. Good supper too. Good gin, good whiskey. Clean bed. Clean clothes, folded neat. I was a good Bwana. I was a hell of a king. Got cheated this time. Other things to do. Damn waste of good hunting. Got sick. Hate being sick. Hate not being there. Not ready to come back. But I'm not in Africa anymore …" his voice trailed off.

I suspected his monologue was his way of apologizing, but I didn't know whether he desired further conversation or he'd rebuke me for saying the wrong thing, so I kept quiet.

"Poor Abigail … I fall asleep as you're opening your gifts. Everyone goes home. You wake in the dead of night, worried, and I insult your intelligence. I was going to tell you about Africa, but there's nothing I want to say that can't wait until tomorrow, or the next day, or never. Go back to bed."

Africa? Now I no longer wanted to leave. It seemed the perfect opportunity to learn what had enticed him to that faraway land. "Is that what you like about Africa? How everybody does what you want?"

"Oh, she talks." He took a sip of his tea. "Of course I like that, but there's more, much more I could tell you."

"Then tell … tell me everything."

"Now that I think about it, I probably shouldn't. You'd think me silly."

"No, I wouldn't," I assured him. "Please, Uncle Jack, I really want to hear your tales of Africa."

He leaned back in the rocker and smiled. "Ah, my tales of Africa; tales of the bwana king … bwana means 'boss' or 'master,' in Swahili. Sounds like a book title, doesn't it? Maybe I'll write one someday."

"You should. *Tales of the Bwana King* sounds even more thrilling than the Tarzan books I've read lately." I smiled back at him. "You'd be famous, Uncle Jack."

"I don't need fame, Abby. Maybe I'll write one, maybe I won't. But I guess I could tell you what it's really like, what it means to me, after I drink and eat a little. I'm starting to feel a bit better."

I waited expectantly as he drank his tea and ate a few crackers. Then he set his cup on the end table and began. His voice, quiet at first, gathered momentum as the story unfolded.

"I'll start at the beginning, when I was young like you … like you, I lived vicariously through my books, reading adventures so fantastic I could hardly believe them: *The Dash for Khartoum*, *With Kitchener in the Sudan*, *The Hunt for the Nile*, *Searching for Victoria*, and many others. The words on the page became alive, and reality and fantasy readily entwined. I was Allan Quatermain in *King Solomon's Mines*. I was Mowgli in *The Jungle Book*.

"I was all of the explorers who ever set foot in Africa. I was Livingstone lost in the bowels of the continent. I was Stanley who found him, and I was Cameron who discovered him dead. I was Lawrence of Arabia, wearing the silk robes of the Sherifs of Mecca. I was Caillie in Timbuktu, and Barth in Tripoli. I was Park who drowned in the Niger. I sailed aboard the *Lady Alice*. I was the first white man to see the rush of the Zambezi and the dust of the Kalahari.

"A thousand tales whirled in my overactive imagination as Africa entrapped me in her haunting web. Katar the Witch lurked in the cistern of our basement, half crushed yet half alive, her moldy claw poised to grab me should I stray within range. From the shadows of our grove, I watched the witch doctors work their magic. Bones rolled from a monkey skull foretold my future, and my future was Africa ... Africa, a place of ultimate adventure, of liberating freedom from our mundane little farm.

"Sometimes the darkness of my bedroom became the mysterious African night, or the patter of rain outside my window transformed into a tropical torrent. Sometimes the ceiling gave way to starlight on the bushveld. My blankets became leopard skins and the decorations on my wall became tribal shields. My BB gun and my slingshot became poisoned arrows and blowguns, and my teddy bears changed into shrunken heads with hollowed sockets where the eyes had been. Paradoxically, I was a happy traveler in Africa long before I ever arrived there ... do you find this odd?"

"Not at all," I said, enchanted.

He smiled again. "Good, because I've just told you things I've never told a living soul. And since you obviously think like me, I'll take you along when I go back."

"And when will that be?"

"When the war's over and you're grown. Travel is too difficult now. I took a chance this time, but I managed."

"But how did you go? Miss Fuhrman said only soldiers can cross the ocean."

"That's true, for the most part. I went on the Grey Ghost, along with many of our brave boys."

"What's the Grey Ghost?"

"It's the wartime name for the *Queen Mary*, an ocean liner that typically sails from New York to all points of the globe, including Africa, wherever our soldiers are needed."

"Oh, that sounds so exciting!" I said.

"It was ... Hitler withdrew most of the U-boats back in '43, but it's a big ocean and danger still lurks. Any German who sinks her would get a quarter of a million dollar bounty."

"That'd be awful, sinking a big ship like that! Hundreds of people would die at the very same time."

"Far more ... fifteen thousand can be aboard at once."

I couldn't fathom fifteen thousand in a town, much less on a boat. I continued the questioning, intent on finding out what I could. "But how could you go when you're not a soldier?"

"Others can be on board. Journalists, diplomats, Red Cross workers. It just has to be arranged by someone in the government or the military. My brother, in my case."

"Daddy?"

"That is correct."

"But I thought he didn't know where you were. In my birthday letter, he wrote you were off 'to parts unknown.'"

"Hell, he always knows where I am these days. He has spies."

"Spies?"

"Stop echoing me, Abigail. Talk about Africa or you're going to bed." My uncle set his jaw and stared into the flickering flames of the stove.

It unnerved me when he was so forthcoming, and then, like a spigot being shut off, nothing. I proceeded cautiously. "Well, if I have to wait for years, can you at least tell me what Africa looks like?"

"It's so vast it has a bit of everything," he said, turning to me again. "Where I've been, for instance, rugged mountains appear purple in the haze rising up from the plains. The plains themselves vary in color, depending on the atmosphere and time of year. Plants that live in pots here grow wild and reach astounding heights there. Africa has steaming jungles, crystal beaches, rich tobacco, potato, sugar cane, and coffee farms, and vast expanses covered with nothing but scrub and rocks. Waterways of the Okavango contrast with the dust of the Kalahari. But everywhere, it seems, there are thorns and bugs … snakes too."

I'd noted the word "sugar."

"Before I got sick," he continued, "there was one particular morning I'll never forget. Rain had fallen during the night, and dawn turned the sky a brilliant blue no artist could ever match. The sun was beginning to warm, and the breeze was like a fairy's breath moving along the tips of the grass. Nate and I settled near a lone acacia beside a water hole. It was an ordinary African morning, but to me it was special because I was exactly where I wanted to be, and I was doing exactly what I wanted to do, and nothing else mattered."

"And what were you hunting?"

"Nothing in particular. My business had been concluded, and the rest was to simply enjoy before my long journey back."

I dared to be bold. "What business? The sugar farm?"

His eyes drilled holes in my affected complacency. "What sugar farm? What are you talking about?"

"The sugar farm you mentioned before."

"That was a generality. Don't lie to me, Abigail. What sugar farm?"

Cornered, I confessed how I'd overheard Aunt Annie damning him and his sugar the morning he left for Africa, causing me to wonder whether he had a sugar farm there.

"I mention a sugar farm in passing, my wife damns the sugar, and somehow you come up with that? Forget it. My business will remain my business."

"But why can't I know? You promised to tell me more if I kept the locket a secret, and I have."

"That has nothing to do with my private business. For now, I'll simply say this: sometimes things happen that can't be explained. Things happen that shouldn't be discussed. Things happen that are best forgotten … now go upstairs so I can sleep."

I slowly undid my blanket. "Do I have to?"

"Yes, and don't whine."

"I'm not whining … but it's so cold up there."

"So? It's cold down here."

My toes languidly sought my slippers. "Can I show you my last birthday present, the one you missed?"

"Fine, then off you go. Agreed?"

"Agreed."

I took the hat from its box, put it on, and stood expectantly before him. Perhaps seeing it again would evoke an explanation of the photograph Darrell and I had found. My uncle recognized it by the way he held his eyes, but he said nothing.

"Daddy sent it," I said. "It's Mother's hat. Gramma and Auntie both said so."

"Really?" he said. "Well, I don't remember it. I don't remember what women wear. Take it off."

I took a step backward. "Why? Doesn't it look good on me?"

"No, it's too big. It looks stupid. Why would my brother send such a thing to you? You, who run around in the summer until you're brown as a nut? Take it off. Take the damn thing off and go to bed!"

I flung the hat back in its box. "Right after I kiss Gramma … please, Uncle Jack, I have to when I get up in the middle of the night. It's a charm. It keeps me safe."

He nodded, redirected his gaze toward the stove, and nestled down in his blankets like an irate mole.

I ran into Gramma's bedroom, leaned over, and kissed her cheek. She remained still. I listened for her breathing. I heard my own. I touched her hand, her arm, her forehead. She seemed cold. I started to cover her with another quilt when it came to me.

An anguished scream pierced the night. A door closed, and behind the door was darkness.

Gramma

The swirling darkness dissipated as I jolted to consciousness. I found myself on the davenport, although I had no recollection of how I got there.

"Gramma's not dead, is she?" I said. "Please tell me she's not dead!"

"I'm sorry, Abby," Uncle Jack replied, his face a reflection of my own anguish. "She died several hours ago, probably before you even came downstairs."

I burst into tears and beseeched God to bring my grandmother back. But even as I sobbed, I knew those who had "gone ahead," as folks delicately referred to the dead, never returned.

My uncle held me until my torrent subsided. Then he placed calls to Aunt Annie, Dr. Jorgenson, Sheriff Branson, and the mortuary. That done, he pulled Gramma's rocker into her bedroom. I heard the click of her bedside lamp as he began to rock. He was watching over her as she'd watched over him. He was saying his good-bye to her. I wanted to say my good-bye to her too, but I didn't dare interrupt him. So I stayed where I was, swathed in my blankets and my sorrow.

Aunt Annie arrived. Uncle Jack appeared from the bedroom. They hugged briefly. He said something to her. She turned to me and attempted a wavering smile.

"Come, Abby. You need to get dressed. You'll have to come home with me now."

Upstairs, I sat on the edge of my bed and did as I was told. I watched her take various items from my dresser and closet and pack them into a suitcase. I felt numb. I felt sick. I felt guilty.

"I did it, Auntie!" I blurted. "I killed Gramma!"

She stared at me as though I'd lost my mind. "What are you talking about? You didn't kill her."

"Yes, I did," I insisted. "You don't know how bad I wore her out. She said so. She couldn't wait for Daddy to come back so she wouldn't have to work so hard—"

Aunt Annie gathered me in her arms. "No, you're wrong. You didn't cause her death, Abby. In fact, you probably helped her live longer than if she'd been all alone. You were the joy of her life. Remember that. She's had heart trouble for years. Dr. Jorgenson couldn't do anything more for her, so it was just a matter of time before she went back to God."

I was stunned. "She did? But why didn't she tell me?"

"She didn't want you to worry. It's just that simple, dear. I hope that makes you feel a little bit better."

I swallowed hard, a lump in my throat as big as Africa. Whenever Gramma had been tired or crabby, I'd never realized she was sick. I'd thought she was just old. How could I have been so stupid?

"Time to go," Aunt Annie said.

I grabbed my pillow and Panda Bear and followed her downstairs.

Uncle Jack was pacing in the kitchen. He looked haggard. The teakettle was whistling on the stove. "Take Abby home," he said to my aunt. "I'll drive Mother's car over after Hanson gets her."

"I'm not leaving until I say good-bye to Gramma," I said.

"Not tonight. Go with Annie."

"After I say good-bye to Gramma."

"I told you no."

"Jack, please," Aunt Annie said. "Let her say good-bye."

"I said no and I mean no! Mother doesn't—well, look right. Abby doesn't need to see that. Will the two of you just go?"

She gave him no further argument. I knew she wouldn't. Frustrated, I took PB and ran outside. She struggled behind me through the drifts, holding aloft my suitcase, pillow, and the rubber boots I'd forgotten.

The snow swirled furiously in the glare of the headlights as she inched the car down the driveway. Much more snow and Hanson, whoever he was, wouldn't be able to make it.

Aunt Annie had to take me upstairs to their spare bedroom and help me undress. I could do nothing for myself. Even with my own pillow beneath my head and PB in my arms, everything felt strange. With the exception of the night I'd destroyed the barn, I'd never gone to sleep without Gramma's goodnight kiss, or without me giving her one if I woke during the night. It'd been the charm to keep me safe. Who would kiss me now?

Out of nowhere, God provided a comforting thought to help me make it through the night: Daddy would be coming home. He'd be coming home to plan Gramma's funeral, and he'd be staying to care for me.

Consoled, I drifted to sleep.

That night, I saw Daddy standing by my bed. I recognized the dark hair, the steady eyes, the long, straight nose, and the curve of the lips from his portrait. Flecks of snow dropped from his overcoat onto my face. He looked at me as tenderly as a mother gazes at her newborn child. Overjoyed, I reached out my arms. "Daddy, you've come back!"

"Not yet, baby," said an unfamiliar voice.

I forced open my eyes. The snow had been tears. My arms had reached for nothing.

"Don't let me give up," I whispered to PB. "Just imagine how distinguished Daddy will look when he gets off the train. The whole town will turn out to greet him. The band will play and the mayor will give a speech … Daddy's a war hero, you know. He'll act like it's nothing, but we'll be so proud. When this awful thing with Gramma is over, we'll be so happy, won't we?"

When I heard Aunt Annie bustling around the kitchen the next morning, I got up and dressed in the nicest outfit in my suitcase. My cousins were already eating when I came downstairs. They were in a sober mood, so I assumed they'd been told of Gramma's passing.

Aunt Annie said my uncle had arrived home at seven and had gone to bed. We needed to keep quiet so we didn't wake him. She was heading to town shortly to make funeral arrangements. She stopped talking for a moment and took a hard look at me. "Why are you so dressed up, Abby?"

"Because Daddy will be coming home and I want to practice looking nice." I reached for the toast. "I look nice, don't I?"

"You look very nice, but who told you he'd be coming home?"

"Well, he is, isn't he?" I didn't want to say God did.

She shook her head. "I don't know where you got that idea, but no, your father's not coming home right now. I'm so sorry."

"He's not?" The toast slipped from my hand.

"No, I'm afraid not. He would if he could, but he's too far away and what he's doing is too important. We'll just have to handle it ourselves. When I go to town, I'll contact him through the Red Cross and we'll be hearing back from him soon … will you be all right while I'm gone?"

She could do what she needed to do, I assured her. I would go back to bed. I hadn't gotten enough sleep anyway.

Darrell came and sat for a while at the foot of my bed, but he didn't say anything. He didn't need to.

Monday afternoon brought a sense of purpose. Baths were taken. Doors and drawers opened and closed. People tramped up and down the stairs. I retreated to my bedroom and locked the door. I knew what was about to happen and I refused to participate. I would not, could not, attend Gramma's wake. The thought of her lying in a satin box made me nauseous.

At six o'clock, Aunt Annie came to my door. I refused to open it. She tried to persuade me to come out. I told her to go away. Then I heard what I'd been dreading: Uncle Jack's heavy footsteps coming up the stairs.

He jiggled the knob. "Why's this door locked?"

"To keep you out. Leave me alone!"

He left. I felt victorious.

Minutes later, he was back. After some rattles and scrapes, the knob turned and the door opened. Attired in a black suit, my uncle loomed in the doorway like a gaunt crow.

"Go away!" I shouted. "I'm not going and you can't make me!"

"Wrong on both accounts."

As he approached my bed, I slid under the blankets and covered my head.

"Due to extenuating circumstances," he said, jabbing my shoulder through the covers for emphasis, "I'll forget what you just said if you get dressed immediately. We leave for the funeral home in half an hour."

"I can't," I whimpered.

"Why not?"

"I'm sick."

"So what? I'm sicker than you and I'm going."

"But you have to go."

"So do you."

"No, I don't."

"Yes, you do. You will go and pay your last respects. You will accept condolences on your bereavement. You'll feel terrible all evening. You'll feel even worse tomorrow at the funeral, but you'll do it anyway. It's your duty. Now get up."

I made no reply and no movement to obey.

"Damn," he muttered.

No sooner had I wondered what he'd do when my bedspread was yanked from my grasp, followed by my blankets, my sheet, and PB. One by one he threw them on the floor. I curled up and shut my eyes.

"Open your eyes or keep them shut; it makes no difference to me," he said, his tone harsh. "Just hear this: I will not be locked out in my own house. I will not be ignored. I will not be defied. And, as is customary when I'm fully dressed, I am wearing a belt. One way or the other, Abigail, you'll be coming with us tonight."

I opened my eyes wide as his hands went for the buckle. "All right, you win!" I lunged for the closet and thrust my nearest church dress in front of me for protection. "Here, is this good enough?"

"Excellent. After you get dressed, make your bed. I never saw such a mess. Be downstairs in twenty minutes." He turned on his heel and shut the door behind him.

"Tyrant!" I hissed. Never had I thought I'd be totally under the tyrant's control. Never had I thought my fairy grandmother would die and leave me imprisoned in the tyrant's castle. Never had I thought I'd be starring in my very own, very sad fairy tale.

Tyrant Jack and Princess Abigail had little chance of a happy ending, but I still had to play my part well. I had to say the right thing, do the right thing, and all at the right times. If I forgot my lines or missed my cue, I could get another licking.

It was a hell of a predicament for a princess.

A single tear dribbled down my cheek as I put on the dress my fairy grandmother had sewn for me. Pinwale corduroy it was, with a crocheted collar and red piping around the cuffs. *Abigail* was embroidered on the tulip-shaped pocket.

"Get down here, Princess Abigail!" The tyrant's voice thundered up the stairs. "The carriage leaves for the village in five minutes."

I assembled my bed, yanked on my glass slippers, and descended the winding staircase. Annie of the Red Hair, a lowly servant who trembled at every word uttered by the tyrant, dutifully brushed my silken tresses and affixed velvet ribbons amid my curls while the tyrant judged the three peasant boys who stood quaking before him.

One, Dennis the Meek, cringed as the tyrant chastised him on the slovenliness of his attire. He was sent upstairs to remedy the situation. We waited. As soon as the piggish peasant returned, we boarded the gray carriage, the tyrant gathered up the reins to the many prancing horses beneath the hood, and we galloped toward town.

I rode in the back of the coach, crammed with the lowliest peasants. Annie of the Red Hair rode in front with Tyrant Jack. *Better her than me,* I thought. Darrell the Dull attempted conversation, but I would not deign to speak to him. He knew only of fields and foolishness, while I was a lady born.

"Are you pretending to be in one of those dumb stories you make up?" he asked.

I arched a regal eyebrow. "Are you addressing me, serf?"

"Good grief." He shook his head and stared out the frosty window of the carriage.

As we neared town, the elegant coach gradually became a common Ford, the three scruffy serfs my irritating cousins, and the trembling servant my Aunt Annie.

Uncle Jack, however, remained a tyrant.

The funeral home was located at the edge of town between Hill House, aptly named as it sat atop the highest elevation in town, which was predominately flat, and the New German Lutheran Church, not to be confused with the

Swedish Lutheran Church that was toward the middle of town and comprised of more Norwegians than Swedes anyway. In the darkness, the funeral home looked forbidding, encompassed by a cluster of naked trees. A single lamp illuminated the front door. No other cars had yet arrived.

"Folks will be coming up to you and extending their sympathies," Uncle Jack said to us kids. "Accept their condolences and make small talk. That's all I expect of you."

Inside the funeral home, he introduced us to Mr. Hanson. Mr. Hanson appeared surprisingly normal, despite what he did for a living. After chatting for a few minutes, he suggested that we go in the adjoining room and look at Gramma. My scalp prickled. I grabbed my aunt's hand. She offered encouragement. We walked in together. My cousins followed. Only Uncle Jack lagged behind.

I approached the casket cautiously. First I looked at Gramma's folded hands. She still wore her wedding ring, and her watch showed the correct time. I held my breath as my eyes traveled upward. Her face appeared peaceful and serene, but there was something strange about her. She looked like Gramma, but she wasn't Gramma. She was a mere shell, an empty body. The inner seed, the spirit, was gone.

The scene dissolved. I was lifted up. I felt the scratchiness of my uncle's mustache against my cheek and inhaled his Old Spice aftershave.

"I can't do this," I sniffled. "I can't."

"You've done it already," he said. "You've done your duty. Now you can stay in the outer room with me." He set me down, took my hand, and somehow the evening passed.

Before I could even begin my prayers that night, someone knocked on my door.

"Go away!" I hollered. Peace was impossible in this house.

Uncle Jack strolled in and sat on my bed. "You can't keep me out if I want to come in." He tucked the bedspread under my chin. "But I guess you know that already."

I rolled over and turned my face to the wall. "I know it, but I don't like it."

"It's hard to talk to you, Abby, if you turn away."

"I don't want to talk."

Rather than leaving, he sat so long in silence that I felt obligated to hear him out. I rolled back and looked at him. "All right … I'm listening."

He hesitated. "I was just thinking … I was wondering whether you wanted to do what you did with your grandmother. Continue the tradition, as it were."

"What tradition?"

"Remember when you said you never went to sleep without first getting a goodnight kiss?"

"I remember."

"Well, I thought you might consider having me do that."

The thought of him invading my privacy to bestow a goodnight kiss struck me as downright unpleasant. "But why you? Why not Auntie?"

"Because I'm your closest relative now, at least until my brother returns. Annie's not related to you by blood, and she has enough to do. I usually roam around a bit at night and it wouldn't take but a moment … so, how about it?"

I understood he wanted to do this, for whatever reason, and it had been difficult for him to ask. What I didn't understand was the conflicting feelings that his strange request stirred up within me. I still despised him, but when I felt my worst, as I had earlier, he'd inexplicably helped me.

"Um … no, I'd rather not," I decided. "It wouldn't be the same."

He sat very still for a full minute without speaking. Then he got up and started for the door.

A powerful emotion overwhelmed me. "Uncle Jack!"

He paused without turning.

"Come back," I said.

"Don't do me any favors."

"I'm not … please, come back."

"Forget it. It was something special between you and your grandmother. It was naïve of me to think I might somehow take her place. After all, you loved her, and I know what you think of me."

I let that pass.

"I thought as much." He reached for the doorknob.

"No, wait, you don't understand!" I said, not understanding myself. "I—I changed my mind. I'm sorry for what I said before … I want you to do it."

"Sure?"

"Yes, I'm sure."

He came back, leaned over me in the darkness, and pecked me gently on the forehead. "Good night, princess."

He'd never called me that in my entire life. What other ironic twists would occur before my fairy tale was done?

A few minutes later, the familiar smell of tobacco wafted through the floor register of my room. He was sitting below, in Gramma's rocker, smoking. I found both the smell of his pipe and the creak of the rocker comforting.

"We might make it yet," I whispered to PB.

All too soon it was Tuesday morning. Another heavy, wet snow had fallen during the night. More was expected. The sky was the color of lead.

We were the first to arrive at the church. Uncle Jack and Aunt Annie paid their final respects to Gramma while I lingered in the vestibule with my cousins. Mr. Hanson and Reverend Richter soon joined us. How Darrell could discuss snowfall with an undertaker and a man in black who scared the devil out of me every Sunday was beyond my comprehension.

Eventually we were ushered to the mourner's pew, at the very front of the church. Uncle Jack seated me between himself and my aunt, as though he feared I might be overcome and require prompt attention.

I concentrated on the stained glass picture portraying Jesus sitting amidst his lambs in a sun-drenched meadow. Was Gramma sitting with the real Jesus in a heavenly meadow at this very moment? Probably not. Gramma never liked doing nothing. More likely she'd be gathering meadow flowers for a bouquet, trimming the grass, or shearing a sheep. I hoped she wouldn't get bored to the extent she created a ruckus that caused her to get thrown out of heaven.

The other place was nothing to be wished on your worst enemy. Reverend Richter had saturated my senses with gruesome descriptions of smoldering sinners from as far back as I could remember. He took his calling seriously, folks said, not like that young Reverend Madsen from the Swedish Lutheran Church, who preached about faith, hope, and charity.

German Lutherans were more into punishment. German Lutherans had it right, I'd been told. But now that I thought about it, faith, hope, and charity seemed far more palatable than more punishment. At ten years of age, I'd had enough of *that* already!

Promptly at eleven o'clock, a deacon closed Gramma's casket. Reverend Richter strode to the front of the church. With a grand sweep of his hands, he motioned the congregation to rise, and the funeral service began.

I tried not to think about the words to Gramma's favorite hymns as Reverend Richter led us through "Sweet Hour of Prayer" and "Just a Closer Walk with Thee." Aunt Annie had a lilting soprano voice, which I already knew, but I was surprised by Uncle Jack's melodious bass. The few times he'd attended church previously, he'd kept his lips tightly closed as though he couldn't read the words or the notes.

When the songs were over, the sermon began. Reverend Richter was uncharacteristically charitable, expounding on Gramma's dedicated service to the church and to the community, as well as touting various aspects of her untarnished character. When he came to the part about her taking me in and raising me as her own, I started to cry. Aunt Annie slid a comforting arm around me. Uncle Jack kept eyeing me as though he expected me to do worse, but I didn't.

After Reverend Richter had finished, Mr. Lilla, the mayor of our little town, sang a cappella Gramma's favorite hymn: "Amazing Grace."

The third stanza went:

Thro' many dangers, toils, and snares,
I have already come.
'Tis grace hath brought me safe thus far,
And grace will lead me home.

Uncle Jack wiped his eyes during the last stanza. I'd thought him to be made of stone. "A Mighty Fortress Is Our God" finished up the service, and the pallbearers took Gramma away.

Snow was again falling by the time our mournful procession arrived at the cemetery. I kept my head downcast as Reverend Richter read the committal service, trying not to see, trying not to hear, trying not to feel.

I couldn't help but wonder whether Gramma's spirit was swirling amid the snowflakes. Or was she sipping heavenly coffee with Grandpa Walter? Or chatting with her parents? It'd been decades since she'd seen any of them. Maybe they were hosting a "Welcome to Heaven" party for her, right now! Gramma had always loved parties.

But what if Reverend Richter was wrong and the spirit didn't go anywhere? What if the spirit just went "poof" at the moment of death, like a candle in the wind? What if Gramma and everyone else who'd ever died were simply dead and dead all over?

I shivered when the casket containing the body of the only mother I'd ever known was lowered into the ground. Gramma always hated to be cold. She'd be so cold there in the ground, wouldn't she?

I thought my agony was over, but instead of heading home, Uncle Jack drove back to town. The Ladies Aid had prepared a bite to eat in the church basement for the mourners, my aunt explained.

I wouldn't have guessed, but apparently funerals whet the appetite. Tuna and chicken sandwiches, macaroni salad, Jell-O in various flavors, sliced pickles, and carrot sticks were in abundance. Lemon bars and thin slices of cake completed the luncheon.

Nearly everyone started visiting loudly. A few even laughed. No one seemed upset about Gramma. It bothered me so much that I couldn't eat a thing. Aunt Annie noticed and I told her what was wrong.

"That's just the way it is," she said. "Everyone's so wrung out, it's rather a relief when the whole thing's over. It doesn't mean we don't care, because we do. We'll grieve, each in our own way, but then life goes on. Maybe it doesn't seem right to you, since you've never experienced this before, but that's the way it is."

Uncle Jack sat down beside me. His plate was heaped high.

"It's true," he said. "Years ago, when your grandpa died, I was barely twelve. I thought I'd never get over it, but eventually the day came when I didn't think about him. Now it's been over twenty years and I still remember him, but I don't dwell on it because nothing can be done about it. You understand, don't you?"

"I guess so." I started picking at my lemon bar. Soon I'd eaten everything.

Uncle Jack expressed his approval. As skinny as I was, he said, I couldn't afford to miss a meal. He'd gotten skinny too, I pointed out, and if he'd stayed in Africa longer, he would've disappeared entirely. He smiled and said I was "spunky."

An RCA Radiogram was affixed to our door when we got home. Uncle Jack opened it on the kitchen table for everyone to see. A big, red advertisement spread across the top of the single sheet: *Fast. Direct. To All the World. Between Important U.S. Cities. To Ships at Sea.* The actual message from Daddy was shorter than the advertisement: *Received sad news. Letters following.*

"He didn't even mention me." I tried to swallow my disappointment.

"Oh, he will," Aunt Annie said. "I'm sure he'll send you a long letter about everything real soon. He just needs time to get to it. He's busy doing his job. You must remember that."

I had remembered. But had Daddy remembered that now I had no real family of my own, except him? Busy or not, a brief "I'm so sorry, Abby," would've eased my mind.

That night, I prayed fervently that Gramma was safe in heaven and Daddy was safe in Italy and wouldn't be killed in the war. It had taken one death for me to realize that another could soon follow.

Primogeniture

THE NEXT MORNING, Aunt Annie began converting their spare bedroom into my very own room. Circumstances had brought me to them, she said, and I might as well settle in. She asked what I needed from Gramma's house.

I had quite a list. Besides the rest of my clothes, I wanted my bow and arrows, knife, tomahawk, spear, and BB gun. I wanted my bike and my other birthday presents. I wanted my Tarzan scrapbooks, comics, books, and Gramma's crazy quilt. I wanted Daddy's letters and his portrait, plus anything else she deemed appropriate.

I worried she'd find Mother's letter, locket, and obituary. My worries compounded when she said my uncle would go through Gramma's house, not herself, as it required the expertise of a man to close the house for winter, remove the livestock, and perform countless other tasks. She assured me that Rover would be brought over in their car so my old dog would know where he belonged. The cats could find their own way. When Daddy returned, a final solution would be agreed upon after taking his wishes into consideration.

Aunt Annie, as busy as she was, performed chores quickly. Uncle Jack, as meticulous as he was, took his time. Mother's letter and locket wouldn't cause a problem since he'd given them to me, but I prayed he wouldn't open Daddy's letters and read every damn one out of curiosity. It was in my father's last letter that I'd hidden the obituary. I couldn't even imagine how I'd explain that one!

I breathed easier when my clothes came, along with my treasures, tossed together in one huge box.

Two weeks later, Daddy's letters arrived, one for me and the other for Uncle Jack. I could hardly contain my excitement as I tore open the envelope.

Dear Baby,

I trust you are being good for Aunt Annie and Uncle Jack. You're fortunate they live nearby so they could make all the arrangements and take you into their home without too much of a problem. I imagine you're missing your grandmother terribly, but nothing can be done about it. Cope the best you can. I was quite distraught (look it up) at the bad news myself, and I would've preferred to have come home, but that was impossible, which I'm sure was explained to you. Sometimes we all have to endure trials—

"Damn!" Uncle Jack shouted. "Goddamn everything!" Livid, he crushed Daddy's letter in his fist.

"Jack!" Aunt Annie reprimanded. "Don't talk like that in front of the children."

"I'll talk any way I damn please. You don't know what's happened. You don't know what she—what he's done now!"

"No, I don't, so why don't you stop swearing and tell me?"

My uncle glared at me sitting transfixed at the table and at Darrell across from me, a half-eaten sandwich suspended in his hand. "Not now."

"Go upstairs," Aunt Annie said to us.

"No, leave them alone. They can stay." He shoved the crumpled letter in his pocket and grabbed his hat and overcoat.

"And where do you think you're going?" Aunt Annie said.

"To town." He picked up the car keys.

"To town? What for?"

"What do you think for?"

She positioned herself between him and the back door. "No, Jack, not so soon after the funeral. Think of what people will say!"

"I don't give a shit what people will say."

"Talk to me," she pleaded. "Tell me what's wrong. Nothing's so bad it can't be worked out."

"I don't want to talk, and you're wrong. It *is* so bad it can't be worked out."

"What? What's so bad?"

"Everything." He put his hands on her shoulders and moved her firmly out of his way.

She stood by the window, hands on her hips, and watched him leave. "Men!" she fumed. She untied her apron and flung it to the floor. She kicked off her shoes and pulled on her boots. She yanked on her coat and reached for her scarf and mittens. She was still dressing as she stormed outside.

"What was that all about?" Darrell asked. He crammed the rest of the sandwich in his mouth.

"Like I could guess," I said. "Where's she going?"

Darrell swallowed before answering. "Walking … he gets her mad and she goes out and stomps around for a while. Nothing to worry about."

"So why'd he go to town?"

"To get drunk."

"To get drunk? No kidding?"

"No kidding."

"I didn't know he ever did that. Gramma never mentioned it."

"She probably didn't know. He doesn't exactly advertise, and the bums at the liquor store wouldn't be spreading it around."

"But he's got a cabinet full of liquor right here," I said.

"It's not the same. When he goes nuts, he drinks in town. Maybe he needs the company of other drunks … wonder what was in that letter that set him off like a keg of dynamite."

"We'll never know."

"Oh, we'll know. Might take a while, but we'll know. We'll read the letter."

"How?" I had to laugh. "Good grief, he didn't even show it to your mom! What makes you think he'll show it to us?"

My query was met with a sly grin. "He won't, not intentionally. But he stuffed it in his pocket. Unless he throws it away on his way to town, I, as head of Snoop and Company, will somehow read that letter and another mystery will be solved."

"Sure … when pigs fly."

Dennis was stricken with stomach flu during the night. As a precaution, Aunt Annie also kept Duane home from school because what one twin had, the other usually got hours later.

Without his brothers tagging along to eavesdrop, Darrell hadn't taken three steps out the door the next morning before he announced, "Pigs flew last night, Watson. I did it!"

"Did what?"

"I read the letter.

"Daddy's letter?"

"Yes, Daddy's letter," Darrell mimicked.

I could've fallen over in the snow, I was so amazed. "Really? I don't believe it!"

"Believe it. Want to know what it said?"

"Do ducks quack?" I hollered. "Of course I do!"

"First I'll tell you how I did it so you can be more impressed than you already are," Darrell said, looking smug. "Dad came home really late. He tried to be quiet, but nothing's noisier than a drunk trying to be quiet. Mom didn't hear him because she keeps their door shut at night. Actually he didn't wake me up either, because I woke up having to pee and I was deciding whether I really had to pee or if it could wait till morning—"

"Hang your pee story!" I said. "Get to the point."

Darrell made a face. "As I was saying, I was trying to decide about peeing when I heard Dad puking in the bathroom downstairs. I snuck down to snoop on him when I saw his sweater lying on the floor. I tiptoed over, reached in the pocket, and would you believe—"

"No!"

"Yes! Just where he'd stuffed it. I flattened it out enough to read before he got done being sick. What a chance I was taking! Can you imagine what would've happened if he'd opened the door—"

"And then?"

"And then I found out what made him so mad."

"What?"

"Don't yell in my face."

I resisted the urge to punch him. "Sorry."

"That's better. You need to appreciate my brilliance, you really do. Anyway, it was a really nasty letter. I didn't understand some of those hard words your dad uses, but what I got out of it was that my dad isn't getting anything of Gramma's."

"So who is?"

Darrell rolled his eyes. "Your dad, of course."

"Wow, that's great! Then after he comes back, we'll have loads of money and we'll live together at Gramma's house and everything will be wonderful."

"Maybe for you, but it's not wonderful for my dad. It didn't make him happy, did it?"

"No, but he has lots of money already. Why would he care?"

"Maybe he feels cheated. I've heard things usually get divided equally after somebody dies."

I felt a tad less thrilled. "Oh … do you feel cheated too?"

"No. Why should I care who gets Gramma's dinky little farm?"

"Thanks."

Darrell smiled. "You're welcome … by the way, that letter had an odd ending. My memory isn't as good as yours, but at the end your dad wrote:

Three times you've taken what wasn't yours, and this is one payback and more are coming. How far do the apples fall, little brother?"

"What do you think it means?" I said.

Darrell shrugged. "Beats me, but we'll find out."

After he sobered up, Uncle Jack ignored me for three days. I felt as welcome as a wart. He did, however, continue his ritual of bestowing my bedtime kiss. It might as well have been coming from a penguin, it was so cold.

Friday brought a welcome thaw. My uncle said he'd been to town again, this time to see the lawyer. He laid a copy of Gramma's will on the dining room table and gathered everyone together to listen to his explanation of how things were.

Gramma had willed five hundred dollars to each of her grandchildren, he said, to be invested and used for our higher education or to be handed over when we were twenty-one, if we foolishly chose not to be educated. That news created quite a stir, since Darrell and the twins had access to very little money, while I had none at all.

After we settled down, he said my aunt was to receive Gramma's collection of Red Wing vases because they'd shared a love of flowers. He paused. Aunt Annie looked at him expectantly, but he said that was it. She nodded and studied her hands folded on her lap.

I felt sorry for her. She'd been so good to Gramma and me, and vases were all the thanks she got?

Uncle Jack was doing fine up to that point, but I saw the situation getting difficult for him. Gramma's savings, the farm, and all it entailed had been willed solely to his older brother, he managed to say, and after him, to me. He cleared his throat, saying he'd expected to receive an equal share, but Gramma had added a codicil to her will, unbeknownst to himself, that excluded him. He didn't need the land or the money, but since he'd shouldered the responsibility of looking after Gramma and me, attending to our every need for years, while his brother pursued a career—

He stopped talking and walked to the window where, beyond the stark white of frozen fields, the shadows of the grove surrounding Gramma's house could be plainly seen, the house where he'd been born and rightfully expected to inherit a portion thereof, according to the natural order of things.

Aunt Annie slipped her arms around his waist. "It's all right, Jack. Don't let it make you bitter. It's not worth it."

He remained silent.

I was well acquainted with disappointment, so I ran to his other side. "Uncle Jack, that's not fair! I don't know whose fault it is, but as soon as I get Gramma's farm, I'll give you half."

He nodded and drew both of us close. "Seems I've gained far more than I've lost. I lost a piece of property and gained what money can't buy: the love and support of two fine women."

I glowed at his referring to me in such a grand manner, but Aunt Annie shook her head.

"That's not exactly accurate, Jack. I've always loved and supported you. Why, for over a decade I've loved and supported you, even when you've acted like a horse's behind!"

He grimaced. "Yes, and for that I thank you ... I gather you expect me to apologize for the behavior I've exhibited lately?"

"Yes, and apologize to Abby too. You've been treating her like she was somehow to blame for all this."

That night, when Uncle Jack came to kiss me goodnight, the warmth was back. "I'd never accept half your inheritance," he said, "but if I live to be a hundred, I'll never forget you offered."

After he left and I thought about it, I regretted offering him my inheritance so hastily. I needed to learn to protect my own interests. Gramma had willed everything to Daddy for a reason, and I had no business tampering with her intent. But no harm had been done, as my proposal hadn't been accepted. And Uncle Jack appreciated my offer, which was a good thing, since I was stuck living in his house.

What I couldn't fathom was why he'd made public the contents of Gramma's will. As secretive as he was, no plausible reason came to mind, unless he'd had no choice.

What had Daddy actually written in that letter? Had he threatened my uncle? I wished I'd had the chance to read it, rather than Darrell. "I would've gotten to the bottom of it. I would've remembered exactly what Daddy wrote," I said to PB.

My panda agreed wholeheartedly.

December arrived almost before I knew it. Darrell and I decorated the Christmas tree with strands of popcorn, tinsel, and shiny ornaments. Uncle Jack directed our efforts from the comfort of his easy chair. Aunt Annie commandeered my help to bake dozens of gingerbread men, pumpkin bars, and butter cookies with colored sprinkles. It wasn't my idea to slave away in her kitchen, but I hadn't any choice.

Christmas Eve brought us together at church. Darrell played Joseph in the Nativity pageant, while I played one of the townsfolk. I'd have fainted if I had to utter so much as a word in front of so many people.

Afterward, Uncle Jack hitched up two of the draft horses and we sledded to neighboring farms to pass out a generous assortment of the cookies we'd made. We laughed, sang carols, and acted giddy. The night air was so crisp and so cold, and the countless stars so clear, I prayed nothing would ever make me feel sad again.

That night, Aunt Annie gave me Daddy's Christmas letter. It had arrived days earlier with instructions not to give it to me until Christmas Eve. After my goodnight kiss from my uncle, I snuggled down in my bed to read.

Dear Baby,

Tonight is Christmas Eve. Undoubtedly you've been to church and gotten your treats and perhaps a ride behind the horses through the snow. Minnesota always has snow for Christmas; it's merely a question of how much.

Here we don't have much snow, except in the mountains, and I'm not in the mountains. Where I am, we have cold rain. It rains so much the roads become half-frozen rivers of ruts and puddles, making it difficult to navigate.

I took ten days R and R to Capri recently. Capri is a beautiful island, comprised of two mountains that rise abruptly from the sea, with a small valley between. The city lies where the valley touches the sea. While there, I did the usual tourist things. I rode a donkey up the mountainside to view the ruins of Tiberius's Castle. The walls are mostly gone, but the tile mosaic (look it up) floor is in good condition, and quite lovely. On the trip back down the mountain, I chose to walk, as donkeys have a rather bony ridge for a backbone, which is not the most comfortable!

I also visited the Blue Grotto, a unique work of nature accessible only by boat. Beyond the entrance is a domed cavern about a hundred feet across. The morning sun shining through the water turns the entire cavern a heavenly blue; hence the name. I bought a bottle of Blue Grotto water as a souvenir, but when I got back outside, the water contained therein looked the same as any other.

I did a little shopping and have sent you some things for Christmas. I'll go ahead and tell you what they are, as you'll be opening the package in the morning anyway. I bought you a cribbage board, inlaid with rosewood and ivory. Do you know how to play? If not, ask my brother. Jack is a lousy player, but he can at least teach you the basics. I much prefer chess myself, but Jack does not possess that skill as far as I know, so cribbage it must be. After you learn, you can trounce (look it up) him for me!

I also sent some leather goods, which need no explanation. Lastly, I sent you a silver bell, made in Capri. They're supposed to bring good luck, so I bought one for myself too. At night, after you say your prayers, hold your bell for a moment and think of me, and I will do the same for you.

My eyes misted as I pictured Daddy, so far away, holding his silver bell and thinking of me. I continued reading.

Thank you for the cookies you and Annie made. They arrived in pieces, but I ate every crumb. I get plenty to eat here, but it doesn't taste like the food from home. I especially miss beef roasts and big, juicy steaks. I plan to eat a lot of meat after I come back, and I hope it'll be soon.

Be a good girl, and write me a long letter next time instead of your usual short one. As you may have noticed, I didn't include many vocabulary words for you to learn this time. I've given you a holiday reprieve (look it up)! Ha, ha.

Merry Christmas.

Love, Daddy

As usual, I had a letter instead of a father. What good was that? Could a letter comfort me? Could a letter hug me?

He hadn't asked whether I was still missing Gramma. Nor did he mention his inheritance. At least he was starting to tell me what he saw and did. But ten days R and R? He could've come home to see me in that length of time, if only for a few days.

Through my floor register, I heard Uncle Jack laugh about something Aunt Annie said downstairs. I contemplated Daddy's portrait, hanging on the wall opposite my bed. It was the first thing I saw in the morning and the last thing I saw when I turned out my lamp at night.

Although the hour was late, I dutifully took paper, pen, and my dictionary from my dresser drawer and began my reply. At the bottom of the page, I quit.

I would compose a second page when I felt better.

Spring 1945

Changes

Arranging my room took a mere day or two. What took far longer was finding my niche, a place where I could suspend without a wobble.

Even Darrell didn't smooth the process. One spring afternoon, as I helped him search for rock specimens for his science project, he suddenly turned on me.

"I'm older and I'm their real son. I'm sick and tired of you prancing around like you're so special. When your precious daddy comes back you can act like the little princess, but not on my turf!"

Fortunately I knew the meaning of "turf." Darrell had begun looking up odd words to use when I least expected it. "Well, I'd rather be Tarzan than a princess," I said.

My cousin snorted in derision. "Some Tarzan you'd make, you with your silly dresses and bows in your hair. Even Cheetah would laugh at you."

Those were fighting words. "Can I help your mom keeps buying me dresses and bows?" I yelled. "And your dad insists I wear the damn dresses and bows?"

"Oh, so you'd be happier naked?" Darrell taunted. "How about food? Do you like stuffing your face at our table or would you rather starve? And how about that room of yours? It's bigger than mine, did you know that? I should've gotten that room, not you. Bet you'll blame my folks for the roof over your head next!"

I was stunned by his vehemence. "That's not what I meant, Darrell."

"So what *did* you mean?"

"I just want to dress how I like and do the things I used to," I said, my feelings hurt. "What's wrong with that? How'd you like it if your folks died and you had to move in with somebody else and all the rules changed overnight?"

He paused, looking at me. "I guess I'd feel lousy."

"Well, that's exactly how I feel. And I didn't get a choice about any of it, did I?"

"No … I was thinking you were lucky you had somewhere to go after Gramma died, but I guess that doesn't make it any easier."

"No, it doesn't." I walked away so he wouldn't see my lips quiver.

He followed me. "Well, as far as the dresses and bows go, Abby, I think you'll have to put up with it for a while. Maybe my folks will get over it. And maybe your dad won't care if you wear my old clothes again."

"Maybe … if he ever comes back."

"Of course he will. The war's practically over … I'm sorry I made fun of you."

I plopped down on the side of the road. I'd get scolded for muddying my skirt, but I didn't care. "I just can't seem to get used to all the changes."

"In case you haven't noticed, things have changed for me too." Darrell sat next to me, but on his gunnysack so his school pants would stay clean. "Seems like my folks always wanted a girl. Dad's never paid so much attention to me in my whole life as he does to you in a single week. The only time he notices I'm alive is when I've done something wrong. It does Mom good, though, having you to keep her company."

"I don't want to keep her company. I'm so sick of working in her kitchen I could puke."

"I can understand that, but I can't change it."

"I know you can't, but at least your dad goes to town or goes riding and you get a break. Your mom's after me constantly. If she's not making me do dishes or clean up something, it's baking. I didn't know helping with those Christmas cookies would lead to baking all year long."

"At least you don't have to do smelly things like Dad makes me do. Baking cookies is lots nicer than shoveling horseshit."

"He only makes you do that when you've made him mad. Charlie and Ole do most of it. I slave in the kitchen whether I've made anybody mad or not."

Darrell shrugged. "Then I guess you're sunk."

Exactly … I was a tiny bathtub toy, swirling helplessly in circles, heading toward the drain.

As difficult as it was to come to terms with Darrell, it was impossible with Duane and Dennis. I tried to stay out of their way, but they seldom stayed out of mine. Our paths collided time after time, and I didn't have to guess how they felt about me.

"Die, Abby!" I'd hear as they scampered past. At seven years of age, they probably didn't realize the implication of those words, but that was cold comfort. I hoped they'd slip up and be overheard, but they were unerringly careful.

Darrell dismissed my concerns. His brothers were nincompoops and should be ignored. But ignoring those two brats was difficult when my natural inclination was to punch them clear into next week.

As though Aunt Annie and my cousins weren't tribulation enough, Uncle Jack wore me out completely. He was so erratic; I never knew how he'd react to any given situation. One minute he'd be ranting and the next he'd be giving me a hug.

Darrell said I caused much of my own upheaval, but I didn't believe him.

All I knew was that I tended to act either my best or my worst around my uncle, seldom even keel. For a time I'd be polite, obedient, and cheerful. Then something beyond my control would erupt inside me and I'd pout, complain, and argue. I'd do my chores sloppily or not at all. Aunt Annie would endure my antics for as long as possible before calling on Uncle Jack.

Then I'd vanish. I'd stay gone until whatever work I'd tried to avoid would be done by someone else. I'd stay gone until the volcano settled again. I'd stay gone until six o'clock, because I never wanted to miss my supper.

But once I stayed gone longer than six. Uncle Jack actually saddled Banat and came looking for me. I watched him saunter under the haymow where I was nestled, but then a sixth sense made him wheel Banat around and make toward the barn. I barely had time to run out the back before he came in the front. I darted from one outbuilding to another, and when I looked back, he was checking each in turn. I raced into the grove, which he surveyed as well. When he got too close, I raced in a zigzag fashion from one stand of trees to another. Finally I tore as fast as I could to my hidey-hole in the slough. I had to cover some open ground to get to it, but it couldn't be helped. Tyrant Jack would never find me there!

He found me in ten minutes. He said later that he'd seen me from his vantage point astride Banat and had let me settle in before quietly picking his way toward me. By then I felt so defeated I couldn't run further. When I saw him dismount and stride toward me, I had no defense but tears.

"I came looking for you because I thought you'd hurt yourself and couldn't make it home." He slapped the crop against his boot. "But from the way you can run, nothing's wrong, is there?"

"Everything's wrong," I sobbed.

He never did hit me. Maybe he felt sorry for me. God knows, I felt sorry enough for myself. My new life wasn't my life. It shouldn't have been my life. I hadn't chosen it. I was outside, looking in, a stranger amid family.

Then Aunt Annie tried to force cooking on me. Baking I was used to. You baked, you cleaned up. A day or so later, you baked again. But cooking was perpetual. You labored for hours. The food was wolfed down in minutes. The second you cleaned up, you were back to cooking. Nope, meal preparation was her job, not mine.

Aunt Annie appealed to Uncle Jack to make me cooperate. I appealed to him to make her leave me alone. He did neither. The situation deteriorated. I told him I was being worked to death. He said I'd never looked healthier. I told him he needed to hire a cook or a maid, or both. He smiled and said that's what Annie and I were for. I told him I was sick of being a girl and I was going to quit. He laughed and said the most wonderful women he'd ever known started out as girls, and I should be proud of what nature made me.

I blew up. I told him I intended to live at Gramma's farm so I could have time for myself. I knew he couldn't take anything more off the place without Daddy's permission, including me. He did not look amused when he agreed I should go.

That bothered me. I never expected his permission. I thought about it while hanging from the apple tree as the wind whipped through my hair, sending my hair bows sailing. I didn't retrieve them. I thought about it while playing with a litter of newborn kittens and getting dirt and kitty pee all over my pretty dress. I thought about it as I trudged three-quarters of the way to Gramma's house. Just past the slough, as the house became clearly discernable, I stopped. The trees surrounding the house hadn't yet leafed out, so they appeared naked and sinister without their summer mantle. The house windows, with their shades partially pulled down, resembled dark eyes with drooping lids.

Then I remembered all the trips Uncle Jack had made to the farm in the weeks following Gramma's death. He'd sold the livestock and the poultry, so nothing alive remained. Even Ole was gone. He now puttered around my uncle's farm, helping Charlie, because he was too old to find another job elsewhere.

Inside the house, the cupboards and the refrigerator would be bare. The stove had to be lit and I didn't know how. The electricity might be turned off. Bugs and snakes and maybe worse had moved in and taken over. I'd have to clean for days to make the place livable again. What would I eat? I was already hungry. What would I wear? I was already dirty.

If I lived alone at Gramma's house, who'd buy me the things I needed and most of the things I wanted? Who'd patch me up when I fell off my bike or out of a tree? Who'd yell me awake in the morning and kiss me to bed at night? On whose lap would I crawl when I was feeling my lowest?

My resolve faltering, I took several more steps toward my goal. A pheasant fluttered skyward from nearly beneath my feet, propelling my heart to my throat. I turned and ran back from where I'd come. I slowed to a walk when I saw Uncle Jack watching me from the front steps.

"Come here, Abigail."

I came, but I refused to look at him.

"Are you done being a pain now?"

Grudgingly I nodded.

"Answer me properly!"

"Yes, sir," I mumbled.

"I won't tolerate ingratitude. I've had enough of that already."

"I'm sorry." I worried an ant with my shoe, hoping for permission to go. It was not forthcoming.

"The last time I saw you, you looked fine. Now you're a mess. What have you been doing with yourself?"

"Stuff."

"What stuff?"

"Well, first I climbed the apple tree, and then I found Penny's new kittens in the haymow, and I gave them all names—"

"I was wondering what that was on your dress."

I looked at the yellow stain Comet had caused. "I'm sorry," I said again. Mostly I was sorry Aunt Annie had bought me the dress I was wearing. I was sorry I had any dresses at all.

"You need to be more careful."

"Yes, sir."

"Now go upstairs and clean up. It's almost time for supper."

As I went past him, he caught my arm. "There's a new pair of jeans on your bed. If they fit, I'll buy you more. Except for school and church, you don't have to wear dresses anymore."

I should've been ecstatic, but right away I wanted more. "What about the hair bows? I hate hair bows. I look like Little Orphan Annie in hair bows."

He shook his head. "I'm not getting involved in that one. Talk to your aunt."

"Well, what about the cooking? I absolutely hate cooking."

"You like eating, don't you? Somebody has to cook what you eat. No time like the present to learn."

My mistake came when I tried to win the second concession on my own. I cut my hair and I cajoled Darrell into helping me.

"I don't think I should," he said when I first asked.

"Why not? It's my hair, and if I want my hair short, what's it to you?"

"Nothing, but I bet it'll be something to my folks … nope, count me out."

So I propped Uncle Jack's shaving mirror on a bale in the haymow and wielded the scissors with cocky abandon. Penny and her kittens watched. Comet even applauded, in her cute little kitten way. I cut my bangs a bit crooked, so I did it a second time. When it turned out the same degree of crookedness as the first, I moved on. In an attempt to even the sides, I hacked off more than I'd originally intended. The results still looked preferable to having dark curls cascading past my shoulders like Rapunzel, that pitiable damsel who waited years for a prince to climb her tresses and rescue her from her prison tower. Nobody was going to rescue me from my particular prison, and cutting my hair so short that Auntie couldn't put a bow in it made me feel powerful.

I waylaid Darrell shuffling to the horse barn. I flipped my head from side to side to show off. "Hey, look what I did already! You've got to help me finish because I can't see the back."

Darrell stopped in his tracks. "Good grief."

I was taken aback. "What's the matter? It looks great, doesn't it?"

He laughed.

"Why are you laughing? Is it bad? Is it?"

"Yeah, it's really bad. Why'd you even try? You don't know anything about cutting hair."

I studied my efforts again in the mirror. My bangs went up at a slant and then down again. The left side appeared considerably shorter than my right. Or was it the other way around? Everything in a mirror was backward. And ragged tufts of hair jutted out in all directions. Why hadn't I noticed *that* before?

I panicked. "You've got to help me now. I can't go up to the house looking like this!"

"Don't you go talking me into this. Ain't any of my business."

"Darrell, please … "

"I'm supposed to shovel in the horse barn for an hour before supper. Dad caught me punching Duane. If I don't get it done because of you, I'll get two hours tomorrow."

"I'll give you anything if you'll help me."

"You don't have anything to give."

I began to cry because it was true and because I was desperate.

"Oh, shut up, will you?" he said testily. "All right, I'll try. You can't go traipsing around like a scarecrow. But you'll owe me, Abby. You'll owe me a really big favor one day."

"You name it; I'll do it."

"Sure."

He plunked me down on a bale and got to work, snipping a bit here, a bit there. Right side, left side, right side again, back, left side again. I sat motionless, worried he'd nick an ear.

"What are you doing?" I said. "What's taking so long?"

"I'm trying to get it even, you doorknob. If you hadn't chopped everything all crooked, it wouldn't take so much time."

"Well, hurry up. It must be nearly six. I don't want to miss supper."

"Like I want to miss supper?"

"No, but hurry up anyway."

"Abby … "

"What?"

"Shut up! This wasn't my idea and if you try to hurry me when I'm trying to fix your mess, I'm going to throw these scissors in a cow pie and you're on your own."

I shut up.

Minutes later the supper bell clanged.

"That's it, I'm done!" Darrell shouted. "I'm out of time and I never even started shoveling. I'll get two hours tomorrow, thanks to you." He stalked off with the scissors.

When I entered the kitchen, Aunt Annie took one look at me and shrieked. Uncle Jack ran in from another room, as though expecting catastrophe. Both stared at me. Duane and Dennis sniggered. Darrell slunk to his chair.

"What the h—" Aunt Annie caught herself in time. "I mean, what on earth happened to your hair, Abby? You look ridiculous."

I wished the floor would open up and swallow me. "I cut it … Darrell tried to fix it."

Aunt Annie turned indignantly to my uncle. "You know what this means, don't you?"

"She wanted short hair?" He kept a straight face.

"No, try again."

"She wanted a new look?"

"No, and that's the same thing anyway."

"I give up."

"She's flaunting our authority, Jack. It's as plain as the nose on your face. She doesn't like her clothes. She doesn't like her hair. She doesn't do her chores. She doesn't want to learn anything. She keeps running off. She hates living with us—"

"Oh, don't blow things out of proportion, Annie. She's still adjusting. I don't think cutting her hair means much of anything. She probably just wanted a change. You do that yourself."

"Without asking?"

"All right; she should've asked."

"Yes, and I'd have taken her to town and had it done correctly."

"You would have?" He arched an eyebrow.

"Well, yes ... yes, I'm sure I would've. And now I'll have to. I'll have to take her to town and get that *disaster* redone. And you know what you have to do now, don't you, Jack?"

"What?"

"You ask me *what*? You have to remedy the situation, that's what!"

"How, Annie? I don't think there's glue for bungled haircuts."

My aunt appeared so flustered I would've laughed if it hadn't been me she was flustered about.

"No, that's not what I meant, Jack. I mean you have to take them to the woodshed!"

"The woodshed? Why? Using a scissors without permission?"

"No, for flying in the face of authority, that's why! Abby knows we want her to look pretty and she did this simply to defy us. And Darrell, instead of telling us or stopping her, he assists her. I told you when you started letting her run around in jeans and cast-offs again there'd be no end to it."

"Oh, there'll be an end to it ... you heard her, you little pups," he said to Darrell and me. "Her wish is my command. To the woodshed with you—march."

I walked behind Darrell. Uncle Jack walked behind me. I couldn't believe what was about to happen. Aunt Annie seldom demanded anyone punished. In fact, she often asked my uncle to excuse even blatant misbehavior.

Darrell opened the door to the woodshed. Uncle Jack shut it. He took the belt off its nail and doubled it.

"Who gets it first?" he said.

"Me." Darrell skewered me with a glance of pure hate.

"Bend over."

Darrell leaned over the toolbox. Uncle Jack raised the belt. I turned away and shut my eyes. Darrell yelped as the belt came down on his rump.

"Get out of the way and keep yelling," Uncle Jack said.

"What?" Darrell said.

I opened my eyes and turned around to see what was happening.

"I said move out of the way. I'm going to whip the toolbox, not you, but you need to holler like it's you," Uncle Jack explained. "Of course, if you prefer—"

Darrell moved as quickly as I'd ever seen. The toolbox took a hard licking, and my cousin squawked at all the appropriate intervals.

"Your mother said I should ... haul you to the woodshed ... but she didn't explicitly say ...what I had to do ... when I got you there." Uncle Jack timed his phrases between licks. "Punishing stupidity is rather ... pointless because kids … are always acting stupid … one way or the other … Abby, your turn."

I obligingly hollered from the safety of my corner.

"Not good enough. Like Darrell, you're getting a real lick so I can truthfully say you've been punished." He grabbed me, flipped me over the toolbox, and whacked me once with the belt. It stung sufficiently to get my hollering off to a believable start.

Darrell stood off to the side, watching. "I don't understand why we're all pretending."

"Because your mother's listening. She stepped outside … as we came in here … for some reason, she's madder … than a hornet about this … Abby, stop yelling so loud … or she'll be running out here … to offer you clemency because … you sound like you're being killed!"

Uncle Jack hung up the belt. "Look teary when you come in the house. You'll get your supper, even if it's gone cold … Abby, I'm warning you. Don't ever mangle your hair again. I won't be repeating this little charade."

Jeanette Kramer, proprietor and sole employee of Jeanette's Cut and Curl, straightened out my debacle the next morning. To even the sides, she had to cut my hair nearly as short as a boy's. She said I had wonderful hair and it would grow out in no time, but she strongly advised against me shearing it myself.

After Aunt Annie paid, she took a blue bow from her purse and fixed it to the top of my head. Without saying a word, she fixed that damn bow to the top of my head.

I pouted all the way home.

My morning deteriorated further when Uncle Jack made me help Darrell for two hours.

"Fair is fair," he said. "Darrell tried to help you, now you have to help him." Then he went riding.

Charlie greeted me with a cockeyed grin as I eased into the horse barn. "Oh, oh … looks like somebody else's been bad. Guess with two kids doing my work and the boss gone, think I'll get a little shut-eye in my truck. Wake me up when he comes back … what happened to your hair, Miss Abby? Didn't you used to have some?"

Without answering, I gingerly sidestepped a plop of shit, grabbed Charlie's pitchfork, and started shoveling.

It was a long and smelly morning. Darrell the Dull wasn't talking to me. Annie of the Red Hair wasn't talking to me. Tyrant Jack, as usual, talked entirely too much.

And I talked only to the cats. They wouldn't tell how my blue hair bow somehow ended up at the bottom of the manure spreader.

Nope, changes sure didn't come easy, not for Princess Abigail.

Rover

As THOUGH I hadn't enough to deal with, Rover disappeared a week later. I suspected something was wrong when I received no welcoming wag or happy bark of greeting as I trudged up the drive after a hard day at school. I called him when I set his supper on the back porch, but he didn't come. By nightfall, the cats had eaten his food, and still he hadn't come. I told my uncle when he strolled in to bestow my goodnight kiss.

"Well, it's not unusual for dogs to wander off for a day or so," he said. "Rover might've found a new girlfriend. Last year, the Swanson's cocker had a litter of pups that resembled you-know-who."

"But Rover was in better shape then. Now he can barely walk. You just don't want me to worry."

"True enough. If Rover hasn't come back by tomorrow afternoon, we'll go looking for him."

"All right. Good night, Uncle Jack."

"Good night, Princess."

Rover was chasing a rabbit through the darkness. The rabbit ran faster and faster, laughing at poor Rover, who never could quite catch him. Rover chased the laughing rabbit into a culvert. The rabbit slipped out the far side, but Rover got stuck. He wiggled and he yelped, but he couldn't crawl forward and he couldn't back up. His lips curled against his teeth as he howled for help.

And then the rain began. The culvert began to fill. The rushing water covered Rover's body and crept past his neck. Exhausted, he struggled to hold his nose clear of the rising water. He howled one last time when lightning sheared the night asunder.

I sat bolt upright in bed. Thunder reverberated. The house shook. I tried to switch on my lamp, but the electricity had gone out. Aided by flashes of lightning, I felt my way downstairs. I flung open the back door and called. The slashing rain mocked me. Hoping Rover had crawled down the coal hole, his usual refuge from rain or cold, I cracked the cellar door and yelled into the blackness. No answer. Thunder crashed. I slammed the door against the crawling, slithering creatures who lurked there during the night.

Rover was out there in the storm, trapped! I could hear him. He was nearby. I had to hurry. I slipped on my galoshes and raincoat. I tied my uncle's rain hat tight with my scarf. The Coleman lantern was in my hand. Where were the matches? *Where the hell were the matches?*

"Where do you think you're going?" Uncle Jack fixed me in the beam of his flashlight as he loomed in the doorway.

"To look for Rover!" I shouted over the thunder.

"What? Now?"

"Yes, now!"

"The hell you are. You're not going anywhere in this storm."

"But Rover's drowning in the culvert! I dreamt it. He's stuck and he's drowning. Help me find the damn matches … shit, give me that!" I lunged for his flashlight.

He moved it away and caught me around the wrist. "Settle down, Abigail. You're not going anywhere."

"Let go, Rover needs me!" I pulled, yanked, and flailed in desperation. I didn't dare bite him, but I did something else that got his attention.

"Kick me again and you'll be sorry!" he said in a tone I'd heard a hundred times. "Stop fighting me and stop it right now."

Struggling was futile. I went limp. He leaned me against him, took off my raincoat, undid my scarf, and slipped his hat from my head. I stepped out of my galoshes when he told me to. He took me inside and sat with me on the davenport as I grieved for my lost friend.

Rover was dead. I knew it. I hadn't been able to save him.

I'd gone to sleep in the winter and Gramma had died.

I'd gone to school in the spring and Rover had died.

Where would I be in the summer when Daddy died?

The storm ebbed as dawn broke pale and pink. Through the window, I saw shattered tree limbs and other debris scattered amid the farm buildings.

"Are you all right now?" Uncle Jack asked.

"Yes … no … oh, I don't know. Why didn't you just let me go?"

"I couldn't, Abby. The lightning was too dangerous."

"But it wouldn't have taken long. The culvert's at the end of the driveway."

"And a dozen other places. Not to mention those on neighboring farms. Not that Rover's stuck in one anyway. I don't hold much stock in dreams."

"I do."

"That's your privilege."

"I'm sorry I kicked you."

"No harm done. Just don't do it again."

"I won't." With my finger, I idly traced the curve of his moustache. I didn't understand why I'd started doing it, but he seemed to tolerate it well.

"How come you didn't get mad when I cried this time? You always get mad when I cry."

"You had a reason this time."

"I always have a reason … Rover's dead, isn't he?"

"Maybe. We'll go looking for him today, right after school."

"School?" I made a gagging sound. "Don't tell me that you're making me go to school after the terrible night I've had!"

"Of course … I don't have time to crawl back in the sack, so why should you?"

"But you could if you wanted to. I have a test in arithmetic, another in spelling, and I'm too damn tired to even think and—"

He held a finger over my mouth. "No more complaints. And no more saying words like 'damn' and 'shit.' Such language hardly befits a young lady."

"You say them. You say lots worse."

"I'm not a young lady."

"Darrell says them."

"He does? Then I'll crack down on him too … although he's not a young lady either."

"Neither am I … I'm Tarzan."

He chuckled. "Oh? I thought you were a princess. A princess, of necessity, is also a young lady."

"Well, I'm sick of being a princess. Why do you think I hate wearing dresses? I'd rather be Tarzan. He wears a rag around his butt and yells whatever he wants."

Uncle Jack's smile faded. "I'm sorry to be the bearer of bad tidings, Abigail, but the closest you'll ever get to Tarzan is Jane, so clean up your language. Understand?"

"Fine." I sighed.

Jane? What a horrific thought! I was as fast and hard as any boy. I could scream and fight and come up victorious, at least sometimes. Studying myself in the full-length mirror in the upstairs bathroom, I lifted my nightgown. My legs were lithe and long, with shapely calves. I shoved up my sleeves and flexed my arms. My shoulders were small but my biceps were clearly defined. Not bad, I thought. If I weighed more I'd have bigger muscles. I would start eating more … maybe even some god-awful vegetables.

Jane? Not if I could help it!

I looked again in the mirror. I studied my lips that were full, my nose that ended delicately, my ears that were small and evenly placed, and my eyes that were large and dark and rimmed with thick lashes. Even with cropped hair, I did not resemble any boy I'd ever seen.

Uncle Jack was right. I would be Jane. I would grow up to be Jane who swept the tree house with a twig broom and cooked the impala meat for Tarzan's supper.

Damn! Damnation all to hell!

After Darrell peeked in the culvert as we waited for the bus, and Rover wasn't stuck there, I still didn't have a good day at school. I got my spelling words right, but I botched my arithmetic test. Billy Hartmann bumped into me on purpose in the hall and made *me* apologize. I closed my eyes for a moment during geography and the next thing I heard was Miss Fuhrman rapping my desk with her ruler, which made me jump and everyone else laugh.

I was glad when the dismissal bell finally rang, although I had nothing to look forward to at home. Try as I might, I couldn't even disappear into one of the stories I made up constantly inside my head, complete with nonstop action and breathtaking dialogue. I was not, nor would I ever be, Tarzan or anyone else of heroic dimensions. Nor was I a princess. I was simply an insignificant young girl and I could no longer ignore the fact, thanks to Uncle Jack, who had no more dreams and took delight in ruining mine.

Uncle Jack, Charlie, and Ole were seated at the kitchen table, partaking of coffee and doughnuts, when we kids walked in from school.

"How'd your day go?" Uncle Jack asked me. "Fall asleep?"

"Rotten. Yes." I went upstairs to change.

Ole and Charlie were back at work when I came down again. Uncle Jack was outside, astride Banat. The mare was anticipating the exercise. Her slender ears were pricked forward and she pranced in a circle as I approached.

"Do you want to ride Peaches or climb up here with me?"

"You."

"Then hurry up, she's ready to rip!" He slipped his boot out of the left stirrup for me and I swung myself up.

Minutes later, I saw what I'd been dreading: a black-and-white ball of fur, curled on the front step of Gramma's house. Uncle Jack slowed Banat to a stop. I slid off and watched as a gust of wind ruffled the fur. I prayed for further movement. There was none.

My throat tightened. "How'd you know?"

"I didn't. I just guessed." My uncle dismounted and tied Banat to the cottonwood in the front yard.

"But why did Rover come here? Why didn't he stay home with me?"

"This was his home, Abby, except for the last five months. He knew his time was at an end, and he came here to die. It must've taken considerable effort for him to get here, but he certainly was determined."

"Do you think he was looking for Gramma?"

"No. He never came here before, as far as I know. I think he just wanted to die where he'd lived."

I let that sink in for a while. "I need to say good-bye."

"I wouldn't do that if I were you."

"Why not?"

"You can, if you want. I won't stop you. But he's probably been dead for two days. The flies will have found him."

As I approached, I saw it was so. I backed off, weeping.

Uncle Jack gave me his handkerchief. "I'd like to bury him here rather than take him back. But you have the last word on that. He was your dog."

I nodded. Much as I wanted to bury Rover at my uncle's farm, where I could visit his grave daily and tell him what he was missing, it wouldn't be advisable to haul him anywhere after two days of mild weather.

I watched as my uncle brought a gunnysack and a shovel from the barn. He eased Rover into the sack and dug a large hole by the edge of the grove. The rain had softened the ground, but still it took a long time. Rover was not a small dog and it wouldn't be proper to have him dug up by another animal. After my uncle finished, I piled several stones, as large as I could carry, from the rock pile to mark the spot.

"Good-bye, Rover." I ran my hands along the damp mound of earth covering my friend. "You always were a good dog. You were the best dog ever. I'll call your name every night at suppertime so you'll know I haven't forgotten you. Keep Gramma company for me."

I wanted to leave then, but Uncle Jack said he needed to rest. He rinsed his hands under the pump, lit a Chesterfield, and sat on the front steps. I sat beside him.

He exhaled slowly. "It's been a long time since I've had to do this."

"Do what?"

"Bury a dog. When I was a kid, we had a dog named Nippy. My job was to feed him every night, same as you did for Rover. He didn't have the best personality, so I had to set his bowl down and back away. If I turned too soon, he'd nip me. But one day I turned around without thinking and that miserable dog tore into me. Ripped my pants, took a chunk out of my leg, blood all over. I screamed until my brother ran up and saw what had happened. He grabbed a baseball bat and beat that dog senseless. I thought he'd kill old Nippy, and I wouldn't have cared if he had. You'd think that would've taught Nippy a lesson, but his temperament grew even worse. Dad finally shot him. James and I buried him, though … took us half an afternoon."

"That's not a very nice story," I said.

"No, it's not. At least Rover never bit anybody. He was a good dog."

"I meant Daddy beating Nippy. I can't imagine anyone doing that."

"He had it coming."

"But Nippy didn't understand, did he? He didn't change. He didn't know why he was getting hit, did he?"

Uncle Jack ground out his cigarette on the steps. "It's you who doesn't understand. Come on, we're going home."

Aunt Annie was waiting for us on the porch. "Jack, Abby!" she called. "You won't believe what just happened—President Roosevelt is dead! Mr. Truman took the oath of office a few minutes ago!"

After supper, we gathered around the Philco. Uncle Jack dialed from one station to another, gleaning the latest news reports. On WCCO, we heard the announcer say:

A shocked nation is in mourning tonight for Franklin Delano Roosevelt. The President died this afternoon at the Little White House in Warm Springs, Georgia. Vice president Harry S. Truman was on Capitol Hill when the president died. He was rushed to the White House, where he offered his condolences to Mrs. Roosevelt before he was sworn in as the thirty-second president of the United States. Doctors say Roosevelt passed away at 3:35 this afternoon, two hours after suffering a cerebral hemorrhage. Grace Tully, his private secretary, is quoted as saying, "The shock was unexpected and the actuality of the event was outside belief." In recent days, Roosevelt appeared to be recuperating from the stresses of war and the Yalta Conference. After Mrs. Roosevelt was informed of her husband's death, she said, "I am more sorry for the people of this country and of the world than I am for ourselves." When Truman asked the First Lady what he could do for her, she replied, "Is there anything we can do for you? You are the one in trouble now."

Stay tuned for updates as we receive them … now for a word from one of our sponsors.

Uncle Jack turned the dial to KNUJ for the war news from both fronts. After Cal Karnstedt's *Farm News Time* on KSTP, he switched off the radio and reached for his pipe. "Time for bed, kids," he said. "Plenty more to hear tomorrow."

As we started upstairs, Aunt Annie said to him, "Well, at least your brother will make it home now."

She sounded so confident that I paused to listen.

"What … makes you … say that?" he asked, lighting his pipe.

"As you know, Jack, deaths usually come in threes. We've had our three now: Mother, Rover, and now President Roosevelt. That means James will be coming back just fine."

"Good Lord, Annie! By what stretch of your imagination can you possibly link the death of my mother with the death of an old dog with the death of a Democrat we've never voted for?"

I knew they were headed for one of their prolonged discussions where he would attempt to persuade and overwhelm her with logic and reason. She would listen politely before she'd shrug her shoulders and say, "Trust me, Jack. I'm right. I'm always right."

I trusted her. She hadn't been right about my dresses and hair bows, but this time she was right. Daddy would be coming back.

But after my prayers and my goodnight kiss from Uncle Jack, who stomped upstairs after giving up the argument in exasperation, I held my silver bell of Capri and wondered what kind of boy would beat a dog.

I wondered what kind of man that boy had become.

I wondered whether a boy who beat a dog had become a man who killed his wife.

Wax Lips and Hot Dots

SHORTLY AFTER ROVER'S death, Aunt Annie extended peace overtures to me. Hair bows were mandatory only for church, she said, and she stopped carping about my slovenly attire and curtailed her demands for my help in the kitchen. Had Uncle Jack influenced her change of heart?

I missed Rover less after my uncle surprised Darrell and me with two mongrel puppies. We promptly baptized Ranger and Molly in a cow tank dunking like the Baptists did instead of sprinkling their fuzzy heads like the Lutherans did. The experience also taught them to swim.

Then two events of supreme significance happened within days of each other. The first was so glorious it was accompanied by the peal of church bells all over town: we had won the war in Europe!

Uncle Jack purchased a special issue of the *New York Times*, as though the *St. Paul Pioneer Press* and the news bulletins emanating from WCCO, KNUJ, and KSTP weren't quite sufficient.

Nazis Give Up! screamed the headline, followed by *Surrender to Allies and Russia Announced*. As the rest of the family sat in rapt attention, I was allowed to do the honors by reading the newspaper aloud. I stumbled over just a few words, mostly proper nouns.

Berlin, May 8th. Adolf Hitler is dead, his Thousand Year Reich is destroyed, and the war in Europe is over. The beginning of the end for Germany was the Russian drive that began on April 16th. Soviet troops reached Berlin by the 22nd and surrounded the city a few days later. Hitler and his mistress, Eva Braun, the Goebbels family, and a few faithful remained in an underground bunker where the Fuehrer played with non-existent armies on a large war map. Above ground, the Russians were blasting into rubble what Allied planes had failed to destroy. On May 2nd, Russians soldiers took the beleaguered city and hoisted the hammer and sickle atop the Brandenburg Gate. The leadership of the ruined Reich was turned over to Grand Admiral Karl Doenitz, who quickly moved to end the suffering of Germany. The Germans attempted to surrender to the Western Allies alone but the effort was spurned. Finally on May 7th at 2:41 a.m., local time, Field Marshal Jodl, at SHAEF advanced headquarters in a boys' school in Rheims, France, signed an unconditional surrender to General Eisenhower. The surrender was ratified in the ruins of Berlin today, thus making May 8th VE Day: Victory in Europe.

The article ended. Time stood still.

Uncle Jack broke the spell. "We're living a moment in history that must never be forgotten. Remember this day forever. And when we're victorious in the Pacific, good surely will have triumphed over evil."

The twins looked blank, as they often did, but Darrell and I nodded solemnly. The war had always been a part of our lives. We couldn't remember when metal, rag, paper, and junk weren't collected for the war effort and when rationing didn't exist. We couldn't remember when signs such as *Schools at War: We are Ready, What about You? Save! Serve! Conserve!* weren't plastered along the halls. We couldn't remember a holiday without first making cards of greeting and appreciation to send overseas or to the wounded in hospitals, or when *Shoulder a Gun, or the Cost of One: Buy War Bonds* wasn't touted as *Your Means of Getting into the Fight.* We couldn't remember when ladies in our community weren't knitting khaki-colored sweaters, assembling Kit Bags, or organizing blood drives and donations to the Red Cross. Banners in windows had always proclaimed a son in the Army, and the possibility of that soldier's life ending prematurely had always been the nightmare of every family.

"Good reading, Abby," Aunt Annie said. "You've learned your words well."

"Thank you, Auntie." I basked in her infrequent praise.

"You're very welcome … oh, I just thought of something else!" She smiled. "Now that we've won Europe, it can't be much longer before your father comes home. We'll throw him such a grand party. I can't wait to get started, can you?"

I saw Uncle Jack wince at her comment, as though experiencing physical pain.

The next significant event in my life happened simply because I wanted wax lips and hot dots. I'd had plenty of opportunities to snatch a nickel here or a dime there, but I always worried it might be a trap, so I had resisted the temptation.

"I need two quarters today," I told my uncle at breakfast.

He peered at me over his pancakes. "What do you need that for?"

"School."

"Why? Isn't everything provided?"

I hadn't expected an interrogation. My mind raced. If I said it was for a gift for someone moving away, he'd ask who. If I said it was to buy supplies, he'd ask what. If I said the truth, he'd say wax lips and hot dots were unnecessary.

"Billy Hartmann," I said.

Uncle Jack stopped chewing. "Billy Hartmann? What does he need your quarters for?"

"Um … he said I swiped fifty cents from his lunchbox yesterday, and I'd better replace it today." I prayed I wasn't digging myself into a deep hole with a big shovel.

"And did you steal his money?"

Darrell kicked me under the table. I tried not to react. Everyone stared at me.

My uncle set down his fork. "Well, did you?"

"Of course not!"

"Then why do you feel the need to give him two quarters?"

"Because he thinks I took it, that's why! Billy's had it in for me forever. Why, he even bumped me in the hall the other day, on purpose, and made *me* apologize!"

"Why didn't you tell me he was bothering you? Sounds like I need to go up to that school and have a talk with—"

"No, don't do that! You can't protect me every day. I have to get along by myself, don't you see? Billy hasn't really bothered me much lately, and if I give him the money he thinks I took, he'll leave me alone. So please, can I just have it?"

"Well, I don't—"

"Give her the money," Aunt Annie said. "If Abby thinks it'll solve the problem for now, it's worth it."

"But who's to say he'll stop at fifty cents? What if he wants a buck next? And two bucks after that? Abby will be forever funneling my money to a liar and a thief!"

"School will be out soon, and by next year it'll all be forgotten. If you won't give her the money, Jack, then I will."

I got the quarters.

And Darrell got the truth.

"You made up that whole dipshit story just because you wanted wax lips and hot dots?" Darrell ridiculed me as we sat together in the back of the school bus. "What's wrong with you? You saw what Dad did. He takes anything you say and runs away with it like a dog with a bone!"

"Shut up," I said. "Everybody can hear you."

"So what? You're an idiot." Darrell pointed at me. "Hey, everybody, see what an idiot looks like!"

I shrunk down in the seat. "Stop calling me an idiot."

"Idiot, idiot … *idiot.*"

"Hey, what's going on back there?" Mr. Wall, hardly one to tolerate disturbances along his route, stopped the bus and ordered Darrell to come forward.

"Prepare to be awed," Darrell said. After conferred briefly with our bus driver, he returned to our seat and the bus began moving again.

"What was that all about?" I asked.

"Oh, I just told him I was mad because you forgot the library books I let you borrow, and today is library day, and I'll miss recess because of it."

My mouth fell open. "That's such a lie! After the crap you gave me over those stupid quarters, you really make me mad."

"Like I've told you a hundred times, lie to folks who don't care or who are too dumb to know the difference, but don't lie to Dad."

"Why should it make any difference to you?"

"Because if he catches you in lies, he'll be checking me out too. Guilt by association. Save your lies for the important stuff and tell the truth about the piddly stuff … remember, things are going to start heating up again."

"What things? You talk in riddles."

Darrell rolled his eyes. "I can't believe I'm related to you, you're so dense! Think about it. The war's over in Europe. Where's your mysterious daddy? Europe. And where are you? Here. When he comes back for you, we'll pester him for clues before he realizes what we're doing. We'll find out what happened to your mom and everything else. Snoop and Company will be snooping overtime."

"Oh … is that all?"

"Is that all? That's all you used to think about, not so long ago."

"You're right," I admitted. Adapting to the present had taken precedent over the past. "It's been months."

"Well, don't give up now."

"I'm not giving up. I'm more interested than ever."

"Good." Darrell smiled. "After all, there's nothing more fun than a good mystery. Think I'll be a detective when I grow up, like Dick Tracy or Mickey Spillane. Can you imagine me sneaking down alleys, my collar drawn up to hide my identity, hand in pocket, ready with the old .38? Pretty exciting, huh?"

"Yeah, pretty exciting," I muttered. Boys had all the luck. Boys grew up to be men and men could do anything. What could I do? Be his Girl Friday? Answer his phone? Brew his coffee? Fetch his doughnuts? Hell, no! I needed to expand my horizons.

So what if I'd never be Tarzan. Jungles were too hot and steamy anyway.

So what if I'd never be a princess. Glass slippers had to be really uncomfortable.

I had plenty of other options, like along the lines Darrell had mentioned. I'd be Abigail Adams, private investigator. Undercover agents always gave themselves catchy names, and Adams sounded nice. I'd buy a lovely raincoat. I'd pack my own .38. I'd be cunning and beautiful like Ingrid Bergman. Crooks would bare their souls to me. I'd be incredibly successful, and I'd take pity on Darrell and offer him a mediocre job in my office so he wouldn't have to stand in a soup line after he'd lost job after job for being such a smart aleck.

One minute after I walked into class, I bribed Ruth into accompanying me to Ludwig's Variety Store during lunch. I'd treat her to fingernail polish while I bought my wax lips and hot dots.

Reading, spelling, and arithmetic crawled. Geography was more interesting, as Miss Fuhrman reviewed where our troops were, where the Nazis had been, and where the Japs still were.

"We can't allow ourselves as a nation to go lax," she cautioned. "Remember, children, the war's not over till it's over everywhere!"

I yawned. I had more important things on my mind.

Ruth and I gobbled our sandwiches and bolted from the school yard as soon as the coast was clear. We darted behind the house on the corner, cut through the yard, and came out on Main Street. We ran past the Texaco station, the Grand Theatre, the lawyer's office, the post office, Dr. Jorgenson's clinic, a cross street, Cathy's Café, a vacant lot, the *Weekly Times* office, the liquor store that Uncle Jack frequented infrequently, the Eat Shoppe (whose proprietor apparently couldn't spell), and finally, Ludwig's.

Irma Ludwig herself waited on us. She hovered close, presumably so nothing we hadn't paid for found its way into our pockets. I preferred her husband Klaus, who added a penny candy free with every purchase. He was sitting near the back of the store, eating what smelled like cabbage.

While Ruth agonized over Pink Pearl or Jungle Berry, I studied the luscious assortment of wax lips, wax fingers, wax teeth, and the newest addition to the wax line: wax Dracula fangs.

"What you touch, you buy," Irma said. "Nobody else wants what you've put your dirty hands on."

I was tempted by the Dracula fangs, but settled for the wax lips I'd wanted to begin with. I'd wear them until my lips turned red from the artificial coloring, and then I'd bite off a corner of the wax smile, savor the syrupy liquid, and chew the rest like gum.

Next I studied the Tootsie Rolls, licorice whips, lollipops, cream pops, orange slices, and everything else on the candy shelf. Many of my favorites had been scarce for the last year or so, but Ludwig's had located a new supply since I'd last frequented their store.

"Come on, come on," Irma groused. "You only got fifty cents and it shouldn't take all day to spend it. My food's getting cold in the back … Klaus? Cover my plate, will you? These two are spending the day here, seems like."

I was tempted to dawdle longer to make sure her food got cold, but we had to get back to school. So I grabbed a Blackjack, a Sugar Daddy, a licorice whip, and a roll of hot dots for her to stick in my sack along with my wax lips and Ruth's Jungle Berry polish. I was due a penny in change, but my quarters disappeared into her pocket as she stalked off, presumably to eat.

"Talk about crabby!" Ruth said.

"No, she's really a sweet old thing," I said.

"Sweet like the witch in *Hansel and Gretel*."

"Or the one in *The Wizard of Oz* … she kept my penny, too, the old fart. I'll get even. I'll swipe something when she waits on Auntie next time."

Ruth looked aghast. "Abby! You wouldn't really steal something, would you?"

I didn't have a chance to answer in the affirmative. I heard my name being called as we hurried past the post office. I turned and recognized our mailman, Mr. Story.

"And what are you girls doing uptown in the middle of the school day?" His eyes crinkled at the corners to match the smile on his cheerful face.

"Skipping out to buy candy," I said. It wouldn't be prudent to lie to someone who knew both the correct answer and my uncle.

"Don't worry, I won't tell." Mr. Story reached into his mail pouch. "School's hard enough, nothing like a bite of candy to sweeten the process … here, I've been carrying this around for three days, wondering what to do with it."

I took the envelope and recognized Daddy's handwriting. "But it's addressed to Gramma. I don't understand."

"It got lost in the mail. After all these months, it showed up. I didn't know what to do with it, other than give it to you. My job is to deliver the mail, so that's what I'm doing." Mr. Story cleared his throat. "Don't let it bother you too much."

"It won't."

Ruth and I got back to school late. Miss Fuhrman sat us in separate corners while she taught the rest of the class science. Sitting in the corner allowed me to daydream, but to Ruth it was the utmost humiliation. When the urge for wax lips and hot dots hit me again, I knew I'd have to find another companion or go by myself.

During the bus ride home, with Darrell as my witness, I read what had been intended for Gramma's eyes only.

Dear Mother,

I trust this letter finds you feeling better. Shortness of breath and constant fatigue can mean many things, but as long as you are following doctor's orders, I hope you find relief.

Try not to become too stressed. Make Abby pitch in and help you as much as possible. She seems naturally inclined to laziness and to following her own pursuits without thinking of others, so harder discipline might be in order. If I were there, I'd attend to it, but as a last resort, you can always call on Jack. He's got three hell-raisers of his own, so I'm sure he'll know what to do.

Darrell and I looked at each other. "Harder discipline?" I said. "And this is someone I want to come home so much?"

"Hell-raisers?" Darrell said. "And this is someone who doesn't even know us?"

"Once he does, he'll know he was right."

"He's right about you, too. When he gets back, you'll be in for it."

"Shut up," I said. "Let's finish this before we get home."

As for myself, I've been kept busy here at headquarters, although I led an attack on the Piave-Susequana railroad yard a few days ago when Captain Cushing came down with a bug. No anti-aircraft emplacements were reported to be in the area, so I decided to bomb visually from a comparatively low altitude of eighteen thousand feet. My group reached the I.P., opened the bay doors, and we started down the run. It'd been a clear day, but just as my bombardier was about to zero in on the target, a small cloud appeared and blocked his view. I pulled up, banked a forty-five degree turn to the right for five minutes, made a one-eighty, and dropped down to bomb from the opposite direction at the same altitude. By this time the cloud had moved, and the target was in plain sight.

We were almost at the release point when all hell broke loose. Flak exploded everywhere! Number two took a direct hit, bursting into a gigantic fireball. Number three suffered a hit in the right wing and spiraled out of control. Flak scored on five and six and both disappeared in flames.

God, I thought it was the end! Four planes gone within seconds. Only Emil, myself, and Tail End Charlie were still in the air. We dropped our presents and got the hell out of there. It took more than a few drinks at the club to settle my nerves that night, I can tell you that.

Darrell whistled under his breath. "Wow, what a story! What guts!"

I glared at him. "Daddy could've been killed. That's nothing to be thrilled about."

"You're right … sorry."

But don't worry about me, Mother. That's the last mission I'll ever lead, so the worst is over. I'll be chained to my desk after this, so the closest I'll come to death is lead poisoning from pushing around too many pencils, ha, ha.

"That's a relief," I said.

"Sounds boring," Darrell said.

Anyway, here's a check for eighty dollars to get Abby whatever she needs and the other three hundred is for your expenses. I have enough in my account to cover both checks. I apologize for not sending you money earlier to get her ready for school. With all I've had to do here, it simply slipped my mind.

I hope you got by without selling the corn from the schoolhouse. Remember you are not to do that, no matter what. When I come back, I'll dispose of what's in that room, and then you can do with the corn as you wish.

Write back soon and tell me all the news.

Love, James

"He didn't even remember school starting," I said. "Your dad bought my clothes because Daddy didn't remember and Gramma didn't have any extra money."

"So, who cares about that?" Darrell said. "Look what he wrote: *When I come back, I'll dispose of what's in that room.* What's that mean?"

"I have no idea."

"Sounds like there's a secret room in the schoolhouse where he's stashed something he doesn't want anybody to see. Gramma knew, but nobody else did."

I said it sounded the same to me, and I forgot my hurt over Daddy forgetting about me.

"Well?" Darrell prodded. "Is there a secret room in the schoolhouse or not?"

"I don't know. I haven't been inside for ages … wait a minute, Gramma sold that corn Daddy was talking about. She sold it already last fall."

"She did?" Darrell's eyes widened with excitement.

"Yes, it was after school started, but before my birthday. Ole hauled a bunch of loads to town. I bet Gramma sold it because she needed the money."

"Then all we have to do is go over there and have a look. No telling what's hidden in there."

"Sure we will, but in the meantime, I'm rich!" I boasted. "I have three hundred and eighty dollars. What do you think of that, poor boy?"

"I think you'd better tear up those checks and throw the pieces out the window."

"Are you insane? I'm not throwing three hundred and eighty dollars out no window. You're just jealous. You don't want me to be rich."

"I don't want you to go to jail, you ninny. Those checks aren't made out to you. If you try to cash them at the bank, you'll end up a jailbird."

"How do you know that?"

"I know because I know everything."

He looked damned confident, even for Darrell. But I checked with Miss Fuhrman the next morning after swearing her to secrecy. She said I wouldn't have gone to jail because I was a child and didn't know any better, but I wouldn't have gotten my money. Questions would've been raised at the bank and my guardians would've been notified—that much was for certain.

After school I took PB with me deep into the grove. As I ripped up my checks and watched the pieces flutter away in the wind, I felt as impoverished as ever.

"This stinks," I said. "This really, really stinks."

PB sadly agreed.

Summer 1945

Black Crow of Death

FINDING THE TIME to snoop inside the schoolhouse proved easier said than done. We kids hopped off the bus the next day and ran up the driveway into a major crisis: Charlie had quit being Uncle Jack's hired man simply because he'd been offered a position at a munitions factory for twice the pay. My uncle had tried to talk him out of it, of course, arguing that the war was nearly over and the job would vanish with the signing of the peace treaty, but Charlie had taken the wages due him and waved good-bye.

"Dumb Polack," Uncle Jack complained over supper.

"Be nice now," Aunt Annie said. "And please pass the potatoes."

"Well, he *is* a dumb Polack," Uncle Jack insisted, passing the dish requested. "Charlie's worked for me since '38, and all of a sudden, when the whole damn shooting match is nearly over, he gets a wild hair up his ass—"

"Jack! The children are listening!"

"—hole and takes off. And where does that leave me? Ole's past seventy. Can't push him too hard. Everyone else worth a tinker's damn is off soldiering or farming their own places—"

"Or working factory jobs for good money."

"Like I need reminding … as I was saying, Annie, where's that leave me? That wire I bought before the war is still waiting to run on those fence posts, there's brush to clear, and I wanted to add on the horse barn yet this summer. Plus all the outbuildings need a coat of paint, if I can find paint. Must be a decade since we last did that … who the hell's going to do all the work around here?"

There was a meaningful pause as he surveyed those of us sitting at his table.

School let out the following week. Uncle Jack kept my cousins busier than they'd ever been. Darrell and I had no opportunity to sneak off to Gramma's farm to investigate the schoolhouse. And Uncle Jack worked harder than I'd ever seen. A saunter on Banat and a smoke on the porch became a special treat rather than the norm. Only Ole poked along as he always had, doing whatever he felt like doing on any given day.

As for me, I spent my time helping my aunt. I maintained her victory garden and flower garden. I helped her can fruits and vegetables. I learned to make jelly and jam. And I helped spring-clean the house.

June ended before we finished the inside. Then we started sprucing up the outside. That's when I got sick. I'd been feeling puny for several days and I'd started coughing, mostly at night, so no one knew. But one morning as Auntie and I were washing windows, I hacked until I threw up. She hustled me inside, laid a cold compress on my forehead, and brought a bowl in case I vomited again.

The next day, I was burning up. She sponged me off every few hours, trying to control my fever. I'd feel better for a while, but then I'd feel worse again.

Always I coughed. I coughed until my lungs ached and my stomach emptied. Cold food and scratchy food, like crackers, were impossible. I could sip tea and warm water. I could eat a little soup. I learned to lie perfectly still after eating to avoid throwing everything up.

After I'd been sick a week, even that didn't help. I lost weight. My lips cracked. Uncle Jack decided I should see Dr. Jorgenson. As neither he nor my aunt held much faith in doctors, subscribing to the belief that the body either heals itself or dies—doctors being useful mainly for births or accidents—his decision left no doubt in my mind that I was fast approaching my end.

For the final time, Aunt Annie helped me bathe. At least my hair had grown sufficiently so I'd no longer resemble a boy when I was laid out in my casket. Somberly I selected my funeral garments: new overalls and a pink blouse. Uncle Jack carried me to the car and tucked a blanket around me, although the day was warm. I imagined my cousins assembling to bid me farewell.

Eyes brimming, Darrell begged forgiveness for all the times he'd called me "stupid," or "idiot," or worse. I lifted my hand and magnanimously absolved him of his iniquities.

Duane and Dennis likewise whimpered their apologies. "We didn't want you to die, Cousin Abigail. We didn't know it would really happen. We'll miss you so much."

Sure, I thought. Difficult as it was, I knew I'd be gaining two additional stars in my heavenly crown if I forgave those rotten brats all the shit they'd pulled on me during my short sojourn on earth. God would punish them later anyway.

But Uncle Jack appeared not to recognize the gravity of the situation. "Tell that old pill-pusher to get her well, and he better not charge me an arm and a leg to do it. We'll be painting the barn when you get back, so come tell me what happened."

Aunt Annie told him that she would.

When she stopped the car at the end of the drive to check for oncoming vehicles, I asked her to drive to Gramma's farm.

"Why?" she said. "That's the opposite way from town."

"Please, Auntie. I want to see it one more time."

She gave me a puzzled look, but turned the proper direction.

Gramma's flowers trailed across the picket fence that had been their prison. Yellow dandelions, creamy milkweed, purple thistle, clover, and a dozen other kinds of weeds sprouted helter-skelter throughout the yard, although someone had recently mowed.

The outbuildings particularly tugged at my heart. Empty and forlorn, they stood silently. Like them, I'd seen my better days. Never would I gladden the barn with the complacent lowing of cattle. No newborn kittens would ever cuddle together in the haymow. No silly puppies would chase each other around the silo. The rural schoolhouse that had serviced my grandmother's education and had been purchased by her, partly from nostalgia but mostly from the need for additional storage years ago when the school closed, stood apart from the rest. Now I would leave this earth without solving the mystery hidden within its clapboard walls.

With the black crow of death perching on my shoulder, it would seem I'd welcome the attention of the learned and venerable Dr. Jorgenson.

Not so. I hated doctors.

My aunt had no sooner exchanged pleasantries with the esteemed man and explained the peculiarities of my perplexing malady when he started poking me in embarrassing places. He stuck a pointy thing in my ears. He shone a light in my eyes and up my nose. He aimed a Popsicle stick so far down my throat I nearly barfed up a lung. He thumped my chest and back. His icy fingers explored my neck and armpits. He prodded my innards so hard I thought I'd pee right there on the table. He stuck a thermometer in my mouth and forgot it for a full five minutes until I coughed it out.

He squinted at the thermometer. "Hmm … she's sick, all right."

"What is it?" Aunt Annie asked.

"Elevated." He wiped the thermometer with alcohol and rummaged in a cabinet at the far end of the room.

"No, what I meant is, what is she sick with?"

"Oh, that … nothing that can't be fixed."

"You mean she's going to be all right?"

"For sure." He focused on whatever he was doing.

My aunt gave an audible sigh of relief, but it was nothing compared to the wave of emotion flooding through me. Thank God! Praise heaven! I was going to live!

Then Dr. Jorgenson turned around. He held the scariest thing I'd ever seen. He tapped the long needle twice with his forefinger and advanced on me.

"Okay," he said. "Turn over on your stomach and I'll be done in a jiffy."

"Done with what?" I said, my mouth dry with fear.

"The injection. You need it to get better."

"Won't I get better without it?"

He shrugged. "Maybe. Maybe not."

"I'll take the maybe." I rolled off the examining table, having gained considerable strength since seeing the needle.

His grizzled eyebrows lifted in surprise. "I beg your pardon?"

"No way are you sticking that thing in me. I'm leaving."

Aunt Annie rose from her chair. "Abby, you'll do no such thing."

"Listen to your aunt and do as you're told, because I'm not finished with you, young lady." Dr. Jorgenson spoke imperiously, as though his authority was rarely, if ever, questioned.

"No. Get that damn thing away from me."

"Abby, how dare you embarrass me, and yourself. As sick as you've been, you do what Dr. Jorgenson says and you do it now."

I shook my head and positioned the examining table between us.

"Doctor, I'm so sorry." She gestured helplessly. "I don't know what's got into Abby. She usually doesn't act like—"

"Do you want her to have the shot or not?"

"No!" I shouted.

"Yes!" Aunt Annie's mouth firmed into such a thin line that her lipstick disappeared.

"Then it will be done." Dr. Jorgenson blocked my way to freedom and called for his nurse.

She came through the second door, the one marked "Private." She was all starch and whiteness. *Ingrid* was embroidered on the pocket of her massive smock. Her shoulders would've made Tarzan proud. Her beady eyes fastened on me. "Ja, Doctor?"

"Our little patient is shy about the shot. Could you assist me for a moment?"

She smiled. "Ja, Doctor."

She lunged across the table and grabbed me. With astounding dexterity, she hoisted me onto the table, flipped me over, and lowered my overalls and panties. She held my ankles so I couldn't kick while my aunt pinioned my wrists. I clenched my teeth as Dr. Jorgenson dabbed the appropriate area with alcohol.

"If you'd relax a bit, it won't hurt as much," he said.

I shrieked a totally unacceptable word.

"Have it your way, then." He plunged the needle into my defenseless little bottom.

The shot stung like fire. I yelled. He probably held in the needle extra long to torture me, but finally he pulled it out and covered the damage with a Band-Aid. Humiliated, I scrambled off the table and yanked myself together.

Dr. Jorgenson scribbled a prescription. Aunt Annie apologized again. He patted her arm. She stopped at Ingrid's desk and paid my bill. She stopped at Schneider's Drugstore and bought my medicine. She was not speaking to me. She was not looking at me. She drove out of town faster than was normal for her.

My rump hurt. After we got home and I spied Uncle Jack on a ladder priming a window, it hurt even more. Sick or not, I was in big trouble.

Leaving me to fend for myself, my aunt marched purposefully across the yard to tell him what I'd done. Summoning my remaining reserves, I flung open the car door and ran for the house. If I had been stronger, I would've run further. I looked back through the kitchen window to gauge his reaction. He was laughing.

She backed off a step or two, put her hands on her hips, and said something more to him. Still he laughed. She threw her purse at him and stomped off on one of her long walks.

I breathed easier, a lot easier.

But late that afternoon, Ingrid called. My throat swab indicated I was sicker than the good doctor first thought. Another shot in the morning was mandatory.

It was a hell of a long night.

Right after breakfast—his, not mine, as I was too distraught to eat—Uncle Jack hauled me to the car. He said while he thought my first stunt was pretty funny, if I was planning a second, he was going to do whatever necessary to reverse my intended course of action.

What choice did I have but to assure him I would be good?

Dr. Jorgenson could've been wearing a polka-dotted clown suit and I wouldn't have noticed. I kept my head down as I answered his questions. I kept my eyes shut as he re-examined me. When the awful moment drew nigh, Ingrid appeared. Uncle Jack leaned against the door, chatting with her about African witch doctor potions, as I endured the dreaded shot.

"Make sure she takes her pills as prescribed, Jack," Dr. Jorgenson said. "I don't want to see her back for this."

That makes two of us, I thought. I put myself together with what little dignity I had left, and hoped to God I'd never get sick again.

Aunt Annie was all aglow when we arrived home. "You won't believe what happened, Jack. Guess!"

"We're having another baby?" he deadpanned.

"That's not funny. Guess again."

"I'm lousy at guessing, Annie. Just tell me."

"The mail came and I've got wonderful news. Abby, your father will be coming home in a little over a week! Isn't that exciting, Jack? I told you he'd be back safely."

Uncle Jack stared at her without saying a single word.

Night Trek

I RECOVERED FROM my illness in time to help Aunt Annie decorate the house and hang a "Welcome Home" banner from the porch in preparation for Daddy's party.

"Oh, it'll be such a festive event!" she gushed. "Those Red Wing vases will be a lovely touch, but it's far too early to cut and arrange the flowers. I'll do that at the last minute or they'll droop, and we can't have that, can we?"

"No," I said, weary of her unending quest for perfection. When I noticed her recipe file and cookbooks spread on the table, I quickly proposed an evasion tactic: helping Ole and Darrell paint the barn. Laboring under the hot sun was preferable to laboring over a hot stove.

Uncle Jack approved my request, despite Aunt Annie's protests. In contrast to her, he had done nothing to prepare for Daddy's homecoming. And all the projects occupying his physical and mental capacities of late were suddenly and inexplicably abandoned.

Without my uncle's diligent surveillance, the twins returned to their usual sloth. Darrell slacked off considerably. Ole accomplished little even on a good day.

Who was I to buck the tide? We'd paint for an hour and loaf for an hour. We drank lemonade while resting in the shade. Ole picked his ukulele and sang ditties. Sometimes we napped. We invented tall tales for our "Liar's Contest." Ole told Norwegian jokes, in English, so we'd laugh at the punch line. When we'd dawdled to the extent that I worried Aunt Annie might check on me, we went back to painting.

Uncle Jack never ventured near the barn to assess our progress. Rather, he'd ride off on Banat and be gone for hours. When at home, he'd sit on the porch and drink. He spurned his pipe in favor of cigarettes. Sometimes he'd be so distracted that the ash would burn clear to his knuckles.

He became irascible and irritable. His nervous energy became misdirected. He seldom slept. I'd smell his cigarette smoke when I got up to use the bathroom in the middle of the night.

He ate little. He looked terrible. His entire psychological state seemed to be in a state of suspension, as though he expected something horrendous to happen that he was powerless to prevent. And the waiting appeared to be his chief torment.

These changes in him were not lost on Aunt Annie. I overheard her trying to talk to him one night after supper.

"Jack, what's wrong? Is it about the farm? Are you still angry about that?"

"Damn the farm … damn everything!" He got up from his rocker. A few steps took him beyond the illumination of the yard light, and he disappeared into the darkness.

I walked out on the porch and took my aunt's hand. "What's the matter with Uncle Jack?"

She sighed. "Oh, Abby, I have no idea."

"He's mad because Daddy's coming back, isn't he?"

"I guess so."

"Why?"

"That's the part I have no idea about."

"Is something wrong with Daddy?"

"Nothing's wrong with your father, at least nothing serious."

"You said once that I'd like him," I said, seeking reassurance. "Has something changed?"

"Not that I know of."

"But you haven't seen him for a long time, have you?"

"No."

"When did you see him last?"

"Let me think … 1939, I believe it was. He visited for nearly a month. I don't think Jack saw him, though … no, that was the summer Jack went to Wyoming on a horse-buying trip. He came back after James left … well, that's interesting."

"What's interesting?"

"Nothing."

"Can I sit with you awhile?" I asked my uncle the following night. Since the arrival of summer, I usually joined him on the porch for a private conversation before I went to bed. Mindful of his ill temper of late, I thought it prudent to ask permission.

He bolted his drink. "Why? Did my wife send you out to pick my brain or are you here of your own volition?"

"Just me … well, can I?" "Volition" was an unfamiliar word, but it didn't seem an appropriate time to ask its meaning.

"Suit yourself."

I got comfortable in the other rocker and started to rock. I liked how it creaked, just a little, with the motion.

"Stop that racket," he said. "What's on your mind?"

I hesitated.

"Well?"

"Why do you hate my daddy?" I said, fearing his response.

My uncle crushed his cigarette in the ashtray. "Oh, I don't hate him, Abby. Don't you see? Doesn't anybody see? I'm afraid of him ... I'm afraid of my own bother."

And then he laughed.

I suffered my obligatory goodnight kiss, as he reeked of whiskey and smoke, and ran upstairs. I wasn't halfway through my prayers when I excused myself to God, slipped into Darrell's room, and told him everything.

"Now why would Dad say that? He's afraid of nothing. Maybe it's the liquor ... drunks say the dumbest things. Remember that W. C. Fields movie we saw last month?"

"Yes, but this is no movie. Your dad's been acting strange all week, even when he's not drinking. Haven't you noticed?"

"Of course I've noticed ... seems like we have another mystery on our hands."

"Don't we have enough already? I'd like to solve the last one before another gets added."

"Are you talking about the schoolhouse?"

"What else? We read Daddy's letter weeks ago."

"I know. I've been thinking about it too. In fact, I've come up with a plan for going there."

"When? Daddy's back in two days. Ole will tattle if we run off on him tomorrow."

Darrell dismissed my concerns. "I know. Tomorrow's out ... that leaves tonight."

"Tonight?" I had to laugh. "That's impossible! Your dad's sitting on the porch right now and he hardly ever sleeps."

"Leave it to me. Are you with me, Watson?"

"Of course I'm with you, Sherlock." I latched my right forefinger with Darrell's for a count of three to seal our pact. "So what's the plan?"

With typical assuredness, he detailed my instructions.

Two hours later, I dressed, fashioned a convincing lump in my bed, and placed an opened book near my pillow. I turned off my lamp and tiptoed to Darrell's room, where he'd taken similar precautions.

The hall was dark. The door to the main bedroom was shut. The twins' door was ajar. One of them was snoring. Darrell went downstairs and checked the lower level and the porch. He reappeared a minute later.

"Dad's finally gone to bed. Let's go!"

On the back porch, we found but one lantern on the shelf. Usually there were two. Darrell said he thought it'd been left in the barn.

"One's enough," I said, taking a flashlight for myself.

"We'll walk to the road before we use a light," Darrell said. "Can't be too careful."

As we started down the drive, we were joined almost immediately by Ranger and Molly.

"Damn dogs," Darrell grumbled. "Go home, you mangy mutts, go home!" They interpreted his wild gesturing as playing and responded accordingly—running, jumping, and falling over one another.

"Stop waving your arms," I said. "Maybe they'll get bored and leave."

"Fat chance … the three-ring circus heads for Gramma's house. All that's missing is dancing elephants and the alligator man."

"Well, we can't go back and tie them up. They'd bark like crazy. Let's keep going."

As Darrell had no viable alternative, we continued on our way. Our dogs soon quieted and fell into a slow amble behind us.

The sky was a yawning chasm of infinite blackness. There was no moon. Even the stars had hidden their faces. I could barely make out Darrell, who walked ahead of me, judging from the sound of his feet. Several times I strayed from the gravel into the weeds. Once I stubbed my big toe on something. I wished I'd worn shoes, although bare feet were far quieter.

The breeze rustled eerily through the trees. It was a fickle breeze, inhaling first one way, holding its breath, and then exhaling the other. As a result, the branches of the willows at the end of the drive seemed to dip and sway, reaching toward us, ever reaching.

Suddenly Ranger and Molly yipped, turned tail, and raced for home.

"Why'd they run?" I felt my pulse accelerating. "I'd rather have them with us."

"How the hell would I know? Am I a dog?" Darrell knelt next to his lantern. "Don't worry about it. Give me a match."

I handed him the matches. "I'm not worried, but dogs can sense things. They see things better than us, and they hear things—"

"Shut up, you're giving me the creeps … damn, why doesn't this thing light? Shine your flashlight down here so I can see."

I held the beam on the proper spot. Darrell fiddled for a minute before he started taking the lantern apart.

"Hurry up. The wind's picking up and I'm getting a funny feeling."

"Stuff your funny feelings. And I am hurrying … here, hold this."

I squatted down to help. So intent was my concentration that I heard only a single footstep crunch the gravel before I was yanked to my feet. I shrieked and dropped the flashlight on Darrell's head. With a yelp of pain, he lunged upward and was likewise corralled.

"What the hell are you up to now?" Uncle Jack slurred. "Well? Don't be shy, boys and girls, speak up!"

As I struggled for something plausible to say, his fingers dug into my shoulder. Darrell gasped. Apparently he was suffering the same rough treatment.

"This is your last chance." Uncle Jack gave us both a meaningful jerk. "Say your piece and say it now or I'll be getting it out of you the hard way."

Darrell crumbled. He repeated Daddy's curious letter. He backed up and told how I'd skipped out of school for wax lips and hot dots. He jumped ahead and said we were positive something mysterious was hidden in the schoolhouse. He concluded his confession with a plea for us to escape lickings if we'd promise to mind our own business forever more.

"You wouldn't be inventing that stupid story to throw me off the track, would you?" Uncle Jack said. "You really were headed to the farm tonight?"

"Yes," Darrell said.

"Stay put while I think on this a minute." My uncle released us, knelt, and deftly assembled Darrell's lantern with the light from his own lantern. My flashlight and the matches I'd dropped found a new home in his pocket. He stood up and faced us. "All right, I've decided. Since that letter was never meant for you, it's none of your damn business. I forbid you to go anywhere near that schoolhouse. Ever. Understand?"

Our promises came easy, given the circumstances.

"Good. Now go back to bed and stay there. More nocturnal wanderings out of you and I won't be so tolerant."

Darrell and I headed for the house. Uncle Jack, carrying both lanterns, walked toward the horse barn.

"Why'd you tell him the truth?" I whispered.

"You didn't exactly come up with anything better, did you? You should thank me for saving your butt."

"Maybe not. Maybe when he sobers up, he'll remember I lied for quarters and skipped out of school that day."

"He remembers it now. He's not that drunk. I know because he got my lantern together so quick. He just ignored it because he's got more important things on his mind. After he thinks we're asleep, he'll head over there himself."

"Why? He must know what's in the schoolhouse already. He went to Gramma's at least twenty times after she died."

"That was to winterize the house and load up the livestock. He had no reason to investigate the schoolhouse."

"Even if you're right, he won't go tonight. He'll ride over there tomorrow."

"No, he won't. I'm telling you, Abby, he'll go tonight. Tomorrow he'll stay home all day and act innocent."

"Have it your way."

As we climbed the stairs to our bedrooms, Darrell turned to me. "I'm sick of mysteries, and I'm solving one tonight. When Dad leaves, I'm following him. You can come, if you have the nerve."

"If you're going, then I'm going." Afraid as I was of my uncle's belt, I was more afraid of missing the only opportunity I might ever have.

"Good decision." Darrell paused at the door to his room. "Go to bed now. Dad will check on us soon. When he does, pretend you're sleeping. Afterward, Snoop and Company will go on its greatest adventure ever."

I pulled my nightgown over my clothes and jumped in bed. I lay there, heady with exhilaration, waiting. As the clock downstairs chimed midnight, Uncle Jack opened my door and walked over to my bed. I continued my steady breathing pattern. He eased out of the room. Moments later, I heard the screen door squeak downstairs.

Darrell also heard. He slipped into my room. With windows facing two directions, my bedroom gave us a clear view of the farm buildings and the driveway. We stood as sentinels, each to a window, straining to see through the darkness.

"The light's on in the woodshed," I said. "He's getting something … he's done already. He shut the light off."

"Keep watching."

"Now he's in the garage … he's starting the car."

"I can hear. Damn it, Abby, we're sunk. I hoped he'd ride or even walk. We could've ridden Peaches or walked behind him, but we sure can't follow him now. We'd be still on our way over when he's already coming back."

My hopes faded as fast as the rumble of the Ford's engine, already growing faint in the distance. "To think the schoolhouse is just a mile away and we can't even get there!"

"Complaining won't help," Darrell said. "Stay here while I check the shed. You know how Dad has everything organized? I'll see what's missing."

My cousin was back within minutes. "Dad took a crowbar and the bolt cutter, so he thinks something's worth going after. And he's breaking in where he doesn't belong, too, or else he'd have a key."

"So now what?"

"We'll get some sleep. He'll come back as soon as possible. He won't want to explain to Mom where he's been if she wakes up without him. We'll be snug in our beds when he checks on us again. I'll set my alarm for a quarter to five, we'll ride over, see what there's to see, and we'll be back long before anybody's up. How's that for a plan?"

"It's a plan. But if we get caught—" I stopped, the consequences too dire to articulate.

Five minutes later, it seemed, Darrell shook me awake. "Dad's back, hurry!"

Half asleep, I stumbled outside and followed him to the horse barn. He quickly saddled Peaches. Once on the county road, he urged the pony into a run.

Dawn pierced the darkness with a soft bluish haze. The deepest shadows were lifting by the time Darrell tied Peaches to the tree in Gramma's front yard.

I was struck by the peace and the solitude. But when I glanced toward the schoolhouse, I immediately became disquieted. What would we discover on the far side of those peeling walls? Would we find answers? Or more mysteries? Or nothing?

Abruptly I sensed that we weren't alone. "Darrell," I said.

He was already a dozen steps away. "What?"

"There's someone here."

"There's nobody here but us. Come on!"

"No, wait … I can feel it. Look around." I stood motionless, my heart pounding.

"Shut up, will you?" Darrell said. "You're as bad as those dogs last night, hearing things that can't be heard, seeing things that can't be seen … oh, my God."

"What?"

"There's someone on the porch! Someone's watching us—"

"Who?"

"I can't tell … let's get out of here!"

I raced to where Peaches was tied and vaulted on her back, expecting Darrell to be right behind me, but instead he sprinted toward the safety of the grove.

"Run!" he shouted.

"Darrell!"

"Run!"

I was poised to follow when I heard a man laugh. I peered into the gloom. The man got up from where he'd been sitting. Slowly he began to walk toward me.

I knew I should flee before this stranger, but for some reason I couldn't. I sat astride a pony firmly tethered, paralyzed by indecision.

The man came closer. He was tall, older than Uncle Jack, but fit. He walked erectly and easily, as though he were accustomed to a great deal of walking. He had the bearing of one in charge. He was dressed in khaki trousers, khaki tie, and an olive drab four-pocket flared jacket. I recognized his garb as the uniform of an Army officer from the newsreels I'd seen. In the dim light, he and his clothes blended together and assumed a subtle pinkish cast, a color akin to an overheated gun barrel or a stormy sky at dusk.

He took the cigarette from his lips and tossed it away as he neared. His face became more defined. He was clean-shaven. He had a strong jaw and a long, aquiline nose like that of a Roman emperor in the ancient history book Miss Fuhrman kept on her shelf. His hair was dark and wavy like my own, but his eyes were distinctly different. They were pale blue, heavily lidded, and framed by imposing brows.

The man stopped within an arm's length of me. "You can't ride far on a pony that's hitched."

I felt like such a fool. "I know."

"Your little friend should stay and protect you from the fearsome stranger rather than abandon you with such unseemly haste. I will speak to his father about him, that I will."

Something in his manner eased my fear. Something in his voice stirred a memory. The voice was rich, mellow—a voice that would lull me to sleep if he read me too many fairy tales.

"I'm Abby," I said, emboldened. "That was Darrell, my cousin. Who are you?"

"Oh, I think you know who I am. Just as I knew who you were before you confirmed it … I'm Colonel Stahl, the new lord of the manor. I am your father, Abigail."

Daddy

How can one greet a dream? Or a nightmare? I slid off Peaches, slipped on the dewy grass, and fell against my father. Embarrassed, I wrapped my arms around his waist and buried my face in his jacket front. I had so much bottled inside that I'd waited years to say, but words failed me. I started to cry instead.

Daddy held me tightly for a moment before he pried my arms loose. "No more of that," he chided. "After all these years, this should be a happy occasion. Come on now, I want to see your smile. Pull yourself together."

"I'm sorry." I sniffled.

"Sorry? For what?" He wiped my tears with his hand. "Don't be afraid to look at me. I don't bite, at least not a little daughter … ah, that's better. You can smile, after all. Now let's get a better look at you."

"Not now, Daddy," I said, mindful of my disheveled appearance. "I just got up. I need a bath, and I have better clothes—"

"Stop the excuses, Abigail. This isn't an inspection. I just want to see how you're grown and who you've come to resemble."

I tentatively met his eyes. "Of course I've grown a lot, but nobody's ever told me who I look like … who do I look like, Daddy?" I knew the answer, judging from Mother's photograph in the locket, but his opinion would make it official.

He held me at arm's length. "Well, let's see … overall, I'd say you favor your mother. You've inherited her eyes and delicate build, although your hair and the shape of your face could be from either of us. Last time I was here I had no inkling how you'd turn out."

"And when was that?"

"August of '39. I stayed several weeks with Mother and you."

"Did you see Uncle Jack then?"

"No."

"Why not?"

"He wasn't home."

"Did you see Aunt Annie?"

"Yes, many times."

"How come you saw her?"

"She was home."

So far his answers matched what my aunt had told me. "Oh … well, why didn't you come back and see me after that?"

"I was busy. After the war started, I was even busier."

"Doing what?"

"My job."

"Other fathers had jobs and they came back to see their kids."

"Not jobs like mine."

"I wish you'd had one of theirs, then." I tried not to sound bitter. "How'd you get here so soon? There's no train this early."

"I hitchhiked from St. Paul … why do you have so many questions?"

"Because nobody's ever told me anything, what do you think?"

"I think that's good."

"Why?" I shot back. "I don't think it's been good at all."

"It's good because you didn't need your head filled with false information while I was gone. I'm here now, and I'll tell you whatever you need to know."

"Well, it's about time. So why didn't you send pictures in any of your letters? Why did Gramma only have that one picture of you over her bed? And how come nobody has pictures of Mother?"

Daddy frowned. "You seem to be obsessed with pictures. We better get comfortable if your questions are going to keep coming like machine-gun fire."

He guided me to the porch steps and sat down. I sat, very purposefully, on the far end of the steps. As much as I longed to pour out my heart to him, it was far too soon.

"Well?" I said.

"The answer is simple, Abigail. I removed all the photographs. Your grandmother refused to part with the one you mentioned, so it stayed where it was."

His straightforward reply took me by surprise. "You did? Why?"

"I thought if I didn't return from the war, it'd be better if you hadn't formed an attachment to me. Without photographs, I wouldn't be someone you could look at, identify with."

"But that makes no sense. If you didn't want me to think about you, why'd you write? And why'd you make me write back?"

"Good question … I hadn't really planned on it, but as the war dragged on, I changed my mind. Other men got mail from their wives and family. I had no wife, just you. So I started writing, and I began the vocabulary lessons to encourage you to learn."

"And it worked too. But I can't use those fancy words in regular conversation, Daddy. Everyone would think I was a show-off. You can stop all that stuff now."

"Stuff? To what does that refer? The process of inserting a mixture inside a roasted bird? Or the filling a taxidermist uses to give form to a creature? For all I've taught you, Abigail, surely you could select a more appropriate word. Contrary to your opinion, you shouldn't be hesitant about exhibiting your knowledge either."

"Fine. Just for you, Daddy, I'll utilize a grandiloquent vocabulary, but only when we're together."

My father's brow arched. "Grandiloquent was never one of your 'look it up' words ... could it be that, to use the vernacular, you're making fun?"

I was, but I denied it. Could I help that "grandiloquent" was on the same page as "grandeur"? It had been one of my words, and I'd studied those nearby, knowing he'd get to them all sooner or later. To my way of thinking, Daddy fit the description of "grandeur," with his propensity toward "moral or intellectual greatness," with a bit of "grandiose" thrown in for good measure.

He seemed, in essence, his letters. I shouldn't have been surprised, but I was. And I was disappointed. I'd hoped to mesh comfortably, converse easily with him, but our relationship already seemed out of joint, our conversation stilted.

And it bothered me that he hadn't displayed any affection past his initial greeting. Where was the concern, the caring? Why hadn't he asked me about myself? Must I ingratiate (he'd like that word, wouldn't he?) myself to him, rather than expect his love to shower down naturally, like rain?

I watched him take a cigarette from a silver case. No half-squashed smokes for him, unlike how my uncle carried his. A Zippo lit Daddy's cigarette. Uncle Jack used ordinary matches. But Virgil had acquired a Zippo during his brief stint in the army, so I recognized the brand.

"What you said doesn't explain why there are no pictures of Mother," I said, intent on steering the conversation back to where it'd been before he lambasted my linguistic shortcomings.

"That's a whole different story, Abby."

I waited expectantly.

"No, not now."

"Why not?"

"Because it's complicated, and I don't want to get into it right now."

"When will you?"

He paused to exhale. "When the time is right."

"And when will that be?"

"When I decide it is."

I'd heard similar delaying tactics from my uncle, so I revisited my original complaint. "Well, it wouldn't have killed you to send a picture of yourself, you know. Carol Jensen's dad sends her pictures all the time. He came home to see her too. And he only left last year, not a whole lifetime ago."

"My intentions were honorable."

"That's no excuse, Daddy. I had an old picture on the wall. I had some letters. I really had nothing." This time I meant to sound bitter. "You were gone. Mother was gone. Everybody says she's dead ... is she really dead?"

"Yes."

"Are you sure?"

The pale eyes leveled me in a cold stare. "Of course I'm sure! What kind of question is that?"

"Oh, I was just hoping she left for some reason and was living somewhere far away, and she'd come back eventually." I tried to ignore the pain rising in my chest. "After all, you did."

The stare turned glacial. "The living can return. The dead cannot. Let me be very clear, Abigail. You have a father and he is all you have."

Stung by his sharp words, I said nothing. Darrell had been wrong.

"And where might you be getting these strange ideas? Have you heard gossip about your mother?"

I shook my head.

"Then stop speculating. If it's the truth you want, come directly to me."

"I'm doing that, Daddy. You've already explained some things, but there's something else ... something I've wondered about for such a long time already—"

"What now?"

"Tell me how Mother died."

Daddy's face turned as hard as his words. "That? I've only just returned and already you're quizzing me about *that*? It strikes me as bizarre, Abigail, and I refuse to continue this discussion!"

Accustomed as I was to flashes of anger from my uncle, Daddy's response seemed more calculated, designed to terminate dialogue.

And it did. I was at a loss how to proceed.

I turned away and saw the sun spreading its crimson glory along the eastern horizon. A beautiful July morning was in the offing, but my reunion with my father had fallen apart. I'd bombarded him with too many questions. I'd needed too much. I'd expected too much. I longed to be asleep at his brother's house, and not here.

Better anywhere than here.

He broke the silence. "I've been too harsh. We need to start over, go slower. After all, you're hardly the little girl who tied her doll to the cat. You've been alone far too long with your questions. Questions for which you think I have the answers."

I kept my eyes downcast. "I didn't mean to make you mad."

"I know you didn't. And I didn't mean to lash out at you without provocation, either … I'm not what you expected, am I? No, don't answer that. I already know I'm not. You've conceptualized an ideal, and reality cannot fail to disappoint. The fact is that I'm unused to children, Abby. In my life, I am not questioned. I am obeyed. I'm a father who does not react as a father should … I think we should get to know one another before more is expected. Is that agreeable to you?"

I nodded.

"Then there's hope." He tossed away the cigarette, settled in one of the rockers on the porch, and beckoned to me. "Come sit on my lap, or have you already outgrown this sort of thing?"

I assured him that I had not. He didn't shift to accommodate me, as did my uncle, but I managed to snuggle against him. I became as four again, remembering how he'd lifted me from the washtub, dressed me in a yellow shift, and carried me upstairs to take my nap. Again I luxuriated in the warmth of his chest, the crisp starch of his collar, and the solidity of his shoulder beneath my head.

"I used to hold my silver bell and pray you'd come back," I murmured. "And now you have … I love you so much, Daddy."

He smiled. "I appreciate the sentiment, Abby, but what you said is impossible. You can't love whom you don't know, and you don't know me. You don't know anything about me. But after you do, I hope you'll still say that you love me … yes, I hope that very much."

"And do you love me, Daddy?" I searched his face.

"Yes, I do."

I sought clarification. "But how can you? You just said you can't love whom you don't know, and you don't know me, Daddy. You don't know me at all."

His smile broadened. "Ah, but as a child, that is your process. It doesn't apply to me. I don't need to get to know you. I already know enough. I love you because you're mine, Abigail. I always love what is mine."

I heard what I wanted to hear: *you're mine, Abigail* … I was his. I belonged. I belonged to him. I had a father. I had a family!

With those few words, Daddy gained my allegiance. So he hadn't sent pictures. So he'd absconded with the existing ones. So he'd refused to answer my most crucial question. So what? He would get to it, in time.

My ecstasy was, predictably, interrupted by Darrell. From the corner of my eye, I saw him ambling across the yard. Peeved, I stuck out my tongue.

"What's the meaning of that, Abigail?" Daddy said.

"Nothing."

"Then keep your tongue in your mouth. It's the apex of rudeness ... come in," he said to Darrell, who hesitated at the door.

My cousin entered the screened porch, avoided my withering stare, and stuck out his hand. "Good morning, sir. I assume you're Uncle James?"

"That I am, Darrell." Daddy eased me off his lap, stood up, and shook hands.

Darrell appeared wary. "How'd you know me?"

"How could I not? Abby screamed your name as you were running off. You shouldn't abandon her, you know. Running away is cowardly. I won't tolerate cowardice."

"I'm sorry. I won't do it again."

"Yes, you will. Given similar circumstances, you'd do it again. Abby has more courage than you. She didn't turn tail when she saw me."

"But she knew who you were."

"I doubt it ... Abby, did you know who I was?"

"No."

"See? I told you she didn't." Daddy casually placed his right hand on his hip. With the movement, his unbuttoned jacket fell open.

I saw a gun, encased in a polished leather holster. Darrell saw it as well.

Daddy followed our eyes. "Like it? It's a German Luger ... took it off the dead bastard myself."

"Love it," Darrell said. "Did you kill the German yourself too?"

"Of course. I shouldn't have taken his Luger if I hadn't. He wasn't a coward either. He gave me all the trouble he could before I did him in. What do you think of that, Darrell?"

"I wouldn't know."

"You wouldn't know?" Daddy took the offensive. "So what do you know? Or is there a vacuum between your ears?"

Darrell reddened. "No, there isn't. Okay, how's this for a question: how'd you manage to kill a German and take his gun? I thought you've been either in a plane or at headquarters. You wouldn't be coming face to face with a German either way."

"I withdraw my previous comment." Daddy smiled, but it was not a pleasant smile. "That's all true, Darrell, but on occasion I've been otherwise engaged. How I got this is a story in itself, involving wire and a knee to the back. I'll withhold additional details in deference to your tender years ... let's just say Jerry crossed me."

"What's that supposed to mean?"

"Our paths crossed. I caught him in the wrong place at the wrong time. Which leads me to the obvious question: why were you and Abby trespassing before dawn on my property?"

Darrell looked at me. I looked at him.

"What's your answer, son? Cat got your tongue?"

My cousin looked blank. He looked downright stupid.

"Abby?"

I studied the dirt lodged in the cracks of the floorboards and tried to think of something plausible. Nothing came to mind.

Daddy resumed his seat in the rocker and smoothed his jacket over the Luger. "I could easily force a confession out of either of you, but I'd rather not … at least not yet. I'll mention it to my brother. Perhaps he can enlighten me."

Nearly imperceptibly, Darrell sucked in his breath.

Daddy noticed, as he seemed to notice everything. "Ah, so you'd rather I didn't mention this?"

Darrell shifted his weight, a nervous habit. "No, sir."

"Why not?"

"Um … because Dad thinks we poke around where we don't belong and he doesn't like it."

Daddy leaned forward. "You don't say! Tell you what—either you spill the truth right now or I'll find out the hard way … talk."

Darrell confessed our intentions for the second time within hours. He added how my uncle had left at midnight with tools suitable for breaking and entering.

Long before the narrative's end, my father's eyes narrowed and his lips pressed together. I would've hated to be the recipient of that glare, and Darrell was faring no better.

"So you read a letter not addressed to you, you jump to conclusions, and then you trespass with the objective of breaking into my schoolhouse? Do I have it straight?"

Darrell nodded.

"And you told my brother about my letter already last night?"

"Yes."

"Why?"

"Because he threatened me … us." Darrell glanced at me.

"Look at me when I'm talking to you! I'm addressing your behavior, Darrell, not hers. Abby's out of this discussion since she apparently follows your lead. Once again, you've proven yourself a coward!"

I expected the inquisition to continue, but instead my father sat ramrod straight in his chair and stared down my cousin without saying another word. The ominous silence was broken by a cricket's single chirp. More silence. Then a dove began cooing complacently from somewhere in the yard.

"Quiet," Daddy said.

The dove, in mid-song, fell silent.

Then it was over. Like a cat that chooses to purr rather than pounce, my father began to visibly relax. The stony countenance softened. The beginnings of a smile played about the lips. The pale eyes blinked several times in rapid succession, lingering briefly on me before shifting focus to my cousin.

"Well, I'm sure Jack just had something to do last night, something he didn't feel the need to explain to you. For once, I'll be magnanimous. I'll overlook your little indiscretion as long as you don't come sneaking around here again. How about it?"

Darrell went pathetic with relief. If he'd been a puppy, he would've slobbered all over my father.

"Is this agreeable to you also?"

"Yes," I said, as relieved as Darrell.

"I thought it would be. Now go back to my brother's, both of you, and pretend this morning never happened. That way you won't get in trouble with him, and I'll retain my element of surprise when I show up later at the house."

Before I could say good-bye, Darrell yanked me from the porch. He hustled me so fast across the yard that I could hardly keep up without stumbling.

"What's the hurry?" I said.

"How dumb are you?" Darrell hissed. "Just because that nutcase on the porch decided not to rat on us, think of what'll happen if Dad catches us sneaking back!"

A certain woodshed came to mind, and we galloped off as though both our fathers were after us. But as we neared the slough, Darrell pulled Peaches up short.

"Why are you stopping? We have to get back."

My cousin pointed at Gramma's farmyard, a half mile away. "Just as I thought. Look who's heading to the schoolhouse. Your dad gives me the creeps, Abby. He's a dangerous man, a real loony."

"He is not!" I said, taking umbrage. "You just don't like him because he talked mean to you."

Darrell bristled. "Mean hardly describes it. I don't like my smarts questioned, and I sure don't like being called a coward, because I'm not."

"Don't run off on me, then. And there's nothing dangerous about Daddy, nothing at all."

Darrell turned in the saddle and shook his head. "If you believe that, Abby, you must believe in fairy tales."

The problem was that I still did.

War Stories

Luckily no one was yet awake when Darrell and I returned. After releasing Peaches to the pasture, we undressed, climbed in our beds, and waited until it was time to get up again.

At seven o'clock, I padded quietly to my closet, opened my suitcase, and packed enough clothes for a week. Aunt Annie could wash when I ran out; surely Daddy and I would visit at least that often. Soon I heard muffled voices emanating from the main bedroom, followed by the creak of a door and footsteps going down the steps. I dressed, went downstairs, and volunteered to help with breakfast.

Later, as the whole family was eating around the kitchen table, Ranger and Molly began barking.

"Damn yapping," Uncle Jack grumbled. He hadn't shaved and the shadows along his jaw were matched by dark circles beneath his eyes.

"Please don't swear for no reason," Aunt Annie said.

"So I can swear if I have a reason?"

"That's not what I meant and you know it."

"Well, I wish I'd never gotten those brainless mutts. Rover never made so much infernal racket."

"They're really going at it. Must be somebody coming," Darrell suggested.

"Nobody's coming. It's tomorrow he's coming." Uncle Jack rolled his last bite of pancake around the plate to gather the syrup. "They must've cornered something. Get the .22, Darrell, and go look."

The barking ceased abruptly as my father strode into the kitchen with the energy of a whirlwind.

Aunt Annie rose from her chair. "James! How'd you get here so soon? We didn't expect you until—"

Daddy grabbed her by the waist and swung her around the kitchen in a display of giddiness I'd never before witnessed between two adults. He was laughing and she was laughing, and suddenly he bent down and kissed her. Full on the lips he kissed her.

My eyes nearly dropped from my head. Darrell's mouth fell open. Uncle Jack's fork hung suspended in midair.

"Oh, that's quite a greeting!" Aunt Annie furtively wiped her mouth, but she couldn't wipe away the blush on her cheeks. She straightened her dress and smoothed her hair.

"Uncle James, Uncle James!" the twins chorused. They'd been well primed for Daddy's arrival by my aunt.

"Did you bring me a present?" Dennis hollered. He always was the bolder one.

"Hush, don't you go asking for things," Aunt Annie said. "Can I get you some breakfast, James?"

"Just coffee, thanks. I ate at a truck stop early this morning." Daddy pulled a chair to the table. "Now that I've got that out of my system, I think I'll get reacquainted with your lovely family, Annie … my, it's been ages, hasn't it? All right, don't tell me, but this young man who begs for presents must be Duane."

"No, I'm Dennis!" Dennis corrected.

"Please don't scream," Aunt Annie said.

"That's all right. At least they look happy to see me. To answer your question, yes, I brought presents. I'll bring them over after I've unpacked … now let me continue the guessing game, which has gotten considerably easier. This young man is Duane."

Duane grinned. "Yes, sir. We look alike but you can always tell me from Dennis because he has stinky ears he never cleans until Mom sticks a rag down there and drags out the goo. I'm the tidy one."

"You are not, pig!" Dennis said.

"You're a sow in slop!"

"Oh, yeah? Well, you're a—"

"Stop it, you two!" Aunt Annie shook a finger at them both. "Get out of here before you find yourselves in the corner, or worse!"

They ran outside, still arguing.

I thought it odd how Uncle Jack had remained tight-lipped throughout the altercation, when he never failed to maintain proper discipline at the table and elsewhere. What I did not think odd was how Daddy seemed to be making a fuss over everyone but me. He was simply saving the best for last.

My analysis proved correct as Daddy turned his attention to Darrell. With nary a trace of the antagonism he'd exhibited earlier, he shook my cousin's hand and conversed briefly in a friendly manner. Then the pale eyes settled on me.

"And this, of course, must be Abby, grown so tall … my, how the years bring such changes. You probably don't remember me, but I remember you." He flashed an ingratiating smile. "Unless you're shy, come give your father a hug."

Shy? That was a funny one. I vaulted from my chair, clambered on his lap, and flung my arms around his neck. I wanted to prove he was mine and mine alone, but apparently I overdid it.

"Whoa, there." Daddy chuckled as he loosened my grip. "I'm thrilled by your enthusiasm, Abby, but I think you had a wrestling hold on my neck."

"Oh, I'm sorry," I bubbled. "I'm just so happy to finally see you. Are you happy to see me too?"

"Of course. Why would I return, if not for you? Now I'm sure you've a lot to tell me, Abby, but it'll have to wait until after I talk to my brother. Finish your breakfast and we'll catch up later, okay?"

"Okay." I slid off his lap and went back to my pancakes.

Then an inexplicable thing happened. In three steps, my father's expression transformed from amiable light-heartedness to ill-concealed malevolence. He placed a hand on his brother's shoulder, and I could've sworn my uncle shrank visibly from his touch.

"You haven't uttered a word of greeting to me, Jack. Is something the matter?"

"Nothing's the matter," Uncle Jack said.

"Are you sure?"

"I'm sure."

"You don't look at all well. Are you sick, Jack?"

"No, I'm fine."

"I'm relieved to hear that. Perhaps you're just not sleeping much ... are you sleeping much, Jack?"

"I sleep enough."

"Oh? And did you sleep enough last night?"

"Yes."

"Are you sure?" Daddy sneered. "Dust, once disturbed, cannot be put back."

Uncle Jack sat very still and made no reply.

"Well, enough of this ... come, little brother, we have business to discuss." My father turned on his heel and stalked out the back door.

My uncle followed, but he did not appear to follow willingly. Aunt Annie went to the window and watched them. Darrell and I watched her. Her brow wrinkled in puzzlement. She turned and caught us staring.

"Do the dishes," she said and went upstairs.

Darrell filled the sink with soapy water. "Did you notice how Dad jumped when your dad touched him?"

"Yes," I said. "It was so weird."

"Not really. Dad broke in the schoolhouse last night, and he knows he's been found out."

"How do you know?"

"What Uncle James said about dust, you dimwit. The dust got disturbed when Dad either took or moved something. Your dad noticed and he's mad as hell about it. Remember when I said he's dangerous?"

"Wash the dishes and stop theorizing."

"Theorizing?" Darrell smirked. "Guess you'll be using lots of fancy talk, now that crazy daddy's home."

I grabbed the dishtowel. "Shut up, Darrell! Shut the hell up! Is that simple enough talk for you?"

When Aunt Annie came downstairs, she'd changed from her everyday dress to a green polka-dotted number with a neckline that dipped too low, in my opinion. It was a dress better suited for garnering a man's attention than for frying chicken. She'd applied rouge and lipstick too. The dress clung in all the right places, the makeup complemented her creamy complexion and her luxurious red hair, and I knew I couldn't compete.

I finished drying the dishes and stomped upstairs to comb my ridiculously short hair. Combing didn't improve matters. Then I smeared my aunt's lipstick on my mouth, but the effect was startling. I wiped it off with toilet paper and flushed the evidence. When I dabbed her rouge on my cheeks, I resembled a clown more than I did her. More toilet paper. Another flush. I washed my face. I stomped downstairs.

Darrell glanced up from my Tarzan anthology. "So what's wrong with you?"

"Nothing," I seethed. "Let's play checkers."

We started a game in the dining room. Darrell trounced me twice because I couldn't concentrate. Daddy returned as I was going down for the third time. I started to get up, but he shook his head and motioned for me to continue playing.

Aunt Annie poured him a fresh cup of coffee and offered him toast and jam. They huddled together at the kitchen table and conversed in low voices, but Darrell and I managed to overhear every word.

"Where's Jack?" my aunt asked. "Didn't he come back with you?"

"Yes, but he wanted to go riding for a while, clear his head," Daddy said. "I noticed he's got some nice horses now, much nicer than the ones he had years ago."

"Yes, he does, but I can't imagine why he went riding now. After all, you've only just returned."

"Oh, I don't mind. He got a little unhinged when I popped in this morning. He doesn't like surprises, as you well know. He'll be back soon."

"I hope so … James, could I ask you a personal question?"

"You can ask me anything, Annie. You know that."

"What was the meaning of that exchange between you and Jack?"

"What exchange? I did most of the talking. He barely said a word."

"That's what I mean. I've never seen Jack that way."

"What way?"

"Oh, I don't know … upset, for want of a better word."

"Yes, he did seem upset. You should ask him."

"He won't tell me. He's been acting peculiar ever since you wrote you were coming back, and he won't discuss it."

"Is that so? I wonder why?"

"Please, James, let's not play those kind of games." Her voice was barely audible. "I'm not blind and I'm not stupid. Something is terribly wrong between the two of you, and I wish you'd tell me what it is rather than pretending such innocence at the very same time you threaten him."

Mild surprise followed by a condescending smile flitted across my father's face. "Oh, I'm not threatening him, Annie. Whatever gave you that idea?"

"How you talk to him, for one. Sarcasm followed by an order like you'd give a dog." She spooned sugar in her coffee and stirred. "He's your brother. Please remember that, for my sake, if for no other."

Daddy patted her arm. "I've always remembered that, Annie. Rest assured I'm not threatening him. If I came across that way, I apologize. Perhaps the stress of war has left me rather inept in familial situations. I'll make things right when he gets back … nothing to worry about."

"But I am worried." She kept her eyes downcast. "You don't know what it's been like around here lately."

I strained to listen so I wouldn't miss a word. Darrell did likewise.

"Why? What's been going on?"

"Nothing I can talk about right now."

"Later, then."

"You could clear up one thing, though. What did you mean when you talked about dust that can't be put back?"

Daddy shrugged. "I was simply referring to Jack's cleaning up the house for me."

Darrell paused with his king in mid-jump. "That's such a lie!" he mouthed.

"Could be," I whispered.

"Jack did that?" Aunt Annie said. "Oh, I didn't know. That seems rather nice of him."

"Maybe he thought so too, but I don't. He's to stay off the place. Vinnie's looking after things for me. If there's dusting to be done, he'll do it."

"I'm sorry, I didn't realize you felt so strongly about it. I'll tell him."

"No need, Annie. I've made it crystal clear."

She sighed and caressed her cup. "Well, I hope the two of you can have a better visit, now that you've reached your understanding. It'd be a shame to have it otherwise, since you've so little time to spend with us."

Daddy looked up and caught me eavesdropping. He scowled at my indiscretion.

"Why do you have so little time here, Daddy?" I said. "Aren't you home to stay?"

"No. I'm just home on furlough."

"Oh … I didn't know," I faltered.

"I told you that in my last letter. Didn't you get it?"

I shook my head, fighting tears.

Daddy came and sat next to me. "That's the way it is, Abby. I'm sorry you're disappointed."

"I thought you'd stay forever." I clasped one of his large hands with my small ones.

"No, the war's still going in the Pacific. I'm in the fight till it's over everywhere." He took his hand back.

He doesn't want me yet, I thought. *Would he later?*

"When the war's over, then where will I live?" I asked.

"I suppose you'll live with me wherever I am. Maybe it'll be here or somewhere else. By then, you might like somewhere else better than here."

"I'll never like anywhere better than right here."

"You've never tried."

"I don't need to try, Daddy. I don't want to try. Promise you'll come back and then we can live together forever?"

"Until you're grown and even afterward."

I felt more confident after hearing his promise. My fairy tale life would happen, just not yet.

"Well, I'm glad that's settled," Aunt Annie said, characteristically cheerful again. "Let's go in the living room where we can visit more comfortably. I'm sure the children would be fascinated by a few of your war stories, James, as long as they're not too gory."

"War stories are always gory, Mom," Darrell said.

"Not always, but a good share of them are," Daddy said. "In deference to my audience, I'll keep them as humane as possible."

As we moved into the living room for our share of humanely gory war stories, he whispered to my aunt, "I can't believe you didn't tell Abby that I wasn't staying."

"It's hard to know what to say and not say around here," she whispered back.

So they shared secrets too. It figured.

Daddy swung a leg over the piano bench and got comfortable. I sat on the floor, closer to him than anyone else. Darrell commandeered my uncle's easy chair. Aunt Annie perched on the ottoman, crossed her slim legs at the ankle, and laughed at Daddy's stories that were funny and went "oh" with her hand to her mouth at the ones that weren't. I spent nearly as much time watching her as I did him.

He began yet another tale. "If you've ever wondered what it's like being up in a B-24, I've got a good one to tell you. Before I was assigned to headquarters, I had the closest call of my life when I returned from a bomb run over Moosbierbaum. That's in Austria, if you don't know. Our mission was to obliterate its huge oil refinery, a major supplier to the Krauts. My flight engineer was down with a bug, so I took on another guy who'd likewise been sick while the rest of his crew finished their missions and went back to the good old US of A. He'd been floating around base for a while, trying to fulfill his requirements so he could get the hell out of there himself.

"I briefed my new engineer as to his duties and what was expected of him should an emergency arise and so forth. The guy nodded like everything was clear as a bell. He seemed a decent enough fellow, so I didn't give him a second thought.

"We bombed the target with little interference in the way of flak, fighters, or ground fire, and as we're crossing the Alps on our way back, I called him over the intercom for the usual fuel check.

"A minute or two passed. I started to wonder what the holdup was. When he finally got back to me, he said, 'I don't know how much fuel is left, sir. I can't seem to read the gauges.'

"I thought he was making a stupid joke, and I was hardly in the mood for jokes. I repeated my request. He called me back the second time and said we were extremely low on fuel.

"I gave the controls to my copilot and crawled over to verify. The fuel level was barely visible in the gauge—the goddamn fool had pumped nearly all of our fuel overboard!

"I called him a few choice names on the spot, but I didn't have time to pitch a major fit because we were barreling along at twenty thousand feet, burning up our remaining fuel at a rate we could scarcely afford. I climbed back in the cockpit and radioed the plane on my right, explaining I had a fuel emergency and was dropping out of formation, and for him to take the lead. I slowed the plane, leaned out the gas mixture as much as possible, lowered the flaps ten degrees, called my navigator for an exact position, and asked how far to the nearest landing strip.

"He said the Isle of Vis, off the coast of Yugoslavia, would be our best bet.

My hopes sunk. I knew Vis had a short runway, barely three thousand feet. Landing a plane already in distress with no margin for error on a runway of that length, or should I say lack of it, would tax my abilities to the limit. Even worse, one end of the runway lies at the water's edge, while the other butts up against the base of the mountains.

"While I was thinking it over, I dropped to ten thousand feet and hugged the coastline as tight as a lonely guy on R and R hugs the nearest girl. Suddenly my navigator yells, 'Vis straight out thirty miles off the right wing!'

"Still so far away! Now I really had a tough decision. We could either bail over Yugoslavia or chance reaching Vis. No fuel showed in our gauges. I sure as hell didn't want to drop into the hands of the Krauts, but if I opted for Vis and fell short, we'd be bailing over the Adriatic, and that cold water would freeze a man in thirty minutes. If a friendly fishing boat wasn't nearby to rescue us, we'd bob around like frozen corks until the scavengers finished us off."

"What a horrible way to die!" Aunt Annie said.

"What'd you do?" Darrell sat at the edge of his chair.

Daddy smiled, enjoying his rapt audience. "Well, I was between hell and a hard place, and time was running out. I flipped the proverbial coin and opted for Vis. We were almost there when the number four engine on the right side sputtered and died. I feathered the prop to stop it from windmilling, reducing drag on the plane. A few minutes later, we were at sixty-five hundred feet and over Vis.

"Hallelujah! Now all I had to do was land. Normally I'd drop in from about five hundred feet, but from the direction I was coming, I had to fly past the island, make a one-eighty, and drop the entire sixty-five hundred feet. If my descent was too steep, we'd fall short of the runway and hit the water like crap hitting concrete. If too shallow, we'd overshoot the coast, crash into the mountains, and turn ourselves into toast.

"There was absolutely no margin for error. Normally I'm not a praying man, but I can tell you I had a nonstop monologue with the Almighty right about then!

"Just as I was making the one-eighty, the number one engine quit dead, on the left side this time, which at least balanced the plane and made it somewhat easier to handle. I lowered the flaps, stayed just above a stall, about one-ten, and descended like a rock. Luckily my angle was perfect. I touched down at the very start of the runway. As the landing gear made contact, the third engine quit. By the time we stopped rolling, they were all stone dead."

"Wow!" Darrell exclaimed. "That was really something!"

"You were so lucky, Daddy," I breathed.

"It was a miracle, James," Aunt Annie said. "And what happened to your flight engineer, the one who caused all the trouble?"

"Nothing good. I called him into my office as soon as we got back to Spinazzola. He was sweating bullets. He figured I was going to slap him with a court-martial for damn idiocy or at the very least, chew him a new one. But I was nice as pie. I said shit happens and as long as he didn't screw up his next and final mission, I wouldn't even write him up. God, he was grateful. He was blubbering grateful. After he left, I looked over the list of available aircraft and assigned him to the worst bucket of bolts I had on hand. He flew off the next morning and never came back … I hated like hell to lose the other nine men, though."

Aunt Annie gasped. "You didn't send him to his death on purpose? Tell me you didn't!"

"No, I didn't send him to his death on purpose. I merely sent him. The Krauts did the rest."

"But you assigned him the worst plane!"

"It was on the list, Annie. Somebody had to take it up."

She rose from the ottoman. "Oh, dear … I think I'll put on a pot of fresh coffee."

"That would be nice." Daddy watched her leave.

"She doesn't understand why you did that," Darrell said.

"Women never understand war."

"That wasn't about war."

Daddy folded his arms and looked down his nose at my cousin. "Then what was it about, in your exalted opinion?"

"Revenge."

"Revenge? No, son, you're wrong. Revenge has its place in the civilian world, but not in war. In war, revenge clouds the mind and muddies the judgment. Results are what matters … results."

"Oh," Darrell said.

"Are you going to tell more stories?" I said to rescue Darrell.

"No … I've already said too much. Unless you were there, you wouldn't understand the situation anyway. Stay here, Abby, while I salvage what remains of my reputation."

I curled up on the davenport and pretended to read a book, remembering what my father had told me that morning. I didn't know him. I didn't know him at all. What else had he done in the years we'd been apart? Had he been empowered on another occasion to chose death over life?

By the time Daddy emerged from the kitchen and announced it was our time to visit, just the two of us, I'd swept those worries aside. I raced upstairs to snatch my little suitcase, and I was all ready to go.

"What's the significance of that?" he asked. "Are you going on a trip?"

"Don't tease, Daddy. I'm going with you, of course. We're going to live together at our farm until you have to leave again ... aren't we?"

"Ah ... well, I hadn't really thought about it. I suppose it would be all right, if Annie can spare you."

"It's all right with me," Aunt Annie said.

"But I'm not ready for her yet," he hedged. "Jack's cleaned up a bit, but there's still so much to do, plus I need groceries."

"That's no problem, Daddy," I piped up. "Auntie can pack us enough food for today and tomorrow. The next day's your party and then you can shop. So, can I come with you?"

"I guess so."

His lack of enthusiasm didn't bother me. Obviously he hadn't planned on me living with him already, but how else could he learn to be my full-time daddy? Besides, I had my own plan. I planned to tell him every detail of my life in the hope that he'd share with me every detail of his. I planned to keep him talking until I had no more questions and there were no more mysteries.

As we hiked along, me carrying my suitcase and him toting the picnic basket, I began by chatting about Rover's death and what my uncle had said about Nippy.

Daddy said his brother had the story wrong. He'd never hit Nippy with a bat. Jack had suffered only a scratch. And their father hadn't shot Nippy sometime later. He'd shot Nippy as soon as he patched up Jack. But they had buried the dog together, and it had taken a long time, so a bit of the story was correct.

Daddy went on to explain that Grandpa Walter had been absent for long periods during his formative years. Each harvest season, Grandpa hired on with a threshing crew around the Dakotas to supplement the family income. Winters he labored in a cabinet shop in New Ulm. If he were particularly busy and the roads were bad, he often didn't return home for weeks at a time. But he learned well, replacing Gramma's battered kitchen cabinets with quarter-sawn oak ones. He most enjoyed making chairs. All of the rockers in the Stahl family were fashioned by him.

Low prices, drought, or grasshoppers made for a meager existence on their little farm some years, although no one ever went hungry. Gramma's bountiful garden always produced, even during dry spells when Daddy pumped and carried pails of water to the thirsty vegetables. Money seemed plentiful in other years. A new car would appear in the garage, or the family would enjoy a road trip to the Badlands or a fishing trip up north.

Daddy said that by age sixteen he made the majority of the decisions concerning both the farm and the raising of his brother, a decade younger than himself. Jack tended to be a lazy dreamer from a young age, and Daddy confessed to taking a belt to him on occasion for motivational purposes. With their father gone and their mother so tenderhearted, there'd been no one else to do it.

"Is that why he's afraid of you?" I took perverse pleasure in learning that Uncle Jack had once been on the receiving end of the punishment he now so readily inflicted on others.

Daddy chuckled. "Oh, that's all in the past. What makes you think he's afraid of me?"

"How he looks when you're around. He nearly hopped out of his chair this morning when you touched him. Didn't you notice?"

"I noticed something, but I didn't know it was fear."

"Well, it was. I know it for a fact because he told me."

"Hmm." Daddy looked thoughtful. "I wonder why he'd be afraid of me."

"Well, you do try to scare people on purpose. Intimidate—that's what you do. You've intimidated the hell out of Darrell already."

"Good. Maybe then he won't be so cocky. I hate cocky. And don't say 'hell' to me, by the way."

He'd said far worse during the telling of his war stories, but I didn't mention it. Better to bide my time until I knew him better.

"Well, Uncle Jack's afraid of you for a reason. Is it because you got the farm and he got nothing?"

Daddy stopped walking. "He told you that?"

"Yes, he showed us Gramma's will and he told us everything."

"Good." I saw a hint of a smile. "But he didn't tell you everything … now you listen to me, Abigail. My relationship with my brother is complex. I won't enlighten you further, but even if I did, you'd get it wrong, like Jack did with his dog story. I don't want to hear another thing about it. Promise?"

I promised with my fingers crossed. Any kid worth a bag of marbles would've checked to see whether I slid by with a cross-fingered promise, but adults never seemed to catch on.

But as we neared the house, I thought again about the Luger, and how my uncle had acted around my father, and I was overwhelmed by a sense of foreboding. "Daddy, I really think Uncle Jack's worried you're going to hurt him."

"What did I just tell you?" The pale eyes narrowed as he seized my arm. "One minute ago I told you to leave it alone!"

I tried not to wince. "But I need to know, Daddy. If you're mad at each other, something might happen, and I'd hate for anything to happen—"

"Oh, I see." He released me. "Jack would be pleased, I think, to have a champion in this matter, especially one who is totally in the dark about who deserves said champion. To address your concerns, Abigail, I'm not going to hurt him. At least not physically. Jack's my brother and we're bound by blood, albeit bitter blood. I seek results, not revenge, as I mentioned this afternoon in another context. But considering the frenzied way his mind churns, both results and revenge are easily attained without me lifting a finger to harm him. He's adroitly capable of providing his own torment … there, are you satisfied?"

He stared at me expectantly, so I said I was satisfied.

Still, I couldn't stop ruminating about Daddy's flight engineer. The war had killed him, I reminded myself. The war had killed a lot of people.

But how could I rationalize away Billy Hartmann's terrible accusation? How would I dare confront my father with that?

The Old Farmstead

THE OLD FARMHOUSE appeared far more inviting than it had at dawn. Daddy had opened the windows, and the breeze flapped the gingham curtains against the screens as though Gramma and I still lived there.

Inside, the table and counters were wiped, but dust layered everything else. If my uncle had cleaned, as Daddy maintained, he'd done a poor job. A profusion of yellow, red, and purple flowers from Gramma's garden were bunched in a mason jar on the table. She'd won ribbons at the Brown County fair for such as these.

I felt my grandmother's presence. She had watched when Daddy arranged her flowers. She watched me now. I longed to take her by the hand like I used to. But now I couldn't. I couldn't ever see her again in my whole life. A lump formed in my throat and I began to weep.

Daddy led me to a chair and sat beside me. "You sure cry a lot … it's being here again, isn't it? Yes, of course … Mother's things are still here. Even her flowers have outlived her."

I saw my sorrow mirrored in his eyes. "I won't cry anymore, Daddy. I didn't mean to make you sad too."

"No, sadness is too shallow, too fleeting. What I suffer is called melancholy. That's a new word for you, isn't it? Yes, I thought so. Melancholy means an abnormal state characterized by irascibility or depression of mind and spirit. The ancients attributed it to an excess of black bile in the body, but now we know better. I believe it's caused by an obsessive dwelling on the past, by constantly struggling with the 'what ifs' and the 'should haves' in one's life, rather than concentrating on the present or anticipating the future … do you understand what I'm saying?"

I shook my head.

"No, of course not. You're too young to have regrets."

"You're wrong," I said, eager to prove his assessment of me false. "I regret I don't have a mother, and that you haven't been here all my life, and I regret smoking with Darrell and burning—" I stopped, regretting what I'd just said.

"Yes, the barn," Daddy finished. "That barn cost me."

"I'm sorry," I said in a small voice. "Uncle Jack already punished us, so you don't have to do anything more. We learned our lesson and we haven't smoked since."

"I should hope not. You better be a good girl for me, Abigail, because I won't tolerate any more foolishness."

As I promised to be an angel, my fingers were again crossed. How could I be totally virtuous when I hadn't yet learned the secrets of the schoolhouse, forty yards away?

I delved into the picnic basket to redirect Daddy's attention from my past sins. Fried chicken, potato salad, deviled eggs, rolls, and bread-and-butter pickles were leftovers from last night's supper. Baby carrots and radishes had been hastily added from the garden.

I grabbed a chicken leg. "We got lots better food because you're here. If it was only me, I'd get a ham sandwich and a cookie."

"Nothing wrong with that."

"No, but Auntie's trying to impress you, if you haven't noticed."

"I have noticed, and she does impress me. She's a wonderful cook. She works like a slave. She's produced three healthy children. She's honest, optimistic, kindhearted, and she's even nice to look at. Jack's lucky to have kept her ... damn lucky."

"Maybe you think she's nice, but she hasn't been nice to me." I wished he hadn't ladled on the praise like gravy. "She works me too hard. She thinks I have nothing better to do than help her."

"Good."

"No, it's not. I'm way behind on all the things I want to do. Besides, she made me wear horrible dresses until Uncle Jack finally bought me some jeans. Even worse, she kept fiddling with my hair."

"Your hair's far too short to fiddle with. What happened?"

I told Daddy about my self-haircut, making the episode as amusing as possible.

He was not amused. "You grow that thatch out. I want to see bows in your hair when I come back again."

"How'd you know I used to wear bows?"

"Photographs."

"You mean you got pictures of me and I never got pictures of you?"

"Correct."

"But that's not fair!"

"I never said it was."

I finished my chicken leg in silence.

"I like to see little girls wearing dresses too."

"I hate dresses. And I cut my hair short on purpose so Auntie couldn't put those dumb bows in it."

"I had that part figured out already."

I tossed my head back. "Well, it's my hair. I like it this way. I looked stupid the other way."

"No, you looked pretty the other way. Stupid is a mental condition, Abigail, and not the least bit affected by one's hair length. And I don't care whether you hate dresses. I expect you to wear one to my party, and ask Annie to do something with what's left on your head."

I resented being told what I'd intended to do all along, but I particularly resented him sticking up for my aunt over me.

"Don't pout," he said. "I can't stand pouting."

"I'm not."

"Don't give me that. Pull in your lip. Then eat your pickles."

"But I hate pickles! You didn't have to dump them all over my plate. Uncle Jack doesn't make me eat them." I conveniently omitted how he made me eat nearly everything else.

"I only gave you two. Stop fussing like it's a bushel's worth. And if you haven't noticed, I'm not your Uncle Jack."

I choked down the ghastly green slices. Throwing up on my plate would serve him right. But then I'd be hungry before morning. Bad plan.

"Do you want anything else?"

"No."

"Then I'm going upstairs to take a nap. I thought I could make it until bedtime, but I'm already so tired, I'm getting testy. You can behave yourself while I'm sleeping, can't you?"

I nodded.

"Good. We'll talk later."

I sat for a while and brooded. Daddy was a tyrant, the same as his brother. But Uncle Jack's tyranny was diluted by the presence of my three cousins. Misdeeds sometimes went undetected; even the most observant tyrant couldn't look four ways at once. Now, being alone, my mistakes were certain to be noticed and dealt with accordingly.

With no particular purpose in mind, I began wandering the house. In the kitchen, my Shirley Temple cup sat by the water pail where it'd been the awful night Gramma died. I peered in the cloudy mirror above the wash stand, purposely hung low so I could comb my hair without standing on a stool. Each New Year's, Gramma had ceremoniously moved the mirror appropriately higher. Now the lowest nail hole showed on the wall below it. I bent down to judge my size. Had I really been that short?

On the faded wallpaper behind the dining room door, I touched the faint pencil lines that recorded my height on each successive birthday, from my first through my tenth. Would Daddy return to measure me on my eleventh and draw the line higher on the wall?

On the buffet, my birthday cards still stood in rows. I blew off the dust and placed them in the center drawer, next to the embroidered napkins. Would Daddy return to display them next year?

In the living room, I snuggled down momentarily in the maroon davenport. Here Gramma had taught me to read, write, and spell. Here I'd deciphered Daddy's letters and looked up his endless vocabulary words. Here I'd cut my Tarzan comic strips from the newspaper and pasted them in my scrapbook.

Now Gramma had passed away. Daddy would leave again, and I was starting to lose interest in Tarzan. Why did things have to change so?

Feeling melancholy, I ran outside for a breath of fresh air. With nothing better to do, I visited each outbuilding in turn to see whether anything had changed there.

Gramma's old Ford, enveloped in dust, remained parked in the converted shed she'd used for a garage. With my finger, I drew a dog on the driver's door to honor Rover, and a multitude of nameless cats on the passenger doors. I depicted farm animals of various species on the hood and birds in flight on the windows. I scrawled my name across the trunk, finishing with a grand flourish.

Next I peeked in the woodshed that had doubled as our workshop. The vise held a tin can lid I'd been turning into an arrowhead. A chipped rock lay on the worktable, suspended by circumstance between being an ordinary stone and becoming a spear head. Grandpa Walter's razor strop still hung on the far wall, along with pieces of harness. License plates, dating from 1928, were nailed to the support beam, a mute testament to the passage of time. Wire, twine, glass, and dowels were strewn haphazardly. Nails, screws, and things I didn't know the names of were separated in shallow drawers of a wooden cabinet. A steamer trunk sat in one corner. Two years earlier, I'd discovered a sizable cache of pinup girl calendars and racy magazines inside the trunk. Darrell and I had subsequently read the magazines, and more than once. Whether they'd been stashed there by Grandpa Walter, Ole, or by someone else, I'd never dared ask.

I latched the door and walked on.

The chicken house was silent except for a mouse's skittering when I first opened the door. Uncle Jack had sold the hens to the processing plant in St. James within days of Gramma's death. Now their water jars stood dry and their feeders sat empty. Dehydrated excrement on the roosts no longer stunk. Mummified eggs lay amid the straw of the nests.

I picked up an egg and flung it against the wall. It shattered with a hollow pop, stirring up dust motes that whirled crazily in the shaft of light filtering through the nearest dirty window. I wouldn't miss gathering eggs and getting my hand pecked for my efforts. I wouldn't miss washing eggs and packing them into cartons in the spooky basement. I threw eggs until none remained.

I hadn't consciously planned to investigate the schoolhouse without Darrell, but something intangible drew me to the door. I paused, vacillating between curiosity and dread. I surveyed the upstairs window, behind which Daddy lay sleeping.

Or was he, like Gramma, watching?

As though by accident, I placed my hand on the doorknob and turned. The heavy door opened with a creak—not a creak at the beginning followed by silence, but a drawn-out, tortuous creak that lasted until I grabbed the doorknob and stopped the door from moving.

Holy cow, Daddy would have to be completely deaf not to have heard that creak! It'd been the loudest, longest creak that'd ever creaked since hinges had been attached to doors!

I debated what to do. No movement caught my eye from the upstairs window. No shout reverberated across the yard, demanding to know what the hell I was doing with my trembling hand clutching the rusted doorknob attached to the creaking door of the forbidden schoolhouse.

So I slipped inside.

I couldn't remember when I'd been in the main room without corn being piled high. For years, I'd played "quicksand" in the corn, enacting fantasies of danger and derring-do. For years, I'd seen only the top of the blackboard and the upper portion of the map of the world.

Now the interior was empty except for scattered kernels and husks swept into a corner. A row of hooks bisected the wall on my left, whereupon children, now grown old, had hung their belongings. Bookshelves, partially filled with mildewed textbooks, stood to my right. Ahead was the entirety of the blackboard. Erasers and bits of chalk still lay on the grooved ledge. The caption on the stained map read: *Our World Today—1913*. A darkened print of *The Father of Our Country* hung askew in a cracked frame adjacent to a door at the back of the room. That small door, which had always been hidden from view, drew my interest like a cow patty draws flies.

The door was thick, solid, lacking neither window nor ornament. A chain and padlock, stretched tight and fastened by heavy screws embedded into the casing on either end, prevented the door from being opened. I ran my fingers along the old chain and checked for a weak link. My hands were dark with rust when I pulled them away. Then I examined the padlock. Untarnished, it looked new. With growing excitement, I felt along the top of the casing for a key, but found none.

Defeated, I chanced to look down and saw the dust on the floor had been scraped aside in the shape of a fan: the track of the recently opened door. Had Uncle Jack opened it, with his crowbar and bolt cutter, at midnight? Or had Daddy, at dawn? Or had both of them?

There was nothing more I could do. I ran outside and flung the main door shut behind me. The resultant creak resonated clear to the patch of willows behind the schoolhouse, where I paused to gather my wits.

As my rotten luck would have it, I heard my name being called a minute later. I darted in a circuitous fashion through the grove, intent on putting distance between me and the schoolhouse. Emerging from the trees adjacent to the outhouse, I saw Daddy standing on the back porch, searching in the opposite direction for me.

I caught my breath before sauntering down the well-used path toward the house. "What, Daddy?" I feigned innocence.

He turned. "Where the hell have you been? I've been calling you for at least five minutes!"

"The outhouse."

"All this time?"

"Not all," I hedged. "Before that I looked at the car, and then I poked around the shop, and then—"

"I don't need your itinerary. You're here now, so come inside. I want to tell you something."

Daddy plunked me down on the davenport and told me his plans for our farm. He and his brother would meet with Gramma's lawyer the morning after his party to draw up a rent agreement, subject to yearly revision. While he hated involving Jack in his affairs, he could hardly locate suitable renters from overseas, while his brother knew farmers in three counties. Two-thirds of the proceeds would funnel into his own account, as taxes and expenses needed to be paid, while one-third would go into a trust in my name.

As far as the house and buildings were concerned, he intended to sort, organize, and dispose of everything portable. I could select a few keepsakes for myself. He'd offer whatever Annie wanted for her years of tending to Gramma and me. The remainder, along with the car and machinery, would be sold at auction.

The new math teacher at the high school and his young family would soon be occupying our farmstead. Daddy was amazed that my aunt had found a suitable renter on such short notice, but she did have her ways.

I'd kept silent throughout his long monologue. How he could callously speak of rents, trusts, and auctions was beyond me. How he could invite strangers to live in Gramma's house was enough to make me sick.

Didn't he realize that they would erase the pencil lines on the wall, place their own cup by another water pail, and position a new washstand mirror to the height that suited them? Didn't he realize that Gramma's spirit permeated the house, the furniture, the decorations, the very walls? Didn't he realize that if he implemented his coldhearted plan, she'd have no place to be?

"I'll come over every week and clean," I implored him. "I want the house to stay like it is until you come back. I don't care whether it stands empty. I want it to be empty. I don't want other people moving in. Please, Daddy, do this for me ... do this one thing for me, if you love me. The house will wait for us to come back."

"I understand your point of view. Really I do. But your grandmother's gone, Abby. You only feel she's here because this house reminds you so strongly of her. But most feelings fade with time. And you're wrong about the house waiting for us. It won't. It'll fall to ruin if it sits empty and unheated another winter. My decision stands ... besides, I need the money."

I started to cry. Sometimes Uncle Jack gave in to my tears, if I caught him in a receptive mood.

"I'm on to you." Daddy walked to the kitchen, located a bottle of whiskey, and poured himself a drink.

I was heading outside to shriek my frustration when I passed an advertisement on Gramma's sewing machine. I picked up the clipping and read:

F. Enger, Licensed Auctioneer. Experienced in Crying Farm, Livestock & Furniture Sales. Dial 2540, Butterfield, for dates.

Auctioneers cry too? I stuffed the ad in my pocket.

"I've already called," Daddy said, watching me from the doorway.

I pushed past him and ran to the barn. I climbed the ladder to the haymow, but I was too disheartened to bother sobbing or screaming. What benefit would I gain? My thoughts, my feelings, my wishes, didn't matter. The sun hung red and low by the time I climbed down again. Daddy had turned on the lights in the house, inviting me back. *Let him wait,* I thought.

First I had something more important to do. I knelt at Rover's grave beneath the willows and remembered happier days. "You get to stay here, but I don't," I said. After further reflection, I added, "But you don't get a choice. You're dead."

My father glanced up from his magazine as I entered the living room. "Oh, there you are. I thought maybe you'd gone back to my brother's."

"No," I muttered.

"Well, at least you know where you belong. Now get ready for bed. I'm tired. I'll make up the davenport for you."

Belong? That's right—I belonged to him. But was that entirely a good thing?

After I'd washed, brushed my teeth, and changed into my pajamas in front of the cloudy mirror, I came back to find that he'd already gone upstairs.

A single daffodil and a note lay on my pillow: *It'll be all right, Abby. I promise everything will be all right.*

Promises came easy to Daddy.

The Italian

I WASN'T THE slightest bit sleepy, so I propped myself on my elbow and read Daddy's *True* magazine. How Theodore Roosevelt, Jr., crippled from arthritis and armed only with a pistol, calmed his soldiers by reciting poetry before leading them inland from Utah Beach on D-day enthralled me. The harrowing tale of a British spy tortured by the SS before he executed a daredevil escape made my pulse thump. For a change of topic, I read how the Plains Indians used to drive herds of hapless buffalo off a thousand foot cliff called "Head-Smashed-In Buffalo Jump" in Alberta. I grimaced. Heads and everything else! A more mundane article reported how Eskimos hunted on ice floes and subsisted on blubber and blood … ugh. A nail-biting narrative about a Baptist missionary nearly devoured by cannibals in the 1890s contained more ugh. I skipped to the last paragraph to make sure God had snatched him to safety to preach another day, hopefully where the congregants were more appreciative!

After I finished reading, I switched off my lamp, but I couldn't switch off my mind. The shadows deepened to an inky blackness. The clock ticked. The hours crawled. Fleeting images of Rover waxed and waned.

Once I thought I heard Gramma invoking the blessing in her guttural German accent. I turned on the light, half expecting to see her spirit seated at the table. It wasn't, but I couldn't shake the sensation of her being nearby. The feeling comforted rather than frightened. Gramma was simply looking out for me, like she'd always done.

Out of nowhere, I got a brilliant idea. I knelt and prayed for Gramma (with God's permission) to haunt the new math teacher and his family until they vacated the premises, thereby keeping our house solely for me, since Daddy didn't seem to give a damn … darn … hoot. (It wasn't judicious to say "damn" to God, but it slipped out before I'd thought of an acceptable substitution.)

Then my musings shifted to the schoolhouse. What had Daddy hidden from me, from his brother, from everyone?

And what would happen to Daddy after he returned to the war? Would his luck run out? What would happen to me if something happened to him? I realized an awful truth: if I had no father, I'd have no hope.

Eventually I fell asleep, but the davenport was narrow and uncomfortable. Twice I nearly slid to the floor when I changed position.

Daddy did not sleep soundly either. Several times, as I hovered between sleep and consciousness, I smelled his cigarette smoke and heard the clink of ice in a glass. I longed to join him on the porch, but I couldn't rouse myself.

I awoke at dawn, shivering. The weather had turned unseasonably cold. A brisk wind gusted though the open windows. I shut them, retrieved my blanket from the floor, and tried to go back to sleep.

No chance of that. My feet were icy and I had to pee. I trudged outside and squatted by the drain spout; the outhouse seemed too far for just a number one. That accomplished, I came back, washed my hands, and got a drink of water. Now I was fully awake and still cold to the bone.

I crept upstairs. Daddy was sleeping heavily in my former bed. His wallet, some loose change, a ring, a key, and a letter were on the dresser. The coins were all from Italy. The ring was wide and plain—a man's ring, judging from its size. Initials were carved inside, but it was too dark for me to make them out. His wallet I didn't touch, but the letter begged closer inspection when I noticed the unsealed envelope. I shook out the contents. Written in a foreign language, the letter smelled faintly of perfume. Disgusted, I put it back the way I'd found it.

Then I lifted the covers and crawled into bed. Daddy stirred and mumbled something unintelligible. I waited until he settled before I nestled down and eased myself against him. My feet gradually thawed, my breathing fell into a natural rhythm with his, and I drifted off.

We awoke simultaneously at mid-morning. I'd rolled against him, waking him with a start, which in turn woke me up.

"What are you doing here?" His voice was thick.

I yawned and stretched. "Isn't it obvious? I was sleeping—until you woke me up."

"You shouldn't be here. It's not proper. I made a bed for you downstairs for a reason."

"But I don't like the davenport, Daddy. It's lumpy. The cushions bunch together in all the wrong places, and it's so narrow I almost fell off. Besides, I got cold. I'd much rather be here with you."

Daddy scowled. "I said it's not proper. If you don't like the davenport, you can have this bed tonight and I'll sleep downstairs."

"But I want to be next to you. You're so nice and warm … what's the matter? Why are you looking so grumpy? Don't you want me around?"

"Not while we're sleeping. If you can't abide by my rules, you'll be spending your nights at my brother's house."

I sighed for effect. "Oh, all right, but I don't know what the problem is."

"You would if you were older." He glanced at the Baby Ben clock on the nightstand. "Good Lord, it's nearly nine o'clock! Leave so I can get dressed."

"Get dressed with me here."

"No, I'd rather not."

"Why not?" I teased, already knowing the answer. Living on a farm with three male cousins and a host of animals hadn't left many surprises.

"Because I don't have much on, if you must know," he said.

That wasn't entirely accurate, but I figured he wouldn't want me correcting him. I rolled out of bed and picked up one of the coins lying by his wallet. "Can I have some of these for show-and-tell when school starts again?"

"Take as many as you like. They're no good here, and I'll get plenty more when I go back home."

"I thought home is here."

"I stand corrected. I meant when I go back to Italy."

I selected the shiniest coin of each denomination before I held up the golden ring for closer inspection. "I never saw this before. Was it Grandpa's?"

"No, it's mine."

"I didn't see it yesterday. Where was it yesterday?"

"It was packed, but I'll wear it from now on."

"It looks expensive. Is it?"

"I wouldn't know. It was a present."

"I should get such nice presents."

"You do. I gave you a charm bracelet for your birthday, among other things. Don't tell me you've lost it already?"

"No, I still have it." I tried on his ring. "Look, your finger is bigger than my thumb!"

"I see that. Now leave so I can get up."

"After you tell me who wrote this letter," I stalled. "It doesn't have a stamp. All letters have stamps, except for your V-mail ones. What, did somebody write it and then hand it to you instead of mailing it? It's got an Evening in Paris smell too … Evening in Paris was Gramma's favorite perfume, you know."

Daddy threw off the blanket and sat up on the edge of the bed, keeping himself covered with the sheet. "Enough questions! You're irritating me beyond endurance, and from that smirk on your face, you know it too. Now get out. I'll tell you later, if I feel like it."

My father had a nice chest, well-muscled, with dark, curly hair, but not too much. I wouldn't have liked if he were as hairy as Tarzan's chimp.

"Tell me now."

"No. I'll tell you later, but not now."

"Why not?" I suddenly felt combative. "What's the big, fat secret now?

It's just a letter, Daddy. How bad can it be? What, do you have a lady friend? Is that it? Please, Daddy, I'm growing up. I'll understand. Just tell me!"

He gave me the strangest look. "It's not from a lady friend."

I felt a surge of relief. "Good."

"It's from my wife."

"Your wife?" The coins slipped from my fingers. "You have a wife? Daddy, how could you? How could you come back without telling me? How could you do this to me? How could you let me think about, dream about—"

"Abby, I—"

I shut my ears and I shut my mind and I tore down the stairs. I twisted my ankle near the bottom, but my rage was so white hot I barely noticed.

"Abby, come back here!"

"No, I hate you, Daddy! I hate you so much!"

I was beyond the barn and far into the pasture before I heard him shout again, "Come back, Abigail! I can't explain if you won't listen!"

I whirled around and saw him standing in the yard with just his trousers on. "Explain what?" I screamed. "You can't explain her! I don't want to hear about her! I don't want to talk to you, ever again! I wish you'd never come back!"

He gestured with his hands in the air and went inside the house.

I ran back to my uncle's farm. A whole mile I ran with my ankle throbbing. If my father really loved me, he would've come after me and made me listen. The fact that he'd given up so easily proved he didn't. And the fact that he didn't made me bawl my eyes out.

I burst into the kitchen where Aunt Annie was canning and Uncle Jack was reading the newspaper. Thankfully none of my cousins were present.

My uncle took one look at me and leaped from his chair. "Good God, girl, what's wrong? What happened? Did he hurt you?"

It took me a while to calm down sufficiently so I could tell them.

Uncle Jack seemed disappointed it wasn't worse. "Is that all? You've told us everything? Are you sure?"

"Is that all?" I screeched. "Why, it's terrible what Daddy's done! He doesn't love me and he doesn't love Mother! He's gone and replaced her with a—an Italian!" I spat out the word as though an Italian were seven levels below Lucifer.

"Did he tell you that?" Aunt Annie asked. "A letter in a foreign language doesn't necessarily mean his new wife is Italian."

"Well, he's been living in Italy, hasn't he?" It wasn't the Italian part that tormented me anyway—it was the wife part.

The telephone rang. My aunt answered. She covered the mouthpiece with her hand, but I could still overhear. After a lengthy conversation, she hung up.

"That was Daddy," I said.

"Yes, and he's very concerned about you."

"I bet."

"Well, he is. You were wrong to run away just when he was trying to explain things."

"Sure."

"That's no attitude to have, Abby. He could've smoothed things over, if you'd given him half a chance."

"He's had years of chances."

"No, he hasn't. You're wrong about that."

"I'm not wrong, I'm right!" I exploded. "He's wrong, you're wrong, and I'm right!"

"Stop it," Uncle Jack warned.

I ignored him and plunged ahead. "And you know I'm right, too, but it's just like you to take his side. I see how you look at him, Auntie. I know what you think of him, you and your lipstick and rouge and fancy dress. I'm so sick and tired—"

"—of hearing you shoot your mouth off!" Uncle Jack grabbed me and positioned me purposefully to his right. "Apologize before I turn you over my knee right here and now!"

Whoops. I'd made a tactical error by standing within easy reach while throwing my fit. Quickly I apologized. Then I had to repeat myself because I hadn't sounded sincere.

"Don't turn sullen on me, young lady," he said.

I swallowed my resentment. "I'm not."

"Could've fooled me."

"You've made your point, Jack," Aunt Annie said. "Abby, come with me to the porch. We need to talk."

Noting the residual thunder in my uncle's eyes, I trailed her to the porch, hoping she'd explain the lipstick, the rouge, and the polka-dotted dress, hoping she'd assure me she was not in love with my father, but she only asked about the events of the morning.

Reluctantly I told her.

"Obviously he didn't want to tell you yet, but the way you were badgering him, he either had to lie, evade, or tell the truth," she concluded. "He chose the truth. That's commendable of him."

"But I didn't expect it, Auntie. It hurt."

Her voice moderated. "Of course you didn't, and of course it hurt. Here you've wanted him all to yourself and now you find out, in the worst possible way, that he has a wife and a whole other life in Italy you knew nothing about."

"What makes you think I want him all to myself?"

She smiled. "Oh, Abby, you wear your heart on your sleeve. I can look at you and practically read your mind."

"Well, he could have written," I said in my own defense.

"True, but he probably wanted to tell you in person so he could deal with your reaction. You forget he's been back for only a day. You scarcely gave the poor man time to unpack, much less do things the way he thought best, did you?"

"No." I hated how she could pile on the guilt in only three sentences.

"I just hope you didn't say anything really awful to him … oh, no, you did! What'd you say?"

"I said I hated him," I admitted. "I said I never wanted to talk to him again and I wished he'd never come back."

My aunt's green eyes flashed an indignation typically reserved for tracks on freshly waxed floors or filthy toilets. "Shame on you, Abby! Such hateful words to your own father! What on earth were you thinking?"

"Nothing." It had been a reaction, not a thought process. "I didn't really mean it, Auntie."

"I certainly hope not, but he doesn't know that. You must tell him as soon as possible."

I felt as small as the ant crawling across the arm of my rocker. "Maybe it won't do any good. Maybe he hates me now."

"I doubt it. But you need to apologize and be on your best behavior, Abby. He thinks the world of you."

"I should hope so … after all, I'm all he has, except for that dumb Italian."

"Thinking so highly of yourself sets you up for a fall."

I switched subjects, hoping to avoid further censure. "Did you know he was married again? You didn't seem very surprised."

"No, but I had my suspicions. While he was telling those stories yesterday, I noticed a white mark around the third finger of his left hand, like a ring was missing. The rest of his hand is so deeply tanned, I couldn't help but notice."

"I didn't notice."

"You wouldn't have known what it meant even if you had."

She was correct on that point. "Do you think he's been married for a while, or just recently?"

"Oh, I'd guess for a while … really, Abby, you should be happy for him. He's a relatively young man, barely forty-six—"

I wrinkled my nose. "But that's old, Auntie. Daddy's old as dirt!"

She smiled and shook her head. "Don't be silly. He's still young, and Lord knows, he's handsome enough. You should be glad he's found someone to share his life with."

"He was supposed to share his life with me."

"And he will. But he deserves a wife as well as a daughter. I'm sure he has enough love for two, and it's selfish for you to wish him less."

I hardened my heart. Reverend Richter expounded upon a whole list of horrendous sins each and every Sunday, and selfishness seldom made the top ten. But hearing that she favored my father's remarriage came as a relief. Perhaps her infatuation with him was nothing more than a passing fancy—like the new kid at school whom everybody wants for their best friend until the novelty wears off.

Daddy's new wife, however, posed a thornier problem. A wife was permanent, more or less. She'd have to be really spectacular for me to willingly share him with her. But what if she didn't want to share him with me? What if she viewed me as a biological mishap of yesteryear? What if she hated me? I already hated her. Would I win Daddy or would she? All of a sudden I wasn't so sure of anything.

"You're going back to him today, aren't you?" Aunt Annie said. "You need to apologize, and the sooner the better. Procrastinating won't improve matters."

Today? I'd be walking into a hornet's nest!

"I can't, Auntie. My bike has a flat, and I can't walk that far because I twisted my ankle running here."

"That's no excuse. Darrell can pump up your tire and I'll get you some ice. Lie on the davenport until we eat and your ankle will feel better soon. But if not, I'll drive you over."

As it turned out, my tire needed a patch and my ankle still throbbed. While she was backing the car out of the garage, I hobbled into the grove and disappeared.

I slunk back just before suppertime. No matter how sorry I felt for myself, I would not miss my meal.

"Brat," Uncle Jack said, his mouth tight.

"Set the table," Aunt Annie said, her mouth tighter.

I made it through supper by keeping my head down and my words to myself. Since it was the twins' turn to do the dishes, I fled to my room immediately afterward and began reading *Out of Africa*. The first line went: *I had a farm in Africa, at the foot of the Ngong Hills.* I plodded along for thirty pages, skipping the unfamiliar words without looking up a single one, before setting it aside.

Then I turned my chair around and glared at Daddy's portrait. I imagined a woman standing next to him: a very dark, very ugly, Italian woman, gaudily dressed, laden with golden chains, reeking of cheap perfume. I balled up a bunch of my socks from my dresser and methodically bombarded his picture with them.

Uncle Jack sauntered in just as one hit Daddy squarely on the nose. "Darts would be more effective. They're in the basement if you'd like to borrow them."

I felt dumb as a board.

"I just came to kiss you goodnight. But, since you're busy—"

I flopped in bed. "Then do it."

"Well, you're certainly in a lovely mood. You wait all your life for my brother to return, and the very next morning you run back here anyway. What's wrong now?"

"He got married."

"Are you still mad about that? Hell, I figured you'd be mad about something else by now. Well, get over it. He should be married. Everybody should be married. I'm thrilled he got married … gives me hope."

"Hope for what?"

"Hope he can be happy again. If he's happy, I can be happy, Annie can be happy, we all can be happy. He's married and you can't change it, Abby. Change what you can—you."

Change myself? What a fabulous idea!

Tomorrow I'd change into a bright and shiny Abby. Tomorrow I'd win my father back. Tomorrow I'd win him back and make him forget all about his dark, gaudy, Italian wife.

Oh, there'd be lots of changes before I was through!

The Party

THE NEXT MORNING, I iced my ankle again. It no longer hurt, but I pretended it did. From the comfort of the davenport, I watched Darrell vacuum, the twins dust, and my aunt arrange the flowers. After the work was finished, I scampered upstairs, took a bubble bath, washed my hair, and happily donned a frilly, white dress.

Then I watched for cars from my bedroom window. Uncle Ben, Aunt Evelyn, and their three kids arrived first. Uncle Ben joined Uncle Jack for a smoke on the porch. Aunt Evelyn toted in two covered dishes. Ardell and Judy raced to my room. Gary, their older brother, ran off with Darrell. Soon Uncle Vic, Aunt Emma, Virgil, and Mr. and Mrs. Swanson came, and the party gathered momentum. Virgil drove off and returned shortly with Daddy.

My father looked imposing in his dress uniform, resplendent with ribbons and medals. The war hero was home; the war hero was my father; and the last thing my father the war hero had heard out of me was that I hated him!

A cheer erupted from downstairs as he and Virgil entered. Then Ruth arrived, brought over by the Olsens, and our welcome home party for Daddy was complete.

"Come on down, girls, we're almost ready to eat," Aunt Annie hollered up the stairs.

"It's about time!" Judy dashed from my room. Ardell followed her little sister, as did Ruth.

I dawdled, checking my appearance in the mirror from every angle. Would Daddy like my dress? My shoes? My hair? Granted, Ardell hadn't had much to work with. Taking a deep breath in an attempt to negate the knots in my stomach, I headed downstairs.

I assumed my rightful place next to Daddy, but he barely acknowledged my presence. He was engrossed in one of Aunt Emma's stories, and he burst out laughing at the end.

Uncle Jack stood at the head of the table and rapped a spoon on the side of a glass to get everyone's attention. "Okay, all you short folks, get in here and line up!" he called toward the kitchen.

A momentary jostling for position ensued as Darrell tried to stand next to Ardell, who didn't want to stand next to him.

"Settle down," Uncle Jack admonished. "Let's say grace."

"Grace," Duane mimicked. A ripple of snickers arose from the line of kids.

"Silence!" My uncle skewered Duane with a glare, then folded his hands and bowed his head.

What was happening? Uncle Jack never prayed! Aunt Annie did all the praying at their house and often, I knew, she prayed about my uncle. I remembered well the Thanksgiving she'd nagged him into asking the blessing and he'd said, "Thank you, God, for this food, which I've planted, cultivated, and harvested. If you had done more, I could've done less."

I closed my eyes as Uncle Jack began the prayer.

"Thank you, Heavenly Father, for bringing us together on this memorable occasion. Thank you also for delivering my brother from the dangerous skies of Europe and seeing him safely home.

"Those of us who labor on the home front in the comparative safety of farms, towns, and factories cannot possibly comprehend the infinite horrors of war. Would that the conflict soon be over, and all who are engaged in the overthrow of the enemy be successful, and be brought home to their families forthwith.

"I pray for the continued safety of my brother, who will soon be returning to Italy, and from there will be reassigned to the Pacific. And I pray for Jimmy Swanson, who is on a destroyer somewhere off Pearl, and for Ben's nephew Bradley, who is piloting a B-29 in bombing raids over Japan, and for all others on the side of righteousness in this struggle against the forces of evil.

"We will now observe a minute of silence to honor our fallen heroes. You know all their names, Lord. In Jesus's name we pray … amen."

"Amen," we repeated. Silence followed for the appropriate time.

Uncle Jack cleared his throat and sat down. "Well, folks, time to eat."

"Thank you, Jack," Daddy said.

My uncle acknowledged the comment with a nod.

"Yes, thank you," Vinnie Swanson echoed. "In a year of Sundays, I never heard a better prayer."

Mrs. Swanson nodded agreement. She blew her nose gently in her handkerchief. A single tear wandered unheeded down her cheek. Jimmy was their only son.

Aunt Annie was staring at Uncle Jack as though she'd witnessed the Second Coming. He asked her to pass the roast. He had to ask a second time before she responded.

Our feast then began in earnest. Besides the roast beef, we enjoyed fried chicken, smothered pork chops, mashed potatoes, and gravy. Early peas, baby carrots, lettuce in cream, and radishes came from my aunt's victory garden. Aunt Evelyn contributed a green bean casserole and a wriggly

Jell-O concoction topped with whipped cream. Aunt Emma brought her incomparable sour cream chocolate cake, plus both apple and rhubarb pies. The desserts would be served with coffee later in the afternoon, after the main meal had settled. I felt a twinge of pity for city dwellers who suffered from the rationing of so many items, while we country folk circumvented many shortages by growing our own.

Daddy finally addressed me when I covered my entire plate with meat, potatoes, and a smattering of carrots. "Eat another vegetable," he said. When I singled out the smallest radish in the relish tray, he shook his head but said nothing more.

I was anxious to make amends, but he began a long conversation with Mr. Swanson across the table. Then he told Virgil one of his lengthy war stories. When he finished, I tugged at his sleeve. He leaned down, his manner grave.

"Daddy, I'm sorry for what I said yesterday," I whispered.

"You should be."

"I didn't mean any of it."

"Then you shouldn't have said it."

"I know. That's what Auntie said."

"She's correct."

"She said you had a perfect right to get married again."

"Yes, I do."

"But without asking me?" I said, mindful of the hurt he'd caused me.

"I don't have to ask your permission for anything."

"Well, you could've mentioned it before I found out the way I did."

"I intended to tell you in a more appropriate way, but you were harassing me." He turned away to pass a dish to Mrs. Swanson.

I pulled on his arm to regain his attention.

"What now?"

"Daddy, please … I said I was sorry."

"Are you? Are you really? You say horrible, terrible things and then you expect instant forgiveness. I can't forgive and forget as easy as that, Abigail."

"Daddy, I can't stand it if you don't forgive me." A lump formed in my throat. "Aren't you ever going to forgive me?"

"I don't know … maybe."

I felt a glimmer of hope for the first time during our surreptitious exchange. "I wish you would. I got all dressed up, just for you. Didn't you notice?"

"Of course I noticed. I'm not blind, even if I am old."

"Who said you were old?"

"You did."

"When?"

"When your aunt said I had a perfect right to get married, that's when. You might think I'm old as dirt, Abigail, but I'm still above it. Keep that in mind."

"I didn't mean anything by it, Daddy."

"Then you shouldn't have said that either."

The conversation was going in circles. I stared at my plate. My lip quivered. I longed to be with the rest of the kids. At least they were having a wonderful time, judging from the frequent gales of laughter emanating from the kitchen.

And what kind of time was I having? Was Princess Abigail doomed to grovel for an eternity before the tyrant James Albert Stahl, previously known as Daddy? I wiped away an unwelcome tear. When I looked to see whether anyone had noticed, my father was watching.

"That's better," he said, appearing less severe. "I wondered whether you were sincere and apparently you are. Finish your meal and we'll continue this later." He resumed a discussion about the Office of Price Administration with Uncle Vic.

I ate my food, the lone radish included. It wasn't too awful drenched with salt. Aunt Emma noticed my disgruntlement and tried hard to keep me entertained, but it wasn't the same as being the apple of my daddy's eye.

After supper, the men retired to the porch to smoke and argue politics, the women cleared the table, and I joined the rest of the kids.

Altogether we were six boys and four girls, so whatever the boys wanted to do, that is what we did. First we pitched horseshoes in the back yard. Ardell won, which caused the boys to lose interest. Then Gary whipped out a pack of Lucky Strikes to share with everyone except Ardell. I was reaching for a smoke when Darrell smacked my hand and made Gary put them away. We played tag briefly, but the boys could run like rabbits, so we girls quit in protest. Hide-and-seek wasn't much fun because it wasn't dark.

Then Darrell suggested going to the slough and playing war. None of us had any idea of what that entailed, but we followed him anyway. Once there, he defined the perimeters of the war zone by pointing out this cottonwood and that willow. He and Gary would be Army snipers and the rest of us would be Japs. He told us to scatter and hide within the boundaries he'd indicated, and the last one discovered would win a silver dollar.

"Prove it," Judy challenged. "I'm not dirtying my dress for nothing."

Darrell obligingly held up a shiny dollar. "See, what'd I tell you? Think I'd lie?"

"Hey, where'd you get that?" Dennis demanded. "That looks like the one I got last year for Christmas!"

"Not so fast!" Darrell held it beyond his brother's reach. "They all look the same except for the year. If you think it's yours, tell me what year it is."

"How would I know?" Dennis wailed. "It's mine, though. I bet it's mine!"

"Oh, shut your pie hole," Darrell sneered. "I say it's mine. But you can win it, you little puke, if you're the last one found today."

With the exception of Dennis, who continued to dispute the ownership of the silver dollar, the rest of us scattered like hens before the fox. I wasn't the only one intent on attaining the prize.

The ground was soggy and would become more so, the deeper I went into the slough. I yanked off my leather shoes, crammed my anklets inside, and stuck them by a clump of cattails where I could easily locate them later. Then I darted through the reeds, avoiding the thistles and burrs, and headed for my secret place: a large, gaping hole beneath the upended roots of a rotting cottonwood that had been dislodged by a tornado years ago. I tossed a clump of dirt in the hole to make certain nothing was lurking within and crawled inside. I yanked some twigs and slough grasses over my head and I was completely hidden.

That silver dollar was as good as mine.

"Ready or not, here we come!" Darrell shouted in the distance.

Several minutes passed. Then Raymond Olsen hollered, not fifty yards away, "Hey, stop throwing mud all over my good shirt!"

"But we're snipers, you idiot," Gary jeered. "We have to hit you with something to make it legal."

"Yeah, but the good news is that now you're one of us," Darrell added. "You can help us hunt everyone else down and throw mud balls at them, as many as you like."

"Oh, yeah?" Raymond changed his tune. "Well, let's go, 'cause I saw where some of those dumb girls went. We'll plaster 'em!"

I heard both Ruth and Judy scream, a minute apart, followed by raucous laughter. Ardell, Kenneth, Dennis, and Duane took longer, but were eventually found and pummeled as well.

As the search party moved off in the wrong direction, judging from the cacophony of yells and laughs, I crept out of my hole to stretch my legs. As I did, my heel sunk in the muck and pressed against something sharp. Scraping the object loose, I pulled up an old Prince Albert tobacco can. Something rattled inside. Curious, I pried open the rusted lid with a stick and discovered a tiny key like one from a diary, and a note wrapped in tin foil.

Here is the key to my heart. No matter what the future holds, you have a lock on my love forever. Ellen.

I'd stumbled, literally, upon the exact spot where Mother had secreted love notes to Daddy so long ago! But why? Had their love been forbidden? Had they been forced to rendezvous clandestinely, here by the gaping hole beneath the upended roots of a rotting cottonwood tree, deep in Gramma's slough? I got all choked up as I imagined my parents enjoying a picnic on this exact spot or just sitting together to watch the clouds and dream.

My father would be similarly touched when I showed him my treasure. I reassembled the contents of the can and slipped it in my pocket. So focused had I been on my discovery that I failed to realize I'd been spotted. When I stood up again, I was pelted by a barrage of mud.

I shrieked and tried to brush off the sludge. The boys convulsed with laughter. Even Ardell giggled. Only Ruth and Judy looked sorry for me. Unlike the other kids, who had two or three dark spots staining their clothes, I was covered in mud. My beautiful party dress was ruined!

I plucked a glob from my hair and flung it at Gary, who was laughing the loudest. "Shut up and I mean it!"

"Oh, don't get your panties in a bunch," Darrell said. "Mud washes out. Smile—you're the winner of my hard-earned silver dollar that I found somewhere. Let's hear it for Abby, the Mud Princess: hip, hip, hooray!"

Amid the cheering, I heard Gary snort, "Princess? You must mean Abby, the Mud Piggy!"

I put up my fists. "I heard that, Gary! You started all this mud throwing."

Gary backed up as I advanced. Evidently he was hesitant to hit a girl, especially a girl cousin. I started to rush him when Darrell stepped between us and grabbed my hands.

"Knock it off, stupid," he said. "You don't pick a fight with somebody who's twelve."

Darrell had a point. Gary wouldn't back up forever, and he was taller than Billy Hartmann, and I'd already had the snot beat out of me by him.

"Let go," I said, reconsidering.

"You okay?"

"I'm okay."

Darrell released me and pressed the silver dollar into my palm. "Okay, everybody, fun's over. Let's head back for dessert."

The money felt good in my right hand until I remembered my shoes. "Wait, Darrell! I took off my shoes when I went to hide, and I can't go home without them. Help me look first."

"Oh, hell … where'd you put them?"

"By some cattails."

"The slough is nothing but cattails, you dipstick. Where exactly?"

I looked around. I'd never noticed so many cattails before. "I don't know!"

"Then you should've carried them with you, because I'm sure not wasting my pie time helping you look." He ran off, followed by the rest of the boys.

"Well, thanks a lot!" I yelled after them.

Ardell, Judy, and Ruth helped me search, but we soon realized that one clump of cattails looked like the next. Our collective fear of missing dessert far outweighed my individual fear of rebuke, so we headed home.

The boys were devouring huge pieces of pie as we entered the kitchen. The twins had changed their shirts, and Raymond and Kenneth had borrowed a couple of Darrell's.

Daddy stood by the stove, pouring a cup of coffee. He frowned at the sight of my girlfriends, but he reserved his darkest frown for me. "Was there a mudslide in the area? Or were you exploring a pig wallow in your party dress?"

The boys giggled.

Color rose on my cheeks. "Neither," I said.

"I was being facetious."

"Um … I don't know what that means, Daddy." What I did know was that I was about to be lectured in the presence of my peers.

"It means levity, wit, a sly humor, but I'm using the wrong word, as I see nothing humorous about your appearance or that of your friends, although you seem to have borne the brunt of the matter … what happened?"

I sidled next to him for privacy as I explained our game and showed him my prize. The treasure in my pocket I'd show him later, when he was in a better mood.

Daddy was hardly impressed by my cleverness, but demanded to know what had happened to the shoes and socks he'd last seen on the ends of my legs.

I told him how I'd taken them off to keep them clean and they were lost, but only temporarily. I'd look for them in the morning or right after I ate my dessert, if he insisted.

He insisted nothing. Locating my belongings was up to me. But if I couldn't find them, I owed him my silver dollar to help replace them.

I nearly said they couldn't be replaced because I'd already received my allotted two pairs of leather shoes for the year, but I stopped myself in time. Instead I nodded my acceptance of his terms, eyeing what little remained of Aunt Emma's tantalizing cake, mere inches away on the counter. Both pie plates were already empty.

"Now go take a bath and wash your hair. Hopefully Annie can salvage the mess on your back."

"But my dessert—"

"Now, Abigail. You're not fit to be seen."

I had no choice but to bow to the will of the tyrant.

I sauntered downstairs at my leisure, comfortably attired in shirt and jeans, knowing everything would be gone. I was standing by myself in the kitchen, fuming over the injustice of it all, when Darrell appeared at my side.

"Did you hear?" He kept his voice low. "Our dads are going to town in the morning to meet Gramma's lawyer. It'll be our chance to explore the schoolhouse."

"I know that already, but listen to this." Hastily I told him about the corn being gone, the rusted chain, and the new lock barring a secret chamber.

"Wow, that's amazing!" Darrell said under his breath. "Why didn't you tell me sooner?"

"I never got a chance. You weren't here when I came yesterday, and today you ran off with Gary … I hate him, by the way. He makes fun of me and every time you're with him, you make fun of me too. What was that 'don't get your panties in a bunch' crap anyway?"

Darrell brushed aside my complaints. "Oh, never mind … now here's the plan. When my dad picks up your dad, call me. I'll ride over lickety-split and we'll figure out how to get past that door."

"You haven't seen that door."

"Leave it to me."

"Like I left the dessert to you and those other oinks," I grumbled. "There wasn't a damn crumb left."

The party ended at dusk. Daddy said I could search for my shoes in the morning and I agreed. Darrell and I would have to make quick work of the schoolhouse to enable me to make good my pledge.

My father was again in a jocular mood. The conversation had been stimulating, the food delicious, and the desserts heavenly. I reminded him that I didn't get any. He shrugged and said that was truly unfortunate. Then I asked whether I could accompany him back to our farm, since he hadn't offered.

"Well, I'm not sure. I don't know if you can behave yourself."

"I'll behave." My cross-fingered promises were getting repetitious.

"No more tantrums about my wife?"

"No."

"No more sneaking upstairs?"

"The lumpy davenport suits me just fine, Daddy."

"No more nagging about things I don't want to talk about?"

"No." I wished he hadn't included that.

"Fine, you can come along."

Aunt Annie stopped putting away the party dishes long enough to pack us a breakfast. "I can drive you over," she offered. "Or would you rather take them, Jack?"

Uncle Jack sat at the table, watching the proceedings. "No."

"I'll get the car then." She bustled out with our picnic basket.

As we started to leave, Daddy paused in front of his brother. "That was a hell of a party, Jack."

"I hope that's a compliment. I thought it turned out very well."

"I do and it did. And that was a hell of a prayer too. I didn't know you had it in you, Jack. Since when did you find religion?"

"Recently."

"How odd, I returned just recently … could it be a coincidence? That was rhetorical. Be careful, Jack, or people might start viewing you in a new light."

"I want to be viewed in a new light."

"Is that so? Well, I'm sure that prayer greatly impressed those for whom it was intended."

Uncle Jack's jaw twitched. "I intended it for you."

"Really?" Daddy scoffed. "In that case, forgive my incredulity."

My uncle slammed his fist on the table. "My God, James, what more can I do? What more do you want? I'm trying, damn it, I'm really trying!"

"Are you? Are you really? Well, keep on trying, Jack. Keep on trying and keep on praying until you get it right. Of all the people I know, little brother, you'd benefit the most from a closer walk with the Almighty … come along, Abigail."

I followed him dutifully, but I felt sorry for my uncle.

Uncle Jack, a strong, proud man, scolded as though he were a child … or less.

Revelations

As soon as Daddy left for town the next morning, I telephoned Darrell. He arrived within minutes, armed with crowbar, bolt cutter, and enthusiasm. But he had neither the strength nor the expertise to breach anything approaching the stoutness of the door leading to the secret chamber. Next he tried turning the heavy screws, but they held fast. We were debating what to try next when I remembered the key upstairs on Daddy's dresser.

Snoop and Company thus experienced a true miracle: the key still lay where I'd last seen it *and* it fit the padlock!

"You do the honors," Darrell said, flushed with excitement. "It's your life and your mystery."

I held my breath as I pulled open the heavy door. As my eyes adjusted to the dimness, I saw the secret room was small in size but of soaring height. A menagerie was mounted on the walls, interspersed at various levels.

"Why, it's nothing but a trophy room," Darrell said. "Why'd your dad bother to lock up a bunch of stuffed animals?"

"Beats me," I said, deeply disappointed. "Guess we got all excited about nothing."

"Maybe, but we might as well look around. We might find a clue."

"A clue to what?"

Darrell shrugged. "Maybe it'll become obvious."

"If we're not too late. Both our dads were here before us."

"We can't back up time. There's a reason that door was chained, so let's try to find it … are you with me, Watson?"

"I'm with you, Sherlock," I pledged.

I initiated my search, hoping to recognize anything of significance, anything out of the ordinary. Most of the trophies were identical to Uncle Jack's: an impala, a bushbuck, and a sable. Some were small: a delicate duiker and a klipspringer. Others were huge: a spiral-horned kudu and a wildebeest. A dusty lion skin was stretched across the far wall, its cavernous mouth opened in a silent roar, mute testimony to the taxidermist's skill.

A hulking black beast I'd never before seen caught my attention. Its dirty head was nearly engulfed by massive curved horns. The staring eyes I knew to be glass, but they looked evil nonetheless. Oddly, the bullet holes hadn't been patched before mounting. Ragged rips through the right nostril and under the left staring eye remained.

"It's a Cape buffalo," Darrell said. "It's in Dad's *African Game Animals* book. Now stop staring at moldy trophies and help me look. We don't have much time."

For once I didn't argue. While he zeroed in on the firearms and hunting paraphernalia, I was drawn to a group of framed photographs arranged on the far wall, adjacent to the lion skin. Additional pictures were strewn on a large table. All appeared to have been taken in Africa, as they portrayed the same trio of hunters, two men and a woman, posing in front of various kills.

My breath caught in my throat. "Darrell, I just found pictures of Mother! Look, she's wearing the same hat Daddy sent for my birthday." I recognized her from the locket, too, but I couldn't tell him that.

Darrell dropped what he was doing and ran to my side. "Wow, she sure was pretty. My dad looks thinner, but yours looks much the same. Just think, Watson, you've always wanted pictures of your folks and here's a whole bunch in one place!"

We proceeded to waste precious minutes by congratulating ourselves on accessing the secret chamber, our egos expanding with each "I told you we'd find something wonderful, Watson," and "I always knew it too, Sherlock."

Suddenly Darrell's eyes darted toward the open door.

"Did you hear something?" I stood shock still.

"I thought I did, but I didn't … keep looking."

Quickly I rummaged through the stack of loose photographs, miscellaneous papers, and other small items on the table, hoping to find correspondence between my parents. It'd be revealing to read something Mother wrote beside her farewell note, and another letter might yield a clue as to why she'd written that one. But I found no letters and no answers.

Most of what I touched was layered in dust, although a clean patch on the surface of the table belied the fact that something had recently been moved, or removed. Had it been by Daddy? Or Uncle Jack? But why would anything in this room be of interest to my uncle? He had his own trophies. And he probably had his own African photographs stashed somewhere too.

Unexpectedly I found a treasure: a leather-bound album, wrapped in a flour sack. Within were dozens of pictures of Daddy. I didn't recognize him as a baby, but his identity soon became apparent.

Later pages held numerous photographs of him with an exquisite young woman; my mother. In one photograph, my parents were seated in a rowboat. She was holding aloft a cane pole as he baited her hook. In another, she was riding bareback. Her hair had been tucked beneath a flowered scarf, but much had come loose and was blowing freely. Daddy was shirtless and running alongside the horse. In another, my parents had built a humongous snowman without a head or arms. Daddy's head and arms jutted appropriately from behind the snowman. He clenched a corncob pipe between his teeth as Mother snapped his picture. She did the same, sans pipe, while he took hers. I was struck by how incredibly happy they both looked.

Another page held a series of petite head-and-shoulder portraits, the kind taken in a carnival booth. Daddy sported a fake moustache and wore a dapper beret. A cigarette dangled from his lips. Mother's curly hair was slicked down, flapper style, and she'd tucked a rose behind one ear. She was mugging for the camera, blowing kisses, pouting, or grinning mightily.

The final page held my parent's wedding photograph: he so proud in his officer's uniform, she so adoring in her bridal dress. So much love had once been bestowed by a youthful James Albert Stahl upon a lovely Ellen Elizabeth Coetzee.

What had gone wrong? Why did no one want to speak of her? Why was my heritage gathering dust in this strange place? And why had Daddy hidden all the pictures of her? And of himself? There had to be another reason beyond what he'd already told me, but how could I ever ask? We weren't supposed to be here!

"Look at this, Abby." Darrell held up a khaki dress. A brackish stain darkened the bodice of the dress, from collar to waist, with a hole sufficient to put a fist through, dead center.

"What's that stain?" I asked.

Darrell peered closer. "I'd say blood. Blood dries black and stiff like this … whose do you suppose it was?"

I felt a chill worthy of a grave. "Mother's."

There was a long pause before Darrell spoke again. "Of course … no other lady was with them in Africa."

Horror jolted through me. "Then the picture we found behind the chimney cover—"

"The picture of the tall man—"

"—holding the gun! Do you think—"

"I do!" Darrell flung away the bloody dress as though he'd been bitten. "Your mom was shot by the tall man and the tall man's your father! Billy Hartmann was telling the truth!"

"No, Billy can't be right!" My pulse pounded in my temples like a fresh wound.

"Then how else would you explain this? This is how your mom died, Abby, and this room exists to hide the secret. That's why nobody ever talked about it. Nobody knew what happened because they weren't there, and they sure didn't know she was murdered!"

"But your dad knew!" I gasped for air like I was drowning. "He was in

Africa. He could've stopped it. Even if you're right, why would he let Daddy get away with it all these years? No, Darrell, I don't believe it. I can't!"

"Believe it! Awful as it is, you have to believe it!" Darrell's eyes sunk like boreholes into my own as he shook me. "My dad couldn't stop a bullet, and afterward he didn't do anything about it because he couldn't. He's scared to death of your dad. I told you before, the man's crazy. Now do you believe me?"

"No!" I twisted away from him. "If Daddy killed Mother, why'd he keep her dress? And why'd he keep all this other stuff that would remind him of her? It makes no sense!"

"Why would he?" Darrell shouted. "Guilt, maybe? But if it's like I said, that's sick! What kind of sick person would do such a thing, keep such a thing?"

"I would," said a deep voice.

I shrieked before I realized the voice belonged to Daddy, and I shrieked again after I did.

We whirled around to see him hulking down to fit through the small door of the chamber. Once inside, he filled the doorway with his bulk. There was no escape.

Like a fiend from a nightmare, he loomed over us, his face contorted. "You certainly waste no time breaking and entering, do you?" he snarled. "Did you enjoy yourselves, digging for clues in my little chamber of horrors? Yes? No? Cat got your tongue?"

Darrell flattened himself against the wall. I clung to him in mute terror.

"Nothing to say? Well, I'll say it for you! You'll pay for this, and right now! Tell me, what punishment do you prefer? Poison? Dynamite? Hanging from the yardarms? Or best of all: a bullet through the heart?"

Darrell's eyes bugged. His mouth gaped.

Snoop and Company was on the brink of annihilation! If Daddy had killed my precious mother, his own wife, surely he'd be capable of killing my cousin—and me!

A terrible half minute passed before Daddy took a single step away from the door and waved a forefinger at Darrell. "Or would you rather save your skin, boy? Would you rather go and never return? Would you rather forget what you saw here? Forget this ever happened?"

My cousin managed a nod.

"Well, what are you waiting for?" Daddy thundered as he took a second step away from the door. "Run—before I change my mind. Run to your father. Fools, the both of you!"

My cousin shot from the room as though hurled by a catapult. I tried to follow, but Daddy blocked my way.

"Darrell?" I screamed. "Darrell, help me!" The pounding of hooves, fading fast away, mocked the pounding of my heart. I evaded Daddy's grasp and shrank to the far side of the room. Even there, barely twelve feet separated us.

Then the strangest thing happened.

"Well," Daddy said in a normal tone, "I got rid of Darrell rather easily, don't you think? For all his bravado, he's proven himself a coward once again. Tell me—is he still your best friend, when he abandons you so easily and so frequently?"

I stood staring. Was my father mad?

"I should hope not," he answered for me. "But he probably is, since you have so little of quality to choose from."

I found my voice and asked the only question I could, given the peculiar twist of circumstances: "Are you going to hurt me, Daddy?"

My father blinked several times, rapidly, and his demeanor reverted to the rage he'd initially displayed. "Well, I should, shouldn't I?" He advanced on me. "After all, you blatantly disobeyed me. I told you to stay away from here, but no, the first chance—"

"I know we did wrong, but don't hurt me," I begged. "You let Darrell go and I'm your daughter, Daddy. Don't hurt me! Don't kill me! I don't want to die! I'm just a little girl—I don't want to die!"

He looked at me as though I were the mad one. "Die? What are you talking about? I'm not going to kill you."

"But what you said: poison, hanging—"

"Oh, that was just to scare you. I said whatever popped into my head. Now I'm over it. I'm in control again. So you can stop looking so scared, Abby. You're safe—"

"I am?" I blurted. "And was Mother safe from you too?"

"Who? Your mother?"

"Of course my mother! I only had one, didn't I?"

"What the hell are you talking about now?"

"The picture, Daddy! Explain the picture!"

"What picture?"

"The picture of you aiming your gun at Mother and Uncle Jack!" I yelled, forgetting the photograph in question hadn't been found within these dusty walls.

Daddy looked blank. "I have no idea what you're talking about."

It was too late to retract my question, so I forged ahead. "Darrell and I found a photograph of you, taken in Africa, aiming your gun at Mother and Uncle Jack. They're smiling for the camera, and you're standing in the background by a hut and Darrell said you—you—" I stopped, repulsed at the accusation I was about to hurl against my own father.

"What? If you think it, damn it, say it!"

"Shot … her." The words left me weak.

"Shot her? Shot my own wife? Is that what you think? Dear God!" Turning his back to me, Daddy passed his hands over his face as a low, guttural moan escaped him.

Did his reaction equate guilt? Or would an innocent man, unfairly accused, react similarly? I didn't know him well enough to judge. "Daddy, are you all right?" I said, thinking I should say something.

"No!" But he had regained his composure by the time he walked across the dusty floor and picked up the dress. He held it for a moment before placing it on the table and seating himself in the only chair in the room. "Come here, Abby. I'm sorry I scared you, but try to understand. I simply can't think about those days, much less talk about them. And now I must or you'll continue to think unspeakable evil of me … how did you find that photograph you just mentioned?"

"Darrell found it upstairs at their house." I approached him with caution.

"Oh, I see. You were snooping, same as here. You find a photograph that looks incriminating and you jump to conclusions." He paused. "Now that I think about it, I do remember the incident, although I'd forgotten Tony had the camera out."

"Who's Tony?"

"Our guide, the white hunter."

"So what really happened?" I wondered whether I'd hear the truth, partial truth, or outright fabrication. The discrepancies of the Nippy story still bothered me, and that hadn't even been important.

This was.

"I did fire my rifle that day, but I didn't shoot at them," Daddy said, his expression inscrutable. "I shot over their heads at a snake, a very poisonous snake, laid out on a limb directly above your mother and Jack. One or both of them likely would've died a hideously painful death if I hadn't killed it before it dropped."

"You shot a snake, Daddy?" The enormity of my mistake made me reel.

"I shot a snake, a damn snake. Feel free to ask my brother, if you dare confess how you found that photograph. I'm sure he'd love to hear about your prying. You should be ashamed of yourself, Abigail, so ashamed."

For a moment, it was as though the sun shone again, deep inside the dusty chamber. Then I remembered the second incident that begged an explanation. I stepped closer and touched my father's hand by way of an apology.

"There's something else, Daddy. Somebody at school said something terrible about you and I was hoping you could explain that too."

"Who's accusing me now—a teacher or a pupil?"

"A pupil, although he's real dumb, so that's a stretch."

"What student would know enough about me to say something derogatory?"

"He doesn't. He probably repeated something he heard." I went on and told Daddy how I'd fought the good fight to uphold his honor.

"And what did Billy Hartmann say that provoked such a melee?"

I prayed for a plausible answer to dispel the remaining cloud on my father's character and set my world right. "Billy said … " I faltered. Then I gathered my courage and started again. "Billy said you killed Mother and everybody knows it, but nobody can prove it because nobody saw it happen."

Outright shock registered in the pale eyes. "What? Now I'm expected to defend myself against a lie perpetuated by some phantom? Someone I don't know and who doesn't know me? Who exactly is this little shit? And who are his family, his father in particular?"

"There's a bunch of Hartmanns living north of town. I don't know his dad's name … why?"

"Because the name sounds familiar. Let me think."

I waited for what seemed an interminable time before Daddy spoke again.

"I remember now … it was back in '42, at Maxwell Field. A Hartmann—I forget the first name—was in pre-flight, and I was in charge of training. I remember him being from my hometown. He got caught cheating on an exam, a breach of the Honor Code. I drummed him out of school, a stigma that'd follow him throughout his military service. He blew off steam before he bused out, but I let it slide … basically he vowed revenge. I assume he started this outrageous slander and his son, Billy, picked up on it. I always told Jack that putting your mother's obit in the paper would give the gossips a field day around here, but did he listen? Hell no, he's never listened to me … but I don't think Hartmann's lie has gotten widespread attention or Annie would've heard and told me. You don't need to give it a second thought."

"I just knew you'd have a good explanation!" Impulsively I gave my father a big hug. "I won't think about it ever again!"

He smiled thinly. "Good … now is there anything else bothering you, since I'm shedding light on lies, deceptions, and mysteries?"

I took his invitation literally. "Yes, tell me how Mother really died."

The smile faded. "Not now."

"Daddy, please."

"I'd rather tell you how she lived."

"I'd like that, too, but it's the other thing I need to know about."

"Some other time."

"I saw the dress, Daddy."

"What of it?"

"It had a bullet hole and a lot of blood."

"I can't deny the obvious. I guess I'll have to explain that … later. I hear a car coming. See who it is."

I ran to look. "It's Uncle Jack."

"Well, I'll be damned." Daddy eased through the chamber opening and closed the door behind him. "Your yellow-bellied cousin didn't forget you after all. He sent the cavalry to the rescue … is Jack alone?"

"No, Auntie's with him."

"Hiding behind a woman. No surprise there."

Daddy sauntered to the veranda of the schoolhouse, leaned against a column, crossed his arms, and waited. I took my place at his side. Whatever was going to happen, I wasn't going to miss a thing.

Uncle Jack and Aunt Annie flew out of the car as though they had expected me to be dead. I'd never seen such concern.

"Abby, are you all right?" Uncle Jack called.

"Yeah, I'm fine. Why?"

He looked taken aback. "But from what Darrell said—"

"And what did Darrell say?" Daddy interrupted. "Did the meddling mess of your loins repeat exactly what I said or just hit the high points? Let me recall—was it something about poison? Being hung? Shot? Wait, I think I missed one! Do you remember, Abby? Or were you as traumatized as Darrell?"

"Dynamite," I chirped. "And no, I remember everything."

"See? Abby understood what I said. Put your hackles down, Jack. It was a joke. Can I help if Darrell misunderstood and blew everything out of proportion?"

"No, I don't think he misunderstood," Aunt Annie countered. "Darrell doesn't scare easily, and he was scared out of his wits. And he doesn't lie either."

"Then today he was a disappointment on two fronts," Daddy stated. "Abby, were you scared at any time during the last hour?"

"No." The lie shivered down my spine.

"There, you've heard it with your own ears. Abby's perfectly fine. We have things to do now, so the two of you can go … Jack, schedule an appointment at the lawyer's for Thursday around the same time. I won't be available tomorrow."

Uncle Jack hesitated, looking at me. I looked back nonchalantly.

"Well, get going!" Daddy snapped. "And do try harder to corral your wandering son. These stealthy excursions to my property are becoming quite repetitive, don't you think?"

My uncle shot Daddy an angry look as he got in the car. From the way my aunt slammed her door, he'd have ample opportunity to explain to her what my father meant.

"You see how it works?" Daddy said to me as he watched them leave. "Keep your head. Think. Don't say too much, just say the right thing. Darrell's in trouble now. He made his father out to be a fool. Jack can't stand that. And Annie, she'll be hounding him all day, trying to get to the bottom of everything. It's just perfect."

"No, it's not. You made me lie for you."

"I didn't make you do anything. You said what you wanted to say."

"But you were standing right there."

"So were they. You could've contradicted me and left with them. I couldn't have stopped you. You backed me up because you wanted me to finish answering your questions. I'm right, aren't I?"

"Yes," I admitted. *At what cost would those answers come?*

But I felt better when Daddy suggested we return to the secret room and he'd explain what he could, after we ate breakfast. He set out the Post Toasties and the other groceries he'd bought, combined with the boiled eggs and the cinnamon rolls my aunt had packed the night before. As I began to eat, I asked how he'd known Darrell and I were inside the schoolhouse but my uncle hadn't. Didn't they come back together?

"Yes, but it was such a nice morning I had Jack drop me off at the mailbox. When I walked up the drive, I saw the pony right away."

"Oh … how'd you get back so soon? Darrell thought you'd be gone at least an hour."

"The law office was closed with a note on the door. Shopping took just minutes."

"Oh … why did Uncle Jack have to break in the other night if there was a key? We didn't have to break in."

"How do you know he broke in?"

"Because the lock seemed new, while the chain looked old and rusty."

"Acute observation. So why don't you answer your own question?"

I pondered the mystery as I finished my cereal. "I can't, Daddy. I can't figure out the rest."

"Then you'd make a poor detective." He looked amused. "Okay, I'll explain what happened. Jack had to break in because I had the original key. He returned a second time the same night and replaced the lock he'd broken with one similar. He hung the new key on the rack as though I'd left it there myself the last time I was here. After I heard Darrell's confession that first morning, I saw the new key, used it, and put it up on my dresser. This morning I neglected to take it along. I wasn't certain you'd noticed it, but I'm not surprised you put the two together, as precocious as you are."

"So what did Uncle Jack take?"

"Who said he took anything?"

"You said dust was disturbed—and it was. I could tell, Daddy."

"He took what was important to him."

"And what was that?"

"Enough questions. Do the dishes."

At least Daddy made good on his promise to explain my early life. He began with basic facts about my mother, some of which I already knew, but I didn't let on for fear of interrupting his monologue.

Ellen, he said, was orphaned in 1918 by the flu epidemic that had killed millions. He didn't know how it had come about, but she got adopted by the banker and his wife from New Ulm. She arrived on a train from Brooklyn in 1919 as a frightened ten-year-old to begin her new life. Being a decade older, he was unaware of her existence until he returned on furlough in the summer of 1928.

When he went to town to make a deposit to his bank account, Ellen was behind the teller's cage. She'd charmed him immediately with her dark-eyed beauty and easy laugh. He asked around town and discovered that she already had a bevy of beaus, so he tried to forget her. But he found himself returning to the bank to add five dollars to his account, to take five dollars out, just for another opportunity to talk with her.

He went back to the army. Six months later, when he returned, she was engaged. He was home three weeks that time. Ever hopeful, he continued going to the bank, time and time again. One day, he noticed the diamond was gone and she appeared to have been crying. He asked her out and dried her tears. For two weeks, they were inseparable. For six months, he was gone again. He thought that he would die from the absence of her, but she waited for him. They were married as soon as he returned in the autumn of 1929, when she was twenty and he thirty.

They lived in several states as he ascended the chain of command. She wanted children from the onset, but it didn't happen. Then he was assigned a temporary duty post where she could not follow. He left her with my grandmother so she wouldn't be lonely. They were helpful to one another—

Ellen with the garden, flowers, and chickens, while Gramma passed on her skills of sewing and needlecraft. He came home on furlough when his assignment was extended. When he returned the second time, Ellen shared the joyous news that she was expecting me.

Then Daddy went through the photograph album, page by page, explaining the circumstances behind each picture. My grandmother had taken a lot of baby pictures of him. He was her first child. And he'd taken a lot of pictures of Ellen. She was his first too … wife, that is. The fishing photograph was taken on Wood Lake. The damn bullheads were biting that day, but the crappies weren't. The horse was in Tennessee where they drove for a short honeymoon. Ellen went bareback riding on a dare and he ran alongside to catch her when she fell, but she never did. The snowman was built beyond the barn. He took me outside and pointed to the exact spot. The snowfall had been unbelievable that year. And the carnival booth photographs had been taken in the summer of 1931, during a visit home.

Daddy's memory was phenomenal. I couldn't have remembered my own short life with such detail. At last we came to the final page. The wedding photograph had been taken in St. James, he said. Our town had no studio. Ellen had caught the hem of her dress with her heel getting out of his car and torn it, but it hadn't shown in the picture.

I closed the album reverently. "She was so beautiful, Daddy."

"Yes, she was."

"So why did you hide all these pictures from me? I loved looking at them and hearing all about her."

"She's dead, Abby."

"What does that have to do with it?"

"It's no good to dwell on the past. The past has to be buried."

"Then why'd you save all these things in this room?"

He pursed his lips momentarily. "I couldn't bury her. I just put her out of sight."

"Well, I'm glad you showed me everything today, Daddy. Pictures can't take the place of a person, but at least they're something … how old was I when she died?" I hoped he'd add something to what I already knew.

"Seven months."

"What made her go to Africa?"

The pale eyes darkened, like clouds scuttling past the surface of the moon. "Insanity … we were all insane, those days."

"I don't understand."

"No, and I'm not explaining it. Take whatever you want to keep up to the house or you'll never see any of it again."

His mood swing took me by surprise. "Why? Are you getting rid of everything?"

"Yes, I'm cleaning house. Schoolhouse, in this case. Three people have already invaded my privacy and I'm putting an end to it ... plus my new renters might want the space."

Both reasons struck me as peculiar, but I didn't waste time arguing. I rescued the photo album and the Africa pictures. Daddy took his guns. When he asked if I wanted any of his trophies, I said the impala. After I grew up, I wanted to hunt my own trophies with him. My own would hold more meaning for me. Daddy said that was a wise assessment, but he would never, under any circumstance, return to Africa. Given that information, I also took his sable. When I thought to look for the dress, between trips to the house, it had disappeared.

We rested on the porch after our exertions. I reminded Daddy that he hadn't told me about Mother's death or explained the significance of the dress. I'd stood by him when he'd gotten rid of my aunt and uncle and it was time to make good on his end of the deal.

"What deal? Haven't I already told you enough? You think you can make me say what I'd rather not?"

"But I thought—"

"You thought what?"

"Nothing ... "

After he smoked a cigarette, he changed his mind. "I suppose I'll have to, after what you've seen today. But when I'm done, I'm done. I'll never speak of it again and I don't want you bringing it up again. Understand?"

"Yes, Daddy ... I'm listening."

He leaned his head back against the rocker as his face lost its freshness. "Not now. Not when the sun is shining and the world is bright. I couldn't even begin it now. I couldn't even think about it now. No, this is a story for darkness. Tonight you will hear about your mother."

The remainder of the day seemed a week, but finally the sun went down on my ignorance and the moon stayed hidden for the telling of the story.

When I went to him, he was standing in the kitchen. A bottle of Canadian Club and a tray of ice sat on the counter. He reached into the cupboard for a glass.

"Is it time already? Is the night ripe for my confession? Are you my priest? What penance must I suffer to purge myself? What darkness must I endure, to gain again the light?"

I didn't know now to respond, so I sat at the table and waited.

He broke open the ice tray. "Tell me, Abigail. Have you ever seen a drunken man?"

"Yes."

"Good … no, bad. You shouldn't keep company with a man who imbibes to the point of intoxication, Abigail. Plainly speaking, you shouldn't keep company with me tonight, because I'll need far more than a few drinks to even think about it. Mind you, I don't habitually get drunk in front of children, but this must be an exception. If you insist on hearing this hellacious story, I must overindulge and you must forgive me."

I shrugged. "I don't mind. Uncle Jack drinks around me, so I'm used to it."

"Does he now? Well, I'm in good company then." I saw my father's hand tremble as he poured the whiskey. "Well, here goes the first one … drinking to forget comes fast and easy, but drinking to remember requires a delicate balance. Too little and I won't be able to tell the story. Too much and I'll lose my way totally."

I nodded, afraid of what he'd say and afraid of what he'd leave out.

He finished his drink. "Seems there's a hole in this glass. It's empty already." He held the glass aloft as if toasting something, or someone, unseen.

I watched as he mixed and drank the second, the third, and the fourth. Not too much ice, not too little. The correct amount of whiskey versus water. I knew how it was done from watching my uncle. Daddy was drinking heavily. I knew that too. When he ran out of ice for the fifth, he drank it without. He seemed to neither taste nor enjoy. He was drinking to get the job done.

Finally, he turned to me. "I'm properly fortified, I think, but if not, it's not for lack of trying. Come with me to the porch. Keep the light off. I'll talk and you'll listen. No matter what, don't interrupt. Don't comment. Don't question. If you say anything, anything at all, I'll stop wherever I am. And don't say anything after I'm done. Go to sleep, if you can. And if you can't, just lie there and think what hell it was for me to relive this all over again, when all I've done since it happened was try to forget. I'll probably drink more afterward, if I can still navigate. Don't worry about it. And if I fall asleep somewhere other than my bed, don't worry about that either. Just leave me alone, understand?"

"Yes." I assumed my appointed place.

He began speaking in a strangely detached manner. "It happened on our first hunt. And for me it was the last hunt, the hunt of a lifetime. Jack had always wanted to go; him and his goddamned fascination with Africa, ever since he was a kid, ever since I can remember.

"I don't recall how I got involved in the whole scheme. Maybe it was because as soon as he wanted to go, she wanted to go too, and I'd be damned if I got left behind … or maybe it was the other way around. Regardless, Jack and I took the money we'd inherited from our father—money that should've been put to a thousand better uses—combined with the money Ellen inherited from her adoptive parents, and we went.

"Mother was upset, I tell you. Jack told me how she tried to talk him out of it, and I could well imagine. Ellen and I were living out East at the time, and her letters had enough of an impact. Nothing good can come of this, she warned. But Jack turned a deaf ear to her and so did I … if he could go, hell, so could I.

"Getting there was a story in itself … anyway, we got there. But before we started hunting, we poked around a few days in the region where Ellen's folks had emigrated from. She always thought it'd be fun to see whether she had any relatives left. We checked some names and dates at a couple of churches and graveyards and put a few pieces of the puzzle together.

"At one of the churches, an old Afrikaner recognized the Coetzee name and steered us to a certain lawyer in Nairobi. Come to find out not only did she have kin, but they'd been looking for anyone left on the American side. The whole damn bunch was rich as sin, with holdings all over southern and eastern Africa, from Nairobi clear down to the Cape. Seemed she'd been bequeathed a sizable fortune by somebody or other. After much discussion, papers were signed … the joke was on me, except I didn't know it yet.

"Then we hired a guide, one of the best hunters on the continent. A Brit, Tony … I forget the last name, doesn't matter. He was good, real good. Good hunter, good drinker, good with the camera, good with the ladies … we only had one lady with us, maybe not so good there. We hunted all day and drank gin all night … well, most of the night. Gin and tonic—supposed to prevent malaria. Mostly it prevented sleep, at least in some of us.

"As far as the hunting went, we did very well, considering we were novices. Jack and I were both excellent shots, although it was hard to pick out the best of the bunch when they were all milling about. But we learned quickly, cutting our teeth on impala and moving on to wildebeest, kudu, and a half dozen other spiral-horned antelopes. Then we switched to cats, and I bagged a lion and Jack his leopard."

Daddy paused and bolted the last of his drink. His voice changed, becoming more intense, hurried. "Then the day came when we went after buffalo. Cape buffalo—those damnable black devils. We'd seen them before while hunting other things. I had no desire to go after one, but Jack was of a different mind. So when Tony glassed the herd that morning and said there were several great bulls and we ought to collect them, what could I do but agree? You can bet the farm I wasn't about to let Jack nail one all by himself and hog the glory. I'd get one too, by God, and mine would be bigger than his by at least five inches!

"So off we went. The herd numbered a hundred or maybe two, feeding near the edge of an immense area of tall grass, intersected at regular intervals by hippo trails. We hiked in a circuitous fashion, trying to get within range without being spotted. When we were close enough, we hid behind a clump of thorn bushes and caught our breath while Tony picked our targets.

"I'd never known anything could look so ugly. I don't mean just in physical appearance, although that's bad enough. Buffs are covered with ticks and they smell of dirt and dung and their horns are massive enough to—"

Daddy stopped for a moment, then continued grimly. "The thing about a buff, he looks like he hates you personally. I was tempted to change my mind when Tony pointed out the two good bulls Jack and I were to shoot. There was the old chieftain with a fine sweep of heavy horns, and a younger bull, with horns nearly as good. We tossed a coin to see who got what. I got Grandpa.

"Tony advised your mother to stay back by the thorn bushes. I seconded the notion, but she wouldn't hear of it. She'd stuck with us every step of the way and there was no reasoning with her. She picked the worst damn time to defy me, of course ... " Daddy's voice trailed off. He caressed his empty glass and took a deep breath before resuming.

"The herd was milling about and becoming restless, and the time for discussion was over. Tony and I dropped. Jack and Ellen followed suit. I crawled along on my belly, pushing my gun ahead of me, keeping the barrel out of the dirt. The thorns ripped my clothes and hands. The sun was high and hot. Sweat stung my eyes. I worried how I could place a shot with my eyes burning like that. Several times I looked back to see how Ellen was faring. She'd always give me the thumbs up, so we continued pressing forward.

"By the time we were alongside the herd, my exhilaration was incalculable. It was an incredible sight! Imagine a couple of hundred animals weighing from fifteen hundred to nineteen hundred pounds each, capable of killing you just as dead accidentally in a stampede as on purpose in a charge.

"I kept rehearsing in my mind what Tony had said, about how fast a buff could turn and how he'd plunge through bush if wounded. I had to shoot and keep on shooting until he died. If I only wounded him, he'd charge. Then I'd have to stand my ground and aim for the nose or the eye and pray the bullet reached the brain. And when he finally went down, he'd probably get back up and come at me again, and I'd damned well better have at least one slug left to finish him off.

"All this was running through my head as I crawled and sweated and wondered how I'd gotten myself in such a predicament. Then Tony stopped, gestured at me, and pointed at Grandpa. He singled out Grandpa's progeny for Jack. We positioned ourselves and shot within a heartbeat of each other. My rifle slammed into my shoulder and I knew I'd scored because the report thudded to a stop. Grandpa flinched. As fast as I could, I fired off another round and so did Jack."

My father's words ran together now, like a torrent. "All hell broke loose. Buffalo exploded past us and around us, walling their black eyes at us in sheer panic. We found ourselves in the midst of a goddamned stampede and Grandpa was leading! I hoisted gun to shoulder and nothing happened. My God, I'd forgotten to reload! Tony got off another shot and I think Jack did too, but Grandpa kept on coming. The others weren't so much charging us but rather swarming in all directions like termites after their mound is kicked.

"Grandpa was closing ground as I broke open my gun and shoved in the rounds. I couldn't see for the dust. I couldn't breathe. Everything was happening so fast, too fast! Then Ellen screamed and I saw her in front of me. *In front of me, for God's sake!* She looked like she was waving at Grandpa! She had her hands flung over her head and for a split second I remember thinking she looked so ridiculous. Several shots rang out but I can't remember for the life of me whether the others came before or after mine. Then all descended into madness, with more screaming and more shooting! Tony tried to turn the stampede, to no avail. He slammed backward into me, grabbed Jack out of harm's way in passing, and we fell together into a hippo trail. I can still see the tall grass closing over our heads and all I could think was that *Ellen was still out there!*

"I clambered out of the water in time to see that buff, that goddamn beast from hell, trample her! But somehow it seemed she'd fallen even before he reached her, and I ran at him, screaming and shooting, until he finally went down. But even after he went down, he kept bellowing and pawing the dirt, trying to drag himself up to kill the rest of us. Tony finished him off as the herd parted way around Grandpa and thundered off with the mindlessness of a runaway train.

"I threw away my rifle and ran to where she was lying. I clawed her free of the muck and wiped off her face. Her eyes were open and she was staring straight at me, but she couldn't move. She couldn't speak. She couldn't even blink. Something hot and sticky was running through my fingers and I looked down and saw blood spurting from a hole in her breast and I tried to stop it, I tried so hard to stop it … but I couldn't, I just couldn't … " Daddy's voice broke.

I gripped the arms of my rocker and shut my eyes against the horror.

He began again, his breathing fast and shallow. "I don't remember what happened next, until Tony started hitting me to get my attention. 'She'd dead, man! She's dead, oh God, she's dead!' he kept repeating. I looked up at him, his face caked with dirt and sweat, and I thought it couldn't have happened. It just couldn't have happened!

"Then I heard the strangest noise. I turned around, and I saw Jack squatting back on his heels with his arms wrapped around his knees, keening and carrying on something frightful. What right did he have to carry on like that when she was *my* wife? I didn't give a shit about him. I was tempted to shoot him right then and there—him and his goddamned safari!"

Daddy paused to light a cigarette. He tried several times before he succeeded, his hands were shaking so badly. After a long exhalation, he resumed the narrative.

"When the dust cleared, Kidoggo and the rest of the boys came back from wherever the miserable cowards had been hiding when the stampede started. We headed back, bearing Ellen with us in a makeshift litter. We broke camp and struck out for the nearest village, which wasn't far how the crow flies, but we weren't crows and it took till the next morning.

"The three of us went straight to the local police, and I use the term loosely. An hour or so of animated gibberish followed, with Tony pleading our case, partly in their native tongue and partly in pantomime. They'd point to me or Jack when someone ran out of breath and the bargaining would resume full force. The matter was settled when Tony offered them most of the money we'd paid him for our hunt. He said bribing the bastards was preferable to risking an appearance before one of their kangaroo courts.

"No funeral home existed in the area so we sent word to one of Ellen's relatives. He insisted we hold the funeral at their nearest farm, with burial in the family plot behind the house. Considering the logistics involved in returning Ellen to the States—not to mention the daily temperatures in the area—I agreed ... can I find peace now? Is it done? Is it finished?"

Before I could respond, Daddy turned to me, his words brittle. "I forbid you to repeat or discuss with anyone what I've told you, under duress, this night. The death of your mother will not be the subject of our next family gathering. Am I making myself clear?"

"Yes."

"Remember that, because if you ever repeat what I've said, I'll find out. Don't think I won't, because I always find out, and you don't want that."

"I won't say a word," I assured him.

"Good. Three people saw your mother die, Abigail. You've heard my version. Jack can't tell a dog story true, so don't bother. Tony is somewhere in Africa—if he hasn't already met his fate in the bush—so you'll never hear his. The subject is closed."

He walked unsteadily toward the kitchen, leaving me alone in the darkness to grieve.

Inferno

I HELD MY panda for comfort as I tried to sleep. Daddy staggered past me several times, ignoring both my presence and my tears. I needed a hug but he probably had nothing left to give, so I didn't ask. PB and I would make it through the night.

I couldn't help but marvel how Daddy had kept his concentration for the entirety of the terrible tale—no meanderings, misspoken words, backtracking, or repetition. Uncle Jack would've been rendered incoherent with far less alcohol.

Had my father rehearsed his story? No, he simply must be a practiced drinker. For as much as he consumed before he quieted, I knew this was not the first time he'd been drunk. I also knew that I would forgive his indifference and his inebriation in the morning.

After all, what I'd forced him to relive hadn't been his choice. No wonder he'd locked his memories in his secret room! But he had loved Mother—that much was clear. For him not to have loved her would've been beyond my endurance.

His explanations of the photograph and Billy Hartmann's accusation had come as a huge relief. And all he'd told me about Mother! I tried not to dwell on her hideous death, although her being shot bothered me more than the rampaging beast. But three guns had been at the scene. Undoubtedly her death had been accidental, and the shooter himself may not have known whether his bullet had ended her life.

But I continued to wonder why Daddy so detested his brother. Did he still blame my uncle for instigating the safari that resulted in Mother's death? Or was there something more?

Daddy's oblique references to gin and papers being signed confused me until I experienced a genuine revelation: Mother had willed her newfound wealth to Uncle Jack instead of Daddy! It would explain both my uncle's money and my father's lack. And it would explain my father's bitterness. I'd already seen how upset Uncle Jack had been when Gramma willed her farm solely to Daddy. Had she attempted to right part of the wrong done to my father earlier?

But why would Mother wrong my father to begin with?

I awoke in the dead of night to the smell of smoke. Not the familiar smell of cigarettes, but a heavy, thick, acrid smoke, billowing and roiling on the night winds. A pinkish light filtered through the living room window, so I stumbled from the davenport to look.

The schoolhouse was ablaze!

Several cars were barreling up our drive, their headlights glaring bright and then dimming whenever a particularly heavy concentration of smoke was encountered. The fire truck clanged behind them.

"Daddy, where are you?"

No answer.

I raced upstairs. His bed hadn't been slept in. Down again, I tore through the house until I literally stumbled over him in the porch. I switched on the lamp and saw him sprawled on the floor near the empty whiskey bottle, the shattered fragments of his glass, and a spilled box of Blue Diamond matches.

"Oh, Daddy," I chided. "Why'd you do that? Don't think you should've been playing with matches tonight, no, sir." I shut off the lamp to give him privacy, not that he cared, but I did. Then I stepped over his prone body and ran outside to experience the excitement.

Our neighbors stood front and center at our fire, shouting to each other above the crackling of the flames: "How the heck do you think it started?"

"Didn't see any lightning tonight, though it was dark as a gravedigger's spade!"

"It shouldn't be burning so fast. Didn't we have rain last week?"

"Maybe spontaneous combustion. What was stored in there?"

"Corn or grain, I think."

"Do you think it could've exploded—from dust or something?"

I hoped no one had seen me hide the empty container of gasoline beneath the lilacs prior to stepping out of the shadows to join the spectators.

Mrs. Swanson was the first to spot me. "Abby! Where's your father?"

"He's inside, sick as a dog. We woke up and saw everything going up in smoke. Think they can save it?"

Mr. Swanson and everyone else greeted me over the next minute and inquired about Daddy's health. My stretch of truth had traveled faster than the flames licking through the schoolhouse walls. I prayed Daddy wouldn't wake up just then, lurch outside, and add a recycled fifth of Canadian Club to the heroic efforts of the Brown County volunteer firemen!

The blaze soon reached the roof, threatening the integrity of the school bell. Enthralled, I was watching the efforts of the firefighters versus the inferno when a horse wheeled to a halt behind me. Uncle Jack slid off Banat and grabbed my arm so hard it nearly came loose from the socket.

"Where's my brother?" he shouted. "Is he in there? Has anybody checked? Somebody—"

He lunged toward the fire, but I managed to grab his shirt. "No, Daddy's not in there! He's in the house."

My uncle turned and broke my grip. "Are you sure?"

"I'm positive. He's sick."

"Sick? What kind of sick?"

I beckoned him down. "He's not sick, Uncle Jack—he's drunk. He passed out. He told me how Mother died, and it was so awful that he got drunk so he could forget again."

The glare of the fire illuminated my uncle's astonishment. "What? He told you that?"

"Yes, and he said you'd tell me your side of the story too."

"He'd never say that … so how'd this fire start?"

I shrugged. "Don't ask me. Ask Daddy when he's feeling better."

"As if he'd tell me."

"Sometimes things happen."

"Bullshit. Like my barn, this was no accident."

"Don't say that so loud, Uncle Jack. Somebody could hear."

He glanced at the house. "Well, that would be a damn shame, wouldn't it?"

"If you say so." I wanted him to go away so I could concentrate on the grand finale, when the roof would collapse, the chimney would topple, and the bell would crash through whatever remained.

"Listen, Abby." He took my arm again. "It's a total loss here. Another half hour and everyone will be gone. You need to come home with me if he's passed out. You should be with family."

"Daddy is family," I reminded him.

"That's not what I meant. Annie and I were concerned for you earlier, and we're concerned for you now."

"No need to be." I twisted free and ran for the house before he could insist. I stepped over my father and curled up in my rocker in time for the final conflagration. It was spectacular.

Eventually the flames died down to a heavy smolder. The onlookers left after the firemen secured the perimeter of the fire zone by watering down a circle of grass around the charred remnants of our schoolhouse. Uncle Jack was the last to leave.

The night became quiet again, and I started to think. How had my uncle arrived nearly as fast as our neighbors and the fire truck? And why had he been on horseback? Had he been lurking nearby, watching out for me? I'd never known him to go riding after dark. Banat could step in a hole and break a leg. It made no sense.

And he'd been willing to risk his own life to save my father. Either he was truly a fool, as Daddy maintained, or he possessed heroic qualities that had been somehow overlooked. Given the bad blood between them, his lunge toward the inferno made no sense.

What did make sense was Daddy's torching the schoolhouse. Darrell had pegged him correctly: my father was crazy. Was I up to the challenge of unraveling his mind?

At dawn, I left my post and made coffee. I'd no sooner returned when Daddy moaned and opened his eyes. I peered at him with interest. "Oh good, you're awake. Did you sleep well?"

"Damn." He pulled himself to a sitting position. "I'm barely conscious and already I hear sarcasm … shit!"

"What's shit, Daddy?"

"I cut my hand. There's glass all over the floor."

"Yes, I know." I smiled. "And I'm not cleaning it up either. Whoever makes the mess, cleans up the mess."

"Then I need a maid." He attempted to pick a sliver out of his palm. "My God, I can barely see … stop staring at me. Go make coffee, if you can manage to be useful."

"It's already made."

"Good. Bring me some."

"Why? Can't you walk to the kitchen?"

"No."

"Why not?"

"Because I feel like shit, if you must know."

"You say 'shit' an awful lot. Uncle Jack would get mad if I said 'shit' twice in one minute. Does that mean I can say 'shit' as much as I like around you, Daddy?"

"No. That's my prerogative, not yours."

"What's prerogative mean?"

"An exclusive right or privilege. Now go."

"Well, I wish I had your exclusive rights and privileges. I'd say 'shit' all the time, just like you do. By the way, Uncle Jack drinks better than you. He gets tight as a tick, pukes in the pot, sleeps all morning, and he's right as rain by suppertime."

"Thank you kindly for that astute comparison." Daddy looked like Ranger did once after gobbling the entire contents of the slop bucket. "Now get me that coffee—and a Band-Aid, if there's any."

"Another new word! What's 'astute' mean, Daddy?" I leaned forward and smirked.

"Not now, Abby. Just go!"

"You don't have get cranky just because you're turning green … after all, nobody held a knife to your throat and forced you to suck down a whole bottle of Canadian Club."

Daddy glared at me in such a way that I vacated the premises rather quickly. By the time I located a Band-Aid and poured his coffee, he was in the front yard doing a convincing imitation of his younger brother.

I rolled my eyes and waited for him to finish. "So, how do you feel now?" I said when he returned.

"Successful." He wiped his mouth with his handkerchief.

"What do you mean?"

"I burned that sucker down, right to the ground."

"Yes, you did. You can really be proud of yourself too, because by the time anybody noticed, it was too late. Too bad you slept through all the excitement, though. It was really something over here. The neighbors came, and the fire truck—"

"But it was the middle of the night! I thought nobody would notice."

I giggled. "Not notice? When flames are shooting a hundred feet in the air? You've been gone too long, Daddy. Don't you remember anything? One neighbor sees and calls the next one, and pretty soon it's a regular party over here, all gawking and yapping about how it got started."

"Ah … yes." Daddy sank into his rocker. "Did you talk to anyone?"

"About what?"

"About how it got started." He glanced at the matches scattered on the floor.

"No … and I hid your gasoline can too."

"Thank you … and did anyone ask about me?"

"Everybody asked about you."

"I'm almost afraid to ask, but what did you say?"

"Not to worry, Daddy. I said you were sick and you'd sent me out to see whether our schoolhouse could be saved. Of course I knew the answer already. Anybody with half a brain could see it was a goner."

"I guess you'd know, since you have previous experience with that sort of thing."

I prudently made no comment.

"Well, besides feeling sick, I'm feeling rather stupid right now. I'm left with a mess that'll take weeks to clean up—and I don't have weeks."

"Should've thought of that before you did it."

"I appreciate your accurate analysis of my behavior, Abby, but brain function ceases when a drunk meets a box of matches … good coffee. Did I buy juice yesterday?"

I brought him the juice. The next hour, I brought more coffee, more juice, a lot of water, and four aspirin. Nothing was more boring than watching a soak sobering up, so I told how Uncle Jack had tried to charge into the burning schoolhouse when he feared Daddy was inside.

That woke my father up. "He did *what*?"

I repeated what I'd just said.

"Well, I'll be damned."

After dozing intermittently throughout the morning, Daddy became more talkative in the afternoon. He originally intended to drag the remaining items from the secret chamber and set them ablaze, he said, but after all he'd drunk, burning down the whole shebang seemed the way to go. He'd located the spare gallon of gasoline Gramma kept for emergencies, found the matches, and next thing he knew, he'd put the two together.

"I don't know why you think fire's the answer to everything. You could've locked up that room and sorted it out next time."

"I wanted to be done with it, once and for all."

"So you don't have to think about Mother. You want everything about her gone since you're married again."

"That's not true, Abby."

"Of course it's true. You burned the schoolhouse so her memory has no place to be. Now you're itching to clear out Gramma's house so *her* memory has no place to be either!"

"Memories don't need a place to be. Memories just are. Don't impute motives when you don't understand."

"Oh, I understand plenty!" I flounced into the kitchen and made myself breakfast. Rather than following me to make amends, which is what I wanted, he shuffled upstairs and took another nap.

When he came down, I started in again. "So what happened to Mother's dress?"

"It's gone."

"Gone where?"

"Up in flames. Why would I keep it?"

"For the same reason you kept it this long."

"I don't know why I kept it this long. It's gone now."

"You didn't offer it to me."

"I didn't want you to have it. It's a horrible thing, that dress."

I agreed with his statement, but I continued to pick. "How come I never found any letters from you to Mother in the schoolhouse? You write everyone letters."

"She threw them away because she had no particular reason to save them."

"Oh … how about from her to you?"

"Same thing."

"So you don't have a single letter from her?"

"Correct."

"Well, I have a letter from her," I boasted.

Daddy riveted me in a cold stare. "What letter could you possibly have? Explain yourself."

Big mistake. "Um … it's a farewell letter. She wrote it to me before she went to Africa."

"I see. … and how did you get it?"

"Uncle Jack gave it to me before he left for Africa." Bigger mistake: I'd mentioned my uncle.

A long pause. "And how did Jack come to have it?"

"Um … I don't know. He was only thinking of me, Daddy."

"I think of you too. I want to see it."

"It's at their house. I'll show you later." With my father's propensity toward fire, I'd show him only the copy.

"Do that."

"Please don't be mad at Uncle Jack. He didn't mean to do anything wrong."

"No, he never means to," Daddy said with a sigh. "That's the frustrating thing about him."

Daddy took a walk in the afternoon to clear his head. I went with him and asked his help to find my lost shoes. He found them readily. Then I showed him the gaping hole beneath the upended roots of the rotting cottonwood tree where I'd unearthed the Prince Albert can containing a love note, written to him by Mother.

"See?" I produced the evidence I'd taken along for maximum impact. "You said you didn't have a single letter written by her, and now you do. Isn't it wonderful?"

As my father read the note, shock hit him. A tremor. A spasm of the mouth. Then he stood so still not even his eyes moved.

"Did I do something wrong?" I searched his face.

No response.

"Daddy?"

He moved then, folding his arms around himself as though holding something inside.

"Not you," he said.

One Hand

"KEEP YOUR MOUTH shut about your mother's death," Daddy warned the next morning before he granted me permission to visit Darrell while he and his brother were in town. My father had been in a touchy mood since I showed him the Prince Albert can, which he'd pocketed on site and hadn't returned. I sensed the faint tremors of a quake building far below his surface, so I'd guarded my tongue during breakfast.

"I will," I said. My fingers were again crossed.

Twenty minutes later, I walked into Aunt Annie's kitchen just as Darrell finished washing dishes. She and the twins were working in the garden, so we could talk freely. I was relieved to learn that Darrell hadn't been punished for breaking into the schoolhouse with me. He wasn't even upset that I'd sided with Daddy against his folks. I was supposed to stick up for my own blood. He'd have done the same.

After swearing him to secrecy fifty ways to Sunday, I recounted what Daddy had told me about Mother. For once, I didn't need to embellish—the tale was harrowing enough!

"Buffalo stampedes in Africa, bullets going haywire ... who would've guessed?" Darrell shook his head in amazement. "I'm terribly sorry about your mom, though."

"It's better than not knowing."

He nodded. "True ... not many mysteries left now. Snoop and Company might be out of business soon."

"I suppose so." I found myself on the verge of tears. "Mother's death was horrible, but we'll have to accept Daddy's story as fact. We'll never hear Tony's side of things, and unless your dad tells us his—"

"He won't. Let's stop talking about it for now. You can't be crying when Mom walks in ... hey, I heard the schoolhouse burned down last night. What happened?"

"Daddy got drunk and turned firebug."

"No lie? He burned it on purpose?"

"Right to the ground."

"Did you save anything?"

"The African pictures, the album, and two trophies. Daddy took the guns and some other stuff. We did that already in the afternoon. I sure didn't know he'd torch the rest."

"What happened to the dress?"

"It's ashes."

"There goes the evidence." Darrell looked glum.

"That dress was no evidence of anything. Mother's death was an accident."

"I disagree, but you can think that way if it makes you feel better … you know your dad's nuts, don't you?"

"A little bit, but I feel perfectly safe with him."

"You're safe enough, but I'm not sure my dad is."

"Daddy promised he'd never hurt him … oh, and I told Daddy about Mother's farewell letter. Don't think I should've done that."

"No, you shouldn't have. How'd he react?"

"He froze up like an icicle."

"Something odd is going on, and I think it has to do with your mom."

"I don't want to think about it, Darrell." I'd wanted to tell him about the Prince Albert can, but I changed my mind. I didn't need additional criticism.

"So don't. All I'm saying is if you manage to stick out the rest of the month with your dad, he's bound to let something slip."

"I hope so. I want to find out everything before he goes away again, unless it's about Maria. All I want to hear about her is that he's divorcing her."

"You can always hope." Darrell poured two glasses of milk and opened the cookie jar. "Oops, Mom needs to bake again. You better run before she finds you in her kitchen and gets ideas." He grinned.

I grinned back. "I'll be long gone by then." As we divvied up the remaining cookies, I repeated Daddy's explanation of the photograph from behind the chimney cover.

Darrell chuckled. "I've got to hand it to Uncle James. He's crazy, but he's as smart as they come."

"What do you mean by that?"

"Think about it, Abby. How are we supposed to confirm that snake story? Ask my dad? Get a licking for snooping to see whether it's true?"

"No, but I believe it."

"Your privilege."

"Then listen to what Daddy said about Billy Hartmann's lie." I confidently launched into the story.

Darrell listened to the end, then shook his head. "I hate to tell you bad news, Abby, but that story just isn't possible."

"Why not? It made perfect sense to me."

"Do you know what old man Hartmann looks like?"

"No. Why?"

"Well, I do. He only has one hand. He lost the left one in a farm accident years ago. The Army Air Corps would never take a man like that. He was never at Maxwell Field or anywhere else. Your dad made that whole bullshit story up."

"Are you saying he lied?" I said as my world tottered and fell. "Billy was actually telling the truth? Like maybe that stampede didn't end the way Daddy said?"

"Hell, I don't know." Darrell avoided my eyes. "All I know is that story can't possibly be true."

"Oh, my God, what can I say now? What can I do now?" I couldn't breathe. I couldn't think. I couldn't finish my last cookie. *My father was a murderer!*

Darrell seized my shoulders and willed me back from the brink. "Nothing. You can't do anything but wait. It'll become clear one day … I'll help you, Abby, I swear. You're not in this alone."

"But how can I go back to Daddy?" My voice came as a squeak. "How can I pretend I don't know he lied?"

"Easy, that's how. You like to pretend. You love to pretend. Just pretend everything's perfect. Pretend you don't know the truth … besides, you have to go back or you'll never get to the bottom of it, will you?"

"No … "

"Maybe there's another explanation. Maybe he made a mistake. Who knows? After all, it was a long time ago." Darrell munched thoughtfully on the cookie from my plate.

Just then Uncle Jack burst into the kitchen, looking as angry as I'd ever seen him. I took his abrupt entrance as my cue to leave. For better or worse, James Albert Stahl was still my father.

But Darrell had to be wrong—because I couldn't stand for him to be right.

Tempted as I was to turn back and seek refuge in my uncle's house, I knew my destiny lay ahead … one step, two steps, three. Princess Abigail courageously trudged onward.

I trudged all the way to the castle of King James, formerly the abode of my Fairy Grandmother. The king was bustling about the scullery when I arrived, searching for an appropriate pot. Apparently he'd made Tyrant Jack tarry in the village after their business had been concluded, because he'd looted all the ingredients needed for our supper.

"Oh good, you're back in time to help," King James said, rather pleasantly.

I dropped a brief curtsy. "What are you doing in the scullery, if I may be so bold as to ask?"

"The cook is dead," he simply said.

"Dead? But Ellen was our best cook! You didn't kill another one, did you?"

"Of course not, my dear Princess Abigail." He flourished aloft a red-stained knife.

"Then what is that red on the knife, pray tell?"

"Tomatoes."

"Tomatoes?"

"Yes, tomatoes. What did you think it was, blood? Or more accurately, dried blood?"

I studied him for a moment. For an omnipotent monarch with an uncertain history, he resembled neither a liar nor a killer. He actually looked quite innocuous.

"Never have I doubted thee, but of thee I beg a humble pardon!" I covered both ends of the spectrum before judiciously changing the subject. "And what is to be our supper this night?"

"I'm making an Italian meal."

"I do not wish to partake of anything Italian." I wrinkled my elegant nose at the assortment of vegetables spread on the counter. "Italy was our enemy in the last war."

"The hostilities have ceased," King James pointed out. "Methinks you object not to the sustenance, but to—"

"No, my King and Father! Do not speak the name of—"

"Maria!" King James thundered. "Your stepmother's name is Queen Maria and methinks you damned well better get used to it!"

I sank to the floor in a swoon.

"Oh, stop being so theatrical." He lifted me as though I were a feather and deposited me on a dining throne to recover. "I'm certain you'll *like* your new stepmother. You'll also *like* what I'm cooking tonight. It's her recipe for spaghetti."

Even I knew when it was useless to argue. When my Father the King said I would *like* something, I had to at least pretend. Dungeons existed for a purpose.

"Again I beg thy pardon." I spoke sagaciously. "May I help?"

"Forsooth," King James replied with rare benevolence. "Methinks it's high time you crawled out of the meat, spud, and gravy rut you and everyone else in this kingdom is mired in … chop the onions for the sauce. I'll assemble the meatballs."

While I helped him, my Father the King told me more about my new stepmother than I'd ever wanted to know. The upstart Maria was a widow with no heirs. Her first husband, King Paul, had disappeared somewhere in Gaul during the early stages of the conflict. Her sire, now deceased, had been a diplomat from the New World. Her mother's family dealt in jewelry and precious gems. They'd been very wealthy before the war and doubtless would be again. He'd met his future queen when he sought to buy ruby earrings for me.

Upon hearing that, I reached for my goblet of wine. I had to suffer an evil stepmother for the rest of my life because my Father the King went *shopping*? Why hadn't he *pillaged*, like any proper despot?

Queen Maria would be ensconced in Stahl Castle as soon as the war was over everywhere, he said, reiterating that I would *like* her. She would be my new mother. At that, I nearly gagged. Annie of the Red Hair could be my new mother too, I said. After all, I was accustomed to her. Annie of the Red Hair wore sensible cloaks and baked me treats. She didn't traipse around bedecked in golden ornaments and ermine-trimmed gowns, smelling of Evening in Rome, which is how I imagined Queen Maria must look and smell.

That lapse of propriety prompted King James to banish me to the Great Hall in lieu of the dungeon, currently crammed with prisoners awaiting execution. I moaned and groaned piteously. Noting a dearth of dining companions, he pardoned me mere minutes later. We sat at opposite ends of the lavish dining table.

To my astonishment, he was a superlative cook, far better than Ellen, Eloise, Martina, Lorena, Corrine, Rena, or Kathryn had ever been; God rest their hapless souls. His meatballs were delectable and his sauce sublime. He set the stage properly too. He draped my Fairy Grandmother's best lace tablecloth over the table and laid out her silver candlesticks, as well as her lavish china and silver plate.

"I don't know why you went to all the bother, my King and Father," I grumbled. "Wooden bowls and fingers would be adequate. It's not Christmas Mass, or even the solstice."

"Are we heathen swine? Are we boorish peasants? Why bother to steal it if we don't use it?" he scorned. "In Queen Maria's family, they use their best *every* day!"

I had no snappy comeback, but it just didn't seem right, dining with the soft glow of candles illuminating a meal I could've seen far better if he'd simply flung open the shutters. Perhaps the dimness was to blame and not me when, three bites into my meal, a meatball slipped and deposited a blood red stain by the side of my plate. Aghast, I feared my Fairy Grandmother was rolling over in her crypt, horrified that her best tablecloth had been desecrated by the likes of me and my Father the King because he had to marry an Italian and then start cooking like one.

"Not to worry." He briefly assessed the damage. "I can get that out … happens all the time. Why, should a person be limited to eating food that won't show on a fancy tablecloth if it misses the mark? Like spuds or rice or, God forbid, lutefisk?"

Even I could see the desirability of spaghetti over lutefisk. I obligingly leaned back as he hacked away the offending section of my Fairy Grandmother's tablecloth with his sword and tossed it in the fireplace.

"See? Stain's gone!" he said in triumph.

I dutifully clapped my approval. When I spent extended hours in his company, my palms stung from so much clapping, but it was obligatory. Branding irons and dunking tanks encouraged even the most disinclined to clap heartily.

Returning to my meal, I dared bridge the Mystery of One Hand. "My King and Father, during the Italian Campaign, did you chance the acquaintance of a knight lacking his left hand?"

"A knight lacking but a single part? Aye, I knew many!" He laughed uproariously. "Left hands, right hands, left legs, right legs. Even eyes, ears, and noses! If they could somehow straddle a horse, I sent them into battle … why?"

"Oh, nothing." Somehow his answer didn't surprise me.

Then I pondered the inevitability of him uniting with a dowager I'd never met or wanted to meet, and I had to ask, "My King and Father, am I as pretty as her?"

"As pretty as whom? Annie of the Red Hair?"

"No, that upstart woman you went and married."

King James's pale eyes flashed daggers. "For the last time, Princess Abigail, that woman has a name and it is Queen Maria, Queen Maria of the Stahl! From this moment forward, whenever you speak of her, you *will* refer to her by her proper name and title! And, after she lives at my castle, if you fail to grovel appropriately, you *will* be replaced!"

"Replaced?"

"Yes, replaced! You're only a princess, after all. A girl, the sad opposite of a boy. Methinks the Queen Maria will produce for me a rightful heir, a namesake, a Prince James … and no, you're not as pretty as she is anyway."

"Oh." I stared at my plate, crestfallen. As though I hadn't enough tribulations, I stood to be replaced by a rotten royal in putrid pants.

"But you might be, after you're grown. You'll be sufficient for a political alliance, at the least. But for right now, there's a distinct difference in the beauty of a princess and the beauty of a queen. A queen shines brightly, while a princess shimmers but slightly."

"Oh," I said again, unable to decide whether I should feel better or not. Looking up, I dared my final, most important question: "My King and Father, do you love me as much as you love Queen Maria?"

King James arched an eyebrow regally. "Again, there's a difference between the love of a king for his queen and the affection of a king for his princess ... but enough of this trivial prattle. Finish your spaghetti before it gets cold."

I felt a malevolent chill that had nothing to do with my supper. And the chill swirled forth from the Great Hall, whispering a warning as it scraped along the floors and walls of the castle of King James, permeating my heart and enveloping my soul.

"Abby!"

"I desire thy love, my King and Father!" I blurted out.

"What's wrong with you tonight?" Daddy's scowl shattered like glass the most unsettling fairy tale I'd ever imagined. "You ate your spaghetti like you were in a trance, and now you're babbling nonsense."

Inheritance

I HOPED DADDY would divulge more about Mother, the photograph, Billy Hartmann, or the Prince Albert tin during the ensuing days, but not one iota of information escaped his lips. Nor did he talk much about other matters. There was work to be done. Daddy honed to the task like a blade to the whetstone. And he demanded my help. No more lollygagging at his brother's house; he'd teach me to be productive, by gum.

We'd sort through the outbuildings first because the house had to be kept livable until the last. He told me to wipe each item with a rag to remove the dirt so a potential buyer could see it was in good condition. Then I was to fill boxes with like items. If I came across something I wanted to keep, I was to ask. If he agreed, it could be set aside.

While I wiped and packed, he did all the things I couldn't do. He shoveled the barn and the chicken house. He hauled out feeders, brooders, pieces of harness, bottles and cans, leftover lumber and paint, wire and fencing, and assorted junk. Grandpa Walter had saved odds and ends for decades on the notion it might someday come in handy. Now, years later, Daddy suffered accordingly from his decision.

When items that couldn't be affected by rain were lined up outside and items that could be affected were lined up inside the barn, Daddy moved on to the shop. I barely had time to grab the arrowhead I'd started making before he sorted everything into boxes and swept the floors clean.

He did pause when he discovered the pinup girl calendars and the racy magazines. I pretended indifference as he flipped through them for several minutes. "Filth," he muttered and added them to the burn barrel in the yard.

He made me scrub my artistry off Gramma's car. My arms were limp with fatigue by the time I got the old Ford clean enough to suit him. Then he told me to wax it until it shone.

He started up the tractor and the rest of the farm machinery, each in turn, making repairs as needed. He oiled everything, even the push mower, to get top dollar at the auction.

For the duration of my servitude, Daddy cooked little to nothing. I began to beg for his spaghetti and meatballs, or anything beyond what we'd been eating. He refused, saying work came first. So we continued to subsist on cereal, milk, canned soup, macaroni and cheese, crackers, tuna, hot dogs, and

Spam. We also devoured the peaches, pears, plums, and applesauce Gramma had canned. With each bite I was reminded that she would never fill her mason jars again, and my heart ached.

Daddy worked me so hard I tried to rebel, but I didn't succeed. Complaints brought rebuke. Once I started to cry. He ordered me to stop sniveling. As though I hadn't enough to do, I had to look up "sniveling" in his pocket dictionary before I knew how I'd been insulted.

Finally, praise heaven, Princess Abigail was allowed a day of rest!

But the next morning came far too soon. I hadn't even gotten another fairy tale spinning inside my head, starring myself as the hapless prisoner of Stahl Castle, when the tyrant informed me that we were starting on the house as soon as I decided what I wanted.

I mulled over my choices while lounging on the davenport. He grew impatient. I dawdled further. He gave me ten additional seconds and started a countdown. At the count of "two," I asked for Gramma's good china, her silver plate, the candlesticks that had illuminated our table the last time I'd eaten something worth a damn, plus the lace tablecloth he'd somehow gotten clean. Only in my fantasy had he hacked out the stain. I wanted my Shirley Temple cup from the washstand, the old mirror above it, and Gramma's coverlet, hand-quilted by her before I was born.

I wanted Grandpa Walter's shotgun and rifle, along with his father's sword from the Civil War era. I wanted Grandpa's collection of Sioux arrowheads, his coin collection, and his stamp collection.

I wanted my own collection of all the birthday cards I'd ever received, and the buffet wherein they were kept. I wanted the *Gone with the Wind* lamp, the two remaining rockers, the oak dining table, the chairs and—

"Stop!" Daddy held up his pencil. "This is ridiculous. You're naming nearly everything in the house. You've no need for it and nearly no place to put it. Start over and limit yourself to just a few things."

"Why?" I seethed with hostility. "Are you planning to give everything I want to Auntie? Or worse, to that god-awful Italian you married?"

No sooner had the words passed my lips when my father flung down the pencil, grabbed my arm, and marched me a whole mile across field and pasture, from our house to theirs. If I wanted to be such an ingrate—and I could look that up at my leisure—I could just sit at his brother's house and worry what he was saving for me, what he was giving away, and what he was throwing in the fire.

He opened the screen door and hustled me inside. I was banished until further notice. I was not to call. I was not to write. I was not to show up uninvited. I was persona non grata, and I could look that up too.

I burst into tears as I watched him stride to where my aunt was hoeing the garden. They conversed briefly. He entered the horse barn. Minutes later, he emerged with two Arabians, saddled and ready. He helped her mount, swung himself up on the second horse, and they galloped off together.

Uncle Jack walked in. "Looks like I've gotten the short end of the stick again," he said in disgust. "I lose a perfectly adequate wife and two incredibly expensive Arabians and in return, I get you."

I'd never viewed myself as the short end of anybody's stick. I wiped my runny nose with my palm and took a hesitant step toward him. I needed comforting, and I needed comforting bad. Even he would do. "Uncle Jack—"

He held up a hand. "Not now, Abby. Whatever you've done to get dumped in my kitchen, I don't want to hear about it. Frankly, I'm surprised it took him so long."

"But—"

"No buts about it. I don't want to hear anything out of you. I don't want to hear your problems or your fears. I don't even want to hear your apologies, as if you'd offer me any. I still believe Darrell over you, the other morning at the schoolhouse. You lied to me. And while I can't turn you out if you have nowhere else to go, I want you to leave me alone. Leave me the hell alone!"

He left me alone that time. I watched him stomp to the horse barn. Soon he was riding Banat in the opposite direction of Gramma's farm.

Why did I have to be so afraid of the Arabians? Everyone seemed to be galloping off in one direction or another. Maybe riding soothed the soul. Maybe riding cleared one's head. Maybe—

The screen door slammed. Darrell appeared. "What's wrong now? What are you doing back?"

I flushed with embarrassment. "Um … Daddy felt I was working too hard so he brought me back so I could rest up."

"Hello? This is Darrell you're talking to!" He snorted in derision. "Your dad drags you up our driveway. Then he and Mom take off. Then my dad takes off. You're left bawling in our kitchen. What, do you have polio? Or did you just do something really stupid again?"

Those were the two reasons Darrell was my best friend: I couldn't con him and he accepted my behaving badly. In fact, he expected it. It saved a lot of time between us, when I could simply confess what I'd done without trying to justify it.

"Well, I think you've hit a new low, you dumb bunny," he said after hearing my sad tale. "Remember how you wanted to find out about your mom? Your dad's now told you. Then you wanted to find out about him. He's now told you. And he was going to give you stuff from the house until you got all greedy.

"And what did he get from you in return? Whining about helping, when he's working his ass off? Bellyaching about food from the shelf, instead of fancy suppers? Snotty comments about his wife, when he just wants you to accept he's married? Squawking about him giving away some of the junk you wanted? Good grief, where were you when God passed out brains—the end of the line?"

I hadn't been in line at all. I was such a disappointment to everyone. Daddy had thrown me out. Uncle Jack had taken me in, but grudgingly. Even Darrell was disgusted. Who was left that mattered?

"I wish I was dead."

"That would sure do a lot of good."

"Maybe not, but I don't know what to do to fix things."

"Don't worry, it'll blow over." Darrell shrugged. "Everything does. Butter up Mom when she gets back. Tell her how sorry you are about everything. She'll tell your dad and soon everything will be okay again."

"You think so?"

"Sure." He opened the fridge and peered inside. "Hey, are you hungry? I see a bunch of fried chicken left over from last night."

Fried chicken? My world suddenly appeared a lot brighter.

It dimmed again at supper. Duane picked a fight, and instead of listening to my side of the story, Uncle Jack laid the blame squarely on me and made me sit by myself in the dining room. But it could've been worse—at least my plate was full. This was quite a feat because my aunt had arrived home at five thirty. She'd never worked so hard in her life, she said, and her headache was excruciating.

Uncle Jack, of course, was sitting like his butt was glued to his chair, waiting for his supper. So were the rest of us—all dogs waiting to be fed. She whipped open the refrigerator and saw that a substantial portion of the leftovers were gone, devoured, down the hatch. She glanced at Darrell, who looked as innocent as a newborn babe, then at me, and I tried my best to imitate him.

"Great! Somebody's gotten into what I planned for supper, and I won't bother trying to figure out whom. You'll just have to wait while I add something to it."

She hastily boiled hot dogs, prepared two packages of macaroni and cheese, and opened a quart of canned green beans and another of peaches. Daddy had been feeding me similar crap, but since I'd been so involved in my own pity party to think about her having to feed us after all she'd done that day, I could scarcely complain.

During supper, she updated my uncle on the situation at the farm. James had already sorted the contents of the outbuildings. The machinery and the car were in running order. Much more work was needed inside the house.

He'd offered her anything she wanted, but she wasn't sure what she should take. Did he have any suggestions?

"That's entirely your decision. Take as little or as much as you wish. I know I'd appreciate that sword from the Civil War, and those two guns Pa had, and his stamp and coin collections ... Abby, stop that infernal noise!"

I had strangled on my hotdog, listening to what he'd said.

"Abby, are you all right?" Aunt Annie called.

I hacked the offending chunk into my napkin. "Yes."

"Do be more careful. Supper doesn't have to be a race ... and Jack, you shouldn't yell at someone who's choking."

"You're absolutely right, but can I yell at her now, since she's finished choking?" His voice rose with every word. "Hey, slow down the eating in there! Didn't you and Darrell already have plenty, wolfing down what we were all supposed to share?"

Tears welled in my eyes. I'd been banished by Daddy, rebuked by Uncle Jack, chastised by Darrell, wronged by Duane, and admonished by Aunt Annie. Now insult was added to injury; my uncle would be the happy recipient of what I'd wanted for myself. Before supper ended, I half expected him to turn to my aunt and say, "Oh, and those arrowheads too ... always did like those arrowheads."

I waited until he retired to the porch before I cleared my place and helped with the dishes. My aunt seemed preoccupied. She rinsed our glasses more than once and forgot to wipe the counters. I asked whether Daddy had mentioned me.

"Not much. He just said you were tired out and that's why he brought you over." She banged around the pots and pans in the sink.

Amazed he'd covered for me, I said, "Could you tell him I'm rested now and I'd be glad to help again?"

"I'll tell him tomorrow." She finished up.

Uncle Jack walked into the kitchen and heard her. "Don't tell me you're spending the whole damn day over there again? And leaving us all to fend for ourselves?"

"Yes, I am," she said. "And you can fend just fine, if you put your mind to it."

He looked petulant, like a child. "Well, what if I don't want to fend? What if nobody here wants to fend? What if I don't give you a choice? What if I put my foot down and tell you that you're staying home tomorrow?"

She whirled to face him. "You can put your foot down anywhere you like, Jackson Stahl, but not near me! I've already made that choice once before, remember? And I may have to do it again, so don't antagonize me. Now, if you can manage to move out of my way, I'm taking a bath!"

What was that all about? I watched her clomp up the stairs.

Uncle Jack smiled crookedly at me. "I think we've both been shit on today … how about a game of cribbage? I feel like giving somebody a good beating."

My scalp prickled. Beating? In cribbage, or literally? Who, Aunt Annie? He'd never laid a hand on her, as far as anyone knew. Daddy? My uncle wouldn't stand a chance. Me? I hadn't been around for nearly two weeks and he'd never punished anyone—ever—for snacking before supper. I got out the board and the cards and tried not to think about it.

Cribbage and Casseroles

UNCLE JACK HAD taught me to play shortly after Daddy sent my beautiful cribbage board for Christmas. Minnesota winters were long and cold, and games helped pass the season. I'd caught on fast. I had the rules down within an hour and the quirks soon after. The game was about fifty-fifty between luck and skill, so I always stood a chance.

I liked to play my uncle because he paid me. He'd never given me an allowance as he did his biological children; perhaps he thought attending to my needs was enough.

He liked to play me because I played as aggressively as he did. Losing in cribbage and death were nearly one and the same to Uncle Jack. He'd slap the table and yell "fifteen for two!" or "thirty-one!" in a voice loud enough to scare the dogs. Or he'd sit, quiet as a mummy, while I counted my points. After I pegged, he'd chuckle at what I'd missed and peg them for himself. Only when he drank heavily during the game would he miss points, usually "nobs." If he degenerated into foolishness, such as throwing a five in my crib when he held face cards, he'd finally call it a night.

He followed a definite protocol for every game. I'd get two quarters to get started. If I won a game, I'd get another. If I skunked him, I'd get a fourth. If he won, I'd have to pay back one. If he skunked me, I'd forfeit two. On a good night, I'd amass enough money for all the wax lips and hot dots I could want.

He had a set pattern for drinking during the game as well. When he brought his evening brandy to the table, he was content. When he brought his bourbon, he was upset. But when he brought a full bottle of bourbon and shoved his brandy toward me, I knew I shouldn't be playing cribbage with him this night.

"Go ahead, drink it," he urged. "You've always wanted a taste, so here's your chance ... I've already cut. Now deal."

I dealt.

And I drank his brandy. After a few minutes, the warmth spread from my stomach upward to my cheeks. When I mentioned it, he laughed.

"Now I'm contributing to the delinquency of a child, along with all my other sins ... good thing my wife appears to have retired after her soak in the tub. She wouldn't approve of this." He poured a stiff drink and bolted it.

"And to think she went to bed without giving me a goodnight kiss … did she give one to you?"

"She doesn't give me a goodnight kiss. You do."

"Ah, you are so right." He refilled his glass.

He was playing as quickly as he was drinking. The bourbon hadn't caught up with him yet because he wasn't making any mistakes. My cards had been wretched, and I'd made numerous miscalculations. I wondered what Daddy would think of me sitting up till all hours, drinking a glass of the finest brandy money could buy, and then playing cribbage for quarters until his brother fell out of his chair. Even that was going poorly. I was only up a quarter for two hours' effort.

The tide turned in my favor the third hour. Uncle Jack began to waver. Now our dance had begun in earnest. How many quarters could I accumulate before he folded?

"Ha! Another queen for six!" he hollered.

"Not so loud, Uncle Jack," I shushed him. "Everyone's asleep upstairs."

"Again, you're right … so right."

The telephone rang, startling both of us.

"What the hell?" He glanced at the clock as he lurched to his feet. "It's nearly eleven o'clock. Too damn late for howdy dos. Guess somebody's dead … who's dead … who do I know that could be dead … hello?"

The caller did all of the talking, but for less than a minute. From my uncle's changed expression, I felt certain someone had indeed passed.

"All right." He hung up.

I rushed to his side in case he needed comforting, or in case I did. "Who died?"

He chuckled mirthlessly. "Oh, nobody died. It's my lord and master calling, and I must obey. I'm going out for a little while … wipe that concern off your face, Abby. Nothing will happen. The screws just need a little tightening. You'd think they could be turned in the daytime though, not in the middle of the goddamned night. Let's see … decision time. I'm drunk, I think … am I drunk?"

I nodded.

"Okay, the child says I'm drunk and the child is never wrong … where was I?"

"Decision time." I wished he would simply go to bed. If he went out, I would stay awake all night, bothering God. And I didn't want to bother God, or worry, but I would do both until I knew he was safe again.

"Decision time." He set his glass on the table with exaggerated care. "Should I drive, although I'm nearly out of gas and could mistake the ditch for the road? Or should I ask Banat to pretty please wake up and convey my sorry ass over there? Or should I walk and hope I won't fall in a hole and break my silly neck along the way? Damn … where was I?"

"Drive, ride, or walk," I prompted.

"Ah, yes … enough of this shit. I'll walk. And it's not even dark, is it? Full moon, I think … I know it is. Any drunk can manage a mile in the light of the moon."

A mile in the light of the moon? The caller had been Daddy!

I shadowed Uncle Jack as far as the county road, weighing whether I should attempt to stop him. He wasn't a mean drunk, but neither did he tolerate much interference. I let him go.

Then I returned to the house, sat on the porch, and stared into the void. My chest squeezed my heart. My stomach crept into my throat. I could taste my terror. I tried to pray. God would know what peril my uncle was in, if any. But I couldn't get past the salutation: "Dear God in heaven … dear Heavenly Father … oh, God!"

I considered waking Aunt Annie. But what would I say? That I had an absurd premonition Uncle Jack was walking into a trap? That Daddy was hardened from the war and accustomed to killing people? That he held a grudge against her husband? That he'd truly sent his flight engineer to his death? That he possessed a Luger he'd killed a German to acquire? That I'd seen a bullet hole in Mother's dress? That Daddy had been caught in a lie implicating him in her death?

And how would Aunt Annie respond? She'd say Daddy would never harm his own brother. Unfortunate circumstances killed the flight engineer. The war killed the German. Mother's death was accidental. And Daddy would never fabricate lies merely to placate me.

No, I could not wake her.

So I sat, wrapped in my cold blanket of fear, waiting. When the grandfather clock chimed one o'clock, I decided to call. Anyone on the party line who heard the ring would assume, as my uncle and I had earlier, that someone had died. There'd be a rush to listen in, so I had to be careful what I said. Two longs and a short rang over and over until a male voice, thick with drink, answered.

"Uncle Jack?" I was unable to distinguish between the two of them.

"No. Who's this?"

"It's me, Daddy. It's Abby."

His voice cleared. "Is this an emergency?"

"No, I just wondered—"

"You just wondered what, in the middle of the night?"

"I just wondered whether Uncle Jack made it over there."

"Yes, and what concern is it of yours? And why are you calling me? Didn't I tell you not to? Didn't I specifically tell you not to?"

"I know, Daddy, but—"

He slammed down the earpiece.

The next morning I was idling in the tire swing when Uncle Jack walked up the drive and saw me before I could hide. He looked as though he'd slept in his clothes or not slept at all. His breath reeked of liquor.

As he stood over me, I averted my face, awaiting my chastisement. He would say that he didn't appreciate my interference, my concern, or my goddamned phone call in the middle of the night.

He came straight to the point. "Did you call the house early this morning, about one o'clock?"

"Yes."

"What on earth possessed you to do such a thing?"

"I was worried about you," I replied, thinking how ludicrous that must sound.

He took a ragged breath. When I dared look up, his eyes were brimming, the wetness clinging to his dark lashes as he struggled to control something deep within him.

"I'm so grateful you did that. You have no idea what you changed, Abby, and I can't tell you, but thank you so very much."

What he said—and the way he had said it—affected me profoundly. Something had happened, or nearly happened, that I had changed. Had God guided my hand to place the call? Or had my concern simply overcome my fear of disobeying Daddy? Or was I again exaggerating the situation? But if it had been nothing, why had my uncle thanked me?

Aunt Annie left for the farm a few minutes later. She drove the car, undoubtedly to bring back all the things I'd wanted for myself. I hadn't told her what I wanted because my father already knew. His actions would either prove or disprove his love for me.

When Daddy hadn't called by noon, my bitterness escalated. I wanted him to apologize for hanging up on me. I wanted him to ask me back. I wanted him to let slip a clue as to what had transpired during the night.

When Daddy hadn't called by two, I made up my mind to forget him the way he had forgotten me. He'd replaced me with his new wife; I'd replace him with his brother. I would love and receive love from someone who was always there—not from someone who appeared for a month and left again—thinking he could force me to love him from halfway around the world.

But Uncle Jack? Someone who'd ripped into my bottom simply because

I'd burned down his barn? Someone who had a directive, an order, or a reprimand nearly every time he opened his mouth? I wasn't that desperate.

Yes, I was.

I needed love and a lot of it. I needed acceptance. I needed cuddling, hugging, and stroking. I needed soft words and tender encouragement. I needed him to look at me with pride and be glad I was there, not yell at me in exasperation and put up with me because I'd been dumped on him.

I formulated a plan: cribbage and casseroles.

The former was easy because he already loved playing the game with me. The casseroles weren't all that hard either. They just made a big mess, which I'd clean up because I needed Aunt Annie's love too. She'd be so impressed coming home to a nice, hot supper instead of seeing us sitting like dogs with our tongues hanging out like she had before.

Uncle Jack was upstairs, sleeping off the night, when I initiated my plan. I didn't need his arched brows or suspicions that I was up to something.

I proposed to make a casserole everyone would remember, so the usual tuna or hamburger wouldn't do. For ideas, I opened *The New German Lutheran Ladies Aid Cook Book*, published 1943. On the first page I read:

Most careful housewives, 'tis to you
We dedicate this book,
For well we know the art to please
Lies in the art to cook.

Holy cow, I hadn't known the way to the heart was through the stomach! And here I'd avoided cooking like the plague unless I'd been forced to help. Cookies I could bake in my sleep, but the rest of my knowledge remained piecemeal: chop that, peel this, stir that. I'd never assembled a main dish in my life.

I checked the index for casseroles and found nothing. Then I discovered what I was looking for was called "hot dishes." I perused the selections … Norwegian Meatballs … nope, we weren't Norwegian. Huntington Delight called for a fowl. What was a fowl? I noticed a lot of rice dishes, but I'd had my fill of rice. With us still at war with the Japs, it didn't seem patriotic anyway. Baby Porcupines seemed interesting until I saw the rice thing again. Old Fashioned Chicken Pie sounded delicious, if Aunt Annie made it. No way would I cut up a stewing hen with my bare hands. Nasty!

Spanish Chops caught my eye. Our druggist's wife had submitted it, so I figured it must be good. And it sounded foreign. I might use it someday to impress Daddy, since he liked foreign things. As if I *cared* to impress him.

I double-checked to make sure Auntie had plenty of pork chops, the main ingredient.

I followed the instructions the best I could. I fried up the pork chops, arranged them in a casserole dish—why did the recipe say casserole dish rather than hot dish dish?—and topped each with a tablespoon of rice—no getting around the rice—a slice of onion, a slice of tomato, and a strip of green pepper, if desired. I did not desire. I added water, covered it, slid my creation into a 350-degree oven, and ran to the slough with Darrell.

Eventually I thought about my casserole/hot dish. I came in and turned off the oven without checking it. Surely it would be done in three hours, and I knew it needed to keep warm until my aunt got back. I peeled potatoes and carrots, put them on to boil, cleaned up the mess, and set the table. I could hardly wait to see how surprised everyone would be.

Aunt Annie was indeed surprised. She said it was nice I had thought to feed everyone, and she didn't have to rush around like a madwoman to get the job done.

Then Uncle Jack served up our food. I swear he didn't blink an eye when he placed one of those dried, blackened pork chops on each of our plates, along with the watery mashed potatoes and the mushy carrots.

And when Duane said "icky" under his breath, Uncle Jack said, very quietly, that he intended to haul my cousin to the woodshed and whip his little ass until his appetite improved if he heard so much as another negative word.

Aunt Annie again complimented my efforts, even managing to sound sincere. She'd be back in her kitchen in the morning, she said, and hoped I'd assist her in any way appropriate.

Long before the conclusion of the hideous meal, I came to the realization that my uncle and aunt already had started to love me, each in their own peculiar way, and I didn't have to continue to poison the whole family in order to worm my way into their hearts.

I had a second revelation that evening, as though one wasn't enough. After the dishes were done, Aunt Annie told me to look in the car. A surprise awaited me.

I got all choked up when I saw Gramma's coverlet, lace tablecloth, and silver candlesticks on the passenger seat, along with Grandpa Walter's arrowhead collection. The *Gone with the Wind* lamp, my Shirley Temple cup, and the mirror from the washstand were in the back. Tucked beneath were Gramma's silver plate and her set of good china. One of the two rockers from the porch had been wedged in the trunk. Behind it, I found the birthday cards from all of my birthdays had been placed in a box and tied with ribbon.

My aunt smiled. "Your father will give you the oak buffet too, if you can find space for it in your room."

I could. It was a fine piece, handcrafted by Grandpa Walter. My uncle could bring it over later in the stone boat or the hay wagon, along with the remaining rocker.

But Daddy was auctioning off the dining room table and chairs, she said, as they'd been hard used over the years. The Civil War sword, the guns, and the stamp and coin collections would go to Uncle Jack as he'd requested.

I nodded my agreement. Uncle Jack deserved some things from his own father. I hadn't even known Grandpa Walter, as he'd passed away years before I was born.

I also decided that I loved Daddy again when Aunt Annie said he wanted me back in the morning, but only if I wanted.

I wanted … oh, I wanted so very much.

Farewell

AFTER I WENT back to Daddy, it seemed as though the unpleasantness of the last few days had never occurred. He mentioned nothing about his brother or what had precipitated my banishment.

And I refused to think anything bad of him. With only a few days remaining before the auction, I settled into my fantasy role of Daddy's little princess. As he again cooked for us, I chatted amiably about Maria and Italy and how I wanted to see both after the war was over. At first he looked like he suspected I was phony baloney, but when I persisted, I learned a bit more about him and much more about Maria. And I clarified something that was bothering me.

"Daddy, are you and Maria really going to have a baby?"

He paused in the preparation of a chicken destined to become our supper. "A baby? Why in God's name should I want a baby?"

"I thought you'd like a son."

"Well, you thought wrong. Boys grow up to be men. No, I far prefer the female gender. You won't have a sibling ... or a rival, if that's your concern."

"But what if Maria wants a baby?"

"She won't."

"What makes you so sure?"

"Because she's nearly my age. It wouldn't be a good idea."

Relief rolled off me like water off a duck.

Later that evening, I told him about playing cribbage with his brother almost every night. Daddy said cribbage was a foolish game and he didn't want me frittering away endless hours on it. He'd given me a cribbage board for Christmas only because no one in the family could play chess beside himself. Chess was a laudable pursuit. He'd teach me how when he returned.

And then I further upset him when I casually mentioned how Uncle Jack frequently drank to excess and had recently shared his brandy with me.

"What? He'll get a piece of my mind first thing tomorrow!"

"Please don't," I said, ashamed of my loose lips.

"Why not? Don't you realize my brother has a serious drinking problem, as I also have struggled with? And our father before us? We're apples off the same tree, Abigail. Do you think I want you going down the same twisted road?"

"No, and I won't. I won't take another sip. Please don't say anything to Uncle Jack because he'd be mad at me and I have to live there. Don't you see, Daddy? It was different when Gramma was alive. Then it was just her and me and everything was easier. But now she's gone, and soon you'll be gone, and it's so hard for me to go back to them because they already have three kids, and I'm another burden for them, and I need them to want me instead of just putting up with me, and I need you to love me, and not just Maria—"

I stopped. My soul lay bare. I could be destroyed by a word.

Daddy seemed to contemplate what I'd said. "I'm afraid I didn't take your predicament into consideration before. Obviously Jack needs to sort out his demons. In that I wish him well ... fine, as long as you promise to stay away from liquor, I won't say a word."

"I promise, Daddy."

"Then we shall speak of it no more."

I realized later that he hadn't declared his love for me. Had it been an oversight or a purposeful omission? I remembered he had, when we'd first met in the pink dawn that already seemed so long ago, unequivocally and without hesitation.

Perhaps once had been enough for him.

It was hardly enough for me.

The auction was a great success. Farmers actively competed for the machinery, parts, and tools that were either nonexistent or in short supply because of the war. Household items always sold well, so the auctioneer didn't have to exert himself in either arena before Gramma's belongings were happily hauled away by new owners.

While the auction was taking place, I sulked in my room at my uncle's house. I'd already said good-bye to the dining room where my height had been penciled on the wall. I'd already dragged a chair to the porch at dusk to watch the fireflies play as though nothing had changed. I'd already stood by the window of my former bedroom and memorized the landscape within its frame. I'd already nestled deep in Gramma's closet and inhaled her Evening in Paris, but as her clothes had been donated to the church mission months ago, the scent had grown faint.

Before I left the kitchen of my childhood behind, I'd pumped one last basin of water from the cistern and washed my face and hands. I had to let them air dry because the towel on the roller was gone. And I was glad I couldn't see the reflection of myself in the cloudy mirror because it, too, was gone, and I wouldn't have wanted to see myself cry.

Then the time came for my father to leave. He'd been staying with the

Swansons since the auction. Whether anyone thought it strange that Daddy wasn't staying with his brother, I hadn't heard of it. Probably the consensus was that Uncle Jack had one spare room and I was in it. And with Jimmy still gone and Vinnie Swanson being Daddy's best friend from high school, it made perfect sense he'd stay with them.

I didn't miss being with Daddy those last two days. I stayed busy helping Aunt Annie. She said repeatedly how much she appreciated it, which gave me a warm feeling. But I made certain Uncle Jack appreciated my helpfulness too. If he hadn't, I intended to go back to roaming the slough and ignore the whole lot of them.

Uncle Vic, Aunt Emma, and Virgil arrived as Vinnie brought Daddy over to say good-bye. Uncle Ben and his family passed on the invitation because they lived thirty miles away. Daddy would understand.

But when I saw my father getting out of the car, I regretted not spending every second with him. He was again dressed in his officer's garb. A fresh haircut revealed the gray on his temples. He was the epitome of spit and polish as he walked briskly to where we were assembled on the lawn as though he were about to perform an inspection.

If so, only Aunt Annie would have passed. She looked stunning in her fashionable pink dress, with her red hair curled and her lips painted. Duane and Dennis looked ragtag as usual. Darrell was greasy from fiddling with his bike chain. Uncle Jack hovered close to Uncle Vic and Virgil, chain-smoking.

I stayed off to the side and awaited my turn. I wore a blue polka-dotted dress with a matching bow in my hair. The bow I'd added at the last minute to please Daddy.

Uncle Vic, Aunt Emma, and Virgil gave my father hugs and talked with him for several minutes. Aunt Emma planted a wet kiss on Daddy's cheek and wished him Godspeed.

"Time to get back, Emma," Uncle Vic grumbled. "Lots to do today."

It was his way of dealing with the situation. Uncle Vic was the most tender-hearted man I'd ever known. He wept while reading the war casualties. He went soft holding a kitten. He hustled Aunt Emma to the car without looking back, but she and Virgil waved until their car sped out of sight.

Then the twins stepped forward and thanked Daddy for the presents he'd brought them and hoped he'd come back soon. I already knew what they'd say because I'd overheard the rehearsal.

My aunt gave Darrell a poke. He looked nervous, but Daddy graciously shook his hand and told him to be helpful to his parents and to stay out of trouble. My cousin acknowledged the comment and left, taking the twins with him.

Aunt Annie slipped her arms around Daddy's waist. He draped an arm over her shoulder as he bent down and whispered in her ear. She nodded. They conversed in low voices like no one else was present. He kissed her cheek and they parted.

"God be with you, James." She brushed away a tear and hurried toward the house.

Standing alone, Uncle Jack appeared taut as a bowstring. Daddy walked within an arm's length of him. Neither spoke. The tension between them was palpable.

My uncle broke the silence. "I guess everything remains the same."

"You guess correctly."

"But what more can I do? How many ways can I possibly tell you—"

"Hell if I know. You should've thought about that to begin with."

"I can't go back in time. But I am sorry. You know I am."

"I don't want to hear any more about it, Jack. What you did was, and remains, unforgivable … but I do regret the shit I pulled on you the other night. That was beyond the pale, even for me."

Uncle Jack nodded and glanced at me out of the corner of his eye.

"Well, go then, little brother. When I return, we'll continue this—what shall I call it—this discussion? In the meantime, you will take fine care of this daughter." He looked at me with what seemed amusement.

Uncle Jack set his jaw, entered the house, and slammed the screen door loud enough to be heard in the next county.

"I wish you wouldn't have done that," I said to Daddy. "I have to live here, remember?"

"You'll be perfectly fine. Jack won't be mad, at least at you … oh, before I forget, bring me that letter you have from your mother. Hurry up about it."

I could hardly believe he'd remembered something I'd said weeks ago! But as I took Mother's farewell letter from its place of honor in my dresser, I couldn't give it up. Daddy would either keep it or burn it. I put the copy I'd made into the original envelope, tucked the genuine letter back in my drawer, and raced outside.

Daddy was pacing on the lawn, smoking. I held my breath as he glanced at my name on the envelope before shoving it into his pocket.

"I'll read it later," he decided. "Right now I need to go before I miss my train. Would you like to ride along and see me off? Vinnie can bring you back afterward."

"I'd love to, Daddy!" All else was forgotten as I jumped in the backseat with my father and wrapped my arms around his waist. He slid an arm around my shoulder as he had with my aunt, and told me what to expect upon his return.

After the war ended, he said, he would leave the military. He was older now and no longer possessed the edge and the drive that had enabled him to achieve his present rank. He fully intended to assimilate into the civilian world he'd fought so hard to preserve. He also would do whatever necessary to bring Maria to America. He stated again that I'd like her and we would be a little family. But he wanted to clarify something he'd said previously: farm life no longer suited him and it would never suit Maria. She was a jeweler, after all, and for her to pursue her profession, they needed to settle in a larger community. For the remainder of my childhood, I'd be living far from what I'd always known and held dear.

That bit of news unsettled me nearly as much as Maria had. But Daddy said that I had months, perhaps years, to get used to the idea.

What choice did I have? Blood with blood. That was how it must be.

"I'll write you every week," he said.

"I'll answer every week," I said.

"I'm considering including some Italian words for you to memorize. With accompanying translations, of course." He said this with a smile.

"Whatever you say, Daddy." I had to grit my teeth for that promise.

"Good girl. When I come back, we'll pick up where we left off." He paused and gave me a slight squeeze. "This time was too rushed. I had too much to do. Next time will be better … I hope I wasn't too much of a disappointment to you."

The words seemed to come from his heart. And my disappointment came from my heart too. While I'd learned to appreciate his positive qualities, he was far from the father I'd hoped him to be. James Albert Stahl was granite. But over time, even granite develops cracks. I'd seen his lighter side in the early photographs of him with Mother and in his initial playfulness with Aunt Annie. If we'd had more time together, might he have shown that side of himself to me?

But it was too late this time. Would there even be another time?

I removed my arms from his waist and blinked back my tears. "Things will be better next time," I managed to say.

"Yes, it will."

Reaching over, he took my hand, further accentuating the distance between us. Why hadn't he reached out to me before he was already anticipating leaving me? He was thinking of Maria, not me. He was doing what he'd failed to do earlier, and now it was too late.

I was still holding myself tightly together, and he was still holding my hand when we rolled into town. All too soon, Mr. Swanson parked the car by the depot. Daddy got out first and extended his hand to assist me. This time I tried to never let go, but he broke my grip to gather up his belongings.

As we waited for the train, I stood by his side and tried to be brave. The sun warmed my head, but there the warmth stopped. The rest of me was numb, cold.

Daddy said a few words of farewell and I said something back. I couldn't remember what either of us said a moment later.

By the time the train came and the train went, I was so conflicted I couldn't even think. The last touch of my father's hand upon my cheek reverberated all the way to my soul, and I wanted to yell down the departing whistle of the train and will him back.

But I knew his will was stronger than mine.

He was going to meet a war on the far side of the world, and when it was over, he was going to meet someone on the far side of the world whom he loved more than me.

And when he came back—*if* he came back—my life would change forever … and I wanted nothing to ever change.

But I wanted him to be safe, so very safe.

"Be careful, Daddy!" I shouted as the dam within me burst. "I love you! And I know you love me too!" An uncaring wind flung the words back at me as the train emitted a final whistle, rounded the bend by the grain elevator on the east end of town, and disappeared.

I stood, waving and crying at nothing, until Mr. Swanson took my hand, led me to his car, and put me inside. He patted my arm and murmured how sorry he was that I was so unhappy. The war had made so many people unhappy. Mrs. Swanson had cried and he'd cried too, when Jimmy had left on that same train one year, eight months, and nineteen days ago.

When we got back to the farm, Mr. Swanson had to usher me into the house.

Aunt Annie took one look at me and led me to the porch, where Uncle Jack was sitting with a drink in his hand. She took his glass away.

In silence, I crawled on his lap.

In silence, he held me.

Angel Food Cake

I KEPT TO myself until I healed inside. No one mentioned Daddy. No one expected anything of me. I inhaled. I exhaled. I ate. I slept. But I did not cry. I refused to cry.

Then one day, it seemed, everything changed. I had a family again. Uncle Jack's family. I was the daughter they'd never had. I was equal to Darrell and equal to—no, *superior* to—the twins. I was subject to the same expectations and the same discipline. I even received an allowance, although it was pathetic compared to what I used to make playing cribbage.

While I felt more at ease with my overall situation, Darrell began to withdraw from me. When I had something important to tell, he listened halfheartedly. When I needed reassurance, he gave rote responses. When I desired a confidant, he seemed preoccupied.

When I pinned him down, he admitted he no longer wanted to keep steady company with a girl. He cautioned me not to take his change in feelings the wrong way; we'd always remain friends.

"Well, I should hope so. After all we've been through together!"

"Yes, we've been through fire … literally."

"That's right. And if we start solving mysteries again, I still want to be your Watson. Nobody else better take my place."

"Don't worry, Abby, you'll always be my sidekick. But I want you to leave me alone at school. No running up to me like a little sister when I'm with my friends, okay?"

"Okay … what about at home?"

"At home, I'll still be your best buddy, if nobody else is around."

While I got less attention from one cousin, I got more from the other two. The twins developed an addiction for hiding my stuff. And if something went wrong, it was automatically my fault. If I complained or tried to defend myself, they'd ratchet up their antics and I'd endure more torment than ever.

I hoped that Uncle Jack would straighten them out, but he told me to deal with my own problems. I nearly wished that Darrell and I had drowned the twins as babies, when we'd had the chance. Folks drowned excess kittens, why not excess little boys?

The fateful morning I spent making an angel food cake was the last straw. After my Spanish Chops fiasco, turning me into a passable cook had become Aunt Annie's personal goal. She'd hovered over me as I'd methodically warmed, separated, sifted, and beat, turning fourteen egg whites into soft and then stiff peaks. I'd folded, blended, and scraped (utilizing almost every verb in the English language), before I gently turned the batter into an ungreased tube pan and slid my masterpiece into the preheated oven. Then I had to wait about forty minutes for it to bake before inverting the pan over the neck of a bottle to cool. My aunt said she'd be back from town in time to help so I wouldn't accidentally burn myself.

I was guarding my cake like a cluck on a nest when Dennis lured me away with a phony story of newborn kitties in the haymow. By the time I got back, Duane had turned off the oven and was jumping up and down in front of the stove and slamming the oven door, as if just one of those three activities wouldn't suffice to make my cake fall flat on its ass.

And then they both started laughing.

I went ballistic, which also happened to be one of my "look it up" words from Daddy's latest letter. I'd never realized how ballistic in the fullest sense of the word I could get when I grabbed that broom and chased the twins around the house, shrieking at the top of my lungs. I clutched the broom near the straw end and swung the handle toward what would hurt most: ankles, wrists, and heads. I was scoring some good points, judging from the screeching going on, when Darrell ran in from wherever he'd been. As he had no time to properly assess the situation, he decided that since I'd gone berserk—also one of my "look it up" words—I likely had a damn good reason for it. He yanked the biggest, heaviest, wooden spoon out of the cutlery drawer and gleefully assisted in my little punishment party.

My broom froze in mid-swing when Uncle Jack appeared. "What the hell's going on here?" He reached over Darrell's head and wrested the spoon away.

I'd never heard so much blatant lying as Dennis and Duane, tearful and bruised, clamored for his attention. He listened, attempting to sort fact from fiction, for a full minute.

Darrell drew a finger across his throat and shook his head. From hard experience, we knew his father preferred the condensed version of events. The longer the fabrication, the less likely he was to believe the complainant. While it was in our favor for the twins to blab as long as possible, it just didn't look good to have been caught beating two eight-year-olds.

"Okay, shut up," Uncle Jack said. He plucked the broom from my limp fingers and threw it into the kitchen, where it scuttled along the linoleum. He still held the wooden spoon. "Abigail, what do you have to say for yourself?"

I gave him the short version: "They flattened my cake so I tried to flatten them."

His eyebrows lifted momentarily before sinking into a scowl. "And you?" he asked Darrell. "What was your part in this commotion?"

My cousin had even a shorter version: "I hate feeling left out."

"That's just terrific!" Uncle Jack rolled his eyes in exasperation. "Of four children, I've got two whiners and two smart alecks. Two can't get along with the other two, and it's been like this for what—forever? Well, it's coming to an end! I've had all I can stand. I've tried staying out of it, but it's only gotten worse. There's been nit-picking, arguing, and fighting going on all the time, and I don't give a rat damn whose fault it is anymore. I'm going to punish the whole lot of you and if you don't like it, find somewhere else to live. There's a train out of town every morning. I'll even buy you a ticket … any takers?"

Darrell and I knew he wasn't serious, but Dennis and Duane didn't. Their eyes widened with concern as they chorused, "No, sir." But we echoed the twins anyway.

"Since you've all chosen to keep living here, you're going to abide by my rules." Uncle Jack rapped the twins on their shoulders with the spoon for emphasis. "You're to stop baiting Abby. And keep your hands off her stuff. If she can't find something, I'll assume one of you had something to do with it and I will act accordingly. Understand?"

"Yes, sir," they said in unison.

"Remember that, because I'll be watching. And for the idiocy and downright meanness you both exhibited today, get yourselves in the corner." He pointed to the appropriate corners of the dining room.

I felt vindicated, until it was my turn.

"Abigail, come here and look at me."

I found it hard to look him in the eye. He was furious.

"You are never, and I repeat never, to go after Dennis or Duane, or anyone else for that matter, with anything that could be even vaguely construed as a weapon. Did you not understand that hitting someone about the head or on the extremities could cause serious injury?"

"No, sir," I said. In my former ballistic condition, I'd thought of nothing except vengeance.

"But now you understand, don't you?"

"Yes, sir."

"Good. Put your nose in that corner." He indicated my place.

As I turned, he swatted my rump with such force that I nearly jumped into the wall. Was he finished? Or would he continue? I didn't dare look.

Then one of the twins giggled.

Uncle Jack stalked to the far side of the room. "Who did that?" When neither twin answered, he gave them both a resounding whack. "You still think it's funny?"

"No," one of them whimpered.

"I didn't think you would."

Darrell occupied the remaining corner of the room without being told. I saw him out of the corner of my eye, standing rigidly to my right.

My uncle came up behind him. "And you, Darrell. You treat your brothers worse than vermin. You're my oldest, but what kind of an example are you? Well, answer me!"

"Not so good," Darrell mumbled.

"No, I should say not. But that's about to change. From now on, you'll treat your brothers as you want me to treat you. If you forget, you will be reminded, harshly. Understand?"

"Yes, sir."

Uncle Jack drew back his arm and walloped Darrell. "There. I'd so hate for you to feel left out." He proceeded to inform us that we had to stand in our respective corners for two hours.

Two hours? I couldn't believe it! I'd fall over before then! His usual was half an hour, with an hour being the extreme.

We all knew the rules: no talking or looking around. We could shift from one foot to the other, but no jiggling or jumping. We could use the bathroom if necessary, but ten minutes would be tacked onto our sentence. Nothing was more boring than staring at the corner of a wall from a six-inch distance while feet and legs prickled and shoulders and backs ached. An hour crawled, and two hours would seem an eternity.

We weren't five minutes into it when Aunt Annie returned. I heard her put down the groceries and open the oven.

"Oh, dear! What happened here?"

"The angel got killed by two devils," Uncle Jack answered.

"They didn't!"

"Obviously they did."

"But why?"

"How the hell would I know?"

"Well, didn't you ask?"

"Sure I asked, but what good does that do? Four kids produce four answers, Annie."

She walked into the dining room. "Maybe something escapes me, but why are Darrell and Abby being punished too?"

"Because they took matters into their own hands, with broom and spoon. I came in to the sorry spectacle of them chasing down the twins. When I asked the reason, our dear borrowed daughter said, and I quote, 'They flattened my cake so I tried to flatten them.' They could've inflicted some real damage on the twins, Annie, and I won't have it. The vigilantes aren't running this family. I am."

"And I," she said.

"Yes, and you."

He agreed to keep her happy, I supposed. Without him, we'd all be ripping around like animals.

"And how long are they to stand there?"

"Two hours."

"Two hours?"

"Yes."

She was our only hope. She often asked my uncle to lessen a punishment if she thought it too severe. Usually he didn't, but once in a while he did. Since two hours of standing in the corner was without precedent, our chances of a reprieve seemed promising.

"Two hours. That's such a long time, Jack."

"Yes, it is."

"Two hours of peace and quiet."

"Yes, two whole hours of peace and quiet."

"And since when have we enjoyed two whole hours of peace and quiet?"

"Oh, let me think … around 1935, I'd say."

"That's such a long time ago. In fact, I'd quite forgotten the tick of the grandfather clock. It's usually so noisy in here I haven't been able to hear it … have you heard the tick of the grandfather clock lately?"

"Not in years, Annie."

"And will it tick until two hours have passed?"

"Most assuredly."

"Can you slow it down?"

"Of course I can slow it down. How slow would you like it to go?"

She sighed. "Oh, I don't know … can they all stand in the corner until they're grown?"

War's End

THE ANGEL FOOD cake incident brought about permanent changes within the Stahl household. Rather than allowing a continuation of our war, with Darrell and me on one side and the twins on the other, a secession of hostilities was dictated by Tyrant Jack and his red-haired collaborator.

We kids didn't fall into line willingly, but we couldn't buck their combined efforts. Not only did the tyrant assume the roles of judge, jury, and jailer with characteristic relish, but his helpmate assisted him in the most subversive manner. She watched, she listened, and she reported.

While the twins kept their grubby hands off my belongings, they continued to clamor for my premature demise. One day Aunt Annie overheard. I said how I'd been verbally abused for months. She called for assistance. The tyrant came, listened to all sides of the story, believed mine, and promptly caused the twins acute discomfort. Neither brat ever wished me dead again, but if looks could kill, I'd have been buried deep and often.

Darrell kept his head down and his mouth shut, for the most part, during this tumultuous time. He wasn't about to make more mistakes that his parents would notice. At first, he tried to blame me for his role in the cake debacle, saying he tended to lose all semblance of common sense whenever I was involved. I pointed out that he was the oldest and the cleverest, so he had only himself to blame. He eventually agreed, and we remained friends.

We needed our friendship because what we were forced to do in the spirit of cooperation nearly drove us crazy. I was flabbergasted when Aunt Annie made the twins assist me with my second angel food cake. By the time cake entered oven, the mess was indescribable.

And Darrell had to teach his brothers how to ride his bicycle. Even my aunt couldn't find additional ones because of the war. Darrell threw a fit every time another scratch appeared on his cherished bike. Aunt Annie simply smiled and said, "All my furniture would look like new, too, if it weren't for all of you."

Darrell and I were at the breaking point when Aunt Annie decided we needed to give the twins a head start in third grade. When she whipped out the primers, tablets, and pencils she'd purchased for our endeavor, we raised such a commotion that we ended up facing the corner for fifteen minutes while the twins played.

"Damn dumbest thing ever," Darrell grumbled. "The teachers get the corner while their pupils get recess."

I didn't comment because I knew the tyrant could hear us.

"A half hour, Darrell," Uncle Jack said as he strolled past.

Because I got out of my corner first, I was allowed to choose who I wanted to teach. I hated both twins, but thought Dennis might be the brighter of the two. He was, but he was also the most easily frustrated. Then I had to learn something myself: patience. Darrell did his best with Duane, and they were a good fit.

Evenings brought no relief from our enforced togetherness. Uncle Jack would set out the games and the cards before withdrawing to his chair to read. If we started to bicker, he'd slam the book shut and stalk back to the dining room. Then it would get so quiet we all could hear the tick of the grandfather clock.

Complaints were futile. Even God was against us. "Idle hands are the devil's workshop," Uncle Jack stated. He'd taken to reading the Bible and quoted it whenever it suited his purposes. When Darrell asked where exactly that was found in the Bible, my uncle said God intended such a statement. As God's intentions were good enough for him, it damned well better be good enough for us.

One sweltering afternoon in August, our petty problems paled in comparison to astounding news from the war front. We gathered around the Philco and listened as President Truman announced: "Sixteen hours ago, an American airplane dropped one bomb on Hiroshima … the force from which the sun draws its power has been loosed against those who brought war to the Far East." Within two minutes, four square miles of civilization had been vaporized, leaving thousands upon thousands of people either dead or missing.

Aunt Annie lay aside her embroidery. "This is just so unimaginable, Jack. How it is even possible? And what does it mean?"

"Armageddon. Now we have the capability of destroying the world."

"But it will hasten the end of the war, won't it?"

"That is the intention. A land invasion of Japan would claim thousands of lives, on both sides. Truman will want to avoid that, if at all possible."

"And your brother? Where is James, in all of this?"

"I have no idea … Abby, do you know?"

"No, Daddy hasn't written me in three weeks." I added that nothing he'd written from the Pacific had revealed either his job or his location.

Worry creased my aunt's brow. "I think this calls for a prayer, Jack."

He obligingly switched off the radio. "Kids, do as your mother says."

"Heavenly Father," she began. "Such a terrible thing has happened. Only you know the extent of the devastation. Please bring about an end to this awful war that has caused so much suffering for so long. Please lead the Japanese to the peace table so such a thing never happens again. Grace be unto those who died in this conflagration yesterday. Amen."

"And grace be unto those thousands of our brave soldiers who got slaughtered by the Japs prior to our government taking the decisive and necessary action aforementioned by my wife," Uncle Jack said crisply. "Amen for the second time."

My aunt looked at him with disgust. "That goes without saying, Jack. Must you always have the last word?"

"No."

But he did. He always did.

When he came to my room that night, I said, "Auntie didn't pray for Daddy's safety."

"Of course she did." He pecked my forehead and tucked the sheet under my chin. "She asked God to end the war and the suffering. Bringing everyone home safely is implicit."

I knew what "implicit" meant, but it wasn't good enough. I needed to ask God to specifically safeguard my father, and I wanted my uncle to stay with me for emotional support while I prayed aloud. I rambled for a minute or two before arriving at the crux of the matter: "God, please bring Daddy back so I can have a home of my own at last." I chanced to open my eyes before I ended with the obligatory "amen."

Uncle Jack was sitting rigidly on the edge of my bed, head unbowed, hands unfolded, staring at the portrait of my father. His expression was one I could not adequately describe.

A few nights later, after the second bomb dropped, I dreamt of a purple-red fire that expanded into a hellish fireball a half-mile wide. The whole monstrous seething mass of purple and red fire rose, accompanied by vast smoke rings encircling the column of flames, until it roiled outward to form a mushroom cloud. At the base, the column sucked what remained toward its center and cremated everything inside with a heat so intense it seared the very shadows of the people it incinerated into the concrete. And, at the end of my dream, I heard my president say, "If they do not now accept our terms, they may expect a rain of ruin from the air, the like of which has never been seen on this earth … "

"Daddy," I whispered, damp with sweat and fear, "wherever you are, be safe." I willed him safe. He would be safe. He had not been at Hiroshima or

Nagasaki. He would not be among the casualties. He would be coming home to me, after all.

On August 15, 1945, my prayers and the prayers of millions of others were answered when President Truman announced to a waiting nation: "I have received this afternoon a message from the Japanese government, a full acceptance of the Potsdam Declaration, which specifies the unconditional surrender of Japan."

The war was over, everywhere.

But Daddy did not come. Several weeks later, he wrote that he was on his way to Italy to find Maria. He'd come when he could. In the meantime, I was to remain where I was, doing what I did, living my life without him.

Fine, I thought. *Take your time, take your damn time.*

But the ache was too great to keep inside, so I brought my letter to Uncle Jack. I crawled on his lap for the second time in as many months as he sat on the porch that evening, smoking his pipe and drinking his brandy.

"Well, if it isn't my dear borrowed daughter." He shifted in the rocker to accommodate me.

"Why do you keep calling me that?" I snuggled against him.

"Because I have to remind myself that I'll have to give you back one day."

"Don't you want to give me back?"

"I'm not going to answer that, Abby. It's not up to me."

"Well, I wish you would."

"Would what? Answer you or want to keep you?"

"Both."

"I can't. It's not my decision."

"I'd think you'd want to get rid of me since you have three of your own."

He chuckled. "How little you know … and besides, after three, what's another?"

"Twenty-five per cent more. I learned that in school."

"That's right, but percentages apply to numbers, not people. People are another matter entirely … what's the letter? Did you bring it to show me?"

"Yes, it's from Daddy."

"I figured as much. Annie said one came for you today. What does it say? Or should I read it for myself?"

"No," I said, changing my mind. "Daddy just says he's on his way to Italy to find that woman and he'll get me when he's good and ready and not a second sooner."

"Sounds like you're anxious for him to come. I thought you were settled here, so what difference does it make how long it takes him?"

"Oh, I don't know … maybe because he's taking forever." How could I tell him being settled wasn't enough? That I longed for permanence?

"So what'd you expect? The end of a war brings confusion, Abby, and the paperwork is nearly endless when a man separates from the military. Getting Maria here will take even more time and paperwork. But eventually, I suppose, the three of you will be just one happy little family."

The phrase sounded suspiciously like what Daddy had told me. I hadn't believed it then and I didn't believe it now. "No, I don't think so. I don't think we'll be happy."

"Why not?"

"Because he'll be happy enough when he gets her back. She's all he talked about, when I'd let him. I don't think he needs me to be happy. I don't think he needs me at all … Uncle Jack?"

"Hmm?"

"Why doesn't my daddy love me? He told me once he did, but it was only once, and I don't think I believe it anymore." Those were the words I'd come to say, but the hurt was so deep I could hardly say them.

My uncle shifted his eyes. "No, you're wrong about that. He does love you. In fact, he loves you very much."

"No, he doesn't. I've been with Daddy less than a month out of my whole life that I can remember. You can't be with somebody for a month out of years and years and still love them. That's simply not possible."

"It is possible." This time, Uncle Jack looked directly at me. "You can be with someone for just a short time, Abby, but love them for years before and years afterward because love doesn't stop when people are apart. It continues, sometimes more strongly than when they were together … and he will come to get you, in case you're wondering."

"Are you sure?"

"Yes, I'm very sure."

"What makes you so sure?"

"Because if he didn't, then I would've w—"

"Would've what?"

"Would've nothing … it's the brandy. I lost my train of thought."

"You did not. You're not the slightest bit drunk."

"No, and I think I should be congratulated." He smiled his crooked smile before he drained his glass.

I sat with him in the gathering darkness, listening to our breathing and our two hearts beating in perfect rhythm. Then I eased away from him and went inside the house.

He hadn't made me feel better. Physically we'd been close, but emotionally he'd kept me at a distance. What was he talking about, love when people are apart? I found it hard to love Daddy when he was with me and even harder to love him when he wasn't. But I needed him to love me unconditionally.

And I needed Uncle Jack to love me unconditionally too. I cared about him, I was accustomed to him, but I didn't love him. I just needed him to take care of me. I needed him to tell me what I wanted to hear. I needed him to tell me that he wanted me to stay, although I knew I couldn't.

Blood with blood. That was how it must be.

Suddenly I filled in the blank: "Because if he didn't, then I would've won."

When I told Darrell the next morning, he was neither concerned nor mystified.

"Won you, dummy," he said. "What's so hard to figure out? Our dads hate each other, remember? Maybe my dad bet yours that he's not coming back to get you. Then my dad will take care of you."

"I know, but would he want to?"

Darrell shrugged. "Who the hell cares? He has and he will. That's all that matters."

"Well, I care and that's not all that matters."

"Will you stop? Honest to God, Abby, I can't take much more of this! All this whining about whether folks like you and want you is driving me nuts. You used to be fun, but you've turned into a regular worrywart."

"Easy for you to talk—your bed didn't change location four times in a single year."

Darrell made a face. "Fine, I give up. I was trying to keep this a secret, little cousin, but now I'll have to let the cat out of the bag so you'll stop torturing yourself. The twins probably still hate your guts, but the rest of us are wild about you, okay? You're the reason we get up in the morning. You're the sun in the daytime and the moon at night. You're the prize in the Cracker Jack box. You're—"

"Oh, shut up."

But as much as I wished it were true, neither Uncle Jack nor Aunt Annie ever treated me as though I were a prize of any consequence. I was simply another one of their "short folks," although my uncle continued to refer to me as his "dear borrowed daughter" when he wandered in at bedtime or at random moments when the phrase seemed totally out of context.

Instead of being part of their family, which I now was, I wanted even more.

I wanted to feel special.

Winter 1945

Fairy Tale Ending

Mrs. Margaret Monson, my sixth-grade teacher, turned every lesson into a revelation, an adventure. For the first time, I loved school. Karen, who lived with her folks on the old Monson place down the road from us, had failed to mention over the summer that her mom was returning to teaching, so it was a genuine surprise when the familiar face of our neighbor appeared in my classroom to facilitate my education.

But when the chill of September slid into the fleeting warmth of October's Indian summer, and the turning of the calendar to November changed everything back again, with savage winds indicative of a harsh and early winter, and my eleventh birthday came and went, and the postmarks on Daddy's intermittent letters changed from foreign to domestic and still he had not come, I knew I'd been abandoned.

And one afternoon in late November when Mrs. Monson ordered me to the corner in lieu of recess after she'd warned me innumerable times to keep my chatty comments to myself during her geography lesson, my disappointment bubbled to the surface.

Mrs. Monson rose from her desk. "Don't cry, Abby. It's only fifteen minutes. I'm not sending you to the office or even writing a note home to your uncle."

When I kept sobbing, she produced a clean handkerchief. I used it and handed her Daddy's latest letter, which I kept in my blouse pocket, the better to bore a hole into my heart.

"Do you want me to read this? Is this why you're so upset?"

I managed a nod and a honk into her handkerchief that would've made Virgil proud.

She read the letter meticulously before giving it back to me. "I don't see anything here to upset you, or am I missing something?"

"Daddy's been back for over a month," I sniffled. "He could've come to my birthday. He's never been to any of my birthdays."

"I imagine that's true, but it appears he's been busy searching for a house for the two of you—"

"Three. You forgot Maria, that Italian he went and married."

"Oh, that's right. Annie said he'd gotten married again. She didn't know any details, though. Did he tell you all about her when he was home?"

I narrowed my eyes. "More than I ever wanted to know. I hate her. I want him to divorce her."

"And then come back and get you? So the two of you can live happily ever after?"

I looked at her with suspicion. "That sounds like the ending to a fairy tale."

Mrs. Monson's mouth curled into a gentle smile. "But isn't that what you're trying to achieve, Abby? Aren't you seeking a fairy tale life with a fairy tale ending?"

She knew me too well. I'd spent numerous days each summer at the Monson farm, playing with Karen, enjoying treats around their kitchen table, talking about whatever popped into my mind, from as far back as I could remember. Mrs. Monson knew, as Darrell did, that often I had a whole other life going on inside my head.

"Yes," I admitted.

"You want to be first in someone's life instead of having to share the attention. That's the whole problem, isn't it?"

I swallowed hard. "Yes."

She pulled up a chair and took my hands. "Listen to me, Abby. Life is no fairy tale. Life has no fairy tale ending. It can be hard. It can be unfair. Your father must care for you or he wouldn't have written to you all these years. As to whether or not he loves you, I can't answer for him, but I suspect he does. But there's another person in his life now. If she were your mother, you wouldn't harbor the negative feelings you do. You must realize that Maria fills the same role for him as your mother once did. You must accept her as your father's wife, Abby. I can't stress that enough. You'll never be happy if you continue to hate. Don't force him to choose between the two of you. You may lose … no, don't turn away. Listen to me, for your own good, for your own future happiness. And there's another thing—"

Reluctantly I met her eyes. "What?"

"Whatever happens, it may be for the best. If he doesn't come for you, for whatever reason, perhaps you'd be happier growing up with your uncle and aunt. And if he comes, but he comes late, in your opinion, he probably had a good reason. From this letter, it appears he does. What benefit is there for you to tag along as he and Maria search for a house and shop for its many furnishings? None. Turning a house into a home is stressful in and of itself without the added challenge of blending the three of you into a cohesive family unit simultaneously. Trust me. You're better off right here, living where you do, attending school the way you always have, until he has everything arranged. Don't you agree?"

"Maybe." At least it sounded plausible.

"And this is the most important point I want to make," she continued. "Whether your life turns out the way you want or whether it doesn't, you have worth. Whether your father, whom you obviously love, loves you back, or whether you have to seek love from someone else, you will find what you're looking for. You are worthy of love, Abby. The fact you're alive, that God created you, gives you worth and makes you worthy of love. Do you understand?"

I nodded.

"My advice to you, Abby, is to be accepting of your circumstances. When your father comes for you, and I believe he will, do not reproach him. Be accepting of him and be accepting of Maria. You never know—she might be a wonderful person. After all, he chose to marry her. She may be what you're missing in your life."

I nodded again, although I was tempted to argue.

"What's she doing in the corner?" a loud voice boomed.

I whirled around in my chair. Uncle Jack stood in the doorway. *Great,* I thought. *First time I get the corner this year and he already knows about it.*

Mrs. Monson gave him one of her arched looks. "Sitting out recess."

"Why?"

"Talking out of turn."

"Imagine that!" He chuckled sarcastically. "Little Abigail, blabbing in class."

"Yes, little Abigail, blabbing in class. And you should be glad about it too. At the start of the school year, she was still so shy about speaking in front of her classmates that I could hardly get her to answer a direct question. The way she's blossomed lately, it's simply wonderful."

"If it's so wonderful, Margaret, I'll ask again: what's she doing in the corner?"

"Now she talks too much. Moderation, Jack, everything in moderation … you should practice that yourself."

To what she was alluding, I had no idea, but she was not intimidated by him. That impressed me. Everyone was intimidated by him, in my limited experience, with the notable exception of Daddy. And she'd stuck up for me. I had worth.

He ignored the barb. "So, has she finished her penalty or do I need to continue it at home?"

"She's finished. You can take her along now." Mrs. Monson's sharp tone softened as she turned to me. "Gather up your things, Abby, and remember what I told you."

"I will … and thank you."

"What did you thank her for?" Uncle Jack asked as he escorted me outside and opened the car door. Aunt Annie scooted over to give me room. Darrell and the twins were already squashed in the backseat.

"It's a secret," I said, climbing in. "Where are we going?"

"It's a secret," he said, closing the door.

"It's no secret, Jack. Why on earth would you say that? We're going to meet the three o'clock train, Abby … Jimmy Swanson finally got released from that Percy Jones Convalescent Hospital in Michigan and he's coming home this afternoon. We thought it'd be nice to join his folks in welcoming him back and save all of you the long, cold trip home on the bus. You're only missing the last hour of school anyway … oh, I do hope a lot of people show up to see Jimmy, for all the pain and misery he's been through! Elsie said they patched his lung up pretty good at Fitzsimmons in Denver first, so from the sounds of it, he'll be all right. I certainly hope so. He's such a nice young man. I've missed seeing him around since he volunteered for the navy … well, not nearly as much as Vinnie and Elsie have, but that's to be expected, since they're his folks … oh, here we are! That didn't take but a minute, did it? And look at all the people here! Goodness gracious, there must be thirty, maybe forty, and on such a raw day too. I'm so glad there's such a big turnout … why are you so quiet, Jack? It's not like you to be quiet. Is something wrong?"

"Nothing's wrong, Annie. I'm just practicing moderation." He eased the car into an available spot near the depot. "Margaret said I should. I figure if you talk incessantly, I'll have to keep quiet to balance things out."

"Don't tell me you got all snippy with Margaret in the time it took to pick Abby up, did you?"

"No, I didn't, Annie. I was nice as pie. But I can't help if she thinks I need improvement now, can I?"

"You do, now that you mention it, but I doubt Margaret was referring to your speech habits."

He changed the subject as we kids piled out of the car. "Okay, all you short folks, listen up. We're only staying a few minutes after the train comes to say our howdy do and then we're leaving. If I can't find you when I'm ready to go, you'll be walking home, and it'll be one hell of a cold hike."

He'd barely finished his admonition before the twins raced to Ludwig's, while Darrell headed for a trio of boys lounging near the station. I hung back, trying to see whether any of my friends had been let out early to greet the train. The way everyone was bundled up, I had to recognize coats and hats rather than actual faces.

"Oh, damnation, Annie, look who else is here!" Uncle Jack blurted.

"I don't know where you're looking," Aunt Annie said.

As short as she was, she often had difficulty seeing what he saw. I looked but didn't see anyone out of the ordinary, just a cluster of townsfolk standing near the tracks looking north, from where the train was expected momentarily.

"Over there." My uncle indicated the direction with a tilt of his head. "It's that Hartmann bunch. I guess Vernon's back on this train too. Those people disgust me."

"Do be tolerant, Jack."

"I *am* tolerant. I'm so tolerant I disgust myself. I'm disgustingly tolerant."

"Then you should act tolerant. Any soldier who took a bullet for our country deserves a welcome home, same as the rest."

"Well, I bet he took it in the ass, running. Can't imagine he'd take it in the chest like Swanson did." Uncle Jack spoke loudly enough to be overheard.

"That's enough, Jack! You don't always have to broadcast your opinions. I have my opinion too, and I give Vernon credit for joining the infantry after he washed out of flight school. Not everyone would pick up a gun after that."

"He didn't wash out of flight school," Uncle Jack snapped. "Where the hell did you hear that? He got drummed out. That's kicked out, in civilian terms. I know it for a fact. My own brother kicked him out at Maxwell for cheating, lying, and I don't know what all. And Vernon didn't get a choice about joining the infantry either. That's what happens when you screw up. They put you where they need you, which usually means carrying a gun into the line of fire."

"Oh, I didn't know."

"No, you wouldn't," he said, sounding conciliatory. "But now you do, and that's what happened. I don't like that bunch and that's just one of the many reasons why … good, the damn train's finally coming. I'm about to freeze to death just standing here … did you hear the whistle, Abby?"

I didn't hear the whistle, and I didn't see Jimmy Swanson get off the train.

I only heard what Uncle Jack had said.

And I only saw Billy Hartmann and his one-handed father and the rest of the Hartmann bunch clamber to greet Vernon Hartmann, the infantry veteran who'd taken a bullet in the ass after being kicked out of flight school by my very own father, whose only mistake was in assuming that Vernon was Billy Hartmann's father instead of his uncle.

Darrell had been wrong: Daddy hadn't lied.

My daddy hadn't lied to me, after all.

Dead Animals and Golden Chains

Now that Billy Hartmann's accusation had been disproved, I focused on contentment. My change of attitude circled outward, like a thrown stone rippling a pond. Uncle Jack hollered less and hugged more. Aunt Annie spent "girl time" with me. Darrell paid me more attention. Even the twins acted with guarded civility. Gradually a faint yearning evolved into a full-fledged wish: I hoped my father would leave me right where I was.

Shortly afterward, of course, Daddy wrote that his preparations for our life together were nearly complete. I'd be notified of his arrival in time to pack.

In the interim, he ignored my pleas for a photograph of Maria. Darrell theorized that she was a freak. I said that Daddy would hardly marry a freak with so many normal ladies to choose from. Darrell countered with, "Then why did he marry an Italian with so many Americans to choose from?" I hated when my cousin funneled more worries into my head besides the ones I already had.

Daddy did write in detail about the house he'd purchased in south Minneapolis, near Minnehaha Creek, with its towering elms, tiered garden, and screened gazebo. He described the interior furnishings as "baroque" and "gaudily ornate." My future home sounded so strange, so outlandish. How could I be comfortable in such a place? Concerned, I shared his letters with Aunt Annie to glean her opinion.

She started laughing midway through the second letter. "I think he's writing this to pique your interest, Abby. Your father has simple tastes. On the other hand, Maria might've selected their furniture. You'll just have to see for yourself … has he said when he's coming for you?"

"The day after Christmas."

She frowned. "I'd think he'd want to celebrate the holiday itself with you."

"No, they don't intend to do much at all this year. Not even a tree. Here we have the pageant, the sledding, and the party. He didn't want me to miss any of it."

"And I was so hoping they'd join us this year. Maybe next year … "

The sadness in her eyes reminded me that if the hateful situation between Daddy and Uncle Jack persisted, I'd never spend another holiday at the farm. Somehow I'd gotten so accustomed to their household I couldn't fathom living anywhere else.

And the closer it got to leaving it behind, the more wretched I became. I developed headaches. My stomach cramped. I lost my appetite. I couldn't finish half of what Uncle Jack gave me at supper. At first, he let it slide, but one night he made me sit at the table until I finished everything, saying I was being obstinate. I'd no sooner downed the last mouthful when I puked right on my plate. Mortified, I burst into tears and ran to my room.

Aunt Annie followed me. She sympathized and she advised. She was glad I enjoyed staying with them, but suggested I might enjoy living with Daddy and Maria as much, if not more. After all, new experiences with different people were "the spice of life." When she went downstairs to explain my trepidations to my uncle, I eavesdropped from the landing.

"That's ridiculous!" he exclaimed. "For months, she wasn't happy here, but now she's so happy she's made herself sick because she hates to leave? Sounds like I should've been harder on her."

"Oh, Jack, you're all bluster and wind. You've been plenty hard on her, but you love her as much as I do, and you don't want her to leave any more than she does. Isn't that true?"

"Of course it's true, but we don't have a choice in the matter, do we? And if she persists in not wanting to go with my brother, who'll he blame? Me. He'll think I talked against him, and I've got enough problems with him the way it is."

"Which I wish you'd settle, or at least confide in me. Maybe I could help?"

"No, you can't … as I was saying, Abby's got to straighten herself out. She needs to at least pretend she's happy he's coming. And sometimes pretense is self-fulfilling. Sometimes it becomes fact. I don't think she'll have a miserable life with him, but it probably boils down to Maria. If Abby accepts her and vice versa, things will be dandy. If not, Abby will stew in her own vinegar, so to speak."

"But what if she's miserable? We'd have to do something then, wouldn't we?"

"What could we do? Snatch her away? Not hardly."

"I realize that, but you would think of something, wouldn't you?"

"I would if I had to, Annie … if I absolutely had to."

He sounded as though he were nearing the stairs, so I tiptoed to my room, sat on my bed, and pondered what he'd said. Maybe he was right. Maybe living with Daddy would work out. After all, living here had worked out.

And Daddy *had* promised things would be better than last time. But what did that entail? Would he cook so I didn't have to? Would he let me wear Darrell's old clothes? Would he buy my heart's desires? Would he devote himself entirely to me? Undoubtedly, yes! And my adoring Italian stepmother would similarly share his dedication!

Or would she? What if she was more evil than Cinderella's stepmother? What if she dressed me in tatters and made me scrub their floors? She'd force me to eat beets *and* cauliflower if I missed a spot!

I shuddered. Then I remembered that Uncle Jack had promised to rescue me if my fairy tale life turned disastrous. And President Roosevelt said once the only thing we had to fear is fear itself. *Buck up,* I told myself. *Stop being such a scaredy-cat.* I rolled off my bed and started packing. A minute later, I quit. Auntie could finish. I had something more important to do, something that would bond me forever to this farm, to this family, and to Darrell.

I barged into his room as he was getting ready for bed.

"I like you plenty, Abby, but not enough to bleed for you," Darrell said after hearing what I wanted.

"Oh, come on."

"Nope, you've got a weak stomach. Seeing you toss your cookies at supper was enough for me. You might do it again."

"I will not!"

After ten minutes of cajoling, Darrell accompanied me outside. We climbed to the top of the haystack. For my special moment, I wanted to be close to God.

"You want to do it soon?" he asked. "My butt is freezing to the snow."

"Not yet … just look at it," I marveled. "It's the most beautiful night ever."

"It's certainly one of coldest."

"I'm not cold."

"The thermometer reads ten below zero."

"I'm still not cold."

"Well, I am. It's now or never, Abby."

"You're not very patient, Darrell."

"Turning blue might have something to do with it." He yanked off his mittens and opened his pocketknife. "Here, hold the flashlight with your right hand and give me your left."

I held the Ray-O-Vac as instructed, but I didn't offer my hand. "First I want to know where that knife's been lately. It doesn't look very clean."

"It doesn't? Then I'll spit on it."

"Ugh!" I grimaced as he spit. "Do you know how many germs live in spit?"

"Who says?"

"Miss Fuhrman did, last year. She was always telling Billy Hartmann not to spit."

"Then you spit on it. Maybe your spit's cleaner."

I spat a cleansing glob and Darrell wiped the excess on his jacket. "Ready?" he asked.

Bravely I extended my finger to the blade and stared into the heavens. "By this blood that we mix, we will be forever joined as one, blood to blood, cousin to cousin, throughout eternity … damn it, that hurt!"

"Don't whine." Darrell deftly slit his own finger. "I don't want to mix blood with a whiner."

"I was swearing, not whining."

We sat with our forefingers intertwined, blending our essence. When I judged the mix sufficient, I let go. My cousin immediately donned his mittens, but I squeezed my finger until a single droplet of blood fell. I pointed the flashlight on the spot and watched the crimson speck melt a few crystals of snow.

I felt near to tears. "I don't want you to forget me, Darrell."

"It's not like you're dying, Abby."

"Moving away is sort of like dying. If you're gone too long, people will forget you."

"I won't forget you."

"Promise?"

"I promise."

"But I don't want to leave here. I'm used to it here."

"I know, but maybe it'll turn out good. Maybe it'll turn out great."

"I hope so."

"I hope so too … can we go in now?"

Before I could respond, the yard light flooded the outbuildings, the haystack, and us with unwelcome illumination. Uncle Jack stood on the back porch.

"What the hell are you doing up there?" he shouted. "It's way past your bedtime!"

"Stargazing!" Darrell shouted back. With a wry grin he added, "Well, if you needed a good reason to leave here, little cousin, one just showed up."

Christmas came. For me, at least, the festivities were bittersweet.

And then came the day after. I dressed again in the velveteen dress I'd worn for the pageant at church. My aunt tamed my curly hair, and I let her fix the sides with red bows to match my dress. I felt like a belated Christmas present, all dolled up for Daddy.

When Aunt Annie spied my father's sedan ascending our long driveway, I ran to a dining room window to watch. Uncle Jack assumed a stance at the other window. Daddy parked, emerged from the car, and waved. I was unable to return the gesture. He paused, looking at me, and opened her door.

Then *she* stepped out.

I squinted into the sparkles of sunshine bouncing off the drifts to see. She was shorter than I'd imagined and a little plumper. She wore a type of coat and hat I'd seen only in periodicals.

"Why, she's wearing dead animals!" I said in amazement.

"That's mink, if I'm not mistaken," Uncle Jack said.

The wind whipped the hat from her head. It went tumbling into a snow bank as her hair escaped its confines. Her hair was dark like my own, but straight instead of curly.

"She has dark hair," I said.

"She's Italian," Uncle Jack said. "Most do."

Daddy retrieved her hat and jammed it down unbecomingly on her head. She laughed. He said something to her and she laughed again.

"She laughs," I said, mesmerized.

"Most people do," Uncle Jack said.

And then a gust of wind blew open her dead animal coat, revealing layers upon layers of golden chains around her neck.

I gasped. "I knew it! I just knew it—she's a jewelry store on legs!"

My worst nightmare approached the house, gloved hand in Daddy's hand, laden with golden chains and undoubtedly smelling as though an Evening in Paris bottle had spilled behind her ears. Losing my nerve, I clomped up the stairs, two at a bound.

"Damnation, girl, don't you do this to me!" Uncle Jack started after me but stopped on the landing as the back door opened and Daddy and Maria cheerily hollered their hellos.

Frantic, I searched for a hiding place. Lacking time to be choosy, I dove into my mostly empty closet and pulled some extra bedding over my head. Covered and cowering, I hid from a dark-haired Italian dressed in dead animals and golden chains.

After several minutes, the hunt for me began. Footsteps thumped back and forth. Various doors opened and closed. Even the attic was searched. Eventually someone walked in my room and sat down on my bed.

"Abby … Abigail?" Her voice was musical, soothing. "I know you're in here because we've looked everywhere else. Your father's told me so much about you, and I've waited such a long time to make your acquaintance. Please, Abby … please come and talk to me."

I crawled out from the closet and held up a pillow. "I—I was just looking for this."

She smiled. "And you found it too."

"You speak English." I looked her over while trying not to. She did not appear freakish. She did not appear evil. A stylish grey suit with a pink blouse enveloped an ample but attractive figure.

Her brown eyes crinkled at the corners as her smile broadened. "Of course. My father was an American diplomat. Didn't James tell you?"

I felt dumber than ever. "Um … I don't remember."

"Perhaps he forgot. It's not important, really, but I speak three languages and another just a tad. What made you think I didn't know English?"

I felt myself blush. "I—I saw a letter once that you wrote to Daddy. It—it wasn't in English, it—"

"Oh that," she said with a light wave of a manicured hand. "I used to write him in Italian and sometimes in French. He wanted to learn those languages and it motivated him to learn quickly. He'd spend hours with his translations just to find out what I cooked for dinner, how the weather was, or what I did that day … I believe he used letters as a tool of learning for you as well?"

"Yes. It worked too."

"And it worked for him also … what are you staring at, Abby?"

Again I flushed. "Um … all those necklaces you're wearing."

"Oh, those … yes, I do have on a bunch, don't I? James says I look like I'm wearing the whole jewelry store. But I have lots more at home, if you can imagine."

"No, I can't imagine."

Her expression changed from lighthearted to somber. "No, you probably can't. It's a habit of mine; probably a silly habit these days. I started wearing so many during the war, but under my clothes rather than on the top of my blouse like now. It was a way of hiding our valuables from those who'd take them from my family. Once I even used some as a bribe to get myself out of a bad circumstance … but you don't need to hear about that. Those days are gone and best forgotten."

I sat next to her and put the pillow aside, no longer needing something between us. "What's a bribe?" The word sounded familiar, but I couldn't recall its meaning.

"It's something valuable that one person offers another when they need a favor. As an example, you could offer me a bribe to leave your room and pretend I never found you."

"But I don't have anything to give you. All my stuff is downstairs for Daddy to load in the car."

She looked intently at me. "And if you did, would you offer it to me and your father? Would you want us to go away and pretend we never came here today?"

I was taken aback. "You mean I have a choice?"

"Answer my question."

I intended to tell her that I didn't want her; that I didn't want to be part of her life; that I wanted them both to go away, but I couldn't. I couldn't express my innermost feelings without hurting her. Hurt cut deep and hurt cut forever.

"Well, that wasn't—I mean, I don't—" I shook my head, at a loss for words.

She tentatively touched my arm. "Wait, stop a moment … before you say anything more, let me tell you something. The war was horrible for your father. In the beginning, he faced death daily from bombs, accidents, incompetence. As he rose in rank, his responsibilities increased—terrible responsibilities. He tallied the dead and the missing. Because he had no choice, he sent men—mere boys, really—up in planes needing repair, even needing replacement, knowing that in the best conditions, with the best equipment, some would not return. He had to write letters of condolence to the families of those who paid the ultimate price. When we first met, he was on the edge, physically and mentally. He hid it well, of course, or his career would've been over. But I recognized his pain because—" she hesitated as her eyes filled—"I was suffering as well. You see, my husband had been part of the resistance. He was presumed dead and my daughter … my daughter as well."

"I'm so sorry," I murmured. "I didn't know that about Daddy, or you … and I didn't know you had a daughter once. He never said."

"He never says all that he knows, and I really can't talk anymore about it either … I guess what I'm trying to say is that your father has waited years for the war to end so he could make plans for the future, plans he could see to fruition. And now he's come back for you. You, his daughter. He wants a new life, a civilian life. He wants us to be a family. You'd be special, Abby. You'd be so special to us."

I looked at Maria's open, hopeful face and at her dark eyes, rimmed with tears. To endure the loss of both a husband and a daughter was beyond my comprehension.

And now she wanted a new beginning.

As did Daddy.

As did I … unbelievably, as did I.

I nodded, my own eyes brimming. "I didn't mean to sound like I didn't want to go with you before. I was just so afraid … I was afraid you wouldn't like me."

Without saying a word, she gathered me in her arms. To my relief, my new stepmother felt warm and comfortable. She didn't smell like Evening in Paris at all. She smelled clean and fresh like Aunt Annie did on a Saturday night after her bubble bath.

Daddy was conversing with my aunt when Maria and I came downstairs. He looked far different than when I last saw him. His hair was longer and grayer. He'd gained weight. He wore jeans, a blue shirt, a tweedy sport coat, and the most intricately tooled cowboy boots imaginable. I'd never seen clothes like that on a man in my life. Could it be high fashion in Minneapolis?

"Hello, Daddy." I sidled up to him for a hug.

"Well, if it isn't Abigail—at long last." He didn't hug me and he didn't appear pleased that his new wife had to fetch his new daughter. Apparently he'd expected her to be successful, though; my bags were gone from where they'd been piled.

He didn't say anything more to me, and I didn't know what to say to him. Maria glanced between the two of us. *Forget the happy reunion,* I thought.

Aunt Annie smoothed over the situation by calling for my cousins. When they arrived, she lined them up like little soldiers to say their good-byes.

"I'm sorry I wanted you dead before," Duane mumbled. "I'm really glad you could live here a while."

"Me too," Dennis said. "I sort of liked you for a teacher."

I decided to be gracious. "It was fun."

Darrell shook my hand as our eyes met. "So long, see you soon." He headed upstairs, taking the twins with him.

Uncle Jack stood stone-faced with his hands thrust deep in his pockets. He offered no farewell nor did he make any gesture toward me.

Aunt Annie glanced at him out of the corner of her eye, then wrapped me in a long, tight hug. "Be sure to write, Abby. And call now and then, collect if need be. Tell us what you're doing, how you like your new home, and all about your new school."

I could only nod. If I said anything, I'd cry.

Maria came to my rescue. "Oh, I just hate good-byes, don't you? They're just too hard. Much better to say, 'See you soon,' like Darrell did. Come on, Abby, let's get our wraps … whenever you're ready, James."

She didn't hustle me out of the room fast enough. As I struggled with my coat, which caught on the long sleeves of my dress, Daddy stepped up to Uncle Jack. In his face, he stepped up to him.

"Well, little brother," my father said. "Payback can be hell, don't you think?"

Uncle Jack's hands flew from his pockets and clenched into fists. "Why, you vindictive ass!"

Aunt Annie grabbed his nearest arm. "Jack, don't!"

"Jack, do!" Daddy mocked. "Go ahead, see what it gets you. Punch me in front of the women, or would you rather do it in the barn? I've an inch and twenty pounds on you, but as mad as you are, it'd be fairly even. Tell you what. If you win, I talk. And if I win, I talk … how about it, Jack?"

At the challenge, my uncle lowered his fists and stormed upstairs.

We stood staring at Daddy: Maria, holding my coat; Aunt Annie, her mouth agape; and me, wondering what else could go wrong in a single morning.

My aunt recovered quickly. "Really, James! How dare you pick a fight with your own brother. What's going on here?"

"I didn't pick a fight, Annie," Daddy said through his teeth. "He threatened to punch me, remember?"

"But you started it."

"No, I was merely stating facts. Can I help if he blew up?"

"Maybe he had good reason. You certainly didn't help matters, did you?"

"No, but you don't need to worry about him. He'll be all right … someday."

"Will he? Well, I *am* worried about him!" She stomped upstairs after my uncle.

Daddy turned and caught Maria and me staring. "Don't just stand there gawking, you two. Come on, we've got places to go."

She helped me with my coat and threw on her mink. Hand in hand, we followed him outside. He flung open both doors for us, jumped in the car, and revved the engine.

"What was that all about?" Maria said to me.

"I have no idea."

"He'll have some explaining to do, later."

For being his wife, I thought, *she didn't know much about Daddy. Unless it was his idea, he'd never explain anything.*

As he drove faster than was prudent down the icy road, I mulled over the events preceding my departure. Why hadn't Uncle Jack said good-bye? That hurt. Even the twins managed to say something nice.

What had Daddy meant by "payback"? It must be really awful for Uncle Jack to attempt to punch my father! And why had he backed down so readily when Daddy threatened to talk? Talking things over during a confrontation was generally helpful … unless a secret would be revealed.

That was it: a secret! Just when Snoop and Company had ended their investigation, here came more mysteries. And now I was alone, without Darrell, without my Sherlock. I was weary of secrets, weary of mysteries, weary of everything.

I had wanted a smooth transition from my old life to my new, but I'd been unceremoniously snatched away. What was wrong with Daddy? And Uncle

Jack? They were two of the rudest, most abrasive people I'd ever known. My classmates in school displayed more social acuity than they did. And my life would, of necessity, continue to revolve around them.

I made a promise to myself, as I huddled in the backseat of my father's sensible black sedan, that one day I would surprise them both. I'd do something so amazing, so insightful, so clever, that I'd shock them into settling the dark secret that caused them to hate.

Yes, I would.

As it turned out, Maria knew how to handle my father's moods. At first she kept quiet. Then she talked innocuously about the driving conditions. Daddy added a few terse comments.

By the time we got to New Ulm, he was calm again. "Are you hungry, Abby? Do you need a restroom break?" he asked as he drove along Minnesota Street.

"Yes twice," I said.

Daddy parked at the Kaiserhoff and ordered ribs for me and Maria and a steak and a Schell's beer for himself. Maria said she was starving. She'd been so nervous about meeting me that she hadn't been able to eat a solitary thing for breakfast. I confessed the same thing. She laughed and gave me a big hug, right there in the restaurant. Then we started yakking about everything, anything, and nothing.

Daddy watched us, a bemused expression on his face.

"A penny for your thoughts, James," Maria said during an infrequent lull in our conversation.

"Oh, I'm just taking it all in."

"Taking what in?"

"Everything ... this café, for instance. It's so warm and safe and so very different from what I experienced during the war. And here I am, all warm and safe too, looking at my wife and my daughter. I can hardly believe it. But I can believe it, because I'm listening to the two of you jabbering like you've known each other for years. I'll probably never get a word in edgewise."

Maria slid an arm through one of his and smiled. "You'll get plenty of words in. You always do."

"Oh, I suppose ... but can you guess the best part?"

"What?" I said, hoping he'd say me.

"Beef." Daddy eyed his plate as the waitress served our food. "Big, brown, delicious, good old American beef. Steaks, roasts, patties—makes no difference. I used to lie on my bunk and dream about beef ... shovel down, ladies."

My New Life

THREE HOURS LATER, we arrived in Minneapolis. Daddy said several inches of snow had fallen since morning. Now, in the gathering dusk of late afternoon, the snow clung ghostlike to the skeletal branches of the elms lining the streets. Slanting drifts deepened to gloom amid thick stands of trees bordering Minnehaha Creek. Christmas lights twinkled from house windows. Decorations protruded from whitened lawns and graced both porch and portal. Couples strolled, oblivious to the cold, along the illuminated parkway.

Daddy slowed the car to a crawl several times, asking whether I liked this house or preferred that one, whether I wanted to live in this one or that one. All looked wondrous to my country eyes, so I always answered "yes." After a pause, he'd chuckle and drive on.

Finally he turned down an alley and parked. A narrow, shoveled path led from the garage to the back door of the house. "Well, here we are, boys and girls. Whoops, no boys in this car, unless you count me." Daddy was evidently enjoying the drama he'd created.

I jumped out of the sedan and looked up. The house was unlike anything I'd ever seen. Two stories plus an attic wasn't unusual, but what focused my attention was a soaring circular section of house topped by a conical section of roof. At the apex perched a rooster weathervane.

"Why, that looks like the tower of a castle," I said. "It even has a round window looking out toward the creek."

"It's the window of your room," Daddy said. "Would you like the grand tour?"

"Yes!" I nearly shouted. Princess Abigail now lived in a castle!

He unlocked the door. Maria and I piled inside and stamped the snow from our feet. I noticed how my father swept out the snow before he put away his overcoat. Following Maria's example, I took off my galoshes and hung my outerwear next to hers.

Daddy insisted on showing me the main floor before allowing me upstairs. The house was Tudor in style, he said, with some Craftsman modifications. Several details had been botched by a previous owner that he intended to rectify. I paid scant attention, noting only the word "stucco," which he explained rather than telling me to look it up.

The kitchen was immaculate, all green and pink and white, with chicken decorations—Maria's idea. The towels perfectly matched the dish cloths, the potholders, and the wallpaper border. Meals would be eaten in the dining room, Daddy said, as the kitchen was so tiny. I'd have to guard against spilling on the beige carpet.

"Then I guess I'll eat over the sink," I teased. Maria stifled a giggle, but Daddy looked as though he were considering the notion.

I quickly said how I liked the paneling halfway up the dining room walls. "Wainscoting," I was told. I also complimented the arched window with a view of the back yard and the chandelier shaped like an opening flower. Silver candlesticks decorated the buffet on either side of an ornate clock. Daddy said he'd found the clock in an antique store in France. With its chips and wear, I'd have tossed it ages ago and bought a new one.

The living room floor was dark wood, the better to obscure my messes, with a sumptuous rug by the davenport. "Persian," Maria said. Three upholstered chairs, each with a side table and lamp, accommodated the serious reader. A coffee table was laden with history and travel books, artfully arranged. Several silver pieces adorned the mantle of the fireplace. Two landscapes, painted by my father, hung on the walls, and that was all.

"Where's the fancy stuff you described in your letters?" I asked. "Or aren't you finished decorating?"

"I wrote that simply to entice you. And yes, I'm finished. A person doesn't need so much junk."

Next he showed me the main bedroom and bath. Both were very clean and very masculine. A white chenille bedspread and a heart-shaped pillow provided the only soft touches. "James and Maria" was embroidered on the pillow, along with the date of their marriage, nearly two years ago. My father was certainly adept at keeping secrets.

Across the hall, a closed door barred the only room I hadn't seen. As I reached for the doorknob, Daddy's hand came down on mine so fast I startled.

"That's my office," he said. "You're not to go in that room."

"Why not?" I said. "I thought you were showing me everything."

"Not everything. My office is private. Sometimes I need my privacy."

I looked to Maria for a further explanation.

"Your father's a private man," she said.

Her comment fueled my initial curiosity. What had Daddy hidden this time? I'd have to find out as soon as possible.

"Forget about snooping. I keep it locked … why don't you go up and see your room now?"

"Well, it's about time!" I smiled and ran upstairs. I'd learned from Darrell to pretend I wasn't interested in what I was interested in, but Daddy would be hard to fool. His ability to decipher my thoughts was uncanny.

I shifted focus as I explored my bedroom. The dark walls seemed oppressive. Could someone paint? The patterned rug on the wood floor looked like it came from Woolworth's, not Persia. The closet was miniscule, but so were my belongings. I opened the door to what I hoped to be a second closet and discovered my very own bathroom. I clapped with delight. My own toilet! No more waiting to poop!

My furniture seemed adequate: bed, chest, nightstand, lamp, and a vanity with a bench where I'd sit while grooming myself … grooming myself? I wasn't a cat! But the dresser set Auntie had given me for my tenth birthday would look perfect on the vanity … ugh, I was thinking like a girl again. How sad was that? But how could I be a princess if I wasn't a girl? I certainly couldn't be a prince. Far too late for that … I needed to rethink myself, when I had more time.

"So, what do you think of your new room?" Maria asked from behind me. I hadn't heard her ascend the stairs. Folks who stomped around so you knew their whereabouts made snooping a lot safer than folks who walked like a whisper; I needed to keep that in mind.

"Oh, it's wonderful, simply wonderful!" I gushed before reeling in my enthusiasm. "But it's a little bare. It needs more stuff. Daddy wrote in one of his letters that I could choose my own things."

"Yes, I know." She produced a pencil and a notepad from her pocket. "What more would you like?"

I rethought myself, right on the spot, and combined my two favorite fantasies: I'd be an African princess. I already felt like a princess and I wanted my room to look like Africa, at least how Africa must look, given my limited knowledge. I wanted a leopard print bedspread and the vanity bench recovered to match, pillows in spots and stripes, and an easy chair upholstered in fur. I wanted carved masks to decorate the walls, along with spears and arrows, but no shrunken heads. I wanted Daddy's sable hung here and his impala hung there. I pointed to the appropriate walls. I wanted the hunting photographs I'd rescued from the schoolhouse arranged on the wall by my closet. I wanted a map of the Dark Continent and a painting of elephants or lions to finish everything off.

In essence, I wanted a room in which Uncle Jack would feel completely at home, if he ever dared a visit, but I kept that sentiment to myself. My father wouldn't like me thinking of his brother fifteen minutes after crossing the threshold to my new life.

Maria went downstairs and showed my list to Daddy.

"What? Is she crazy?" I heard him exclaim.

Yup, that was me: Crazy Abigail, the African Princess.

Over the next couple of weeks, my room gradually took shape. Maria couldn't find what I wanted for the bedspread, vanity cushion, and pillows, so she bought fabric and sewed them herself. She also fashioned a faux fur throw to enliven my thrift shop easy chair.

Daddy painted a pride of lions and hung it on my north wall. Spears and masks of dubious origin he mounted on the south wall. His trophies and the hunting photographs he arranged on whatever space remained. After considerable searching, he located a map of the Dark Continent in a dusty antique store off Hennepin Avenue, framed it for over my bed, and proclaimed my room finished.

In addition to refurbishing my room, Daddy and Maria tried to show me a good time in the big city before school resumed. One afternoon we toured the Walker Art Center, where I saw more pictures than I ever knew existed.

"Um … I think I like your paintings better, Daddy," I said, trying to understand why a particular picture had a blue nose sticking crossways out of an ear.

"It's a Picasso," he said. "This particular work is worth multiple thousands of dollars."

I laughed out loud. "For that piece of crap?"

"Pipe down, Abigail!" Daddy shook a forefinger at me.

Several well-dressed matrons turned and stared. I blushed red as a ripe tomato. But when my father moved on to the next painting, Maria slipped her arm around me and whispered, "I think it looks like crap too."

The next day, we took a streetcar downtown. I'd never been on a streetcar, and I certainly hadn't seen a building taller than three stories before. I could hardly believe the height of the Foshay Tower: thirty-two stories! Daddy insisted we go to the top, as though looking up didn't make me dizzy enough. I had to grab Maria when the elevator lady started pushing buttons, fearing my breakfast would remain on the ground floor.

"Nothing to worry about," Maria said, but she held me tight anyway.

"The Foshay Tower was the first skyscraper west of the Mississippi, built in 1929 by Wilbur Foshay," Daddy said as we enjoyed the spectacular view. "John Philip Sousa composed a march for its grand opening. Do you know who he was, Abby?"

"Of course I do," I said, seeking to vindicate myself. "He wrote 'Stars and Stripes Forever' and a hundred others. Sousa marches are all the band ever plays on Independence Day."

"I'm glad to hear your education hasn't been totally lacking." Daddy went on to explain how Mr. Foshay's fortune vanished during the Great Depression and his check to Sousa bounced at the bank. Sousa retaliated by prohibiting his march from ever being played again.

"What a waste of Sousa's time," I said after being told what "bounced" meant.

Daddy smiled. "I concur with that statement."

He didn't smile the following day when we toured the grandest department store imaginable: Dayton's. Maria would begin working there after the holidays, selling jewelry and repairing watches. I succumbed to my excitement and rode the escalator up and down numerous times, along with a little boy who seemed determined to escape his mother. My travels ended when Daddy positioned Maria at the top of the escalator while he waited at the bottom.

He took me firmly by the arm. "Stop it, Abigail. You act like you're four."

"I wish I was," I mumbled. I remembered being completely happy at four because I didn't know any different. Being happy at eleven was proving a challenge.

"Oh, let her have fun," Maria said.

"I thought I was," Daddy said.

I contented myself with looking but not touching, until he released me. Then I made a beeline to the jewelry counter.

"Can I try that one on?" I pointed to a sparkly ring.

"I'm afraid not," the black-suited man behind the counter replied. "These rings are not for children … oh, Mrs. Stahl. I didn't see you before. Is this young lady your daughter? Yes? In that case, she may try on a ring." To me he cautioned, "Be careful. You mustn't drop or scratch it."

"I won't." I positioned my hand to catch the light. "Um … no, this one isn't quite right. Besides, it's way too big."

"Any ring can be sized to fit the finger perfectly, even a child's finger," the clerk said with chilly civility.

"Oh … well, I don't like this one. How about that one?" I tried on nine or ten sparkly rings although I only had a quarter in my pocket and Dayton's didn't sell so much as a barrette for a quarter. But I refused to be rushed. I was a princess in my treasure trove, and I ignored both the haughty attitude of the penguin behind the counter and my father's growing irritation.

"Abby," Daddy said, "it's time to move along."

"In a minute, Daddy … I think I prefer this red one," I said to the clerk. "It's so pretty. How much is it?"

The penguin snatched it from me and methodically checked the price in his book before he announced, "This ruby ring is a real buy at one hundred and nine dollars and ninety-five cents."

"Holy shit!" I blurted. "You're wrong. It'd be a real buy at nine dollars and ninety-five cents!"

Daddy unceremoniously hauled me away. "What kind of language is that for a young lady? What's wrong with you? Were you raised in a barn?"

"Pretty much," I said.

Then Maria giggled. "That was my boss."

"Dear Lord," Daddy said with a roll of his eyes. "We're going home."

We continued on course, me trying to ignore my father's tourniquet grip on my arm, Maria trying to match his stride, trying to hide her amusement. But on the way out, we had to pass the perfume counter and the scent drew her in like a rose draws bees.

"Oh, James, can we stop for just a moment? I'd like to try some of the new perfumes … please, dear?"

Daddy obliged her but kept me corralled. Apparently "please, dear" worked far better with him than "holy shit."

She diddled around far longer than I had at the jewelry counter, but he showed no signs of impatience. "How about this one?" She held up her wrist for him to sniff. "I think I like this one."

"I like it too," he said and bought it for her. I watched the cash register. For the price, I'd have thought the bottle would've been a whole lot bigger.

Daddy again headed for the street, but Maria successfully detoured through the fur department.

"Oh, there's nothing in the world like sheared beaver," she said, trying on a three-quarter-length jacket. She pirouetted in front of the mirror, admiring herself from all possible angles. "Just feel this, Abby."

"It's wonderful," I agreed. Sheared beaver was even softer than a newborn kitty.

"But you've already got a mink," Daddy said.

"It doesn't cost to look, James."

"But looking too often leads to buying."

"Not always … thank you, it's simply lovely, but we're just looking today," Maria said to the saleslady as she handed back the beaver. "Can we look again next Christmas?" she asked Daddy. "I'll have my employee discount by then."

"Where's Abby?" he said, ignoring her query.

I'd been poking around nearby, calculating a rough guess of the price of Maria's mink coat. Whew, was it expensive! I ran up when I heard my name, but I wasn't fast enough.

"Can't you stay put?" Daddy took hold of me again. "I let you go for one minute and you disappear!"

I assumed my best sad face. "I'm sorry, Daddy. I'll stay put. Don't be mad at me."

"I've good reason to be mad at you. You've been a real nuisance today, do you know that?"

"But she's never been to a store like Dayton's before," Maria said. "She wouldn't be normal if she didn't get excited."

"Excited?" Daddy said. "Going amok would be a more apt description! And that wouldn't excuse her foul language, lack of propriety at the museum, or her spooking inside the elevator the other day anyway."

"Those were all new experiences for her. Remember, dear, Abby's from the country and she's still a child. Please have patience with her."

I hung my head and bit my lip and liked my new stepmother even more.

Daddy sighed. "Fine, have it your way ... well, at the risk of more public humiliation, I'd like to go eat at the Red Dragon. Is anyone hungry besides me?"

Maria and I answered in the affirmative, and I breathed easier. If Daddy was thinking about his stomach, he wasn't thinking about disciplining me.

Minutes later, we arrived at the Red Dragon, a genuine Chinese restaurant. Sitting in a darkened booth decorated with red dragons and illuminated by paper lanterns and being served by a little yellow man in black pajamas and a funny accent thrilled me as much as Dayton's. But I stifled my exhilaration, determined not to cause my father further embarrassment.

Daddy and Maria quickly made their selections, but I perused the menu carefully. Darrell had told me that the Chinese cook dog, and no way in hell did I want to accidently eat somebody's Ranger or Molly.

"What's taking you so long?" Daddy asked. "Chang won't take our order until you close your menu."

"I don't want to accidentally order dog," I said in a low voice. "Chinese people eat dogs, you know."

For a moment, my father looked as though his hearing was suspect. Then he threw back his head and laughed. It was the first time I'd made him laugh since he'd kidnapped me from the farm. Maria laughed too.

"What?" I demanded. "What's so funny?"

"You won't accidentally order dog. Dog might be on the menu in China, but here it's the usual beef, chicken, pork, or seafood. So make up your mind, Abby. I'm starving."

I believed him, but I still ordered a chicken dish after making sure the pieces arrived whole. I had plenty of experience with poultry and I could tell a chicken leg from a terrier leg … Chang wasn't going to slip one by me!

That night, Daddy laid down the rules that would govern my life. I'd been under his roof nearly two weeks, he said, doing what I pleased. Now it was time for me to do as he pleased.

"I've been watching, listening, figuring you out. I don't know you as well as I'm going to, but some things are apparent. You're spirited to a fault. You have few social graces. Your language is often abominable. Your work ethic is lacking. You're impulsive. Your overall knowledge is deficient, due to the narrow scope of your education.

"On the positive side, you're imaginative and intelligent. You possess, thanks to my efforts, although you seldom utilize, a rather impressive vocabulary. You have a desire to fit in, to please. The latter is essential for us being a family, so I'm glad about that. And you've already attached yourself to Maria. That's good. Nothing could make me happier. In disposition you're generally cheerful, but you tend to worry, often needlessly.

"You also tend to forget or ignore rules, so I wrote down the basics. Read them over. I'll be back in a few minutes to discuss any questions you might have. Their order is not linked to importance. They're all important." He handed me a typed list and went downstairs.

A list? My conduct was to be governed by a damned *list*? Did Colonel James Albert Stahl somehow think he was again in the military and I was one of his underlings? Had Tyrant James learned about the power of lists in Tyrant School? Was my Father the King demanding the complete subjugation of Princess Abigail?

I felt like running away. But where could I go so late at night?

So I read the list.

1. Cleanliness is not optional. Your Saturday night bath is insufficient. You will bathe daily. You will wash your hair twice weekly in the winter and every other day in the summer.
2. You will refrain from foul language except in the most extenuating circumstances. Swearing when you cannot locate your shoes is unacceptable. Swearing when you are bleeding profusely is acceptable.
3. If you don't know what to do in a social situation, watch others. It is more acceptable to do nothing than to do the wrong thing.
4. Snooping will not be tolerated. My office is locked for a reason. You will not enter even if I forget to lock it. Similarly, you will not scrutinize Maria's possessions simply for your own amusement.

5. You will keep your room and bath tidy, set and clear the table, and do the dishes. In other parts of the house, you are to return to its proper location whatever you move out of place. In addition, you are to do whatever else you are asked to do.
6. You will be transported to the library each Saturday for a book selected specifically to improve your vocabulary and general knowledge. Each Friday you will be quizzed on its contents.
7. Breakfast is optional, lunch is at one, dinner at seven. If you are late, you will not eat.
8. Your whereabouts will be known at all times. You will not leave the house without permission. You will return from school directly.
9. You will be at all times respectful and compliant.
10. Mistakes will be corrected, ignorance will be addressed, and defiance will be punished.

I couldn't believe it. I just couldn't believe it! Uncle Jack had rules for everything, too, but he never felt compelled to write them down, like I had mush between my ears!

I did the only thing I could: I tore them up. Into teeny, tiny bits of paper I ripped up the tyrant's dictates and piled the pieces on my nightstand, nice and neat. Then I used the bathroom so I'd be ready for anything.

Daddy returned and saw what I'd done. His jaw set. His eyes grew cold. His hands moved meaningfully toward his belt buckle. I blanched.

"Why'd you do that?" His thumbs hooked on his belt.

"I—I don't know."

"Do you think the rules will go away if you tear them up?"

"No."

"What is so unfair about my rules that you would do that?"

"Nothing."

"Are they in any way unusual, unjust, or untenable?"

"No."

"Did you read rule ten?"

"Yes."

"Do you remember what it said?"

I swallowed hard. "Not really."

"Defiance will be punished. Do you think tearing up my rules is an act of defiance, Abby?"

My voice came as a whisper. "Yes."

"Then why did you do it?"

I crumbled. "I don't know … I'm sorry, Daddy. I won't do it again. I don't know what got into me … don't spank me. Please don't."

An agonizing minute elapsed.

"Stay put, I'll be right back." He left but returned a minute later with a carbon copy. "I thought you might pull a stunt like this … do you still feel the urge to rip up my list?"

"No," I said, chastened.

"Good. In a contest of wills, Abigail, you'll never win. Tape this to your wall so you can refer to it readily."

Obediently I took it from his hand and taped it to the wall next to my closet.

Then I began to plot my recourse.

The next night, over dinner, I handed Daddy my own list, handwritten on tablet paper. Like him, I'd made an extra.

"It's in no particular order," I said. "I wrote it down as it occurred to me."

As he began to read, I watched his expression. If he erupted and Maria couldn't protect me, I intended to call Uncle Jack and request transfer back to the farm.

Somehow I hoped it wouldn't come to that.

Abby's List:

1. Tell me you love me. You've only said it once and that's not enough.
2. Don't yell. I have really good hearing.
3. Don't threaten. I already know what can happen.
4. Do things with me. I want your attention.
5. Don't expect me to be perfect. I'm trying.
6. Don't keep me busy every minute. I need time to do nothing.
7. Encourage what I'm good at instead of pointing out what I'm not good at.
8. Don't make me go hungry if I'm late. Maybe I had a good reason.
9. Knock on my door before you come in. I need privacy too.
10. Kiss me goodnight when I go to bed. It's the charm that keeps me safe.

"Are you mocking me, Abigail?" Daddy's pale eyes penetrated my affected complacency. "Do you think this is funny?"

"No," I said, my heart pounding wildly.

Just when retribution seemed imminent, he handed my list to Maria. After she read it, she daubed her eyes with her napkin and said, very softly, "Oh, James."

Daddy looked from her to me and back again. "Well, I guess there's just one thing to do now." He got up from the table, walked into the kitchen, and affixed my list to the refrigerator with magnets.

The Fourth Commandment

My list was a mere beginning, as time and effort was needed to turn James Albert Stahl into a real father. The changes he made seemed to go against his grain, but change he did. My bedtime kiss was the most easily accomplished of my ten demands.

"I don't know why this is so important to you, but if it makes you feel more secure, it's fine by me," he said the first night he came to my room.

"Gramma always did. And after she died, Uncle Jack did."

"Is that so?" He started to leave.

"Wait, Daddy! You're not going without saying you love me, are you?"

"Of course I love you, Abby. Why else would I want you here?"

"Because I'm yours. That's what you said when I first met you. You need a better reason though, because kids aren't like something you own."

"No, they're not," he said and went downstairs.

I lay in my bed, holding PB and remembering another man whose profession of love I had to overhear rather than being told outright. Why was it so difficult for people to say they loved me? Mrs. Monson said I was worthy of love. Maybe I should I ask her to write a letter to Daddy and explain love. He liked letters. Perhaps he'd learn something from reading hers.

The second night, Daddy proclaimed his love without prompting.

"Why? Why do you love me?"

"Do I need a reason? I just do." Then he went downstairs.

He was simply saying what was expected of him, I thought. So I switched on my lamp and dashed off a short note to Mrs. Monson, stating my problem. I checked my spelling and punctuation like she'd taught me. I did have one cross out, but I didn't bother rewriting. Maria could mail it for me in the morning.

The third night, Daddy lingered for a while, and I cautiously began to share my heart with him. While I was getting to know him, he was easier to talk to there in the darkness than in the cold, gray light of morning.

But after he left, I remembered another man with whom I'd begun sharing my heart. I remembered soft summer nights, two rocking chairs, an old porch, lightning bugs, and drinking lemonade while the man drank his brandy. I missed being there.

I missed it even more when Darrell's first letter arrived. I'd nearly given up hope as he'd promised to write weekly, which made his first letter three weeks late. Eagerly I ripped it open.

Dear Abby,

Great news! Gary got a .16 gauge Browning for Christmas! We went over there last weekend and I got to shoot it. We'll really be able to whack those pheasants next fall. He's a lot better shot than you, but you were okay last year, for a girl. I'm going to nag Dad for a .16 gauge of my own. Won't do any good, but I'll nag anyway.

Both the twins got the chicken pox. Glad I can't get that again. They look as ugly as what you drop in the toilet! (I only said that because Mom says I shouldn't say shit so much.)

Banat stepped in a hole and hurt her leg last week. Dad worried he'd have to shoot her, but the vet patched her up. She won't run as fast, but she'll be good enough to ride so Dad's happy about that. He likes that horse better than he likes any of us, that's for sure.

Here's what's going on at school. Ruth had a sleepover last Saturday. Too bad you missed it. Yesterday Karen got caught smoking in the girl's restroom. Mrs. Monson threw a fit at her in the hall, saw it with my own eyes! Billy Hartmann got thrown out for a week for I don't know what reason, but the dumbass is back already.

Other than that, school's boring. How's it for you? Must be really exciting not knowing anybody. You can invent a whole new you! Well, hope you're doing okay there in the big city.

Mom says hi, wishes you were here to bake cookies. Oh, she says she wishes you were here for lots of other reasons too.

Got to go, Dad's yelling about something I forgot (on purpose) to do!

Your blood brother, Darrell

My eyes lingered on his signature. Nearly a month had passed since we'd blended our blood atop my uncle's snow-encrusted haystack, gazing at the heavens, mouthing platitudes. When would I see Darrell next? Or anyone else at the farm?

I was wallowing in self-pity when Daddy emerged from his office.

"Why the face?"

"Darrell's letter."

"You're sad when he didn't write and now you're sad when he does? Seems he could've saved himself the trouble."

"But everybody's having fun without me, Daddy. I'm missing everything."

"It might seem that way, but Darrell's condensing the past three weeks. You've had some fun yourself the past three weeks, haven't you?"

I had, but not since school started. City kids were just plain mean. When I said I'd lived on a farm, one nasty boy actually wanted to see the bottoms of my shoes to check for manure. When everyone laughed, I could've fit in a thimble with room to spare. Lunch was the absolute worst. I ate alone, as the whole school was already segregated into the popular, the bookworms, and the outcasts. I was in a class by myself: a pariah, one of my father's latest vocabulary words.

"What you need is an outside activity so you can make new friends," Daddy said. He took a pad and pencil from the telephone stand and pulled up a chair next to me.

I watched with suspicion. "What's that for?"

"I'm making a list."

"No, Daddy, not another damn list!"

"You'll write your fifty sentences as soon as we're done with the list."

"But I wrote fifty sentences three times just yesterday! That's a hundred and fifty sentences. And I got a whole bunch of schoolwork to do tonight. I don't have time for more da—dumb sentences!" I caught myself in the nick of time. Scribbling "I will not swear" fifty times for every swearing slipup was getting downright tedious.

"Dumb? Why do you call everything I make you do *dumb*?" Daddy exercised his forefinger in my face again. "Well, too bad, Abigail! Maybe when your fingers cramp from so much writing, you'll learn to control your mouth!"

My father was negative sympathy. If I were a filly, wild as the west wind, he'd break me by jumping on my back, spurring my flanks, and riding me until I frothed. And I was determined not to be broke … easily anyway.

I took a cleansing breath. "So what's the list, Daddy?"

"Activities you can do here in the city."

"I don't want to do anything."

"Don't be difficult. Of course you do. It's better than carping about school and other things that can't be changed … so, what do you like to do besides your extracurricular reading and vocabulary exercises?"

"Who said I like those?" I muttered. "You make me do them, that's all."

"What I make you do, Abigail, I make you do for your own good."

I averted my eyes, hating him. He could give me back to his brother. That would be for my own good too.

"Well, if you're determined to be miserable, there's not much I can do about it."

"Guess not." I stood up to leave.

"Sit down!"

I sat where he pointed and willed myself not to cry.

He started over. "There must be something you'd like to learn, Abby. How about music lessons? Voice? Piano? I could buy you a piano."

"No. I can't sing and my coordination stinks."

"Who said that?"

"My second-grade teacher."

"I'll be the judge of that. Sing something."

Self-consciously I sang "Twinkle, Twinkle, Little Star."

Daddy looked impressed, but not favorably. "Now tap twice with your left hand while you tap once with your right, like you're beating a drum."

I watched while he demonstrated. It seemed simple enough.

It was impossible.

He leaned back in his chair and cleared his throat. "Maybe music lessons would be a waste of money... how about dance lessons? Learning to dance would improve both your social graces and your coordination."

"I'd rather be dead."

My father slammed the pad on the table. "Abigail, you're impossible!"

"I am not! All right, you asked for it—I want to learn fencing!"

Daddy's eyebrows lifted so high they nearly touched his hairline. "Like Errol Flynn? Or the post and barbed wire version?"

"Do you think I'm talking about fencing fields?" I hollered. "Of course I mean like Errol Flynn!"

"Don't be preposterous, Abigail. You're seeing way too many movies."

"Like that's my fault? If you went to church like you're supposed to, I wouldn't be seeing so many movies!" Daddy had been raised German Lutheran and Maria Roman Catholic. Neither would attend the other's church, so we went to the movies instead. While I enjoyed the Sunday matinees more than I had Reverend Richter's thundering about fire and brimstone, I continued to pray. I prayed God would forgive us for seeing Errol Flynn, Clark Gable, Gary Cooper, or Spencer Tracy up on the silver screen rather than his earthly representative up in a pulpit.

"No ... definitely not," Daddy decided, ignoring my accusation. "The very notion of you waving around a foil is ludicrous."

"So how about riding lessons?"

"Why? You're afraid of horses."

"You're always telling me not to be afraid, Daddy, and I want to stop being afraid." *Uncle Jack could teach me the finer points of horsemanship later,* I thought. He'd be so impressed ... if I ever saw him again, that is.

"Fine. There's a stable near Shakopee that probably gives riding lessons. We'll check it out on Saturday."

"Instead of our trip to the library?"

"We can skip the library for a week … anything else?"

"Yes, I want to learn to shoot better. I want shooting lessons."

"No, you've way too much interest in guns the way it is. Why, the next thing you'll want to do is to go hunting!"

"But I already want to go hunting." I wondered how he'd react if I whipped out my pheasant photos. I'd kept them secret because I could keep secrets too. Hunting was fun, but mostly I wanted to shoot better than Gary so I could impress Darrell.

"Forget it. There are no opportunities for shooting around here. Riding lessons are enough. Now write your sentences." He went inside his office and closed the door firmly behind him.

After I dashed off my fifty sentences, I checked the telephone book and found numerous advertisements for gun sales, gun repairs, and one gun club. Might a gun club offer lessons? Lowering my voice in hope of sounding older, I dialed the number and asked.

"Yes," said the man who answered. "We offer a course in gun safety and practice sessions for boys and girls ages ten to fourteen. Are you at least ten?"

My voice ascended to normal range. "I was eleven last November."

"Good. Then stop in with a parent and we'll sign you up. Our next course starts the first Saturday in March."

"Thank you! Oh, thank so you much!" In my excitement, I inadvertently broke Daddy's Fourth Commandment: I barged into his office. Afterward, I couldn't remember putting my hand on the doorknob, or opening the door, or stepping inside, but suddenly I found myself surrounded by photographs, clothing, objects of all sorts, and a pervasive odor of stale perfume. Heavy drapes, closed tightly, prevented me from seeing details with clarity.

"Abigail!" Daddy bellowed as he snapped off a small lamp. He rose from behind a massive desk. "Haven't I told you never to come in here? Haven't I? *Haven't I?*"

He swooped down on me, grabbed me, and whirled me around. I was propelled into the hall before I could take my next breath. I was headed to my room a moment later, with a hard swat on my rump hastening my scramble up the stairs.

"And stay there!" he raged from below me.

I flung the doors to my room and my bathroom shut behind me and shakily took a pee. A minute passed, then another. I kept expecting him to stamp up the stairs. What was taking him so long? After fifteen minutes, I attempted to do my homework, but how could I memorize Lincoln's

Gettysburg Address, short as it was, when all I could think about was what I'd seen in his office, short as my stay had been?

I recalled a heaviness, not of dust or dirt or even of antiquity, but of atmosphere. Of the multitude of furnishings, I couldn't remember specifics beyond the heavy drapes, the gilded lamp on Daddy's desk, and the journal spread out before him.

But I did recall the fire in my father's eyes as he rose from his chair, like a raptor rising from its kill, and lunged at me. But I shouldn't have been able to see the fire in his eyes, given the dimness of the room, but I had … hadn't I?

And the stale odor of perfume … where had I smelled that before?

I'd accomplished nothing but fretting and scribbling more sentences in preparation for my next inevitable swear word when a bus squealed to a stop outside. I ran to my tower window and watched Maria get out. She waved. I waved back. With her home, Daddy was unlikely to punish me now.

I heard him greet her at the back door. I knew he'd hang up her coat and handbag, give her a welcoming kiss, and pour her a glass of wine while he finished cooking our dinner. She'd kick off her heels, sip the wine, and tell him about her busy day. Occasionally she'd giggle about someone, usually her boss, whom she'd nicknamed "The Penguin," in honor of my own less-than-stellar performance at the jewelry counter.

Then she would inquire about his day.

And what would he say? That their new daughter still swore a blue streak, sang like a dying frog, and couldn't tap a simple rhythm to save her life? That she preferred death over dance? That she sought to thrust and parry, ride horses, and shoot? That she demanded her own dictates be followed while blatantly disobeying the simple rule of a closed door?

Then I heard what I'd been dreading: footsteps coming up the stairs, down the hall, at my door. My stomach nearly eclipsed itself. I retreated to my bed as the knock came.

"Come in," I wavered.

Maria entered my room and sat on the edge of my bed. Her manner was grave. "Your father told me what happened this afternoon."

"What part?"

"Oh, probably everything, but it's the last part that concerns me. You shouldn't have run into his office, Abby."

"I didn't mean to. I just got so excited about telling him something that I forgot."

"He realizes that. That's why he didn't come after you."

I nodded, thankful Daddy had accepted my mistake as such.

"But he wants you to understand it's never to happen again."

"It won't … Maria, do you know what he has in that room?"

"I know some. The rest is none of my business. Understand one thing, Abby. Your father and I had past lives when we met, and we both carry some of that into the present. As a result, we ask no questions and we respect each other's privacy. You must too."

All of a sudden I remembered where I'd smelled the perfume before—very faint in a letter, slightly stronger in the schoolhouse. "It's about my mother."

Maria's face remained expressionless. "I'm not going to comment."

"But he's hiding more secrets."

"I said I'm not discussing it. Stop thinking about it."

Seeing that she couldn't be swayed, I pretended to agree. "You're probably right. I'll stop thinking about it … is Daddy still mad at me? Can I come downstairs now?"

"That's the reason he sent me up here. You're to stay in your room for the rest of the night."

"And miss supper? I mean dinner?" I kept forgetting that "supper" didn't exist as a word in my father's lexicon.

"I'm afraid so."

"But I'm hungry. I didn't eat much at school today, and I know Daddy's frying chicken. I've smelled it for a half hour already, and I just love his fried chicken."

She patted my arm. "I'll see what I can do."

An hour later, Maria appeared with my measly dinner: one chicken wing, four carrot sticks, and a generous helping of beets. I reacted with revulsion.

"He said hunger makes beets more palatable … I'm sorry, Abby."

I'd have taken a lick or two with the belt if I could've eaten all the fried chicken I wanted that night. As it was, I savored the lone wing and devoured the carrots. The beets I flushed down the toilet. Modern conveniences had novel uses.

I tore through my homework, took my required bath, jumped in bed, and waited for my goodnight kiss.

My father did not come.

I could hear snippets of conversation from below. They were sitting together on the davenport, having a drink. His arm was draped around her and she was leaning back against him. I knew because the exact scene repeated itself every night after dinner.

On an ordinary night, after I finished the dishes, Maria would often invite me to sit between them, calling me the baloney in their sandwich. This would cause Daddy to grimace and pronounce us both silly geese.

But tonight they'd washed the dishes themselves and their baloney was upstairs, alone, wondering why their sandwich was so content without her.

Morning brought forgiveness. Daddy was cooking my favorite breakfast of pancakes and sausage when I came downstairs. It was his way of making things right between us.

"Is Maria gone already?" I said, testing his mood.

"Yes. Dayton's is starting inventory today, so she went in early."

"Here are my fifty sentences."

"Good." He gave my efforts a cursory glance, knowing how many lines to a page, and crumpled it up.

"I did my schoolwork … I took a bath … I'm sorry I ran into your office … I waited for you to come upstairs … last night so I could tell you," I said between bites.

"I couldn't. Better not to come than make things worse."

"You've made another secret room, like you had in the schoolhouse. Why'd you do that?"

"What I do has no explanation. Finish your breakfast; it's nearly time for the bus."

I finished eating in silence.

As I was packing my school bag, he said, "Bring me that farewell letter you have from your mother."

I froze. "But you've already read it."

"I didn't say I wanted to read it. I've already read the copy. I want the original."

"Will I get it back?" I hadn't had the foresight to make a second copy.

"Yes."

"Are you sure? You get mad and you burn things."

"Get it and get it now!" he erupted. "Remember, Abigail, you're gone seven hours a day. I can find whatever I'm looking for in a fraction of that time. You'd be wise not to make me look!"

I got it because I didn't want him finding the obituary, the locket, the hunting pictures, and my diary filled with complaints, chiefly about him. But I agonized over the safety of my letter until the natural course of the day's events superseded my concern.

I returned from school in a rage. "I hate school! I hate those kids! I hate everybody and everything about it!" I threw my books on the floor for maximum effect. One slid all the way to the dining room where Daddy sat with his afternoon coffee.

He kicked it back at me. "Then I'll teach you at home. If you can't fit in, you can't fit in. No sense screaming about it."

I suspended my theatrics, thinking I'd heard wrong. "But you can't teach me at home, Daddy. You're no teacher."

"No, but other parents teach their children at home. Why can't I?"

"I've never known anybody who did."

"It's usually done because the child has special problems or the parents are religious types who think public schools teach the wrong values. I'll call your school tomorrow and see what I need to do to get you out. By next week, Abigail, it should be just you and me."

"Really?"

"Really. I promise."

Calm again, I trudged upstairs and changed into my jeans.

Just like that, I could be done with that lousy school forever.

Just like that, I could be done with those fancy-pants snotty city kids who looked down their noses at me.

Just like that, I could be free from all of it.

Just like that, I could spend the next six years memorizing obscure vocabulary words and studying ponderous volumes of knowledge, courtesy of Daddy and the Hennepin County Library.

Just like that, my father would become my teacher, my mentor, my jailor. I would never get away from him, not for thirty-five hours a week, but never.

Never!

I tore downstairs and said I'd like to give my new school another chance. Maybe I wasn't trying to fit in. Maybe I wasn't trying to make new friends. Maybe if another new girl moved in, I could be friends with her. Maybe everything would be better next year.

"Are you sure? I was *so* looking forward to teaching you."

"Me, too … but I really think I should give it another try."

"Fine, as long as you stop complaining about it … oh, I nearly forgot." He produced a letter from his pocket. "Here, you can have this back."

I was greatly relieved to see Mother's letter whole and not ashes. "It's real, isn't it? It's her writing?"

"Yes, it's genuine."

"Why do you think she wrote it?"

"In case something happened to her in Africa."

"And something did."

"Yes, something did."

"But why didn't you have it, Daddy? Why did Uncle Jack have it?"

"I suppose she gave it to him for safekeeping."

"Wouldn't it have been safe with you?"

He paused. "Of course … but if I'd read it sooner, I would've stopped her."

"Stopped her from what? Going to Africa?"

"Yes … from going to Africa."

I detected a nearly indiscernible tremor in his voice. He was no longer looking at me. He was no longer telling me the truth.

Three days later, Commandment Eleven was added to Daddy's list. I had just walked in the door from school.

"Explain this!" Daddy clenched a letter in his hand. He was livid.

I pretended innocence. "Who's that from?"

"Margaret Monson!"

"Um … I thought you liked letters."

"Sure, I like letters. I like letters from meddling former teachers who take it upon themselves to instruct me on how to treat my own daughter! Don't ever pull this shit again, Abigail. What happens in this family, stays in this family, understand?"

"Yes." I edged away from him.

He followed me. "And what drivel are you writing to Annie? And Darrell? Are you complaining about me to them too?"

"No. I promise, Daddy, I haven't!" To them, I was still pretending my new life was perfect.

"I'll bet! From now on, I want to see all your letters. Put them right here on the table. After I read them, I'll stamp and mail them. Understand?"

"Yes." I understood censorship.

I also understood that I'd gone too far. The filly, wild as the west wind, had been reigned in, sharply.

Summer 1946

Mrs. Jack Stahl

By spring, my fairy tale existence with my father had edged closer to reality. Apparently we both had required a period of adjustment. Maria served as mediator, smoothing over our frequent altercations with gentle persuasion and wry humor.

Daddy turned out to be a competent, albeit overbearing, teacher. Whatever I wanted to know, he provided an answer. If he didn't know, he found out. Gradually my horizons expanded to include his interests—art and history. And he allowed me time for my own pursuits. Creative writing swiftly became my passion, putting to good use my extensive vocabulary.

My riding lessons progressed satisfactorily. No longer was I sentenced to the gentlest of nags, but to a younger mare with spirit. Daisy and I came to an abrupt understanding one day when she reared and I reacted the way I'd been taught, rather than panicking.

School remained an ordeal, although I learned to ignore my tormentors and made friends with another new girl. Only on occasion, usually after a letter from Darrell, did I cave to self-pity. Then I'd climb to my Africa room, curl up in my easy chair, and have a good cry.

Aunt Annie had corresponded faithfully with Daddy and me throughout the winter and spring. I found the closing paragraphs of her May nineteenth letter to be of particular interest.

We're hoping Abby can come down for a month or so this summer. She'd have fun, as the kids don't have so much work to do since Jack hired two brothers to help around here. Maybe you know them, Ron and Rueben Simon? They work for us weekday mornings and help Maynard farm the home place the rest of the time. It's been wonderful for everyone. Did I mention before that Ole retired? As Jack says, "He's sleeping in his own bed now instead of on the job!"

We've had the strangest weather this spring: thunderstorms, heavy rains, even a tornado touchdown at St. James that ripped the roof off the pool hall and damaged the Ben Franklin, but no loss of life. Nothing severe around here, so far, and I hope it stays that way.

If you decide to bring Abby, you and Maria are welcome to stay and eat with us. I'd like to get to know her better. But if you'd rather drop Abby off and go again, that's okay too, but please bring her either way. We really miss having her here, but I'm glad she's happy there with you. I was praying she would be.

Let me know what you decide.

Love, Annie

"Oh, Daddy, can I? Will you drive me down for a visit?"

"I don't know … I hadn't planned on it." He tucked the letter back in its envelope to reread later. "Well, I suppose I'll have to or that sparkle in your eyes will turn to tears."

"Then it's a yes? Oh, thank you, Daddy! Thank you a million times!" I flung my arms around his neck and then ran upstairs to pack, three weeks early.

Daddy drove me down alone, as Maria had to work, but at least he took me. He greeted Aunt Annie at the back door, tarried long enough for a beer, and left. Uncle Jack was predictably absent. He'd gone to town a half hour before we arrived.

"Hey, city slicker; thought you'd be too good for the likes of us," Darrell teased when he saw me. His copper hair was awry. His hands were grimy. He wore ragged jeans and nothing else. I could hardly wait to change from my matching outfit, kick off my shoes, and be like him.

Dennis wrinkled his nose when he passed me on the stairs. "Don't tell me you're going to be my teacher again!"

I shook my head, noting how he'd matured in only six months. "No, I'm just here on vacation for a few weeks."

"Good." His freckles spread across his cheeks as he grinned.

After a few minutes of awkwardness, it seemed like old times between me and Darrell. We explored the slough. We played checkers and cribbage. After supper, we drank lemonade on the porch far into the night, watching fireflies and telling lies. Since it was my first night back, Uncle Jack had waived our bedtime.

"Find anything interesting since I've been gone?" I asked.

"Like more mysterious letters or pictures?"

I nodded.

"Nope, I think Dad got rid of that stuff … how about you?"

"I thought Daddy had too, when he burned the schoolhouse, but he's hiding more in his office. Creepy, musty, dark things. I got a quick look once when I barged in there by accident. I've been racking my brain ever since, trying to figure how to get inside long enough to snoop."

"I bet he keeps a lock on the door."

"Of course."

"You can pick a lock, if you know how," Darrell suggested.

"You mean open it without the key?"

"That's exactly what I mean."

"Sounds complicated."

"Probably, but locksmiths learn how … burglars too."

"Well, Daddy sure won't be sending me to locksmith school." I snickered. "I can't get near that door. He hovers like a broody hen every minute I'm home."

"Even broody hens get off the nest now and then. Sherlock has faith in his Watson."

More than I do in myself, I thought.

Molly, asleep at my feet, yipped softly, her legs jerking in rhythm. She'd worn herself out tearing around the yard in happiness from seeing me again, and now she was dream-chasing rabbits. I closed my eyes and relished the chirp of the crickets and the creak of my own rocker. Far away, on the Monson farm, a dog barked. Another answered from the Swanson's … familiar sounds, comforting sounds.

Sounds I had missed.

The next morning, Uncle Jack took Darrell and me fishing on Wood Lake. Between his stabbing our many bullheads and adding our few crappies to the stringer, I told him how I'd finished beginning riding lessons.

He was impressed. So much so, that when we got home, he immediately offered me Banat so we could go riding.

"But she's too fast!"

"Oh, you'll be fine. She doesn't run nearly as fast since she hurt her leg."

I accepted his offer. If I hadn't, my lessons had been for nothing. Riding Banat was akin to straddling a rocket, but I managed. Uncle Jack rode Chestnut, a bay stallion, while Darrell rode Profit, a recently acquired mare. When I questioned the odd name, my uncle said he intended to breed her and make a tidy profit from her offspring.

It was only the first of many rides I enjoyed during my month at the farm. Besides the riding and the fishing, the gardening and the visiting, I practiced with my new .22, a gift from Uncle Jack. He said I was to keep it at the farm so his brother wouldn't find out.

All too soon, my vacation came to a close. Daddy called early that morning, saying Maria had to cover for someone who was sick, so he was driving down alone. He planned to arrive at the Swansons by noon, visit with Vinnie, and pick me up first thing the following morning.

After a leisurely breakfast, my last at the farm for the summer, Uncle Jack went outside to tend the horses. Aunt Annie assembled a casserole for our noon meal and started a fruit pie. Dennis rode his new bike to a neighbor's to play, promising to be back in time to eat. Duane flopped on the davenport with one of my Tarzan comics, while Darrell and I started a game of checkers.

Being a Saturday, neither hired man was available when Uncle Jack decided that he needed something from town. He stuck his head in the kitchen for a moment and asked whether my aunt wanted him to pick anything up, since he was driving in.

"I don't think you should, Jack. The sky looks pretty dark. We might be in for another storm."

"Oh, it doesn't look so bad. I'll be back before you know it."

"In that case, get me some tapioca. I'm making pie for dessert tonight, and I noticed I'm out."

"Okay, back soon."

Aunt Annie had just remarked how unsettled Molly and Ranger were acting when the wind picked up and it began to rain. Soon the wind and rain escalated into a violent thunderstorm, not fifteen minutes after my uncle had left. My aunt flitted from one window to another, keeping a watchful eye on the cottonwoods near the house as they bent in the strong winds. Lightning flashed, causing the electricity to flicker twice, but both times it came back again.

"Well, at least Jack made it to town before it hit and Dennis will stay where he's at," she said to no one in particular.

"Yeah, Mom, everybody's fine," Darrell said. "Hey, look at this, Abby! I've got your kings cornered. You're going down."

"I hate you, Darrell." I didn't really, but I sure hated how lucky he was.

The rain stopped as abruptly as it had started.

"Good, that's over." Aunt Annie poured herself a cup of coffee and sat down at the table. "Sudden storms make me nervous. You never know whether they'll lead to something worse or when they're going to end."

"Well, this one's ended." I made a final, desperate jump.

"You're right two ways. The storm's done and you're done." Darrell jumped my remaining king. "Pay up, little cousin."

I slapped my last dime on the table. "There, you jackass, I hope you're happy!"

"Abby!" Aunt Annie said. "Does your father permit you to say words like that?"

"Um … not really," I said, hoping she wouldn't tell him.

"I didn't think so, and I don't like to hear them either. It's bad enough the words some people use around here, but for you to—"

I stifled a grin. "I'm sorry, Auntie. I won't call Darrell a jackass anymore."

She shook her head and let it go. She probably knew she was bucking the tide, the way her husband and my father expressed themselves.

While Darrell put our game away, I poured milk and dug the last of the oatmeal cookies out of the cookie jar for us to enjoy.

"Looks like I need to bake again," Aunt Annie said. "What's that?" She cocked her head to the side.

"What's what?" Darrell mumbled, his mouth already full.

"That noise … listen."

A rumble in the distance grew sharper and louder. We ran to the porch and saw that the low, indistinct form roiling across the Swansons' cornfield was neither rain nor a patch of fog, but a grayish cloud rotating beneath a heavier, darker mass extending from the southwest corner of what appeared to be another fast-approaching thunderstorm.

"Dear God, it's a tornado and it's coming right at us!" Aunt Annie effectively combined prayer with panic. She hustled Darrell and me through the main part of the house and grabbed Duane along her route. *"To the cellar, now!"* She flicked on the basement light as we kids scrambled down the creaking steps. When we had reached the bottom, she tossed Darrell a flashlight. "Here, catch! Keep it off unless you need it; I'll be there in a minute!"

At Darrell's insistence, we sought refuge next to the rock wall of the old cistern. Duane had wanted to sit at the bottom of the stairs, but Darrell overruled him, saying the cistern would keep the house from crushing us, if all collapsed.

Duane burst into tears. "I don't want to get squashed! I want to find Mommy! Where's she? Why doesn't she come?"

He tried to stand, but Darrell roughly yanked him down. "Stay here, you idiot! Mom went to shut the windows, that's all. Tell him, Abby!"

"She'll come after she shuts the windows," I said. "Stop crying. She'll be coming, just you wait and—"

The storm whistling outside intensified to a deafening roar. The lightbulb dangling over our heads exploded. Everything went black.

Duane screamed. I screamed.

"Turn on the flashlight!" I groped for the light, but found Darrell's arm instead. "Turn it on, I'm scared!"

"Not yet!" Darrell twisted his arm free. "This storm could last for hours.

We have to save the battery to help Mom down the steps. We can sit in the dark for now … shut up, Duane! Shut up before I punch you!"

There was nothing I could do. Darrell had the flashlight and I didn't. Duane found my lap, wrapped his thin arms around my shoulders, and cried on my neck. His small chest heaved. His heart pounded maniacally. Or was it my own?

Where was Aunt Annie? She wasn't shutting windows—even I knew that! What was she really doing? And what was that hideous noise? What was happening upstairs? And outside?

The very air seemed to vibrate with unearthly sound, howling and wailing, as the tornado approached the house, sucking at windows and walls, peeling away whatever it could. As my eyes adjusted to the dim light, I saw debris tumbling past the small basement window. Above us, the house groaned and cracked, its foundation shifting in the brutal wind. A barrage of hail began, hail the size of plums. Ice accumulated on the ground outside and piled against the window.

I wanted to cover my ears against the horrific sound, but Duane was clutching me in a death grip and I couldn't move, I couldn't move at all, but I could pray: *Oh God, I don't want to die this way, none of us wants to die this way, dear God make it stop, make it stop, save Auntie, where is she, what's she doing up there with the house coming apart over our heads, oh God, make her come back, make her come, oh dear God help us all!*

The hail ended. A moment later the rain returned; menacing swirls of water, dark and fierce. It seemed to go on forever.

Then the world fell silent.

Until we heard the screaming.

The screams catapulted the three of us from the cellar. We'd been waiting to see whether the tornado had indeed passed or more was yet to come. We raced up the stairs, through the kitchen, which by some miracle seemed intact, and out to the yard.

There we saw Dennis kneeling by a blue dress.

We picked our way over and around the broken limbs of a shattered cottonwood, near what remained of the porch. Mrs. Jack Stahl lay sprawled on the ground, her mouth open with the start of a shriek, her eyes wide as though with surprise. A shard of glass had pierced her throat. A crimson rivulet bubbled from the jagged wound. More blood had already pooled beneath her head.

"No, no, no!" Duane cried. "Wake up, Mommy, wake up!"

Dennis stopped his screams and started to sob. I saw him rub his mother's hands, but he never looked at her face. He never looked at her eyes—her eyes that had last seen him, and then had seen nothing.

I stood mute, unable to process the unspeakable horror before me. *Oh God, why'd you let this happen, Auntie didn't deserve this, she didn't, she never hurt anybody, my cousins need her, my uncle needs her, and this isn't fair, it just isn't fair!*

Darrell's face went white. Standing stoically by my side, he began to sway. I reached out to steady him. *I couldn't be the strong one,* I thought, *I couldn't …*

Thankfully I didn't have to be. Brakes squealed as two cars ground to an abrupt halt beyond the fallen branches. Daddy and Uncle Jack raced from their respective cars toward us.

My uncle reached her first. Darrell and I made way for him as he fell to his knees beside the twins. Gathering her up, he cradled her in his arms. "Oh, my God … oh, my God, Annie … Annie," he moaned as he rocked her back and forth. "Please God, no … no.…"

He was crying. He was actually *crying.* It was the most horrible sight I'd ever seen: Uncle Jack rocking Aunt Annie in her blue dress within a sea of broken green. I stood mesmerized, staring but not wanting to stare, overwhelmed with compassion but at the same time feeling somehow removed from the tragedy, as though it weren't real, as though it couldn't be real.

But it was. I felt Daddy's hand on my shoulder. Darrell, looking sick, stepped back of his own volition and ran for the house. Daddy pulled back the twins, both of whom continued to cry profusely. Duane rushed after Darrell, but Dennis slumped to the ground near my feet.

My father scooped him up and held him tightly. "Nothing you can do, son. There's nothing you can do for her now."

"But I … killed her … I killed her!" Dennis choked on his tears.

"No, you didn't kill her. The tornado killed her."

"But she ran outside … yelling for me to get off my bike and hide in the culvert … she'd be alive if it wasn't for me … I thought I could beat the storm … I never thought—I never thought—I'd kill her … "

Daddy's pale eyes flashed anger, but his voice remained low, soothing. "You didn't know a twister was coming when you went out on the road, did you?"

"No … "

"Then you didn't do anything on purpose that caused her to die. It just happened. Bad things happen sometimes. The tornado killed her, Dennis. I never want to hear you blame yourself ever again. Understand?"

"Yes … "

"Remember what I said. All you can do now is be brave and carry on the best you can. You have to be brave for your brothers and your father, especially your father. It's harder for a man to lose his wife than for a child to lose his mother because a man expects to grow old with his wife, while the child will simply grow and be gone … do you understand me?"

My cousin's reply was muffled against my father's shoulder.

"No, of course you don't," Daddy said. "I'm talking way over your head."

Several cars and the fire truck had gradually lined up behind one another at the end of our driveway. Friends and neighbors clustered in small groups, keeping a respectful distance, conversing in hushed tones.

"Daddy." I tugged at his arm.

"Not now, Abby … here, take care of Dennis."

I wrapped my arms around my cousin and felt him quiver as he tried to be brave, as he tried to carry on the best he could. I couldn't think of anything to say to him.

Daddy took charge. He asked someone to notify the funeral home and Reverend Richter. He told the volunteer firemen to go and see whether others might need their help. He made arrangements for my cousins to spend the night with Uncle Vic and Aunt Emma and for me to leave with the Swansons. He said he planned to stay with his brother throughout the long night ahead.

Uncle Jack had finally grown quiet. He lay Aunt Annie down, gently, for the last time. With trembling fingers, he closed her green eyes. He caressed her cheek and kissed her parted lips for the last time. Then he drew his hands across his face and tried to compose himself. After several minutes, he got to his feet and walked toward us. As one oblivious to the earth beneath him or the carnage surrounding him, he walked.

Our friends and neighbors immediately encircled him. Handkerchiefs appeared from pockets. Aprons blotted eyes. Condolences were murmured. Aunt Emma embraced him. So did Mrs. Swanson. Sympathies were extended to Darrell and Duane, who had reappeared. Dennis clung to me like a tick until Uncle Vic, with tears streaming down his own face, pried him off.

Aunt Emma sought me out. Enveloped in her ample arms, I dissolved. She matched me tear for tear. She understood my pain. She knew how much Auntie had meant to me.

Apparently Daddy did not, as he made no effort to comfort me. As before, he was all business. He told Vinnie Swanson to arrange for the repair of the electric and telephone lines. When Rueben and Ron arrived, having seen the tornado touch down from their own farm, he asked them to check the livestock. When they reported numerous missing cattle, one dead horse, and the total loss of the henhouse, Daddy said the collateral damage didn't seem too bad, considering.

Reverend Richter and Dr. Jorgenson arrived. Minutes later, the car from the funeral home came and bore Aunt Annie away.

By this time, Uncle Jack's initial shock had worn off. His agitation grew. He interrupted Daddy's discussion with the reverend. Dr. Jorgenson recommended a sedative. Uncle Jack rebuked him. Daddy concurred with the good doctor. Uncle Jack unleashed a tirade against my father. Daddy walked away. Dr. Jorgenson shook his head and drove off. Reverend Richter tried to calm my uncle with appropriate, although largely ineffectual, platitudes.

Daddy instructed us kids to get our things together for overnight and leave with those he'd designated to care for us. Uncle Vic shepherded Dennis. Darrell took Duane's hand. I followed them, walking as though in a dream, a very sad and awful dream.

But I had no intention of leaving. If my father was too busy to give me his undivided attention now, I'd stay and await my turn. I procrastinated until everyone had gone except the Swansons, who continued to wait for me at the end of the driveway. I could see their car from my bedroom window.

Apparently no one realized I was still in the house, because as Uncle Jack and Daddy entered, they were already engaged in a heated exchange. I'd never heard such hateful words pass between two people, least of all two brothers.

"Get the hell away from me!" Uncle Jack was shouting.

"No, I'm not leaving," Daddy told him. "And this is hardly the time for arguments. You can't be alone—"

"I can and I will. Get out!"

"Forget it, Jack. I'm staying the night, whether you like it or not."

"Is that so?"

"Yes, that's so."

"Well, you're not calling the shots now, are you? You've nothing on me now, do you?"

"This is hardly the time to talk about that."

"You'll talk about whatever I goddamn well want to talk about! And all I want to hear out of you right now is that you're leaving!"

"For the second time, Jack, you can't be alone, at least not yet. Maybe later, after you're feeling better—"

"Feeling better?" Uncle Jack mocked. "Listen to you! I've just lost Annie and already you talk about feeling better?"

"That's not what I meant and you know it."

"I don't give a damn what you meant. I don't have to listen to you. I don't have to do what you want. My life is ruined, but you've wanted that for years, haven't you?"

Uncle Jack was pacing, judging from the varying direction of his shouted words. Daddy was following, trying to placate him. Appalled as I was by their confrontation, I couldn't help but hope to learn the problem between them. I crept halfway down the steps to listen.

"No, you're wrong," Daddy said. "I never wanted that. I just wanted—"

"For me to suffer? Was that it, James? That goddamn little game you liked to play, the turning of the screws? You wanted it to go on forever, but now it's over. With Annie gone, I've nothing left to lose."

"I'm so sorry about her. I really and truly am. Annie was a wonderful—"

"Don't say her name!" Uncle Jack spat. "Don't even say her name, after that shit you tried! Refresh my memory—was it once or was it twice? Didn't think I knew, did you? But she was better than you. She was far better than either of us."

"Yes, and for what it's worth, I'm sorry about my end of it."

Uncle Jack laughed—a mirthless, hollow laugh that set my hair on end. "What, you're sorry? You're actually sorry about something? To think of all the years I've waited to hear that—I can hardly believe it."

"Believe it, and I think we should take it to the next logical level."

"Which is what?"

"Forgiveness."

"Shit, you couldn't forgive me if I were roasting in hell like a chestnut."

"Maybe not, but I'm willing to try. We've both made mistakes—terrible mistakes—but we're still brothers, Jack. It's time to forgive and forget."

"Oh, come now. Surely you can do better than that. 'Forgive and forget' just sounds so goddamn trite, doesn't it?"

"Yes," Daddy admitted. "But it's appropriate."

"Tell you what," Uncle Jack said. "We'll settle the score and we'll settle it for good."

"How?"

"Did you bring your Luger with you?"

"Of course."

"Where is it?"

"My car."

"Get it."

"Why?"

"I want you to kill me."

My gasp nearly gave me away. I heard a similar reaction from downstairs, followed by a prolonged pause.

"Don't be ridiculous," Daddy said finally.

"I'm not. I mean it. You've held it to my head before. Instead of just scaring the piss out of me, you can finish me off this time."

"You're out of your mind, Jack."

"My mind's fine."

"No, it's not. It's your grief talking. I'm not doing that."

"But you nearly did it before."

"I was blind drunk. I didn't know what I was doing, except I knew enough not to pull the trigger."

"Then I'll help you over the hump. We'll both get drunk, starting right now. I've got a cabinet full of whatever soaks your head these days. The damn tornado didn't touch it. Suck enough down and you'll be able to do it. You can hold that gun to my head and reminisce about all the shit I've pulled on you—"

"Stop it, Jack."

"—and you can fill in the juicy little details, however you like—"

"Stop it, I said."

"—and if there's something you've been wondering about, just ask—"

"Shut your goddamned mouth!"

"I knew I could get you going," Uncle Jack said. "To think of all the time I've wasted. I've lost sleep. I've drunk too much. I've worried myself sick, all to keep you from blowing your stack. Now I'm doing it on purpose … rather funny, if you think about it. Don't you think it's funny?"

"No," Daddy said. "Nothing you're saying is the least bit funny."

"Then let's change the subject … when would you like to bump me off? How about tonight, after I've sweetened the pot?"

"Shut up, you're making me sick."

"Be sick then. You can't make me shut up. Not until you shoot me. Won't that be a relief? All that goddamned peace and quiet. Almost make you forget I was ever here … oh hell, I'm getting maudlin. That's a good word, isn't it?"

"Shut up, Jack."

"All right, I'll shut up … we'll just quietly start imbibing. That's a good word too, isn't it? We'll drink until I'm dead. You can do it tonight, in the dark. You've done other things, haven't you, without even waiting for dark?"

"You don't know what you're talking about."

"Oh, I do … I really do. But that's not the topic of the hour now, is it? For once in your life, you're going to listen to me, James. … are you listening?"

"I'm listening."

"Good. Then understand this: I don't want to live. I can't go on without her. I can't. It's too much."

"It's not too much. I survived and so will you. Don't be such a goddamned coward."

"You're right, I am a coward. I want to die, but I'm afraid of the process. I want it done right, and I know you won't hesitate. You won't botch it. You're my chosen executioner, James. You're perfect for the job because you've killed before, haven't you?"

"In war."

"And not in war?"

"Again, you don't know what the hell you're talking about."

"Don't I?"

"No, you don't! For God's sake, Jack, stop talking about it! Stop talking about what's past and start talking about right now!"

"Fine ... what's your pleasure?"

From my perch on the landing, I heard the clink of glass.

"Nothing," Daddy said.

"That's a first. I'll have both yours and mine then."

"Have as many as you like as long as you come to your senses."

"Like I told you before, my senses are fine. Maybe it's my way of punishing myself for what I did, but I want to be with her, even if we're just dirt in the ground. I'll make it easy for you, James. I'll point your gun at my own head. You make the minor adjustments. Then you pull the trigger. No one will ever suspect. Bereaved widower finds brother's gun, kills self, a double tragedy. Slant my obit any way you damn please."

"I can't believe what I'm hearing."

"Believe it. Do it and it'll pay off too. My will left everything to Annie, but now she's gone. I've bypassed my kids in favor of you. Think of it as my pathetic little way of making up, James. You'll be so rich you'll stink. You'll have everything, even my kids."

"I don't want any of it. I don't need any of it. As for your kids—think about them, will you? I'm too old to raise your family. I'm not their father. They need you, not me. You'll destroy them if you persist with this insane idea of yours."

"Oh, but I *have* thought about them. You're always the good soldier. You'll step in and do your duty. You always do. They'll have you, Maria, and all that lovely money. And you'll take such good care of them. I know you will. After all, haven't you started already? How does it feel being a daddy?"

"Go to hell."

"I probably will, but I won't be there alone. You'll be coming to see me, won't you?"

"Not if I can help it."

"You will. We're both apples off the same tree, aren't we? Rotten apples."

"Stop all this stupid talk. Talk about something that makes sense. Talk about getting through this and getting your kids back."

"No … here. You do need a drink."

"No, not until—"

The screen door slammed as Vinnie Swanson walked into the house and asked for me. I clutched the newel post to avoid falling down the steps. *I had forgotten about them still waiting for me!*

An ominous silence prevailed in the room below. Vinnie repeated his request.

"Abby?" Daddy said, sounding peculiar. "I thought she'd already left."

"No. We've been waiting in the car while she got her things together. I saw her go in the house, but I never saw her come out. Is she still upstairs?"

"Upstairs?" Uncle Jack repeated.

How could I escape? The trellis? I fled to my room and peered out the shattered window. The trellis was gone! I swallowed my pounding heart, grabbed my bag, and decided to saunter past Daddy and Uncle Jack like I hadn't heard a thing. I promptly lost my nerve, flew down the steps, and raced outside. Down the driveway I ran, dodging fallen branches, until I hopped in Mr. Swanson's car. I started crying, I was so scared.

"Oh, you poor dear," Mrs. Swanson commiserated. "Go ahead, cry it out. You'll feel better for it. Such a wonderful person your aunt was, taken from us far too soon … "

I neglected to correct the misunderstanding. The truth would be more than the old lady could bear. It certainly was more than I could bear. Minutes later, I sat on the Swansons' porch and filled several of Mr. Swanson's red handkerchiefs. Wallowing in grief was beneficial, I'd been told, so I wallowed mightily. But I scarcely thought of Aunt Annie. I thought of two men, a gun, and the inevitability of night.

Eventually Mrs. Swanson summoned me to supper. Their farm had escaped with only minor damage from the tornado, so the utilities still worked. She knew fried chicken was my favorite, so she'd prepared it especially for me, with sides of German potatoes and baked beans.

Oddly enough, the tragedy had little effect on my appetite. I'd just sat down to partake when we heard a car coming up the drive.

Mrs. Swanson went to the back door. "It's your father, dear."

I lost my appetite with those four words. I heard her extend an invitation for Daddy and Uncle Jack, if he was able, to join us for supper, but Daddy declined. He only wanted to talk to me.

I came to the door as calmly as possible. Without saying a word, he took me by the arm and marched me to the far side of the Swansons' barn. Not a good omen. He plunked me down on a bale and stood glowering over me.

"How dare you eavesdrop on us! What the hell's wrong with you?"

"I'm sorry, Daddy," I whimpered. "I was upstairs when you and Uncle Jack came in yelling, and I didn't know how to get away."

"And you didn't know how to alert us to your presence either? Don't give me that shit! You're not that stupid!"

I cringed. I was that stupid or I wouldn't be in the predicament I was in.

My father lit a cigarette and paced briefly before zeroing in on me again. "All right, Abigail. I want to know how much you overheard."

"Everything, from the time you came in." It didn't seem prudent to lie, crossed fingers or not.

"That's what I figured." He took a deep drag on the cigarette. "And what did you understand from all of that?"

I thought for a minute, sorting the facts from the cursing and shouting. What seemed so clear at the time had already gotten muddled, although a few things stood out.

"Well?" Daddy said.

"That Uncle Jack thinks he doesn't have to listen to you anymore."

"And why does he think that?"

"Um … I don't know."

"What else?"

"You wanted to forgive and forget, but he didn't."

"What were we supposed to forgive?"

"Each other."

"That's not what I meant. Specifically, what did we do that needed forgiveness?"

"I don't know, Daddy."

"Good … and then what did Jack ask me to do?"

I paused, unwilling to think about that part.

"I know you heard, because it went on for a long time. What did Jack ask me to do?"

"Shoot him," I whispered.

"And why would he ask such a thing?"

"He's lonely and sad. He doesn't want to live without Auntie."

"Correct. And what did I say to his awful request?"

"You said no."

"Correct again. What else do you remember?"

"Nothing much, until Uncle Jack wanted you to start drinking and you didn't want to. That's when Mr. Swanson walked in." I had realized the less

I seemed to have remembered or understood, the better my chances of being forgiven. In actuality, I remembered Uncle Jack saying Daddy had held a gun to his head once before and he'd accused Daddy of killing someone not in war. The first could explain why my uncle thanked me so profusely for my middle-of-the-night phone call last summer. The second reminded me again of my mother's dress with the bullet hole.

"Have you mentioned any of this to the Swansons?"

I shook my head.

"Are you sure? Was there anything—anything at all—you've repeated?"

"No. I didn't want to think about it, much less talk about it."

He stamped out the cigarette and sat next to me on the bale. "Thank God, because if you had, it'd be all over town in five minutes. The Swansons are fine people, but they carry news better than a pail carries water. And this doesn't need to be spread around … in fact, nothing needs to be said because nothing is going to happen."

I looked at him in surprise. "Then Uncle Jack—"

"—isn't going to do what he said."

"He changed his mind?"

"I'm not sure. I don't think he was totally serious to begin with. A man intending to end his own life will generally do it himself, not ask for assistance." Daddy appeared to weigh his words. "He knew I wouldn't do it. That was all theatrics—a plea for help, so to speak. And I will help him, Abby, as much as he'll let me. I'll do what I can and the rest will be up to him. He's got three sons to rear, and I hope he'll be able to cope again fairly soon."

I slipped my arm around my father's waist. "I'm so glad, Daddy. I was hoping we could stay and help. Please don't be mad at him anymore."

"Whatever I do for him will be a hell of a lot more than he did for me." Daddy pursed his lips and stared past me.

Was he thinking of the time long ago when the trouble started? Would he—could he—forgive? And would his forgiveness heal the festering wound that was tearing our family apart?

I needed forgiveness too. The last words Auntie had heard out of my big mouth had been me calling Darrell a jackass. I wished God would reset his eternal clock and suck the tornado back into the sky so I could apologize to her instead of making fun. I wished she could add the tapioca and bake her pie for the wonderful farewell supper she'd planned for me, and all I'd have to do this evening was eat and enjoy being with them instead of sitting on a bale by Vinnie Swanson's barn beside a father who still hadn't comforted me with the wind blowing through the hole in my soul because I'd lost someone so special to me and I hadn't realized it until it had been too late.

It occurred to me that life went on and on and on, and then suddenly it didn't, and I began weeping.

"Your concern for my brother is rather touching," Daddy said, misreading the cause of my tears. "You'll be relieved to know I've taken him to Dr. Jorgenson. He's gotten a medication to help him sleep. That's what I've been doing since you left—arguing with him, trying to convince him that he needed help to get through the next few days. He finally listened to me."

I accepted Daddy's offering of a handkerchief. "Where is he now?"

"In my car."

"Your car? But I didn't see him before!"

"You weren't looking. As always, you were too concerned for yourself. Why do you think Elsie asked the both of us to supper?"

"But your gun's in the car, Daddy!"

"No, it's locked in the trunk."

"Your car keys?"

"Right here." He patted his pocket. "And I'll be locking up Jack's liquor because he can't be drinking on top of the medication. I've already secured his gun cabinet."

"Good." I breathed easier.

"Like I said, Abby, he's in my car. He's sedated. He may even be asleep. But you need to say something to him. He'll wake up long enough to hear."

"What should I say?"

"Something comforting."

"Why me?"

"Because it would mean the world to him."

I had no idea why my words would mean more to Uncle Jack than the condolences of others, but Daddy knew more about these things than I did. We walked to the car together.

My uncle was slouched in the front passenger seat, asleep. His neck and shirt were smeared with Aunt Annie's blood. His arm rested limply on the door frame of the rolled-down window.

I touched his hand. "Uncle Jack, it's me, Abby."

His eyes opened to slits. "You sneaky little shit."

Even my own father hadn't nailed my eavesdropping with such scathing accuracy! Startled, I turned to Daddy. "What am I supposed to say now?"

"Say the truth."

I wondered what that might be. Uncle Jack remained motionless, but his red-rimmed eyes continued to watch me. Then it occurred to me.

I took his hand again. "Uncle Jack, I'm so sorry about today. It's been the most awful day ever, and I don't want anything else terrible to happen. I'm sorry I listened, but maybe I heard so I could ask you not to do what you said. Please, Uncle Jack, please be safe. I couldn't stand it if something bad happened to you."

His fingers tightened over mine. "Why do you care?"

"Because ... because I love you, Uncle Jack. I do ... I love you."

He closed his eyes and turned away his face.

"You didn't have to go that far, did you?" Daddy muttered as he got in the car.

"You told me to say the truth."

I had to do my best to save my uncle. He'd never know his wife's love again. My paltry expression of affection could never replace hers, but it might help. A medication couldn't shield him from his sorrow, from his loneliness, from himself.

All of us had to band together and love him now—even Daddy.

Aftermath

Daddy retrieved me from the Swansons the next morning. Since I was already cognizant of the situation, my unhappy duty became to shadow my uncle in his own house. Daddy thought his brother wouldn't attempt anything foolish, but he couldn't be positive.

Uncle Jack's medication seemed wholly inadequate, as he alternated between unprovoked belligerence and outbursts of profound grief. My shepherding efforts went unappreciated, and the morning crawled.

Daddy began his duties by sorting through the perishables. He made sure his brother didn't see him dispose of the pie shell my aunt had readied prior to the tornado. As chance would have it, the linemen from the county cobbled together the electric line soon after he'd finished.

Rueben and Ron arrived after church to begin the cleanup. They brought a tuna casserole, biscuits, and an apple pie, courtesy of their mother. Additional sustenance would be delivered by the parishioners later in the day.

Daddy wanted the hired men to start clearing the driveway, but Uncle Jack insisted that they begin with what remained of the porch. He seemed lost without his special place where he'd sat each evening, weather permitting, for as long as he'd owned his home. He even demanded new rockers be purchased immediately to replace the ones that had blown away. To placate him, I offered him the two from my room. Daddy had intended to take them along to Minneapolis at the end of my summer stay, but my uncle's needs surpassed my own.

Uncle Jack accepted readily. Dragging a rocker to a private area on the side of the house, he sat there for hours, smoking. I sat some distance away and watched.

When he came back inside, he laid down the law. He said that he didn't give a damn about the chickens or the chicken house. He'd always hated hearing the roosters crowing at dawn and eggs were a dime a dozen from Mrs. Monson. Neither did he care about the missing Angus or the dead Arabian. Cows were cows, one as dumb as the next, and the horse must've been a brainless mutant to have smashed its head against its stall just because a tornado was roaring outside. It deserved to end up as dog food.

Neither Annie's garden nor her flowers would ever be replanted. He'd purchase his vegetables from the bounteous gardens of others, and he'd had his fill of flowers anyway. Flowers needed nurturing. Bare ground suited him better. Bare ground didn't require water, weeding, fertilizer. My God, he was only one man—he couldn't do everything!

He demanded a timetable of Daddy. The porch would take four, maybe five days? Abruptly he decided that my father was right—the driveway needed clearing first to enable the lumberyard to deliver the materials needed for reconstruction. How long would that take? Two days or three?

Next he rattled off a list of repairs: siding as needed, shingles on the house and barns, windowpanes as needed, a new silo! Plus the grove cleaned up and another garage erected! And he wanted everything done immediately—he had money; he had lots of money! Work Rueben and Ron from sunrise to sundown! Hire additional help: Mennonites, Congregationalists, Lutherans ... hell, hire the Catholics! Hire the whole goddamn town, just get the job done!

When the rant ceased, Daddy simply nodded.

Uncle Jack was wire, becoming unspooled.

After a mid-afternoon meal of casserole, biscuits, and pie, Daddy announced that it was time to go to town to arrange the funeral.

Uncle Jack said he couldn't. Daddy said he must.

Uncle Jack said Daddy should go ahead and do it. Daddy said he must.

Uncle Jack exploded with a barrage of foul language that set my ears to tingling. Then he went to town with Daddy.

I collapsed in my uncle's easy chair. Through the window, I saw Rueben and Ron clearing the driveway, using saws and the John Deere to pull away the larger sections of felled trees. I shut my eyes for a second and didn't open them again until my father and my uncle returned, two hours later.

Both looked haggard. Daddy tossed a pair of new black trousers over a chair. I supposed he'd be borrowing the rest of his funeral clothes from his brother. Uncle Jack carried a brown paper sack. He went upstairs without saying a word.

Daddy unlocked the liquor cabinet and poured himself a double bourbon.

"What's Uncle Jack doing?"

"How should I know? I can't spy on the man in his bedroom. Hopefully he'll go to sleep. That's what I need, God knows."

"What's in the sack?"

"Her dress."

"Whose dress? Auntie's?"

"Of course."

"The dress she was wearing when she died?" Uncle Jack taking her bloody dress into their bedroom struck me as morbid.

"Yes."

"Why did he keep it?"

"Why did I keep your mother's?" Daddy paused to knock back his drink. "Why does a man do whatever he does when he loses his wife? Stop all the damn questions and leave me alone! I'll find you when I need you!"

I slunk outside and raked branches. At least the hired men were appreciative. After they quit for the day, I returned to the house. Daddy had set out my supper, but I ate alone. Both he and Uncle Jack were upstairs sleeping. *Good*, I thought. Maybe things will be better when they awoke.

Or maybe not. The funeral was still to come.

My cousins returned the following afternoon, sober but rested and well fed. Aunt Emma believed wholeheartedly that a good night's sleep and a full stomach made sorrow easier to bear; in fact, it made everything easier to bear.

Uncle Jack brightened when he reunited with his sons. Daddy called a halt to my surveillance, which came as a big relief to me and probably to my uncle as well.

After supper, Uncle Jack methodically flushed his medication. He was fed up with feeling like his brain was encased in fog. While nothing could alleviate his emptiness, he'd faced the fact that he had to forge ahead without her. He had kids to rear. That required a clear head or the little beggars would get the best of him.

He asked for the key to his liquor cabinet, which my father handed over. He poured himself a brandy like the situation was normal and went out to sit on what remained of the porch.

"Well, it looks like Jack's back," Daddy said to me, cautiously pleased. He poured a drink for himself and joined his brother.

Aunt Annie's wake was held the next evening. Mr. Hanson suggested that Uncle Jack go in alone for the initial viewing to make sure everything was to his satisfaction. He'd been doing reasonably well all day, but when the undertaker held open the door and the casket came into view, he faltered. Daddy steadied his brother, and the two of them went in together.

Uncle Jack looked pallid and sick when they emerged. Daddy helped him to the nearest chair. Mr. Hanson said for us kids to go in, if we wanted. Darrell marched in stoically, Duane in tow. Dennis declined and broke into tears. Daddy took him on his lap to comfort him. I hesitated, and then my curiosity got the better of me.

To my surprise, Aunt Annie looked nearly as lovely in death as she had in life. Her red hair cascaded around her shoulders. Her face was pale but perfect. She wore her favorite emerald green dress, but I'd never before seen the coordinating scarf strategically covering her neck.

The three of us broke down. It was so tragic, so irrevocable.

While Gramma's death had affected me deeply, she'd been old, and I knew death often visited the old. But Aunt Annie had not yet lived thirty-three years. I felt nauseous as I came from the viewing room. Daddy led me to a chair. Soon all my cousins were seated along the perimeter of the outer room, adjacent to their father.

Only Daddy stood, as though guarding us, as the mourners began to arrive.

As we were leaving for the funeral the next morning, Uncle Jack grabbed a cup of coffee on his way out the door. When his hand shook so badly that he spilled coffee on his shirt before he'd gone three steps into the yard, Daddy sent me upstairs to fetch him a clean one.

There, on the left side of his closet, I saw my aunt's bloodied blue dress hanging next to my uncle's bloodstained work shirt. The two items hung front to front, with the sleeves of the shirt draped around the waist of the dress in a final, perpetual embrace.

The church was already at capacity when we arrived. Aunt Annie had been much loved and admired on her own, being of sterling character, but her generous contributions of Uncle Jack's money to the church, the library, and other worthy causes had not gone unnoticed or unappreciated in our community.

Reverend Richter outdid himself in preaching her funeral sermon. Not a word was mentioned about damnation. While damnation was his favorite subject for regular sermons, he danced around the word during eulogies, satisfying himself with a vague allusion if the deceased had led a questionable life. But not this time—Aunt Annie was most positively already in heaven, pitying us that we still had to endure the mortal before achieving the immortal. The concept did not appear to be of comfort to either Uncle Jack or Daddy. They sat as pillars on opposing ends of the pew, with us kids wedged between them.

Finally, it was over.

Finally, the sun was allowed to shine again, but not for Uncle Jack. As soon as we returned from church, he bolted several drinks, went upstairs, and did not reappear until the next afternoon.

"Shouldn't he be eating something?" I worried.

"I'll check on him," Daddy said.

To my knowledge, he never did. Rather he took advantage of his brother's absence by making a list of projects and ticking off each in turn. He organized the donated perishables in the refrigerator and told Darrell how long each would stay edible. He oversaw Rueben and Ron's cleanup effort and made my cousins help. He told me to tidy the house and prepare our meals. He calculated the materials needed for the rebuilding of the porch and general repairs and taped the list to the liquor cabinet, where my uncle would be sure to see it. The new silo and garage could come later, he decided.

Most importantly, Daddy contacted Aunt Emma, Mrs. Swanson, and Dorothy Evans, who manned the telephone switchboard in town. Uncle Jack now required a housekeeper and a cook, preferably one and the same person, and Daddy knew those three ladies would make filling his brother's need a personal quest.

Uncle Jack's insistence that no domestic reside under his roof complicated matters by limiting the range of potential help. Still, by two o'clock on the day after the funeral, Daddy managed a temporary fix to his brother's dilemma. Dorothy Evan's niece, Nellie, would come each Monday and Friday to clean and wash. Mrs. Swanson offered to cook supper nightly at her own house, if Darrell would ride over and get it. Aunt Emma, as expected, promised to keep a sharp eye on the overall situation.

Daddy figured he'd come up with a reasonably good solution in such a short time and told me to get my things together. We'd return to Minneapolis in the morning.

His decree took me by surprise. "But Daddy, I thought we'd stay another week or two to help!"

"We've already helped, Abby. You're not the maid and I have other things to do. If we stay much longer, Jack and I will be at each other's throats again. Go pack your clothes."

Uncle Jack came downstairs and heard us. "You're not going back so soon, are you?"

"Yes," Daddy said. "Is that a problem?"

"Well, no … but she can stay, can't she?" Uncle Jack indicated me. "She's been such a help around here. And she's gotten so good with Dennis. He's suffering terribly, I'm afraid. What would it hurt if she stayed a little longer?"

Daddy seemed to waver for just a moment. Then he asked, "Are you reneging already?"

"No, I just thought, under the circumstances—"

"We're both leaving in the morning. Believe me, Jack, it's for the best."

"As you wish … but I'd like to say good-bye to her now. I know how early you like to get going and I won't be up that soon."

"Fine." Daddy's eyes darted between the two of us, lingering on his brother as though in warning. "I'll get my things from Darrell's room and leave you to it."

Uncle Jack watched my father ascend the stairs before telling me how much he appreciated everything I'd done for him. He hoped that I'd visit often, but with nearly a hundred and fifty miles separating us, it wouldn't be often enough. If he didn't see me again for a long time, he hoped that I'd enjoy my next year at school better than I had my last, and he knew my friends would miss me, and Darrell would miss me, and—

"Uncle Jack," I said, searching his face. "Why are you talking like this? I was gone nearly six months before and I came back to visit. And I will again … why are you looking like that? You promised Daddy something, didn't you?"

He turned to pour a brandy, but he wasn't quick enough. Resignation, sadness, desperation: I saw a kaleidoscope of emotions.

"Please, Uncle Jack. I have a right to know if it's about me."

He walked to the window, holding his drink, but not drinking it. He stood there, saying nothing, staring at nothing.

I felt near to tears and I didn't know why. I needed to say something and I didn't know what. He was my Uncle Jack without my Aunt Annie, and now Daddy and I were leaving him and going far away for a long time, and I couldn't make anything better for him because I had to do what Daddy wanted, and it seemed that he had to do what Daddy wanted as well.

"I'm so sorry about everything," I said.

"Yes … "

"I hope you'll be okay."

The dark eyes flashed as he turned around. "Time is both friend and enemy, Abby. Time distances one from sorrow, but also from those one wants to hold dear. Time is swift and merciless, uncaring of either a mistake or a promise … and my time, much anticipated, will soon be gone and gone forever."

"I'm afraid I don't understand," I said, unnerved by his sudden intensity.

"No—and you won't for a very long time."

"Does that mean you'll explain it to me someday?"

He smiled wanly. "Oh, I suppose … well, give me a good-bye hug. The boys will be coming in soon, and I don't want to make a big deal out of this."

He held me longer and tighter than I expected. He caressed my hair and even kissed my forehead. He seemed overwrought. I could feel his heart thudding as he pressed me against him. I was becoming uneasy when I noticed Daddy watching. I hadn't heard him come downstairs.

Uncle Jack looked up, squared his shoulders, and pointedly turned his back.

Daddy walked behind him and put his hand on his brother's shoulder. In a voice so low I could barely hear, he said, "Thank you, Jack."

"*Jacta alea est*," Uncle Jack responded and went upstairs. He did not appear for supper that night nor did I see him in the morning before we left. But this time, I knew Daddy had brought him something to eat and more to drink, and they had talked, however briefly.

"Daddy, can I ask you something?" I said during our long drive home.

"Why? You don't generally ask my permission to speak your mind."

"I thought maybe I should this time … I've been wondering about something."

"Go ahead. I'll answer if I can."

"Why did you thank Uncle Jack and what did he say to you?"

"None of your business. Any other questions?"

For a moment, I felt as defeated as my uncle had looked. Then I shifted my focus. "Did you love Aunt Annie?"

"Of course. Everyone loved her."

"That's not what I meant."

"Oh … well, the answer is still yes."

"Do you love Maria?"

"Naturally … I married her, didn't I?"

"Did you love Mother as much as you love Maria?"

"She was the wife of my youth."

"What's that mean?"

"It means yes."

"And did you love her as much as Uncle Jack loved Aunt Annie?"

"No," Daddy said, keeping his eyes on the road.

I swallowed hard. "No?"

"No … I loved her more."

I let that settle before voicing my final concern: "Do you think Uncle Jack will be all right?"

"Yes."

"Are you sure?"

"Yes, I'm sure."

"What makes you so sure?"

"Because once you've been through fire, Abby, you can never burn again."

It was a statement, not an answer, grim and from the heart.

Hooker

Maria greeted me at the door with a sympathetic hug and expressed her condolences.

"Feeling any better?" Daddy asked when his turn came.

"Yes, that stomach bug finally left. I'm sorry I wasn't able to take the train down in time for the funeral. How'd it go?"

"As well as could be expected. Jack will have one hell of a time. Three motherless sons, rebuilding his own life—he'll have his hands full ... I need a drink. Is anything ready?

"I made you a martini when I saw you pull up. It's on the coffee table."

"Good. It's a start."

I trudged upstairs with my suitcases and let them thump against the stair risers, hoping Daddy would hear and feel remorse because he was drinking his martini with Maria instead of helping me. Once again, I felt alone. Then I remembered how truly alone Uncle Jack was, and I felt ashamed. My life wasn't so bad. Daddy loved me, although he seldom demonstrated it. That's what Maria was for; her effusion balanced his reticence.

After putting my clothes away, I gazed idly out my tower window, waiting for a suitable fantasy to pop into my head. Usually it took only a minute or two. Then I'd jot it down and create a story around my idea. But nothing appeared. My muse was hiding. Aunt Annie's death and the subsequent events at the farm had drained me. And it suddenly seemed trivial to attempt to create lighthearted fiction when I'd just left the most horrible reality imaginable. I was about to curl up with the latest Nancy Drew mystery when a movement from below caught my eye.

A sandy-haired boy about my own age was lying on a hammock in our neighbor's yard. His shirtless chest was tanned and lean. A massive book was spread across his stomach, but he wasn't looking at it. Rather he seemed to be looking up at me.

"Maria, do the Petersons have company?" I called downstairs. "There's a boy over there I've never seen before."

"They moved away last week," she hollered. "Haven't met our new neighbors yet, but we must soon. If the boy's outside, maybe you could say hello?"

"Oh, I intend to." I washed up and strolled next door to see whether the new boy looked as interesting up close as he had from my window. I stopped a few feet from his hammock.

"Hey," I said.

"Hey yourself." He looked me up and down.

"So you're our new neighbor." I did the same to him.

"Yup, and you're so lucky."

"Is that so … why?"

"Because we're the perfect neighbors, that's why. We don't have a cat so your flower beds will stay pristine. We don't have a dog so you won't be bothered by yapping. We don't host loud parties because we don't know anyone yet. But we do have me, which means you'll never be bored again."

I watched the tip of his tongue moving along his lips as though he were anticipating ice cream or something equally delicious. "Well, you're sure being presumptuous," I said with the darkest frown I could muster. "Maybe I don't want to know you."

"Presumptuous is a great vocabulary word." The boy smirked. "I'm impressed."

"Now I'm positive I don't want to know you." Just my rotten luck to have a junior version of Daddy living next door!

"Oh, but you do."

"Is that so? Well, maybe you don't want to know me." I noticed how his eyes seemed bluer than Lake Nokomis on the clearest day of summer.

"Wrong again, dear heart."

"Dear heart? What kind of dumb talk is that? What are you, French?" Daddy told me once that the French were rude, smelly, and to be strictly avoided.

He burst out laughing. "Half … and you?"

What *was* Mother? Maria would have to suffice. "Um … I'm half German and half Italian."

The boy grimaced. "So I have the union of the Axis powers as my new neighbor?"

"So what? The war is over, Frog!" I'd learned that derogatory term, plus many more, from Darrell. This strange boy was not going to get the better of me!

"And so it is, dear heart. But remember, in the fairy tale, the princess always kisses the frog and you know what happens next."

"I know, but it'll never happen to you." I put my hands on my hips and peered down my nose like Daddy always did when he lectured me. "You'll stay a frog and never be the prince."

"No, I won't. You'll kiss me one day, along about … oh, what's appropriate, two or three years from now? And then how much longer will we have to wait till we get married? Say, another four or five years after that?"

I stared at him, lounging on his hammock as languidly as if he'd stated the baseball scores or the price of soybeans. His blue eyes had golden tints in their centers. His ruddy face was cheerful and open. His lips were full, framing perfectly his even teeth. Then I remembered to be incensed.

"Excuse me? How can you talk such drivel? I'll never kiss you. And I'll sure never marry you. I'm not going to marry anyone … besides, you don't even know my name."

The boy leaped from the hammock and executed a grand bow. "Pardon, Madame. I forget my manners—a thousand lashes upon me. And your name is—?"

"Abby."

"Abby? Are you sure?"

I rolled my eyes. "I guess I should know my own name."

"But it's so small, so ordinary, so very mundane, so extremely common. Couldn't it be a bit grander … Abigail, at the very least?"

I had to laugh in spite of myself. "Yes, it is Abigail, as a matter of fact. My full name is Princess Abigail Elizabeth Coetzee Stahl. There, is that better?"

The strange boy with the blue eyes and sandy hair and ruddy complexion pantomimed deep thought. "Oh yes, very much better … but I note no Italian derivation in your name. Stahl is definitely German, but Coetzee? That's not Italian … nope, not even close. Coetzee sounds Boer … or Dutch. And isn't Boer actually Dutch by African descent? Could it be that Princess Abigail is unsure of her own pedigree and is telling her smitten neighbor a little white fib?"

"How do you know about things like that?" I was intrigued.

The boy bent down and picked up the unwieldy book that had fallen to the ground when he bowed. "See my confidant? He was expounding his knowledge to me before I noticed you in the window. I shall make the proper introductions: Mr. Webster, meet Princess Abigail … Abigail, Webster."

"Oh, come on. Nobody actually reads a *Webster's Unabridged Dictionary*. It must have a million words."

"Well, I do … and no, it doesn't have a million words. It just seems so to the poor, the huddled, and the uneducated masses that wouldn't recognize an unabridged *Webster's* if it fell on their faces. But you did, so there's hope for you."

"Thanks. I'm so glad you have hope for me, because I'm sure not poor, huddled, or uneducated!"

"Whoops … stepped on your toes there, didn't I, dear heart?" The boy chuckled. "Well, 'shut my mouth,' as my dear departed mommy from Charleston used to say."

"Your mom's deceased?" I feared condolences were in order.

"Deceased? Oh no, she's very much alive, I'm glad to say, but she *is* departed. Dad threw her out of the house. But she got even. She squeezed every nickel out of him and hung him upside down to shake the pennies from his pockets when they divorced."

The mental image I had of a grown man dangling head down with pennies raining from his pockets was an unsettling one. "Oh … why did she divorce him?"

"Mary Anne."

"So?"

"My mom's Adeline."

"So?" I was tempted to give up this convoluted conversation and go back to my room and read.

"You look confused, dear heart … okay, here's what happened. My mom, Adeline, caught Dad cavorting with Mary Anne, who was his girlfriend at the time. Mom got really pissed and divorced him. Then he married Mary Anne. That was going all right till he liked Kathryn better. So Mary Anne divorced him after she threatened to put a bullet through his noggin. Dad got the divorce instead of the bullet because he bribed her with all the money he'd made since his divorce from Mom. Then he married Kathryn. She left after he forgot to come home a bunch of times. I don't think she could handle the stress … now he's married to Debbie."

I stared at him hard. "Are you kidding me?"

"God's truth, cross my heart and hope to die."

"No wonder you read the dictionary. I wouldn't want to think about your life either."

"Oh, it's not so bad. I just check out Dad's bedroom now and again, see who's going in there with him … actually I like Debbie. She's the best one since Mom, in my unbiased opinion. She can't boil water, but she's a great bartender. Dad loves to drink, so when he's happy—hell, we're all happy."

I didn't know what to think. I didn't know what to say. I couldn't believe what this strange boy had been through. My confused upbringing paled by comparison.

He took up the lag in our conversation. "Anyway, that's my story … well, back to the dictionary. You wouldn't believe all the things you can learn from Mr. Webster. Plus, I'm working my way through the *Encyclopedia Britannica*, every word. I'm on 'E' right now."

I found my voice again: "You're weird."

"No, but you're not the first person who's said that. Actually I'm a prodigy, but only in some things. Do you know what a prodigy is?"

"Of course." I hadn't a clue.

"You're smarter than average to know that, but don't be intimidated. I'm not a prodigy in everything. In mathematics, I'm already quite hopeless ... how old are you?"

"Eleven, almost twelve."

"Me too. Or as Dad says, I'm eleven going on twenty. He should know—he's dated some that age. I mean the twenty, not the eleven. We'll be in the same grade then when school starts. I was hoping to meet someone this summer I'd be in school with ... school is so dull, don't you think?"

"School is terribly dull. But maybe it'll be better this year."

"Not a chance ... come to think of it, maybe it will, because you'll be there with me."

"Since you're looking forward to a better school year with me, it'd be beneficial to know your name. You've introduced your dictionary, but not yourself."

He laughed and tapped his forehead with the heel of his hand. "Oh, I've quite forgotten, haven't I? My name, dear Abigail, is A.J. Sebastien Delalande Hooker. Sebastien and Delalande are French. Mom wanted to honor both sides of her family when I was christened, so hence the ridiculously long name."

"And A.J.—what does that stand for?" I hoped for something I could actually remember.

He grimaced. "I don't want to tell. It's awful ... really awful."

"Come on, *tell.* I won't mention it again if you don't want me to."

"Oh, all right ... against my better judgment, it's Archibald Jeremiah, after my dad, but he goes by Archie."

I giggled. "I see what you mean. What were your folks thinking of?"

"Nothing. They were drunk."

I shrugged off that bit of information as though most parents were drunk while selecting their baby's name. "So what do I call you then, A.J.?"

"That's what most people call me, but my friends call me Hooker. Would you like to be my friend, dear heart?" The corners of his full lips turned up invitingly. "Or would you rather be my best friend?"

I stared again at Hooker, trying to decide whether I wanted to slap him across his cheerful face like I'd seen in the movies when the cad gets fresh with the heroine, or whether I just wished we were both far older so I could deliver on the answer he so obviously desired.

"Oh, I don't know," I hedged. "How long do I have to make up my mind?"

"Till tomorrow … by the way, I've been bored out of my skull ever since we moved in. Do you know how to play cribbage?"

I flashed my best saccharine smile. "Only for quarters."

Two hours later, I climbed the stairs to my room, a jingle in my pocket. As I waltzed past, Daddy said, "Now what do you suppose that look on her face means?"

"Depending on how many years our new neighbors stay our neighbors," Maria answered, "I think it means trouble."

She was so right.

Stirring the Pot

"I LIKE TO be bad," Hooker said. "Do you like to be bad?"

"That depends," I said. I'd known Hooker a month, and he kept surprising me.

"I don't mean doing really nasty things like knocking down old ladies or swiping candy from tots. I mean bending the rules … breaking them too."

"Sounds like fun." I was chafing from the restrictions imposed by my father's continually expanding commandments, currently at twenty. "But I have to be really careful so Daddy won't find out."

"He's one of those strict types, isn't he?" Hooker had taken an instant dislike to my father. The feeling was mutual.

"Horrible. He tries, but he's really a tyrant. His ultimate rule is, 'Do as you please as long as you do as I please.' And he's typed up nineteen more, like I'm too dumb to figure anything out."

"What happens if you break a rule?"

"From nothing much to writing sentences to potentially awful. He's never used the belt, but the threat is always there."

Hooker understood. "Thank God my dad doesn't believe in that. His only rule is no rules at all."

"Lucky you."

"Not always. It's hard knowing what's right when I'm only eleven."

"But you do, don't you? After all, you know when you're being bad."

"True … want to see a show?"

"I'm out of money."

"So?" Hooker smiled beatifically. "Who needs money?"

It wasn't too difficult to access theatres without using money. Hooker and I would position ourselves near the exit when the show let out. As the usher opened the door and patrons poured into the street, we'd race inside like salmon swimming upstream. If the usher barred our way or questioned us, Hooker would dissolve in phony tears. Each performance was worthy of an Academy Award.

"Our kid sister got away from us and ran in here before we could stop her. Did you see where she went? She's real little, but she's really fast. We've got to find her, or Pa will kill us! Susie! Susie, where are you? Stop hiding and come to brother!" And off he'd run, trying not to laugh, with me close behind.

We saw numerous movies that way, limited only by the number of theatres within walking distance or an easy streetcar or bus ride of our homes. Somehow we always had a dime for transportation. I'd tuck popcorn and little bottles of Coca-Cola in my schoolbag, so we lacked for nothing.

The only time we failed to see a movie was when a well-intentioned usher insisted on helping us search. We looked and looked, but little Susie could not be found. We had to run away ourselves when he summoned the police.

"Damn!" Hooker said afterward. "I really liked that theatre."

"What church do you hate?" Hooker asked me a week later.

"You're not supposed to hate any church, you dumbbell. God lives in all churches, and that's like saying you hate God."

"Who told you that?"

"Maria."

"She's Catholic, right?"

"Yes, but what does that have to do with it?"

"Catholics have funny ideas ... okay, pick any church but Catholic. We'll leave the Catholics alone for now."

"Methodist," I said, although I didn't hate Methodists. I had nothing whatever against Methodists—I had never known any Methodists. All I knew was that St. Andrew's Methodist Church was four blocks from our house. More than once, I'd been tempted to slip inside and beg God's forgiveness for sneaking into so many movies.

"Methodist it shall be. Put on a dress and I'll be over at nine-thirty on Sunday."

"Why?"

"So we can go to church."

"But we don't belong to that church."

"So? The sign says services start at ten, newcomers and sinners welcome."

My eyes narrowed with suspicion. "What are you up to? You never go to church."

"Nothing. I'm just an innocent newcomer, dear heart ... and a sinner too."

I had nothing better to do that Sunday, so I asked Daddy. To my surprise, he agreed. He said he'd rather have me attending a Methodist church than popping more popcorn for another mysterious outing with that little shithead from next door.

The singing was uplifting, the sermon was inspiring, and I was contemplating turning Methodist when the collection plate was handed down our pew. I'd planned ahead and dropped in one of Daddy's dimes. Hooker's hand passed over the plate as well.

A moment later, he whispered, "Come with me to the restroom."

"Why, do you need help?" I teased.

"Come on!"

We excused ourselves and made our way to the back of the church. I was heading toward the ladies' room when Hooker grabbed my arm and I found myself outside, squinting into the dazzling sunshine of a sultry August morning.

"What's going on?" I demanded.

Hooker grinned and opened his hand. Crumpled in his palm was a ten-dollar bill.

"Where'd you get that?"

"Where do you think?"

"You stole that? You stole that from the collection plate? You stole that from—from God?"

"Not so loud!"

"You think that's loud? How's *this* for loud?" I screeched. "I don't know you, Hooker! I don't want to know you! You're going straight to hell!" I turned and stomped down the street in righteous indignation. I glanced up several times, expecting a lightning bolt to shear apart the cloudless sky and incinerate Hooker right on the sidewalk.

A block later, he caught up to me. "I gave it back, Abby! I swear I did. I gave it to the usher by the back door."

I stopped momentarily. "Oh, yeah? And what'd you say to him?"

"I said I found it on the floor when I went to the restroom."

"What? Now you *lied* about stealing? You're *still* going straight to hell!" I continued tramping home. Hooker followed at a safe distance.

Daddy looked up from the lunch he was preparing as I burst into the kitchen. "You're sure home early. Did church let out already?"

"No, it wasn't over yet, Daddy. I left because Hooker's a damn fool!"

"Glad you finally realized that … write your fifty sentences, Abigail."

I came down hard on Hooker that time, but I caved to my own greed two weeks later when I decided my stories would improve considerably if I owned a book on creative writing. When I'd asked, Daddy said he'd consider it for my birthday or Christmas. Both were months away. He never bought me presents except for special occasions, and I didn't have the two-and-a-half dollars.

When Hooker suggested, very tentatively, that we attend church again, I smacked him. At least he didn't smack me back like Darrell would've. Hooker was a thief, but he also was a gentleman.

So I went shopping. Borrowing a blouse of Maria's, which had ample room in the bosom area for a book on creative writing, I went shopping. Hooker agreed to act as my lookout.

It wasn't as simple as I'd thought. When Daddy and I had patronized the bookstore previously, we could hardly locate a clerk. This time, clerks hovered attentively and customers were in abundance. I was tempted to abandon the notion and check out a suitable tome from the Hennepin County Library like an upstanding citizen. But I wasn't an upstanding citizen. I was a sneaking, skulking eleven-year-old with larcenous leanings.

Hooker and I circled the book stacks several times, taking books out, perusing them, and putting them back. The object of my desires lay on the middle shelf, within easy reach.

"Now!" Hooker hissed, and my prize went up my blouse. If I kept my arms crossed, it would stay there too!

We sauntered nonchalantly toward the door. Someone else sauntered behind us.

My heart hammered. My stomach knotted.

Hooker eased out the door. I was one step shy of freedom when a hand grabbed me and spun me around. *How to Become a Better Writer* crashed to the floor. I looked up fearfully.

"Why, you little thief!" The male clerk shook me vigorously as though to dislodge additional books from beneath my clothes. "Pat! Over here, Pat!"

I assumed he was calling for assistance from the lady clerk, but I was wrong.

Pat appeared from the far side of the bookstore. Pat was a man. Pat was a cop.

"You mean to tell me all the stealing going on around here is because of you? Well, missy, you're not getting away with it this time!" His beefy face scrunched into a scowl as he twisted my arms behind me. Cold steel pinioned my wrists. "I'll see that you get what's coming to you, you little brat. Where do you live?"

I shook my head. My lips were sealed.

Pat could haul me to the cop station. Pat could throw me in jail. Pat could stick me in reform school. Pat could sell me to the gypsies. Pat could do whatever the hell he wanted, but I'd never tell.

Hooker came back.

And Hooker told.

I was sitting in the back of the cop car, with Hooker seated dejectedly next to me, as Pat drove us to my doom.

"You pinheaded nincompoop! Why'd you tell?" I couldn't slug Hooker with my hands cuffed behind me, so I gave him a kick. "Daddy's going to murder me!"

"Kick me again and I'll kick you back. What the hell was I supposed to do? We can't live under a bridge for the rest of our lives and act like we don't belong anywhere. Somebody would figure it out eventually … and he won't murder you anyway."

"No, he'll think of something worse!" I started to bawl.

Hooker looked out the window and ignored me. My face was covered with tears and snot before he finally dug a handkerchief out of his pocket. He wiped my eyes and held it over my nose. "Blow!"

I blew. And I bawled some more.

"Oh, stop your howling." He wiped my face again. "I'll take your punishment."

I was so astounded I stopped. "What? You can't do that!"

"Why not? It was me who started all this stealing stuff. I'm as guilty as you are."

"I know, but Daddy already hates you. He'd love nothing better than to get his hands on you. Why, he'd use the belt for sure!"

"I know."

"You like me enough to do that?" I asked my light-fingered, misguided best friend.

Hooker nodded, but the fear in his eyes was unmistakable.

Pat was a block from my father's house. Retribution was imminent.

"No," I decided. "I can't let you do that. I survived Uncle Jack when I burned down his barn, and I'll survive this."

I'd hoped for the teeniest, tiniest bit of argument, but Hooker looked pathetically relieved that he wouldn't have to sacrifice his comfort for my sake.

"You burned down a barn? Wow, that's impressive!"

Pat glanced at us in the rearview mirror. "Sounds like I have a career criminal back there."

"It was an accident," I said.

"Sure. That's what they all say." Pat parked the patrol car, marched us up the steps, and rang the doorbell.

Maria opened the door.

Pat explained what I had done. He explained Hooker's role in what I'd done. He removed my handcuffs.

Maria yanked me inside. Then she yanked Hooker inside.

I'd never realized that my good-natured Italian stepmother possessed such a volatile temper. Her face turned crimson. Her eyes blazed. Her arms waved. Her voice shot up two octaves as she upbraided us in three languages. I understood the English version perfectly and the rest in context.

She grabbed her wooden spaghetti spoon and paddled my bottom, warning that if I resisted, I'd be dealing with Daddy the second he returned from his errands.

She did the same to Hooker, with the same caveat. When she finished, she ordered him to stay out of my life until further notice.

He ran out the front door.

When I protested Hooker's banishment, she paddled me again, saying that she must have missed a spot. When she heard Daddy's sedan coming down the alley, she quit. She told me to take off her blouse, stay out of her closet, stay out of bookstores, and let me go.

I raced upstairs as Daddy came in the back door. If Maria couldn't assume her happy face in time, he'd know something was up. I threw her blouse under my bed and donned one of my own. I ran cold water in my sink and washed my face. My eyes were pink and puffy, although I managed to make the rest of my face look fairly normal. My rump felt anything but normal.

Minutes later, I heard Daddy's heavy footsteps coming up the stairs. He knocked once and opened my door.

"Maria said you were back already."

"The roller rink was closed." I hoped to sound blasé instead of petrified.

"You should've known that ... what's the matter?" He came closer. "Your eyes are all red."

"Um ... I was using glitter when I sneezed. I think some got in my eyes." I grasped at anything plausible.

"Oh? Let me look." He set down the sack he'd been holding. He washed his hands in my sink and peered in my eyes, moving the lids around with his fingers. "Hmm ... I don't see anything. Maybe it's out by now."

"Maybe ... "

"Well, let me know whether it keeps bothering you."

"It feels better already, Daddy."

"Good, then you can enjoy your present. I decided this morning to get it for you rather than make you wait for your birthday, since it's educational. One corner's a bit smashed, but I didn't think you'd mind. Somebody tried to run off with it just before I got there, and it got damaged in the scuffle. I got fifty cents off." Smiling expectantly, he reached in the sack and handed me *How to Become a Better Writer*.

"Thank you, Daddy," I managed to say. "It's a wonderful present ... I just wish you'd gotten it for me yesterday."

"That's odd. Maria said the same thing. But I figure a present's a present, no matter when you get it ... isn't that so, Abby?"

"I think our thieving days are over," Hooker said.

"I think so too." I was secretly relieved. My nerves couldn't handle another confrontation with Pat. And being separated from Hooker for an entire week had been hard, although not nearly as hard as my raging stepmother's spaghetti spoon spanking. At least she'd never tattled on us.

"And the theatres all know us by now." Hooker lolled on his back in the hammock. "We've picnicked, explored, played at least a thousand games of cribbage … guess I could always go back to studying Mr. Webster or the encyclopedia … never did get past 'E' since you moved in."

"Go ahead, blame me for your lack of initiative." I lay opposite him, luxuriating in his company, the sun warm on my face.

"Initiative is a good word … is it one of your dad's?"

"Of course. I'm through learning stuff unless he makes me."

"Guess you'll be learning a lot."

I sighed. "I'm afraid so."

"School starts in a few days. We won't have much free time after that."

"I know … what do you want to do until then?"

"Oh, I don't know." He paused thoughtfully. "Everything costs money, and I sure don't have any."

"I can't do much either on what Daddy gives me."

"At least he gives you something. My dad thinks I should earn money if I want money."

"So why don't you?" Daddy had told me, in no uncertain terms, that Hooker was the laziest boy on God's green earth.

"Oh, I will … someday. Nothing much I can do summers except mow yards, and grass makes me sneeze. I've always managed before—until that crabby cop ruined everything."

"I think we ruined it for ourselves."

"Maybe … hey, I just thought of something fun: let's investigate your dad's office!"

"That's impossible. When he's not pestering me, Daddy's always in there, painting or writing or whatever he does. The rest of the time he keeps it locked … he's even installed an extra lock, just in case."

I'd told Hooker my entire life story, from the missing mother to the mysterious letters to the bloodstained dress to the flaming schoolhouse to the forbidden office … and I'd confessed the details about torching my uncle's barn too.

A familiar glint appeared in Hooker's cerulean eyes. "Nothing's impossible. Leave it to me, dear heart … I'll figure it out."

Summer 1947

Uncle Jack's Liver

While I waited for Hooker to figure it out, I celebrated my twelfth birthday, passed my first holiday season with Daddy and Maria, endured the seventh grade, and anticipated my summer trip to the farm, although my father had not yet agreed to it.

I'd kept connected to my former life by conscientiously corresponding with Darrell, Ruth, Judy, Uncle Jack, and Aunt Emma. Daddy still censored my letters, so I didn't write to Mrs. Monson.

Response varied. I hadn't heard from Darrell since Christmas. Ruth and Judy wrote occasionally. Uncle Jack penned sporadic, terse notes describing the rebuilding of his farm and nothing about the rebuilding of his life.

But Aunt Emma wrote as often as I did: lengthy, meandering letters detailing sensational medical maladies and salacious family gossip. Daddy cautioned that Emma had never met a scandal she couldn't improve, which only titillated my interest.

Nellie Evans, she wrote, was doing a poor to middling job of keeping Uncle Jack's house livable. Elsie Swanson still provided supper, although "between you, me, and the gatepost," Annie had been a far better cook. Ron and Rueben came only two mornings a week, as only the horses remained. My uncle had recently shipped the remaining Angus to the auction barn in Sleepy Eye.

I felt a twinge of sadness finding out in such a way that Copper was gone. I'd forgotten to say good-bye to her last summer. Perhaps it was for the best—me leaving without knowing I'd never see my pet again. Then I thought about Uncle Jack leaving for town without knowing he'd never see his wife alive again, and I wept for him.

I wasn't the only one. In early June, Aunt Emma wrote of my uncle's despair:

Vic doesn't think I should involve you in this, but I simply must before it's too late! The twins are on their own much of the time, although Darrell tries his best. That boy has too much responsibility for one so young. Vic and I often take the kids on the weekends to help out, but Jack doesn't seem to care one way or the other. It's all over town that he's hit the bottle again, and I've seen the terrible results with my own eyes. If he keeps it up, he'll ruin his liver. Drinking totally ruined your grandpa's liver, if you didn't know. Sometimes I lie awake nights weeping and worrying about Jack's liver, and him with those three boys to raise! I've begged and begged your father to come down and intervene, but he won't commit to it. I'm sorry to ask this of you, Abby, but if you care at all about your uncle, please try to get him here, because I'm completely at my wit's end!

I took Daddy's medical book from the shelf and read about alcohol's effect on the liver. After looking up the unfamiliar words, I was certain Uncle Jack wouldn't survive the year if I wasn't successful in convincing my father to drive to the farm.

I started my lifesaving campaign over dinner that same night. "Daddy, Uncle Jack really needs your help."

"No, he doesn't ... you've been reading another of Emma's letters, haven't you?"

"She's worried."

"She's always worried."

"Well, she's got me worried."

"You're always worried too."

"But he's drinking like a fish, Daddy. His liver will be ruined, and him with those three boys to raise!" I couldn't improve on Aunt Emma's prose.

"His liver will be fine. Where the hell do you get such ideas?"

"Your *Mayo Clinic Medical Encyclopedia*."

"Remind me to throw the damn thing out."

Maria interjected herself into our conversation. It wasn't accidental that I'd started nagging Daddy in front of her.

"Oh, James, why don't you go? You know how badly Jack must feel since he's lost Annie. If something happened to him, you'd never forgive yourself."

"I would too."

"James ... " Maria gave him one of her looks.

"Don't 'James' me," Daddy muttered. "Stop talking and pass the salad."

She passed the salad. And she talked, far into the evening.

The next morning, Daddy announced he was driving to the farm.

"Wait, Daddy, you can't go without me!" I bolted my cornflakes, nearly choking myself in the process.

"I can and I will."

"James," Maria said again.

Daddy set his jaw and shut his mind as she talked some more.

The following day, my father and I went to the farm. He was in a rotten mood, which I discovered the moment I opened my mouth.

"Just because you're along doesn't mean I want to hear you blab for three and a half hours," he grumbled.

I shot him a look of my own, which thankfully he didn't see. Then I dug out my journal. By the time we reached the farm, another chapter of *The Tyrant Chronicles* had been duly composed.

As Daddy's sedan ascended the long driveway, I was unprepared for what I saw. The lawn had gone to seed, the shrubs needed pruning, and weeds sprouted helter-skelter. Remnants of the reconstruction lay scattered about. The absence of Aunt Annie's colorful flowers accentuated the obvious neglect.

Uncle Jack was slumped in a rocker on the rebuilt porch. He looked up as we passed, but did not acknowledge us.

Daddy parked and stormed in the house. I followed, leaving my suitcase behind in case he refused to let me stay, or in case I chose not to.

Darrell stood in the kitchen, making sandwiches. Leftovers and dirty dishes littered the counter and sink. He appeared as unkempt as everything else.

"Oh, hello," he said. "I didn't know you were coming."

"What the hell's going on here?" Daddy demanded. "Your father's sitting on his ass, drinking. The yard looks like shit. The kitchen looks like shit. You look like shit. Where are the twins? Do they look like shit too?"

"They're at Aunt Emma's," Darrell said, glowering. "She's probably cleaned them up by now. Don't crab at me. I can't do everything."

Daddy studied him for a moment. "That's what I thought … Abigail, stay here with Darrell. I'm going to have a talk with my brother."

Naturally we snuck after him. From our vantage point next to the davenport, we could observe through the living room window without being seen.

I saw in a glance that Uncle Jack was much changed. His clothes were rumpled and dirty. He'd lost weight. His greasy hair had grown past his collar. His darkly handsome face was shrouded by stubble.

"Welcome to hell, James." He gestured with the whiskey bottle as he rose unsteadily. "Want some?"

Daddy backhanded him across the face, hard.

The bottle dropped and spilled. Uncle Jack staggered and fell back into the rocker. He rubbed his cheek. "A simple 'no' would've sufficed."

My father slapped him a second time … and a third.

"Damn you!" Uncle Jack snarled, roused from his lethargy. He stood up and rushed my father, who easily sidestepped him. My uncle tumbled off the porch, managed a sitting position on the grass, but did not rise.

Daddy towered over him, hands on his hips, eyes narrowed in scorn. "Just look at you, Jack! Drunk on your ass with your kids being taken care of by Emma, and everything falling down around you. Where's your pride? Where's your sense of duty? Where's what you used to be?"

"Dead … everything's dead in the ground … with Annie." Uncle Jack moaned and began to weep.

"You're so pathetic, Jack; you're so goddamned pathetic!" Daddy screamed in a black fury. "Stop acting like you're the only man who's ever lost a wife! Stop acting so goddamned sorry for yourself! And stop that goddamned ridiculous noise!" With difficulty, he hoisted my uncle to his feet. "Walk, damn you. Don't make me sorry I didn't shoot you when I had the chance."

Darrell and I fled to the safety of his room as my father opened the screen door and thrust my uncle inside. We heard a lot of shouting and swearing during the next half hour, mostly by Daddy. Finally it stopped. Then we heard the sounds of someone being dragged upstairs. In the main bedroom, bedsprings creaked.

"Sleep it off, Jack." Daddy slammed the door, stomped down the steps, and began clattering around in the kitchen.

"Is this what's been going on?" I asked.

Darrell nodded. "Yes, but it wasn't always this bad. Dad held things together pretty good until around Christmas. Christmas was so special to Mom, and their anniversary came just before. Instead of us going to church and doing the things we used to, Dad got falling down drunk … he's never really come out of it."

"Why, that's five months!" I said, thinking of the damage already done.

"Nearly six. Some days were better, some worse. But I can't remember the last time Dad stayed sober very long. If it weren't for Vic and Emma, we probably would've been taken away by now."

"Taken away where?"

"To live with another family … or to an orphanage, if nobody wanted us."

"Why didn't you write and tell me? Aunt Emma's been writing all along, but I had no idea things were this bad!"

Darrell averted his face. "I couldn't write … I just couldn't. I kept hoping I'd wake up one morning and everything would be better."

I slipped my arm around my blood brother, aching for him. I'd felt the same way my first few months in Minneapolis, but I'd never had to fend for myself, or cared for two younger siblings, or watched helplessly as my father poisoned himself with liquor.

Daddy and I stayed nearly three weeks. He began his duties by drying out my uncle. He locked the liquor cabinet and hid the car keys, saying that if his brother simply had to get drunk, town was four miles away. More than one heated exchange took place about that, but Uncle Jack stayed home.

Once his brother achieved full sobriety, Daddy seldom missed an opportunity to berate him for failing his parental responsibilities. These one-sided harangues took place in private. But due to the volume and intensity of the words, we all overheard.

Conversely, Daddy also attempted to positively motivate his brother, saying he could rise to the challenge if he damn well wanted. Only a spineless fool required solace from the bottle. Uncle Jack promptly called my father a hypocrite, so more than one heated exchange took place about that too.

When he wasn't rehabilitating my uncle, Daddy set out to rectify the sorry mess that the house had become. He compiled chore lists for us kids. The twins attempted to shirk their duties, but only once. My father was not a tyrant to be ignored.

To keep the house as spic-and-span as we'd gotten it, Daddy fired Nellie Evans and replaced her with Margaret Monson, on Aunt Emma's recommendation. Mr. Monson had keeled over shoveling snow back in February, at age fifty-two. Margaret, it was rumored, was too distraught to teach this coming year, but a little extra income would be appreciated.

I listened from around the corner as Daddy interviewed my former teacher, curious how he'd treat someone who had censured him for his past treatment of me. He was extremely solicitous. After extending condolences on her recent loss, he brewed a fresh pot of coffee and offered her a brownie I'd made. When she declined, he offered her a cookie I'd made, which she accepted. All the while, he spoke highly of me. Her duties were mentioned only in passing. Either he was determined to make a good impression or he had no other options.

Mrs. Monson readily accepted the job.

Uncle Jack protested vehemently to Daddy afterward. "Why didn't you tell me you were going to do that? I can't stand that woman! She'll never work out, not in a hundred years!"

"Don't be so crotchety, Jack. She's the ideal solution."

"The hell she is. She hates me."

"You're easy to hate, Jack, although I have no idea why she does."

"That makes two of us ... unless she's still mad I dumped her back in high school."

"Good Lord! You dated Margaret too? Was there anyone you didn't?"

Daddy marveled. "Good thing you dumped her, though. You did her a big favor."

"Keep your damn opinions to yourself," Uncle Jack bristled. "All I'm saying is that Margaret Monson's a judgmental prude and she's had me in her crosshairs for years. Every chance she gets, she picks at me like I'm a scab."

"Good. You need picking. Make the best of it, Jack."

"I'll make the best of it, all right. I'll send her packing the minute she shows up."

"You do and I'm done trying to help you!" Daddy's face turned scarlet as he slammed his fist on the kitchen table. The sugar bowl jumped. Darrell and I jumped. "Live and die in your own filth! Drink till you lose your kids! Drink till you ruin your goddamned liver, same as our father did! See if I give a shit!"

Uncle Jack began a retort, but apparently thought the better of it.

When Mrs. Monson arrived on Friday morning, Uncle Jack slipped out the back door. Daddy told me to see whether he was heading toward town. He wasn't. He simply saddled Chestnut, rode to the slough at breakneck speed, circled it twice, and rode back again. Then he stayed in the horse barn, grooming Chestnut and Banat, until Mrs. Monson finished her work and left.

"Don't be petulant, Jack," Daddy said when his brother came inside.

"Don't be smug, James," Uncle Jack said. The house was spotless, but that didn't stop him from finding fault. "Anybody who cleans my house should know the damn cookie jar doesn't belong on top of the refrigerator." He moved it to the counter with a scowl that made me suspect he wanted to move far more than the cookie jar.

He wanted to move my father out of his house—permanently.

On our second Monday at the farm, dissatisfied with merely reordering everyone's lives, Daddy expanded the duties of Rueben and Ron. By Thursday noon, the grass was cut, the shrubs were pruned, and flowers were planted around the house. Pots of geraniums lined the porch for additional color.

"I hate geraniums," Uncle Jack groused. "They stink."

"And where were you when I picked them out? Riding that goddamned horse! Make the best of it," Daddy said.

Grumbling about Margaret Monson, the cookie jar, and geraniums was only the beginning. Soon Uncle Jack argued about everything.

And Daddy argued. It was as though they were feeding off each other, with all the arguments.

When I asked, Daddy tried to explain the acrimony to me. "Jack's back with a vengeance, but he sure as hell needs a drink."

"I thought he wasn't supposed to drink anymore."

"He shouldn't, but he will. I hope he can regulate himself, same as I do. I can't stay here forever and police what he does."

On our last night at the farm, Daddy produced his brother's car keys and opened the liquor cabinet. He mixed a Seven and Seven and went to sit on the porch. Uncle Jack made another and joined him. As usual, they started in on each other.

Rather than listening to them bicker, Darrell and I took a walk before bedtime. All the way to Gramma's farm we walked, using lanterns to light our way.

It was a perfect July night. The darkness tasted soft, like warm chocolate. The fireflies were out en masse. The earth beneath our bare feet extruded a lingering sweetness of a recent rain.

"Remember the last time we did this?" Darrell said.

"Yes, and it didn't turn out quite the way we wanted."

"Nothing ever does."

I changed the subject before I felt melancholy. "Have you found anything interesting lately? Like letters or more photographs?"

"I found a few burned pieces of some letters. You can take them with you when you leave tomorrow."

"How'd they get burned?" I was astonished that he hadn't mentioned it sooner.

"Dad burned them. On New Year's, he was drinking so hard I called Uncle Vic. He came and took the twins. I told Dad I was leaving too, but I didn't."

"Why not?"

Darrell paused. "Because I was afraid he'd hurt himself. I had to stay behind and try to stop him."

"I'm sorry … "

"Not as sorry as I was … anyway, around midnight Dad started rummaging in the attic. Then he went outside and started a fire and burned some stuff. I worried he'd freeze, but finally he came in and stumbled up to bed. I managed to save a few pieces before they blew away in the wind."

"Maybe that's what happened to the stuff from behind the chimney cover."

"Or what he swiped from the schoolhouse. Nothing much was left. Just fragments. Maybe you and your new pal can make sense of it. I'm done playing Sherlock. Snoop and Company is in the past. I don't have time for that now."

"I know you don't."

"But I hope you keep playing Watson. You still don't know everything that happened in Africa."

"Oh, I intend to. When Hooker and I get inside Daddy's office, maybe everything will become clear."

"Let me know if that ever happens … look, Abby."

As we stood atop the final knoll of the pasture, we saw barren ground where the schoolhouse had been. The barn and the other outbuildings were dark, devoid of life or light. But the new tenants had neglected to draw the curtains, and the windows of the old house glowed like golden eyes within a blackened face. A hound, roused from its slumber, howled briefly, and the night again went quiet.

"I don't know why we came," I said.

"We came to remember," Darrell said.

After I packed for the trip back to Minneapolis, I read the fragments he'd given me:

Stay home or the curse of God will be upon you. Nothing can be gained from taking from one and lying to the other. Astonished, I recognized Gramma's crabbed handwriting.

You deserve far better. No one would blame you if you left and never looked back … opportunity knocks but once, or in this case twice! Let me know what— and the rest of the typed fragment was missing.

The third consisted of only three words: *Poorly differentiated. Prognosis—* and the remainder, in my mother's elegant handwriting, had been consumed by fire.

The fourth was the longest, also Mother's: *Forgive me, my darling. What I do, I must do. Since you refuse to help, I will find another way. And I WILL find another way. It shouldn't be too difficult. After all, aren't my affections easily transferred? I shall soon be proving that one way or the other, won't I? That, my dear one, you must forgive as well. At least I won't—* and the rest was missing.

The fifth and final fragment was again from my mother. *—so much. Kiss her as often as you can. She is my precious one—* and it ended.

I slipped the five pieces in an envelope for safekeeping. How could a few dozen words, plucked from a fire, provide answers, solve mysteries? Still, I couldn't help ruminating.

Was I my mother's precious one?

What was she planning that begged both help *and* forgiveness?

In what context did she write "poorly differentiated" and "prognosis"?

Who thought who deserved better?

And who did Gramma curse?

"Water those geraniums, Jack," Daddy said the next morning.

"They'll be dead by next week," Uncle Jack said.

"I'll do it," Darrell said.

Daddy glared at his brother. "Flowers are one thing, but people are another. You damned well better be nice to Margaret."

"That'll be Darrell's job too. He can sweet talk anybody … thanks for coming, James."

"I can think of no better way to spend three weeks of lovely summer than to drag you back from the brink," Daddy said. "Get in the car, Abby."

I hugged Darrell good-bye. "Things will be better now."

"I'll write if they're not." His words rang hollow.

"I hope you'll be okay," I said to my uncle.

"Of course." His dark eyes met my own. "Do you think I could tolerate him," indicating my father, "here for this long again?"

"No." I jumped in the car before Daddy gunned the engine a second time.

The twins stood by the tire swing and waved as we passed. I waved back. Motherless, and during the past months nearly fatherless as well, they'd won a place in my heart. Unlike them, I'd always had a rock to cling to during my storms. I prayed that my uncle could again be the bulwark for his sons that he'd once been for me.

"Do you think Uncle Jack will be all right?" I looked both ways as Daddy eased the sedan onto the county road. He seemed too preoccupied to do his own looking.

"Hell if I know."

"You thought he would be, after Auntie died."

"Yes, but my brother continues to amaze me with his unerring ability to disappoint."

What Daddy said changed my perspective. For the first time, I realized my chance for happiness surpassed that of my cousins. My final glimpse of Darrell, with his arms draped around the thin shoulders of his small brothers, particularly tugged at my conscience.

I decided to ensure their welfare. If Darrell was too embarrassed to write the truth, Aunt Emma held no such inhibitions. If she even hinted that Uncle Jack was ruining his liver again, I'd take it upon myself to get him help posthaste. Never would *my* cousins end up in an orphanage! My simple strategy comforted me as I left the farm behind.

But not everything was left behind. The remnants of Uncle Jack's secrets traveled with me, hidden deep within my suitcase.

Hooker and I studied the fragments later that afternoon in his room.

"This is your grandma's writing?" Hooker examined the first fragment carefully so it wouldn't crumble.

"I'm positive."

"She wrote this to either your aunt or uncle, or these letters wouldn't have been in his possession … is he religious?"

"When it's convenient."

Hooker smiled. "I assume that's a 'no.' Was your aunt?"

"Very much so."

"Then I think your grandma wrote this to her, not him. You don't threaten someone with a curse unless they're religious enough to heed the warning."

"That makes sense, but Aunt Annie never did a thing wrong in her whole life." I was loath to defame the dead.

"How do you know? Do you know what she did before you were born? Or when you were little? Do you know what she did every minute of every day after that?"

"Cook and clean."

"Okay … how about at night? Did you know what she did at night?"

I grimaced. "Oh, stop it. I don't want to think about that."

"We're trying to piece a puzzle together," Hooker reminded me. "Nothing can be off limits."

"Fine, but that doesn't explain why Gramma would curse her anyway."

"No, it doesn't, so let's go on: *You deserve far better. No one would blame you if you left and never looked back.*" He read the rest silently.

"Well?"

"It's typed, which is curious."

"Why? Lots of folks type letters."

"They type letters, too, if their handwriting is readily recognizable if the letter falls into the wrong hands."

"That makes sense. … how do you get these ideas?"

"I'm your new Sherlock. I'm supposed to get these ideas … did your grandma own a typewriter?"

"No."

"And who does that we both know and love dearly?" Hooker was grinning now.

"Daddy?"

"You win the prize, Watson."

"But there are thousands of typewriters in the world."

"Are there thousands of typists who'd be sending a letter to your uncle's house? I think not. We just need to compare these typed characters to the same characters on your dad's typewriter. Certain ones, like 'j' or 'g' look far different from one to another. I learned that from reading crime novels. If they match, we'll know your dad typed this."

"We'll only know somebody used Daddy's typewriter."

"True, but who's the most likely suspect?"

I conceded the point. "But there's another problem, Hooker. Daddy always keeps the typewriter in his office."

"Borrow it. Ask him to teach you to type, if nothing else. That'll get it out of the cave long enough to make a comparison … what's next?"

"Only three words, in my mother's writing."

"*Poorly differentiated … prognosis*," Hooker read aloud. "I think it's time for Mr. Webster to shine his linguistic light on our latest mystery." He rolled off his bed and hoisted the *Unabridged* from his bookshelf. "No need to look up 'poorly.' Any dummy knows that one … okay, here's 'differentiate.' Several meanings … this might be the one we need: 'in biology, to undergo a differentiation, meaning to make distinct or specialized; acquire a different character.'"

"That's clear as mud," I said.

"I'm not done. 'Differentiation' … 'in biology, the process by which cells or tissues undergo a change toward a more specialized form or function, especially during embryonic development.' Now I'll look up 'embryonic' … the one that best fits is 'an animal in the earliest stages of its development in the uterus or egg.'" Hooker frowned.

"What? What's wrong now?"

"Was your mom pregnant when she died?"

I was taken aback. "Daddy's never said. Why?"

"You could ask, couldn't you?"

"I suppose. He might not answer, but I could ask."

"Do that. Let's go on … *prognosis*. Oh, this doesn't sound good … it means either 'a prediction of the probable course and outcome of a disease,' or 'the likelihood of recovery from a disease,' as well as 'a forecast or prediction.' Expecting a baby isn't considered a disease, is it?"

"Of course not."

"I didn't think so. Then maybe your mom had a disease. Can you ask?"

"Sure, but Daddy would get highly suspicious."

"Oh, you'll think of something … what's next … this long one? Also your mom's writing?"

I nodded.

"Oh, this one's hot! Listen to this: *Forgive me, my darling.* She's writing to your uncle, but it's not just a friendly letter—it's a love letter! She's asking him to help her do something he won't do, but what could it be? Don't hate me for saying this, dear heart, but it fits with the previous clue. What if she was expecting a baby, and she didn't want to have it, and she wanted him to help her get rid of it?"

"She wouldn't get rid of a baby, Hooker! She'd want a baby. After all, she wanted me. She—"

"She might not if it wasn't planned, or—oh, I just thought of something else! What if it wasn't your dad's? What if it was somebody else's? Like your uncle's?"

"Are you nuts? How dare you suggest that my mother—that my mother and Uncle Jack—that her and—" I was too upset to finish my sentence.

"Stop talking so loud!" Hooker held a hand over my mouth. "My window's wide open and your dad's not exactly deaf. Do we want him charging over here?"

I shook my head and pushed his hand away.

"No, you bet we don't, so settle down."

I settled, with difficulty.

He continued. "Now this part is interesting: *after all, aren't my affections easily transferred.* Maybe she found somebody else to do what she wanted … yup, no doubt about it, because right afterward she asks your uncle to forgive that as well. And then this last part: *At least I won't*—won't what? Won't bother him with this anymore? Won't have to explain what happened? Won't be seeing him after this? The possibilities are endless, unfortunately."

I took a deep breath, overwhelmed at what my novice Sherlock could envision from a few fractured phrases.

"And here's the last one," he said. "This one's easy: *Kiss her as often as you can*, and so forth. She's asking Uncle Jack to love you for her, because she knows she won't be there to do it."

"Why not?"

"Because she knows she'll soon be dead."

I shuddered. "I thought you'd say that. But why didn't she ask Daddy to love me for her?"

"Who said she didn't? We don't have those letters. Maybe she asked all the relatives. And maybe this letter wasn't meant for your uncle. It could've been written to your aunt … and I just thought of something else."

"What?"

"Maybe she knew your grandma would raise you after she died. Your uncle and aunt lived nearby, so they'd help out, while your dad would be off pursuing his career, like always."

"And that's exactly what happened," I said.

Hooker took a hard look at me. "What's wrong? You don't look so good."

"My head hurts." I slid the envelope containing the fragments into my pocket. "It's really too much to think about all at one time. I better get home. Daddy gives me the twenty questions if I'm over here too long."

"Okay, just remember to ask if your mom was sick or expecting a baby. And borrow that typewriter."

"No problem. Daddy won't think a thing of it." I marched myself downstairs.

I began my feeble attempt to solve the new mysteries over dinner at the Red Dragon. I began cautiously, saying how nice it was for Darrell to have brothers to share his childhood, and how nearly everyone had siblings but me, and how I would've liked to have had a brother or sister. Maria agreed with my statements, while Daddy was noncommittal.

Then I took the plunge. "Daddy, I've always wondered whether you and Mother ever planned to have more kids, beside me."

"You weren't planned. You just appeared, like an early Christmas present." He kept reading the menu.

"But didn't you want more?"

"No."

"Did Mother?"

"Yes."

"But she never did."

"Obviously not."

"Well, why not?"

He looked up from his menu. "Isn't this an odd topic for dinner conversation?"

"Not really." I tried to sound unconcerned. "I thought maybe she had a disease that made her unable to have more kids … did she?"

Daddy focused more intently on me. "Abigail, where's this bullshit coming from?"

I hoped Maria would intercede, but she wisely kept quiet.

"Nowhere, Daddy … I was just wondering."

"Keep wondering … now, is there anything else? I want to eat without being quizzed about the dead and buried."

"Um … could I borrow your typewriter?"

"That's a bizarre change of subject. What do you want that for?"

"So I can learn to type."

"No need for that. You'll learn next year in school. If you learn too early, it'll become a crutch and your handwriting will go to pot … have you made your selection?"

"What selection?"

"Your meal selection, Abigail! What's wrong with you tonight? Your mind's everywhere but inside your head. Close your menu so Chang will know we're ready … I'm not in the best of moods, in case you haven't noticed."

Actually I had.

That night, after Daddy's perfunctory goodnight kiss, I prayed for God to heal whatever ruination Uncle Jack had wrought upon his liver during his lengthy obsession with the bottle. I prayed that my next letter to Darrell would find him still living at the farm and not be forwarded to the Good Samaritan Home for Orphans, Foundlings, and Indigent Children. I prayed that God would facilitate a safe passage into Daddy's forbidden office for me and Hooker. When I'd run out of requests, I slept fitfully.

I dreamt of unwanted babies and dead babies.

I dreamt of Mother with Uncle Jack, and of Daddy with Aunt Annie.

I dreamt of fresh red blood, dried black blood, slicing knives, and rivers of running blood.

I dreamt the curse of God manifested itself in the form of a diseased finger scuttling along the wooden floor of my bedroom with no hand or body attached, creeping ever closer toward my footboard, creeping closer and closer—

I awoke with a scream. Or had I screamed only in my nightmare?

I switched on my bedside lamp, fearing the febrile finger. It was not there.

And then I noticed it, glowing white upon the dark walls of my room: Daddy's latest list, *typed!* I waited torturous minutes in case someone ascended the stairs in response to my shriek. When no one did, I slipped from my bed, dug the envelope containing the fragments from its hiding place, and made the comparison.

The typed letters matched perfectly.

Daddy had written the letter to Aunt Annie. He was encouraging her to leave and never look back. But leave what: the farm? Uncle Jack? Her children? And when: years ago or more recently?

I'd always felt uncomfortable whenever the two of them had been together, although Uncle Jack hadn't appeared to share my unease. Or had he been powerless to object? I also remembered Daddy never missed an opportunity to compliment my aunt, even admitting he'd loved her … but then, everyone had. He'd said that too.

But Daddy hadn't seemed as upset about her untimely death as others had been … or was he simply a master at concealing his feelings?

He already seemed a master at concealing the truth.

Autumn 1948

The Enigma Journal

THE SEASONS AGAIN came full circle. After school ended in June, I made my usual pilgrimage to the farm. With me nearing fourteen, Daddy figured I could manage the train trip alone, and I did.

Uncle Jack was waiting for me at the depot. His welcome was warm and his demeanor cheerful. Aunt Emma had found little fault with his behavior in her frequent, newsy letters of the past year, and my visit bore out her favorable opinion.

Daddy and Maria attended Uncle Vic and Aunt Emma's Independence Day celebration before taking me back home. It was the party to end all parties, boasting of fried chicken and hot dogs with all the trimmings, root beer floats, fireworks, and a hay ride. Virgil and Jimmy Swanson donned clown costumes to amuse the kids, while kegs of beer amused the men and some of the women too. An impromptu sing-along was instigated by Uncle Jack, beginning with "Mockingbird Hill" and ending with "Too Old to Cut the Mustard." For as much beer as the singers had consumed, the result was akin to hounds baying at the moon. Then Harold Evers pumped his accordion far into the night as everyone who was still able, danced.

Getting in the spirit of things, my cousin Gary and I snuck some beer, drank it, and kissed in the darkness behind the barn. His was my first kiss, and it was bad. When I told him to keep his tongue to himself, the second kiss was better. At least I didn't have to spit afterward. If we'd stuck to the lemonade like the other kids, we never would've kissed because I didn't like him much, although he seemed to like me. I remembered that the next morning when I woke up with a headache.

But Daddy and Uncle Jack fared far worse. Both fell off the wagon, literally and figuratively. On the afternoon of July sixth, after some memorable post-holiday carousing with Vinnie Swanson, Uncle Vic, Uncle Ben, and a couple of bums nobody seemed to know, Uncle Jack wandered home to his sons, and Daddy sobered up sufficiently to haul me and Maria back to Minneapolis.

Maria wasn't speaking to him, but I was. I told Daddy how happy I was to be returning to the city because I'd realized that my new life afforded me more opportunities than had my old one. Daddy mumbled something unintelligible before asking me to dig in the glove box for the aspirin.

But the real draw of home was the boy next door. Once school started, Daddy hoped that Hooker would consume less of my affections, but he hoped in vain. While he agreed that Hooker was brilliant scholastically, he couldn't stomach him personally. This made Hooker perfect, to my way of thinking. I used him to antagonize Daddy, whenever Daddy antagonized me.

"Don't you think Hooker's just wonderful?" I'd say. "He's my best friend. I can tell him everything, and I do. I bet you're glad I've found such a good friend, aren't you, Daddy?"

"No." Daddy would peer at me over his evening newspaper. "Hooker's a conceited, shiftless, weaseling smart aleck. What you see in him is beyond me."

"But he *is* polite," I'd say. Hooker was careful to call my father "Mr. Stahl" or "sir" at every encounter, but what he called Daddy behind his back was something else!

"Yes, he is polite," Daddy would admit.

"And Hooker is very cheerful."

"Yes, he's the most goddamned cheerful boy I've ever run across. I'd like to run across him too … with my car."

"Oh, how can you say such a terrible thing?" I'd react in mock horror. "After all, Hooker's so thoughtful and considerate. Why, he treats me like a real princess!"

That statement rankled Daddy every time. "No, he couldn't possibly, because you're *my* princess."

"Oh, that's right!" I'd laugh and give my father a hug before I ran next door to be with the boy I hoped would become my prince.

And so Hooker and I slid from our fourteen year toward our fifteen, like two silly peas in a crazy pod. Daddy said every gray hair on his head was because of me. And his spike in blood pressure was because of Hooker.

Daddy's only respite came when he disappeared into his office and locked the door. Sometimes I'd hear the click-click-click of his typewriter. Other times I'd hear nothing. Often I would smell the oils, turpentine, and varnish that he used for his paintings. I'd long wanted him to get a regular job, but he preferred to lose himself in his art.

He was a superlative artist. He won prizes at juried shows. His exhibitions sold out. He raised his prices and began accepting commissions, preferring wildlife or landscapes. He painted portraits only if the recompense was high enough. He painted me on several occasions, but I hated the results. I looked pale, troubled, a frail child portrayed stark against a swirling maelstrom of blacks, grays, and purples.

By contrast, his sole painting of Maria did her justice. He accurately captured the tilt of her head, the curve of her nose, the sensuousness of her lips, and the fullness of her bosom. *The Woman from Naples* hung above our fireplace, its backdrop a warm mix of umber and gold.

It happened one day after school, when Hooker and I least expected it: we gained access to Daddy's secrets. He'd been in his office, working on his latest commission before the afternoon light waned and he'd be forced to set his brushes aside. Hooker and I were seated at our dining room table, studying health. The chapter was "The Physiological Differences between Boys and Girls."

"My God, there's a difference?" Hooker sniggered, beginning our study session on an appropriate note.

Daddy demanded that we study together at our house rather than Hooker's, probably the better to overhear our conversations. On this particular afternoon, Hooker was outdoing himself, saying words like "pubescent" and "urethra" unnecessarily loudly. We filled in the gaps with pantomime, interspersed with giggling.

I nearly expected Daddy to charge out of his office, smock askew, brushes at the ready, poised to protect my maidenhood, but he didn't. Apparently he was working against a deadline, which trumped his obsession with my safety.

Daddy had months ago decided that there was something precarious with my continued association with the blue-eyed, sandy-haired, half-French, half-mongrel wastrel from next door, but he hadn't been successful in convincing me. I liked Hooker more than ever. I was just contemplating how much I liked him when the telephone rang.

"Should I answer?" I hollered. Daddy kept a second telephone in the office, but he usually didn't like to be interrupted while working.

"No, I'll get it." His response sounded muffled through the door. Moments later, he appeared, wiping his hands on a rag. He locked the office door behind him. "It's Dayton's. Maria's had an accident. They're taking her to the hospital."

I gasped. "What happened? Will she be okay?"

"I hope so. She fell and broke something. Stay here and finish your work. I'll be back as soon as I can."

"All right, Daddy." I watched through the window as he sped away.

"I hope it's not serious," Hooker said.

"I wouldn't think so. If you break something in a fall, it's usually an arm or a leg. She should heal up in no time."

"I hope so. I like Maria. Other than the time she beat my butt, she's been real nice. She doesn't look at me like I'm heading straight to the penitentiary like you-know-who."

I sighed. "I know, but he can't help it. He's just being Daddy."

"Abby." Hooker broke into a grin. "Here's our chance."

"Our chance for what?"

"Our chance to get inside his office, that's what."

"We can't do that, Hooker. He locked it. I saw him."

"He left in a hurry. He only locked the bottom lock, not the top. I think I can pick the bottom one. I've been practicing."

"You've been practicing for over a year," I scoffed. "You haven't picked a lock yet."

"There's always the first time ... wait here, I'll get my tools."

Hooker returned from his house with a leather pouch, hunkered down, and got to work.

I labeled the male and female parts on my health worksheets while Hooker picked. I memorized my ridiculously easy spelling words while Hooker picked. I summarized Poe's "The Raven" while Hooker picked.

"You better hurry up. Daddy's been gone forty minutes already. Getting a bone set and a cast put on shouldn't take more than another hour or so."

"Like I don't know that? This shit isn't easy, you know, or locksmiths wouldn't have any business."

I was halfway through a chapter on Spain when the office door swung open.

"Eureka!" Hooker clambered to his feet. "I did it!"

"You did! I can hardly believe it, Sherlock, but you really did it!"

Hooker executed an exaggerated bow. "Time's wasting. After you, Watson."

I held my breath as I stepped through the doorway. Through the doorway I stepped, from the present into the past. Daddy had closed the drapes before he left, as he always did to prevent us peeking from outside. I opened them again, and what the late afternoon sun illuminated was peculiar, to say the least.

A tall bookcase stood in one corner, next to the heavy drapes. Arranged on the shelves were a collection of milliner heads and department store hands. The molded eyes of the heads stared at me, all brown, their lashes and brows carefully painted.

Odd, I thought. The milliner heads at Dayton's had blue eyes. Looking closer, I noticed that the eyes had been repainted. The lips had been repainted too, in a shape familiar to me. Daddy had replicated Mother's features on the milliner heads!

Atop each head was a hat, embellished with feathers, beads, and various ornaments. Were they Mother's hats, more than a decade out of style? Costume jewelry adorned each swanlike neck. Neither Gramma nor Aunt Annie had ever owned anything similar. Matching earrings, glued in place, completed each silent ensemble.

The ivory hands rested mid-arm, the fingers thrust upward, reaching toward the shelf above. Some wore kidskin gloves, some rhinestone bracelets and rings, others held dainty handkerchiefs. One, taller than the rest, boasted two rings: a plain, gold band on the ring finger and a much larger ring, also gold, slipped over the thumb. I held the large ring up to the window. E C to J S was carved inside. My father's wedding band.

I put it back and admired a dress worn by a headless, armless manikin. An evening dress, all satin and beads. A second manikin faced the corner, attired in a khaki dress. With foreboding, I turned it around and recognized the brackish hole I could put my fist through—my mother's death dress! Daddy had not burned it after all. I withdrew my hand, trying to understand.

A dozen or more framed photographs of Mother with Daddy hung on the wall nearest the manikins. In one, she was wearing the beaded satin dress, while he was attired in a tuxedo. In another, her face was uplifted to his, as though they were about to kiss. I swallowed the lump forming in my throat and moved on.

An autograph book lay on top of a bureau. Opening it, I saw Gramma had given it to Mother in 1932. I paged through the inscriptions penned by many of our relatives and from some unknown to me. One page caught my eye: *Time is swift and merciless, uncaring of either a mistake or a promise*, followed by the initials J S. I couldn't be certain whether the author was Uncle Jack or Daddy, as they wrote so similarly. The phrase seemed familiar.

Tiny bottles of partially filled perfumes were arranged on a gilt mirror, along with compacts, a hairbrush and comb, dusting powder, and various whatnot. I pried the stopper from one bottle and the scent permeated the room, overwhelming the odor of solvent emanating from Daddy's latest artistic endeavor.

His easel was placed on the far side of the room, in a bright corner next to a window. Only there, with his tubes of paint meticulously arranged on a small table, was I comfortable with the things I was seeing.

The rest of the room seemed stagnant, the atmosphere heavy. I remembered Daddy saying when I first met him that he struggled with bouts of melancholia. If I spent too much time within these walls, I would as well.

Hooker had been poking around in a battered campaign chest, taking things out, looking at them, and putting them back. "What kind of place is this?"

"My father's second shrine."

"That's what I thought … I'm sorry."

"So am I."

On the massive desk, the gilded lamp and the journal I'd seen three years ago were still present. At the top of the opened page of the journal was the present date: the first of December, 1948. Several paragraphs followed. At some point earlier today, Daddy had entered his thoughts.

My dearest Ellen,

Last month was fairly peaceful around here, if any month can be peaceful with Abby in this house. Raising a child of her mercurial temperament continues to be challenging. Her impetuosity and willfulness have mitigated somewhat, however, while I'm encouraging her more positive aspects. You would be gratified to know that she continues to do admirably in school. My insistence on her studying vocabulary from an early age and reading extensively outside of the classroom has already come to fruition.

I've mentioned Hooker to you before … well, not much more I can say about that sorry situation. Hopefully he's a phase she'll eventually outgrow.

As for myself, I'm doing incredibly well with my painting. Funny, you always said I would, if I could somehow tear myself away from the military. If my success continues unabated to the end of this month, I stand to make as much this year as I did as a colonel, and without risking my life! Isn't that a hoot? I remember you liked to use that bit of slang.

My skin prickled on the back of my neck. "Hooker."

"What?"

"Look at this … Daddy's writing to Mother as though she were still alive."

Hooker left what he was doing and read over my shoulder. "You're right. That's *so* creepy … well, would you look at this! So he's hoping I'm just a phase, is he?"

"Don't worry about it. He wasn't all that complimentary to me either … I wonder how far back this goes." I flipped to the beginning of the journal. "August first, 1935 … that's shortly after Mother died." I thumbed through the next few pages before my mind grasped what I was seeing. "Oh, my God! Daddy's made entries in this journal on the first of the month ever since. That's over thirteen years!"

Hooker whistled under his breath. "Then you've found the prize, after all these years. Read it and you'll know everything."

"Grab my notebook so I can take notes." I held the journal tight as though it might vanish if I let go.

"Good idea. Otherwise things get mixed up." Hooker retrieved my health notebook from the dining room and handed it to me. "While you're doing that, I'll read these letters I found in this drawer."

"Pull the drapes first."

"Why? I won't be able to see to read the letters."

"You'll see well enough. We can't take the chance of Daddy driving down the alley and seeing the drapes open when he closed them. How dumb are you?"

"As dumb as you. My butt is on the line, same as yours."

He was right. This time it wouldn't be Maria and her spaghetti spoon. This time it would be Daddy, with a temper like Mount Vesuvius and an arm of iron.

"Sorry, we just can't take the chance." I closed the drapes myself. "We'll just have to listen for his car. Make sure you can put everything back exactly like you found it in one minute. That's probably all the time we'll have."

"No pressure there," Hooker said.

"No pressure at all." I glanced at the clock on Daddy's desk, judging the time I'd have, and began reading the first entry.

Dear Ellen,

How can I continue to call you "dear" after what happened? Other terms, hardly of endearment, come to mind! How could you have disobeyed me, at the worst possible moment? Did you not realize what could happen? Or did you wish it to happen, after the previous night?

God forgive me that! Could I not have believed your explanation, one more time, implausible as it were? I've believed other explanations of yours, haven't I? Even the most ludicrous!

Was our last confrontation designed to twist the knife already in my heart? And the way you laughed, at the end, ridiculing me … my God, even now, I can hear you laughing. I can see you laughing. You are here, with me, inside me, torturing my days, haunting my nights … will I ever know peace? In the end, perhaps, when I've slipped my temporal bounds and returned to dust … then I may find peace, but not before.

And to think it could've ended far differently if only you had not done that, my foolish one. I could hardly be blamed for reacting the way I did. You died with my mark upon you … a mark you did not live long enough to heal.

A growing sense of apprehension made my pencil shake. What was Daddy saying? He loved my mother, but they had a terrible fight about something, and she'd laughed at him? He'd lost control and did something to her that resulted in a mark? What kind of mark? A bruise? Or far worse—a bullet?

"Hooker," I breathed.

He glanced up fearfully. "What? Did you hear the car?"

"No, not the car. It's this journal, Hooker. Daddy didn't write facts I can copy. He wrote opinions and emotions. I'd have to study this for days, maybe weeks, before I'd understand the full story. And I only have about another hour."

"Then all you can do is skim and summarize. Jot down the dates along with whatever details you come across. You never know how things might fit together. After all, I came up with some pretty interesting ideas after reading those few clues from your uncle."

"You're right, that's all I can do." I turned to my task.

An hour and a half passed as I filled page after page of my notebook, writing as fast as I could, hoping I'd be able to read my chicken scratches later. *Write faster, write faster, skim, write, next page, skim, write, next page, get it done, get it done, you won't get another chance, you'll never get another chance, never!*

"This is a really good one," Hooker said. "I'm taking this one."

I startled, my concentration shattered. "What did you say?"

"I'm keeping this letter. Evidence, you know." He smiled and patted his pocket.

"Put it back."

"No, it's the most interesting one I've read. You won't believe what your uncle wrote your dad."

"I don't care. We can't take a chance. Put it back."

"It won't be missed. There's maybe a hundred letters here."

Just then I heard the familiar rumble of my father's sedan. "Daddy's coming! Put everything away! Hurry, Hooker, *hurry!*"

He scooped the letters he'd been reading from the floor, piled them into the bottom of the campaign chest, straightened them with a sweep of his hand, and crammed his notes into his pocket.

I flipped Daddy's journal forward to the present date. After a cursory glance, making sure we hadn't dropped or forgotten anything, I switched off the desk lamp and we dashed from the office.

"Lock the door!" I said.

Hooker froze.

I started to panic. "Don't just stand there! Lock the door!"

"I can't!"

"But you have to!"

"I tell you I can't! I can pick a lock, but I can't relock it!"

"*What?* You idiot! You moron!" As my brief life flashed in front of my eyes like a movie reel gone berserk, I kicked Hooker so hard that the toe of my saddle shoe crumpled.

He lurched and grabbed his shin. "Don't kick me! God, that hurt!"

"Don't tell me what to do, you lock-picking imbecile!" I kicked him again.

He kicked me back, hard enough to cause tears. But I'd need those tears, so I tried not to react.

But Hooker reacted. He raced out our front door, leaving me to face perdition alone.

For a split second, I considered running after him. But Hooker was mad and he might deny me refuge in his house, so I tore up the steps to my room instead. I ripped the notes I'd taken from my health notebook and shoved them between my mattress and box springs.

"Abby, we're home!" Daddy called.

I took a deep breath and sauntered downstairs. My father's mark would be upon me in no time.

"I'm here," I said, like he couldn't see that for himself.

"Good. We'll need your help tonight." He assisted Maria into the living room.

"Oh, Abby, such a day!" Maria sank to the davenport and handed me her crutches. "If only the new girl had put the silver cleaner where it belonged, I never would've been on that ladder looking on the top shelf. All I got for my trouble is a broken ankle … James, would you be a dear and make me a martini?"

"Of course … Abby, make dinner. Anything will do."

I threw together a hamburger casserole and opened a can of corn. Maria drank her martini. Daddy drank several.

After dinner, I started the dishes. Maria went to bed. Daddy went to his office.

I watched him out of the corner of my eye. He put his key to the lock when the door opened slightly. He paused, one hand on the knob, the other holding the key. He stood by the door for what seemed an eternity.

I trembled.

He cocked his head to the side, as though trying to remember. "Well, I could've sworn I'd locked this." He went inside. The click of the lock was unmistakable.

I stood by the sink, hardly daring to breathe.

I wondered whether I'd turned the second manikin back to the corner.

I wondered whether I'd closed Mother's autograph book.

I wondered whether I'd taken my No. 2 pencil off Daddy's desk.

I wondered whether the scent of perfume was still apparent.

I wondered whether Hooker had closed the campaign chest completely.

I wondered whether anything had gotten turned, tilted, left awry, left askew.

After Daddy remained inside his office for five whole minutes, I wondered whether we had gotten away with it.

Miraculously, we had.

The next morning, I went next door and apologized to Hooker for kicking him twice. Once would've been okay, given the circumstances, I said, but twice was plain mean.

Hooker apologized for leaving me to face my father's wrath alone.

Then we made up the grown-up way: we kissed for the first time.

"Um … not bad," I said.

"What do you mean, not bad?"

"Just what I said. Not bad."

"So how would you know? Have you made a comparison? Maybe you've kissed somebody else already?"

I shrugged. "Just Gary."

"Gary? Who the hell's Gary?"

"You know, Gary … my cousin from St. James."

"You're kissing your cousin? Ugh, that's disgusting! You're not supposed to kiss your cousin!"

"You would if you had enough beer."

For as long as it took me to calm Hooker after that statement, I realized that my frog, at last, had become my prince.

That night I peeled away the felt underside of my bedside lamp's base. Within the hollow, I inserted the notes that Hooker and I had taken, along with the purloined letter. I glued the felt back with Elmer's.

I'd read everything, but I hadn't understood everything. I'd have to wait until I was older to fit the pieces of the puzzle together.

Summer 1951

Great White Hunter

AND SO TIME passed, as time does. The mysteries inside my lamp base remained unsolved, waiting for the proper circumstances, while other things and other people occupied my mind.

Uncle Jack thrust himself upon my consciousness rather abruptly the summer of 1951. Not that he said anything, but Aunt Emma sure did. This time it wasn't my uncle's drinking; it was his wandering.

"Daddy, what's wandering?" I wanted to make sure I had the context correct.

"Moving around aimlessly, possibly ending up somewhere other than where you should be." He paused in the preparation of a curried dish destined to become our dinner. "You know that already, so who are we talking about now?"

"Your brother."

"That figures … what does Emma say?"

"How do you know Emma said anything?"

"I just know these things."

I retrieved her letter from my room so I could read him the most tantalizing parts. "First of all, she says your brother was seen at the Hickory Inn with a redhead last Friday."

"Good. He needs companionship. Annie was a redhead."

"And he was seen at the Orchid Inn with a brunette the week before."

"Brunettes are nice … your mother was one."

"And he was seen drinking at the Dew-Drop Inn with a blonde just the other night. Aunt Emma says, and I quote:

Harry was there, meeting an Army chum, so he saw the whole thing. He said she was dressed like a tramp, with her clothes too low on top and too high on the bottom. She was smoking a blue haze and throwing back shots and draping herself all over Jack and he ended up leaving with her. After they left, everybody in the bar started laughing about it. Nobody knew who she was, so she wasn't a local, but everybody agreed she looked like a gold digger and that Jack better check himself afterward.

Daddy's eyebrows shot up a full inch. "Emma wrote *that*?"

"Yes, I'm reading it right here. What's 'check himself afterward' mean?"

"It means—never mind what it means! And where exactly are your cousins while all this is going on? Does Emma say?"

"Of course she does." I resumed reading:

Darrell's taking care of the twins and the home front all over again, because I've found out this has happened before! I called about eleven the night Jack wandered off with the tramp and he hadn't gotten home yet, so I called again the next morning. Same story. We were about to notify the sheriff to go look for him when Darrell called in the afternoon and said he'd showed up, acting like nothing was wrong. We'd all been worried sick!

"Son of a bitch!" Daddy's mixing bowl hit the sink with a bang.

Daddy and I drove to the farm the next day, exactly as Aunt Emma had hoped. After all, someone had to set my uncle straight before a floozy spent all his money and gave him a disease to boot! I'd asked Hooker what "check himself afterward" meant.

Uncle Jack greeted us at the back door with a wry smile. "Looks like the morality lecture has arrived … hello, Abby."

"Hello, Uncle Jack." I gave him a quick hug. He didn't look as though he spent his nights with women of low repute, but Hooker hadn't known how quickly loose living would alter one's appearance.

"Is this a setup?" Daddy inquired, taking the beer his brother offered.

"Naturally. How else would I get you here to discuss what I want to discuss? You never bother answering my letters."

"You mean to tell me you suckered Emma into reporting on you?"

"No, that was quite legitimate … did she do a good job?"

"More than adequate … how was the blonde?"

"More than adequate."

Daddy stifled a smile. "All right, Jack, let's stop the games. What do you want?"

"Why don't you go for a long ride with the twins?" Uncle Jack said to me. It was an order phrased as a question. "They're in the horse barn. Tell them they can stop shoveling."

As the three of us galloped down the driveway, I saw Daddy and Uncle

Jack talking on the porch. Judging from my father's stance, he was not a happy man.

A deal had been struck by the time I returned.

Daddy's face was tightly held. "Good-bye, Abby. I'll see you the end of August."

"August? What's going on here?" He smothered me like a broody hen and suddenly he was letting me go for nearly three months? Impossible!

"He'll fill you in." Daddy indicated his brother. "Remember what I said, Jack. Anything happens to her, you'd better be dead first."

"Everything will be fine."

"It damned well better be."

My father gave me a long hug, and then he got in his car and drove away. He paused by the mailbox, as though looking back. I waved, but he did not reciprocate.

I turned to my uncle. "Now what'd you do? You look like the cat that ate the canary. What's the big secret?"

Uncle Jack chuckled. "No secret. I'm just taking you to Africa."

My eyes nearly fell from my head. "Are you serious?"

"Of course. How many times already this year have you mentioned going?"

"I—I don't know."

"Seven. I've kept your letters and I've kept track, Abby. It's time I show you the continent I love. It's time I take you hunting—and it's time I take you to your mother."

Only after shopping excursions to New Ulm and Mankato did I fully realize that my African dream was, at last, coming true. A man's jacket with plenty of pockets and a shooting vest, both sized small, were purchased at a sporting goods store. Several hats, scarves, slacks, sweaters for nippy nights, and two pairs of boots suitable for hiking completed my ensemble. When my uncle said I wouldn't be returning home before the start of our trip, I also bought underwear, dress clothes, and personal items.

"How'd you get Daddy to let me go?" I asked during one of our first outings.

"Oh, I threatened him like he used to threaten me." Uncle Jack had smiled, but his eyes had not smiled accordingly.

"Threatened him how?"

"That's for me to know and you to find out."

"And will I find out?"

"Most assuredly."

Uncle Jack had asked Darrell to accompany us to Africa, but the invitation had been declined. He'd go next time. This time, he opted to spend his summer behind the soda fountain at Schneider's Drugstore, sweet-talking the girls as they drifted in for their cherry fizzes or their latest movie magazines.

Darrell confided to me that he'd set his sights on Denice Andersen, whose dark eyes and vivacious personality sent shivers up his spine. That she was Catholic to his Lutheran made her all the more delectable. Darrell called her his "forbidden fruit," and I called him stupid. Girls weren't apples waiting to be picked.

Conversely, Uncle Jack had not invited the twins. He said that he needed to take both if he took one, and part of his reason for going in the first place was to get the hell out of Dodge, if I caught his drift.

I did.

Duane and Dennis were like having two additional Uncle Jacks around: sarcastic, opinionated, and a bit squirrelly. They weren't nearly as organized or particular as he, but at thirteen, they were still developing. Neither twin slowed from the time he awoke until he collapsed at night. I found them amusing, but they wore me out. If given a choice, I wouldn't take them roller skating, much less to Africa.

When my expedited passport arrived, I called Daddy and Maria to say good-bye. Maria became very emotional, but my father sounded distant and hard.

"Daddy, what's wrong? Are you still worried? I'll be all right, I promise!"

When he wouldn't elaborate, I got Maria back on the telephone. She told me what he couldn't: he was terrified for me. I nearly cried. I wanted to reassure him, but she said he'd left on a walk. Then I did cry, remembering how I'd felt when Daddy had gone back to the war and I feared I'd never see him alive again. I'd never wanted him to hurt as much as that.

No one answered at Hooker's house, so I called Maria back and asked her to explain the circumstances surrounding my departure. She said she would. Hooker would be glad for me. After all, his curiosity nearly equaled mine. Soon I would find out what really happened to my mother in Africa.

Uncle Jack had promised.

Uncle Vic and Aunt Emma moved into Uncle Jack's house the next morning, while Virgil remained at their home place. Uncle Jack handed Uncle Vic a wad of cash when he thought I wasn't looking.

Mrs. Monson arrived as we were leaving. I hadn't seen her since the previous summer. She was returning to teaching in the fall, she said, but working for my uncle the past four years had been enlightening. Then she gave us a prettily decorated box of sandwiches and cookies to tide us over the first leg of our trip.

Uncle Jack and I waved good-bye and left. We left with our passports and tickets, his clothes, my clothes, his guns, and my gun: a custom 30-06 with my name inscribed on the receiver, in gold, which he said I was to use in Africa and keep forever.

As my uncle drove toward Union Depot in St. Paul, I set aside my regrets about failing to bid Hooker farewell and to speak to Daddy one last time.

Hallelujah, I was going to Africa!

I'd write from Pretoria and Nairobi and Gaborone and Cape Town and Durban. I'd pose in front of the thundering Victoria Falls and sip my tea with my pinkie held high and nibble my cucumber sandwiches on the veranda of the Victoria Falls Hotel. I'd slosh through the Okavango and hunt along the hippo trails. I'd huddle by a campfire with nothing but the embers holding back the ink of the African darkness. I'd shoot my impala and my zebra and thrill to the lion and the hyena when they invaded camp in the dead of the night to shriek and cackle over the moldering carcasses.

And Uncle Jack would calm my fears, as though I'd have any, and show me the Africa he loved.

I don't know what to expect in Africa, but my imagination serves me well. I picture trekking through thorn-covered brush, up stony-pathed mountains, fording rushing rivers dotted with crocs in search of a snack and crazed hippos with an affinity for hunters. I envision rhinos charging from around every bend, leopards dropping from every tree, snakes writhing along every path, insects of differing dimensions and potencies crawling uninvited onto everything and everybody.

Nearly two weeks of exhausting travel follows: by train, by ship, and ship again, and train again, by truck. Uncle Jack waxes ecstatic when our guns arrive safely at each temporary destination. "Things do tend to disappear in Africa," he says.

I am more ecstatic when our battered luggage arrives when we do. To me, our guns are expendable, but my clothes are essential.

Finally we arrive at *The Last Outpost*, as the sign at the edge of a dusty town, whose name I can't pronounce, proclaims. I'm uncertain whether the sign is a boast or a threat. At the Elangeni Hotel, dating from the height of the British Empire, Uncle Jack dines on impala curry while I savor eland cutlets. A string orchestra soothes in the background. A scented bath, drawn deep and hot by the chambermaid, precedes my weary sleep. Uncle Jack spends half the night at the bar, and I again fear for his liver.

Our white hunter, Terry Shaw, arrives the next morning with his lead tracker, Solkwemu. Terry is brown and lean from a lifetime in the bush. He is dressed, appropriately enough, in khaki. A skinning knife dangles from his belt. He flashes a cheerful smile, shakes our hands, and says with a clipped accent, "Good to meet you, Jack. And this is Abigail, I presume? Shit of a trip, isn't it?"

He drives us five hours north to our first camp, where we will eat and sleep before moving further inland. While dodging goats, skinny dogs, and the curious, Terry fills us in on the current political situation, economic conditions, Zulu lore and customs, the flora and fauna of the region, and an overview of African history of the past two hundred years.

The road goes from bad to worse, and we penetrate areas I wouldn't have thought a vehicle could go, up perilous inclines, slipping down the other side, creeping along hairpin curves, hugging the sides of steep hills, looking almost endlessly across the valleys below.

Terry gestures grandly. "M.M.B.A. ... miles and miles of bloody Africa."

In the waning light of late afternoon, the view is breathtaking.

Terry urges Uncle Jack to shoot whatever we chance upon to supply the camp workers with fresh meat. My uncle is pleased to oblige, and dispatches a young impala ram before darkness falls like a blanket.

"*Mashaya Kahle*," Terry says. "He who only needs one shot."

That night I again sleep deeply, but Uncle Jack stays up for hours with Terry, sharing stories and whiskey around the campfire.

Then it is dawn. The first tenuous slivers of light creep across green hills punctuated with low trees and scrub. The chattering of monkeys mixes with the occasional cry of a bush baby, an eerie sound Terry describes as "a baby getting its head screwed off." The air hangs cool and still. The merest of breezes reach this quiet valley sequestered among the many hills. A shout would carry for miles. A rooster crows at a Zulu settlement far up the valley, then another.

A greeting is voiced outside our tent. A slim boy arrives with a tray of hot tea, cookies, rusks, cheese, and honey.

"Ah, the boys." Uncle Jack drizzles honey on his rusk. "What I love most about Africa in the morning. Too bad they don't speak English ... on second thought, if they did, where'd be the intrigue? The romance?"

We resume our northerly trek after breakfast and have a flat along the way, which Solkwemu changes as Terry digs in the cool box for beer. I content myself with a sickly sweet lime drink that does nothing to assuage my thirst.

By afternoon, it is hot, dusty, and flies assume every portion of our exposed bodies is available for their amusement. Just before reaching camp, Uncle Jack shoots an enormous snake draped languidly in the crotch of an acacia near the road. It drops to the dust, writhing, on the passenger side of the Rover, mere inches from my door. I cringe as it curls back along itself, bleeding, dying.

"No worries," Terry says. "Not poisonous."

I think of Daddy shooting a far more lethal snake on another African safari, but for now, the past is past. I'm living in the moment and the moment is magic.

The following day goes better. The weather cools. The drive is long but without incident.

Hunting should be good here, Terry informs us, after we've camped. We begin at first light. Uncle Jack will do the honors on the trophy animals, and I can shoot whatever target of opportunity arises. I decline politely, saying I wish to observe for a few days first.

"No problem," Terry says. "Whenever you're ready."

We walk for miles the next day. The sun is warm and comforting. Breezes ripple the long grass. The only missing components are the distant beat of drums and Humphrey Bogart to lead us. Every Tarzan story I've ever read comes alive.

Never had I believed, when I was a child on Gramma's farm, that one day I'd experience an African adventure with Uncle Jack. Never had I believed I'd actually see what he saw, what my father saw, what my mother saw—before she died.

Since arriving in Africa, I've been feeling her presence. She is with me wherever I am. I am dreaming of her, in the blackness just before dawn, when the stagnant night air weighs most oppressively on me, condensing my dreams. My dreams are so intense I'm thankful Uncle Jack is sleeping on the next cot. He is sleeping, but he is holding up my dreams. If I were alone in the tent, my dreams would crush me.

She knows I am coming to her, at last.

Uncle Jack decides he'd like a trophy bushbuck. But for all our efforts, bushbuck elude us, although we hear one barking in the distance as we come back to camp that evening.

Over the next several days, Uncle Jack bags a bush pig, a duiker, and several impala. None are trophy quality, but he doesn't care. Hunting for sport and meat is fine. We don't see any bushbuck. The good ones have moved north, Terry surmises. We'll catch up to them. No matter, Uncle Jack says. The scenery here is worthwhile for me to see before we move upland.

We eat only the most tender portion of each impala. Terry gives the rest to the boys, and they gleefully hack strips from the bones and hang it high in the trees to dry. But they neglect to haul away the carcasses, and lions visit us during the night. The great beasts cough as they move through the bush and enter our camp. They are very close. Terrified, I clasp my blankets and my eyes dart after the sounds, but I can see nothing in the blackness.

Uncle Jack sleeps through the entire thing.

In the morning, I notice multiple tracks in the dirt around our tent. I'm grateful to be alive, and I ask Terry whether we could be mauled in our cots if the lions return.

He laughs. "No. Lions don't know how to unzip a tent."

Uncle Jack laughs the hardest, and I slink off to get more tea.

Terry follows me. It is his job now to make me feel less the fool. But I am a fool, and his amends will not make me feel better. But he persists, and I soften. His piercing blue eyes look through me, past me, as he talks. I feel myself blush. I wonder whether he thinks I am just another spoiled city girl who knows nothing and dresses the part.

He asks again whether I'm ready to hunt. I reply not yet.

But I practice faithfully whenever we return to camp before dark. My new gun feels good in my hands. I like its heft, its weight, its balance. It is far more suited to me than Aunt Annie's .410 was when I hunted pheasants so long ago. I am consistent at fifty, seventy-five, and a hundred yards, but I'm off center an inch at a hundred and fifty. Terry says I probably won't have to shoot that far. He urges me to try my luck with an impala, as they are cheap and plentiful. I worry I might falter under his scrutiny, or I might miss entirely if my intended target moves, but I don't tell him that.

Uncle Jack continues to shoot whatever he chances upon. I stand in awe of his calm and steady aim under all circumstances. Compared to him, I feel inadequate and ill prepared. I decide to forgo my own hunting indefinitely. I ask Uncle Jack whether he is disappointed in me.

"No, that is such rubbish. Besides, we have plenty of time for you to change your mind. And if you don't—well, more for me."

Rubbish? Terry commonly uses that word, not him. My uncle is becoming part of Africa, right before my eyes. And he need not be disappointed. I am disappointed enough in myself.

Then I ask whether Terry is married.

"He is indeed," Uncle Jack replies. "He is married to Africa."

When my uncle takes a break from hunting, Terry drives us around the countryside. On the banks of a secluded stream, we picnic on biltong, bread, cheese, wine, and various selections of liquor. Terry digs near the water and uncovers a Bushman knife that he says could easily date back ten thousand years, as well as a potsherd. He presses both into my palm and closes my fingers over his offering.

I notice something unsettling in his eyes.

Later, we visit a potato farm and enjoy tea with the managers on their veranda. Visitors are few, and they are loath to see us go. They give us lemons and oranges from their small orchard to enjoy along the way. Terry whips his skinning knife from its sheath, wipes the stained blade across the front of his soiled khakis, and slices some of the lemons into a used cup before drenching the entirety with sugar. He starts up the Rover, and for the next several hours, he and Uncle Jack proceed to throw down shots of vodka followed by the sugared lemon slices.

I eat the oranges.

As the Rover careens from side to side along the dirt road at a very low rate of speed, supposedly to ensure our safety, Terry launches into the most vulgar ditty imaginable. He sings with unabashed gusto. Uncle Jack learns the lyrics and joins in. Together they are raucous enough to drive all game from the entire vicinity.

I refuse to sing, but I wonder aloud whether we'll make it to camp alive. Terry tells me to get the bee out of my bonnet and trust him. I refuse to trust him. I am experiencing Africa with two very bad boys.

But we make it back to camp.

The next day, we stay in camp and are waited on hand and foot. Terry and Uncle Jack feel like hell. At least they look like hell. They insist they feel fine.

I finally have an opportunity to learn about Terry. He's quite talkative as he lolls in a hammock in the shade, nursing his headache with a concoction he calls "the brain banger." He says he's a doctor's son and was headed for medical school himself when he decided it was all such a pile of shit. He'd be damned if he'd spend his life digging in sick people's bodies, trying to discover what was killing them. He'd apprenticed himself to an older white hunter, left for a life in the bush, and never looked back. His decision had come as such a disappointment to his father. He'd never have the wealth, the fine house, the community standing.

But he did have peace of mind. He was happy and would continue to be happy until he made a fatal error and a lion or a buff got him. I say that maybe he will die when a client makes a fatal error. He says that he screens his clients carefully and hopes for the best … but everything dies at some point.

When I broach the subject of marriage, he says that his ended five years ago. He asks about me. I tell him I have a boyfriend, but it isn't serious. He asks why I bother having a boyfriend if it isn't serious. I don't know how to answer, having been caught in a lie, so I mumble something about Hooker being so young and I'm looking for someone more mature.

I notice that unsettling look again.

Uncle Jack is sitting a few yards away, listening. He shakes his head in disgust.

Our sightseeing resumes with tours of a sprawling sugar cane operation and an enormous dairy farm. Privately, Uncle Jack tells me that the sugar cane farm is similar to one he once owned.

"I already guessed that, years ago," I say.

"Then you guessed too damn much, years ago."

When I inquire how he came by it, he responds bitterly, "I won it in a game of chance, but then I lost … "

Again the dark suspicion that I could barely conceive when I was a child claws and clamors inside my mind, but I cannot—will not—give it voice.

After a month in Africa, I never think of Hooker. I still can't hunt. And I'm falling in love with Terry. No doubt about it. I warn Uncle Jack not to laugh before I tell him. He doesn't laugh when he tells me that I'm a fool to even think of it.

Still, I cannot stop watching our white hunter.

In the morning, I watch him as he shaves, stirring his brush in a ceramic cup and squinting into the dimness of a cracked mirror wired to a tree. He pulls his cheek taut for the blade, and in the reflection he sees me watching. A partial smile plays about his lips as though he expects me to fall in love with him.

In the day, I watch him as he walks ahead of us, checking for spoor, judging the wind, looking for tracks, moving easily and confidently. He sees me watching when he turns suddenly to say something to Uncle Jack. To my uncle he speaks, seldom to me.

And in the night, I watch him as he weaves his tales around the ironwood fire. The glow from the embers illuminates his face—the confident glint of his eye, the rough slant of his cheek, the sensuous curve of his mouth. And when Uncle Jack pushes the logs inward or seeks another drink, Terry Shaw locks his eyes with mine, but I can only see his surface.

The rest, the interior of the man, remains in darkness.

All this I hold in my mind.

We did not mean to find them, but perhaps they found us, when we come upon a great herd of Cape buffalo, those horrid beasts that killed my mother. Or those horrid beasts that trampled my mother after she was killed—however it had happened. We both see and hear their shadowy, foreboding masses in heavy brush, lumbering about, breaking branches, snorting.

It has already been a thoroughly miserable day, with both tsetse and mopane flies torturing us, delving into our most tender areas. All afternoon, the salt of my own sweat has stung my eyes and parched my lips, and long sleeves and pants have not saved my skin from the insects.

And now this black evil.

"Let's get out of here," Terry whispers to my uncle when he sees the abject fear on my face.

Uncle Jack nods and takes my arm. We back up as silently and as unobtrusively as possible.

In leaving, Terry points to where vultures are circling, and he fails to stop me in time before I stumble across a sight I never wanted to see: a man—a dead black man—on the ground. He's been gored, trampled into the red sand, destroyed by a buffalo—most likely by one we have just seen.

"Attend to him!" Terry hisses to the gun bearers.

When we are safe again, I collapse against my uncle, weeping for the mother I never knew, weeping for myself.

Much is done for me that evening in camp, but for the first time I think about home. Later that night, my uncle gives me whiskey and honey in water, and I drink it down. The cot drifts and bobs, but I'm able to sleep.

But then I dream. I dream about Daddy seeing Mother die. I dream about Uncle Jack seeing Mother die. I dream about the black evil trampling her into the red earth and the ground oozing blood and the sky raining blood and—

I wake, my mouth gaping with the start of a scream. But I'm able to stop myself. I do not want to cry out again and have these strong men judge my fear.

An hour passes, but I'm unable to go back to sleep. I need more to drink, I decide. I feel my way to Uncle Jack's cot. He's sleeping heavily as he does every night. I grope for the whiskey he keeps on the reed table. When I find it, I twist off the top and gulp a generous mouthful.

Never before have I attempted to drink plain whiskey. I choke, cough, and spit all over my uncle before I have the presence of mind to turn my head.

He sits bolt upright in bed. "Goddamn it! What the hell did you just do, girl?"

When I stop coughing, I tell him.

"Well, hell. Scared the absolute shit out of me, you did." He turns over and goes back to sleep.

I locate the edge of my cot and sit down. I do not belong here. I am too weak for Africa.

I hate Daddy for letting me come, and I hate Uncle Jack for bringing me. But I mostly hate myself.

I crawl back under the blankets until I'm warm again. The night is quiet. All the noise is inside my head.

Enough of this, I tell myself. Tomorrow I will kill something. And whether it feels good or not, I'll kill something more. And whether that feels good or not, I'll kill a third time. Then I'll decide whether to continue or to stop. Killing is the only way to overcome my weakness and my fear, and I will prove myself as good as those two strong men I so admire.

The next morning, Terry notices that I'm not eating. I'm pacing the same as my uncle does when he is stressed. He has not paced since he has been in Africa.

"Good morning, Abigail." Terry's eyes fixate on me as he holds aloft his tea. "Something is troubling you. Is it still the dead man we came across?"

"No. That was the most horrible sight ever, but I refuse to think about it anymore."

"Good, because nothing can be done about him now, the poor bugger. But something is definitely different today … could it be you're going hunting?"

"Yes… do you think I'm ready?"

"No."

"No? Why on earth not?"

"Because you had to ask me. If you were truly ready, you'd say, 'Terry, I'm going hunting today, so set down that goddamn tea cup you're holding like such a priss and get your bloody ass ready to take me.'"

I break into a grin. "I'll say that, if you want."

"Yes, I want." He is smiling and it isn't his habit to smile much to me.

Uncle Jack comes around the corner of the dining tent and hears me. "Now what's going on?"

"I'm going to change," I announce. "Then I'm going hunting!"

Back at our tent, I slip off my fashionable woman's skirt and pull on my khakis. I've lost weight, but my webbed belt cinches it in. I shove the pant legs into my boots to prevent bugs from crawling up my legs. I don my shooting vest over my blouse. My hunting clothes are still pristine. Will they be properly bloodied by day's end? I pocket the appropriate rounds and locate my gun. Peering into the tiny mirror dangling from the tent support, I adjust my hat and scarf at a jaunty angle.

Now I'm ready to kill things.

Uncle Jack looks at me with admiration. "Good, I was starting to wonder whether you'd ever put to use what I bought you."

I am consumed with excitement and bravado as I assume the front seat next to Terry. I hold my gun at the ready, barrel pointing outward. Uncle Jack lounges in my usual backseat. Solkwemu perches on the top of the Rover on his padded platform, driving stick in hand, the better to both sight game and avoid pitfalls in the so-called road. Another tracker and two gun bearers hop in the back, chattering animatedly while looking at me. I wish they'd stop. I have enough on my mind without additional distractions.

"Don't worry, Abigail," Terry says. "I'll make it easy for you."

"Don't do me any favors," I reply.

"But if I don't do you any favors, you won't be getting anything at all."

"If I get nothing at all, you won't be doing your job and my uncle won't pay you."

Uncle Jack kicks the back of my seat so hard that the barrel of my gun clunks against the windscreen. "That's enough, children," he growls.

I glance up at the rearview mirror. He is glaring at me.

Terry's mouth thins. He looks straight ahead and drives.

I wither inside. If I hadn't been so rude, Terry would've put himself out for me, and I could've taken wonderful trophies for as long as I wanted to hunt.

Although my uncle meant his comment for me, Terry has been reminded of his station. Now my white hunter will not be doing anything more for me than he must. I talked myself into this hole and I'll have to talk myself out, I realize, or I won't shoot anything today or any other day. And the only talk either of them wants to hear out of me is an apology.

"I'm sorry," I say.

Terry ignores me.

"I'm sorry. Really I am. I'm so rude sometimes. It's my worst fault. Please don't hold it against me. I can't hunt if you're upset with me, and I've waited so long to hunt."

"Sounds like you're apologizing for how that impacts you, not me," Terry says.

"Yes, I'm afraid you're right, and I'm sorry about that too. Please forgive me, Mr. Shaw." I figure the "Mr. Shaw" is a humble touch. "I know you don't appreciate smart comments from your clients, and I'm sure my uncle will pay you a huge bonus if I say even one more stupid thing."

Uncle Jack mutters something indiscernible. Terry stares at me as though I'm an errant child. I look at him pitifully: the look that has served me well.

Terry glances at the mirror. "Well, what do you think, Jack? Should I forgive her?"

"That's up to you. But if you don't, she'll just nag the whole damn day. And if she nags the whole damn day, one of us will have to get out of the Rover and spank her."

Terry looks as though such a scenario would be appealing.

I cringe. *Thank you so much, Uncle Jack,* I think. *You have such a knack for putting me in my place. And now I'll have to hunt perfectly to make up for what the two of you think of me.*

But it's easy, after I get the hang of it.

Terry glasses all morning for a nice impala for me, but they are skittish and few. Then we startle a trio of warthog. The family has been rolling in a mud puddle. At the sight of us, they take off single file at a steady trot, their tails held high above the waving grass.

"Well, look at the cute little piggies: Papa, Mama, and Junior," Terry says. "And if you don't know, it's Papa you want. He's the big one protecting the rear. Shoot him."

One of the gun bearers thrusts my rifle into my hand. I bring the barrel up and flip off the safety. My heart thumps and my hands shake.

Terry covers his ears with his palms. "Balance your gun on my shoulder. Take your time ... aim just behind the front leg. Slow squeeze, don't jerk, slow—"

My rifle recoils into my shoulder pad as the bullet rips into Papa. He flinches, goes down for a second, then leaps up again. His head and tail lift simultaneously and he starts trotting more quickly—toward me!

"Dumbest pig in Africa!" Terry says with a laugh. "You pepper him and he comes closer for you to finish him off, which you'll have to do now, since he's already sick. Steady, another shot—"

I chamber a second round, squeeze the trigger, and Papa's trotting days are over. But then Mama and Junior stop and circle back to see what has happened to Papa. Mama pokes at Papa with her snout before veering off as we near.

"Look, she knows he's dead," I lament.

Terry merely shrugs. "Who knows what they know? But you did that one a favor, or he'd be hyena or lion lunch soon ... see? Look at the size of these tusks. He's an old one. Better to go quick like this than slow. Hyenas eat their prey while they're still alive, do you know that? Rip the entrails clean out."

"No," I say, "but I'm not surprised."

Africa is a cruel place. Nothing ever lies about. Everything is picked clean in a night. The hunters are always hunting and prey is always being devoured, a cycle from the beginning of time to the end of time. My shooting an old warthog isn't going to make any difference.

I feel better by the time Uncle Jack takes my photograph, kneeling behind my first kill. My 30-06 is cradled in the crook of my arm, and I'm smiling against the burning African sun. Uncle Jack takes several shots from different angles to make sure he gets a good one.

Terry kneels next to me. I feel overwhelmed by his presence. We both smile for the camera as though nothing is going on between us.

And nothing is, which is precisely the problem.

He rises and offers me his hand. I brush the dust from my clothes and hand my rifle to a gun bearer. Solkwemu beams and says something to Terry in his language.

"What did he say?" I ask Terry.

"Oh, he's surprised you shot something. He thought you were just going to talk all day."

"And I'm surprised you let him say things like that about me."

"What's the harm? He has opinions, like me."

I don't venture to guess what those might be. I get back in the Rover, the back seat this time. Little is going the way I'd hoped, and I need to rethink my strategy before I hunt again.

Diana the Huntress

THE THREE OF us stay up until the wee hours as Terry and Uncle Jack partake heavily of whiskey. I nurse the single drink my uncle allows me: a concoction of fruit juice and gin, which tastes like fruit juice and nothing. Within my set parameters, I can scarcely attain their inebriated state where everything is hilarious, nothing is sacred, and morning is a distant uncertainty.

It occurs to me that I will never become one of them. My enforced sobriety further sets me apart. But would it really make me feel better to be whacked on the shoulder when I place a good shot? Or drink until I can barely stagger to my tent? Or be expected to know what to do when my gun jams, misfires, or does the funny little things that guns do on occasion?

No, my only hope is to be what I am, intensified. I am female. Therefore I will be the ultimate female: Diana, the Huntress. Terry Shaw will either notice me or I will shoot an arrow in his foot!

Little do I know that what I think in jest will come scarily close to fact before our next hunt, which occurs on Wednesday as neither Terry nor Uncle Jack assume the vertical until nearly noon on Tuesday.

Since I'm up early, having been awoken at dawn by the antics of frolicking monkeys, I pass Tuesday morning perfecting my aim. I keep Solkwemu busy tacking up targets and taking them down again. When my barrel overheats, I trade off with a rifle of Terry's until mine cools. When I score well, the old tracker's rheumy eyes light up and he chatters in his language. I nod, smile, and hope he is being complimentary. I could use a friend.

Uncle Jack finally puts a stop to my efforts, complaining that each shot reverberates through his brain like a red-hot poker. Terry, who looks nearly as beaten down as my uncle, calls from his hammock in the shade, "Oh, let her be!"

He is overridden.

So I reluctantly case my gun. In my irritation, I make a potentially fatal error.

The next morning, we load the Rover prior to seeking an impala for me. As I uncase my rifle and hand it to Uncle Jack to hold as I climb in, it goes off.

Nothing in the world is louder than a gun going off unexpectedly.

Nothing in the world moves after a gun goes off unexpectedly.

My bullet has missed my uncle's head by a scant six inches, judging from the angle of the barrel. He is temporarily deaf. He stands shock still momentarily, as do we all, before attempting to strike me, but Terry grabs his upraised arm.

"You fool!" Uncle Jack shouts. He yanks his arm free as I back away, horrified at my own carelessness. "What's the matter with you? Is it too much for you to unload the goddamn gun? Or keep the goddamn safety on? Did I bring you here so you could blow my goddamn head off?"

His diatribe lasts for seemingly an eternity, bemoaning my lack of even the most miniscule amount of common sense, in scathing and shockingly virulent language. I take it as long as I can, standing there in the pink dawn of a perfect African morning, tears streaming down my face. He orders me to our tent for the duration of our hunt, but I'm already heading there.

Sobbing on my cot, I am hollow. I am worthless.

I'm no Diana. I'm no huntress. I'm a fool to him, to Terry, and to the boys who'll undoubtedly jabber their gibberish about me. I have traveled thousands of miles and I have come to this. During breaks in my crying, I hear an acerbic exchange between my uncle and Terry.

"Of course it's frightening, Jack, but things like this happen, especially with the inexperienced. No harm was done, and I'd stake my life she'll never forget again."

"You'd stake your life? Well, I wouldn't! There's no excuse for such laxness! She could've blown her own head to kingdom come, or one of the boys, or even you! I'm not even talking about me now!"

Terry tries repeatedly to calm my uncle, with minimal success.

Then my uncle demands that Terry take him out. He will shoot impala in my stead. He feels like killing something, and he feels like killing something immediately.

Terry refuses, saying he takes out no client in such a state.

Uncle Jack repeats his demand, loudly.

Terry says shouting is unnecessary and will not be tolerated.

My uncle relieves Terry of his obligations.

Terry says he will return us to town the following day. Our safari is over. His voice is eerily calm.

Uncle Jack marches to our tent. I cower on my cot, my arms covering my face. He walks up to me and stands there, his breathing ragged. He kicks our tin washbasin so hard that it goes flying out of the tent. He kicks a few other things before stomping away again.

I get up, daub my eyes, blow my nose, and scrape my dignity off the floor.

A few minutes later, I hear him apologize to Terry. Terry apologizes to him.

He asks Terry to consider continuing our safari. Terry accepts my uncle's hope of reinstatement. They go off together to seal their pact with gin. A half hour later, they go off together to hunt.

Men, I groan. *Who can understand them?*

I pray that Uncle Jack will be in a better mood when he returns, undoubtedly with the finest impala in all of Africa. I pray that he will release me from my confinement and grant me a second chance. I've already punished myself beyond anything he could ever do. A little forgiveness would be appreciated.

Uncle Jack returns that night with no impala. He strides to our tent immediately after dinner and goes to bed. He is not talking to me.

But Terry is. I wonder whether he seeks to lessen the impact of my uncle's disgust, or whether he talks to me because there is none other with whom to converse.

I begin by apologizing profusely. Terry indicates his acceptance.

"Do you think my uncle will forgive me tomorrow?"

The glint of Terry's eyes in the glow from the campfire is strangely exhilarating.

"Oh, I think so … or soon after."

"Sometimes I think he hates me, for as mad as he gets at any mistake on my part."

"Nearly blowing his head off wasn't just any mistake. But even so, he doesn't hate you. He might hate himself for not checking up on you more closely, but I think it's more a concern for you, a fear for you, that you could end up as your mother did."

"He told you all about it?"

"No. He mentioned it the day we came across the dead man, and he mentioned it again today, but no details … would you care to fill me in?"

"No, I'm sorry. I simply can't go into it."

"Just as well … one's own life is tragedy enough without wallowing in another's."

"Then you have tragedy you're hiding as well?"

"No, I just said that," he says with a faint smile. "Conversation, you know. My own life's been charmed. No major mistakes, other than my divorce, which I won't discuss."

"Fair enough … I would like to know one thing, though."

"And what's that?"

"How many women fall in love with you during the course of their hunt?"

At that Terry Shaw smiles broadly. "Oh, a good share of them, I would assume."

"Really, a good share of them?" I match his smile with one of my own. "And why is that, do you suppose?"

"Because I'm part of the deal … think of it, here's a woman who wouldn't miss a salon appointment and suddenly she's in Africa with some oaf who's dragged her halfway around the world and she's covered in dust and drinking warm gin and peeing behind bushes, so she figures what the hell, she's doing everything she never thought she'd do anyway, why not bed down with the white hunter after her mate's nodded off? After all, wouldn't *that* be something to crow about during luncheon back at the bridge club!"

"No!" I say. "Don't tell me some women would actually do that and tell? Would boast about it?"

Terry laughs. "Of course they would."

"But that's awful. That's adultery!"

"Of course it's adultery … oh, Abigail, you're so terribly young. You have no idea how some people conduct themselves, and their marriages."

"So you've done this? You've actually given them something to crow about during their luncheons at their bridge clubs?" I hope Terry Shaw will vehemently deny such boorish behavior. But if he denies it, what chance will I have? But if he doesn't, why would I be special? Either way, will he continue to be my perfect white hunter or am I already wishing for something more?

He looks at me intently. "Again, Abigail, you're so young. Better you think what you like of me, rather than have me spell it out for you in so many words."

"That doesn't tell me anything."

Terry leans closer. I smell his aftershave and cologne. He has bathed and shaved. His khakis are clean and pressed. His gun and bloody knife are elsewhere. He neither looks nor smells like a man who kills for a livelihood.

"I'll tell you this much," he says. "I hunt more productively while on my feet than I do while lying down."

"That still doesn't tell me anything." I settle back in my chair, vaguely disappointed.

"Yes, it does … might I get you something to drink?"

"Oh, I'd love something, but you know Uncle Jack doesn't allow it except for one, and one is hardly enough."

"He doesn't allow you to forget the goddamned safety on your goddamned gun either," Terry says with a wink. "Tonight you can have as many as I think you can handle … so, what would you like?"

"Whatever you think I might like." Tentatively, I touch his arm—the strong, lean arm of my white hunter.

Uncle Jack apologizes as soon as his eyes open the next morning. He says that I'd scared the shit out of him, and he tends to react poorly when shit is scared out of him, but he had no right to chew me out in front of Terry. He intends to forget it ever happened and hopes I can as well.

I accept his apology and say how grateful I am that he wasn't harmed. I realize that Daddy is holding him responsible, and I promise never to be so careless again.

"I don't need reminding," he says. "I already know all about repercussions."

"I'm sorry. I shouldn't have mentioned Daddy."

"No, you shouldn't have ... so what happened last night?"

"Nothing." I hope he doesn't quiz Terry, who has an unnerving propensity to tell the absolute truth.

"Well, make sure it stays nothing, because I know what you're up to." He waits for my reaction—a lowering of eyes and a nod of understanding—before granting me permission to hunt again, without him. His stomach is bothering him and he intends to stay in camp for the day.

I can hardly believe my good fortune!

On the way out, I wonder aloud whether a good impala will be found.

"Naturally," Terry says. "Especially if we locate the old one Jack and I happened upon yesterday. He was magnificent."

"But he didn't come back with it last night. Didn't he have a clear shot?"

"He had a perfect shot. Broadside, motionless for nearly a minute. And you thought he hates you just because he lost his temper? If he hated you, Abby, he'd have shot it and rubbed your nose in it. He let it go for you."

Again I feel foolish.

We spend the morning alternately driving and stalking. Rain hasn't fallen in several weeks, but too much tall grass remains. Impala avoid tall grass because carnivores hide in it and eat them, Terry explains. He figures that a thousand impala are somewhere in the area, but we have seen only a few dozen. Each time he glasses a good group, he stops the Rover and we work our way toward them. But I get no chance at a shot before they blend into the bush.

Then we give up stalking and try the waterholes. Again, there are too many waterholes. Hunting will improve as the smaller ones dry up and the game is forced to congregate at the larger, deeper ones.

We eat our lunch at a particularly picturesque one while watching for impala. None come. After we finish, Terry takes a tarp from the back of the Rover and spreads it on the ground. He lies down and covers his face with his hat.

"The impala are napping," he says with a sigh. "They'll come later."

I look at him, thinking he is either very tired or very bored. Why is it more awkward to hunt alone with him than with my uncle along? And what has changed since last night?

My little romance is going nowhere.

My hunting is going nowhere.

So I do what Uncle Jack would do in similar circumstances. I dig the last warmish beer out of the cool box, drink it, bunch up my shooting vest like a pillow, and go to sleep. As I drift off, I remember how much I truly hate beer.

Sometime later, Terry pokes me awake. "It's happy hour in Africa!" he whispers with more excitement in his voice than I've heard all day.

The gun bearers wake too. One hands me my rifle and I ease forward on the embankment for a better look. Terry lies on his stomach next to me, glassing.

Fourteen impala are at the waterhole, dipping their graceful necks forward to drink, popping their heads up to access the breeze. The faintest of sounds will startle them.

Terry shakes his head. The magnificent one is not among them.

They leave and others take their place. A group of wildebeest and their friends the zebra arrive, mill about, spook, and run off. Something in the tall grass on the far side of the waterhole coughs.

I look at Terry.

"Shit," he says. "*Simba* is heading to the bar as well. No need to waste our time here."

The sun is touching the horizon and the air is beginning to nip as we head toward camp. Vast herds of zebra and wildebeest are scattered in the distance. The road dips and wanders, and the numerous hills meet and slide down into a concave valley, with reeds of an expansive swamp punctuating the terrain.

It is then that Terry spots him. Scorning the safety of numbers, the magnificent one stands alone on the cusp of a hill, silhouetted against the fading sky. My white hunter kills the engine, and we drift to a noiseless stop.

"There he is, if you can shoot that far," he says in a low voice. "He's about one seventy-five, maybe two hundred yards."

"I'll try," I say.

"Give it a go then."

My heart begins a staccato beat as I chamber a round. "Lean out of the way," I whisper. "I'll shoot from here so I won't spook him."

"You're not shooting from the Rover," Terry says under his breath. "It's not sporting. It's not legal either."

"Who says?"

"Me, I say! Get your rump out of my truck and shoot over the bonnet, if you're going to shoot at all. And hurry up—he's starting to quarter away!"

At least I know what a bonnet is. I ease from the truck, brace my elbows against the bonnet, flick off the safety, and center the crosshairs on the shoulder. My magnificent impala stops cooperatively and stares at me.

I hold my breath and slowly squeeze the trigger. The roar of my rifle is deafening. The sound stops with a dull thud, as though the bullet has connected with a bag of wet cement. My impala leaps in the air, runs perhaps fifty yards, and collapses. I watch the horns through my scope, but there is no further movement from my second African trophy.

"Good girl!" Terry lowers his binoculars. He jumps out of the Rover and claps me on the back, the same as he does when Uncle Jack places a good shot.

"I got it?" I already know the answer.

"Of course you got it! That was a hell of a shot! You pulled it off in the nick of time too. I was starting to wonder whether you were ever getting out of the truck."

"Was there any doubt?" I glow in the warmth of his praise. Apparently nothing pleases my white hunter as much as success at the end of a tedious day.

"With women, there's always doubt."

"I'm sorry I argued with you about that. I got so excited I couldn't think."

"You're forgiven. I forgive women very easily … especially you." He grins and locates the camera he keeps in his duffle. "Well, let's get your pictures before the light fades."

He cuts away the impala's protruding tongue—that I cannot watch—wipes the blood from the mouth with tufts of grass, wipes the wound with additional grass, and demonstrates how to hold the horns so my trophy looks as large as possible for the camera.

My impala does not need much enhancement. It is indeed large. Terry says it's the largest impala he's seen in five seasons. He takes numerous photographs: with my hat on, with my hat off, with my gun cradled in the crook of my arm, with my gun propped beside me.

Unlike my warthog, I feel no guilt about cutting this impala's life short. It would've been devoured by nightfall if it hadn't located its kinfolk, Terry says. When he and my uncle had seen it yesterday, it had nine companions along.

Uncle Jack is waiting when we arrive at camp, the soft, black night already upon us. The fire blazes cheerfully and a boy appears with two drinks. Uncle Jack is already holding his.

"For me?" I ask.

"Of course," he says. "A hunter always drinks a toast to the animal he's made a part of himself in his memory. I heard the shot and I figured you got it. By the looks on both your faces, I know I'm right … cheers."

"Cheers." I touch my glass to theirs.

After dinner, more tales are woven amid the glow of the ironwood fire, and more drinks are served as my own small tale becomes a miniscule part of the intricate tapestry that is Africa.

Finally, I feel acceptance by the two men I so admire.

I am, at last, a hunter.

Bananas are Silent

ONE MORNING, I show Terry the journal in which I've been writing stories about my sojourn in Africa. He thumbs through it with much interest.

"I've never had a writer among my clients before," he says. "Do you intend to publish these and make me famous?"

"That's the general idea."

He leans back in his chair. "So … if you get these published, I'll either become very successful or I'll be ruined?"

"You'll become more successful than you already are, whether anyone pays even the slightest attention to my writing, I'd never say anything derogatory about you. It wouldn't be true, and it wouldn't be sporting even if it were true … sort of like shooting from the truck."

"Ah." He sounds relieved.

I locate a particular section for him. "This one's about my uncle's lion and our celebration afterward. If you like, you can skim through it and tell me when I'm in error."

He reads my story thoroughly. "It's very good. No obvious errors. Acute observations on your part. I didn't know you were listening to half of what I said."

"And you? What do you think about my portrayal of you?"

"Competent hunter … nice chap. Runs a tight camp, but a bit loose with the liquor … good with the tales, not much with the ladies." He says this in all seriousness.

I smile. "Not so far, but he may progress."

"Progress to what?"

"Oh, you know—progress to the 'give them something to crow about during luncheon back at the bridge club.'"

"Dear God!" Terry Shaw nearly drops his teacup. "Don't you go writing that rubbish about me! Didn't you realize that was *my* story? I'm a professional hunter and I have a reputation to uphold! I don't go bedding down with anybody's wife or sweetheart while on safari; hell, I'd get my bloody ass blown apart by someone unwilling to share!"

"Even though you'd like to?"

"Even though I'd like to."

"Oh, so if a love-struck lady on safari stripped herself naked and lounged across the bonnet of your truck, you wouldn't do a thing about it?"

Terry looks appalled. "Of course I'd do something about it. I'd ask her to please move her lovely naked body off my bonnet so I could see the bloody trail in order to bloody drive!"

"Well, if that's the case," I say with a laugh, "I'll need to create an alternate story that will progress the way I want, and it'll have nothing to do with you. The setting will be a safari such as this, and the characters will engage in a fantastic love story … let's see, I think I'll name my heroine Rita and the white hunter will be Rodney … no, Percival."

"Percival?" Terry grimaces. "What kind of asinine name is that? Sounds like either a humping dick or a boring prick … how about Shelby? Now Shelby's a nice proper Brit name, if that's what you're after."

"Shelby it is." Terry thinks he's such a clever hunter, but I'm the one hunting and he's already nibbled my bait. Even if our little romance never ignites, I can still enjoy titillating him with the exploits of Rita and Shelby.

It works like a charm.

"Well, how's our man Shelby doing tonight? Has he achieved union yet?" Terry asks the next evening around the campfire.

"Oh no, much too soon for that. But he has managed a gander at her through the flaps of the shower tent."

"So he's already resorted to being a peeping Tom? Then I shall maintain high hopes for him … I assume she hasn't yet flung herself naked across his bonnet for him to admire openly?"

"Never!" I reply in mock horror. "Rita's a lady, after all. The fire's under the ice."

Uncle Jack returns with his drink and hears us. "What kind of degenerates are these people? And how the devil do you know them?"

We laugh and neglect to answer him.

A few nights later, Terry says, "Has Shelby progressed to puritanical handholding at least? Wouldn't want too much passion to build up inside him now, would we?"

My uncle is in the bath tent, so I can say what I please. "Oh, Shelby's gone a bit further than that."

"Well, tell me … or is it secret?"

"Oh, it's sort of a secret. With Rita anyway … you see, she's insanely in love with Shelby, but she's unsure of herself because she's so much younger and relatively inexperienced, while Shelby's a man of the world. She figures if she lays all her cards on the table too readily, she'll lose the only thing she has to offer him. He'll have a good laugh about it afterward, go about his next conquest, and forget all about her. After all, her safari will end far sooner than her thoughts of him."

Other than the calls of the nightjars and the chattering of something in the trees overhead, all is silent around our campfire in deepest Africa. I catch my breath as I realize what I've said. Unless Terry's stark solid between the ears, he now sees through my ruse of Rita and Shelby … if he hadn't previously.

Terry looks from me to the fire for the longest time and finally back to me.

"Well, if he took her offering and then laughed about it, he'd be a cad of the lowest order and I'd fancy shooting him for it. So what is this 'bit further' you mentioned?"

"Oh, he's just taken her in his arms one afternoon while he was guiding her hunt," I say, grateful for his gracious response. "That and some personal, intimate sort of talk … they're still getting to know one another. They're taking it slow."

"Not so slow that her safari ends before anything happens, I should hope?"

"No. That wouldn't make much of a story."

"It sure wouldn't. I think they should be encouraged, don't you?"

"I intend to give them all the encouragement necessary."

With two weeks remaining in our safari, I remind Uncle Jack that I'd wanted to hunt three animals and I've only hunted two, while he has achieved all his trophies.

"Not entirely," he says. "I still want a leopard."

"You have one already, back home."

"That one is representative. I'd like a bigger one."

"But leopard take too long. Terry allows two weeks to get a good one."

"We have two weeks."

"But if you hog the entire two weeks, I won't get my chance."

"You'll get your chance."

"Even if I get my chance, I'll be too tired by then. I'm already tired of being dirty and sunburned. I'm tired of bouncing around in the truck until I'm black and blue, providing a smorgasbord for bugs, and kicking snakes out of bushes so I can pee."

"So stay in camp and miss the dirt, sun, bruises, bugs, and snakes," he says with a shrug. "Stay in camp and pamper yourself. I'm going after leopard."

I'm waiting in the truck before he is the next morning. For being a good sport, he lets me shoot the bait.

Five days later, my leopard story is partially written. My journal entry reads:

One who has never tried cannot possibly imagine the physical stress of attempting to sit stone still for two or three or more hours; of simultaneously endeavoring to ignore the hardness of the rocks beneath, the internal forces surging within, and the gradual and insidious numbing of the lower extremities.

As minutes drag with agonizing slowness, only the mind remains alert as the eyes seek to penetrate the gathering dusk of an African evening. The ears strain to hear the distant snap of a twig, the crackle of a disturbed leaf, the low, guttural cough of an approaching prowler, the scratch of unsheathed claws upon bark, and the unmistakable rip of raw flesh.

But too often the wait is in vain, and it becomes painfully apparent that the leopard will not come. And then, the next afternoon, the process has to be repeated.

A leopard blind certainly is not designed for human comfort, professional hunter Terry Shaw maintains as he works wonders with a scraggly length of camouflage netting, broken branches, and a generous helping of omnipresent thorns. He is again weaving a nest for three on a rugged portion of Artie Guillaumes's mountainous farm, where several leopards have been wreaking havoc with the livestock of late, killing eight goats and a calf.

Uncle Jack is hoping to rectify the problem.

I had been initiated into the fine art of leopard hunting the previous night, spending nearly three motionless hours in our first blind, which seemed to be attached to the mountain's side solely by sheer tenacity. A chill, daunting wind had tested both our fortitude and our perseverance.

Talk about togetherness! We hadn't room to move if we had wanted. Uncle Jack's chair had been slanted backward at a precarious angle, Terry had kept his legs rigidly braced the entire time to avoid sliding off his rock, and I'd done likewise.

And the leopard had not come.

This time, Terry is constructing a second blind in a slightly more accessible area, where a leopard has made a visit to our springbuck bait while we waited in vain on our mountainous perch the evening before.

I'm in for another long wait, but I can't complain. Since I want to experience my uncle's leopard hunt, sitting, waiting, and hoping is just part of the deal. Terry has made it clear from the onset that whining would not be appreciated. Three in a leopard blind is one too many, and I can either like it or lump it.

So I've decided to like it. Although the experience won't grow hair on my chest, and I probably won't feel more masculine at the end than I did at the beginning, I figure I can sit as still, keep as quiet, and hold my water as long as any man.

Blind complete, we ease off and amuse ourselves by glassing warthog, kudu, and innumerable impala at a waterhole several miles away. We return in mid-afternoon, just as the warming sun starts to waver behind the parched crags.

For the second time, I settle in, arranging my limbs and my clothes with comfort in mind, declining both the offered drink and the banana from Terry's rucksack. One can eat a banana in a leopard blind, he says, because bananas are silent. But with my limited capacity, I find it more prudent not to drink or eat anything until the wait is over.

All is in readiness by three o'clock. Uncle Jack sits in a folding chair above and to my left. He takes a practice bead on the bait lashed in a fork of a gnarled tree some forty yards upwind.

Satisfied, he sits back to wait. Terry perches on a rock across from me, a loaded shotgun by his side. His eyes close periodically, his head bobs, and then he wakes with a start.

We'd been joking on the drive out about the size of the leopard we hoped for, wishing for an obscenely large beast, so gigantic he would be a genetic aberration of his kind. But now the mere thought of a leopard of any size whatever, slinking out of the mountains and approaching us with glinting eye and hungry belly, makes my heart race.

As twilight settles in with the softness of a falling blanket, I feel insignificant and exposed. Facing the rear of the blind, with only a few hewn branches separating me from a hundred and seventy pounds of ravenous cat, I feel as France must have felt during the war, when the enemy sneaked across the border from around and behind the Maginot Line, with all the guns facing the wrong direction.

Oddly enough, I had experienced no such trepidation our first night out. I knew leopards typically do not attack humans unless cornered or wounded. But I also know the leopard we are hunting has been identified as a problem animal, killing domestic livestock rather than its usual wild prey. It has also been spotted during daylight hours, which is highly unusual, near where we are hiding.

I can't help but wonder: is this leopard wounded? Is this leopard typical? And most of all, does this leopard know the rules?

The late afternoon becomes tomb silent, with whispery puffs of breeze so miniscule they seem imaginary. The vast mountainside is barely visible through the thicket of brush and thorns surrounding me. As more minutes pass, the mountains, the brush, and the thorns begin to blend together in an unending mass of gray.

More long minutes pass. Straining to see what I no longer can, I startle at a night bird's call. Then I hear the eerie lowing of cattle, far below in the valley.

Another puff of breeze. A twig snaps, not far distant.

I sense, rather than see, Terry tense. Uncle Jack brings his gun up.

Then it begins: a steady cacophony of coughs and grunts, behind and to my right, as the leopard steadily works its way toward us through the rocks and brush. It is a noisy creature, not content with a single outburst, but vocalizes five to seven grunts at a time. A spooky silence of a minute or more punctuates and separates each effort.

His last coughs are frighteningly near. Unable to see his direction from my nest in the branches, the snap of twigs abruptly ceases as the leopard pauses on the uphill side of our blind as though to assess the situation.

I hear nothing for a time. Then the scratch of lethal nails upon bark is unmistakable as the leopard ascends the forked tree in front of us and begins to feed.

Ripping. Pausing to listen to whatever the breeze brings. Tearing.

Terry rustles on his rock, ever so slightly, as he leans forward to motion to Uncle Jack.

Uncle Jack shifts his weight on the chair, attempting to discern the spotted shape against a backdrop of spotted foliage barely illuminated by the setting sun.

My uncle's breath is labored. I stiffen inside my layers of clothes, expecting the deathlike silence to be ripped asunder by the roar of his rifle at any moment.

But nothing happens.

"Shoot!" Terry mouths.

"Can't!" Uncle Jack whispers back, just as forcefully.

At the exchange, the leopard jumps from the bait and melts into the shadows.

We wait, scarcely daring to breathe, unable to converse as to why my uncle has failed to shoot.

An eternity passes.

Again we hear the crack of twigs, the scratch of claws, the tearing of meat. The leopard is back.

"Shoot!" Terry mouths again.

Uncle Jack shakes his head, and nothing happens.

Abruptly the cat bounds from the bait and fades into the gloom. We wait, hearts pounding, hoping for his return.

He does not.

Terry is beyond frustrated. "Why didn't you shoot, Jack? Two perfect shots, broadside, framed in the crotch of that tree. You had twenty to thirty seconds of opportunity each time."

"I couldn't see the goddamned thing!" Uncle Jack says in such a way that Terry curtails his carping. "I couldn't tell head from ass or cat from branches and everything looked like spots."

Terry stands up and climbs out of the blind, as does my uncle. I scramble after them. Our hunter waves his torch to signal Adam to come with the truck.

We are heavyhearted on the interminable drive back to the Guillaume farmhouse, where we are staying rather than drive half the night back to camp. In retrospect, it seems ludicrous to hinge such importance on the untimely demise of a single leopard, but that is exactly what the three of us did that night. It angered us that somewhere, hidden by the darkness and the crevices and caves of his favorite abodes, Spot had been able to thumb his feline nose at us, and win.

We could almost hear him laughing.

Warming ourselves by the blazing fireplace, Terry tries to ascertain what went wrong. Artie, who at seventy-three has been hunting before the rest of us drew breath, joins our discussion. Narrow, milky scars bisect his face and one ear is partly missing, souvenirs of a youthful leopard hunt. In his experience, he says, a hunter needs to do a dozen things perfectly to get his leopard. Omission of any will likely result in failure.

Terry considers Artie's input. He decides to reposition the shooting rest in relation to the bait, remove a bit of the brush obstructing the view, and situate himself closer to Uncle Jack to facilitate communication. Given my uncle's apparent low vision problem, he also hopes that the leopard shows his spots earlier rather than later.

We check the bait the next morning and find that the leopard had returned after we'd left. Telltale tracks in the dust indicate where it had paced not fifteen feet from the back of our blind, a chilling revelation. Terry points to the depression in the grass where the cat rested after gorging. And he notes the tracks of a second, smaller leopard. A mating pair, he concludes, as leopards do not usually share dinner unless amorous. Since Uncle Jack had not fired, nor had we left noisily, he hopes that the leopard(s) will return that afternoon.

Terry makes the necessary adjustments to the shooting rest, blind, and surrounding area before he drives us to a waterhole several miles away to eat lunch and keep our minds off the leopard business. But we think of little else.

In my journal, I continue my story:

That afternoon we again settle in by three. The grunting and coughing begins promptly at twilight. A sudden sound erupts not twenty feet away, propelling my heart to my throat. I see a flutter of brown as the shape scurries away.

"Bush pig," Terry whispers.

Then a single guttural cough literally paralyzes me. The leopard is on my side of the blind, not a dozen yards from me. No wonder the bush pig left with such haste!

An imaginary line can be drawn from the leopard directly through our blind to the bait. I remember Terry's warning that a leopard that catches a whiff of human scent close to a blind often attacks, assuming if humans are so near, it must be cornered. Stealthily, Terry brings up his double barrel. The safety is off. He points the shotgun above my knees and out the rear of the blind.

Uncle Jack turns his head to check on me. Terry indicates with a jerk of his thumb that he wants him to continue to cover the front of the blind.

The situation is beyond tense. Uncle Jack hunches over his rifle, motionless. Terry's face is drawn and hard. Unarmed, I am two leaps from being leopard lunch.

Several minutes pass.

Suddenly we hear the scratch of claws on bark and the tearing of meat.

For some mysterious reason, the leopard has circled back around the rocky ledge to our left instead sauntering down the easier, more obvious path through our blind to the bait. It has moved nearly sixty yards through dense underbrush without making a single sound.

Uncle Jack brings his rifle up.

A branch cracks loudly and the leopard is gone. A minute of stunned silence follows.

"What the hell?" Uncle Jack asks of Terry.

Terry studies the situation through his binoculars. "Shit! I think the stupid cat put a foot wrong when he shifted his weight. He broke a branch and the snap scared him silly … he won't be back, at least not tonight."

"So now what?" Uncle Jack says.

"So now we're leaving." Terry climbs out of the blind and waves for the truck with his torch.

Our bad luck continues into the next afternoon. Huddled once again in the first blind clinging to the side of the mountain, Uncle Jack sneezes loudly at the precise moment that a great leopard ascends the forked tree and begins to feed.

Spot vanishes in a heartbeat.

I have never seen my uncle so glum. "Terry," he says very softly.

"What?" Terry says.

"Shoot me … I swear to God I'm not kidding. Just shoot me."

"I can't do that, Jack," Terry says, equally glum. "I can leave you here on the mountain and let something eat you, or I can withhold your liquor as punishment for making that goddamn noise at the worst goddamn moment, but I can't legally shoot you. I don't have a license, and the game department takes a negative view of shooting clients without a license."

"Well, I wish they'd make an exception in my case." Uncle Jack clambers slowly to his feet. "I wouldn't have sneezed if that goddamn bug hadn't flown up my nose with the intention of raising a family in my sinus cavities, but it did, and I did, and that's that … I gather there's no reason to wait here anymore?"

"None whatsoever," Terry says. "And as much as I'd like to help Artie out,

it's best we head back to our own camp tonight before things fall apart there. Tomorrow we'll move east to a spot that should be good this time of year. I don't want to keep boarding with the Guillaumes, and this is dragging on too long. He'll get a local to finish his problem."

In silence, Terry drives us three hours back to camp.

In silence, Uncle Jack sits dejectedly until he falls asleep.

In silence, I give thanks that it wasn't me who sneezed.

And somewhere in the mountains behind us, a leopard is laughing.

Uncle Jack reads my story the next morning as we jar down a bone-crushing trail en route to our next camp, from which Terry promises him a leopard.

"Well, why the hell didn't we go there to begin with?" my uncle asks. Not getting a satisfactory answer, he tosses my journal back at me. "Lousy story. Burn it tonight in the campfire. Offer it to the leopard gods."

"Oh, don't denigrate Abigail's story." Terry takes my side although he hasn't read it yet. "I'm sure it's a fine tale. What don't you like about it?"

"The ending."

"She can't write what you haven't done, can she? After you get your leopard, I'm sure the ending will be to your satisfaction."

Uncle Jack sighs with resignation. "Oh, I suppose you're right … or at least I hope you're right."

"Of course I'm right. But if I'm not, that's why it's called hunting."

As the hours drag, I daydream about Shelby and Rita. After a sluggish start, their romance is progressing rapidly and is becoming downright naughty. The lurching of the Rover prevents me from making additional entries in my journal, but at least I know where *that* story is going!

During my more lucid moments, I contemplate the roll of toilet paper, the crumpled box of tissues, and the rusted container of mints on the dash. Beside me resides the chop box, tins of tepid water, a nearly depleted bottle of whiskey, seventeen shell casings, a first aid kit missing many of its components, a torn box of ammunition, a stained machete, an equally stained axe, our rifles in their cases, innumerable rags, Terry's rucksack, tools for repairing the truck, and whatnot. Beneath me is Terry's woolen turtleneck sweater that he wears as protection from the cold or a wounded cat. I've used it as a cushion so long it smells like me instead of him.

And I have been in the Rover so long I have it all memorized.

I've been in the Rover so long I can barely remember anything else.

We reach it, our first permanent campsite in a month, well after dark.

We reach it well after dark because the infallible, unflappable Terry Shaw gets horribly lost, which he doesn't admit until he gets his bearings again after two hours of frenzied backtracking. And he doesn't begin the frenzied backtracking until Solkwemu, from his perch on top of the truck, slaps the windscreen with his pointer, which causes Terry to jam on the brakes. A lengthy discussion takes place between the two of them, none of it in English, accompanied by grunts, gesturing, and arm waving.

Bitterness is added to the brew when, in the darkness, the Rover falls in a rut so deep that it cannot climb out without help. Solkwemu, Adam, and Allabar get down from the truck. Using Terry's torch, they locate enough branches to fashion a ramp for the front wheels to ascend. I watch as they and my uncle put shoulder to rear bumper as Terry stomps on the accelerator.

After several attempts, their combined effort is successful.

But the rut is also a wallow, and the wallow is filled with a foul-smelling muck. And now four men are also covered with a foul-smelling muck. The stench is overwhelming when Uncle Jack climbs back in the Rover.

"You smell like a rose, Jack," Terry says.

"I feel like one, too, scabby and thorny … will I get a bath before I die?"

"In about an hour, now that we're back on track," Terry says cheerily.

Ten minutes later, a front tire blows.

"Goddamn bitch of a truck," Terry says, not cheerily.

Adam and Allabar climb down again and change the tire. Solkwemu squats back on his haunches and holds the torch. Terry and Uncle Jack finish the whiskey. I dig three aspirin from the first aid kit and dispense them with a swig of warmish water from a tin.

Something shrieks like a calliope gone berserk not fifty yards away and is joined by numerous kin. The hair shoots up on the nape of my neck. Forget peeing! I leap back in the truck instead.

Terry bounces the beam of his torch off leering faces, lined up in a ragged semicircle around us. "*Fisi* … hyena. They're hoping to pick one of us off." He heaves a branch at them. "Run, you cowardly beggars!"

"I'll get my gun," Uncle Jack says.

"Don't bother; we're leaving." Terry starts the Rover as the boys ascend to the top of the truck in haste.

It is an eerie night. Stars dust the yawning velvet sky. Distant bush bulks black against the horizon, which seems merely a lighter black. The grass reflects silver from the moon, which hangs as a low crescent. Little bat-eared foxes scamper ahead of us, disorientated in the glare of our headlamps. Unknown things go whoosh and flutter away like ghosts as we lumber past. When it seemed it would go on forever, a dim light ahead catches Terry's eye.

"Ah, there she is," he says. "Shy little mother; our camp! After baths and drinks, we'll have a spot of dinner after I wake up Thomas … or is it too late for dinner?"

"I'll just have a bath and drinks," Uncle Jack says. He lights a cigarette in celebration.

"The same for me," I say.

"She'll just have a bath," he corrects. "She doesn't get to drink again until she gets my leopard."

Never did I dream I'd be sent after leopard. Even Terry seems dumbfounded and asks the reason why. After much cajoling around the campfire, Uncle Jack says his stomach has been bothering him for some time, and it seems to be getting worse. After hearing the symptoms, Terry is convinced that he has an ulcer. My uncle admits that he had one during the war, but shrugs off Terry's diagnosis until he is informed that our white hunter was in his first year of medical school before chucking it all for a life in the bush.

"Well, what should I do now?" Uncle Jack asks. "Can't leave the safari and expect you to drive me two days into town just to see a doc … don't believe in all that witch doctor voodoo, anyway."

"This is 1951," Terry says. "I can find you one who's not a witch doctor, but if you'd rather wait until you get home, throw your cigarette in the fire and give me your drink. I have some antibiotics in my kit, and I'll get Thomas to whip up some food for you."

Uncle Jack must respect Terry Shaw a great deal because he smokes his last cigarette of the night down to his knuckles, and he drinks his last gin of the night down to vapor, but he doesn't light up again and he doesn't wave for a refill. Then he eats bread, cheese, and cold meat, swallows the antibiotic, and goes to bed after a long soak in the canvas bathtub.

While I'm awaiting my turn in the bath tent, I express trepidation about being expected to do what my uncle hadn't.

"Not to worry," Terry says as he shoves the burning logs of our campfire inward. "You know all about it already. Cats are easy to shoot, being thin-skinned, and you don't have to worry about blowing off a horn. As long as Spot comes with enough daylight at your back and poses prettily on the bait, you'll have a rug for your bedroom … and don't sneeze. For God's sake, whatever you do, don't sneeze!"

"I'll put a clothespin on my nose." I smile.

"That's a solution." He smiles back. "And—I've neglected to ask lately—how's our old boy Shelby doing?"

"He's doing very well, thank you. He's stolen a kiss from Rita while they were ensconced in a leopard blind together, and the very next night she visits him while he's in the bath. He'd been working so hard guiding her fabulous safari that the poor man fell completely asleep, until she slips into the water with him."

Terry's reaction is hardly what I expect.

"Really? And did she shoot a good leopard before she did that?"

Two days later, Terry has located three appropriate trees, I've shot the three baits, and Terry and his retinue have constructed the three blinds a short distance downwind of the three trees.

There has been no time for romance. With our safari growing short, my white hunter is devoting every precious hour to making sure that everything is perfect. Whether he's feeling pressure from Uncle Jack, who sits worriedly caressing his tea by the fire every morning and every evening as we're either leaving or coming back, asking a dozen questions about things he already knows the answer to, or whether Terry feels pressured to deliver a fine leopard to me, who no longer asks questions about anything, I am uncertain.

Perhaps he works to perfection merely from pride.

On the drive to check the baits the morning after all is in readiness, Terry drapes an arm along the back of my seat. I think nothing of it, but a few minutes later, his hand caresses my neck. His fingers are surprisingly smooth and pliable.

I'm so shocked I stare straight ahead.

"Am I making you nervous?" he asks.

"No."

"I don't believe you. You've been waiting for some sort of reaction from me for nearly two months now, haven't you?"

"Yes … "

"And now that I'm finally receptive, you're not sure what to do. After all, you're hardly Rita, who plays hard to get but then slips uninvited into Shelby's bath. You'd never do such a thing, at least at sixteen."

"I'm nearly seventeen," I remind him.

He stops the Rover on the edge of a small hill. Dust begins to rise as animals move in the distance, disturbed by the sound of the engine. If I had looked closely, I would've seen zebra, wildebeest, impala, and a lone jackal trailing after them.

But I only see him.

"And I'm thirty-one," Terry says in a thoroughly disarming manner. "I live in the bush. I work my tail off trying to provide an experience my clients will remember for a lifetime. You're not Rita, but I *am* Shelby. I live to see the sun melt away the mists in the morning, and I live for the smell of my dinner cooking in the late afternoon; dinner either I or my client has thoughtfully provided. And I live for my drinks and my visiting around the campfire at night when my work is finished. My soul is entrenched in the thorny bush and the hippo trails and the tangled web of swamps, plains, jungles, and mountains that is Africa … in short, Abby, I wouldn't trade what I do and where I am for anything or anyone. But having said that, sometimes I wake up in the dead of night, when everything is quiet except for a distant cough of a lion with indigestion, and I'm alone in my tent, and alone on my cot, and I still wonder if I'm missing something … if I truly could have it all."

"I think you could," I say.

"I already tried it once."

"You tried it with the wrong person."

For a moment I think he might kiss me, but he hesitates.

"I thought you'd say that," he says instead. He withdraws his arm and turns the Rover back to the trail. "I rather wish you hadn't, but I figured you would. I gave you the perfect opportunity to, and now I'm not certain what to do."

"Then I'll help you out." I lean against him and slip my arms around his waist: the trim, taut waist of the hunter Terry Shaw. "Let's go see whether any of our baits took a hit last night."

"Yes, let's do." The glint of confidence is back in his eyes. "That sort of hunting I'm comfortable with."

And that is how our romance starts.

And that is how our romance ends, temporarily, when I get my fine leopard two evenings later.

And Uncle Jack, miraculously recovered, gets a second leopard the evening after. His leopard is a bit finer than my leopard, and for that I am grateful.

He now likes my leopard story. He likes it very much. Says it's the best hunting story I've ever written.

The Gift

Our safari over, Uncle Jack borrowed Terry's truck so that we could pilgrimage to the final resting place of my mother. We left our white hunter in his office in town, planning the itinerary of his next clients, who were expected in three days.

By then we'd be sailing toward England. After a leisurely hiatus in America's "Mother Country," culminating in Southampton, Uncle Jack had arranged for us to return to New York aboard the *Queen Mary*, retrofitted back to civilian use after the war ended. Her passenger list promised a literal "who's who" of the titled, the moneyed, and the glamorous. My uncle titillated my imagination by saying that Clark Gable might be on board. Mr. Gable had become my not-so-secret passion since I'd thrilled through *Gone with the Wind* five times.

I reminded myself that I had no title, no money, and the little I knew of glamour had been gleaned from advertisements and movie magazines. But, after a week of recuperation in London and a shopping excursion to Harrods, I hoped to somehow pass as one of the "beautiful people."

Today my thoughts were of a different nature. Visiting the grave of my mother had been long-awaited, but as it neared, somewhat dreaded. I hoped my dreams of her would end after I'd come to her, because they had not been good dreams. Uncle Jack said he'd been experiencing similar nightly disturbances.

While he drove to our destination, I looked out the window, assimilating the sights and sounds of Africa. The juxtaposition of the poor and the rich particularly jarred my sensibilities. Gaunt cattle, cobbled-together huts of tin and sticks, hollow-eyed boys herding scrawny goats, and bony-ribbed dogs tottering along the road contrasted sharply with vast cultivated fields and manicured orchards.

At the end of one orchard that had stretched for miles, Uncle Jack turned onto a narrow drive. This was not where his own land had been located, he said, or where Mother had died, but simply where she was buried.

The Coetzee home was a plain, white, colonial-era farmhouse surrounded by a garden of brilliantly-hued flowers and dominated by a great jacaranda. A saucy parrot squawked an alarm as we got out of the Rover, its cage suspended from the cool underside of a spreading tree.

Our hostess was waiting for us on the veranda. She was the wife of a doctor, now retired, who'd lived all his life in the area. Her British husband was a descendant of David Livingstone. They are no relation to the Coetzees, but are simply the managers of this farm. It was a quiet and peaceful life; she stopped talking for a moment and offered us tea.

As we drank our tea and made polite conversation, Uncle Jack seemed preoccupied. He studied his watch, the flowers, the parrot. He tapped a broken cadence on the floor planks with his boot as she talked, as he talked, as I talked, as she talked again. A sudden gust of wind turned the blades of the ceiling fan overhead. The sky darkened.

Our hostess sighed. "Oh, it looks like we're in for it again … as much as I enjoy visiting, Mr. Stahl, you and your daughter better hurry before the rain returns. If you don't remember, it's along that path." She pointed.

"Thank you, Mrs. Livingstone. And thank you for tea … come along, Abby."

When we were well along the path, I said, "I guess she didn't know who you are."

"Of course she knows who I am. She called me by name."

"That's not what I meant. She thought you were my father, not my uncle."

"She's right."

"She's right about what?"

He stopped and turned to me. "She's right about everything, don't you see? Her mistake is your truth, Abigail." His voice rose in defiance. "I am your father. Did you hear me? I *am* your father! You *are* my daughter! My brother is your uncle, not me! I had an affair with your mother while he was overseas. Anything else you'd like to know?"

I took a step backward as I looked at him standing there with the thunderheads gathering over us, and I couldn't believe what I was hearing. I couldn't believe that he was shouting those words to me with such belligerence. I stood stunned, staring at him but not seeing him.

Uncle Jack, my father? Daddy, my uncle?

"Took you by surprise, huh? Guess you were too young to take things to their logical conclusion when you and Darrell found those damnable letters. Wipe that look off your face, daughter, because I guarantee you're not half as surprised as I was when it happened … well, let's go see your mother. It's been one hell of a long time since we've been together: Randy Jack, Eager Ellen, and you, the Big Surprise." He turned on his heel and continued down the path.

I hesitated, my mind reeling, before following.

Around the second bend, nearly enveloped by various succulents and brightly blooming wildflowers, lay a small cemetery. The weathered headstones glared white as bones against the waxy green leaves of the surrounding foliage.

And there I saw my Uncle Jack, my father Jack, kneeling by my mother's grave. I could hear his voice, raspy from tears, but I couldn't make out the words. Every now and again, he would pause and look up.

Was he begging forgiveness from God?

Or her?

Or me?

I waited at a respectful distance until he got to his feet, brushed off his clothes, and wiped his face with his hands. He moved off a short distance and turned his back.

I had begun crying since I'd first seen him at her grave. Trembling, I came forward, knelt, and touched the smooth marble of her gravestone. I read her name, the dates of her birth and death, and the memorial inscription that Darrell and I had so long ago read in the dusty basement of our town's newspaper: *So Young, She Now Resides with the Angels*, and I thought of my father, not of her.

But I cried because of her, because she had loved me, and I hadn't the chance to love her back.

Because she had known me, and I hadn't the chance to know her.

Because she had given me life, and I hadn't the chance to thank her.

Because she had made a mistake with the man who wept at her grave, and I hadn't the chance to tell her I forgave her.

"Mother … Mother, I'm here … " The words were wrung from my depth, my soul. "Your little girl's all grown up, and she's come to see you. Abby loves you … I love you so much … oh, my God, I love you so much … "

Thunder rumbled. The sky opened. I ignored the rain as my fingers caressed the earth covering her. My mother was down there. Beneath me. Dead. For years already. I dared not think how it must be, down there.

The rain pattered softly at first, then harder.

"Abby, come." I heard him. My father's voice.

I felt his hand on my shoulder. My father's touch.

It was too much, too soon. "Don't talk to me! Don't touch me!" I recoiled and huddled closer to Mother's grave.

Several minutes passed. The rain gradually became a deluge.

"Fine," he said. "So drown then."

Water cascaded down my face as I watched him walk away, turning his collar against the rain. He did not look back.

So drown then? That comment was so like … him.

If I lay down and pressed my face into the earth rapidly turning to mud covering my mother's grave and breathed in my tears and the rain and drowned, would he be sorry then?

Would he miss me then? Me, his Big Surprise?

And would Mother welcome me, down below, if I drowned at her grave?

No, she would not. She'd loved me in life, and she wouldn't want me to join her prematurely in death. And because she would not, there really was nothing left to do. And there was really nothing left to say. I'd waited my entire life for this moment and the moment was already past.

I ran my hands along the chiseled words of her headstone, dragged my forefinger through the red mud and scrawled, "Abby loves you," although the rain obliterated the first word before I finished the last, sobbed my final farewell to Ellen Elizabeth Coetzee Stahl, and fled.

He'd started the Rover by the time I arrived. Wordlessly, he handed me Terry's woolen sweater. I pulled it on for warmth. He offered me his handkerchief. I cried for my mother and for him and for me. My agony had to turn liquid and flow out, and if I tried to bottle it inside, I'd die.

Eventually I quieted, but I kept his handkerchief clenched in my hands. It was as though squirrels were running around inside my head, scrambling my thoughts, my feelings. Jack Stahl—*my father!* So many things made sense now, but why had he shouted the truth just as I went to see her?

Why hadn't he knelt by my side at her grave and told me gently? Hadn't he known I would break like glass? Had he bellowed out the fact to get it over with? Like a quick yank to a dangling tooth? Or a swift thrust to a beating heart?

And why now? Why hadn't he told me sooner? Or later? Or never?

And what kind of father would dub his own creation the "Big Surprise?" A callous cad! A libidinous Lothario! Had my arrival spoiled his fun?

I could feel him looking at me, but I wouldn't look back. If I did, I'd feel obligated to say something, and I didn't know what to say.

Five minutes down the road, he said, "I told Darrell just before we left."

"You didn't!" I finally looked at him.

"Yes, I did. I'm tired of living a lie. I told Darrell, and I told him to spread it around. I hope the gossip has died down a little by now."

"But when did you tell him?" I was determined to keep the conversation civil. "Wasn't he at work when we left?"

"That's where I told him."

"I thought we stopped for your cigarettes."

"And my confession."

"But you were in the drugstore only a minute."

"That's all it took. I gave him the condensed version."

"What'd he say?"

"You want the condensed version?"

I nodded.

"He said, and I think this is verbatim, 'Well, I guess I won't have to listen to any sanctimonious sermons from the likes of you.'"

"What was the long version?"

"Same thing, plus 'you conniving bastard.'"

Something struck me funny because I could just picture in my mind's eye Darrell standing behind the soda fountain, mixing up a shake, and Uncle—no, what should I call him now?—Daddy Jack?—barreling in for cigarettes and then beckoning Darrell over to whisper in his ear the fact he had a daughter he'd somehow neglected to tell anyone about for nearly seventeen years and—oh, by the way—drum roll, please—this daughter had been passing as his own brother's girl, and then Darrell probably dropped the shake and raced to the washroom to pound the wall until he split his knuckles because if there was one thing Darrell couldn't tolerate was scandal—and family scandal was beyond intolerable—and then I could picture Daddy Jack waving good-bye and leaving for Africa with that same daughter he'd somehow neglected to tell anyone about for nearly seventeen years, and I started laughing.

I laughed so hard my stomach cramped.

My father stared at me as though I'd lost my mind. "If I'd known you'd think it was so hilarious, I'd have told you years ago."

I was about to refute his comment when my side of the Rover dropped off the road with a thud. A barrage of loose stones pelted my door as the truck slid sideways in the rain-slicked muck. A massive boulder loomed directly ahead.

"Look out!" I screamed.

Daddy Jack cranked the wheel barely in time to avoid a collision. "Hell, I better watch my driving … hate to kill you today, on top of everything else."

"And I'd hate to be killed today, on top of everything else! Don't you know you can't stare at someone and drive like a maniac at the very same time?"

"I can't?" He eased up on the road again. "No, I suppose not. Sorry … so what were you laughing about?"

I'd nearly forgotten I'd been laughing moments earlier. "Oh, I was just picturing Darrell's reaction. I bet he was horrified. You made a big mistake in telling him. You could've just told me and let it go at that."

"Perhaps … but that's a little mistake compared to the rest I've made, don't you think?"

"No. This is worse because this is right now and that was years ago."

"How else was I supposed to get the word out? If I told anybody but Darrell, and he heard it in town, he'd never forgive me. At least now I stand a chance."

My eyes narrowed. "A chance for what? Redemption? There's no reason the whole world has to know what you did. If you absolutely had to salve your conscience, you should've told Reverend Richter. It would've made his day. He probably goes years without hearing a sordid confession like yours."

Daddy Jack lit a cigarette. "So where was your good advice when I needed it?"

"I was your niece before. I had to mind my P's and Q's. Now that I'm your daughter, you'll get more advice than you ever wanted to hear."

"Oh, so that's how it works."

"Yes, that's how it works. And put that cigarette out. Smoking's bad for your ulcer."

"Damn my ulcer."

"It's your ulcer. Maybe when you're oozing blood inside, you'll wish you would've listened."

"Stay on topic, Abigail. You really don't think this is a laughing matter, do you? You just don't know how else to handle it."

"Yes," I admitted. How *could* I handle the fact that he and the truth had long been strangers?

"That's what I thought."

"So what did you expect?" I flared. "Am I supposed to gush 'oh wonderful, I've always wanted you to be my daddy, let's hug'?"

"No … but for what it's worth, Abby, I'm sorry." He took a deep drag on the cigarette. "I'm sorry about everything. Your mother was so vulnerable when my brother was gone, and I was right there to take advantage. What I did was reprehensible."

"Yes, it was. And did you treat Mother like you treat the tramps you pick up in bars now?" I put civility aside. "After she gave you everything, did you dump her for the next one?"

He looked properly affronted. "No, that's not how it was at all."

I continued my attack. "Why should I believe you? Preying on a married woman and you married yourself! Didn't your vows mean anything? Didn't you care what Auntie thought?"

"She didn't know."

"How's that possible?"

"We were careful, that's all I can say."

"No, that's not all you can say! And wasn't she expecting Darrell at the time?"

"Yes."

"And you still did—*that?*" I was unable to say "adultery." The word seemed too sordid, too dirty to apply to my own father. "Wasn't Auntie enough for you? Wasn't being Darrell's dad enough for you?"

"I said what I did was reprehensible … I loved your mother, Abby. She wasn't a one-night stand. Maybe that's worse because it was deliberate and it was ongoing, but I can't go back and change it. I can't change anything. All I can do is get it out in the open, deal with the consequences, and just hope the hell you won't hate me … that would be the worst thing of all, if you'd hate me for it."

"I should, shouldn't I?" I raged. "For stringing me along like some mindless puppet! For taunting me with promises you never intended to keep, dropping those hints over the years! Cruel, that's what you were. Malicious. Egocentric. Give Abby a kiss, give Abby a hug, call her your 'dear borrowed daughter.' Give her just enough love to keep her alive, to keep her hopes up. And then, when you had your final chance to do the right thing, you gave me away. *You gave me away!* My God, didn't you ever give a damn about anyone but yourself?"

"Of course I did! It wasn't—"

"Oh, stop it! I don't want to hear your justifications! I don't want to hear your excuses! I'm so mad I could—I don't know what I could do!" I stopped my rant, twisted his handkerchief in my hands, and willed myself to rise above my anger. I took deep breaths, like one breaking water after nearly drowning. I knew I couldn't stay mad at him for long. The handsome man seated next to me extruded charm at will. If he put his mind to it, he'd win me over in no time. As a character in one of my stories, he'd be fascinating. As my father, he was infuriating!

He remained silent. Was he steeling himself against my next outburst? Or didn't he care enough to comment?

"I should hate you for deceiving me," I finally said. "I should despise you … but somehow I can't."

"Good. That's a relief."

I glared at him. "Don't celebrate yet. You owe me an explanation. A big explanation. I want to know how it happened. I want to know why it happened. I want to know everything I don't already know."

"All right. I guess I owe you that much." He flicked ash out the window. "For as long as it takes us to get home, you can ask me anything. I'll answer the best I can. And after we get back, I'll never speak of it again."

"That sounds exactly like what Daddy said about Mother's death … yes, you heard me correctly. All my life I've viewed your brother as my father, and

I'm not going to rip away his title simply because years later you decide to tell me otherwise."

"I suppose I'll have to accept that ... so, what will you call me? I'm sure Darrell's thought of a few possibilities."

"I assume that's an attempt at levity. Do you actually want me taking suggestions from him?"

"Ah, no ... 'you conniving bastard' has already lost its appeal."

"Appropriate for special occasions, but not for daily use ... you'll be Daddy Jack."

He frowned. "Daddy Jack? Sounds like a card I wouldn't want to be dealt."

"Well, I got dealt a whole hand I didn't want. Take it or leave it."

"I'll take it." He smashed his cigarette in the tray and said nothing more.

I took advantage of the silence by struggling to get my mind around everything. The situation was overwhelming. "So what about me?" I said.

"What about you?"

"What do I have to do now?" I clarified. "Do I have to move in with you and leave my city life behind? Do I have to change everything *again?*" If I did, Daddy and Maria would be heartbroken. So would Hooker, although I hadn't given him much thought since I'd fallen for Terry.

"Naturally I'm hoping you'll want to be with me and your half brothers, but so much time has already passed. You're nearly grown, Abby, so I suppose you can do as you wish."

I heard sadness and resignation in his answer. But it was his own fault, I reminded myself. He could've done the right thing long before now. I couldn't let guilt determine my decision. Living at the farm permanently would've been tempting five years ago, but things had changed. I had changed. And I had no inclination to submit myself to gossip. Even a whisper would be deafening, if the whisper was about me: *Look at her, the poor little bastard ... never knew her mother, never knew who her father was, either ... such a pity, such a shame.*

"What are you thinking?" Daddy Jack asked.

"How this will impact everyone, especially me and Daddy ... does he know he's not my father?"

"Of course. He's the one who told me."

"But how—?"

"Without going into details," Daddy Jack said, lighting up another cigarette—apparently he couldn't divulge much without a crutch—"he couldn't father a child. Yes, you heard me. My brother had his dirty little secret too."

For the second time, I could hardly believe what I was hearing. "Then if it weren't for you, I wouldn't *be?*"

"Correct."

"And Mother, did she know?"

"I don't think so."

"Are you saying only Daddy—that sounds like such a misnomer now, doesn't it?—knew he couldn't be my father and then he told you but not my mother?"

"Correct again."

"But why?"

"Why do you think? She'd been longing for a baby ever since they'd gotten married, and now we were having this torrid love affair, and suddenly she's expecting you. My brother could hardly confront her with his own inadequacies then, could he? After all, he'd been misleading her for years, saying her infertility was her fault, not his, when in fact all she needed was a stallion in her pasture, not a gelding. If he'd forced a showdown, she might've left him, and that's hardly what he wanted … no, better to tell only me and make my life a living hell."

More nuances for me to assimilate: Daddy lying to Mother … Mother cheating on Daddy … Daddy Jack cheating on Auntie and lying to everyone. "But it seems what Daddy did was nearly as bad as what you did. Why didn't you just spill the truth and let whatever happened, happen?"

"Things were never that simple, Abby. He had me where he wanted me and I couldn't say a word."

"Why not?"

"Because of Ellen … and because of something he had on me from before, when I'd stupidly confided in him."

"And what was that?"

"Is there any beer in the cool box?"

I opened the lid and looked. "No, just some water."

"Any whiskey?"

"No."

"Gin?"

"I said just water."

"What good is that? I need a real drink."

"No, you don't. You drink way too much, and I just asked you a question."

"I do need a drink, I don't care whether I drink too much, and I know you just asked me a question." Daddy Jack bore down on the accelerator. "I said I'd tell my side of the story before we got home, and I will, but not now.

Enough revelation for one day … please, Abby, let me enjoy my remaining time in Africa. Let it be for now."

I made a mental note of where he'd balked. "Fine … but I'm wondering how Daddy will react when he finds out you've told me."

"He'll explode. It'll be ugly. I always said I'd tell you the truth when you were grown. That was our agreement. He could have you until then because I'd already taken his wife and the result was all he had left. He wanted a family when he came back from the war, and I felt I owed him. The truth would come later. He envisioned me telling you when you were … oh, thirty or so."

"So he thought me not knowing was a good thing?"

"Of course. He got to play daddy and nobody's the wiser."

"But now I'm wiser … and after Darrell tells, everyone's the wiser."

"Yes. It'll be the final rift between my brother and me."

I knew it to be true. "Did you make your agreement right after Auntie died? I remember the two of you talking for hours that one night out on the ruined porch."

"Yes. I can't believe you remember that, it was so long ago."

"I remember a lot of things."

"Then remember my predicament too. I was a bereaved widower with three sons to rear, and I had no idea how I'd accomplish that, much less you. I didn't want you stuck with the cooking and the housework. You deserved to be simply what you were, a young girl. You deserved to grow up gradually instead of having so much responsibility dumped on you at such a tender age. I knew my brother would raise you right. And as long as you liked Maria and her you, I figured you'd have a good life."

"Nobody ever asked me." I couldn't mask my bitterness.

"And what should've you have been asked? At eleven years of age, you didn't have the wisdom to choose. We did what was best."

I pondered what he said for many miles. He was right. But at least I would've had two from whom to pick. How often in my childhood had I feared no one wanted me at all?

"Then I was a gift," I said.

"What are you talking about?"

"Me. I was a gift from you to your brother."

"Yes … you were the gift that tore my heart out to give."

The Kiss

As IF I didn't have enough to think about, Terry kissed me the night before we left Africa. Daddy Jack had retired early, saying he needed a good rest. We'd taken separate rooms at the hotel, so it was easy to slip out without him knowing.

Terry was at the bar waiting for me. Of my change in paternity, he knew nothing. In public, I'd been careful to refer to my father as Uncle Jack, the way I always had. Terry didn't need to know my business.

And my father did not need to know my business either.

That night, my last in Africa, my bath had been sweet. My freshly washed hair cascaded past my shoulders in curls and ringlets. Earlier, Daddy Jack had given me money to buy personal items and makeup. He hadn't known what anything cost and neither had I, so he gave me plenty and said I could return what was left.

So I bought the most expensive makeup I could find. Studying my face in the mirror, I experimented. I had to experiment because Daddy hadn't allowed me to wear makeup, being of the opinion that girls my age didn't need enhancement. But Daddy wasn't in Africa, so I could do as I pleased.

My first attempt turned tragic. The foundation resembled paint on clapboard. The rouge made me look feverish. My lips seemed crooked. Excess mascara clumped my eyelashes together. A surplus of eye shadow made me appear as though I'd been punched. But by the time I finished, my brows were plucked and arched like Rita Hayworth's, my lips were lush as cherries, and my eyes were lined with mystery.

No more khaki for me. A deep mulberry dress with a plunging neckline that accentuated my bosom, a sash that emphasized my waist, patent pumps for my feet, Maria's pearls for my neck, and my own earrings completed my ensemble.

I'd purchased perfume too. Daddy Jack didn't know about either the dress or the perfume. He'd find out in the morning when I had none of his money left. I applied the perfume before scampering around the room to escape the smell as it dried … phew, had I applied too much? But I knew men liked this one. The saleslady had told me.

I was a sight to behold when I waltzed into that smoky bar and sidled up to Terry like I'd been waltzing into smoky bars dressed to the nines a thousand times before.

The joint smelled of liquor and sin. A few other women, all far older than I, lounged at various tables. A dozen or so men, some in suits but most dressed casually like Terry, turned to stare as I sat down beside him.

To say I looked out of place was an understatement.

"Well, I'll be damned." Terry looked me over approvingly. "You seem familiar … have we met somewhere before?"

"No," I said, playing the game. "I'm Rita, and you are—?"

"Charmed."

I laughed, one of the many times I would laugh that night.

"And what would the lovely lady like to drink?" the bartender asked. He seemed to be peering down my dress. I shifted on my stool to remove his view.

"Oh, I don't know … a martini, perhaps?" I tried to sound worldly. "Do you have martinis here?"

The bartender leaned toward me as though conveying an intimate secret. "Lady, this is Africa, and this is the finest bar in town. If it has alcoholic content, we have it."

"Oh," I said.

Terry stifled a smile. "And have you had a martini before, Rita?"

"By the hundreds," I said. "James and Maria, those two who live with me in the city, make them for me all the time. Why, martinis are my absolute favorite!"

"I see."

My white hunter took my elbow and guided me to a corner table. In the dim light, I was aware of his eyes and little else.

After a few minutes, the bartender brought my martini. It tasted awful. Thinking I wasn't doing something right, I took a big gulp and it tasted worse. I coughed daintily, covering my mouth with my hand.

"Do you like it?" Terry asked.

"Love it. I just had a catch in my throat."

"Cut the crap, Abigail. I happen to know that James and Maria are your father and stepmother, not your hired help. You've never had a martini in your life and you think it tastes like shit. I think they taste like shit too, but since I've paid for the damn thing, I'll finish it off and order you something you'll like better."

"Whatever you say," I mumbled, my worldliness becoming undone.

My first Cosmopolitan went where it should.
My second Cosmopolitan went to my head.
My third Cosmopolitan went everywhere else.

Terry was drinking heavily himself or he wouldn't have ordered me a fourth … and maybe a fifth, although I lost track after four.

All evening long, we'd been huddling and cuddling at the corner table of the finest bar in town, and perhaps in all of Africa, according to our attentive bartender. All evening long, I'd breathed into myself the smoke and the smell of liquor and sin until it became a part of me and me of it. All evening long, Terry had been touching me in some way, caressing my hand, stroking my arm, or fondling my knee under the table as he talked, as I talked, as we both talked at the same time.

I felt peculiar in ways I couldn't describe. I'd never felt anything similar when I'd been with Hooker. But I knew I'd been safe with him. Daddy would've nailed Hooker's ears to the kitchen door, or worse, if he had taken advantage of me.

But was I safe with Terry Shaw, the white hunter, fifteen years my senior? I was alone with this tawny lion from the bush. Daddy Jack was snoozing complacently upstairs, oblivious to my growing peril.

The other women inside the bar looked well accustomed to the ways of men. Lots of men. And the other men inside the bar looked far more dangerous than Terry Shaw, the white hunter, fifteen years my senior.

No matter.

I was just professing my love for him, and he was just professing his love for me, when he slid my hand upward from his thigh and I felt something I hadn't expected. I yanked my hand back with all the indignity I could muster. He started laughing.

"What's so funny?" I demanded.

"You. You're so adorable, but you're such a fraud. Don't you realize I liked you better out there in the bush? But even then you were faking. Trying to kill animals so you'd feel important like us men, but then not knowing which one to kill. Getting all snotty with me and then offering me that phony apology. 'Mr. Shaw,' you simpered, giving me that look. 'Mr. Shaw'—my ass. You should've said, 'Terry, you're pissing me off, so stop it!'

"And now tonight, dolling up like a movie star to impress me. Well, you do impress me, Abby. You're damned beautiful. You're undoubtedly the most beautiful young woman I've ever seen. But you were just as lovely when you were dressed in khakis with your face reddened from the sun and your lips chapped from the wind, dangling half out of the Rover as you looked for something to kill so you could convince yourself that you were a great hunter.

"And another thing. You shouldn't pretend to know about drinking. I've been enjoying your company so much this evening I've let you drink far too much, and your uncle will hold me responsible … and to answer your question, I wanted to make sure. You've never been with a man, have you?"

I kept my eyes downcast. His assessment of me was painfully accurate.

"From your silence, I know I'm right. But don't be ashamed. If you had, I'd be so disappointed."

"Well, it's not too late, is it?" I heard myself asking.

He reached for my hands and began kissing my fingers. "Yes, Abby, it's too late. The hour is too late, and it's too late for us … and even when the hour was early, it was too late for us."

"Whatever do you mean?" I was having difficulty understanding. The smoke-filled bar smelling of liquor and sin was fast closing in.

"I mean it was too late for us when the evening first began, when your uncle went up to bed. He's no fool. He figured we'd be getting together as soon as he retired, so he said to me, 'Terry, if you muck with Abby, I'll blow a bullet up your ass and mount your head on my wall.'"

"Why, that's just awful," I said dreamily. "You shouldn't have listened to him, though. He's all bluster and wind. He didn't mean it."

"He meant it, all right. But I like that about your uncle. He's a no-bullshit kind of man, so you always know where you stand."

I had to give my father credit. Here he'd been sleeping soundly for all these many hours and watching out for me at the same time. Hell, I'd be twenty-five years old before I'd have something to crow about in *my* diary!

And that is when Terry kissed me.

Not like Hooker kissed me, but like a ferocious lion from the bushveld that springs without warning and takes whatever it wants because it is big and because it is powerful and because it can, Terry kissed me.

Caressing my hair, he tilted back my head and pressed my lips into his. He loomed over me, dangerous, possessive, exhilarating me to the very depths of my being. His fingers were strong along the back of my neck and his cheek was unyielding, but his lips were soft and pliable and exploring, and I wanted it never to end.

The Dance

My father and I stood together on the deck of the ship and watched Africa slip away. The multicolored roofs perched at odd angles atop the houses clinging to the clefts of the cliffs, the staggered skyline of the bustling business district, and the boisterous cacophony surrounding the docks slipped away gradually and with finality, and were replaced by the grayish chop of a limitless sea and the emptiness of an unending sky.

"As trite as it sounds," Daddy Jack said, "whenever I leave Africa, I feel like I'm leaving a part of myself behind."

"Then you'll be returning?" I asked.

"Of course. After the twins are grown, I'd like to stay here for a long time, a year or so."

"But that's so far in the future, Daddy Jack. How about next summer? It could be my graduation present."

He appeared dubious. "So soon? Did you have that good of a time?"

"Of course, but I wasn't as prepared for hunting as I should've been. By next summer, I will be."

"Oh, I think your hunting went just fine. Even your hunting of animals went just fine."

I ignored the innuendo. "Well, can we go then?"

"Maybe ... I'm not making any promises. I'll see what's left of the farm."

I kept to the subject. "I'd really like to hunt with Terry again. He helped us collect some nice trophies, and I want a wildebeest and a gemsbok next."

"Seems to me your continued interest in hunting is coupled with your continued interest in Terry ... what happened last night?"

"Nothing." I gave him a little pout. "You should know. You gave him his marching orders."

"That I did."

"He said you threatened to blow a bullet up his rump and mount his head on the wall if he didn't behave himself. Did you really say that?"

Daddy Jack chuckled. "Yes, but I only said it because I like him."

"What if you didn't like him?"

"Not a word ... action without warning."

"Oh, so without warning, you'd shoot a man you didn't like and mount his head on the wall because he messed with me?"

"Only if he were trophy quality. If he wasn't, I'd simply shoot him and be done with it."

"Well, that sounds just like you." I didn't believe a word of it. "By the way, Terry's asked me back."

"Then it's not a one-sided infatuation?" My father looked more dismayed than surprised.

"Not hardly!" I was confident that my white hunter still shared my passion after sobering up, although his chaste peck on my cheek as I boarded ship had provided no hints.

"I was afraid of that."

I felt myself blush. "Why do you say that? Are you going to find fault with Terry like Daddy has with Hooker? Or is it simply against one of your rules to fall in love?"

"Don't be ridiculous."

"I'm not being ridiculous. I'm being truthful, which is more than you've been."

"Don't start in on me."

"I'm not. I'm just asking you to hear me out."

"Fine, I'm listening."

"All I'm saying is that we talked it over last night. We talked about a lot of things."

"I'll bet you did."

"His asking me back was only a small part of it."

"I bet."

"Stop saying that."

"All right, I'll stop," Daddy Jack said. "But now it's your turn to hear me out ... are you listening?"

I nodded grudgingly.

"Good ... so here's Terry, a successful but monetarily deficient man living in the bush. And there's you, a love-addled girl with money who nearly throws herself at him. His wanting you back is highly suspect. Think about it."

"That's a mean thing to say."

"No, it's not. I'm merely being accurate."

"You're not being accurate. Terry Shaw wants to see me again because he loves me. And I have far more to offer him than money."

"You're missing my point entirely."

"I am? Well, whose money are you referring to? I certainly don't have any."

"Mine," Daddy Jack replied. "You'll never be lacking as long as I think you deserve it. And of course you have far more to offer him than money. That's not what I meant. Terry's a fine man, but he's too old for you. His life isn't your life, nor could it ever be. You've come to appreciate the finer amenities of life, I've noticed, and it's preposterous to think you'd be content living in the bush for any length of time."

"But I wouldn't be in the bush. Terry's buying a house in town this fall. I'd live there … after we're married, of course."

"My God, you're talking marriage already? Why, you're not even seventeen!"

"It wouldn't happen until after I graduate, so I'd be seventeen and a half." I strained to recall whether we'd discussed it or not. My evening spent in the finest bar in Africa had left annoying gaps in my memory.

"That's still too damn young."

"Auntie married you when she was seventeen."

"She probably wouldn't have if she'd waited until she was old enough to get the stars out her eyes."

"So? I don't have stars in my eyes. I know exactly what I'm doing."

"You and every other sixteen-year-old."

"Stop belittling me when I'm telling you how I feel. Or would you rather I keep everything secret, like you did?"

"No … so what are you trying to say?"

"That I'm old enough to be a good wife, at least by next summer. I'd keep Terry's ledgers and correspondence up to date while he's attending to his clients. And I'd write stories, Daddy Jack. I've totally filled my journals this summer, and you know they're wonderful stories, simply wonderful!"

"Your talents are beside the point. Even if Terry buys a house in town, how often would he be there? Seldom. A man like Terry Shaw doesn't turn his back on the life he loves and become domesticated. A man like him will follow the trail until the trail ends."

"That's not true!" I said, stung by my father's deprecation of my latest fantasy. "Terry would never marry me and then let me sit home alone."

"Of course he would. The bush is his job, his life. Hard as it may be, Abby, you need to get him out of your head."

"No. I can't."

"You must."

"Why?"

"Because a life with him would never work. It wouldn't have a snowball's chance in hell of working. Your head's full of dreams, daughter. You're far too young to make a mistake like that. It's out of the question. I'd never allow it."

"You'd never allow it?" I tossed my hair back angrily. "Who gave you control over my life? Who are you to judge? I still consider your brother my father, not you!"

"Abby, don't … "

I dug the knife deeper. "I think I'm old enough to make my own decisions. And your brother loves me enough to support those decisions, even if you don't. He'll take me to Africa and make my dreams come true."

"No, he won't. He'll agree with me that you're far too young to make such a mistake."

"So when should I make such a mistake?" I fumed. "Isn't it better to make my mistakes early in life and get them out of the way?"

"Abby, stop … "

"Or would you suggest later, when the impacted years are fewer? Or should I spread them throughout the decades simply to prevent boredom? And isn't there an optimum age for making a major mistake, say, twenty-seven?"

His hand flew off the railing. I flinched.

"That was uncalled for, Abigail." He lowered his hand. "That was completely uncalled for."

If I hadn't been sixteen and so full of myself, I would've apologized immediately. I'd been wrong to throw at him the age at which he'd dallied with my mother. And I knew I'd been wrong because I hadn't shielded my face. If he hadn't reconsidered, I would've taken the full force of his hand across my mouth. And I couldn't remember a single time since the angel food cake fiasco when he'd hit me.

He turned and walked away.

I watched him weave his way between the other passengers who'd gathered on deck as we had, saying farewell to Africa. I caught the concerned stare of an older, smartly dressed woman, who must have witnessed the incident. Mortified, I looked away and alternated between watching the chop of the sea and the flight of a lone gull soaring high above my head and pondered what to do.

After a while, I went below to our cabin. He wasn't there, which didn't surprise me. He seldom had been during our trip over and nothing would've changed. He'd be in the aft smoking lounge or the library, whiling away the time.

I decided to make things right with him over dinner. I took a nap but slept lightly, hoping for his return. I took a lingering bath, locking the door against his return. I dressed for dinner, expecting his return.

When it did not occur, I ventured out by myself, attired in an emerald dress of modest cut with a high neckline. It wasn't a dress for attracting a man's attention, but it was an appropriate dress for an apology.

I walked aimlessly, looking for him but not looking for him. For an hour, I sat in the observation lounge overlooking the bow, sipping a pre-dinner cocktail. I avoided eye contact with several young men who seemed poised to approach me, thus ensuring my privacy.

Then the sun slipped into the sea and it was time.

We had first seating at the captain's table, so I knew exactly where he'd be. Rounding a corner of the dining room, which was decorated with lush palms and tropical flowers, I saw him.

And I saw her. She was seated next to him, her hand on his sleeve, smiling provocatively. She was a slim, elegant creature of indeterminate age, very smartly dressed. Her hair was coiffed in the latest fashion for evening. I couldn't help but notice the sparkle of her diamond choker and dangling earrings. She took a cigarette from her case and brought it to her lips, never taking her eyes from him.

It was enough to make me vomit.

He produced his lighter and held it for her. I was about to make my presence known when he chanced to look up. Rather than smile a greeting or gesture an invitation, he stared at me coldly. She turned around to see who he was staring at. She said something to him. He shrugged and gave back to her his full attention.

No unoccupied chairs remained at the captain's table; I had been replaced.

I ran back to our cabin, threw off my green dress, and had a good cry. Then I ordered a shrimp cocktail, a lobster appetizer, and caviar from room service, plus two Cosmopolitans from the bar, and charged everything. The tip I dug out of my father's travel case, from the secret compartment where he stashed cash for an emergency. I was having an emergency, so I figured it was all right. The caviar made me thirsty, so half an hour later I ordered another Cosmo and a mineral water for health purposes. If there was one thing I'd learned since traveling with Daddy Jack, it was how to spend money.

When he hadn't returned by eleven, I ordered two more Cosmos and plotted my revenge. I dressed again, this time in my deep mulberry number with the plunging neckline. I slopped on my makeup, twirled my hair atop my head, fastened it with rhinestone combs, and loaded up on jewelry. My dress stunk from my memorable evening with Terry, but so much the better.

I walked, albeit unsteadily, back to the dining room and bribed, with more of Daddy Jack's money, an accommodating waiter to figure out who had taken my place. She'd charged a pack of cigarettes during the meal, so within two minutes I learned both her name and cabin number.

Off I went on my little quest. If I was wrong and my father wasn't with her, I planned to act more intoxicated than I was, thus covering my error. But if I was right, he was in for a big surprise from me, his Big Surprise.

Not once did I consider what he might do to me later. In the condition I was in, later never comes.

I knocked on her door, tentatively at first, then harder. Then harder still. I was starting to think no one was inside and all I was accomplishing was annoying those in nearby cabins when the door opened, just a tad.

"Who's there, Jack?" a woman called from the darkened room. "Did our drinks finally come?"

Daddy Jack stood there, attired in undershorts and nothing else. The look on his face was priceless. He was so shocked that he forgot to hang onto the doorknob. I shoved open the door and stepped inside.

"What the hell—?" he started.

I flung my arms around his neck. "Daddy! I've bin lookin' all over for you and so's Momma," I hollered happily in my best *Gone With the Wind* drawl. "Why, Momma's done took to her bed, with the headache she's bin havin' all day an' she says to me—'Abby girl, you git out and find your daddy and git him home right now,' and Lord a Mercy, here you is!" I tried to imitate Scarlett O'Hara, but I might've sounded more like Prissy. I made a hell of an impression, that's for sure.

"Jack, you're married?" the woman questioned from beneath the sheets.

"Oh, Lord, course he is! How you think he's my daddy?" I bubbled. "He's got me and Lizzy and Stella and Jimmy Jack. Why, he's bin married to Momma for near a quarter century, but he still looks fine—a fine lookin' man, that's my daddy!"

Daddy Jack shoved me into the corridor as those words were flying out of my mouth and slammed the door. Muffled voices emanated from within the room, and I started laughing.

Then the voices stopped. I took off my pumps and held them as I raced along like a jackrabbit. I burst into our cabin and locked the door behind me. Then I stopped laughing because I realized he had another key or he could get someone to open the door if he didn't.

Lord a Mercy, Scarlett O'Hara was in deep shit!

I didn't have long to worry because he was back within five minutes. He opened the door, slammed it, locked it, and sat down. In the chair opposite my chair, where I was huddled, he crossed his arms and sat there.

"You little witch."

I didn't say a thing.

A minute passed.

"I can't decide whether to turn you over my knee or hand you an award for that stellar performance back there."

Still I kept quiet.

Another long minute passed. He uncrossed his arms and leaned forward.

I tensed.

"What, aren't you talking now? You ruin my night and now you won't even talk?"

"I'll talk," I said in a small voice. "I just don't want to say anything that'll make you mad."

"You couldn't say or do anything more to make me mad tonight! You've covered all the bases already!"

"Well, you ruined my night too. How do you think I felt when I came to dinner and you looked so hateful and you had that creature taking my place?"

"That cuts both ways. How do you think I felt when you said you intended to do whatever you damn well pleased, and you poked fun at my good advice? And then, to top it all off, you threw my past in my face?"

"Um … about as bad as I did?"

"That is correct. It's high time you realize that others have feelings, too, not just you. And now we'll have to come to some sort of agreement before we both have nothing but ruined nights."

I mulled that over. "I suppose so … like what?"

"Like how about I do what I want and you do what I want?"

"Fine." I yawned.

Something didn't sound quite right about his proposal, but I didn't understand what it was until the next morning when I awoke with the worst headache ever. I'd had a rough night, and it hadn't been from the waves on the Atlantic.

He promptly came up with a new set of rules that weren't much more acceptable than the first, but what could Scarlett O'Hara do?

Lord a Mercy, when Daddy Jack put his foot down, he kept it down!

"You shouldn't run off with tramps," I said when I felt better in the afternoon. Aunt Emma's accounts of his dalliances in Minnesota hadn't bothered me particularly, but seeing him with the floozy at the captain's table had deeply offended my genteel sensibilities. As my father, he must adhere to a higher standard of behavior.

Daddy Jack set aside his *Life* magazine. "Mrs. Edwards is hardly a tramp. She has money and she has—"

"Your rich tramps are married too? What's with you and married women?"

"Mrs. Edwards is divorced, not that it's any of your business. She simply finds it more socially acceptable to retain her title."

"Well, if you'd like to retain *your* title, Daddy Jack, you'd better stop running around! What kind of an example are you? You make rules for me while you act any way you damn please!"

"Rules? Then last night I should've had a rule against you getting tight!" he retorted. "What kind of young lady gets three sheets to the wind, impersonates—badly, I might add—a southern belle, and chases down her own father in the boudoir?"

"One who can't tolerate him acting the way he does!"

"So we're back to that?"

"We've never left the subject!"

Daddy Jack shifted his gaze from me to the mirror behind me, as though reflecting on his fitness as a parent. "I'll be discreet," he decided.

"No, you'll be good."

"Sometimes talking to you is like talking to the wall, Abigail. Try to understand. I've been a widower for years. I'm raising three boys by myself. I need a break. I need some fun. If I have fun back home, I get reported on and all hell breaks loose. Whatever happens here stays here. You're not adverse to fun, I've noticed, so you could be a little more understanding."

"But I don't have fun that way," I needled. "I'm a good girl."

"You're sixteen. You'd damned well better be a good girl. I'm past forty … as I said before, I'll be discreet."

"Oh, so you'll continue doing whatever you want, while I can't?"

"Bingo! You're slow, Abigail, but you're catching on."

"That's not fair."

"What's not fair? Seems to me I already let you do far more than I should, now that I think about it. I let you swear, within reason. I let you rendezvous with Terry. I let you waste my money. I let you buy dresses that turn the head of every man in the room. I even let you drink, but you've certainly abused that privilege lately, haven't you? What exactly do you have to complain about?"

"You … just don't let me see what you do." I began to cry.

"Oh, stop the waterworks. Every time you don't get your way, you start with the tears. It gets old. Really old."

"Well, I can't help it. I think of you with those tramps and I can't stand it!"

He drummed his fingers on the arm of his chair. He consulted his watch. He contemplated the ceiling. He shook his head. He watched me weep.

"Oh, Abby, what shall I ever do with you?"

I didn't answer. If he didn't know what to do, I'd go back to his brother.

But he did … somehow he did. He led me to the davenport, sat me down, and put his arms around me. At first I resisted because I was so angry, but when he persisted, I yielded.

It was the first time he'd held me since telling me the truth. It felt so good and so right I didn't want to stop crying if it meant he would stop holding me. My father was holding me. My *real* father.

"You can quit now," he said.

I nodded and wiped my eyes. Being held had brought back a recollection of another man's chest, the crisp starch of another collar, and the hardness of another shoulder whereon I had, long ago, rested my head.

"Have I ever told you about my first memory?" I said.

"No, what is it?"

"It's of Daddy giving me a bath in the washtub out on the lawn. I remember giggling and him laughing as he dried me with a white towel and dressed me in a yellow nightgown. I've always remembered how safe and warm I felt when he carried me upstairs to take my nap. All my life I've wanted to feel as safe and warm as I did then … right now came pretty close."

I heard his breath catch. I looked up. "Did I say something wrong?"

"No, I was just thinking of all the years that have gone already. That wasn't my brother, Abby. That was me."

"You? Are you sure?"

"I'm very sure. That was the day your grandmother went in for a checkup and Dr. Jorgenson told her she a heart condition. I took care of you that day. In fact, I took care of you whenever possible at her house. It was the only chance I had to demonstrate my affection for you without anyone thinking it odd."

"But didn't Auntie think it odd? Men don't usually babysit."

"She didn't know. She thought I was off riding or working."

"Gramma must've thought it odd then."

"Probably … she never said anything, but I think she guessed the truth."

"So that's why she left the farm to Daddy … "

"Very likely. She knew I didn't need the money at that point, but it would be so like her to cut me out when I expected otherwise … can we talk about this later? I'd like to enjoy my remaining time on the ship."

"Enjoy how?" I hoped he'd heed my entreaties.

"I'll be discreet," he said for the third time.

The remainder of our voyage to England went smoothly. Daddy Jack paid close attention to me whenever we were together, and I was never again replaced at dinner. Once he disappeared afterward, but he returned in the wee hours.

I tried not to think about it.

His rules were simple. He allowed me to drink my Cosmopolitans, for which I'd developed a real affinity, as long as I stopped at two. He wanted to know where I was, who I was with, and I had to be back in our cabin by midnight. My Cinderella coach would turn into a pumpkin then, he said, but he was seldom present at that hour to check on me.

The hussy from beneath the sheets never approached him again, fortunately for her. I would've clawed her eyes out.

After a week's whirlwind tour of England, we boarded the *Queen Mary*, the most magnificent vessel ever built, according to my father. I had to agree. She was a literal floating palace, boasting of thirty types of wood, innumerable marbles, and oriental tapestries. Her flourishes and finishes featured vignettes of mythology and animals in natural settings. The Grand Salon was the epitome of luxury. The public rooms extended the length of the promenade deck, with exclusive shops, a library with Art Deco embellishments, an observation lounge, and a cocktail bar with curved glass windows for a panoramic view.

As first-class passengers, Daddy Jack and I passed through a bronze door each evening to dine beneath a map of the world. A crystal model of the ship inched along the map to indicate her progression across the Atlantic. True to the *Queen's* origins, roast beef and Yorkshire pudding were offered, as well as delicacies from around the world.

Even Daddy Jack was impressed. "How do you keep 'em down on the farm, after they've seen the *Queen*?" he asked, paraphrasing a popular saying.

I could only shake my head in wonderment. My frugal upbringing on Gramma's farm had faded to a distant memory, replaced by glitter and glamour.

With only five days before our arrival in New York, I wasted no time blending into the crowd of beautiful people. I talked. I laughed. I entertained and was in turn entertained.

I changed my attire several times daily, in deference to the social function I was attending and the hour. My dresses from Harrods were "haute couture," a new word for me. All boasted necklines that took full advantage of my natural endowments, and they were all my favorites.

For giggles, I anointed myself with an imaginary title and country. I became Princess Abigail of Stataslova, a tiny principality near Hungary. So tiny, I said, it wasn't even on the map. I invented an entire saga about Stataslova that was nothing but hooey, to see whether I'd be challenged. My new companions were either too dumb or too polite, I never figured out which, to question me. So I babbled about Stataslova being isolated from much of history because it was surrounded by mountains, and how it'd been colonized by lost British brigands around the time of the fall of the Hungarian Empire, so—surprise—they spoke English! I'd have been in real trouble if someone had asked me to speak Stataslovak, so I made that up beforehand.

I wasn't the only royalty on board either. I met a real duchess, an earl, and a peculiar white-haired gentleman who referred to himself as the Count of Monte Cristo. But I'd read that book and I suspected he was playing games too.

After looking around for an entire day, I asked someone in the know whether Clark Gable was on board. He wasn't, but Fred Astaire was. That bit of social trivia sent one matronly acquaintance of mine into pitter-patter heaven, but I didn't care a whit about Fred or his dancing shoes. The dashing Mr. Gable remained *my* dream.

The second day out from port, I enrolled in ballroom dance lessons. At first I felt like a true country bumpkin, but I wasn't the only one whose social graces along those lines had been somehow overlooked. I had fun learning, and I flirted, very successfully, with the young man who taught the class.

Mr. Barry Beauvoir wasn't Hooker, and he certainly wasn't Terry Shaw, but he had the most marvelous grace about him and he bought me drinks and kept me entertained. He especially cracked me up when he made light of certain people's affectations.

Barry was in characteristic form one evening in the first-class bar. "Darling, my sweet, have you fared well on the horses this week?" He spoke loudly to attract attention but not so loud as to sound boorish.

"Oh, fabulously," I answered. "*Racing News* said Bolting Nag came in eight to one. I won a hundred dollars!"

"You won a thousand, my pet," Barry corrected under his breath. "This crowd leaves tips of a hundred."

"Did I say a hundred? Silly me, I meant five thousand!" I blithely upped my purse.

"Five thousand is a right proper return, I dare say. And what will you do with that middling trifle of loose change? More baubles? A vacation on the Riviera? Shopping on Fifth Avenue?"

"Why, give to the poor, of course!" I smiled beatifically. "Our Lady of Perpetual Need is erecting an orphanage, and my winnings will feed and clothe many a good orphan."

"Your charity will be repaid a hundredfold, I should think … come, come, kind friends, join me in giving a hand to the benefactress of Our Lady of Perpetual Need's much-needed orphanage!"

I was astounded when a goodly number of patrons in the bar actually clapped and cheered. I was mortified when I saw Daddy Jack standing off to the side, watching. For once he was alone. Our eyes met.

"What the hell are you doing?" he mouthed.

I ignored him, hoping he'd go away. No such luck. Out of the corner of my eye, I saw him working his way through the throng toward us.

He scowled as he appeared at my side. "Abigail. Explain this damn foolishness."

"Ah, what do we have here, a rival? A bit long in the tooth for you, don't you think, my sweet?" Barry said to me, draping an arm over my father's shoulder. Barry was, by this time, rather drunk. "But on closer inspection, not bad ... not bad at all."

"Take your arm off me, you insect." Daddy Jack fixed my friend with a steely glare. "Can it be you're using my daughter as a beard?"

"You're her father? Oh, my God, pardon me!" Barry withdrew his arm, turned on his heel, and vanished into the crowd.

"What did you just say to him? You certainly were rude."

In a low voice, Daddy Jack explained the situation.

"Holy shit!" I breathed.

"Abigail!"

"Sorry ... but I thought Barry really liked me."

"He did, but he rather fancied me more ... and another thing, don't poke fun of the wealthy. Some are jaded, it's true, but most are hardworking entrepreneurs and businessmen who provide a livelihood for the not-so-wealthy, and many take their philanthropic endeavors very seriously."

"I'm sorry. I guess I have a lot to learn about the stratums of society."

"Apology accepted. You didn't know."

"You'd better stick around so I don't make more social gaffes. After all, being forgiven because I'm dumb as a rock is small comfort."

"I think I'll do just that." Daddy Jack guided me to a table. "Tonight my daughter will take precedence over the ladies of the evening ... Bolting Nag, now that was truly funny!"

After I learned to waltz, I asked Daddy Jack to dance with me, and he obliged. He obliged me many times, and each time was the best, the very best. Whenever he slipped his arm around my waist and we took to the dance floor, I thought I'd faint from happiness.

"Do you love me?" I'd ask.

"I love you, Abby," he'd say.

"Are you proud of me?"

"As proud as I can be."

"Are you happy?"

"As happy as I've ever been."

"And will you remember our dances aboard the *Queen*?"

"I'll remember our dances forever, Abby … will you?"

"I'll remember forever and beyond."

My father looked so fine in his tuxedo with his hair slicked back and the gray starting at the temples and the fine lines beginning around his eyes … well, he simply looked so beautiful. He looked beautiful to me, and I knew he'd looked even more beautiful to my mother. Little wonder she'd fallen in love with him.

The orchestra would play as the two of us floated around the dance floor as though nothing else existed. He'd gaze at me with those dark eyes and he'd smile, just a little.

He was my father and I was his daughter, and during our dances, everything was perfect. Like my first kiss from Terry, I wanted it never to end.

But as all things precious are fleeting, it did.

Looking Back

As we left the *Queen Mary* behind in the harbor, I looked back so long I came close to tears. I wasn't ready to leave the magic behind. Not yet, not ever. My father took my hand as though I were a child.

"Don't ever look back," he said. "It's too hard."

But he spent our long train ride home doing just that. At times he talked steadily, seemingly determined to purge his soul of his mistake by confessing to the one he'd created by his mistake.

I only had to listen, and that was difficult enough.

"It wasn't anything I ever intended," he said of the beginning. "I was married, happily, I thought, and Annie was expecting Darrell. But her pregnancy was more difficult than either of us had expected. In hindsight, I realize I wasn't nearly the help to her that I should've been. With her own mother already deceased, she reached out to my mother for consolation and understanding.

"Ellen had been living with Mother for several months already while James was gone. She wasn't pleased with the arrangement, but she figured she could put up with it. With Annie coming over frequently to discuss her problems with Mother, she became friends with Ellen, in a manner of speaking.

"Annie had no inkling of how envious Ellen was of her condition. Ellen had been longing for a baby ever since she married my brother, and she'd nearly given up hope. Several doctors had told her nothing was wrong, but it hadn't happened. And because it hadn't, she tended to be upset. Of course she was told being upset was part of the problem. She even looked into adoption, but James adamantly refused, saying he'd never raise a child not of his blood."

"But that's exactly what he ended up doing," I said.

"You are of his blood, Abby, but from a generation back."

"That's not quite the same, is it?"

Daddy Jack smiled faintly. "No."

"So what happened then?"

"Summer turned to fall, and James had his orders extended. Ellen was beside herself. She showed me his letter, so matter-of-fact. 'Duty was duty,' he wrote, and she started to cry. How dare he leave her there, bored out of her mind? But she was a military wife, and she was his wife, and she'd have to make the best of it because he controlled everything. That's the way he was, even with her."

And he hasn't much changed, I thought.

"I remember it started with the horses," Daddy Jack continued. "Late that same summer I bought two riding horses. Not Arabians, just ordinary horses with spirit. Annie couldn't ride because of her condition, but I could, and Ellen could.

"As it turned out, the horses weren't even broke. The laugh was on me. You couldn't get a saddle near those hellions before they'd bolt. And here I'd wanted to train them to do tricks like I'd seen in the movies ... whistle and the horse comes, open a gate with their teeth, silly things like that.

"I didn't know how to settle them down, much less train them. Neither did Ellen, although she knew more than me. So together we began to sort it out. It gave her something to do, and it gave me something to look forward to instead of just hearing over and over how rotten Annie was feeling. Of course she felt rotten. She was pregnant, and that was my fault too. Everything that summer was my fault, whether it was or it wasn't.

"Now that I think about it, her being pregnant actually was her fault. She'd nagged me into trying for a baby before I thought we should, so naturally it happened right away. From the start, she constantly worried something was wrong. I sympathized as much as I could, and then I just had to get the hell out of there before I said something I shouldn't. So what happened in the end was worse. I got the hell out of there and I did something I shouldn't." He stopped talking and shooed away a fly.

I waited for him to resume, which he did after a moment.

"Well, I guess it started the way a regular romance does. One person looks at the other, the eyes meet and hold a little too long, and it becomes apparent something's about to start ... and pretty soon something does.

"We had ample opportunity to meet. Mother knew we were training the horses. So did Annie. It was right out there in the open because at first there was no reason to hide anything. After there was, nobody knew how long it took us to accomplish what we wanted with the horses.

"And your mother was marvelous with them, Abby. She had a way about her. Her spirit communicated with their spirit, or some such thing, and they progressed rather quickly. But we pretended they were still giving us trouble, so it made more time for ourselves.

"Spring came. Annie had Darrell and her problems went away. My brother returned home on furlough and then we had to act our parts: me, the happy daddy, and Ellen, the obedient wife. And the thing was, I really wanted to be the happy daddy. Darrell had turned out fine. Annie was so thankful and so apologetic. I forgave her in a heartbeat, but would she ever forgive me? No, and I hate to admit this … God, I hate to admit this, but it had happened before, when we hadn't been married even a year. That time Annie found out, and she said never again. Then I compounded my idiocy by getting drunk and telling James what I'd done and what Annie said. He never divulged a word of it to anyone, but he never forgot it either. And then I did it all over again with Ellen, his own wife … " His voice trailed off as he stared out the window of the train.

I felt no sympathy for him. Gramma had always taught me, "You reap what you sow." Why hadn't her youngest son learned that simple lesson?

He took a deep breath and began again. "Anyway, when I really thought about it, I still loved Annie, and I loved my newborn son so much I ached just holding him in my arms. And I loved Ellen too, and I didn't know what to do about any of it.

"How Ellen played her role those two weeks my brother was home is beyond me, but she did. She said the right thing, did the right thing. She had to because she was afraid. You think he has a bad temper now? Well, it was worse then. He was capable of anything … and they'd been so good together, in the beginning.

"As for me, I'd run around from the time I was able. But him, he stuck to hearth and he stuck to home. Sure, he'd had a few girlfriends, but none who ever caught his interest like her. From the first time he met her, she was all he wanted. And here I'd stepped right into his shoes … and his bed, but he didn't know it yet."

Daddy Jack smashed the fly with his newspaper with more force than necessary. I kept quiet, afraid he'd make some excuse not to tell me the rest.

"And then you came: you, the Big Surprise. Your mother thought you were a miracle that'd evaporate into thin air if she said anything too soon, so she waited three months before she wrote my brother. She was one of those lucky ones who never had nausea or anything. I never suspected a thing. The only difference was that she wouldn't get on a horse. It was too cold, too windy, too something. Then we had to meet clandestinely because we had no more handy excuses. She'd leave me notes in our secret spot in the slough when we had to go a few days without meeting, in that Prince Albert tin you stumbled across that time. I didn't realize there'd been one last note left for me until you found it and showed it to my brother, and hell broke loose all over again."

"I'm sorry. I thought it was written to Daddy. I never meant to cause trouble."

"A natural assumption, given your age … anyway, Annie never knew what I was up to because I was always gone working the farm, running errands, or riding. But Ellen found it more difficult from her end. She felt there was a limit on the number of unexplained absences she could get away with. I think Mother had her suspicions because she sent me a rather cryptic letter at one point."

I wondered whether he was referring to the partially-burned fragment Darrell had rescued from the snow: *Stay home or the curse of God will be upon you. Nothing can be gained by taking from one and lying to the other.* I remembered the wording although I hadn't read it in years.

"Are you listening?" Daddy Jack said. "Your attention seems to have wandered."

"I'm hanging on every word. Please, go on with the story."

"All right … well, after Ellen told the rest of us about you being on the way, I counted backward and her due date was a bit early, but you could have been my brother's, so I tried to put it out of my mind.

"Soon after James left, he wrote and said he had something important to discuss with me, and he didn't want his next letter to fall into anyone's hands but mine. He told me to open a post office box in a town where I wouldn't be recognized, and to use an alias. I had a bad feeling about that, but I felt I had no choice. If he knew something I didn't know he knew, it'd be better to find out privately rather than have a letter show up and Annie open the mail before me. After I provided him with my alias and box number, what he wrote in his next letter nearly drove me out of my mind."

"What?" I couldn't help being morbidly fascinated by the unraveling of Daddy Jack's life.

"What I told you before, Abby, that he couldn't be your father. He'd suffered a terrible accident early in his military career, before he married Ellen. He'd kept it secret because it wasn't the kind of thing a man would advertise. Long story short, he was functional but sterile.

"He said he'd noticed little things about Ellen and me when he was home, and he knew. He just knew. He was deciding what to do about it, which would be in his next letter. He told me to write him back and enclose the letter he'd just sent. He was clever that way because it both eliminated the evidence and proved I'd read his letter. If I failed to follow his instructions, he'd 'take care of business' when he returned. And if I told anyone, Ellen would become part of his 'business.'"

"That sounds like a genuine threat," I said.

"Certainly it was a threat!" Daddy Jack was animated now. "I sent his letter back with a note begging his forgiveness, saying if I had a chance to do it all over again, I'd ship myself to hell first!"

"And he never accepted your apology."

"Of course not. His next letter was blank, except for a terse scrawl near the bottom where he'd written, 'Still thinking it over, you bastard.'

"He was playing mind games with me, and I didn't know what to do. It drove me crazy, seeing your mother so thrilled with her expanding waistline and writing him what he was missing, and what he could expect when the two of them became three. Only I knew how perilously close to the precipice we both were.

"But Ellen was oblivious to everything. Having a baby had been her dream. She thought, or at least hoped, he was the father, so I guess it was natural she started slipping away from me and going back to him. She'd loved me, but it was changing. And with Annie and Darrell taking up so much of my time, it changed for me as well.

"But I'll never forget that day in July when Ellen was resting on the davenport at Mother's and you kicked. She was so excited and had me come over and put my hand on her belly and wait for the next kick. When it happened, all I could think was that a baby was growing inside her, one I'd made, one I could never claim or tell anyone about … well, enough torment for now. I need a drink." He stood up, slid open the door of our private compartment, and left.

I started to breathe again. And I started to think.

During most of his confession, my father had been looking inward, seldom at me, reliving his private hell. But I knew, as he must, that the closer we came to home, the more public it was going to get. At least the gossips would never know the squalid details. It wasn't necessary. In a small town, folks invented their own details.

Then I remembered another fragment, the one where Daddy urged my aunt to leave something behind. It was about her deserving better and opportunity knocking twice. Twice … Daddy was persistent enough to try twice. Had he tried to take Aunt Annie for himself?

The pieces seemed to be drifting together. I couldn't wait to remove the clues from my lamp base and study them as soon as I got home. But what if Maria had redecorated to surprise me? My things *were* looking rather worn after five years. If she had, my clues might've been discovered. Glue didn't hold forever! Or my lamp could've been donated to charity! I reminded myself that Daddy was still frugal. My room would be as I'd left it … it had to be!

While Daddy Jack seemed to be doing a thorough job of explaining things, it was unlikely he'd tell me *everything*. And Daddy had terminated his side of the story when he'd burned the schoolhouse. How many gaps would yet remain when the train rolled into Union Station later today? I needed those fragments more than ever!

With difficulty, I shifted my thoughts back to my father's confession. One fact stood out from the rest. Without his mistake, Daddy Jack would've led a far easier life. Daddy had managed to administer his brother's punishment quite effectively with his menacing letters from overseas, and he'd continued the punishment to varying degrees since. So many irretrievable years had already been wasted by grudges and vitriol. Could my newfound knowledge somehow enable me to heal the rift between the two men I'd come to love?

A headache was starting, slow and insidious. I concentrated on the landscape rolling by my window: a white farmhouse, a red barn, a boy on a bicycle. Heavy-headed grain, undulating fields of grain, picturesque herds of dairy cattle. A little girl with her father—I was positive he wasn't her *uncle*—watching the train from their porch.

Bucolic, serene Wisconsin, so far from the glitz and glamour of the ship, from the wilds of Africa, from the arms of my white hunter. And Minnesota would be even further.

I was coming home and it was tearing me apart.

Daddy Jack returned an hour later, looking worse for the interlude. Rather than resuming the narrative, as I'd hoped, he took a nap.

While waiting impatiently for him to wake, I ordered a Cosmo. He was still sleeping when I finished, so I ordered another and pondered whether my newfound knowledge might alter my relationship with the man I'd always called Daddy.

Although I'd often resisted his many rules, he'd done well by me after a tumultuous start. Without his encouragement, I likely wouldn't have won the awards I'd already received for my writing. He'd been unfailingly vigilant, ferreting out new publications for me to submit my efforts. Without him, my children's book, *The Princess and the Tyrant*, wouldn't be awaiting publication in the fall. I had to smile, remembering his troubled look when he'd first seen the title. I'd allayed his suspicions by telling him the tyrant was based on the character of his brother, not him. Of course I'd told his brother the exact opposite!

Although I owed my existence to Daddy Jack, I couldn't blame Daddy unduly for his punitive treatment of his younger brother. And what Daddy had done in withholding his physical limitation from Mother wasn't as bad as what Daddy Jack had done in pursuing her, I decided. One was a matter of pride, while the other was a matter of lust.

At least Daddy had overcome his pride sufficiently to forgive my origin, and had learned to love me. For that, I was grateful.

But Daddy Jack loved me, too, and I could live with him if I chose. But if I did, would I witness his continued misbehavior, as I had aboard ship? Could a leopard ever change his spots?

And would Darrell find me detestable if I moved in as his sister? Wasn't I the bastard, not Daddy Jack? The "Stallion in the Wrong Pasture" seemed a more fitting name for him! And what would the twins think of me? Unlike their straight-laced brother, Dennis and Duane were quirky enough to think the whole affair hilarious.

But Daddy wouldn't. If I deserted him now, he'd become vehemently angry with his brother … again. And Hooker—how could I not be with Hooker? Terry Shaw was, after all, so very far away.

Oh, the complexities of choices! Life had been so simple three weeks ago.

Daddy Jack opened his eyes. "You're still here."

"Of course I'm here." I stealthily covered my Cosmo glass with my hat. "Where else would I be?"

"In the lounge with your favorite drink."

"I was tempted, but I'll have to stop soon anyway. Daddy will throw a conniption when he finds out you let me drink, and even worse, that I like it."

"If it comes up, tell him you got led astray by the fellows aboard ship and turned barfly without my knowledge. Say I was so involved with the ladies that I failed to pay attention."

"That doesn't sound very good … for you, anyway."

Daddy Jack shrugged. "So what? He can think of me as he likes. He always has."

"And you?" I said. "What do you think of him?"

"When? Then or now?"

"When you were a boy."

"Oh God, I hate to even think of those days."

"He told me once he used to punish you. Did he really do that?"

My father dug for a cigarette, avoiding my eyes. "Yes."

"Why?"

"Because he could … and because I deserved it, I suppose."

"Then the problems between you started long before my mother?"

"Of course." He lit up. "Try to understand, Abby. Our father was gone a lot and he drank heavily when he was home. Things wouldn't have gotten done if James hadn't taken up the slack. He ran the farm from the time he was sixteen."

"And he thought he could run you too."

"Yes, but I gave him all the trouble I could. I'd sneak in from wherever I'd been, and he'd be waiting for me. He'd haul me down to the basement and—"

Thirty-five years of bitterness abruptly altered my father's face. His lips thinned. His eyes clouded. He turned away.

I put my hand on his sleeve. "I'm sorry. It must have been awful."

"James was my brother," he said in a low voice. "He was supposed to teach me how to ride a bike, play ball, help me with my schoolwork. He wasn't supposed to be doing that … he was my brother."

"But it stopped … eventually."

"Sure, when I got old enough to fight back, it stopped." Daddy Jack cleared his throat. "One night I just couldn't take it anymore. I slugged him as hard as I could. I thought he'd beat the shit out of me, but he backed away. I've never forgotten the hate in his eyes. A few days later, he joined the army. We were through with one another until I honed in on his wife, but he got even for that. Tormenting me was pure enjoyment for him."

"And it never got better, even after Auntie died."

"No. Forgiveness is just a three syllable word to him. It doesn't mean a damn thing."

"And you? Have you forgiven him?"

"No."

"Why not? All these things happened years ago, Daddy Jack. If you'd try and he'd try, maybe you could—"

"Stop dreaming. What happened with your mother will always divide us."

"I hope not. And I hope Daddy forgave my mother. It would've been horrible for her to live with him hating her too."

"She didn't live long with him hating her … that is, if he indeed did."

"What are you implying?"

"Nothing. I wasn't privy to his mind then, and I'm certainly not now. There's darkness in him for which I haven't a light and I haven't a clue."

"Nor do I," I said. How else could the artifacts enshrined in the schoolhouse and in Daddy's office be elucidated?

"Suffice it to say we're both flawed. We are what we are and nothing will ever change."

"Except now I know you're my father and not him. That's changed. When will you tell him?"

"As soon as we get back. Assuming my car's still parked where I left it, we'll drive over and have it out. Maria should be at work. He can tell her. I'll have enough trouble dealing with him."

"Maybe it won't be so bad," I hoped. "Maybe he'll be so happy I made it back alive he won't care so much about the rest of it."

"Are we talking about the same person?" Daddy Jack sneered. "It'll be terrible! But you'll be my protection, Abby. He won't commit murder in front of you."

"Merely mayhem."

"At the least."

"That reminds me. How'd you get Daddy's permission to take me to Africa? You said before that you threatened him."

"I threatened to tell you the truth if he didn't let you go."

"And then you told anyway?" I was astonished by his blatant duplicity. "How could you?"

"Easy … I'm tired of living a lie, Abby. I intended to explain everything to you all along, but the threat was the only card I had and I played it. Tonight he'll likely trump me and the wild card will be you."

"I don't understand."

"Plainly speaking, who will you pick? Will you go with me or stay with him?"

"No. I don't have to pick and I won't. I need time to think it over."

"You won't have the luxury. You'll have to choose. By the time the sun sets tonight, there'll be only one winner in this little competition of ours."

He was probably right. I'd need the wisdom of Solomon to know what to do, and I was just a sixteen-year-old girl who'd be torn apart by an impossible choice presented by two egocentrics who despised each other while using me as a pawn in their never-ending rivalry.

Dear Lord, what had my life come to?

"Do you want to hear the rest of my sad story or do prefer to sort out your own thoughts?" Daddy Jack asked. "You can guess where this is going anyway."

"I'd rather hear the rest. This story is so convoluted I could guess wrong."

"True enough … do you remember where I was?"

"Daddy's letter saying he was thinking it over and Mother's feeling me kick."

"Yes … well, those damn letters came every two weeks, like some sort of sick clockwork. I got another one or two of the 'still thinking' ones before he wrote that, after mulling it over for nearly two months, he'd decided to play along. He still loved Ellen, even after what she'd done. She'd always wanted a baby, and goddamn it all, thanks to me, now she was having one. He planned to raise you as his own and fulfill her dream. I was to stay away from her and shut up about our agreement or he'd rat on me to Annie. And if that didn't produce the desired results, he'd proceed with 'business.' I didn't know exactly what he meant, but I could guess.

"He came home as Ellen started her ninth month, decked out in his officer's uniform, but he'd added something. He displayed a Luger prominently on his belt. He never said a word about it, but he didn't have to. I realized the implication."

"Daddy said he shot a German to get that gun," I said.

My father raised his brow. "Don't think he shot one before the war started, do you?"

"No … " I wondered what other lies I'd been told.

"Anyway, after you were born, my brother whisked you and your mother off to his new post. His leaving was such a relief. I was finally able to relax and enjoy my own family for a few months.

"Then I started getting letters from her. His came every two weeks, same as before. Sometimes he'd threaten me. Other times he merely signed his name. I'd given Ellen my alias and box number before she left, in case things didn't work out with him, in case her life fell apart … I'm not sure why.

"Guess she figured what worked for me would work for her, although she never knew why I had mine in the first place. I'd find a half-dozen letters from her during my two-week period. So did I put a stop to it while I still had the chance? Shit, no. I wrote her back."

"Why, if your affair was over?"

"Because of you, Abby. She wrote all about you, and she sent photographs. She seldom wrote Annie or even Mother, so how else could I know how you were? That was so hard, seeing how quickly you grew and changed in those pictures and I couldn't see or hold you in my arms, not even once."

"Yes, that would be hard."

"Then when you were only a few months old, she wrote that she was going to Africa to find her relatives. She'd inherited—"

"I've never understood why she did that. Mother waits years for me and then she takes off on a dangerous trip when I'm just a baby! Why didn't she wait until later?"

Daddy Jack ignored my question as though he hadn't heard it. "She'd inherited money from her adoptive parents, who'd been killed in a car accident. James was dead-set against going, being such a tightwad, but it was her money and she was going. She told him he could stay home if he wanted to be such a stubborn mule. She'd invite me instead.

"I could imagine that scene! I checked my box a few days later rather than waiting the full two weeks, and I had letters from both of them. What a mess. What an unholy mess … but I made my plans to go regardless. I talked the bank into giving me a loan, although I had no idea how I'd repay it. My brother scraped enough together or maybe Ellen helped him, because when we got on the ship in New York, there were three of us, not two."

"Who took care of me?"

"A friend of Ellen's. It was a long trip over, for obvious reasons. Both James and I drank heavily. It was the only way we could tolerate the other.

"As far as your mother and I were concerned, it soon became apparent that our affair wasn't over, at least in her mind. A few private words, a passed note, a meaningful gesture, a momentary encounter, that's all we could manage. My brother watched us like a hawk.

"Then we located what remained of her relatives. They'd been looking for her too. She'd inherited a sizable fortune from her grandfather on her mother's side. I remember she'd been arguing with James about something for most of the week, and in Nairobi, she signed papers passing it on to me, without him knowing."

"And that's how you got your money," I said. "I thought as much when you told me about the land you once owned in Africa. Did she will it to you because she was still in love with you?"

"The reason was in her mind, not mine."

"That's evading the question."

"Oh, so now I owe you a dead woman's story as well as my own?"

"Never mind," I said. "So how did Daddy react when you got what should've been his?"

"How do you think? Do you think he clapped me on the shoulder and said, 'Good going, little brother, you got my pot of gold'?"

"But didn't you try to share with him? You were plenty upset when Gramma bypassed you in favor of him."

Daddy Jack's answer came after a long pause. "No, I did not."

"Why not? Seems to me that would've been the fair thing to do."

"It wasn't a matter of fairness, Abby. It was a matter of—"

"Greed?"

"No, nothing of the sort."

"What then?"

"I'm sorry—not for you, but for me because I can't exonerate myself. I'll have to let you blame me, but I don't deserve it. I really don't."

"You mean you'll never tell me?"

"No … never."

"But you promised to answer all my questions."

"Yes, but some situations are ambiguous. Fact and fiction often slide together in memory, slipping this way and that. Situations don't come all neat and tidy, tied with a bow. That happens only in fairy tales. And the older you get, Abby, you'll realize it's so."

Daddy once said that his brother tended to confuse reality with perception. How much of what I'd already learned had been slanted? Or worse, partially or totally in error? I turned the conversation to a more innocuous topic.

"Be that as it may," I said, "can you tell me why Mother wrote me that farewell letter? Did she suspect something bad was going to happen to her in Africa?"

"Again, I don't know what she thought. She sent it to my post office box prior to us meeting in New York. I found it when I returned. She sent the locket the same way. You can imagine how I felt, with her already dead."

"Awful."

"Yes, awful."

"Maybe she had a premonition."

"Maybe."

It seemed the perfect opportunity to ask whether Mother was either sick or pregnant when she traveled to Africa, but I lost my nerve. Rather I said, "I've always wondered why you kept that picture of Mother and you with Daddy in the background, aiming his gun at the two of you."

"I don't know what you're talking about."

"It's the photograph Darrell and I found behind the chimney cover when we were kids, along with those love letters written to you from Mother, although we didn't know it then. I suppose you knew we'd found them?"

"Oh, that … yes, I figured it out. The answer is simple. It was the only picture I had of your mother beside the one in the locket. After she died, James went to all the relatives and demanded every photograph of her and himself. How did anyone know he'd erect a secret place where he could brood and hate? He'd apparently gone off the deep end, so he got what he wanted. In my own house, he charged in one morning, wild-eyed, waving that damn gun. He ripped pictures off the bookshelf, out of Annie's albums. That particular photo was tucked away, so he never knew about it."

"Not then, but he's known about it ever since he discovered Darrell and me inside the schoolhouse that time."

Daddy Jack looked surprised. "He has? Well, that explains why I'm sitting here, after all these years."

"I don't understand."

"And you won't, because I'm not going to explain it."

"So be stubborn. What happened to the love letters? Darrell looked again afterward and they were gone."

"They sure were."

"You're not going to tell me," I said.

"Correct."

"So keep your little secret. Just tell me why Daddy was aiming his gun your direction to begin with."

"Why don't you ask him?"

"I have. He said he was aiming at a snake in a tree above your head."

"My God, that's clever!" Daddy Jack said with a laugh. "My brother can think of more plausible explanations than anyone."

It was my turn to be surprised. "Well, was there a snake or not?"

"Why don't you ask him again? I'm sure he'd welcome the opportunity to elaborate."

"Oh, stop it!" I said. "Here I'm trying to get to the bottom of everything and you're throwing roadblocks in my way."

"Nothing says I have to make it easy."

"So be smug. It turned out well anyway."

"At least that day."

"Fine, so I'll change the subject," I said. "I've always wondered what you took from the schoolhouse the night you sneaked over there."

"The letters I'd sent your mother. Neither of us took our own advice, to burn our correspondence. I had no idea what I'd find, but I wasn't about to pass up an opportunity to destroy any evidence my brother might have had linking the two of us. Annie was alive at the time and he still threatened to expose me. I took his proof, until you found that last note in the slough."

"I thought it was written to Daddy."

"So you said. My confession is about to end … anything else?"

"Yes, I was wondering whether Mother was sick when she went to Africa." I knew it to be my last opportunity.

"Sick?" My father appeared guarded. "What makes you ask that?"

"Daddy said she was sick in Africa," I lied. "Was she?"

"I can't answer that."

"Why not?"

"Because I have no proof."

"I'm not asking for proof, Daddy Jack. I'm simply asking your opinion."

"I don't have an opinion."

"Or was she expecting another baby?"

"Where are these questions coming from?"

"I was just wondering."

"No, you're not just wondering. Somebody put these ideas in your head and I want to know who."

I hesitated, unsure if I should tell him about the fragments.

"I asked who, Abigail!" His fingers dug into my arm.

"Nobody! It was just an idea I had … I was thinking if she was expecting another baby, maybe she—"

"Maybe she what?"

"Maybe she … please, you're hurting me!" I tried to twist my arm free.

"So it's come down to this, has it? You want to know all about it, don't you? You already think you know why, and now you want to know who. Isn't that right?"

"Yes!" I nearly shouted. "Daddy told me years ago about the buffalo stampede and the bullet hole in Mother's dress. But buffalo don't shoot guns! Why can't I know what really happened?"

"Because it does no earthly good," he said through his teeth and let me go.

"Not to you, because you already know." Angrily I rubbed away the imprint of his fingers. "Even if you don't know her personal situation, you must know whether it was an accident or not. My God, you were there. If you know, Daddy Jack, tell me! I beg you, please!"

"That's it, isn't it?" His eyes narrowed to slits. "Even if I told you it was an accident, you wouldn't believe me, would you? You already think it was murder, don't you?"

"No!" I said, horrified he could so easily voice my deepest fear.

"No, you say? I don't believe you. You're trying to achieve closure by tormenting me. Well, what should I say now? What can I say now?

"If I say I think my brother did, would you turn your back on him and love me the more? If I say I think our white hunter did, in a last-ditch effort to save us, although he had the reputation as the best shot in Africa, would you believe that? Or if I say I fear I did, would you think me worse than Satan? Would you believe my shot went wild as I tried to stop the buffalo, or would you think I craved riches prematurely from the one I'd loved?

"Would you believe one of us capable of murder? Or would you believe, and believe steadfastly, that what happened really and truly was an accident? That we all had guns, and we all shot, and any of our bullets might have gone astray, considering the chaotic scene? Answer me, Abigail!"

I stared at him, my mouth agape.

"Ah, silence from one who is scarcely acquainted with silence. You've answered your own question. The question has no answer … no answer at all." He turned to the window as his fury waned. "Look, Abby. We're crossing the river. We're almost home."

I glanced at the silvery shimmer of the broad Mississippi and at the billowing arcs of cirrus stretching across the azure sky, and then I closed my eyes.

The chasm had not been bridged. My father had taken me to the edge of what his memory and emotions would allow. Beyond it, I could not go. I could never go.

I would have to find a way to cross the abyss on my own.

Resolution

"ABBY!" DADDY WRAPPED me in a hug so tight I could barely breathe.

"I told you I'd be all right," I said, thrilled at seeing him again.

"You look wonderful ... well, maybe a little thinner." He held me at arm's length. "Not that you needed to lose any."

"Wild meat is lean meat. You've trimmed down yourself."

"I'm the same as when I came back from the war. We didn't bother cooking so much with you gone. Maria's slimmer too. You'll be impressed."

"I bet I will. When does she get home?"

"Around six. She tried to get off early so she'd be here when you came, but somebody called in sick. She'll keep you up half the night talking, I'm afraid."

"I don't mind ... and how's Hooker?" I couldn't wait to tell him my African adventures, plus all I'd learned on the train.

"How should I know? He's gone ... oh, hello, Jack." Daddy acknowledged his brother with all the enthusiasm he'd give a pimple.

"Hello, James," Daddy Jack responded in kind.

"Well, don't stand there in the entry like a damn statue," Daddy said, apparently deciding to be hospitable. "Come in, sit down, and tell me all about it."

My father ventured inside his brother's house for the first time. Rather than proceeding straight to the living room, he perused each area as though assessing what objects might be used against him. He paused near the chef's knives arranged in a block on the kitchen counter.

"Henckels," Daddy told him. "They're sharp as razors."

"Undoubtedly," Daddy Jack said. In the dining room, he fixated on the crossed swords hanging above the French clock.

"Union ... the blood grooves are stained with the guts of some unlucky Johnny Rebs."

"So I noticed." Daddy Jack next studied a Kentucky rifle mounted in the hall adjacent to Daddy's office.

"From the 1840s ... I keep my Luger loaded for the unexpected, but this one's unloaded, of course."

"Of course."

"Oh, for God's sake, sit down!" Daddy gestured toward the living room.

"You make me nervous with all this hovering. Abby, get my brother a beer before he falls apart. Get one for me too."

I got their beer and sat in the chair by the side window so I'd notice when Hooker returned. Daddy and Daddy Jack assumed seats on opposite ends of the davenport. Like birds on a wire, space always separated them even if their intercourse remained civil.

I initiated the conversation by expounding upon our long trip over. My father joined the discourse after a second beer. He told about our sightseeing, our hunts, the weather, the food, and the people we'd met. Daddy inquired about the voyage, saying he wanted to take Maria back to Italy for a visit, although he certainly couldn't afford the *Queen*.

I noticed Daddy Jack, and I was careful not address him by that name, failed to mention my romance with Terry, his own dalliances, or drinking. His rendition contained no hangovers, no bugs, no sweat, no sunburn, no missed shots, no bad shots, and nothing about my mother. That came at the end when he recounted our visit to the cemetery. Even then, he omitted the tears, the incriminations, and the rain.

Daddy listened intently, his expression grim. "And you were so close to her, while I was not."

"I'll pay if you want to go."

"A pittance offered from plenty is an affront, Jack. If go, I go on my own terms."

"Then I retract my offer, James. Go to Africa or go to hell."

Here it comes, I thought. The verbal daggers have been unsheathed. Nothing to say now except the truth. I stopped looking for Hooker. Daddy Jack shifted position on the davenport. So did Daddy. Daddy Jack cleared his throat. So did Daddy. I mentally counted the steps to the telephone. I hoped a police car was nearby. Blood on the Persian rug would be difficult to remove.

Daddy lifted his chin as though to slide his arrogance down his nose. "Go home, Jack. As lousy as you look, you shouldn't be driving after dark."

"Thanks for your concern." My father remained seated.

Daddy glanced between the two of us. "What's going on here? Something is, or you'd be out the door already."

Daddy Jack took a deep breath. "I told Abby that I was her father."

A long moment of silence followed his declaration. Then the very air inside the living room was sucked into a black hole before exploding outward with the force of a hydrogen blast.

"You told her? How dare you!" Daddy leaped from the davenport and paced the floor with heavy, staccato steps.

"It was time."

"It was *not* time!" Daddy's face darkened with rage.

"Yes, it was. She deserves to know."

"Like hell she does! You just couldn't leave well enough alone, could you? After nearly seventeen years of living a lie, you just couldn't leave it the hell alone—"

"You've lived it just as long."

"Longer!" Daddy thundered. "Since I knew before you did, or didn't you tell her about that part?"

"I told her everything."

"Damn, that's wonderful!" Daddy jabbed a forefinger in his brother's face as punctuation. "That's simply wonderful news, you pitiful ass! Well, who exactly is this burning bit of knowledge supposed to benefit? Or didn't you think that far ahead? Did you think it'd benefit Abby to learn I was cuckolded by my own brother? That for nearly a year you didn't know the location of your own bed?"

"I really don't give a damn. I told Darrell too, and I told him to let it out. I'm tired of pretense."

"Well, Jack, that's commendable of you, after all these years!" Daddy spat. "Pretense didn't bother you back then, did it?"

"No," Daddy Jack said after a pause.

"You didn't mind pretending to be happily married while at the same time knocking up my wife while I was gone, did you?"

"No."

"And it didn't bother you to correspond surreptitiously with her after I returned, did it?"

"No."

"And you would've started up again, in Africa, if given half a chance, wouldn't you?"

"Yes."

Daddy stopped pacing. "Hell's bells, four times in succession I hear the truth out of you! It's such a novelty, don't you think? Oh, don't bother answering. You don't think. You never think. But I hope you haven't forgotten how to pretend you don't care. You'll need to remember that when everyone's talking about you behind your back and when your children—not this one, but the other three, or do you have even more?—stare at you and wonder what in hell ever possessed you to open your goddamned mouth. Then you'll get plenty of practice pretending you don't care, and I know you do. You care what your sons think, and what this daughter, in particular, thinks."

"You're right. I do care. But I'll be damned if I'll let you continue to talk like this to me," Daddy Jack said, taking the offensive. "So you're pissed.

When it comes to me, you're always pissed. You knew I'd tell her someday. That was our agreement."

"You also agreed it wouldn't be yet. I let you take her to Africa so you'd keep your goddamn trap shut for a few more years, but you told anyway. You lied to me. You're a lying sack of shit, Jack."

"It takes one to know one, doesn't it?"

"Get out!" Daddy pointed to the back door. "You brought her back alive. Your job's done, so get the hell out!"

"Don't repeat yourself. I'm going and I'm not coming back."

"Good. If I never see you again, it's too soon."

Daddy Jack took his time getting to his feet. "Coming?" he said to me.

"Coming where?" I asked.

"I'm your father and your bags are still in my car. Are you coming with me or not?"

"Not," Daddy answered for me. "She's lived all her life as my daughter and she's not going anywhere. Dump her shit on the lawn and go."

"Come for a few days, at least long enough to think it over," Daddy Jack urged, again to me.

"Think what over, Jack? She already knows what it'd be like, with folks pitying her and your sons acting like they've never really seen her before."

"I need you to come," Daddy Jack said. "Darrell—"

"Darrell?" Daddy said. "What's he got to do with it? Do you need help convincing him a surprise sister is a good thing? Or hasn't the shit hit the fan yet? Strange Emma hasn't informed me either way. Have you somehow managed to muzzle her?"

"You must come," my father implored.

"Daddy Jack, I don't really—"

"Daddy Jack? Is *that* your new name? Well, isn't that cute! Damn near brings a tear to my eye," Daddy taunted. "Go to your room, Abby, while Daddy Jack and I hash this out."

They stood within striking distance of each other, both irate, both thinking that they knew the best for me. One felt secure enough in his dominant position to order me upstairs, while the other probably wanted to order me to his car, but couldn't. The best my father could hope was that I'd be sufficiently swayed by his plea to accompany him down the highway without doing due diligence.

If I'd had a lifetime, I couldn't have chosen between them. No matter what I said or did, I was certain to anger one of them. And I didn't want to do that because, as maddening and as flawed as they were, I cared for them both.

But neither had the right to tear me apart like this.

"No, Daddy, I'm not going to my room. And you're not hashing this out—I am. You've been discussing me like I was invisible, and you've been shouting and interrupting, and it's my turn now. Your brother just happens to be my father, so I'd like you to keep that in mind. You owe him a little respect, to my way of thinking."

"Don't you talk that way to me, Abigail." Daddy's finger waved a warning.

I held my ground. "You're forcing me to talk this way, Daddy. You and your brother are like two kids arguing over candy. You both think you're right and neither of you wants to budge. But the thing is, I'm nearly seventeen and I'll be making my own decisions soon. You'd better start getting along with each other before you both lose."

"Abby … "

"Listen to me, both of you." I waved my own finger. "I'm tired of your endless bickering. I'm sick of it. You two make *me* feel like the adult here. And another thing. I don't know why Daddy Jack—and you can stop making fun of his name, Daddy, or I'll be calling you *Uncle James*—wants me to go to the farm right now, but I can guess, so I'm going." Like an exit line from a bad movie, I finished with, "Let's hit the road, Daddy Jack. I'm ready."

Daddy stood stolidly in the center of his living room, hands on his hips, feet apart as though planted. "So what am I supposed to do with the lasagna Maria made for your happy homecoming?"

"Give it to me," I replied sweetly. "I'm sure Daddy Jack and my three new brothers would enjoy it very much tonight for supper."

"Like hell. I'll stick it in the freezer for when you come to your senses."

I felt vindicated as I jumped in my father's car. I'd openly defied Daddy for the first time in my life and had gotten away with it. But as we sped down the street like something from the nether world was chasing us, I made a mistake. I looked back.

Daddy was standing outside the door, watching us go. The expression on his face broke my heart. The pillar of stone was crumbling.

Darrell was waiting for us in the dining room when we arrived at the farm. His scruff of copper hair was slicked back. Rather than a T-shirt and whatever jeans had been nearest when he'd dressed that morning, he sported a pinstripe shirt and dark slacks. A cigarette dangled from his lips. He held an opened beer. He looked really calm, which meant he was really mad.

"Hello, Darrell," I said.

"Hello … sister." He spoke quietly.

Daddy Jack bustled in with our first load of bags. "What, I get no howdy do?"

"Hello, father … of us all," Darrell intoned.

"I don't need any smart mouth from you, Darrell. You might say you're happy we made it back alive."

"I *am* happy you made it back alive, and I'm not smarting off. I'm the good son, in case your memory's failing you again."

"Well, you sure look different these days." Daddy Jack disregarded the comment as he pulled up a chair. "What's with the cigarettes and beer? You hate smoking and beer. And those clothes you're wearing … did somebody die?"

"I smoke and I drink now, and if you didn't want me to start, you should've stayed home. As for the clothes, nobody died. I'm going to instruction tonight, and then I'm going out."

"What instruction?"

"Catholic instruction. I'm converting, Dad."

Daddy Jack looked apoplectic. "What, you're turning Catholic?"

"Yes."

"That's such bullshit! Don't tell me you'll be mumbling over beads, lighting candles to dead folks, praying to more dead folks, and worshiping the pope like he's God? Forget it, Darrell. I forbid it. If you want religion, get your heathen ass back to the Lutheran church. For them, you don't have to do anything special and five bucks a Sunday puts a smile on the reverend's face."

Darrell's fingers tightened around the Schell's bottle until his knuckles shone white. "That's such a pile of sanctimonious crap, Dad. You have no idea what Lutherans believe, much less the Catholics. And you're in no position to forbid anything. You have no moral authority left, unless what you dumped on me as you were traipsing off to Africa was a total fabrication?"

"No, it wasn't … this is about Denice, or am I mistaken?"

"You're not mistaken."

"Then it's serious?"

Darrell glared. "You'll be the last to know—just like I was."

"Well, I guess turning Catholic's better than turning Democrat." Daddy Jack walked to the liquor cabinet and paused with his hand on the door. "Why's this unlocked?"

"You should've hidden your key better," Darrell said.

"You found it?"

"No, one of those hell-raisers you spawned found it. Once it was open, though, I sampled some of everything. I like the whiskey best, especially with 7-Up … don't bother digging for the brandy. Duane and Uncle Vic polished that off."

"Duane drank my brandy? Why, the little shit is barely fourteen! Why did you let him do that?"

"It's your own fault you left Uncle Vic in charge. You know he hates drinking alone. I guess he figured guzzling with a fourteen-year-old little shit was preferable to drinking solo ... and since when is it my responsibility what either of them does?"

For once, Daddy Jack had no sarcastic comeback.

"And beer stinks. I was just pretending, when you walked in. Somebody else drank them. I don't smoke either." Darrell snuffed the butt in the ashtray. "I wanted to make a point."

"Point taken." Daddy Jack rummaged in the cabinet. "Well, at least there's a bit left for the one who bought it ... where's the twins?"

"Hell if I know."

"Why don't you keep track of them?"

"Why don't you stay home and keep track of them yourself?"

Daddy Jack poured a drink and sat down. He started to say something, but then stopped.

I'd been watching from the far end of the table. The initial repartee had not gone well for our father. He seemed tired, deflated, unsure of himself. Darrell was seething under his surface, and the time had long passed when Daddy Jack could order him to the corner or march him to the woodshed. Like his older brother, our father had little leverage left.

"All right, then. You can stop the snide comments, Darrell. You don't like hearing things like what I did, and I shouldn't have told you that way."

Darrell's mouth curled into a sneer. "So you admit you shouldn't have asked for smokes and said I had a surprise sister in the same breath?"

"No, but I did. I'm sorry I told you like that, and I'm sorry I did it, way back when. But that was then and this is now ... so, what's everybody saying about me? Has it blown over yet?"

"No. I never told anybody."

Daddy Jack nearly dropped his drink. "What do you mean you never told anybody? Why not? That's the specific reason I told you before I left!"

"I didn't tell because I wouldn't have been able to stand it," Darrell said, his anger barely controlled. "I couldn't stand for busybodies to be gossiping about shit you did years ago like it happened yesterday. There's no reason to. My God, didn't you ever think about the ramifications? Or do you have a screw loose in your head that you never considered how this would affect me? Or the twins? Or Abby? Tell me the purpose, Dad, if there even is one!"

"So I can live the rest of my life in the open! So I can lay claim to my daughter without people speculating why she's with me so much! I'm sure somebody's wondered why I took her to Africa. It's a little too cozy, isn't it, a niece traveling for months with an uncle?"

"That's a totally asinine reason! You've already lived your life in the open more than anyone else! You've always done what you damned well pleased—gossip or no gossip—even when Mom was alive. Don't you realize how goofy you seem to folks around here? You and your money and your fancy horses and your trips to Africa when the average Joe spends his days on a tractor or behind a store counter, never seeing anything in his whole life past the damned horizon?"

"What the hell does that have to do with Abby?"

"Everything!" Darrell's green eyes narrowed like his mother's used to when she'd get totally fed up with the exasperating man she'd married for God-knows-what reason.

"Everything?"

"Yes, everything!" Darrell slammed his fist on the table. "You've already used up all the forgiveness you'll ever get out of this community. You hit your apex when Mom died and you've been going downhill ever since. Your romping with every tramp in southern Minnesota is bad enough, but if you insist on standing on a street corner now and bellowing out your past sins, I'm leaving! I've got plans for myself and it doesn't include being further humiliated by the likes of you!"

"How dare you!" Our father got to his feet.

Darrell stayed seated. "Before you fly off the handle, Dad, hear me out. There's no need to explain Abby's presence. She's always been here a lot, and I never told anyone she went to Africa with you. The immediate family knows, but they don't blab around town. So, if you want to move Abby back in with us again—if you want to give her an extra hug or kiss or whatever the hell it is you want to do that you haven't already done—I really don't give a shit what, as long as you shut your damn mouth about the rest of it!"

The paragon of tyranny stared at Darrell, me, and then his son again, before recovering sufficiently to speak. "So you're saying hardly anybody knows I took her to Africa, and nobody but you knows she's my daughter? Is that correct?"

"Correct. And I would've been happier not knowing too."

"And you took it completely upon yourself to keep my little secret under wraps?"

"Not entirely. I figured I was making the right decision, but I double-checked with Father Stephen."

"Who's Father Stephen?"

"The new priest at St. Peter's."

"The new priest at St. Peter's? Are you saying there's a Father Stephen in town who doesn't know me from Adam—"

"He does now."

"Oh, he does now ... well, that gives me great comfort, Darrell. You don't want anybody to know what I did, but you confess my sins—not even your own, but *mine*—to the new priest at St. Peter's? And what makes you think he won't tell?"

"He won't. He doesn't want to fry."

"No wonder I drink!" Our father headed toward the liquor cabinet again.

"Better pour a double," Darrell deadpanned. " And call the lawyer in the morning. He has news about the twins ... well, I best get going before I miss my lesson on how to mumble over beads, and how to pray to dead folks, and how to worship the pope like he's God. I'll pass along your howdy do to Father Stephen, who not only knows you from Adam, but he knows your sins better than you do."

Daddy Jack abandoned the drinking notion and stomped upstairs in disgust. Darrell stalked outside. I stifled a giggle before I ran after him.

"Hey, slow down!" I grabbed his arm. "I know you're mad at him and you have every right to be, but I hope you're not mad at me too."

Darrell whirled and thrust my hand away. "Don't touch me!"

I'd never seen such loathing. I felt as though I were standing there naked. I took a step backward, seeing his hands ball into fists. He stood six feet tall, with a muscular build, courtesy of farm work and football. We were no longer children. He could destroy me if he wanted.

"Don't look at me like that," I pleaded. "Don't hate me. It's not my fault. Remember how we used to play? How much we meant to each other? I'm still the same person ... please, don't hold this against me."

He held the glare and said nothing.

"Please, Darrell ... "

His lashes fluttered briefly as he relented. "You're right. You're not to blame. None of us can pick where we come from. But I've been stewing about this all summer, Abby, hating you, hating Dad for hurting Mom—"

"She never knew, Darrell."

"She didn't?" His tone moderated. "Well, I guess that's one good thing, if anything in this mess can be termed good. Maybe it'll help me forgive Dad one day. I'm not there yet. But Father Stephen says I have to accept human frailty for what it is and rise above it ... oh, get yourself over here." He beckoned to me. "You look like you've been through the wringer."

I accepted his hug gratefully. "Thanks for understanding. I was so worried about your reaction. I couldn't stand it if you hated me."

Darrell smiled thinly. "No, Sherlock could never hate his Watson. So I share the will with you. No big deal. But for now, and I'm dead serious about this, Abby, I need your support. This has to be kept secret. Maybe stuff like this won't matter a decade from now, but it matters today. A public confession by that loony father of ours will negatively impact both our futures."

"You can count on me." My future aspirations included attaining a ring for the third finger of my left hand, not political office like Darrell, but I had no proclivity for scandal. "I'm so glad you never told. If he blabs now, I'm catching the first train back to Minneapolis."

"If he blabs now, I'll be sitting next to you. I've saved enough to support myself while I finish school, and Denice will join me as soon as we graduate. I've already said I might be leaving. Big opportunity in the big city, you know the line. She'll find out the real reason, but she'll stick with me regardless."

"Then it really *is* serious?"

Darrell grinned impishly. "Serious as a goat in the garden. Well, I better get going, little ... cousin."

I didn't have the wisdom of Solomon, but I did have the wisdom of Abby, for what it was worth. I informed Daddy Jack of my plan and caught the train to Minneapolis three days later. I needed to salve Daddy's feelings, I longed to visit with Maria, and I was dying to see Hooker. Plus the conditions at the farm had settled down as much as they could. Daddy Jack had finally agreed with Darrell that the secret would remain a secret.

Our father had enough on his mind anyway, after meeting with the lawyer. He learned that, on the twentieth of June, Duane had swiped a car, whose rightful owner had tantalizingly left the keys inside, only to wrap it gently around a telephone pole two miles outside of town. The car belonged to the sheriff's wife, to add interest to the situation. Whatever had possessed Duane to drive a car when all he'd ever driven was the John Deere, nobody could figure out, except it might've had something to do with our father's depleted liquor supply.

Daddy Jack went ballistic when he heard what Duane's escapade would cost him. He grabbed Duane by the neck and thumped him against the kitchen door while screaming expletives. This would've scared straight a normal kid, but Duane was a hardened smart aleck, and paternal violence was like rain off a roof. Afterward, our father grounded him for the rest of the year, which would be effective until Duane really wanted to go somewhere.

Dennis, on the other hand, had behaved himself in June. Around midnight on the Fourth of July, however, his weenie roast for his friends under the football field bleachers had somehow raged out of control. Dennis said he wouldn't have used so much gasoline to get it started if he'd known the wooden bleachers were tinderbox dry. But it wasn't his fault that the fire department was so busy putting out a hog barn fire west of town that they didn't bother showing up. The bleachers had been slated for replacement soon, and Dennis figured the school board would be pleased to accept a check from Daddy Jack a tad early.

But when the wind blew burning embers from the bleacher fire onto the roof of a nearby garage—hell, that was a story in itself! Who would've guessed the garage housed the sheriff's wife's brand-new car? Dennis said that wasn't his fault either, because if the fire department had doused the original fire, the garage wouldn't have gone up in more smoke and flames than Nero's Rome.

Dennis also received an enthusiastic thumping that night. The yelling on Daddy Jack's part and the absurd promises to be good on Dennis's part combined for interesting entertainment. His subsequent grounding would be an effective deterrent until Dennis just had to do something to trump his twin. Darrell and I placed a bet on how many days that would take.

Later, after downing multiple drinks and losing horrendously to me in cribbage as a result, Daddy Jack announced both twins were up for adoption—free to a bad home.

I hailed a taxi from the train station and handed the driver a hefty tip for lugging my Africa bags up all thirteen steps from the sidewalk to Daddy's front door. For once, I had plenty of money in my purse. After what Daddy Jack had been forced to spend paying for damages incurred by his wayward twins, he'd handed a wad to both Darrell and me, saying at least we'd put it to good use.

After worrying about me for nearly three months and anticipating my return just to hear me shoot off my mouth, Daddy needed an apology out of me whether I'd been right or wrong.

So I gave him one. He draped an arm around me as we sat together on the davenport and said if I hadn't come back on my own, he would've gotten me. But he was glad I'd saved him the trouble.

When I told him that the secret was going to stay secret, Daddy expressed considerable relief. He hadn't yet informed Maria and now he wouldn't have to.

Then I told him my plan. I'd continue living with him for the first school term, but at Christmas, I was moving in with my real father until graduation. I'd already checked with both schools and no problem was foreseen. After renewing my friendships with my childhood friends, catching up with my cousins from St. James and the rest of my relatives—whom I hadn't seen nearly enough during the years I'd been in Minneapolis—I intended to walk across the stage and receive my diploma in the town where I'd been born. I hoped that he and Maria would be in the audience that night, applauding my achievement.

"We'll be there," Daddy assured me. "No matter the situation with Jack, we'll be there."

"I'm so glad, Daddy. I just know everything will work out."

"And afterward?"

"I'd like to study journalism at the university."

Daddy nodded his approval. "Good choice. You could always work for the newspaper and write creatively on the side … will you live on campus?"

"I'd rather live here, if that's okay with you."

"Of course." His pale eyes misted.

So did mine.

Maria arrived home at ten after six. She gave a joyous whoop when she saw me. Daddy was right. She'd trimmed down considerably.

"Rabbit food instead of real food," she explained with a laugh. "I never ate so much salad in my life. But tonight we'll feast." After sliding the frozen lasagna in the oven, she whipped up an appetizer tray consisting of fruit, cheese, olives, and crusty rolls.

Daddy popped a bottle of champagne in celebration. I could hardly believe my good fortune when he poured a glass for me.

"Welcome back," he said with feeling. Maria seconded the sentiment.

I was content … I was home.

Autumn 1951

My Triad

CONTENTMENT LASTED UNTIL morning. As soon as the lights popped on at the Hookers, I dolled myself up, went downstairs, started the coffee, and scampered next door while it perked.

But things seemed amiss. Hooker's hammock was absent from between the elms. The planters contained live geraniums, not plastic tulips. A blue Chevy was parked in the driveway instead of a black Mercury. Even so, I wasn't expecting an elderly woman to open the door.

"Um … is Hooker in?" I said, thinking she must be a relative.

"Who?" She cocked her head to the side.

I spoke louder. "Hooker, my boyfriend. Archie's son."

"Oh, they moved away, dear. It's me and Fred now. We've leased this place through an agency." She smiled pleasantly. "Are you a neighbor?"

I turned and ran. Straight into Daddy and Maria's bedroom I ran. "Why didn't you tell me Hooker moved away?" I shrieked. "Where did he go? You better know, Daddy, and you better tell me too! You better have a damn good explanation!"

Daddy assumed a lethal look that meant business and ordered me to my room to calm down while he got dressed.

I stomped upstairs, muttering more profanities. From my tower window, I noticed additional changes next door. The grass was cut. The hedges were trimmed. The garden was flourishing. The barbeque was gone. The patio lights were gone. The boyfriend was gone.

The boyfriend was gone!

After I wrote my fifty sentences for swearing, Daddy made me apologize for flying into their bedroom like a raging harpy. He said it truly had slipped his mind. After all, Hooker had been my fixation, not his. And the Hookers had left more than a month ago, so it wasn't recent news. He seemed smugly pleased while telling me this, so I asked Maria for details.

She said Hooker showed up one morning and asked for his letter jacket. She got it for him. Then he asked for his class ring. She was still rummaging for it when Daddy returned from the store. Hooker's unwanted presence in the kitchen prompted Daddy to demand what was going on. Hooker mumbled something about money troubles and left. Daddy walked next door. Archie was sitting in the living room, ripping up papers. He offered Daddy a beer but not an explanation. Debbie was nowhere in sight, so Daddy figured Archie was headed down the wide road to divorce again. Out of politeness, he asked no more questions.

A letter from Hooker had arrived while I was at the farm, Maria said, handing it to me. Eagerly I ripped it open.

Dear Heart,

Sorry to write you this way, although it's MORE than I got when you left for Africa! Would it have been SO inconvenient for you to explain how THAT happened? Oh, I know we were fishing on Rainy Lake that weekend, but a letter would've eased my mind. Your tyrant father was no help. He was THRILLED you were finally so far away from me, but Maria sympathized with my broken heart and told me what I wanted to know. Still I hoped to hear from you, but a whole month passed without a word. Were the gay fellows on the ship and the white hunters in the bush SO time-consuming that you couldn't pen a line?

Well, can't go into details or Dad will KILL me, but we're gone and that's that. We still own the house, but the way things are, it's doubtful we can hang onto it much longer unless Dad gets his shit straight. I retrieved my letter jacket from Maria, but she couldn't find my ring. If Dad lets me write our new address, can you send it? Or maybe you're so mad you won't?

We had a good six years, didn't we, Dear Heart? Hope you forge ahead and find somebody new because I think I have already. Leslie reminds me a lot of you except she's a blonde. But you know me, OPEN-MINDED! If I get back in town I'll stop by and we'll take a walk around the creek for auld lang syne.

Fondly, Hooker

I bawled till my eyes turned pink like a bunny's, my nose ran rivers, and my face scrunched into something grotesque. Maria called in sick so she could sit on my bed and pet my hair and tell me that Hooker was a horrible, uncaring beast to have done me that way.

Daddy might've felt the teeniest bit of remorse for treating Hooker mean for the six years we'd been together, but he didn't. He did show his concern, however, by threatening to haul me to the doctor for a sedative if I didn't stop caterwauling by nine o'clock. I was still howling at nine-o-five, just to see if he meant it. When I heard him clomp up the stairs, I quit.

I was out of steam anyway.

I couldn't believe what Hooker had done to me. It was one thing for me to go to Africa for a few months without getting in touch with him, but for him to vanish for an eternity was another matter entirely!

And I couldn't believe that Daddy had let the Hookers move without ferreting out the reason or getting their new address. He couldn't ask because he was being polite? Daddy was never polite! He was ecstatic Hooker was gone. Period.

But there wasn't anything I could do about Daddy, and there wasn't anything I could do about Hooker. So I arose from my bed of pain, washed my face, waited for my hiccups to subside, and did the only thing I could: I composed a love letter to Terry Shaw.

My great white hunter,

I've gone without seeing your face for nearly three weeks, but already it seems a year. Our tedious trip home was totally uneventful. It saddened me greatly that every mile of travel further separated us. I trust the hunting is going well and you are staying safe. I would die if anything should happen to you. Uncle Jack is planning to return next summer, but even that is so far away! Perhaps he will send me alone, if it doesn't work for him to come. I cling to the memory of your kiss the last night we were together. Please let me know your thoughts on this.

Fondly, Abby

P.S. I have broken off with my former boyfriend. He's a wonderful man, but it wouldn't be fair to prolong our relationship when all I think about is you.

Terry would either return a letter in kind or he'd have a good laugh and throw it in the fire one night when the lions coughed and the hyenas cackled and darkness covered the whole of Africa, save for the glow of the embers from the ironwood fire.

It was worth a stamp.

I dreaded returning to school in Minneapolis without Hooker. I briefly considered heading to Daddy Jack's four months early, but decided such an abrupt change of plans would be too shallow, even for me.

But when I walked into Newburg High that first day, I felt so lost and vulnerable. Thirty times I explained how Hooker's dad got this really incredible job offer in Chicago that was too good to pass up. Of course we were missing each other terribly, and of course I'd visit over Christmas break, and of course we were writing daily, but for the remainder of my senior year I'd have to make do without him. I withheld the truth because I had no trustworthy friends in the entire school. I hadn't bothered to cultivate any because I'd been completely involved with Hooker since I was eleven years old.

Without Hooker, I knew I'd soon be dropped from the popular crowd.

The jocks and the cheerleaders would fade away. I told myself I didn't care. Their trivial interests revolved around sports, cars, movies, and clothes. I liked those things too, but I wanted to be a writer, hunt, and live in Africa.

Their world was not my world.

Without A. J. Sebastien Delalande Hooker, I finally had the opportunity to return to my true self, rather than acting like a pseudo-popular, letter-jacket-wearing, giggly appendage of my former boyfriend.

Who was I kidding? Without him, I was dirt. And by the end of September, I was tired of being dirt.

I began noticing a new boy who shared several of my classes. As teachers typically seated students alphabetically, and his last name started with an S, we often were across from or behind one another. He seemed introspective, and spoke only when spoken to. Few of the other students bothered with him, being so involved in their own cliques. I liked that he didn't appear to care.

I saw him roll his eyes at a particularly ludicrous answer that Stan Johnson, the captain of our football team, gave one day in American Literature. Had Stan been tackled once too often not to realize *The Scarlet Letter* referred to a punishment for fornication, not a mash note penned in red ink? The new boy raised his hand and set the matter straight, in no uncertain terms! By the time he'd finished expounding on the thesis set forth by Hawthorne, with lucidity worthy of Daddy and sarcasm worthy of Daddy Jack, all the students who worshiped Stan Johnson thoroughly detested the new boy for showing up their hero.

He wasn't as handsome as I preferred, but he was an opportunity. At lunch the following day, when I saw him sitting alone, I swooped in.

"Hey," I said. "Can I join you or are you expecting somebody?"

"Yes and no."

I interpreted his answer as an invitation so I sat down. "You're new, aren't you?"

"No, I'm nearly eighteen." He looked at me with suspicion.

"Oh, that's not what I meant." I tittered politely. "I mean you're new to this school, aren't you?"

"Yes."

"Where did you go before?"

"Nowhere. I was homeschooled."

"My dad thought about doing that once, but he didn't, thank God. Why were you?"

"Because we lived hundreds of miles from a school where anyone spoke the King's English properly and knew more than my folks did," he replied, sounding bored. "I had the option of attending boarding school, but my mum wouldn't hear of it. So she taught me and my father filled in the gaps. He's a missionary so he thinks he knows everything anyway. Mum was a teacher before she married him, so between the two of them, they had it covered."

"Oh, that sounds fascinating," I cooed. "Where were you living?"

"In Africa."

"Where?"

"A place you've never heard of."

"Try me."

"A little village upriver from Garissa."

I nearly choked on my meatloaf. "In Kenya?"

"Yes." The boy set down his fork, a quizzical expression on his face. "How did you know that?"

"Because I've traveled all over southern and eastern Africa with my uncle." I paused to smile winningly. "In fact, we came back less than a month ago. Would you like to hear about it?"

The boy leaned closer to me. "Of course! Is your uncle a missionary too?"

I giggled. "Not hardly."

"What then? Garissa isn't exactly on the beaten path to anywhere. Upriver is worse."

On impulse, I told the truth. "We were on safari. A real safari with guns, not with cameras or scientific journals. I went hunting, and I killed a warthog, a bunch of impala, and a leopard. What do you think of that?"

"Sounds more exciting than sermons."

His freckled face lit up when he smiled, and I decided that he was better looking than I'd initially thought. We spent the rest of lunch getting to know each other. And the next lunch, and the next.

Randy, christened Randolph Scott Simpson after the actor whom his mum adored as much and on occasion more than her missionary husband, told how the Reverend Simpson had picked up, internally not literally, a parasite from the ground when he'd walked barefoot to the latrine one night. His strength ebbed to such a degree that church headquarters called him back to the States to recover. With strong medicines and rest, he was recovering, slowly.

In the meantime, his mother was enjoying civilization. She delighted at the wide variety of foods available in the grocery stores, and she loved the movies. She crisscrossed the city in an effort to see all the Randolph Scott movies she'd missed since they'd been stuck in Africa, but she'd settle for anything starring John Wayne or Gary Cooper too.

Randy had been accompanying her to the Sunday matinees. By the end of our first week of acquaintance, he asked whether I'd like to tag along to see the new Scott flick, *Santa Fe.*

"Why, I'd be thrilled!" I gushed. Attending a matinee with Randolph Scott Simpson and Missionary Mum seemed slightly better than doing nothing.

Randy was five minutes early picking me up. Daddy opened the door and greeted this stranger with his usual disapproving stare.

Randy stuck out his hand. "Good afternoon, sir. Mr. Stahl, I presume?"

"You presume correctly." Daddy shook hands as though Randy harbored a communicable disease.

"Let me introduce myself," Randy said with utmost gravity as he looked Daddy straight in the eye. "I'm Randolph Scott Simpson, and I attend school with your daughter. Abby's had the kindness to lunch with me this past week, as I'm new to this area. My father is the Reverend Maynard Simpson, recently returned from missionary work in Kenya. My mother is Mrs. Mary Simpson. She'll be accompanying us to the movies this afternoon. In fact, she's waiting for us in the car right now. We'll be at the Majestic on Penn Avenue, in case something unexpected occurs and you need to locate your daughter. The movie concludes around five o'clock, and I'll return Abby shortly afterward … is that all right with you, sir?"

I shook my head in wonderment as Randy Simpson procured Daddy's stamp of approval in one minute flat.

Daddy shouldn't have given me up quite so freely, in retrospect, because Randy wasn't as respectful to me as Hooker had been. Randy liked to tease and Randy liked to squeeze. Randy evidently hadn't gotten enough stimulation all those years he'd been growing up a little white boy amid the mud huts and skinny chickens.

But I set my limits and he crashed into my limits, and then he stopped. He had no choice but stop or I'd tell Daddy what a certain missionary's son was trying with me, and Randolph Scott Simpson would've gone missing while attempting action.

That would've made headlines in their church bulletin, sure as bells on Sunday.

In the meantime, of course, I was keeping my options open with Terry Shaw. He'd taken his sweet time writing back, and his first letter seemed carefully phrased. I couldn't tell whether he was encouraging me or not. Mostly it was an account of the clients he'd guided and the trophies they'd taken, along with descriptions of weather, camps, and other humdrum matters.

Only at the end did he write that he'd purchased a house in town, a quaint little abode with tile floors and a picturesque view. He'd painted the interior, tidied the yard, and planted flowers and a garden. He'd turned one bedroom into an office and was in the process of hiring a local woman to answer his phone and do his paperwork.

I hoped that the woman he hired would be very old and very ugly. The notion of sharing a quaint little abode with my white hunter set my heart to palpitating. The notion of sharing his cot as wild creatures grunted and roared outside our tent was even more exhilarating!

I was tempted to show the letter to Daddy Jack to prove he'd been wrong about Terry buying the house. A second later, I reconsidered. I didn't need his censure. Daddy knew I'd gotten a letter from Africa, but he hadn't asked for details. Daddy Jack knew far too many details, but as the brothers weren't communicating, I had nothing to worry about.

Between movie dates with Randy, I composed my second letter to Terry. My words contained the same degree of ardor as my first, but no more. He replied in half the time of his previous letter. And his tone was more cordial. Soon we were exchanging letters as fast as they could cross two continents and an ocean.

We started numbering and dating them to make certain none had gotten lost. I still worried that Daddy might toss them rather than give them to me, while Terry indicated his mail service left much to be desired. But none did, although some arrived slower than snails, and our romance via correspondence budded, blossomed, and then bloomed.

At the beginning of December, I wrote Terry that I was changing my address temporarily to Uncle Jack's farm. I'd nearly written "Daddy Jack's." I had to remind myself that only when we were alone could I call my father what I called him in my heart.

Daddy and Maria were fine with my being gone for five months. They'd be gone more than a month themselves, sailing to Italy as soon as the weather warmed. Maria was so excited at the prospect of seeing her relatives again. She'd saved much of her salary toward the trip, her leave of absence had been approved, and a trusted coworker would be checking the house.

I packed the clues from my lamp base before I left. Hooker couldn't help me assemble the pieces of the puzzle, but Darrell could.

After all these years, Snoop and Company would be together again.

Winter 1951

Snoop and Company

Daddy Jack met me at the train station the day before Christmas. Snow drifted from a pewter sky, settling on the slanted roofs, the frozen ground, and the barren trees. Flecks of white clung to my father's coat, hat, and mustache. He'd been standing in the cold for fifteen minutes, waiting for the train, waiting for me.

"Good trip?" He gave me a hug and kissed my cheek.

"The best." I opened my bag and presented him with a bottle of the finest brandy Daddy's money could buy.

"Oh, you shouldn't have." He looked pleased nonetheless.

"But I wanted to, and Daddy wanted to. He's sorry he blew up at you last summer."

"Oh? Does he want to kiss and make up, or is this a token overture?"

I shrugged. "I'm not sure. He didn't say."

"Then it's a token. If he wanted to make up, he could've written since then, but it's hard for him to bend with all that innate rigidity … oh, before I forget, you have two letters at my house from a certain Mr. Shaw. What the devil are you up to now?"

"Nothing." I hid a smile and jumped in his car.

"Bullshit." He set my luggage in the back and got in himself.

"We're just writing," I assured him. "I have a new boyfriend now, in case you're interested. Hooker moved away while we were in Africa."

"Good riddance."

"Why didn't you like him? You only met him that one time at Aunt Emma's."

"Too suave, too debonair, too handsome … reminded me of me." He said this with a straight face. "What's the new one like?"

"Smart. Good in science and math, panders to Daddy."

"All negatives … anything positive?"

"Nope, more arms than an octopus. Missionary's son. Lived for years in Africa, too much built up inside him."

"What's with you and boys from Africa? What about ones from North

Dakota, if you crave the exotic? Oh, don't answer that. You'd probably find something lacking in a strapping young Scandinavian or Germanic lad from the hinterlands … well, hope the new one keeps his octopus arms to himself. Hate to have to shoot him with all the other troubles I've got."

"Don't worry. You won't have any surprise grandchildren."

"Abby … "

"Yes, father?" I smiled sweetly.

"Stop it, daughter," he said, not smiling.

"Oh, all right. You don't have to get cranky two minutes after I get back."

"I'm not. I just don't want to think about things like that. I have enough on my plate."

"The twins?"

"Who else? Hardly a day goes by where I'm not tempted to pitch them out of the house or run away myself. I wish I were the tyrant you once thought I was, Abby. I'd clamp them in leg irons, toss them in my dungeon, and lose the key. Sure make my life simpler."

"How'd you know I thought that about you?"

"It's a secret." His eyes crinkled at the corners with amusement. "At my age, I know lots of secrets."

"I know you do. And your biggest secret—me—you managed to keep secret too."

"Not by choice." His mood darkened. "But it hardly made sense to gain a daughter only to lose a son."

"I'm sorry I brought it up. You did the right thing. I can enjoy being with Daddy and Maria, and I can enjoy being here. Darrell didn't need to know, but he's accepted it. Believe me, you did the right thing."

"I hope so."

"So what's the latest news?" I prudently changed the topic.

"Nothing good. Jimmy Swanson eloped last week with a girl from Springfield his folks don't like. Bad start to a marriage, if you ask me … nobody asked me. Vic had a heart attack on Tuesday. Saw him yesterday in the hospital, but he's supposed to be home by now. It was a mild one."

"Thank God. We didn't know. Aunt Emma never called."

"She probably will after he's settled. She's been beside herself with worry."

"I'll bet … what was he doing when he was stricken?"

"Shoveling snow. That's why I make the twins shovel mine, for my own safety."

"It must be hard getting those two motivated."

Daddy Jack chuckled. "I'm up to the challenge."

"I'm sure you are ... and how's Darrell doing?"

"Haven't heard any complaints. His lessons are ongoing. Wish he would've stayed Lutheran while courting Denice, though. About time folks around here had something new to discuss. The twins destroying Sheriff Branson's two cars finally petered out, and my own shenanigans are nearly ancient history. I've turned over a new leaf, you'll be happy to know. I'm back to supporting the church in case the reverend is bad-mouthing me to God for neglecting the coffers since Annie died. I handed him a thousand bucks last Sunday. He was so shocked his collar nearly came unscrewed."

"Why'd you do that?" I could imagine Reverend Richter standing in front of the pulpit after concluding a fiery sermon condemning self-indulgence and my father handing him a thousand bucks for his efforts and the good Reverend's pursed lips gaping as he realized he'd have to compose a sermon on tolerance and forgiveness the very next Sunday.

"Oh, just in case ... the sins of the fathers upon the children—you know what the Good Book says. And because of Darrell. I'm making peace with the community so he doesn't cringe when he hears my name bantered about. I used to try and behave myself so I wouldn't embarrass Annie and now I'm trying to behave myself so I won't embarrass Darrell. Funny, isn't it? Especially with the twins embarrassing the hell out of all of us."

"Amazing, but not funny ... by the way, Uncle Jack—I'm practicing your old name—do you have plenty of sugar and butter at the house? I'm thinking of making Christmas cookies this afternoon."

"Don't bother. Darrell and I made six dozen of those rolled-out ones with the frosting and sprinkles yesterday. Damn near drove us crazy. Who knew dough would stick like that just because it warmed up a little? We already had such a mess we made pie afterward. Again, the dough was a bitch, but the filling was easy."

"Now I've heard everything. Giving to the church and then baking! Don't tell me you wore an apron too?"

"No, but I laid one on the floor. Caught most of the crap we dropped."

"At least it'll be easier next year, as long as you don't forget how."

"I've forgotten already. Once and I'm done. Next year either you or Denice can do it. I mean, what are women good for? No, don't answer that."

"They sure weren't baking cookies and pies aboard the ship," I teased.

"I told you not to answer that." But my father chuckled again as he maneuvered the car up the icy driveway, and the snow-encrusted house of many memories came into view.

That evening was special because Daddy Jack knew exactly where the twins were: seated on either side of him in the pew for the Christmas Eve program. We listened as the little kids said their pieces and sang their songs like we'd done ourselves only a few short years ago.

Rather than playing Joseph, Darrell now sat next to me in the darkened audience. He didn't believe in public displays of affection, but I knew that he was holding Denice's hand because each had only one hand free for hymnal holding. Afterward, they'd attend mass together at St. Peter's while the rest of us drove home.

When they arrived back at the house, I served eggnog and Christmas cookies. Except for the messy frosting, the cookies looked as good as the ones I would've made. Then we piled on the sled to pass out gifts to our neighbors. Denice began singing "Good King Wenceslas" in a lovely, lilting voice. Daddy Jack joined in, but he could've used another strong male voice to help him out. I did my best while Darrell sang flat. The twins pretended to be mute.

The night was crisp, cold, and still—pretty enough to be a Currier and Ives print. I loved hearing the clomp of the horses, the jingle of their bells, and seeing the pinpricks of a billion stars sparkling across an infinite heaven and the reflection of the ice moon on the surface of the drifts.

If only Daddy and Maria had been with us. I hoped, if my plan were successful, by next Christmas they would be.

The next afternoon, Darrell and I sat cross-legged on his bed, the clues from beneath my lamp spread across the bedspread. Pages of his last government project were strategically placed on the pillow, poised to cover my notes at the sound of footsteps.

"Are you sure Daddy Jack won't sneak in here to see what we're doing?"

"Remember to call him Uncle Jack. And no, he's off riding."

"Through the snow?"

"Of course not, dummy. He rides down the roads after they're plowed."

"That won't take long."

"It'll take longer than you think. He's not alone."

"Oh … who's with him?"

"Margaret."

"Margaret? Margaret Monson?" My mouth dropped open.

"Yup, our old teacher is Dad's new squeeze. Can you believe it? He chases every skirt in the county, mortifies me half to death in the process, and ends up cavorting with somebody he used to hate!"

"Guess he doesn't hate her now."

"No, but it took five years. When she first starting cleaning our house, Dad said only what he had to. She did her job and left. One day he got mad about something and gave her hell. She gave him hell right back. I figured she'd quit, but she didn't. She probably stayed to antagonize him. Eventually they started acting civil again, and things progressed from there."

"I wondered whether something was going on when she brought over those sandwiches and cookies the day we left for Africa."

"That was the beginning. They went riding a lot after he came back. He pretended nothing was going on, but I could tell."

"And how could you tell, Sherlock?"

Darrell grinned. "Elementary, my dear Watson. The horses would come back looking bored instead of breathless."

"You don't say! Is it serious?"

"As serious as he'll get. Dad says he'll never marry again, but he won't lack for companionship. As long as he keeps it quiet, whatever makes him happy makes me happy."

"Well, it doesn't make me happy. I hate thinking of him with a woman—even if she's one I know and like. I still think of him and your mom as a couple."

"Those days are long gone, unfortunately." Darrell looked pensive. "Everybody needs somebody, especially our father. You need to be more accepting."

"I guess so." Daddy had Maria. Now Daddy Jack had Margaret. I'd fantasized being the only female in my father's life since our return from Africa, but on whom did my own thoughts revolve? Randy, Terry, and Hooker, although the latter had broken my heart.

"Well, let's get to it," Darrell said. "I've been anticipating this ever since you told me about the cemetery in Africa, Dad's confession, and that weird stuff in Uncle James's office. Just think, Watson, we might actually put the pieces together today."

"If we do, it'll be a miracle."

"Miracles are my specialty."

My half brother relished anew his dual role as detective and confidant. He studied the clues as I peered over his shoulder and told him what Hooker and I had deduced, to the best of my recollection.

"Hooker was wrong about whom Gramma cursed, but Dad pretty much told you it was meant for him and not my mom," Darrell stated. "After all, he was the one taking his brother's wife."

"Exactly … and what about '*you deserve far better*?'"

"Composed on Uncle James's typewriter?"

"Yes."

"Obviously written by him. He's making a play for my mom, probably in retaliation for Dad's affair. I always thought he seemed way too friendly with her. He kissed her right on the lips the first time he walked in our kitchen."

"I remember that too … do you think it went further?"

"No way of telling. They had time alone together when they cleaned out Gramma's house, didn't they?"

"A couple of days. By then Daddy was married to Maria."

"Since when did that stand in anyone's way?" Darrell scoffed. "Only if marriage vows meant something to my mom would nothing have happened."

"We'll never know."

"Probably not … now what's this? '*Poorly differentiated, prognosis.*' That'd refer to a disease, but whose? Your mother's? Or someone she knew? Sorry, we need more evidence this time to make a judgment."

"I've already asked our father and Daddy whether Mother was either sick or pregnant when she went to Africa. They both turned hostile, which makes me suspect she was."

"Good deduction. What makes you think she might've been pregnant?"

"Read on."

"Okay … '*forgive me, my darling. What I do, I must do. Since you refuse to help, I will find another way*' and so forth … sounds serious, since she tried to get a third party involved. Are you thinking she didn't want a baby and hoped Dad would help her get rid of it?"

"That's what Hooker thought, but I don't."

"I don't either. He'd never do it … then she must've been sick. Sounds more like … oh, God, I hate to say what I'm thinking this time!" Darrell's complacent demeanor changed to one of alarm.

"What?" I said. "What are you thinking this time?"

"Suicide."

The word hit me like a sucker punch. *My own mother—a suicide?*

"No, she couldn't have wanted that," I managed to say. "She simply couldn't!"

"Why not? If she was really sick, she was going to die anyway. Maybe she wanted to end it quickly. When Dad refused to help her, she got someone else. Maybe she had it all planned, and that's why she wrote that farewell letter to you … and someone did kill her, didn't they?"

"It was accidental. Our father said so … in his confession on the train."

"Did he? You said before his answer was ambiguous."

"It was … let it be for now, Darrell. Let's just go on."

"All right … here's the one about asking Dad to kiss you for her. She'd only say that if she knew he was your father. She knew. She had to know. And she also knew she was going to die. This fragment, together with your farewell letter, proves both." Darrell paused and put his hand on mine. "I'm sorry, Abby. I know this isn't what you wanted to hear."

"No, but I need to get to the truth." I took my hand back and put on a brave face. "It's too late to save Mother, but it's not too late for Daddy and Daddy Jack to get beyond whatever happened to her and mend their own relationship."

"That won't happen if one of them was responsible for her death," Darrell said gently. "And from what I know of Dad, it wasn't him ... are you okay?"

"Sure, I'm okay. Why wouldn't I be? Suicide, murder ... happens in every family." I attempted a wavering smile.

"Bull ... we need to stop. It's too much for you."

"No. We started this and we'll end this ... here, read these notes I took from Daddy's journal. The first one was written right after Mother's death."

I mulled over what Darrell said while he deciphered my scribbles. What if my continued digging unearthed the truth and the truth was unacceptable? I hadn't considered that before. How could I proceed? *Should* I proceed?

"Now this is really interesting," he said. "Uncle James is angry at your mom because she died. He's actually blaming *her!* She disobeyed him and she died ... but how had she disobeyed? And 'disobey' is an odd word to use about your own wife, isn't it? The night before she tried to explain something to him, but he didn't believe her, although he had on previous occasions. When she laughed at him, he did something to her ... *'you died with my mark upon you ... a mark you did not live long enough to heal.'* I know you hate hearing how I think he's got a dark side, Abby, but I've always felt that way about him."

"I know ... just read the rest."

"Guilt," Darrell concluded, minutes later. "He's writing a literal stream of consciousness, and it's all about guilt. He's consumed with it. The emotions here are so raw, so painful, it's truly hard to read. He'll never find peace, not until he's dead himself."

I nodded miserably. "Here's more. Hooker took these notes from actual letters."

Darrell studied the notes for nearly half an hour. In far less time, I nibbled down every fingernail and rejected my half brother's conclusion. After all, Darrell had always disliked Daddy. That alone would skew his opinion. Suspicion wasn't evidence, and I refused to think such a thing of the man who raised me. There would be another explanation. There *had* to be another explanation.

"Well?" I watched as Darrell refolded the notes into their envelope.

"It's interesting who the letters are from, Abby, but it's more interesting who they're not from. What they actually contain doesn't shed much more light on the situation."

"I don't understand."

"Well, he seems to have kept every condolence letter he got after your mom's death, but there's none from our dad. It is merely missing? Or does its absence mean Dad either knew or suspected Uncle James was complicit in her death? You'd hardly send a sympathy card to a murderer, would you?"

"So you're back to that?"

"Yes, unfortunately. And all those letters over the years between my mom and Uncle James raises a red flag to me too. They don't appear to be true love letters though, just unusually friendly."

"That's good, I guess … anything else?"

"There's no letters from your mom to Uncle James, or vice versa."

"I asked him about that once. He said they didn't save their letters to each other because they had no particular reason to. They simply threw them away. If you remember, Darrell, we didn't find any in the schoolhouse either."

"I remember, but it's not logical. Almost everyone keeps a special letter or two as a keepsake."

"Especially when Daddy kept nearly everything else … here's one last letter." I took it from my purse. "Hooker swiped it because he thought it was revealing."

Darrell read the letter out loud, keeping his voice low.

James … I haven't heard a damn word from you since the "incident" and now you dare write such a letter to me? What madness possesses you now? From what depths do you accuse me of a deed only Satan himself could do?

You know how I felt. You know I wouldn't be capable of such a thing. But let's turn the finger around. You could, couldn't you? You could. Revenge is a razor, cruel and sharp, is it not?

And how does it feel now, dear brother? Do you sleep well at night? I don't, but not for the reason you said. By the way, I will never again call you "dear brother." You're no brother of mine, both for what you did in the past and for what you did much more recently.

But I reiterate, once again, that it was not me you saw. You saw a shadow, but the shadow was not mine. Blame your suspicious mind. Blame your lying eyes. Blame your own inadequacies. I was already sleeping.

And another thing, before I close. I will keep what was given me. I'll keep it all. You'll get nothing, not a pittance.

If I'm wrong in this, and I pray I am, I will crawl on my belly for your forgiveness. But if I'm right, and I fear I am, you will reside in hell, both on earth and in the hereafter … Jack.

Darrell whistled under his breath. "This is the most incriminating letter imaginable!"

"When Hooker and I first read it three years ago, it didn't make nearly as much sense as it does now," I said, hating every word of it.

"It makes total sense. It's all here in black and white. Two men are in love with the same woman. She dies and each accuses the other of killing her, but for different reasons. The reason Uncle James thought our dad did it is unclear, unless he thought he did it for the money. But our dad thought Uncle James did it for revenge. And he doesn't want to be next, because he emphasizes that he wasn't the 'shadow.'"

"If we can believe his denial."

"We probably can. Didn't he say Uncle James was always watching them while they were in Africa?"

"Yes, but I can't recall his exact wording. It seemed vague at the time."

"Doesn't matter. Shades of meaning won't enlighten us now. The fact remains that Uncle James thought it was our dad."

"But what if it wasn't? Think of it, Darrell. My own mother, entertaining someone other than Daddy, or even our father, in that tent in Africa … this is so appalling. I used to worship her."

"That was a mistake."

"I know. I used to cry because I'd never known her. I feel like crying now."

"I wish you wouldn't, but you have every reason to."

"I just didn't realize the possibility. Between the two of them, I always thought Daddy would be the one at fault, not her."

"Maybe he was. Maybe he drove her to it. They were both good, in the beginning. Remember that, Abby. They loved each other. Circumstance changes people. Life changes people. We don't know enough about either of them to know how or why, and you shouldn't torture yourself wondering about it."

"I'll always wonder about it."

"That's the difference between you and me. You worry about what you don't know and what you can't change, while I don't worry at all."

"Unless it affects you."

"Exactly. Right now Dad and Margaret are having themselves a good time, but it doesn't affect me. You need to take a lesson from that, Abby. You shouldn't let how your mom acted years ago affect you or you'll end up sick in your head."

"I suppose you're right."

"Of course I'm right. Sherlock is always right."

"Don't break an arm patting yourself on the back," I snapped. "Getting back to the subject, I understand now why our father didn't share the money with Daddy. He didn't want Daddy to profit from Mother's death because he thought Daddy killed her."

"And he wouldn't tell you that on the train because he's still hoping he's wrong. He didn't want to accuse without knowing for certain."

"What I don't understand is why Mother went to Africa to begin with. I asked our dad that question on the train and he totally ignored me. To leave me behind to find her relatives makes no sense. Even if she was sick to the point of being suicidal, that's a long trip to make just to die."

"Maybe she wanted to die where she was born, like Rover did when he crawled all the way to Gramma's house."

"Darrell!" I glared at him with revulsion.

"Sorry." Darrell looked sheepish. "You can hit me for that."

"Never mind." I sighed and let it go. "It's as good a reason as any … all these bits and pieces, snippets and fragments … how can I put it all together? And if I do, how will I know what's true? Before you read that last letter, I had convinced myself that Daddy couldn't have done it, and now I'm wondering if he did, and then I'm thinking our father … I'm overwhelmed, Darrell. I just can't think anymore." I tucked the clues back in my purse and stretched out on his bed.

"I can't either." He reclined the opposite direction. "Maybe it doesn't even matter anymore."

I was reminded of lazy summer afternoons when Hooker and I would lie opposite each other in his hammock, gazing at the clouds, gazing at each other. I missed Hooker. I was thankful my half brother had taken the time to be with me, to help me, like Hooker had done.

But what were the odds that one day our father would have to crawl on his belly before his brother? Remote, unless I had more help than Darrell's.

That night I had two revelations. Whether my mother had been pregnant, sick, or even suicidal, her death might not have been impacted by any of those factors. And, assuming Mother hadn't extended an invitation to a camp boy and Daddy Jack was telling the truth, the "shadow" must have been Tony, the white hunter. I had no last name. But in 1935, how many white hunters named Tony were guiding in Kenya?

Morning brought no progress. While Daddy Jack was only too pleased to give me a personal tour of the trophies hanging on the walls of his vast living room, complete with lengthy anecdotes, he said he'd quite forgotten the guide's surname. I should ask his brother.

"Oh, I will," I said. I didn't mention how Daddy had already glossed over the subject the night he burned the schoolhouse. "A Brit, Tony," he'd said. He'd forgotten the last name because it didn't matter. But now it did matter.

Odd how he'd remembered the unusual name of one of the trackers while forgetting the name of his own guide!

Hardly a memory lapse. It had been a deliberate omission.

My last hope hinged on the knowledge and cooperation of my own white hunter. At midnight, I began writing an impassioned plea for closure. I penned four drafts of my letter in an effort to word it exactly right. When it accurately reflected both my piecemeal knowledge and the contents of my heart, I made a copy for myself and licked the envelope shut at three in the morning.

Terry Shaw, on the far side of the world, would now be privy to my darkest secret.

Summer 1952

Temperature Rising

My last months of high school in my hometown passed quickly. I renewed my childhood friendships, visited with my relatives, and cemented my relationship with Darrell. With every new letter from Terry Shaw, we'd put our heads together and decipher the latest information. Gradually we cobbled together the past with an eye toward the future.

After graduation, I moved back to Minneapolis. The months I'd spent with my father had been sufficient for a while, and everyone was busy anyway.

Darrell was laboring for the second summer behind the soda fountain at Schneider's Drug and canoodling with Denice during his days off. Both would attend the University of Minnesota with me in September, he for pre-law and she for elementary education.

The twins were spending their summer hoeing sugar beets, walking beans, and detasseling corn in the appropriate months. Supposedly this hot and repetitive labor would enervate them to where Daddy Jack could safely indulge himself without worrying what mischief they were plotting.

Sheriff Branson, to his credit, supported my father's attempts to subdue Duane and Dennis with a daily drive-by. The sheriff would sit on his car hood, chat with the supervisor in charge, clean his revolver, or catch up on paperwork while scrutinizing the twins. As a result, both kept working rather than running amok as was their preference.

This fact had been reported to me by Daddy Jack himself. His glee was unmistakable, even over the telephone. He remained mum about Margaret Monson, but he didn't need to say anything.

Aunt Emma's latest letter sat steaming on the buffet. Vinnie Swanson had spied my father and Margaret together from his vantage point atop his John Deere. He told his wife, who promptly told Dorothy Evans, who told Nellie Evans, who told Aunt Emma. Thanks to party lines and the cautionary "keep this under your hat," nearly all of southern Minnesota knew the licentious Lothario of Brown County had scored again. The consensus was that Margaret was getting the short end of the stick … figuratively speaking.

While my father had a love life, I certainly didn't. Randy was spending his summer helping his folks and others from their church erect a school in rural Central America. The Reverend Maynard Simpson, now fully recovered from his parasitic infestation, was spearheading the construction as part of a mission effort. Mary Simpson was in charge of procuring needed textbooks and supplies once building was complete. Both were learning Spanish, plus the local dialect, and were seeking permanent placement rather than a return to Africa.

Randy wrote that the nights were hot and steamy and the days were hotter and steamier and the bugs were as big as frying pans and this was the last summer he'd waste erecting a claptrap school in an equatorial jungle on the south side of hell. The sole positive aspect was the availability of cheap liquor, although he had to pretend not to know about that since the good reverend didn't allow him to drink. But Randy had his ways, and he promised to bring some regional brew back with him in September and whip up a concoction that would knock my bobby socks off.

Despite his travails, Randy found ample time to pen passionate letters nearly every evening, and I unblushingly replied in kind.

I had wanted to work to keep myself occupied during the summer, but Daddy vetoed the idea, saying I needed a break between educational endeavors. He wouldn't admit it, but I suspected that he'd missed me while I'd been away. So we cooked, gardened, played chess, and took meandering walks along Minnehaha Creek on the days Maria worked, and I read my freshman college books ahead of time on the days he worked.

At least he'd taken a real job again, which afforded me breathing space. While I'd been at the farm, he'd developed a tremor in his right hand. The doctors said it was nothing, but for an artist, it *was* something—he could no longer steady his brush. He tried to compensate for a while before he gave up in frustration. He'd hauled his supplies from his office, dumped them in the back yard, and set everything on fire. Canvas, oil, and turpentine burned hot and smoky, and it was hardly a surprise when the fire truck came clanging down the alley.

Maria was furious when she learned what he'd done, but he'd pointed to the ash heap and said he'd been completely successful in his intentions. The next day he paid his fine at city hall, in cash, so she wouldn't see the amount in the checkbook and get mad a second time. I knew the details because he told me. He seemed rather proud of himself, for some strange reason.

The tenth of July dawned warm and humid. I was alone in the house when the mailman slipped something through the slot. I was anticipating a letter from Terry, but this one was thicker than usual. Hoping he'd sent photographs of himself, as I hadn't taken nearly enough of him while I'd been in Africa, I was disappointed to find none inside. Rather, a second letter was enclosed within another envelope, addressed 'To Ellen's daughter.'

Instantly I knew what it was. I read Terry's letter first.

Dear Abby,

I hope you're reading this letter before the other, as it explains the additional enclosure.

Much has happened since I've last written. Nearly two weeks ago, my father was stricken with a stroke of utmost severity. I came to his bedside late, but I came as soon as my office girl could locate me. He is partially paralyzed and has trouble speaking, but manages to scribble notes with difficulty.

I've since maintained a somber vigil at his side, trying to atone for my past indifference, communicating the best I can, attempting to draw close to him after a lapse of nearly a decade. Think of it, Abby—a decade gone, never to come again! And the chasm has been mostly my fault, me and my youthful pride and foolish arrogance!

My father says he forgives me, but can I forgive myself? It is already too late for many things, but he says not to dwell on it. If we have but a week together, it is a week more than we had.

Perhaps at your tender age you will not understand this yet, but somehow I think you will, given the acrimony that has existed within your own family for far longer … well, enough self-pity. I cannot undo the past; I can only impact the future.

Now for the background of the second letter.

After leaving school, I apprenticed myself to a friend of my father's, Tony Tompkins. From this venerable white hunter I learned my skills in the bush, such as they are. He became as a second father to me, as I'd estranged my first. I remained with Tony until I was sufficiently experienced to strike out on my own. (I should mention that Tony and my father had grown up together in Nairobi, keeping in close contact with each other all these years, although their paths diverged widely when my father entered the medical profession.)

Since my father's disability, it has become my habit to fetch the post and read to him whatever is of interest. A few days ago, a letter arrived from Tony. We assumed it to be a get-well wish, but it was nothing of the kind. Tony wrote that he was terminally ill and wished to see my father one last time, if possible. As it was not possible, my father urged me to go in his stead.

This I did.

My serendipitous visit with my old mentor resulted in the most astounding revelation. When he inquired about my business and how things in general were going with me, naturally I mentioned you.

"Stahl?" he responded. "Is she any relation to James or Jack?"

When I replied in the affirmative, such a change came over him that I truly feared he had breathed his last! He waxed apoplectic, and I ran for his nurse. She assured me his seizure would be of short duration, but that I should leave promptly as to not upset him further. But he motioned me stay, and when he could speak again, he asked for a priest.

I summoned a priest, and Tony was given last rites while I waited in an adjoining room. That done, he asked me to witness his confession, written verbatim by the good Father.

I had no idea what I was about to hear. And after I heard, I regretted my hearing, but it was already too late. Abby, I could hardly listen and connect his words back to the man I once thought I'd known so well! I pray you will not blame me for my part in this conveyance, but Tony demanded me as witness, in case this letter was lost in transit. He wanted to set the record straight before he faced his own final judgment.

It may be too little, too late, as such things often are, but hopefully you find some closure in this. I hope it is not a dreadful mistake, me forwarding to you this appalling confession.

One thing; I beg of you, Abby, do not read Tony's letter alone! Have your father with you. (*Which one?* I thought ruefully.) *I cannot stress this too much. I know the curiosity you've had for years concerning the death of your mother, but please heed me. Have your father with you and read this together.*

I wish so much I could be with you.

All my love, Terry

I tucked the letter beneath the newspaper on the coffee table, as if I'd read it and then forgotten to take it upstairs. Daddy always read the paper as soon as he came home, so I was confident Maria would never see it. He would make sure of it.

I shivered although the thermometer on the wall registered eighty-nine degrees. The French clock on the buffet chimed eleven. Maria would be working late, Daddy would be giving flying lessons at the regional airport until five, and Daddy Jack lived nearly four hours away.

The second letter was about Mother. Tony Tompkins knew what had happened to her, and he had dictated the truth from his deathbed.

Never would I wait until Daddy and Daddy Jack arrived. I had already waited far too long. I sat on the davenport, took a deep breath to steady my fingers, and opened the second envelope.

When I'd finished reading, I began to weep. I wept for the misunderstanding, the expenditure of time, the bitterness between two brothers, and for the innocent swept into their maelstrom. Then I composed myself. I knew what I had to do. Tomorrow was a Saturday, so Daddy would be home. Maria would be working. Daddy Jack would be … oh, surely he could tear himself away from his latest passion long enough to drive to Minneapolis!

I placed a call to him.

"What's wrong?" Daddy Jack said, after our initial greeting. "Are you sick?"

"No, at least not that way … can you come up here tomorrow? Say about noon?"

"Why? Has something happened to my brother?"

"No, he's the same."

"That's unfortunate … well, something's the matter because you never call during the day."

"You're right," I said. "Something *is* wrong, very wrong."

"What is it? Spit it out."

"I know who killed my mother."

A lengthy silence followed my statement. Finally he said, "And how the hell would you know that?"

"I got a letter from Africa. It's from Tony Tompkins."

Another prolonged pause. "I'll be there by noon."

Daddy was one of more popular flying instructors at Perryton Field, and his popularity certainly didn't stem from his personality. It was because of his expertise; his tongue remained sharper than most cleavers. The job suited him well. He got to boss and teach. Occasionally, when his bossiness trumped his teaching, he got fired by a flustered student. That suited him too, because he hated expending his precious time on the weak and the nervous.

Flying light aircraft was fun, he said, although he considered them pabulum compared to those B-24 behemoths he used to take up, high in the skies over Europe. God, those were the glory days … I'd heard his stories a hundred times.

He was in an unusually chatty mood when he arrived home.

"Jerry Anderson's coming right along. By the time he's been run through my wringer, he'll able to fly to Whitehorse in a snowstorm though mountains blindfolded. He'll be hauling those hunters and fishermen around those Yukon backwaters in no time flat, thanks to me. I hear they've got some great bear and caribou up there … why the pinched face? What's wrong with you?"

"You noticed," I muttered.

"Of course I noticed, but I was at the start of my self-congratulatory spiel. So, what's the deal? You look like the bearer of bad tidings."

"Maybe I am … I got a letter today."

"Oh? From whom?"

"Tony Tompkins."

Daddy's well tanned features hardened. "Tony Tompkins, from Africa?"

I nodded.

"My God … I'd hoped that bastard would've been devoured ages ago."

"So you remember him?"

"Of course I remember him."

"You didn't remember him the night you burned the schoolhouse."

"My memory's improved since then."

"Apparently."

"So what's he want?"

"To set the record straight."

"About what?"

"About Mother."

"Why now?"

"It's his confession. He's dying."

"Good … what of?"

"Cancer."

"Good. He deserves to suffer."

"You're not very pleasant."

"I'm as pleasant as I want to be."

He didn't appear to be nearly as shocked as he had been initially, but there was something in his eyes that I hadn't seen before: a shadow, a shimmer, a reflection of something very painful. He'd have ample opportunity to display that look while I read Tony's letter.

"I've invited Daddy Jack to come for the reading. He'll be here tomorrow by noon."

"Damn, that's wonderful! The two daddies and the inquisitive little girl—"

"I'm not a little girl—"

"—and the dead mother and the soon-to-be-dead bastard, gathering together for the solving of the Eternal Mystery! Has Darrell been invited too?"

"No."

"What? How can the Eternal Mystery ascend to its breathtaking finale without the insatiable Sherlock?"

"This is hardly a joke."

"Who's making a joke? Tell you what, Abigail, in all seriousness, I think I'll whip up some dainty finger sandwiches and serve tea. Eternal Mysteries do whet the appetite, do they not? Or should I just buy a keg so we can all toast the truth as Tony Tompkins, the great white hunter, perceived it and simply get drunk?"

I rolled my eyes. "Daddy, don't be such an ass."

"Guilty as charged." He flung open the refrigerator and rummaged amid the condiments. "An ass has its head so far into its feedbag it can't see where it's going, Abigail, and I can't for the life of me see where this is going."

"No, you can't, and how does it feel, Daddy? I've spent most of my life not knowing where I came from or where I'm going!"

"Let's not go into all that shit again."

In the position he was in, I was tempted to kick him in the pants. But if I did, I'd have to run and I'd have to keep running, and I was just too tired. So I said, "What are you looking for?"

"Beer."

"You drank the last one last night."

"How would you know? Are you guzzling behind my back?"

"No, but I looked for one after I read that letter."

He straightened up. "Well, if that's the situation, I'd better buy more."

"Do that, but you don't have to drink them tonight. Save them for tomorrow."

"Oh?" His face remained expressionless. "Are you saying I can sleep well tonight? No libations required?"

"You can sleep fine, Daddy. What Tony Tompkins says never has to go further than the three of us. It's far too late to punish the guilty anyway."

"Good."

"But I'd think you'd be curious about what it says."

"Why? I already know what happened, and the last rant of some dying fool won't add anything to it."

"Don't bet on it."

He grunted a reply and drove off to buy beer.

I timed a leisurely walk to coincide with when I thought he'd be returning. I paused to watch some boys playing softball in the park, which afforded Daddy ample time to take the bait.

Upon my return, I saw Terry's first letter had been refolded and placed on the steps for me to take upstairs. I nonchalantly curled up in a living room chair with Maria's latest romance novel and awaited his response.

There was no response. Daddy seemed engrossed in his newspaper. He read the sports section. He hated sports. He did the crossword puzzle. He hated crossword puzzles. He didn't speak to me. He didn't look at me. He did not switch on the evening news.

Eventually he wandered in the kitchen and made a light supper for the two of us: finger sandwiches and tea. For dessert, he drank beer. I still detested beer, but I could've used one … or more.

But for all of his bluster, Daddy didn't sleep well that night. Around midnight, I heard him moving around downstairs. The refrigerator opened, ice tinkled in a glass, the back door opened and closed. He was sitting in the gazebo, drink in hand, awaiting the judgment.

I didn't sleep well either. As the temperature kept rising, along with the humidity, I paced upstairs in my room, weighing the wisdom of what I was about to do.

Voices from the Grave

All was in readiness by one o'clock the next day. Daddy Jack stood by the living room window, holding a glass of lemonade. He was dressed appropriately in black, as tense as a coiled spring.

"Go ahead, sit down," I said.

"You better know what you're doing." He assumed a seat on the davenport.

"Daddy," I said.

"I'm not too feeble to stand." Daddy lingered by the front door, attempting to catch a breeze. "This won't take too long, I hope?"

"That depends on how many times you interrupt."

"Smart aleck."

I ignored him, unfolded the second letter, and began to read.

To Ellen's daughter ... let me first say that if I digress, it may be because I am so ill, or it may be because I am having difficulty staying on topic, considering the topic is the death of your mother.

As Terry Shaw is my witness, this is my confession before God Almighty, begging His forgiveness as I beg yours ... I should mention this is being written as I speak by Father Gutter.

"Appropriate name, given the subject matter," Daddy said. "He'll be hearing and writing nothing but swill."

"Daddy, please!"

He turned his back and focused his attention on the robins outside as I resumed reading.

In early May of 1935, I had the unfortunate experience of guiding a hunt for James and Ellen Stahl, as well as his brother, Jack Stahl. We made the arrangements through the usual channels, but as soon as I met them, I should've called the whole thing off.

I'd never met three more unhappy people in my life. There was a tension, a bitterness, a something I couldn't adequately describe, going on between all of them, all of the time.

Not that they weren't good shots and I thought their hunt wouldn't be successful. No, that wasn't the case at all. Ellen practiced but decided against hunting, which was fine by me. I didn't need any more theatrics. There was enough of that already. Jack was a passable shot, for a farmer, and James … well, James was another matter entirely. Unless the gun malfunctioned, he never missed. He simply never missed. Not only that, but there was something else going on with him, inside his head. With Jack I could relax a bit and drink around the campfire, but with James …

I saw Daddy cock his head to the side. He was no longer fixated on the birds.

We hadn't gotten two weeks into it when the problem became apparent. Ellen herself confirmed it, one night when both men were so drunk I wondered whether either of them would wake up alive, which of course they did.

She caught me unawares, with her little ways … "Oh, you brave, beautiful man," she said to me as we found ourselves alone in front of the campfire.

"That's such bullshit!" Daddy erupted. "She never talked like that!"

"She did, but apparently not to you," Daddy Jack said.

"How dare you!" Daddy took a menacing step toward the davenport.

"I dare, so don't threaten me. The situation is beyond your control, James, so put your goddamned hackles down and listen."

"To what, more lies?"

"Lies are merely truth enhanced by perception."

"You should know."

My father raised his glass in mock salute. "So should you."

"Please, just hear me out," I said.

"I'll try." Daddy retreated to the arched doorway.

"Let's get this over with," Daddy Jack said to me. "My brother has a short fuse when confronted with the unknown."

As do you, I thought.

I was startled, to say the least, when it happened that night … I had enough on my plate, trying to keep the hunt going without the complications of a woman. I was still drinking their whiskey, meaning the hunt had gone sour and there was nothing left to do but endure to the end … I was hardly prepared for her advances because I knew she'd already tried taking up with Jack again—

"I didn't! I swear to God, James, I didn't," Daddy Jack insisted.

"Why should I believe you?" Daddy replied in a voice like ice. "This isn't your confession."

"Stop it," I said. "Save your arguments for the end … please."

The air snapped electric between them, but both fell silent, glowering. I cleared my throat and read on.

Whether or not she was successful, I never knew … it would've been difficult, with James dogging Jack's every move, but even he had to bathe and do what all people do. She was quick and she was determined, at least with me. When she'd be too closely watched, she'd borrow a rifle and I'd take her target practicing. It was such a clever ruse … we'd go off by ourselves for a half hour or so, usually during the time her husband and Jack would be cleaning up for dinner, and we'd shoot off a few rounds and laugh while we went at it.

"My God," Daddy said.

And then the day came when I was taking a photograph of the two of them, Ellen and Jack, per Jack's request. James saw them with their arms around each other just as I snapped the picture and he stepped from the shadow of the dining hut and shot. We all hit the ground, hearing that heavy load flying past, mere inches over our heads.

"What the hell are you trying to do, kill us?" I remember Jack yelling as he scrambled to his feet.

"If I was, you'd both be dead," James said as he strolled over. "No one touches my wife but me."

"That's a goddamn lie!" Daddy flared. "I never said that last part!"

"You did. That's exactly what you said," Daddy Jack stated.

"Can I finish?" I noted neither had mentioned a snake in the tree overhead.

"Is it worth finishing?" Daddy said to me.

"Very much so."

"Proceed. I'll shut up for this idiocy, if I can."

I told James if he pulled another stunt like that, the safari was over. He could take his problems with his brother elsewhere. I didn't care for his overall demeanor as I said this, but he appeared to listen.

And then I got careless, thinking I'd gotten the upper hand. A couple of weeks later, James caught a glimpse of me leaving their tent when he came back from his bath a trifle early—

"Then you weren't the one I saw that night?" Daddy said.

"I always told you I wasn't," Daddy Jack said.

"I never believed you."

"You should have."

"On what basis? After all, you were with her more than I was those last two years, weren't you?"

My father finished his lemonade and slammed the glass down in lieu of an answer.

"Your silence is your affirmation, Jack. At least you didn't lie about it."

"Can I go on?" I asked.

"Don't bother. I'm bored already."

"You're anything but bored, Daddy. You just want this over with so you don't have to hear something you don't want to hear."

"On the contrary, Abigail. I simply love hearing again what should've been buried along with your mother. I love dragging it all up from the grave and airing it out. It's stimulating. It's fun. Pray, tell us more!"

"Thank you, I will." I resumed with what was certain to incite a reaction from both of them.

Ellen told me in early June that she was pregnant again and it wasn't her husband's, because she hadn't slept with him since she'd had Abigail. She said she—

"She was not pregnant!" Daddy said with sudden vehemence. "Maybe I didn't know everything, but at least I knew that!"

"For a change, you're absolutely right." Daddy Jack stared balefully at me before addressing his brother. "She wasn't pregnant; she was sick. In fact, she was terminally ill."

Daddy looked dumbfounded. "What are you saying? She wasn't sick. And she sure as hell wasn't terminal. Where are you getting these asinine ideas, Jack?"

"From her. She told me."

"When?"

"She wrote just prior to our trip to Africa."

"What was she doing writing you?"

"She needed a friend, James."

"Well, why didn't she tell me?"

My father narrowed his eyes. "Like I said … she needed a friend."

"You're insufferable, Jack. Are you telling me my own wife was sick with a terminal disease and I didn't even know?"

"That's exactly what I'm telling you."

"No, she couldn't have hidden that from me," Daddy said. "I'd have noticed something. It's simply impossible!"

"It's not impossible. She hid plenty of other things from you."

"I could kill you for that, Jack!" Daddy lunged toward his brother.

"Like you killed *her,* perhaps?" My father leaped to his feet. "You had reason, didn't you?"

I vaulted from my chair and stepped between them. "Stop it! Please, stop!"

"I did, but I never killed my own wife!" Daddy shouted past me.

"Well, neither did I!" Daddy Jack shouted back.

"Please sit down," I implored. "The neighbors don't need to hear this."

"Damn the neighbors," Daddy said.

"Please, Daddy."

He scowled in a way that made me wish I'd never started any of this. He hated not knowing what was yet to come down the pike, but it served him right.

"All right, Abigail." He slumped in a chair on the far side of the room. "I'll save the beating for the end."

Whose? Mine? Did he already suspect?

"Mine," Daddy Jack said.

"Sometimes you're a regular goddamn mind reader, Jack," Daddy said. "So what did she have?"

"Cancer."

"I guessed that already. What kind?"

"She never said. I asked once, but she wouldn't discuss it."

"Uh huh ... where did she go to the doctor?"

"At your post."

"Oh? And did she go for a second opinion?"

"Of course. For that, she went to a civilian doctor."

"Where?"

"In the same town."

"What was his name?"

"How the hell would I know?"

"Uh huh ... you say she was terminally ill, but you don't know the specifics and you don't know the doctor."

"That's significantly more than you knew."

"You'd better be right, Jack, because I can check."

"Go ahead, do that."

Daddy appeared surprised his brother had so readily acquiesced. "Well, I don't remember her looking any different."

"Not when we went, but she'd lost weight by June. How could you not notice?"

"Why would I? So she was thin. She always kept herself thin. She was vain that way."

"But she didn't have the energy she once had."

"She had enough to traipse all over Africa with us. If she felt bad, why'd she bother going? Why didn't she stay home and take care of herself?"

"Don't you get it yet?" Daddy Jack said. "Because it wouldn't have made any difference, that's why! Better she did something she'd always wanted to do rather than sit home and wait for the lid to be nailed down!"

"But in going, she cheated herself out of those last months with Abby." Daddy's voice betrayed rare emotion. To me he added, "She loved you so much."

I nodded, not trusting myself to speak.

"Maybe it was easier for her to leave," Daddy Jack said. "Maybe it would've been too heartbreaking to try and care for a baby when she no longer could."

"You seem to know an awful lot about my wife."

"And you seem to know precious little."

"Please stop," I said. While I found their exchange fascinating, I had to control the situation. There'd be opportunity enough for accusations and squabbling later.

"I'll stop when I'm good and ready," Daddy said. Addressing his brother, he asked, "Don't you think it's curious she told Tony she was pregnant? We both agree she wasn't, so who's lying now? Was Ellen lying to Tony? Or is Tony lying to us? Or could this entire so-called 'confession' be a lie from start to finish? Did you ever think of that?"

"No." But my father looked as though the seed of suspicion had found fertile ground.

"Maybe it's a setup, composed by our darling daughter here, to squeeze the juice out of us bitter lemons?" Daddy said.

"It's not, Daddy!" I protested. "How can you even think such things, much less say them?"

"Because I'm old and I'm suspicious, and I thought it damned peculiar how you left Terry's letter lying beneath the newspaper for me to find. The only reason you'd want me to read it ahead of time was to plant worry in my mind. You figured I'd say more than I intended, to clear myself of wrongdoing."

Before I could respond, Daddy Jack said, "Since we've started down this road of revelation, James, we might as well finish. Tony Tompkins didn't know everything, but neither of us knew the full story either. We should let Abby finish."

"Then you don't think it's fabricated?" Daddy queried.

"I'll decide at the end."

Daddy pursed his lips. "I guess I can endure the rest of this fairy tale … proceed."

I repeated the last sentence and forged ahead.

Ellen told me in early June that she was pregnant again and it wasn't her husband's, because she hadn't slept with him since she'd had Abigail. She said she was afraid he'd blame Jack because he always blamed Jack, although they'd had little opportunity to get together.

"As in none," Daddy Jack said.

"You said that already," Daddy said. "Often you protest too much."

"So do you."

I quickly resumed reading.

But I was afraid; no, I was certain James would blame me, not Jack. He was always watching Jack.

"He'll kill you when I tell him," she told me, confirming my supposition. "He has the most atrocious temper."

"Then don't tell him," I said.

"Well, he'll figure it out, won't he?" she said. "He'll notice something's growing inside me. He'll demand to know whose it is, and I'll laugh at him and he'll hit me. I already suffered enough that night when he caught a glimpse of you outside our tent. I covered for you that time, but next time I won't. I'll crumble before he hurts me too much. I'll tell him all about you, darling. I'll even embellish it a little. I'm certainly not going to let Jack get killed over this."

I paused and glanced at Daddy. His eyes were closed, his lips pressed tightly together. At least he didn't doubt the veracity of this portion of the confession.

Neither did Daddy Jack, judging from his expression.

I had no idea of where this was going, except I knew my days were numbered if she told. I hadn't a clue what I was going to do about it when she took ill a few days later, although she did her best to hide it.

"I need new boots," she told her husband. "My feet have been hurting for ages and Jonah's driving me into town. We'll be back sometime tomorrow … you and Jack and Tony have a lovely day killing things, all right, darling?"

I knew she was seeing a doctor and a lawyer concerning the money she'd recently inherited and wasn't shopping for boots at all, but I played along and told her where the shoe shop was located.

She returned late the next day, pale and fatigued. "I couldn't find any to fit," she complained. "Just a wasted trip."

Hoping she'd done the practical thing, as soon as I got her alone, I asked, "Did you get rid of the baby?"

"No … there's no baby," she said and collapsed against me. I remember looking around, wondering where James was, wondering where his gun was, wondering where my own was, but thankfully I saw both brothers sitting by the campfire, doing what they did best: drinking.

"No baby? What is it, then?" I asked, perplexed.

"I have a tumor," she answered. "I found out just before I came to Africa … there's nothing that can be done. I've been to several doctors … I'm dying, Tony. I'll be dead by Christmas, maybe Thanksgiving."

I paused for effect, but neither Daddy nor Daddy Jack said a word. When I expected drama, when I anticipated enlightenment, neither said a word. "Mother had a tumor that was growing like a baby," I prompted. "She had only months to live."

My father fastened his dark eyes on me. "You don't have to repeat yourself, Abigail. We have ears. We can hear."

I could feel his loathing. I'd unearthed facts that only he knew and had never wanted to share. I'd violated a trust between him and my mother. The letter felt heavy in my hand. Would reading the remainder serve any purpose?

Daddy broke the silence. "I remember her going to town that one day. She's dying so she pretends to shop for boots … how incredibly calculating. Who else would do such a thing?"

"You would," Daddy Jack said. "She learned deceit from the master."

Daddy arched his brow. "Are you saying she learned it from you?"

"I, too, learned from the master."

Daddy cleared his throat. "Let's stay on subject, Jack. So she goes to town to cut me out of her will."

"And more pain pills."

"And she tells Tony the truth, but she tells him late … it's curious why she'd invent a phony story about a baby."

"I know the answer to that," Daddy Jack said.

"Which is?"

"I'll tell you at the end, if he gets it wrong."

"I think I know already," Daddy said. "If this confession has any basis in fact, I know where this is going."

"So do I … continue, Abigail."

Unlike the two of them, I had no idea where this was going.

"But I can't die that way," Ellen said to me. "I just can't ... it's too dreadful. You'll have to do it for me."

"What are you saying?" I asked her.

"What do you think I'm saying? You'd kill a charging lion or buffalo to save your own life. Surely you can kill me for the same reason, can't you?"

"You want me to kill you—on purpose? Don't be absurd," I said, aghast at the very idea. "My profession demands that I jeopardize myself to safeguard my clients, and my morality ensures that I act honorably. It cannot be any other way!"

She didn't buy it for a minute. "Well, you sure haven't acted honorably with me, have you, my brave, beautiful man? Where's your bravery now? And where's your beauty?" she taunted me. "Very well, I'll tell my husband how you took me shooting and you ravaged me in the bush and now I'm having your baby. He'll believe me because he loves me. Why, I'm not sure, unless he still thinks of me as his and he always loves what is his."

"But none of that is true!" I said in disbelief. "There's no baby, and I only did what I did with your full consent. I'll tell him so myself!"

"You'll tell him nothing," she said. "Dead men can't talk. When I tell him what you did, he's certain to kill you, slowly. You'll feel the bullets rip through your leg, your arm, your shoulder ... you'll cry, you'll scream, you'll beg for death before he delivers the coup de grace. He won't care about the consequences, only that you've been punished ... enjoy the day, Tony Tompkins. You're a dead man already." And then she laughed.

I begged her to quiet down before we were overheard, which she finally did.

"You'll get your chance to do it," she said, abruptly very calm, very analytical. "I'll do something incredibly stupid in the next few days, and in the confusion you'll shoot me ... right through the heart. I don't want to get it through the lungs; I'd be aware of that, wouldn't I? And I don't want to be shot in the head. I want to look pretty, there in my casket with James, Jack, and perhaps even you weeping over me. But I want to die instantly ... a shot through the heart won't hurt, will it?"

"Embarras de choix," Daddy muttered. "Embarrassing variety of choice ... "

Daddy Jack poisoned his brother with a single glance.

It was the only time I saw her cry. I assured her she wouldn't feel a thing, but reiterated that I wasn't going to do it.

"Oh, but you must," she said. "It's either you or me, and I'm going to die soon anyway ... don't be such a damn fool, Tony. There's no one else. Jack can't do it; I've already asked. James could, but somehow I don't think he would either. He'd

prefer me going painfully, miserably, for all the years of hurt I've caused him. Jack wasn't the first, you see, although he was by far my favorite ... and you wouldn't be my last, my dear Tony, if it weren't for this ... this thing."

"Corruptio optima pessima," Daddy breathed, and closed his eyes.

"The corruption of the best is the worst of all," Daddy Jack translated for me. "I took high school Latin too. Apparently my brother is still capable of emotion, shockingly enough, and what he's feeling at this very moment can't be adequately expressed in ordinary, mundane English ... isn't that so, James?"

Daddy had no reaction to his cruel comment, no reaction at all.

I took a deep breath and finished.

And that was how it happened, dear daughter of Ellen. In the confusion of the stampede a few days later, I shot ... James shot ... Jack shot, and she died. Just like that. She died. A perfect heart shot. She felt nothing. And no one ever knew, for certain. It was the perfect murder because it was the perfect accident. It could have been any of us. Even an official inquiry was avoided. Questions were avoided, when we went to the local authorities. I knew the officials could be bought off, most happily so. With the language barrier confusing the issue, neither the husband nor his brother ever suspected that I had saved myself.

I worked for another decade in my profession. I never touched another client's wife. This is my confession to God and to you. I took from you your mother, prematurely, to prolong my own life. I pray for, but do not expect, your forgiveness.

As Terry Shaw is my witness,

Tony Tompkins

Daddy slumped forward in his chair, his head supported by his large hands. My father sat stone-faced, staring at him, at me, and then at nothing.

"It's done," I said. "It's over." I tossed the confession on the coffee table and climbed the stairs to my room, thankful I'd not been witness to any of the ugliness I'd been recounting.

But two brothers had been witness. How were they feeling now, after hearing my mother's and her paramour's voices from the grave?

I hadn't meant to fall asleep, but I did. When I awoke, I was alone in the house. While heating some leftover minestrone for an early dinner, I noticed Daddy sitting outside in the gazebo. I went out to him. "Where's your brother?"

"I sent him home."

"After such a terrible day? Couldn't you have put him up for one night?"

"No."

"The minestrone's hot," I said gently. "Would you like some? I'll bring it out to you, if you like."

"No."

His thoughts were elsewhere, so I went inside and ate alone. While eating, I envisioned the idealized aftermath if the letter had made a difference:

Daddy and Daddy Jack were drinking beer in the kitchen. A cribbage board lay between them, with a pile of quarters already on Daddy Jack's side.

"About time you woke up," Daddy said to me. "I was just thinking of checking on you."

"What's going on?" I frowned, seeing the bottles, peanut shells, crackers, and an opened jar of pickled herring littering the counter.

"Eating and drinking," Daddy Jack said. "Want something?"

I shook my head. "I don't believe this! I go through hell reading a confession explaining Mother's death, and two hours later you're sitting here drinking beer together?"

Daddy shrugged. "We decided to bury the hatchet."

"Not in each other," Daddy Jack added.

"We had a good talk after you went upstairs," Daddy explained. "We've decided that what happened with your mother is in the past. That letter was wrong in places, but since neither of us knew the whole story, a few errors can be overlooked. At least it cleared up one thing. I always wondered whether Jack killed her to get the money, and he always wondered whether I killed her to get revenge. Neither of us ever considered it might have been Tony's response to Ellen's blackmail. So that's that … would you like me to make you a Cosmopolitan? My brother tells me you've taken quite a liking to them."

The scenario was a stretch, even for me. But the wonderful thing about stories is that they turn out the way the author wants them to.

But life doesn't, because life has no author. Life is lived on a whim, with one decision signifying nothing and another decision signifying everything, and who can discern one from the other in time to dodge disaster?

My reading of Tony's confession had been a bad decision. It had changed nothing.

I dialed the stove burner to low and set a place for Maria, who was due home momentarily, and for Daddy, in case he changed his mind about eating, and went out for an evening walk along the creek. I hadn't gone twenty yards before the tears came.

I awoke in the middle of the night to the sounds of destruction. Either a herd of buffalo had entered the house or Daddy was on a rampage. I threw on my robe as I ran downstairs. Maria was standing by the office door, similarly attired.

"James! Let me in!" she hollered, banging on the door.

Glass was breaking inside, cracking sharply at the onset, tinkling eerily at the end, accompanied by unintelligible mutterings.

I moved Maria aside and pounded the door with my fists. "Open up, Daddy, we need to talk!"

He hurled something heavy against the far side. The door shuddered.

"He's going to hurt himself in there!" I worried. "Can't you do something?"

"Like what?" Maria said. "Come on, let's have coffee while he runs out of temper and things to smash."

I dutifully followed her to the kitchen, eyeing the Kentucky rifle and the Union swords in their proper fittings. The kitchen knives were present in their block.

"Where's his Luger?" I asked.

Maria patted the bulge in the pocket of her housecoat. "I thought of that too, although he generally threatens to kill others, never himself. He's quite consistent that way."

I filled the percolator and plugged it in. "So what brought this on?"

"That confession you read, of course." She took two mugs from the cupboard. "After thinking it over half the night, he told me he's been captivated by the memory of a devil, not a woman. He's performing an exorcism of sorts in there." Her hand flew to her mouth. "Oh, I'm terribly sorry, Abby. I shouldn't have said that. Please forgive me."

I shrugged. "It doesn't matter. She wasn't who I thought she was."

"No one ever is."

I sat calmly, drinking my Folgers at three in the morning as Daddy reduced the contents of an entire room to rubble and shards. I'd never have another chance to study his journal. Or read the letters in the campaign chest or the entries in the autograph book. Or wear Mother's evening dress, hats, jewelry, perfume. What stunned me was that I no longer cared. The whole situation seemed surreal.

I refilled Maria's cup. "Daddy's crazy, isn't he?"

She shrugged. "Sometimes."

"Do you ever regret marrying him?"

"No."

"I'd think you would, at a time like this."

"Well, you thought wrong. Remember, Abby, I'd lost everything in the war. Your father walked into my life and we filled a need in each other. And we fell in love. He's not an easy man to live with, but he's never dull … oh, I do hope he's leaving the bookcase and the desk intact."

"Probably. The furniture had nothing to do with my mother." I located Daddy's Irish whiskey, added a generous shot to my coffee, dropped in three sugar cubes, and stirred briskly before pouring cream over the back of a spoon into my mug. I'd learned how from Randy.

Maria watched without comment.

Daddy emerged from his office. Blood covered his hands. His face was flushed but inscrutable. "You're drinking my whiskey," he said to me on his way to the sink.

"You drive me to it … so, how do you feel now?"

"Better." He picked a sliver from his palm and washed the blood down the drain. "Maria, get me some Band-Aids, would you?"

She made a face at him. "Get them yourself, dear. I'm going to bed."

"Love you too," Daddy said under his breath. Returning from the bathroom, he poured a whiskey for himself, added ice and a splash of water, stirred it with a bandaged forefinger, and sat down across from me. "Don't let me catch you drinking that again."

"You should talk. You drink all the time."

"Don't push me," he growled. "I'm past fifty, and I can drink if I want."

I finished my Irish coffee before he had a mind to take it away. "I'm not cleaning up that mess you made in your office."

"I didn't ask you to … that was some story you came up with yesterday."

"I didn't come up with it. Tony Tompkins came up with it."

"That's what I meant. And what exactly would you like me to do about it?"

"Do about what?"

"Stop the evasion, Abigail. I'm not gullible and I'm not stupid. Terry Shaw, Tony Tompkins, and you pieced that story together in an attempt to broker peace between me and Jack."

I feigned surprise. "What makes you say that?"

"Because it's the only thing that makes sense. You portray Tony as a villain and your mother as a harlot, and when the former removes the latter, who's left? Jack and me."

"You're right," I said, ignoring his first conclusion while addressing his second. "Of course that's what I want, what I've always wanted. Is it too much to ask that we be a normal family?"

"No, but this isn't likely to end the way you want."

"Why not?"

"Because big mistakes don't come with big erasers."

"No, but you could try, Daddy. Nothing will ever happen unless you try. And the first move has to come from you."

He nursed his drink contemplatively. I waited, alternating between hope and despair. I couldn't read his face. I couldn't guess his thoughts. He sat there, a clever, complex, maddening man. He'd raised me, but I didn't know him. I loved him, but I couldn't understand him. He was an enigma, like his journal.

He looked up, the decision made. "Fine … I'll drive to the farm in the morning, have a talk with Jack, and see what I can do."

"You will? Are you sure?"

"I will and I'm sure. Hell, if I don't do something, you'll keep picking that same scab over and over until we all bleed to death. You're not the only one who'd like to bury the past and move on. What do you think my rampage in there was about?"

I got all teary, slipped my arms around his neck, and kissed his cheek. He patted my back. He seemed so reflective, so solemn. Daddy Jack once said how difficult it was for his brother to bend, but now he was bending, for me. For me, James Albert Stahl would forgive. For me, he would unite our family.

"Thank you, Daddy," I murmured. "I love you. I love you so much."

"And I love you, Abby."

"Do you love me because I'm yours?" I couldn't help asking.

"No, I love you in spite of the fact you're not."

"That is even more commendable."

"Enough sentimentality." He untangled my arms from his neck. "You might be getting your hopes up for nothing, you know. Jack might view our relationship as irrevocably broken."

"No, he won't. I have faith in you, Daddy. When you put your mind to it, you always get your way."

He shook his head. "No, during the most pivotal points of my life, I did not get my way … go to bed now or you'll be as exhausted as I'll be in the morning."

"All right, Daddy … good night." I set my mug in the sink and headed for the stairs.

"Oh, by the way," he said from behind me. "Jack might've believed that letter, but I didn't. It really wasn't a very good story."

I turned, hardly daring to meet his eyes; the pale eyes that could see clear to my conniving soul.

"But it was good enough." And then he smiled.

Mission Accomplie

DADDY RETURNED FROM the farm late the next day. I greeted him with fresh lemonade and chocolate chip cookies, anticipating a reason to celebrate.

There was, to a degree.

"Jack didn't seem very surprised to see me," Daddy said, settling in his favorite chair in the gazebo. "He had things to discuss with me too. Some of it got straightened out by the time Margaret showed up … good cookies."

I poured his lemonade. "Margaret came over again? Or does she live there now?"

"No, but she will soon."

"What's that supposed to mean?"

"It means they're getting married next month."

"Oh, no!" I blurted.

Daddy frowned his disapproval. "That's a selfish attitude, Abby. You ought to be happy for him. Margaret's a fine woman, and she'll keep him in line better than Annie did. The twins will benefit from having a mother in the home again, although she comes too late for Darrell."

"I suppose … " Then I considered the larger picture. "We'll be invited to the wedding, won't we?"

"I think so."

Already I planned on wearing one of my low-cut dresses I'd worn aboard the *Queen*. I'd have a last dance with my father before I gave him up. But he wasn't mine to give. Why couldn't I remember that? And the dance came after the vows, not before!

"What about my birthday?" I said, moving on. "It's a big one this year: eighteen. You'll invite Daddy Jack and Margaret to my party, won't you? And surely we'll spend the holidays together."

"You're putting the cart before the horse. Jack and I are barely on speaking terms and you're already setting the table for eight."

"I know, but you'll keep trying, won't you?"

"I will as long as he does."

"Then it'll happen. Maybe not right away, but it will. And when it does, we'll make up for lost time."

"Unless Margaret and Maria detest each other."

"Oh, don't tease me, Daddy. They'll simply love each other. You know they will. They're not at all like you and your brother." Instantly I regretted what I'd said, but he took it the proper way.

"Yes, I suppose we're just a couple of prickly people … prickly people, but with deep roots to weather the storm; the storm we created ourselves."

Sleep was impossible. After Daddy and Maria retired for the night, I sat on my bed and composed a letter of gratitude to Terry Shaw.

Dearest Terry,

I am still uncertain of the ultimate outcome, but I believe our ruse worked! I'm so hopeful right now, and I've never had cause to be hopeful before, that I can hardly concentrate sufficiently to write this letter to you. But I will, as I'm sure you're anxious to hear what happened.

It was my—or should I say OUR—best effort, and for the best of purposes, and you did your part fabulously. Compiling what I'd learned on this end with the information you gleaned from Tony's journals on your end, has FINALLY compelled my father and uncle to begin the arduous task of reconciliation. Daddy actually drove to the farm today to begin the process!

Oh, how easily everything could have backfired! Time after time Daddy interrupted me as I read. Once he got so mad he nearly punched his brother. But my slant on the story, plus the fortuitous details you provided, combined to make a compelling tale. The part about Mother going off target practicing, Daddy shooting toward Uncle Jack and Mother, Mother's illness and her going to town for new boots—the boot story, I think, sucked them both in. What else could they say after that? They both realized events had taken place that neither of them knew about. And Mother's confiding to Tony that she hadn't had relations with Daddy since I was born and still held strong feelings for my uncle—well, it all fell into place like pieces in a puzzle.

But I feel terrible I had to denigrate the memory of my mother to the men who'd loved her. Putting those words into her mouth—"oh, you brave, beautiful man"—I cringed just repeating them! And the part about the "shadow"—I'm SO thankful I decided to pin the blame for that on Tony, because Uncle Jack did NOT need the truth to come out! He himself denied it so very convincingly, both in that letter I'd found and again straight to Daddy's face.

But the part about Daddy hitting Mother tore my heart. It was true, too, because when I read it, such a change came over him. He nearly wept. Yes, I know he had reason, considering her adulterous liaisons, but STILL.

Those last paragraphs were so awful, when I related how my mother begged Tony to kill her so she wouldn't suffer the agonizing death she'd otherwise face. That finally brought Daddy down. The ending, where Tony says, "I took from you your mother, prematurely, to prolong my own life … I pray for, but do not expect, your forgiveness," was truly a showstopper!

But then I doubted we'd made a difference. I came downstairs after a nap and Daddy wasn't talking and he'd already sent my uncle home. I feared all our efforts had come to naught.

The climax came in the middle of the night, when Daddy went stark crazy, destroying all the memorabilia he still had of Mother's. He turned his office into an absolute shambles. Afterward he told me that although my uncle believed our story, he didn't, saying it wasn't very good. But then he said the strangest thing—"it was good enough." Terry, that means he's using it as a convenient excuse to make peace with his brother, to bring us all together as a family again! What do you make of that? Isn't it an amazing twist?

On a far more serious note, I sincerely hope your father is recovering. I've been praying for him. I am most gratified the two of you have also reconciled your differences.

I'm also thankful Tony willed his camp journals to your father upon his untimely death during the war. Who could've foreseen that his diaries would not only provide your father with countless hours of entertainment in his later years, but solve an age-old mystery as well?

Perhaps I should be incensed with Tony for the part he played in my mother's demise, but she brought it upon herself, didn't she? My whole perspective of her has changed since the reading of your letter. To find out she really was incurably ill was horrible enough, but to learn of her affair with Tony, not to mention how analytically she planned her final days—! Didn't she realize Daddy and his brother would blame each other, or themselves? Or didn't she care? I hate to think poorly of my own mother, but it seems there was not one villain in our story, but two.

At least Tony has vindicated himself somewhat in my mind, since what he did ultimately was a mercy killing. And his heroic exploits with the RAF in defense of London during the Blitz proved he possessed at least some admirable qualities, although being shot down by the Luftwaffe put him in the wrong place at the wrong time, again!

To change the subject rather dramatically—Uncle Jack is bringing me back to Africa next summer, for certain. I'll be nearly nineteen then, so you know what THAT means! If you don't, I'll show you … or maybe a proper girl shouldn't be so bold as to say that?

On that note, I'll seal this up now so Daddy doesn't see it. That WOULD be impossible to explain, wouldn't it? I'll mail it from the post office first thing in the morning. Thank you for doing your part so well. If life in the bush ever fails to please you, you've a definite talent for writing fiction. Write soon, to my box rather than the house until we're done discussing this, and this time write only the truth!

Love you so much, Abby

"Write only the truth" ... oh, wouldn't Terry be shocked to learn my final secret? Maybe in my next letter I'd reveal the identity of my true father ... or maybe not.

Several weeks later, a reply arrived from Africa. After retrieving the letter from my box, I sidled to an area of the lobby devoid of postal patrons to read, as I was far too excited to wait until I got home.

Dear Abby,

I am so gratified at the success of your mission. Congratulations for pulling it off! I can only imagine the tension in the room as you read Tony's "confession." I would've liked to have been a mouse in the corner, or is that not befitting your white hunter? Better to have been a lion in the corner?

Regardless, I am happy to hear that your family is on the road to becoming united again. My own relationship with my father had been the cause of so much ill feeling, but now it continues to bring me great joy.

Notice I said NOW, as my father is recovering from his stroke! His speech is returning and he is able to take a few steps unaided. A nurse comes to the house daily, helping him with hygiene and therapy. To fill his days, he continues to read Tony's journals. My father never was a hunter, but he has always been a bona fide armchair adventurer.

Now I must explain something that will alter greatly your perception of both Tony and your mother. I'm not sure how this happened, with the innumerable exchanging of letters between us, but somehow pretence has turned to fact in your mind and you have gotten confused. In that last letter I wrote, the one you read to your father and uncle, there were some key elements that I assumed you knew NOT to be true. Apparently you've gone off track somewhere during this long, convoluted journey of revelation, so I must set the record straight.

To summarize the facts: your mother had cancer and she had not long to live when she arrived in Africa. She did suffer at the hands of her husband. She loved you and she loved your uncle to the day she died, which was the reason she willed her wealth to him. The small details: the shooting while Tony was taking the photograph, the boots, and the drunkenness of both brothers, all likewise were true.

Now to summarize what was not true, which you've somehow taken as fact: Tony NEVER had an affair with your mother. That was simply how I wrote that part of the story, but you were not to believe it yourself. Tony was not that kind of man and I verified this with my father. He was morality itself, upstanding, deeply religious. He was merely your mother's confidant. That is how he came to know of her life, writing it down in excruciating detail.

An episode I did not mention before is where your mother walked away from camp one evening and Tony found her standing by a water hole, waiting for something to kill her. Tony did not relay this incident to either her husband or his brother, as she begged him not to. I include it now simply as proof that your mother had truly become suicidal.

In the confusion of the stampede two days after this particular incident, Tony states explicitly in his journal that he did not fire at the buffalo. He was reserving his shot if your father and uncle missed, as a professional hunter should. As it turned out, his shot was unnecessary, as the buff went down. Horribly, so did your mother. Tony did not insist on an investigation because he knew her standing in front of the buffalo was hardly accidental, although her getting shot WAS accidental. It was no one's fault, and he convinced the authorities to let the matter go.

Do not agonize from whose gun the fatal shot came. It is unlikely the shooter himself knows. And remember this also: your mother wanted to die. She died quickly, as she wished. She went out on her terms. Do not grieve unduly. As I told you when we first met, all that lives dies at some point. Cherish her memory.

All my love, Terry

I sank to a bench in the lobby and pressed the letter to my heart.

Mother, my precious mother, forgive me! How could I have misunderstood? How could I have believed such wantonness of you? You were sick. You were dying. You scarcely could have pursued an affair with anyone under those horrendous circumstances.

No wonder Daddy hadn't believed my story; putting those vile words in your mouth, characterizing you so falsely! But he said Daddy Jack *had* believed my story, or was it just another instance of my father doing the expedient thing: lying?

But someone *did* pull the trigger the day you died. If not Tony, was it Daddy, in a final act of retribution? Tony said Daddy never missed—he simply never missed. It hardly would've been an accident if he shot you during the stampede, would it?

Or did the bullet originate with my father, who acted upon your final request? Had you finally convinced him, the night he was "the shadow," to assume the role in reality that Tony played fictively in my erroneous story? That would be reason enough for him to accept my story as fact, since it pinned blame on someone other than himself!

But why had Daddy said my story was "good enough?" So I'd stop my digging short of the truth? But what *is* the truth, Mother? Are you the only one who really knows? Or is the truth unknowable?

Conflicting thoughts swirled through my mind like a tempest. What should I do now? Would my mother want me to continue to pursue the matter, suspecting one brother over the other? Or would she want me to put the situation behind me, as Terry said I should, and go on?

And could I allow my uncle and my father to put the matter behind them, as I said they should, and go on?

Yes, I could. I must. For my own peace of mind, I must.

To encourage two brothers to heal, I first had to heal myself.

I slipped the letter in my purse and waited until I was strong enough to walk home.

Life Yet to Come

A MONTH LATER, I was wading through *Main Street* by Sinclair Lewis, at Daddy's insistence, when the doorbell rang.

"Expecting anyone?" Daddy peered at me over the top of his newspaper.

"Nope."

The doorbell rang again.

"Well, hell. Who do you suppose it is: Mormons, Jehovah's Witnesses, or sales slime? And if sales slime, is it vacuums, cleaning products, or encyclopedias?"

"No clue, Daddy."

The doorbell rang for a third time. He went to answer, as I knew he would. He relished the chance to tell whomever it was to get a "real job" and stop bothering folks. Only with shy little Girl Scouts selling cookies would he be affable.

As soon as he left, I picked up my preferred reading, *Horn of the Hunter*. Numerous books of similar genre lay on the coffee table. Daddy deplored that hunting and death on the Dark Continent still captivated my imagination, but there wasn't much he could do about it. At least I'd finally stopped pestering him about Mother.

"Oh damn, you're back," I heard Daddy say, from around the corner.

"I certainly am," confirmed a cheerful, very familiar voice.

Horn of the Hunter fell from my lap as I ran to the window. I saw Debbie Hooker, carrying the most garish table lamp imaginable, walk from a United Van Lines truck, which was idling noisily on the corner, to the entrance of the house next door. Apparently she had not divorced Archie, as Daddy had assumed.

Next I both saw and heard Archie Hooker, beer in hand, hollering directions and gesticulating wildly to the truck driver who was, according to Archie, the most incompetent, incongruous, incomprehensible, inconsequential idiot behind a steering wheel in the entire nation, bar none.

And the only boy who had ever broken my heart was at our back door.

I eavesdropped while watching the proceedings outside.

"Is Abby in?" Hooker was asking.

"No," Daddy said.

"Oh ... when will she be back?"

"Never."

"What do you mean, never? How's that possible?"

"Easily, that's how."

"Well, where is she?"

"Gone. Disappeared. Vanished."

"Vanished? Where?"

"Africa. Went and never came back."

"She did?"

"Yes, she did."

"But I wanted to make things up to her!" Hooker sounded distraught, which pleased me immensely.

"Well, you're too damn late."

"It's never too late, as long as I can write and explain. You'll give me her address, won't you? She can receive mail where she's at, can't she?"

"Yes, but her husband won't like it."

"Husband? What husband?"

I had to snicker, very quietly, of course.

"She up and married that white hunter she met in Africa last summer. Hot nights in the thorny bush, as it were. My brother couldn't keep her corralled. She's Mrs. Terry Shaw now."

"My God, that's just awful!"

"Awful?" Daddy mimicked. "Hell, I think it's just wonderful, her married off to a real man!"

"And what exactly do you mean by that, Mr. Stahl?"

"You know damn well what I mean, Mr. Hooker. A real man. Has a big gun and a big—"

"—I get your drift," Hooker said. The perpetual cheer had left his voice.

"Well, be that as it may, I'll get her address for you. I'm sure she and the kids will be thrilled to hear from—"

"—kids? He had kids, from before?"

"No, she does."

"She does?"

"Not by herself. They do. Together."

"Together?"

"Yes, together … is there a parrot in the house?"

"No, there isn't. And you don't have to be insulting, Mr. Stahl."

"Me? Insulting? Why do you say that?"

"Because you are! Before we terminate this inane conversation, you said 'kids,' as in more than one. How's it possible that Abby could produce two children in less than a year?"

"Twins, my dear Hooker!" Daddy crowed. "Twins run in our family. And here I thought you were so damned brilliant. What, did you flunk biology? Or was it probabilities in mathematics that you failed to understand?"

"No, I did not!" Hooker's voice rose. "I misunderstood, that's all. And you know what else? I'm thinking that you're making all of this crap up. I'm thinking this is just another one of your devious methods to keep me from your daughter, which I don't understand, which I've never understood. If you can actually be truthful for once, what exactly is it about me that you don't like?"

"You mean besides my thinking you're an opportunist?"

"Besides that."

"And besides my thinking you'll never have a pot to piss in?"

"Besides that."

"Well, I'm not sure, Hooker ... I just can't seem to put my finger on it. Perhaps if we were to go into the basement and lock the door, just you and me, alone together for say, half an hour, I might be able to answer that question ... well, how about it?"

Hooker turned on his heel and strode down our sidewalk so fast I barely caught a glimpse of him before he disappeared into his own house. From his militant deportment, I wasn't certain he would attempt to speak to me again.

Daddy, looking smug, returned to the living room. "Well, that was fun."

"Fun? You call that fun?" I momentarily forgot what Hooker had done to me. "You're so bad, Daddy. You lied through your teeth and you treated Hooker like sh—manure. Years ago, you'd have yelled till you went purple in the face and yanked my privileges for doing half what you just did!"

Daddy picked *Main Street* from the floor and tossed it back at me. "Oh, don't get all riled up. It was for a good cause."

"What good cause? Making Hooker grovel, just because you could?"

"No. I did what I did for a reason, Abby. I wanted to see how far I could push him. I wanted to see how much abuse he'd take before he'd either punch me or walk away. I wanted to see if he had a limit, a core. And I wanted to see at what point you'd rush in and rescue him."

"And?"

"Well, I found out he'll take quite a bit, but he does have a limit. That's good. And you didn't rescue him. That's good too, because it means you're no longer in love with him."

I hadn't thought of it quite that way. Perhaps Daddy was right. Until I looked deep in Hooker's limpid blue eyes and heard his apologies and his regrets, would I know whether I still loved him.

And Randy was attending the university with me next month. How would I feel about him then?

And I thought about the last letter I'd received at the post office. Neither Daddy Jack nor Daddy knew about it—yet. Someone in Africa had a proposition for me. I truly could have hot nights in the thorny bush, if I wanted. I truly could become Mrs. Terry Shaw, if I wanted.

Daddy thought it funny when he told his fiction as fact. Would he think my fact as funny as his fiction?

Later that afternoon, as I waited for my casserole to finish cooking so I could bring it next door to the Hookers, I contemplated my life thus far.

My earliest recollections were of a mysteriously deceased mother, a distant but demanding father, and a benignly tyrannical uncle.

In actuality, I had been blessed with an adoring mother who'd loved me for as long as she lived, a doting grandmother who took up the reins of my upbringing for another nine years, followed by Aunt Annie, who did a commendable job until God gave her a rest. Now I had Maria. Warm, comfortable, happy Maria.

And instead of one father, I had two. They were both a gigantic pain in the ass, but they did their best and they both loved me. I could count on them to be after me: supporting, correcting, nagging. I could keep them busy for years … maybe forever.

Life.

So much to sort out. So much to think about.

So many mistakes to be made while trying not to make any mistakes.

I could hardly wait to see what would happen next.